ALSO BY FÉLIX J. PALMA

The Map of Time

the MAP _of the_ SKY

A Novel

FÉLIX J. PALMA

TRANSLATED BY NICK CAISTOR

ATRIA PAPERBACK

NEW YORK   LONDON   TORONTO   SYDNEY   NEW DELHI

ATRIA PAPERBACK
A Division of Simon & Schuster, Inc.
1230 Avenue of the Americas
New York, NY 10020

First Atria Paperback edition June 2013

ATRIA PAPERBACK and colophon are trademarks of Simon & Schuster, Inc.

For information about special discounts for bulk purchases,
please contact Simon & Schuster Special Sales at
1-866-506-1949 or business@simonandschuster.com.

The Simon & Schuster Speakers Bureau can bring authors to your live event. For more information or to book an event, contact the Simon & Schuster Speakers Bureau at 1-866-248-3049 or visit our website at www.simonspeakers.com.

Designed by Suet Y. Chong

Manufactured in the United States of America

10 9 8 7 6 5 4 3 2 1

Library of Congress Cataloging-in-Publication Data

Palma, Félix J.
[Mapa del cielo. English]
The map of the sky : a novel / by Félix J. Palma. — 1st Atria Books hardcover ed.
p. cm.
1. Writers—Fiction. 2. Wells, H. G. (Herbert George),
1866–1946—Fiction. 3. Time travel—Fiction. I. Title.
PQ6666.A3965M3413 2012
863'.64—dc23   2012028794

ISBN 978-1-4516-6031-9
ISBN 978-1-4516-6032-6 (pbk)
ISBN 978-1-4516-6033-3 (ebook)

ON THE COSMIC SCALE, ONLY THE FANTASTIC
HAS A POSSIBILITY OF BEING TRUE.

Teilhard de Chardin

IT IS A STUPID PRESUMPTION TO GO ABOUT
DESPISING AND CONDEMNING AS FALSE
ANYTHING THAT SEEMS TO US IMPROBABLE.

Montaigne

"WHAT DO WE KNOW ABOUT MARS?" ASKED
GUSEV. "IS IT INHABITED BY PEOPLE OR
MONSTERS?"

Aleksey Tolstoy

CONTENTS

the MAP of the SKY

PART ONE

WELCOME, DEAR READER, AS YOU
PLUNGE VALIANTLY INTO THE THRILLING
PAGES OF OUR MELODRAMA, WHERE YOU
WILL FIND ADVENTURES THAT TEST YOUR
SPIRIT AND POSSIBLY YOUR SANITY!

IF YOU BELIEVE OUR PLANET HAS NOTHING
TO FEAR AS IT SPINS IN THE VAST
UNIVERSE, YOU WILL PRESENTLY LEARN
THAT THE MOST UNIMAGINABLE TERROR
CAN REACH US FROM THE STARS.

IT IS MY DUTY TO WARN YOU, BRAVE READER,
THAT YOU WILL ENCOUNTER HORRORS THERE,
WHICH YOUR INNOCENT SOUL COULD NEVER
HAVE IMAGINED WERE GOD'S CREATIONS.

IF OUR TALE DOES NOT TAKE YOU TO THE
DIZZIEST HEIGHTS OF EXHILARATION, WE
WILL REFUND YOUR FIVE CENTS SO YOU
MAY SPEND THEM ON A MORE EXCITING
ADVENTURE, IF SUCH A THING EXISTS!

"What do you suppose that thing is, Peters?" asked one of the other sailors, a man called Carson.

The Indian remained silent for a few moments before replying, contemplating whether his companions were ready for the revelation he was about to share with them.

"A devil," he said in a grave voice. "And it came from the stars."

I

HERBERT GEORGE WELLS WOULD HAVE PRE-
ferred to live in a fairer, more considerate world, a
world where a kind of artistic code of ethics prevented people from ex-
ploiting others' ideas for their own gain, one where the so-called talent of those wretches who had the effrontery to do so would dry up
overnight, condemning them to a life of drudgery like ordinary men.
But, unfortunately, the world he lived in was not like that. In his world
everything was permissible, or at least that is what Wells thought. And
not without reason, for only a few months after his book *The War of the
Worlds* had been published, an American scribbler by the name of Garrett P. Serviss had the audacity to write a sequel to it, without so much
as informing him of the fact, and even assuming he would be delighted.

That is why on a warm June day the author known as H. G. Wells
was walking somewhat absentmindedly along the streets of London, the
greatest and proudest city in the world. He was strolling through Soho
on his way to the Crown and Anchor. Mr. Serviss, who was visiting
England, had invited him there for luncheon in the sincere belief that,
with the aid of beer and good food, their minds would be able to com-
mune at the level he deemed appropriate. However, if everything went
according to plan, the luncheon wouldn't turn out the way the ingenu-
ous Mr. Serviss had imagined, for Wells had quite a different idea, which
had nothing to do with the union of like minds the American had envisaged. Not that Wells was proposing to turn what might otherwise be
a pleasant meal into a council of war because he considered his novel a

masterpiece whose intrinsic worth would inevitably be compromised by the appearance of a hastily written sequel. No, Wells's real fear was that another author might make better use of his own idea. This prospect churned him up inside, causing no end of ripples in the tranquil pool to which he was fond of likening his soul.

In truth, as with all his previous novels, Wells considered *The War of the Worlds* an unsatisfactory work, which had once again failed in its aims. The story described how Martians possessing a technology superior to that of human beings conquered Earth. Wells had emulated the realism with which Sir George Chesney had imbued his novel *The Battle of Dorking,* an imaginary account of a German invasion of England, unstinting in its gory detail. Employing a similar realism bolstered by descriptions as elaborate as they were gruesome, Wells had narrated the destruction of London, which the Martians achieved with no trace of compassion, as though humans deserved no more consideration than cockroaches. Within a matter of days, our neighbors in space had trampled on the Earth dwellers' values and self-respect with the same disdain the British showed toward the native populations in their empire. They had taken control of the entire planet, enslaving the inhabitants and transforming Earth into something resembling a spa for Martian elites. Nothing whatsoever had been able to stand in their way. Wells had intended this dark fantasy as an excoriating attack on the excessive zeal of British imperialism, which he found loathsome. But the fact was that now people believed Mars was inhabited. New, more powerful telescopes like that of the Italian Giovanni Schiaparelli had revealed furrows on the planet's red surface, which some astronomers had quickly declared, as if they had been there for a stroll, to be canals constructed by an intelligent civilization. This had instilled in people a fear of Martian invasion, exactly as Wells had described it. However, this didn't come as much of a surprise to Wells, for something similar had happened with *The Time Machine,* in which the eponymous artifact had eclipsed Wells's veiled attack on class society.

And now Serviss, who apparently enjoyed something of a reputation as a science journalist in his own country, had published a sequel to it: *Edison's Conquest of Mars*. And what was Serviss's novel about? The title fooled no one: the hero was Thomas Edison, whose innumerable inventions had made him into something of a hero in the eyes of his fellow Americans, and subsequently into the wearisome protagonist of every species of novel. In Serviss's sequel, the ineffable Edison invented a powerful ray gun and, with the help of the world's nations, built a flotilla of ships equipped with antigravitational engines, which set sail for Mars driven by a thirst for revenge.

When Serviss sent Wells his novel, together with a letter praising Wells's work with nauseating fervor and almost demanding that he give the sequel his blessing, Wells had not deigned to reply. Nor had he responded to the half dozen other letters doggedly seeking Wells's approval. Serviss even had the nerve to suggest, based upon the similarities and common interests he perceived in their works, that they write a novel together. After reading Serviss's tale, all Wells could feel was a mixture of irritation and disgust. That utterly childish, clumsy piece of prose was a shameless insult to other writers who, like himself, did their best to fill the bookshop shelves with more or less worthy creations. However, Wells's silence did not stanch the flow of letters, which if anything appeared to intensify. In the latest of these, the indefatigable Serviss begged Wells to be so kind as to lunch with him the following week during his two-day visit to London. Nothing, he said, would make him happier than to be able to enjoy a pleasant discussion with the esteemed author, with whom he had so much in common. And so, Wells had made up his mind to end his dissuasive silence, which had evidently done no good, and to accept Serviss's invitation. Here was the perfect opportunity to sit down with Serviss and tell him what he really thought of his novel. So the man wanted his opinion, did he? Well, he'd give it to him, then. Wells could imagine how the luncheon would go: he would sit opposite Serviss, with unflappable composure, and in a calm voice politely masking his rage, would tell him how appalled he was that Serviss had chosen an idealized version of Edison as the hero of his novel. In

Wells's view, the inventor of the electric lightbulb was an untrustworthy, bad-tempered fellow who created his inventions at the expense of others and who had a penchant for designing lethal weapons. Wells would tell Serviss that from any point of view the novel's complete lack of literary merit and its diabolical plot made it an unworthy successor to his own. He would tell him that the message contained in its meager, repugnant pages was diametrically opposed to his and had more in common with a jingoistic pamphlet, since its childish moral boiled down to this: it was unwise to step on the toes of Thomas Edison or of the United States of America. And furthermore he would tell him all this with the added satisfaction of knowing that after he had unburdened himself, the excoriated Serviss would be the one paying for his lunch.

The author had been so wrapped up in his own thoughts that when he returned to reality he discovered his feet had taken him into Greek Street, where he found himself standing in front of the old, forgotten theater at number twelve. But do not be taken in by the look of surprise on Wells's face: this was no coincidence, for in his life every action had a purpose; nothing was left to chance or impulse. However much he now tried to blame his innocent feet, Wells had gone there with the precise intention of finding that very theater, whose façade he now contemplated with what could only be described as somber rage. Consider yourselves welcome, then, and prepare for a tale packed with thrills and excitement, both for those ladies of a sentimental nature who will enjoy the romantic exploits of the charming and skeptical Miss Harlow, to whom I will have the pleasure of introducing you later on, and for the more intrepid gentlemen, who will undoubtedly tremble at the weird and wonderful adventures of our characters, such as this thin little man with a birdlike face, solemnly contemplating the theater. Observe him carefully, then. Observe his thin blond mustache with which he attempts to impose a more adult appearance on his childlike features, his finely drawn mouth and bright, lively eyes, behind which it is impossible not to perceive a sparkling intellect as sharp as it is impractical. In spite of his ordinary, less-than-heroic looks, Wells will play the most important role in this tale, the exact beginning of which is difficult to pinpoint, but which for him (and for our purposes) begins on this quiet morning in 1898, an unusually glorious morning, in which, as you can see, there is nothing to suggest to the author that in less than two hours' time, he will discover something so astonishing that it will forever alter his deepest-held beliefs.

But I will stop beating about the bush and reveal to you what you have no doubt been puzzling over for the past few minutes: why has Wells paused? Is he perhaps regretting the closure of the venue where he had spent so many nights enjoying the best stage plays of the time? Not a bit. As you will discover, Wells was not easily prone to nostalgia. He had come to a halt outside that old theater because, some years earlier, it had become home to a very special company: Murray's Time Travel. Do the smiles playing on the lips of some of you mean the aforementioned establishment is already familiar to you? However, I must show consideration to the rest of my readers, and since, along with the knowing smiles, I noticed more than a few raised eyebrows, no doubt occasioned by the company's curious name, I must hasten to explain to any newcomers that this extravagant enterprise had opened its doors to the public with the intention of realizing what is perhaps Man's most ambitious dream: traveling in time. A desire that Wells himself had awoken in the public with his first novel, *The Time Machine*. Murray's Time Travel's introductory offer consisted of a trip to the future: to the twentieth of May in the year 2000, to be precise, the day when the decisive battle for the future of the world would take place, as depicted on the billboard still attached to the side of the building. This showed the brave Captain Shackleton brandishing his sword against his arch enemy Solomon, king of the automatons. It would be a century before that memorable battle took place, in which the captain would succeed in saving the human race from extinction, although, thanks to Murray's Time Travel, almost the whole of England had already witnessed it. Regardless of the exorbitant cost of the tickets, people had thronged outside the old theater, eager to watch the battle their wretched mortal existences would have prevented them from seeing, as though it were a fashionable new opera. Wells must have been the only man on Earth who hadn't shed a tear for that over-sized braggart, in whose memory a statue had been erected in a nearby square. There he stood, on a pedestal shaped like a clock, smiling self-importantly, one huge paw tickling the air, as though conjuring a spell, the other resting on the head of Eternal, his dog, for whom Wells couldn't help feeling a similar aversion.

And so, Wells had come to a halt there because that theater reminded him of the consequences he had already unleashed by giving someone his true opinion of his novel. For, prior to becoming the Master of Time, Gilliam Murray had been a young man with somewhat more modest pretensions: he had wanted to become a writer. That was the time when Wells had first met him, three years earlier. The future millionaire had petitioned Wells to help him publish a turgid novel he had written, but Wells had refused and, unable to help himself, had told Murray per-haps rather more bluntly than necessary what he thought of his work. Not surprisingly, his brutal sincerity had turned the two men into en-emies. Wells had learned a lesson from the experience: in certain situa-tions it was better to lie. What good had come of telling Murray what he thought? And what good would come of telling Serviss the truth? he now wondered. Lying was undoubtedly preferable. Yet while Wells was able to lie unhesitatingly in many situations, there was one thing he couldn't help being honest about: if he didn't like a novel, he was incapa-ble of pretending he did. He believed taste defined who he was, and he couldn't bear to be taken for someone whose taste was appalling enough for him to enjoy *Edison's Conquest of Mars*.

LOOKING DOWN AT HIS watch, the author realized he had no time to dawdle at the theater or he would be late for his appointment. He cast a final glance at the building and made his way down Charing Cross Road, leaving Soho behind as he headed for the Strand and the pub where he was to meet Serviss. Wells had planned to keep the journalist waiting in order to make it clear from the start he despised what he had done, but if there was one thing Wells hated more than lying about his likes and dislikes, it was being late for an appointment. This was because he somehow believed that owing to a cosmic law of equilibrium, if he was punctual, he in turn would not be made to wait. However, until then he had been unable to prove that the one thing influenced the other, and more than once he had been forced to stand on a corner like a sad fool or sit like an impoverished diner in a busy restaurant. And so, Wells strode briskly across the noisy Strand, where the hurly-burly of the whole universe appeared to be concentrated, and trotted down the alleyway to the pub, enabling him to arrive at the meeting with irreproachable punctuality, if a little short of breath.

Since he had no idea what Serviss looked like, he did not waste time peering through the windows—a routine he had developed to establish whether whomever he was meeting had arrived or not: if he hadn't, Wells would rush off down the nearest street and return a few moments later at a calm pace, thus avoiding the need to wait inside and be subjected to the pitiful looks of the other diners. As there was no point in going through this procedure today, Wells entered the pub with a look of urbane assurance, pausing in the middle of the room so that Serviss might easily spot him, and glanced with vague curiosity about the crowded room, hoping the American had already arrived and that he would be spared the need to wander round the tavern with everyone staring at him. As luck would have it, almost at once, a skinny, diminutive man of about fifty, with the look of someone to whom life has been unkind, raised his right arm to greet Wells, while beneath his bushy whiskers his lips produced a wan smile. Realizing this must be Serviss, Wells stifled a grimace of dismay. He would rather his enemy had an intimidating and arrogant appearance, incapable of arousing pity, than this destitute air of an undernourished buzzard. In order to rid himself of the inevitable feeling of pity the scrawny little fellow inspired, Wells had to remind himself of what the man had done, and he walked over to the table in an alcove where the man was waiting. Seeing Wells approach, Serviss opened his arms wide and a grotesque smile spread across his face, like that of an orphan wanting to be adopted.

"What an honor and a pleasure, Mr. Wells!" he exclaimed, performing a series of reverential gestures, stopping just short of bowing. "You don't know how glad I am to meet you. Take a seat, won't you. How about a pint? Waiter, another round, please; we should drink properly to this meeting of literary giants. The world would never forgive itself if our lofty reflections were allowed to run dry for lack of a drink." After this clumsy speech, which caused the waiter, a fellow who unequivocally earned his living in the physical world, to look at them with the disdain he reserved for those working in such airy-fairy matters as the arts, Serviss gazed at Wells with his rather small eyes. "Tell me, George—I can call you George, right?—how does it feel when one of your novels makes the whole world tremble in its shoes? What's your secret? Do you write with a pen from another planet? Ha, ha, ha . . ."

Wells did not deign to laugh at his joke. Leaning back in his chair he waited for Serviss's shrill laughter to die out, adopting an expression more befitting a pallbearer than someone about to have lunch with an acquaintance.

"Well, well, I didn't mean to upset you, George," Serviss went on, pretending to be put out by Wells's coldness. "I just can't help showing my admiration."

"As far as I am concerned you can save your praise," Wells retorted, resolving to take charge of the conversation. "The fact that you have written a sequel to my latest novel speaks for itself, Mr. Ser—"

"Call me Garrett, George, please."

"Very well, Garrett," Wells agreed, annoyed at Serviss for forcing this familiarity on him, which was inappropriate to an ear bashing, and for the jolly air he insisted on imposing on the conversation. "As I was saying—"

"But there's no such thing as too much praise, right, George?" the American interrupted once more. "Especially when it's deserved, as in your case. I confess my admiration for you isn't an overnight thing. It began . . . when? A couple of years back, at least, after I read *The Time Machine,* an even more extraordinary work for being your first."

Wells nodded indifferently, taking advantage of Serviss having stopped his salesman's patter to take a swig of beer. He had to find a way of breaking off Serviss's incessant prattle to tell him what he thought of his novel. The longer he waited, the more awkward it would be for them both. But the American was unrelenting.

"And what a happy coincidence that just after you published your novel, someone found a way of traveling in time," he said, bobbing his head in an exaggerated fashion, as though he were still recovering from the shock. "I guess you took a trip to the year two thousand to witness the epic battle for the future of mankind, right?"

"No, I never traveled in time."

"You didn't? Why ever not?" the other man asked, astonished.

Wells paused for a few moments, remembering how during the days when Murray's Time Travel was still open for business he had been forced to maintain an impassive silence whenever someone alluded to it with an ecstatic smile on his or her face. On such occasions, which occurred with exasperating regularity, Wells invariably responded with a couple of sarcastic remarks aimed at puncturing the enthusiasm of the person addressing him, as though he himself were above reality, or one step ahead of it, but in any event unaffected by its vagaries. And wasn't that what the hoi polloi expected of writers, to whom by default they attributed loftier interests than their own more pedestrian ones? On other occasions, when he wasn't in the mood for sarcasm, Wells pretended to take exception to the exorbitant price of the tickets. This was the approach he decided to adopt with Serviss, who, being a writer himself, was likely to be unconvinced by the former.

"Because the future belongs to all of us, and I don't believe the price of a ticket should deprive anyone of seeing it."

Serviss looked at him, puzzled, then rubbed his face with a sudden gesture, as though a cobweb had stuck to it.

"Ah, of course! Forgive my tactlessness, George: the tickets were too dear for poor writers like us," he said, misinterpreting Wells's remark. "To be honest, I couldn't afford one myself. Although I did begin saving up in order to be able to climb aboard the famous *Cronotilus,* you know? I wanted to see the battle for the future. I really did. I even planned mischievously to break away from the group once I was there, in order to shake Captain Shackleton's hand and thank him for making sure all our prayers didn't fall on deaf ears. For could we have carried on inventing things and producing works of art had we known that in the year two thousand no human being would be left alive on Earth to enjoy them—that because of those evil automatons, Man and everything he had ever achieved would have been wiped away as though it had never even existed?" With this, Serviss appeared to sink back into his chair, before continuing in a melancholy voice. "As it is, you and I will no longer be able to travel to the future, George. A great shame, as I expect you could more than afford it now. I guess it must have pained you as much as it did me to find out that the time travel company closed down after Mr. Murray passed away."

"Yes, a great pity," Wells replied sardonically.

"The newspapers said he'd been eaten alive by one of those dragons in the fourth dimension," Serviss recalled mournfully, "in front of several of his employees, who could do nothing to save him. It must have been awful."

Yes, thought Wells, Murray certainly engineered a dramatic death for himself.

"And how will we get into the fourth dimension now?" asked Serviss. "Do you think it will remain sealed off forever?"

"I've no idea," Wells replied coldly.

"Well, perhaps we'll witness other things. Perhaps our fate will be to travel in space, not time," Serviss consoled himself, finishing up his pint. "The sky is a vast and infinite place. And full of surprises, isn't that right, George?"

"Possibly," Wells agreed, stirring uneasily in his seat, as though his buttocks were scalding. "But I'd like to talk to you about your novel, Mr. Ser— Garrett."

Serviss suddenly sat bolt upright and stared at Wells attentively, like a beagle scenting a trail. Relieved to have finally caught the man's attention, Wells downed the last of his beer in order to give himself the courage and composure he needed to broach the subject. His gesture did not escape Serviss's notice.

"Waiter, another round, please, the world's greatest living writer is thirsty!" he cried, waving his arms about frantically to catch the waiter's eye. Then he looked back at Wells full of anticipation. "So, my friend, did you like my novel?"

Wells remained silent while the waiter placed two more tankards on the table and cast him an admiring glance. Realizing he was under scrutiny, Wells automatically sat up straight, surreptitiously puffing out his chest, as though his greatness as a writer must be evinced not only in his books but in his physical appearance.

"Well . . . ," Wells began, once the waiter had moved away, noticing that Serviss was watching him anxiously.

"Well, what?" the other man inquired with childlike anticipation.

"Some of it is . . ." The two men's eyes met for a moment and a cavernous silence grew between them before Wells continued: ". . . excellent."

"Some. Of. It. Is. Excellent," Serviss repeated, savoring each word dreamily. "Such as what, for instance?"

Wells took another swig of his beer to buy himself time. What the devil was there of any excellence in Serviss's novel?

"The space suits. Or the oxygen pills," he replied, because the only salvageable thing in the novel was its paraphernalia. "They are very . . . ingenious."

"Why, thank you, George! I knew you'd love my story," Serviss trilled, almost in raptures. "Could it have been otherwise? I doubt it. You and I are twin souls, in a literary sense, of course. Although who knows in what other ways . . . Oh, my friend, don't you see we're creating something hitherto unknown? Our stories will soon move away from the common path of literature and forge a new one of their own. You and I are making History, George. We'll be considered the fathers of a new genre. Together with Jules Verne, of course. We mustn't forget the Frenchman. The three of us, the three of us together are changing the course of literature."

"I have no interest in creating a new genre," Wells interrupted, increasingly annoyed at himself for his failure to steer the conversation in the direction he wanted.

"Well, I don't think we have much choice in the matter," objected Serviss with finality. "Let's talk about your latest novel, George. Those Martian ships like stingrays floating over London are so startling . . . But first I'd like to ask you something: aren't you afraid that if, after you wrote *The Time Machine,* someone discovered a way of traveling in time, then the next thing will be a Martian invasion?"

Wells stared at him blankly, trying to decide whether he was in earnest or whether this was another of his crazy ideas, but Serviss waited solemnly for him to reply.

"The fact that I wrote about a Martian invasion doesn't mean I believe in life on Mars, Garrett," he explained frostily. "It's a simple allegory. I chose Mars more as a metaphor, to lay emphasis on the god of war, and because of its redness."

"Ah, the iron oxide in the volcanic basalt rock covering its surface like damned lichen and giving it that disconcerting appearance," Serviss replied, airing his knowledge.

"My sole intention was to criticize Europe's colonization of Africa," Wells resumed, ignoring him, "and to warn of the perils of developing new weapons at a time when Germany is engaging in a process of militarization, which seems to me unsettling to say the least. But above all, Garrett, I wanted to warn mankind that everything around us, our science, our religion, could prove ineffectual in the face of something as unimaginable as an attack by a superior race."

He failed to add that, while he had been at it, he had allowed himself to settle a few old scores: the first scenes of Martian destruction, such as

Horsell and Addlestone, were places where he had spent his rather un-happy childhood.

"And boy, did you succeed, George!" Serviss acknowledged with gloomy admiration. "That's why I had to write my sequel: I had to give back the hope you took away from Man."

And that hope was Edison? Wells thought, grudgingly amused, as he felt a vague sense of well-being course through him. He couldn't tell whether this was a result of the tankards starting to clutter the table-top, or the little man's delightful habit of agreeing with every word he said. Whatever the reason, he couldn't deny he was beginning to feel at ease. He wasn't sure how they had succeeded in discussing the subject of Serviss's novel without incident, but they had. Although how could it have been otherwise, he asked himself, if the only word he had man-aged to mutter was "excellent"? Consequently, Serviss now believed this was Wells's true opinion of his novel, and he hadn't the energy to take issue with his own words. He didn't want to do that to Serviss. The man might deserve some punishment for having the nerve to write a sequel to his novel, but Wells didn't think he would derive any pleasure from exacting it. Then he recalled how the novel's outlandish humor, which, although clearly unintentional, had brought a fleeting smile to his lips several times while he was reading it. And although on various occasions he had hurled the thing against the wall, exasperated at such exemplary inelegance and stupidity, he had always picked it up and carried on read-ing. He found something oddly likable about the way Serviss wrote. It was the same with his absurd letters. Wells invariably ended up throw-ing them on the fire, yet he couldn't help reading them first.

"Didn't it occur to you at some point to give the story a different ending, one in which we managed to defeat the Martians?" said Serviss, interrupting his reverie.

"What?" Wells declared. "What hope do we Earthlings have of de-feating the Martian technology I described?"

Serviss shrugged, unable to reply.

"In any event, I felt it was my duty to offer an alternative, a ray of hope . . . ," Serviss finally muttered, contemplating with a faint smile the crowd in the pub. "Like any other man here, I'd like to think that if someday we were invaded from the sky, we'd have some hope of survival."

"Perhaps we would," Wells said, softening. "But my mistrust of Man is too great, Garrett. If there was a way of defeating the Martians, I'm sure it would be no thanks to us. Who knows, perhaps help would come from the most unexpected quarter. Besides, why does it worry you so much? Do you really believe our neighbors from Mars are going to invade us?"

"Of course I do, George," Serviss replied solemnly. "Although I suppose it'll happen after the year two thousand. First we have to deal with the automatons."

"The automatons? Oh yes, of course . . . the automatons."

"But there's no question in my mind that sooner or later they'll invade," Serviss insisted. "Don't you believe, as Lowell maintains in his book, that the canals on Mars were built by an intelligent life-form?"

Wells had read Percival Lowell's book *Mars,* in which he set out this idea; in fact he had used it to substantiate his own novel, but it was a long way from there to believing in life on Mars.

"I don't suppose the purpose of the many millions of planets in the universe is simply to create a pretty backdrop," replied Wells, who considered discussions about the existence of life on other planets a pointless exercise. "Nor is it unreasonable to imagine that hundreds of them probably enjoy the conditions essential for supporting life. However, if Mars is anything to go by . . ."

"And they don't necessarily need oxygen or water," Serviss observed excitedly. "Here on our planet we have creatures, like anaerobic bacteria, that can live without oxygen. That would already double the number of planets able to support life. There could be more than a hundred thousand civilizations out there that are more advanced than ours, George. And I'm sure generations to come will discover abundant and unexpected life on other planets, although we won't live to see it, and they'll come to accept with resignation that they aren't the only intelligent, let alone the oldest, life-form in the Cosmos."

"I agree, Garrett," Wells conceded, "but I am also convinced that such 'civilizations' would have nothing in common with ours. We would be as hard put to understand them as a dog would the workings of a steam engine. For example, they may have no desire to explore space at all, while we gaze endlessly at the stars and wonder if we are alone in the universe, as Galileo himself did."

"Yes, although he was careful not to do it too audibly, for fear of upsetting the church," Serviss quipped.

A smile fluttered across Wells's lips, and he discovered that the drink had relaxed his facial muscles. Serviss had extracted a smile from him fair and square, and there it must stay.

"Of course, what we can't deny is Man's eagerness to communicate with supposed creatures from outer space," Serviss said, after managing to make two fresh pints brimming with beer appear on the table, as if out of nowhere. "Do you remember the attempts by that German mathematician to reflect light from the sun onto other planets with a device he invented called a heliotrope? What was the fellow's name again? Grove?"

"Grau. Or Gauss," Wells ventured.

"That's it, Gauss. His name was Karl Gauss."

"He also suggested planting an enormous right-angled triangle of pine trees on the Russian steppe, so that observers from other worlds would know there were beings on Earth capable of understanding the Pythagorean theorem," Wells recalled.

"Yes, that's right," Serviss added. "He claimed no geometrical shape could be interpreted as an unintentional construction."

"And what about that astronomer who had the bright idea of digging a circular canal in the Sahara Desert, then filling it with kerosene and lighting it at night to show our location?"

"Yes, and a perfect target!"

Wells gave a slight chuckle. Serviss responded by downing the rest of his beer and urged Wells to do the same. Wells obeyed, somewhat abashed.

"The last I heard they are going to hang reflectors on the Eiffel Tower to shine light from the Sun onto Mars," he remarked, while Serviss ordered another round.

"Good heavens, they never give up!" Serviss exclaimed, thrusting another pint toward Wells.

"You can say that again," Wells seconded, noticing with alarm that he was beginning to have difficulty speaking without slurring his words. "We seem to think here on Earth that beings in space will be able to see anything we come up with."

"As if they spend all their money on telescopes!" Serviss joked.

Wells couldn't help letting out a guffaw. Infected by his laughter, Serviss began slapping his hand on the tabletop, causing enough din to elicit a few disapproving looks from the waiter and some of the other diners. These censorious looks, however, appeared not to intimidate Serviss, who slapped the table even harder, a defiant expression on his face. Wells gazed at him contentedly, like a proud father admiring his son's antics.

"Well, well . . . so, you don't think anyone would go to the trouble of invading a tiny planet like ours, lost in the infinity of the Cosmos, is that it, George?" Serviss said, trying to sum up once he had managed to calm down.

"I think it unlikely. Bear in mind that things never turn out the way we imagine. It is almost a mathematical law. Accordingly, Earth will never be invaded by Martians like it was in my book, for example."

"Won't it?"

"Never," Wells said resolutely. "Look at all the novels currently being churned out about contact with other worlds, Garrett. Apparently, anyone can write one. If future encounters were to take place with beings from outer space identical to the ones we authors have written about, it would be a case of literary premonition, don't you think?"

At this, he took a swig of beer, with the nagging impression that what he had just said was no more than harebrained nonsense.

"Yes," agreed Serviss, giving no sign that he considered Wells's disquisition outlandish. "Our naïve rulers will quite possibly end up believing that evil beings from outer space have filled our subconscious minds with these imaginings, by means of ultrasonic rays or hypnosis, perhaps in preparation for a future invasion."

"In all likelihood!" Wells burst out laughing, at which Serviss began slapping the table once more, to the despair of the waiter and the nearest customers.

"Consequently, as I was saying," Wells resumed after Serviss stopped making a din, "even if there is life on Mars or on some other planet in our vast solar system . . ." He made a grandiose gesture toward the sky and seemed annoyed to encounter the tavern ceiling with its plain wooden beams. He gazed at it in dismay for a few moments. "Damnation . . . what was I saying?"

"Something about Mars . . . I think," Serviss added, looking up at the ceiling with equal misgivings.

"Oh, yes, Mars," Wells remembered at last. "I mean, assuming there was life there, it would probably be impossible to compare it with life here, and therefore envisaging spaceships engineered by Martians is absurd."

"All right. But what if I told you," Serviss said, trying to keep a straight face, "that you're mistaken?"

"Mistaken? You *could not* say I am mistaken, my dear Garrett."

"Unless I was able to back it up, my dear George."

Wells nodded, and Serviss leaned back in his seat, smiling enigmatically.

"Did you know that as a youth I was obsessed with the idea of life on other planets?" he confessed.

"You don't say?" Wells retorted, a foolish grin on his face.

"Yes, I hunted through newspapers, treatises, and old essays looking for"—he pondered the best word to use—"signs. Did you know, for example, that in 1518 something described as 'a kind of star' appeared in the sky above the conquistador Juan de Grijalva's ship, before moving away leaving a trail of fire and throwing a beam of light down to Earth?"

Wells feigned surprise: "Heavens, I had no idea!"

Serviss smiled disdainfully in response to Wells's mockery.

"I could cite dozens of similar examples from my compilation of past sightings of flying machines from other worlds, George," he assured him, the smile still on his lips. "But that isn't why I'm convinced beings from the sky have already visited Earth."

"Why then?"

Serviss leaned across the table, lowering his voice to a whisper: "Because I've seen a Martian."

"Ho, ho, ho . . . Where, at the theater perhaps? Or walking along the street? Perhaps it is the queen's new pet dog?"

"I mean it, George," Serviss said, straightening up and beaming at him. "I've seen one."

"You're drunk!"

"I'm not drunk, George! Not enough not to know what I'm talking about at any rate. And I tell you I saw a darned Martian. Right in front of my very eyes. Why, I even touched it with my own hands," he insisted, holding them aloft.

Wells looked at him gravely for a few moments before bursting into loud peals of laughter, causing half the other customers to jump.

"You are a terribly amusing fellow, Garrett," he declared after he had recovered. "Why, I think I might even forgive you for writing a novel in order to profit from—"

"It was about ten years ago, I forget the exact date," Serviss said, ignoring Wells's banter. "I was spending a few days in London at the time, carrying out some research at the Natural History Museum for a series of articles I was writing."

Realizing that Serviss wasn't joking, Wells sat up straight in his chair and listened attentively, while he felt the pub floor rock gently beneath him, as though they were drinking beer on a boat sailing down a river. Had this fellow really seen a Martian?

"As you know, the museum was built to house an increasingly large number of fossils and skeletons that wouldn't fit in the British Museum," Serviss went on dreamily. "The whole place looked new, and the exhibits were wonderfully informative, as though they really wanted to show visitors what the world was about in an orderly but entertaining fashion. I would stroll happily through the rooms and corridors, aware of the fact that numerous explorers had risked life and limb so that a handful of West End ladies could feel a thrill of excitement as they watched a procession of marabunta ants. A whole host of marvels beckoned from the display cases, stirring in me a longing for adventure, a desire to discover distant lands, which, fortunately, my affection for the comforts of civilization ended up stifling. Was it worth missing the whole theater season just to see a gibbon swinging from branch to branch? Why travel so far when others were willing to endure hammering rain, freezing temperatures, and bizarre diseases to bring back almost every exotic object under the sun? And so I contented myself with observing the varied contents of the display cases like any other philistine. Although what really interested me wasn't exhibited in any of them."

Wells gazed at Serviss in respectful silence, not wishing to interrupt him until he had heard the end of the story. He had experienced something similar himself on his first visit to the museum.

"On the second or third day, I began to notice that, from time to time, the head curator of the museum would discreetly lead groups of visitors down to the basement. And I have to tell you that among those groups I recognized a few eminent scientists and even the odd minister. As well as the head curator, two Scotland Yard inspectors always accompanied the visitors. As you can imagine, these strange and regular processions to the basement aroused my curiosity, so that one afternoon, I stopped what I was doing and took the risk of following them downstairs. The procession walked through a maze of corridors until it reached a locked door. When the group came to a halt, the older of the inspectors, a stout fellow with a conspicuous patch over one eye, gave a command to the other one, a mere stripling. The younger man assiduously removed a key from a chain around his neck, unlocked the door, and ushered the group inside, closing the door behind him. I questioned several museum employees and found out that no one was completely sure what was inside the room, which they dubbed the Chamber of Marvels. When I asked the head curator what it contained, his response took me aback. "Things people would never have thought existed," he said with a self-satisfied grin, and then he suggested I carry on marveling at the plants and insects in the display cases, for there were some frontiers beyond which not everybody was ready to cross. As you will understand, his response angered me, as did the fact that he never extended me the courtesy of inviting me to join one of the groups that were so regularly given access to the unknown. Apparently I wasn't as important as all those great men of science who deserved a guided tour. And so I swallowed my pride and got used to the idea of returning to the States having only discovered what a group of insensitive bureaucrats wanted me to know about the world. However, unlike the museum's head curator, Fate must have considered it important for me to find out what was inside that chamber. Otherwise I can't understand how I got in there so easily."

"How did you get in?" Wells asked, astonished.

"On my last day in London, I happened to find myself in the elevator with the younger of the two Scotland Yard inspectors. I tried to persuade him to talk about the chamber he was guarding, but to no avail. The youth would give nothing away. He even refused my invitation to have a beer at a nearby pub, with the excuse that he only drank sarsaparilla. Well, who drinks sarsaparilla these days? Anyway, as we stepped out of the elevator, he said good-bye politely and began walking down the corridor toward the exit, oblivious to the deeply resentful look I was giving him. Then, to my astonishment, I saw him pause, his legs swaying beneath him as though he were suddenly unsure of where he was going, before collapsing like a marionette with its strings cut. I was in shock, as you can imagine. I thought he had dropped dead before my eyes, from a massive heart attack or something. I ran over and unbuttoned his shirt collar with the idea of testing his pulse, only to find to my great relief that he was still alive. He had simply fainted like a lady whose corset is too tight. Blood was streaming down his face, but I soon realized it came from a cut on his eyebrow, which must have happened when he fell."

"Perhaps he had a sudden drop in blood pressure. Or was suffering from heat stroke," Wells suggested.

"Possibly, possibly," Serviss replied distractedly. "And then—"

"Or low blood sugar. Although I am inclined to think—"

"What the hell does it matter what it was, George! He fainted and that's that!" Serviss said, irritated, keen to go on with his story.

"I'm sorry, Garrett," said Wells, somewhat cowed. "Do carry on."

"Good, where was I?" muttered Serviss. "Oh, yes, I was concerned. But that concern soon gave way to something more like greed when I noticed a strange gold key decorated with a pair of pretty little angel's wings hanging from the inspector's neck. I immediately realized that the charming key was the one he had used to open the Chamber of Marvels."

"And you stole it from him!" Wells said, shocked.

"Well . . ." Serviss shrugged, unbuttoning his shirt collar to reveal a delicate chain from which hung the key he had just described.

"I couldn't resist it, George," he explained, with theatrical remorse. "It wasn't as if I was stealing a pair of shoes from a dead man. After all, the inspector had only fainted."

Wells shook his head in disapproval. Considering the liberal amounts of alcohol he had imbibed, this proved a perilous gesture, as his head began to spin even more, giving him the impression he was sitting on a merry-go-round horse.

Serviss went on. "That's how I got into the room where, for many reasons, they hide away all the things they don't want the world to know about. And, take my word for it, George, if you saw what they've got hidden in there, you'd never write another fantasy novel."

Wells looked at him skeptically, straightening in his chair.

"But that's the least of it," Serviss went on. "What really mattered stood in the corner of the room on a pedestal. An enormous flying machine. Very strange looking. And whether or not it could actually fly was a mere suspicion in the minds of the scientists who had been privileged to examine it, as far as I could gather from reading the notebooks and papers listing all the details of the discovery, which I found lying on a nearby table. Unlike the *Albatross* in Verne's *Robur the Conqueror*, this machine had neither wings nor propellers. And no balloon either. In fact it looked more like a plate."

"A plate?" Wells asked in astonishment.

"Yes, a soup plate. Or to be more precise a saucer. Like the ones you Britishers use under your teacups," Serviss added.

"In short, a flying saucer," Wells said, eager for him to go on.

"Precisely. According to what I read in the notebooks, an expedition of some years past to the South Pole found the machine buried in the Antarctic ice. It appeared to have crashed into a mountain range inland, which is what led them to believe the thing could fly. Except they were unable to open it, because there was no hatch or anything resembling a door."

"I see. But what made them think it came from another planet?" Wells asked. "Couldn't it have been built in Germany? The Germans are always experimenting with—"

"No, George." Serviss butted in forcefully. "One look was enough to see the thing had been built using technology far superior to anything the Germans, or for that matter any country on Earth, could possibly possess. For example, there's nothing to suggest it is steam driven. But in any case, it wasn't only its appearance that made them think it came from space."

"Really? What then?"

Serviss paused for dramatic effect, using the opportunity to take a swig of beer.

"They found the machine not far from a vessel, the *Annawan,* that had set sail from New York Harbor on October 15, 1829, on an exploratory voyage from which she never returned. The ship had caught fire, and the crew had perished. The frozen bodies of the sailors lay scattered about, half buried in the ice. Most were charred, but those that weren't still wore a look of terror on their faces, as if they had been fleeing the fire . . . or who knows what other horrors. They also found the bodies of several dogs, their limbs mysteriously torn off. The members of the expedition described the scene as gruesome. But the real discovery came a few days later, when they found the probable pilot of the machine buried in the ice nearby. And I can assure you he wasn't German, George: I knew that as soon as I opened the casket where he's kept."

Serviss paused once more and gave Wells a warm, almost affectionate smile, as if to apologize for scaring him. Wells looked at him with as much trepidation as his drunkenness would allow.

"And what did he look like . . . ?" he asked in a faint voice.

"Needless to say, nothing like the Martians you describe in your novel, George. In fact, he reminded me of a darker, more sophisticated version of Spring-Heeled Jack. Have you heard of Spring-Heeled Jack, that peculiar jumping creature that terrorized London about sixty years ago?"

Wells nodded, unable to fathom what possible similarity there might be between the two.

"Yes, they said he had springs on his feet, which allowed him to take great leaps."

"And that he would spring out of nowhere in front of young girls, and caress their bodies lasciviously before disappearing again. Many depicted him as diabolical, with pointed ears and clawed hands."

"I suppose that was a result of the hysteria at the time," Wells reflected. "The man was probably a circus acrobat who decided to use his skills to sate his appetites."

"Probably, George, probably. But the thing in the museum reminded me of the monstrous version the illustrators of the more salacious newspapers and magazines produced. I saw copies of those old newspapers when I was a child, and Jack's appearance made my blood run cold. But, yes, perhaps that similarity is only visible to me, and it comes from my deepest fears."

"So what you are saying," Wells said, attempting to sum up, "is that there is a Martian in the Natural History Museum?"

"Yes. Only it's dead, of course," Serviss replied, as though somehow that made it less appealing. "Actually, it's little more than a dried-up kind of humanoid. The only thing that might offer some interesting revelations is the inside of the machine. Maybe it contains a clue as to the Martian's origins, or some maps of space, or something. Who knows? And we mustn't forget what a step forward it would be for human science if we were able to figure out how it worked. But unfortunately they can't open it. I don't know whether they're still trying, or whether they've given up and both machine and Martian are gathering dust in the museum. Whatever happens, the fact is, my dear George, that thing didn't come from Earth."

"A Martian!" Wells said, finally giving free rein to his bewilderment when he realized Serviss had come to the end of his story. "Good God in Heaven!"

"That's right, George, a Martian, a hideous, horrible Martian," Serviss confirmed. "And this key can take us to him. Although I only saw him that one time; I haven't used the key since. I just keep it round my neck like a lucky charm, to remind me that there are more impossible things in the world than we story writers could ever imagine."

He unfastened the chain and handed it to Wells ceremoniously, like someone surrendering a sacred object. Wells examined it carefully with the same solemnity.

"I'm convinced the true history of our time isn't what we read in newspapers or books," he rambled, while Wells went on examining the key. "True history is almost invisible. It flows like an underground spring. It takes place in the shadows, and in silence, George. And only a chosen few know what that history is."

He deftly snatched the key from Wells and placed it in his jacket pocket. Then he said with a mischievous grin: "Do you want to see the Martian?"

"Right now?"

"Why not? I doubt you'll have another chance, George."

Wells looked at him uneasily. He needed time to digest what Serviss had told him. Or to be more precise, he needed a couple of hours for everything to stop spinning, for his head to clear so that he could judge the American's story rationally. Perhaps he might then refute it, for it was true that in his present alcoholic haze it felt extremely pleasant to believe that the impossible could form part of reality. Indeed, in his current state of calm euphoria, Wells rejoiced at the thought that the world he was compelled to live in had a hidden dimension, and that the frontiers erected by Man's reason to define its boundaries might suddenly collapse, mingling the two worlds to form a new reality, a reality where magic floated in the air and fantasy novels were simply true accounts of their authors' experiences. Is that what Serviss was saying? Was that nondescript little man guiding him, like the White Rabbit in *Alice in Wonderland,* to his warren, where Wells would enter a world in which anything was possible? A world ruled over by a far more imaginative God than the current one? Yet that reality did not exist, it *could not* exist, much as it seemed to him now the most natural thing in the world.

"Are you afraid?" Serviss inquired, surprised. "Ah, I see, perhaps this is all too much for you, George. Perhaps you prefer your monsters to stay safely within the confines of your imagination, where the most they can do is send a shiver down the spines of your readers. Perhaps you haven't the courage to face them in reality, off the page."

"Of course I have, Garrett," Wells retorted, irritated at Serviss's presumption. "It is just that—"

"Don't worry, George. I understand, I really do." Serviss tried to console him. "Seeing a Martian is a terrifying experience. It's one thing to write about them, and quite another to—"

"Of course I can face them in reality, confound it!" Wells cried, leaping unsteadily to his feet. "We shall go to the museum this instant, Garrett, and you can show me your Martian!"

Serviss looked up at him with amusement, then rose to his feet with the same gusto.

"All right, George, it's up to you!" he roared, barely able to stand up straight. "Waiter, the bill! And be quick about it, my friend and I have an appointment with a creature from the stars!"

Wells tried to dissuade him from another outburst, but Serviss had already turned toward the other tables.

"Does anyone here wish to accompany us? Does anyone else wish to see a Martian?" he declared to the astonished customers, spreading his arms. "If so, come with me, and I'll show you a bona fide inhabitant of the planet Mars!"

"Shut your mouth, tosspot!" someone bawled from the back of the room.

"Go home and sleep it off, leave us to eat in peace!" another man suggested.

"You see, George?" Serviss said, disheartened, hurling a handful of coins onto the table and weaving his way over to the door, head held high. "Nobody wants to know, nobody. People prefer living in ignorance. Well, let them!" He paused at the door, jabbing a finger at the customers as he tried not to fall over. "Go on with your miserable lives, fools! Stay in your rotten reality!"

Wells noticed a few burly looking characters making as if to get up, with what seemed like a none-too-friendly attitude. He leapt forward and began wrestling Serviss's skinny frame out of the pub, gesturing to the locals to keep calm. Out in the street, he stopped the first cab he saw, pushed Serviss inside, and shouted their destination to the driver. The American fell sideways onto the seat. He remained in that position for a while, his head propped against the window, grinning foolishly at Wells, who had sat down opposite him in an equally graceless posture. The jolting of the coach as it went round Green Park sobered them slightly.

They began laughing over the spectacle they had created in the pub, and, still fueled by drink, spent the rest of the journey inventing crazy theories as to why beings from Mars, or from some other planet, would want to visit Earth. The carriage pulled up in the Cromwell Road in front of a magnificent Romanesque Revival structure whose façade was decorated with friezes of plants and animals. Wells and Serviss got out and tottered toward the entrance, while the driver stared after them aghast. The man's name was Neal Hamilton, he was approximately forty years of age, and his life would never be the same again. For he had just overheard those two respectable, sophisticated-looking gentlemen confirm that life had been brought to Earth in vast flying machines by intelligent beings from outer space, whose responsibility it was to populate the universe and make it flourish. Neal cracked his whip and headed home, where a few hours later, glass in hand, he would gaze up at the starry sky and wonder for the first time in his life who he was, where he came from, and even why he had chosen to be a cabdriver.

ENVELOPED IN A THICK haze, Wells allowed Serviss to lead him through the galleries. In his current state, he was scarcely aware of what was going on. The world had taken on a surreal quality: objects had lost their meaning, and everything was at once familiar and alien. One moment he had the impression of walking through the famous whale room, filled with skeletons and life-sized models of cetaceans, and the next he was surprised to find himself kneeling beside Serviss in the midst of a group of primates to escape the watchful eye of the guards. Eventually, he found himself staggering behind Serviss along the corridors in the basement until they reached the door the American had told him about at lunch, whereupon Serviss plucked the stolen key from his pocket. Unlocking the door with a ceremonious gesture, he bowed somewhat unsteadily and ushered Wells into the realm of the impossible.

Some things I would rather see sober, Wells lamented to himself, stepping cautiously over the threshold. The Chamber of Marvels was exactly as the American had described: a vast room crammed with the most wondrous things in the world, like a vast pirate's treasure trove. There was such an array of curiosities scattered about that Wells did not know where to look first, and the irritating little prods Serviss kept giving him to speed him along through the fantastic display did not help matters. He observed that a great deal of what was there had been labeled. One revelation succeeded another as Wells found himself gazing at a fin belonging to the Loch Ness monster, what looked like a curled-up kitten inside a glass jar marked FUR OF THE YETI, the purported skeleton of a mermaid, dozens of photographs of tiny, glowing fairies, a crown made of phoenix feathers, a giant bull's head allegedly from a minotaur, and a hundred other marvels. The fantastical tour came to an end when, suddenly, he found himself standing before a painting of a hideously deformed old man labeled PORTRAIT OF DORIAN GRAY.

Still recovering from the shock, he noticed some familiar objects next to him: a chemical flask containing a reddish liquid, and a small sachet of white crystals. The label on it said: "Last batch of chemicals salvaged from the warehouse of Messrs. Maw, indispensable for making Doctor Henry Jekyll's potion." Almost without thinking, the astonished Wells grasped the glass beaker: he needed to touch some of these wonders simply to be sure they were not a figment of his drunken imagination, inflamed by Serviss's storytelling. He needed to know they existed outside books, tales, and myths. As he held the beaker, he could smell the sharp odor of the blood-colored liquid. What would he change into if he drank the mixture? he wondered. What would his evil side be like? Would he suddenly get smaller, would he acquire the strength of a dozen men, a brilliant mind, and an overwhelming desire for wicked pleasures, as had happened to Stevenson's Doctor Jekyll, in what he had always assumed was a made-up story?

"Hurry up, George, we haven't got all day!" the American barked, yanking Wells's arm and giving him such a fright that the beaker slipped from his hand and shattered on the floor. Wells watched the red liquid spread over the tiles. He knelt down to try to clean up the mess but only succeeded in cutting his hand on one of the shards of glass.

"I broke it, Garrett!" he exclaimed in dismay. "I broke Doctor Jekyll's potion!"

"Bah! Forget about that and come with me, George," Serviss replied, gesturing to him to follow. "These are nothing more than fanciful baubles compared to what I want to show you."

Wells obeyed, threading his way through the hoard of objects as he tried to stanch the cut. Serviss guided him to a corner of the large room, where the flying saucer awaited. The machine rested horizontally on its stand, exactly as Serviss had described, like an enormous upside-down soup plate, tapered at the edges and crowned with a dome. Wells approached the object timidly, overawed by its sheer size and the strange shiny material it was made from, which gave it the appearance of being both solid and light. Then he noticed the peculiar carvings that dotted the surface and gave off a faint coppery glow. They reminded him of Asian characters, though more intricate. What did they symbolize?

"It doesn't look like they've managed to open it yet," Serviss remarked over his shoulder. "As you can see, there are no openings, and it doesn't seem to have any engine either. Although it looks like it must be extremely easy to fly, and probably incredibly fast."

Wells nodded absentmindedly. He had just noticed the large table piled high with papers beside the machine. This was where Serviss had told him he had found the files documenting the amazing discovery. He approached it, mesmerized, and began rummaging through the piles of notebooks and documents. Among them two thick albums containing photographs and newspaper clippings stood out. During his random search, Wells came across the burnt vessel's logbook, kept by the captain, a man by the name of MacReady. The handwriting was plain, devoid of any flourishes, and suggested a man with a stern, no-nonsense character, in complete contrast to that of Jeremiah Reynolds, who had been in charge of that expedition to the South Pole, whose diary seemed much more rambling and unmethodical. Wells browsed through the numerous articles in one of the albums describing the terrible fate of what the press had nicknamed the Ill-Fated Expedition, which had set sail from New York bound for the Antarctic on October 15, 1829. With some alarm, Wells read a few of the lurid front-page headlines, accompanied by bloodcurdling photographs of the sailors' bodies and the remains of the vessel: "Who or *what* slaughtered the crew of the *Annawan*? What horrors are buried beneath the Antarctic ice?" Yet, as far as he could make out, none of the articles mentioned the two main discoveries: the flying machine and the Martian. In the second album, however, he found several photographs of the strange machine half buried in the ice, glistening against the menacing grey sky, as if a giant had dropped a shiny coin from a great height. Next to these was a pile of scientific reports, which Wells could scarcely make sense of, and which by all appearances were secret and consequently had been kept from journalists and the public alike.

"Don't waste time on that, George. The important thing is in there," Serviss declared, breaking Wells's intense concentration and walking over to what looked like a wooden trunk covered in copper rivets, to which a small refrigerator had been attached. He placed his hands solemnly on the lid, turned to Wells, and said, with a mischievous grin, "Are you ready to see a Martian?"

Needless to say Wells was not ready, but he nodded and swallowed hard. Then, with exasperating slowness and a conspiratorial air, Serviss began lifting the lid, which let out a blast of icy vapor. When at last it was open, Serviss stood back to allow Wells to look inside. With gritted teeth, Wells leaned gingerly over the edge. For a few moments, he could not understand what the devil he was seeing, for the thing in front of him resisted any known form of biological classification. Unable to describe the indescribable, in his novel Wells had placed the Martians somewhere on the spectrum between amoebas and reptiles. He had depicted them as slimy, amorphous lumps, loosely related to the octopus family and thus intelligible to the human mind. But the strange creature in the coffin defied his attempts to classify it, or to use familiar words to describe it—which, by definition, was impossible. All the same, Wells endeavored to do so, aware that however precise he aimed to be, his portrayal of that creature's appearance would be nowhere near the truth. The Martian had a greyish hue, reminiscent of a moth, although darker in places. He must have been at least ten feet tall, and his body was long and thin, like an evening shadow. He was encased in a kind of skinlike membrane, which appeared to be part of his structure. This sprouted from his shoulders, covering his body down to the tops of his slender legs, which were made of three segments, like a praying mantis. His equally slender upper limbs also poked out from beneath the mantle, ending in what looked to Wells like a pair of sharp spikes. But the most remarkable thing of all was the Martian's head, which seemed to be tucked inside a hood of the same textured cartilaginous skin as the mantle. Although it was scarcely visible among the enveloping folds, Wells could make out a triangular shape, devoid, of course, of any recognizable features, except for a couple of slits, possibly the eyes. The presumed face was dark and terrifying and covered in protrusions. He thought he saw a thick cluster of cilia around the creature's jaw, from which emerged a kind of proboscis, like that of a fly, which now lay inert along his long throat. Naturally, the Martian looked nothing like how he remembered the phantasmagoric Spring-Heeled Jack, Wells thought. Unable to stop himself, he reached over and stroked one of the Martian's arms, curious to know what the incredibly alien skin felt like. Yet he could not tell whether it was smooth or rough, moist or dry, repulsive or pleasant. Strange as it seemed, it was all those things at once. But at least he could be sure of one thing, Wells thought: judging from his expressionless face and lifeless eyes, the terrifying creature was dead.

"All right, George, it's time for us to get out of here now," Serviss announced, closing the casket lid. "It won't do to stay here too long."

Wells nodded, still a little light-headed, and took care to avoid knocking over any of the wondrous objects as he followed Serviss toward the door.

"Remember everything you've seen, George," Serviss recommended, "and whether you believe these marvels are real or fake, depending on your intellectual daring, never mention this room to anyone you wouldn't trust with your life."

Serviss opened the door and, after making sure the coast was clear, told Wells to step outside. They walked through the interminable corridors of the basement until they finally emerged on the ground floor. There they slipped in among the crowd, unaware that beneath their unsteady feet, inside the wooden casket, the skin of the creature from the stars was absorbing the drops of blood Wells had left on its arm. Like a clay figure dissolving in the rain, his shape began to change, taking on the appearance of an extraordinarily thin, pale, youngish man with a birdlike face, identical to the one who at that very moment was leaving the museum like an ordinary visitor.

ONCE OUTSIDE, SERVISS SUGGESTED to Wells that they dine together, but Wells refused, claiming the journey back to Worcester Park was a long one and he would prefer to set off as soon as possible. He had already gathered that meals with Serviss were conspicuous by their lack of food, and he felt too inebriated to go on drinking. Besides, he was keen to be alone so that he could reflect calmly about everything he had seen. They bade each other farewell, with a vague promise of meeting again the next time Serviss was in London, and Wells flagged down the first cab he saw. Once inside, after giving the driver the address, he tried to clear his mind and reflect on the day's astonishing events, but he was too drowsy from drink and soon fell asleep.

And as the eyes of that somnolent, light-headed Wells closed, inside a casket in the basement of the Natural History Museum, those of another Wells opened.

II

ROM THE LOOK OF ASTONISHMENT ON YOUR faces, I can tell you are wondering what really happened to the *Annawan* and her crew at the South Pole. Is the Martian in the Chamber of Marvels really alive? Is our world threatened by a strange and sinister danger? It will give me the greatest pleasure to provide you with the answers as we go along, but in order to so in a proper, orderly fashion, I ought to go back in time to the very beginning of this tale. Since I have to begin somewhere, I think it would be best to travel back in time and place to the year of our Lord 1830 and the frozen wasteland of the Antarctic. As you will recall if you were paying attention to the clippings Wells browsed through in the museum's basement, that was where the ill-fated *Annawan* became icebound, and her valiant crew had the misfortune to be the first to welcome the Martian when it landed on Earth, a role for which undoubtedly none of them was prepared.

Let us repair to the South Pole, then, where we shall see that as the flying machine shaped like a saucer was hurtling through space toward our planet, Jeremiah Reynolds, the leader of the disastrous polar expedition, was examining the ice that had trapped his vessel and wondering how they would get out of there, unaware that this would soon be the very least of his worries. It occurred to the explorer that in all likelihood no other human being had ever set eyes on this place before. He wished he were in love so that he could baptize it in the name of a woman, as was the custom; the sea ice he was standing on, for example, or the distant mountain range to the south, or the bay sweeping away to his right, blurred by snow, or even one of the many icebergs. It was important for the world to see that his heart belonged to someone. But unfortunately, Reynolds had never experienced anything remotely resembling love, and the only name he could have used would be that of Josephine, the wealthy young woman from Baltimore whom he had been courting for several different reasons. And, frankly, he could not imagine saying to her as they took tea under her mother's watchful gaze, "Incidentally, my dear, I have named a continent in the polar circle after you. I hope you are pleased." No, Josephine would be incapable of appreciating such a gift. Josephine only valued what she could wear on her fingers or around her wrist or neck—provided they were not shackles, of course. What use would she have for a gift she could never see or touch? It was too subtle an offering for someone like her, impervious to subtleties. Stuck there in the middle of the ice, in temperatures under forty degrees below zero, Reynolds made a decision he could never have made anywhere else: he firmly resolved to stop courting Josephine. It was unlikely he would ever return to New York, but if by some miracle he did, he solemnly promised he would only marry a woman sensitive enough to be inspired by having a frozen wasteland in the South Pole named after her. Although, in case fortune failed to smile upon him, his uncompromising pragmatism insisted on adding, it would not be a bad thing if the woman in question had enough money to be able to excuse him for that remote island being all he could offer her.

Reynolds shook his head to rid himself of those romantic visitations, which seemed out of place there, as if they belonged to a strange, distant world he could scarcely believe existed. He gazed at the infinite expanse of ice imprisoning them, that landscape far from civilization, which even the Creator Himself had forgotten to adorn with living creatures. The ship and her crew had set sail from New York in the fall of 1829 hoping to reach the South Pole three months later, in the middle of the Antarctic summer; but a series of unfortunate mishaps, which had dogged them almost as soon as they weighed anchor, fatally delayed the voyage. By the time they had passed the South Sandwich Islands heading for

Bouvet Island, even the lowliest kitchen boy knew they would be lucky to arrive before the end of summer. However, the voyage had involved great expense, and they had gone too far for the option of turning back to be feasible. And so Captain MacReady had resolved to continue until they reached the Kerguelen Islands, in the hope that the sailors' rabbit's-foot charms would prove effective in the polar circle. Heading south-west at eleven knots in a fair wind, they had soon found themselves dodging the first icebergs, which seemed to guard the Antarctic coastline like hostile sentinels. They navigated the channels between the icebergs and the pack ice, pounded by fierce hailstorms, making good headway without further incident, until they realized from the expanse of solid ice almost covering the water that the long Antarctic winter had arrived in mid-February that year, much earlier than usual. Even so, they forged on with naïve zeal, trusting in the double hull of African hardwood with which Reynolds had insisted the old whaling boat be reinforced. It was a long and arduous struggle, which came to be fruitless when at last the indestructible pack ice closed in around them. Captain MacReady proved resourceful in a crisis: he gave the order to scatter hot coals on the encroaching ice to melt it more quickly, and to furl the topsails. He even sent a gang of men down armed with spikes, shovels, pickaxes, and any other sharp tools they could find in the hold. He did everything in his power except try to push the vessel himself, like a god of Olympus. But all that activity did not succeed in rendering their situation less dire. They were doomed from the moment they ventured onto that sea strewn with icy snares, perhaps from the moment Reynolds had planned the expedition. And so, no longer able to move forward, the *Annawan* became gradually hemmed in by sea ice until she was stuck fast in the immensity of the Antarctic, and the crew had to accept their situation, like warriors accepting defeat, as the ice encroached hourly upon the narrow channel of water behind them, crushing any hopes they had of survival.

When they had managed to clamber off the ship, which was slightly tilted to her starboard side, MacReady ordered one of his men to climb to the top of the nearest iceberg and report what he saw. After hacking out a few steps in the ice with a pickax, the lookout peered through his brass spyglass and confirmed Reynolds's fears: for them, the world was now no more than a vast frozen desert spreading in all directions, dotted with mountain peaks and icebergs. A white expanse without shelter or refuge, it rendered them instantly insignificant. Whether they lived or died was of no consequence in the face of that immensity, cut adrift from the world.

Two weeks later their situation was no better. The stubborn ice holding the *Annawan* prisoner had not yielded an inch. On the contrary, they could only deduce from the alarming groaning sounds the ship's hull made that the ice was wrapping itself even more tightly around it. It would be eight or nine months, perhaps even longer, before the return of summer, when the ice would begin to melt, and then only if they were lucky, for Reynolds had heard many similar stories in which the long-awaited thaw never came. In fact, once Man ventured into those icy domains, however experienced he was, everything became unpredictable. The expedition Sir John Franklin had led in 1819 to map the north coast of Canada, for example, had not been able to rely on a kind fate. The wretched explorers had spent so long in the ice that Franklin had been forced to eat his own boots as the only way of staving off extreme hunger. Although, unlike some of the others, he at least had made it home. Reynolds looked down uneasily at his frost-covered boots and wondered whether their names would also be added to the already lengthy list, carefully kept by the Admiralty, of doomed expeditions, ships that had vanished, dreams swallowed up by the unknown. He cast a mournful eye over the *Annawan,* which despite all her reinforcements had been taken hostage quickly. The enormous whaler had formerly been used to hunt sperm and yubarta whales in the South Atlantic Ocean. All that remained of those glory days were half a dozen harpoons and spears that were kept in the armory as terrifying souvenirs of those brave harpooners, who would skewer the huge whales during epic duels. And now the *Annawan* lay absurdly tilted on what looked like a marble pedestal, her prow sticking up in the air. To reduce the likelihood of her capsizing, MacReady had ordered the crew to strip her two topsails and rigging and to shore up her starboard side with a mound of ice that would act as a ramp. The sun hovered just above the horizon, where it would remain for a few more weeks, spinning out the dusk, until April came and it vanished completely, heralding the endless southern winter night. For the moment it still cast a dim light over the *Annawan*. Like it or not, the explorer thought to himself, that phantom-like vessel would be his home for the foreseeable future. Perhaps his very last home.

Tired of being confined to the ship's narrow hold, of banging their heads on the utensils hanging like vines from the ceiling, and of being hemmed in by bunk beds and piles of provisions, a few of the men had huddled in a group at the foot of the *Annawan,* braving the fierce cold that played at forming crystals from their vaporous breath. Besides Reynolds himself, who was the titular leader of that reckless expedition, the ship's company under Captain MacReady consisted of two officers, a quartermaster, two gunners, a surgeon, a cook, two kitchen boys, two carpenters, two electricians, and a dozen sailors. One of these was Peters, a huge, silent Indian, the offspring of an Absaroka woman and a white man, who was responsible for looking after the sled dogs. As far as Reynolds could tell, none of the men seemed overly concerned about their fate, instead showing a kind of hardened resignation. Still, the explorer hoped that however long the coal and victuals lasted, the store of rum would never run out: Reynolds had heard that in such situations there was nothing to worry about so long as there was plenty to drink. But once the rum was finished, things would change drastically: insanity, which had been content thus far to hover in the wings like a timid lover, would begin to tempt the crew, luring the weakest of them, and it would not be long before one placed a pistol to his head and pulled the trigger. Then, like some macabre ritual, the sound of gunshots from different parts of the ship would become their only form of entertainment throughout the long polar winter. Reynolds wondered how many gallons of rum remained. MacReady—who, judging from the smell of his breath, had his own reserves of brandy—had ordered Simmons, one of the kitchen boys, to dilute the daily grog rations with water to make it last as long as possible. Thus far none of the sailors had complained, as if they also knew that so long as they had their rum they would be safe from themselves.

Reynolds contemplated Captain MacReady, who seemed to have been infected by the same air of indifference as the others. At that moment, the officer was also off the ship, sitting on a bundle next to the iron dog cage that Peters had installed on the ice. Like the other men, MacReady was wearing several layers of wool under his oilskin, and one of those woolly hats with earflaps jokingly known as a Welsh wig. As he studied the burly captain, so motionless he might have been posing for a photograph, Reynolds realized he had to shake the men out of their stupor at once, before the whole ship's company fell into a state of hopeless lethargy. Yes, they had become icebound, but that did not mean nothing mattered anymore. It was time for him to ask MacReady to organize teams of men to explore the area, with the aim of continuing the mission that had brought them there, the mission that would shower them with more glory and riches than they could ever imagine: the discovery of the entrance to the center of the Earth.

And yet, despite his intention, Reynolds did not move a muscle. He stayed where he was, watching the captain from a distance, still hesitating to approach him. He disliked the captain. He considered him coarse, cynical, and hotheaded, the kind of fellow you could sooner imagine comforting a hound caught in a trap than a man suffering from a broken heart. Anyone could see that MacReady harbored mutual feelings, and, owing to the onboard hierarchy, his loathing had spread to the other men, so that Reynolds soon found himself leading an expedition in which he had no allies, except for Allan, the gunner who dreamed of being a poet. The two men were the youngest in the crew. Perhaps because the sergeant was the only one who did not see Reynolds as an impulsive young fop, something resembling a friendship had grown up between them. However, Allan was doubtless in his cabin, scattering words onto paper as he so often did, his quill scarcely touching the page, like a cloud skimming the surface of a river. And so Reynolds began scuffing the snow with the tip of his boot, trying to pluck up the courage to challenge MacReady alone, for that was what their recent conversations had seemed like to him, swordless duels in which the captain attempted, metaphorically speaking, to pierce him through the heart. Ten more minutes passed before he thrust his fists into the pockets of his oilskin and strode resolutely toward the captain. After all the effort it had taken him to get there, he had no intention of letting some arrogant numbskull stop him from finishing what he had begun, no matter that the man was a head higher than he and looked strong enough to tear him limb from limb with his bare hands.

"Captain MacReady," the explorer ventured.

"What is it, Reynolds?" the captain asked, annoyed at being interrupted in the middle of an important task, which appeared to be none other than feeling the cold in his bones and making sure the snow was still white.

"I would like us to begin exploring the area today," Reynolds replied, undeterred. "I don't think we should just sit around waiting for the ice to thaw."

The captain smiled to himself for a few moments. Then, with calculated slowness, he got up from where he was sitting, his imposing bulk rising before the young explorer.

"So that's what you think we're doing, is it, waiting for the ice to thaw?" he asked.

"If you are engaged in some other activity, then you could have fooled me," Reynolds replied sarcastically.

MacReady gave a disdainful laugh.

"I don't think you've quite understood the situation, Reynolds. Let me explain it to you. Being stuck in the ice in this godforsaken place isn't our only problem. Do you know what those sporadic groans are that wake us up at night? That's the ice, Reynolds. The accursed ice, slowly crushing our poor ship so that when it finally releases her, assuming it does, her hull will be so damaged she'll probably no longer be seaworthy. That's the exact situation. I haven't told my men because I don't want to alarm them, although I imagine most of them suspect that those groans don't bode well. But since you are in charge of this expedition, I thought you ought to know. And what can we do about it? I'll tell you before you ask: we can abandon ship and cross the frozen sea until we reach the coast, taking with us the team of dogs, the provisions, the lifeboats, and at least two iron stoves with enough coal to keep us from freezing along the way. Tell me, does that strike you as a plan that could succeed?"

Reynolds made no reply. Naturally, this suggestion struck him as crazy. No one knew for certain how far the coast was or in what direction, and traipsing blindly across that landscape bristling with icy peaks, which they would have to circumnavigate with their loaded sleds, would only exhaust them. Except for that crazy plan, the only one Reynolds could think of was crazier still. He had heard that, in similar situations, some captains had ordered their men to build makeshift camps on a block of ice and then let those improvised vessels be pushed by the currents, although the number of times a far-fetched plan of this sort had actually worked could be counted on the fingers of one hand. The storm-wracked waves and winds had drowned the rest, without the slightest sympathy for those amusing examples of human ingenuity. Reynolds did not dare even mention this option to MacReady. Perhaps it was preferable to stay in the shelter of the ship and just drink rum while they waited for something—anything—to happen. But he did not intend to simply do nothing while awaiting a miracle. It was preposterous to come all that way and not explore the area.

"What about the mission?" Reynolds asked, at the risk of angering the captain. "I see no reason why we cannot proceed with it. It might be the best way to cope with the boredom, which I am sure you know can quickly turn to madness."

"Oh, yes . . . your mission," MacReady responded sardonically. "Your attempt to find the opening that leads to the center of the Earth, which you believe is inhabited and illuminated by a sun smaller than our own, or is it two suns?"

Hearing MacReady scoff at his ideas, Reynolds could not help being reminded of his partner Symmes and the laughter they had endured during their exhausting lecture tour concerning the Hollow Earth.

"Believe it or not, Captain, that is the aim of this expedition," Reynolds replied, undeterred.

MacReady let out a guffaw that echoed across the white desert.

"Your naïveté is touching, Reynolds. Do you really believe the aim of this expedition is that altruistic? Mr. Watson of the Scientific Corps doesn't give a fig about finding your entrance to the Earth's core."

"What are you implying?" the explorer demanded.

The captain smiled contemptuously.

"We didn't organize all this to prove or disprove your ludicrous theory, Reynolds. Our sponsor wants what all the world powers want: to determine the strategic importance of the last unconquered territory."

The explorer looked at the captain with feigned disbelief, while smiling to himself contentedly. With these last words, MacReady had confirmed that he had taken the bait. Reynolds knew that John Frampton Watson believed wholeheartedly in his Hollow Earth theory, as did the politicians, the government institutions secretly supporting them, and the handful of private backers who preferred to remain anonymous. But they had all decided to be cautious and to conceal their true aims, at least for the time being. If the expedition turned out to be a disaster, Reynolds would be the only one publicly disgraced, mocked, and humiliated. Those who remained in the shadows, on the other hand, stood to lose only a few dollars: they could wash their hands of the matter, claiming they had quite different aims, that they had never given that poor lunatic much credit and had simply used him for their own ends. As things stood, it was preferable not to let the public think they were wasting money on such reckless ventures. And Reynolds had accepted the role of scapegoat in exchange for a confidential agreement. If he succeeded in finding that other world, which he was convinced he would, his dreams of wealth and glory would be amply fulfilled, for tucked away in his lawyers' safe was a document, inspired by the Capitulations of Santa Fe between Christopher Columbus and the Catholic monarchs, stating that Reynolds would be named admiral viceroy and governor general of all the land discovered beneath the Earth's crust, as well as receive a tenth of any riches found in the conquered territories. So MacReady could carry on thinking Reynolds was a puppet manipulated by obscure masters. Actually, it was preferable: the less the captain knew the better. Reynolds did not trust MacReady. In fact, he did not trust anyone: the world was full of men who had usurped the discoveries of others, stealing all the glory for themselves and dooming the true pioneers to obscurity. Reynolds did not want to run that risk. Thus the more stupid MacReady thought he was, the greater the advantage Reynolds had over him.

The captain observed Reynolds's silence with a mocking smile, awaiting a response. Having confirmed his role as naïve idealist, Reynolds was about to say something else about the businessman when a huge noise from the sky shook the earth beneath them. Reynolds and MacReady looked up, stunned. The other members of the crew also gazed at the sky, convinced the thunderous roar could only mean that it was falling in on them.

If the flying saucer had managed to impress a man like Wells, with his vast scientific knowledge and an imagination capable of dreaming up similar artifacts, imagine the fright it must have given that handful of rough sailors as it suddenly appeared on the horizon. It hurtled toward them, passing above their horrified heads and deafening them before disappearing toward the distant mountains, leaving behind a thin slash of light on the dark stain of the sky. They had only been able to see it clearly when it flew over them, but evidently none of them understood what the huge, flat, circular object was that seemed to spin on its own axis as it thundered through the air. Shortly after it disappeared behind the frozen peaks, they heard a tremendous bang, as though a ten-ton object, possibly made of iron or some equally heavy material, had crashed into the ice. It was a couple of minutes before the echo from the collision died away. When it did, the ensuing silence felt intolerable, as if they were all submerged at the bottom of the ocean. Only then did MacReady dare to speak.

"What the d-devil was that . . . ?" he stammered, not bothering to hide his bewilderment.

"My God, I've no idea . . . A meteorite, I imagine," Reynolds replied, his mystified gaze fixed on the distant ridge.

"I don't think so," someone disagreed.

It was a skinny sailor by the name of Griffin. Reynolds wheeled round and looked at him curiously, surprised by the conviction with which the man had contradicted him.

"Its path was too . . . erratic," the sailor explained, somewhat uncomfortable at feeling all eyes suddenly upon him. "When it reached the mountains it turned sharply and tried to gain height, as though wishing to avoid the fatal collision."

"What are you trying to say?" asked MacReady, who was not one for riddles.

Griffin turned to the captain and answered his question, a little hesitantly. "Well, it looked as though someone was trying to guide it in a particular direction, Captain. As though it was being . . . steered."

"Steered?" MacReady exclaimed.

Griffin nodded.

"He's right, Captain. That's what it looked like to me, too," agreed Wallace, one of the other sailors.

MacReady looked at Griffin without saying anything, trying to digest what he had just heard. Alarmed by the noise, the rest of the men still aboard the *Annawan* had descended the ramp and were gathering round their fellow crew members, asking what had happened.

"Perhaps it is some kind of . . . flying object," Griffin ventured, ignoring the others and addressing the captain, who was deep in thought.

The sailor's assertion surprised Reynolds. A flying object? But what sort of object might that be? he wondered. Not a balloon, clearly. It had crossed the sky at a devilish rate, as though something was propelling it, although he had seen no steam engine attached to it. Looking more like the statue of an explorer, Captain MacReady surveyed the distant mountains as if he were planning to build a house there.

"Well, there's only one way to find out," he declared at last. "We shall go to where it fell."

With a rush of energy, as though he had suddenly remembered he was the captain of the ship, he studied his men, called out a list of names, and within seconds had organized a search party. He left Lieutenant Blair in command of the *Annawan* and of the remaining sailors. Then he gave the explorer another of his condescending smiles.

"You're welcome to join us if you wish, Reynolds. Perhaps we'll come across your hole on the way."

Reynolds did not deign to respond to the gibe. He bobbed his head as if to say yes, then followed the other men aboard to kit himself out with everything needed for a journey across the ice. Reynolds attempted to ignore the wave of heat from the stoves and kitchen that hit him as he descended to the lower deck. He dodged the confusion of beds and hammocks and, guided by the faint light of the lanterns, managed to reach the narrow passageway leading to the officers' quarters. Once inside his cramped dwelling, dimly lit by the pale rays filtering through the porthole, Reynolds cast a melancholy eye over the uncomfortable room where he now spent his days: the built-in bunk with its lumpy horsehair mattress, the tiny desk, the table and two stools, the armchair he had insisted on bringing from home, the small larder, containing mainly bottles of brandy and a couple of cheeses, the washbasin in the corner, its water now frozen, and a few shelves lined with books, which he scarcely dared displace, for he had discovered a new use for the great classics that had never occurred to him before: as insulation from the cold on the other side of the wall. As soon as he was properly outfitted, Reynolds went back on deck.

Twenty minutes later, the men MacReady had picked were outside on the ice once more, warmly wrapped up, armed, and accompanied by a couple of sleds and a handful of dogs. In addition to Reynolds and the captain himself, the group consisted of Doctor Walker, Gunnery Sergeant Allan, and seven ordinary seamen with whom Reynolds scarcely had any association: Griffin, Wallace, Foster, Carson, Shepard, Ringwald, and the Indian Peters. After making sure they were all present, MacReady gestured energetically in the direction of the mountains, and without further ado the group set off.

III

URING THE JOURNEY, REYNOLDS AVOIDED PO-
sitioning himself next to the captain, although that was
the most appropriate place for him. He did not want to be drawn into
a verbal battle with MacReady while they crossed the ice, so he deliberately hung back, until he found himself walking beside Griffin, the
scrawny sailor whose remarks had aroused his curiosity. He remembered that Griffin had signed up for the *Annawan* at the last moment,
when the ship's crew was already complete, overcoming MacReady's
misgivings with his insistence on joining the discovery team and proving that not only was he genuinely passionate about the voyage but also
able to surmount obstacles, including a boorish, stubborn captain. But,
Reynolds wondered, why was it so important to Griffin to be there now,
in that freezing cold?

"I think you're right, Griffin," he said as they drew level. "No doubt
we will find some kind of flying machine in those mountains."

Griffin was surprised that the man leading the expedition, who
scarcely fraternized with the sailors, should address him in the tone of
someone wanting to engage in pleasant chitchat. Visibly awkward, Griffin simply nodded his head, reduced to a ball of kerchiefs and scarves
with a frozen nose and mustache poking out. But Reynolds was not put
off by his reticence and resolved to strike up a conversation with the
mysterious sailor, whether he liked it or not.

"Why were you so keen on joining our expedition, Griffin?" he asked
him outright. "Do you believe in my Hollow Earth theory?"

The sailor looked at him for a moment, aghast. His thin mustache was caked with frost, and it occurred to Reynolds that when they returned to the ship, Griffin would have no choice but to chop off the frozen hair. This was precisely why Reynolds himself insisted on continuing to shave, even though he had to do it with a basin of melted ice. Clearly Griffin preferred not to put himself through that torture every morning.

"The idea is very poetic, sir," the sailor replied at last.

"Very poetic, yes . . . But you don't believe it," Reynolds deduced, looking askance at Griffin. "I suppose like all the others you are here because of the money. But in that case, tell me why you were so keen to come aboard the *Annawan*. The wages are the same on any other ship, possibly higher, and the conditions less dangerous."

Griffin, who seemed increasingly upset about being questioned, reflected for a moment before replying.

"I needed to board a ship that offered no guarantee of return, sir," he said at last.

Reynolds was unable to conceal his confusion. He recalled the advertisement MacReady had posted in the various New York newspapers in order to attract recruits, which when he had read it had made his blood run cold:

Crewmen wanted for Antarctic expedition in search of
the passage to the center of the Earth. Perilous conditions:
extreme cold and constant risk. No guarantee of return. Honor,
fame, and a handsome bonus if the mission is successful.

"I never imagined that would tempt anyone," said Reynolds, glancing at the little man with an expression bordering on respect.

Up until then he had thought Griffin was no different from the others, whom he assumed had been enticed to join the *Annawan* by the advertisement's last sentence. Yet for this skinny sailor it had been the penultimate one. Apparently, the ways of the human heart were as inscrutable as God's own designs. Griffin shrugged and walked on in silence, until Reynolds's quizzical gaze forced him to speak, "I don't know what reasons the others had for embarking, sir," he confessed, continuing to stare straight ahead, "but I am here to get away from a woman. At least for a while."

"From a woman?" the explorer asked, intrigued.

With a heavy sigh, the sailor continued.

"I had been courting a young lady for a little over four months, when suddenly, I'm not quite sure how, I found myself engaged to be married." Griffin appeared to smile resignedly beneath the layers of cloth wrapped around his face. "And I'm not ready for marriage yet. I'm only thirty-two, sir! I still have so much I want to see!"

Reynolds nodded, pretending to comprehend.

"The day after I plighted my troth," the sailor went on, "I signed up for this expedition. I detest the cold, but as I said before, the *Annawan* was the only ship that did not guarantee my return. That way I would have enough time to decide what I really wanted to do with my life."

"I understand," said Reynolds, who did not understand at all. "And what about her?" he added, assuming the woman in question would have broken off her engagement to someone who prior to their nuptials would embark upon a suicide mission.

"As you can imagine, she did not take kindly to this sudden postponement of our wedding for months, possibly years. Yet she understood my . . . my need for adventure."

"I understand," Reynolds repeated mechanically.

Griffin nodded, grateful for the explorer's sympathy. As though having squandered the better part of the store of words he had brought with him for the voyage, he broke off the conversation, sinking once more into an unassailable silence. Reynolds gave up any further attempt at conversation and continued walking alongside Griffin, sharing his silence. An untimely fog closed in around them, the cold seeming to intensify.

In order to take his mind off his frigid extremities, Reynolds tried to recall the strange machine's vertiginous descent. It struck him as particularly odd that it had occurred precisely when they were there, as though arranged for their entertainment. If they had not become icebound, no one would have seen the machine, and its occupant, assuming someone really was steering the thing, would have perished alone. Then he wondered what country had the scientific capability to produce a machine like the one that had hurtled through the air at such an incredible speed, but he promptly shook his head. There was no point in speculating. In less than an hour he would find out for himself, he thought, and so he focused instead on the majestic beauty of the landscape, that neverending expanse of pristine whiteness surrounding him on all sides, like an imitation marble palace. As he did so, he thought it ironical that the very qualities that gave the landscape its beauty would probably be the same ones that killed them.

DESPITE THE THICKENING FOG, they soon caught sight of the machine. The object that had fallen from the sky was so enormous it stood out ominously in the distance, like a beacon lighting their way. When they finally reached the site of the accident, they could see it was indeed some kind of flying machine. Almost as big as a tram, but round and domed, the machine stuck up from the ice like an idol from some unknown religion. It appeared undamaged, although the impact had cracked the ice in a thirty-yard radius, so that they had to tread carefully as they approached. The object was made of a shiny material, sleek as a dolphin's skin, and seemed to have no door or hatch. The only blemish on the glossy fuselage was a cluster of strange embossed symbols from which a faint coppery light emanated.

"Does anyone have any idea what the devil it is?" MacReady asked, glancing about inquiringly.

No one spoke, although the captain was not really expecting a reply. They were all mesmerized by the machine's gleaming surface, which mirrored their astonished faces. Reynolds studied his reflection as if it were a stranger's. He was so used to seeing himself broken up into what looked like lopsided fragments in the tiny mirror he used for shaving that he was surprised to discover the pitiful result when they all came together. No one could deny he was impeccably clean shaven, yet his eyes had a weary, feverish look from lack of sleep, and he seemed as slender as a wraith. Apart from that, the face peering back at him from the machine's silky surface still had that same childish air that made it difficult for him to compete in the adult world, those plump lips that failed to command authority.

Reynolds sighed resignedly and looked away from his reflection in order to examine the nearest cluster of markings. Most of these were finely drawn symbols, vaguely reminiscent of Asian characters, framed by what looked like geometric shapes. He could not resist stretching his right hand toward one of them, with the aim of running his finger along their wavy spirals. Although he was curious to know what that peculiar shimmering material felt like, he chose to keep his glove on for fear his hand might freeze. When he touched the symbol, a strange plume of smoke began to rise slowly into the air, and as Reynolds looked on in wonder, a tiny blue flame sprouted from his glove like an unexpected bloom. The explorer felt a stabbing pain, which instantly radiated through his whole body. He withdrew his hand, unable to stop the excruciating agony from emerging as a terrible roar. Reynolds caught a sudden whiff of singed fabric and flesh and amid the pain was scarcely able to grasp that on touching the strange symbol, his glove had caught fire, despite the subzero temperatures. The sailors standing next to him recoiled in horror, while Reynolds, his face screwed up in pain, fell to his knees on the ice, holding up his right hand, now wrapped in shreds of charred cloth, blackened and smoking like a witch's claw.

"Good God!" Doctor Walker exclaimed, hurrying to his aid.

"No one is to touch the outside of that thing!" MacReady roared. "Damnation, if anyone touches anything without my permission I'll string him from the yardarm!"

The surgeon ordered Shepard, the sailor nearest him, to dig a hole in the ice as quickly as possible. Shepard took out his pickax and struck obstinately at the brittle crust until he managed to make a kind of burrow. As Walker thrust Reynolds's arm down the hole, they all heard a noise like a red-hot iron being plunged into a bucket of water. When Walker deemed that was enough, or perhaps when he felt his own fingers begin to freeze through his glove, he yanked Reynolds's hand out. The explorer, half stunned by the sudden contrast of fire and ice, put up no resistance.

"I must take him back to the infirmary immediately," Walker declared. "I have nothing to bandage his hand with."

"Captain!" cried Peters, before MacReady had time to respond.

MacReady turned his head toward the Indian, who was standing about ten yards from the machine, pointing at the ice.

"I've found some tracks, sir!"

The captain opened his mouth in surprise, then collected himself and strode over to Peters, a few of the other sailors following behind.

"It looks like something came out of the machine," the Indian surmised.

MacReady glared at Peters, as though he were to blame for everything, when clearly what he was angry about were the endless surprises that prevented him from showing his men the imperturbable calm every captain should possess. The Indian knelt by the prints, studied them in silence, then explained to the others what he saw in those scratches in the snow.

"The prints are huge, too big for an animal, at least any I know," he said, pointing at the outline. "Do you see? They're almost as long as a man's arm. And strangely oval shaped and deep, as if what made them weighed several tons. But the funniest thing is there are no toe prints in the snow. These look more like claw marks."

"Are you sure about that, Peters?" Wallace said, leaning over them. "They look more like hoofprints to me."

"Hoofprints? Since when did you become a tracker, Wallace?" Shepard scoffed.

"I don't know, Shepard, but I have goats and those prints are—"

"Shut up, both of you!" MacReady bellowed at the two men. He turned to the Indian, who, rather than argue with them, was scowling silently, aggrieved perhaps that anyone should question his vast knowledge in this area. "Continue, please, Peters . . . You were saying the prints aren't human?"

"I'm afraid so, sir," Peters confirmed.

"But that's impossible!" MacReady exclaimed. "What else could they be?"

"Footprints never lie, Captain," Peters replied. "Whatever came out of that machine is a creature that walks upright, but it isn't human."

A deathly hush fell as the others leaned over the strange tracks.

"And the prints are fresh," he added. "I would say about twenty minutes old, possibly less."

Peters's words alarmed the men, who glanced around anxiously, peering into the white void. All of a sudden, they were not alone.

"And the next set of prints?" MacReady asked, trying to appear unruffled. "Which direction did this . . . creature take?"

"That's the odd thing, Captain," said Peters, leading them a few yards farther on. "The next prints are over here, nearly six feet from the first. That means that in one stride the creature can cover a distance impossible for any other animal. And the next lot must be even farther away, because I can't see them."

"Are you saying the creature moves in leaps?"

"It seems so, Captain. In bigger and bigger leaps, which makes it very difficult to follow even without this fog. Unless we comb the area, we can't know which direction it took. It could have gone anywhere."

"You see, Wallace?" Shepard piped up. "Could one of your goats do that?"

The captain gave Shepard a black look and told him to shut up.

"What do you suppose that thing is, Peters?" asked one of the other sailors, a man called Carson.

The Indian remained silent for a few moments before replying, contemplating whether his companions were ready for the revelation he was about to share with them.

"A devil," he said in a grave voice. "And it came from the stars."

Inevitably, his words caused a great stir among the men. The captain raised his hand to quiet them down, then desisted. Did he have a better theory, one that might put his men's minds at rest?

"All right," he said at last, trying to keep control of the situation. "Let's not jump to conclusions. Whatever this thing is, it may still be in the vicinity. We'll go and see. Doctor Walker, you and Foster take Mr. Reynolds back to the ship, dress his wound, and when he's recovered, remind him to stop and think before touching anything. Even a child knows that."

The doctor nodded. He helped the sobbing Reynolds to his feet, while MacReady continued giving orders.

"It's best if we split up into pairs; that way we can cover the whole area around the machine. Peters and Shepard, you take one of the sleds and go south. Carson and Ringwald, you take the other sled and go north. Griffin and Allan, you go east, and you, Wallace, come with me. If you don't find anything within a two-mile radius, come back here. This will be the meeting place. Any questions?"

"I have a question, Captain," said Carson. "What if we find the . . . demon?"

"If you find it and it behaves in a threatening way, don't hesitate to use your musket, Carson. And then finish it off."

Everyone nodded.

"Good," said the captain, taking a deep breath. "Now let's get going. Let's find that thing!"

IV

CRADLING HIS BANDAGED HAND, REYNOLDS WATCHED from the deck of the *Annawan* as the reddish-purple hues of dusk bled onto the ice fields, giving him the impression he was on the surface of the planet Mars. However hard he looked, he was incapable of seeing where the frozen ocean ended and the land began, for the snow had wiped away all trace of its union like a skillful tailor's invisible seam. Reynolds only knew that MacReady had prohibited them from walking around the outside of the ship as well as on the port side. Although it did not look like it, the ice there was much thinner, scarcely eight inches thick, and could easily break under their weight, since what they would in fact be walking on was the waterway, now layered with ice, that had brought them there. Consequently, he had ordered those sailors who were in the habit of emptying their bowels overboard to do so over the port side, with the result that enjoying the majestic frozen landscape from that part of the ship was not advisable.

Looking away from the frozen desert, Reynolds tilted his head up toward the handful of stars that were out and contemplated them with the habitual reverence he reserved for the Creator's majestic handiwork. If what Peters said was true, the machine that had fallen from the sky and landed on the ice must have come from up there. In fact, it was not such a crazy idea, he told himself; no more so than believing that the center of the Earth was inhabited, as he did. Although it might be more precise to say that he wanted to believe it, for the only path he had discovered that could lead to immortality was to become the last great conqueror of the last great undiscovered territory. But now another completely unexpected vista had opened before his eyes, one that contained an infinitely bolder promise of eternal glory. How many planets in the firmament were inhabited? And how much glory would go to the person who succeeded in conquering them?

Reynolds was so absorbed in these thoughts that he nearly leaned on the metal handrail. He stopped himself just in time and gazed at it in disbelief for a few seconds, alarmed by what would have happened if he had touched it. He had been told that metal was a lethal substance in subzero temperatures, even when wearing gloves, and Reynolds had no wish to put that theory to the test. He gave a weary sigh. This accursedly hostile place allowed no respite. Everywhere was fraught with danger: at that very moment, in order to stop the ship from capsizing, a group of men with hatchets and pickaxes was hewing off the ice that had built up on the masts, and chunks of it were dropping onto the deck with loud thuds, like the sound of cannon fire. If Reynolds wanted to gaze up at the starry sky, he was obliged to dodge the lethal shower of icy shards capable of dashing his brains out. Yet, despite the perils, the explorer preferred being on deck, occasionally pacing up and down to get the circulation going in his numb legs, rather than in the infirmary, where the groan of the ice as it crushed the ship's hull prevented him from falling asleep. That relentless creaking had become a dreadful lullaby, forcing him to ponder each passing hour in that ghastly, interminable twilight.

It was more than five hours since Captain MacReady and his group had returned from their exploratory trip, having found nothing. Only Carson and Ringwald, who had gone north, had failed to show up at the meeting point. MacReady and the others had waited for almost an hour until finally, tired, cold, and hungry, they had decided to return to the *Annawan*. No one had drawn any conclusions about their absence, and yet the question everyone was silently asking himself was whether those two poor wretches had stumbled upon what the crew had begun referring to as "the monster from the stars." They could not know for sure, of course, but it was the most likely explanation. However, even though the captain and most of the rest of the crew had apparently given the two men up for dead, Reynolds imagined that, as soon as MacReady thought they had rested enough, he would organize a fresh search party.

Earlier, while Foster and Doctor Walker were dragging him back to the ship, reeling with pain, Reynolds had regretted his recklessness, not simply because it made him look foolish in front of the crew, and would fuel the captain's mockery, but because it had prevented him from exploring the surrounding area as he had been longing to do from the moment they became icebound. But now he was glad of his foolish act because, as Sergeant Allan had pointed out, it would have been impossible in that dense fog to find his longed-for passage to the center of the Earth unless he had fallen directly into it. Not to mention the threat posed by the creature from the machine, which had almost certainly ended the wretched lives of Carson and Ringwald. On hearing that, Reynolds decided that a burn seemed a modest price to pay for having avoided putting his life in peril.

However, he had to admit that the expedition was not turning out quite as he had expected, and after the recent events it was difficult to predict what would happen next. He remembered the series of obstacles he had been obliged to overcome in order to get this far and the enemies he had made because of his persistence. It had not been easy to find backers for such an expedition, owing to the fact that the vast majority of people gave no thought whatsoever to whether the Earth might be hollow. Needless to say, Reynolds did. Indeed, he could almost claim he had been inside it, albeit only in his dreams.

IT HAD ALL BEGUN on a distant afternoon when, by sheer chance, one man had changed Jeremiah Reynolds's fate. From that day on, he had ceased drifting and had set off along a single pathway, whose end was very clearly mapped out.

He had been passing by a public lecture hall in Wilmington, Ohio, when he heard loud guffaws coming from within. And if Reynolds needed anything after a disappointing day's work at the newspaper he edited, it was laughter. To understand his state of mind that day, you would need to know a little more about him, and so allow me to interrupt our story to give you a brief tour of the explorer's soul. Like many others before and after, Reynolds was born into abject poverty. He had been obliged to start work young to pay for all his needs, from resoling his boots to enrolling at university. From a tender age, although that may not be the most suitable expression in this case, he had been an avid reader. But he was more interested in accounts of voyages and discoveries than in novels. With astonishing zeal he had devoured Marco Polo's tales, the flattering biography of Columbus written by the explorer's own son, the heroic epics of those who first ventured to the North and South poles, and into darkest Africa.

Understandably, all these daring exploits had shaped Reynolds's youthful fantasies, and he had grown up dreaming of emulating those men, who had carved their names on the tablet of History and, more important, had won untold wealth and fame for themselves and their descendants. Reynolds despised mediocrity and very early on had begun to feel superior to everyone around him, although even he was unable to define what exactly that superiority was based upon, for it was plain to see he had no outstanding talent, nor any extraordinary physical attributes, nor was he of above average intelligence. Up until then, Reynolds could not be said to differ much from other young men, not even in this persistent belief in his own superiority, so natural in Man. In what way, for example, was he any different from the accountant who lived in the same building and whom he looked down on scornfully whenever they met on the stairs? The thing that made him stand out from his neighbors was his belief in himself, the absolute conviction that he was destined for a life of grand, heroic exploits. For Reynolds sensed he had not come into the world to live such a shamefully dull life. And yet the years went by without anything happening to suggest he could unearth the astonishing secret destiny that awaited him. It is true that he soon stopped suffering hardship, since he managed to finish his studies and even became editor of a newspaper, but these worldly successes, within anyone's reach, did not quench his thirst for glory. Deep down, Reynolds felt he was wasting his life, the only life he had, a life that, when it ended, he would care so little about that he might as well have been carried off as a child by the smallpox. In short, he was fed up with wallowing in mediocrity while relating the heroic deeds of others, recounting miracles that never happened to him. That was not why he had been born. He had been born so that his brave exploits would be splashed all over the newspapers, exploits that would make him the envy of his fellow men, causing their wives to swoon and their mothers to sigh with admiration; even their lapdogs would bark, for his extraordinary prowess would not go unnoticed even in the animal kingdom.

Unfortunately, he had no idea how to achieve his dreams, and it should therefore come as no surprise that his nights were as close to torture as it is possible to imagine. Lying in the dark, waiting for the oblivion of sleep, Reynolds would torment himself by recalling epic passages he had read in his books about explorers, and when he grew tired of that, he would puncture the gloom with what sounded like his last gasps, bemoaning the fact that everything worth discovering had already been discovered. For it was clearly not enough simply to discover something. What glory and riches could be gained from mapping out each cranny in the Antarctic's frozen coastline, for example? None. It took far more ingenuity to be able to discover something that both changed History and guaranteed one immortality, while at the same time, if possible, lining one's pockets. However, he had to proceed with great caution, for in the years between Marco Polo's return in 1295 and Columbus's departure in 1492, dozens of explorers had made important discoveries, and yet their names had been virtually forgotten, eclipsed by the discovery of the Americas. And what was worse, almost none of those brave adventurers had obtained more than a pittance and a lifetime of fevers. Who remembered Brother Oderico da Pordenone, for example, who fought his way into deepest China through India and Malaysia? Or the Arab Ibn Battuta, who explored Central Asia and North Africa? Not even the renowned Christopher Columbus had played his cards right. He managed to convince the royal court that the Earth was much smaller than the ancient Greek Eratosthenes' calculations had suggested, and that he, Columbus, would discover a sea route to the East Indies that would assure a flourishing spice trade—although what most impressed Reynolds were the advantageous terms he had negotiated for himself. Unfortunately, in the wake of his fabulous success, he acquired some powerful enemies, who were quick to denounce his mistreatment of the native populations. In the end, the deplorable way he governed his viceroyalty had gradually meant the loss of his prestige and power. Yes, the profession of discoverer was clearly fraught with dangers, and not merely the ones lurking in the jungle undergrowth.

Reynolds was confident he could manage things better, if the occasion ever presented itself. After all, he was a seasoned newspaperman, and he had political contacts and a nose for business. True, his knowledge of geography and navigation was limited, but most frustratingly of all there was no territory left for him to discover. And so, he had little choice but to wait patiently and hope for some miracle that would rescue him from mediocrity. And if not, then he could always marry Josephine. Whilst this was no heroic feat that would guarantee him a place in the history books, it would at least fill his pockets. Although as things stood, Reynolds was not even sure he could still count on that, for the girl seemed more and more immune to his very limited charms. In short, such were the anxieties eating away at the explorer as he walked past the lecture hall and heard those loud guffaws. Therefore it was no surprise that he flung open the door: Reynolds needed to laugh at someone else in order not to feel like a joke himself.

Yet as soon as he walked in, he discovered with amazement that the man onstage who was producing all that mirth was no comedian at all. On the contrary, the ex–army captain John Cleves Symmes Jr. appeared very serious about his subject, which, incredible as it sounded, was that the Earth was like a gigantic hollow shell. In fact, it was like an egg, in which shell, white, and yolk were quite separate. It was possible to enter this shell through two immense holes, one at each pole, and at its core four equally hollow spheres floated in a kind of gelatinous fluid that was responsible for gravity. But what most astonished Reynolds was that it was deep inside the Earth that the miracle of life had occurred. Symmes claimed that underneath them, a second warmer and more diverse world existed, where plants, animals, and possibly even human life thrived. Predictably, this comment unleashed more peals of laughter from the audience, and Reynolds, who had taken a seat in the back row, joined in heartily.

Symmes tried to silence the guffaws by explaining that his ideas had their origin in the writings of some of the most celebrated scholars of the past. He cited Edmond Halley, who had also envisaged the Earth's interior as teeming with life and illuminated by an iridescent gas that occasionally seeped through the fine crust at its poles, coloring our night skies with the aurora borealis. He mentioned many more besides, whose extravagant theories only made the audience laugh even louder, including Reynolds, who chortled in his seat as though possessed, exorcising his life's frustrations. Meanwhile, Symmes went on describing the center of the Earth, where vast four-hundred-year-old herbivores dwelled, and creatures who communicated their thoughts to one another through the airwaves, albino dwarves who traveled in antigravitational trains, and mammoths and other animals that Man had long ago thought extinct. The belly of the Earth, according to Symmes, was a very crowded place. But all of a sudden, while the audience's guffaws crescendoed, Reynolds's laughter dried up in his throat, and while his mouth remained fixed in an amused smile, his eyes began to narrow, and he leaned forward, like a slowly falling tree, in order to hear more clearly what the pitiful little man was saying. His words plummeted like raindrops as they tried to pierce the noise of the jeering crowd.

Even so, hardly daring to breathe, his pulse quickening, Reynolds managed to catch the scientist Trevor Glynn's theories about the Earth's subterranean deposits. As everyone knew, Man labored hard to reach them, boring inch by inch through the thick rock upon whose surface he lived, digging coal, diamond, and other mines, risking life and limb to plunder those precious metals from an Earth whose crust seemed to offer them an almost motherly protection. However, once Man reached the center of the Earth through one of its poles, access to such deposits was easy. For it seemed (and here Symmes displayed a vast collection of corroborative charts, maps, and complex diagrams) there were hundreds of deposits deep inside the Earth that were infinitely richer and more plentiful than those closer to the surface. For the inhabitants of the hollow planet, those caverns were as easy to reach as the apples on the trees were for us; it was not difficult to imagine them using gold, diamonds, and other precious stones with the same insouciance as their outside neighbors used clay. No doubt those minerals, of inestimable value on the Earth's surface, were commonly used to help make their cities, roads, and even their clothes. This meant that finding the path to the center of the Earth was equivalent to discovering the path to all those riches. Symmes's last words were scarcely audible amid the peals of laughter, but by now Reynolds was no longer listening. He was stunned, hands clutching the sides of the chair, throat dry and burning. This was the answer to all his prayers. Not everything had been discovered. Perhaps no one had much interest anymore in the Earth's surface, but beneath it a new world was waiting to be conquered. A world in which whoever arrived first would be able to consolidate his power and even establish a new Spice Route, a route that would pour gold, coal, minerals, and precious stones out to the Earth's surface, creating one of the greatest enterprises the world had ever known. And clearly whoever set up that business would control it in the name of his country, with all the attendant privileges.

Reynolds could not help but begin to daydream, lulled like a baby in his cradle by the public's laughter. How would people refer to those new territories—as the Other New World, the Inside World? And of course this new trade route would not be across the seas. A new term would have to be coined: Intra-Terrestrial Trade? The Route of the Depths? He imagined the turmoil all of this would create in society: As happened after the discovery of the Americas, an endless stream of eager adventurers would travel to the new territories, drawn by the promise of wealth. But only the person who got there first and knew how to play his cards right would be singled out for glory. All at once, Reynolds could not bear the thought of someone beating him there. He had to approach the little man and contrive to glean as much information as he could in order to find out if this was another crackpot idea or if it had the makings of a successful venture. Reynolds had his misgivings, but nevertheless he imagined he could feel a slight tremor beneath his feet that emanated from the Earth's entrails: a sign of the mysterious life going on below, busily yet calmly, oblivious to the debates about its existence.

And so, when the audience had left the hall, shaking their heads at the gibberish they'd heard, and Symmes, with the helpless air of a drowning man, began to collect the drawings he had used to illustrate his lecture, Reynolds approached the chubby-faced speaker, congratulated him on his lecture, and offered to help him gather up his things. The delighted lecturer accepted, eager to go on spouting his ideas to this unexpected listener that Fate had sent his way. Reynolds soon found out that after the captain had quit the army, he had spent ten years traveling around the country like a zealous preacher, proclaiming his theory from every kind of pulpit, greeted with either roars of laughter or pitying smiles.

"The evidence substantiating my theory is overwhelming," Symmes declared as he took down the drawings he had placed on various easels. "What else causes hurricanes and tornados if not the air sucked into the polar openings? And why do thousands of tropical birds migrate north in winter?"

Reynolds saw these as rhetorical questions and let them dissolve like snowflakes. He was not sure whether Symmes was saying that the migrating birds flew into the polar openings in order to nest inside the Earth, or something completely different, but either way he did not care. He decided to nod enthusiastically, pretending to listen to Symmes's grating voice while he feverishly examined the jumble of papers, maps, illustrations, and charts with which the captain tried to give his ideas some credence. Most of them looked like serious articles, many by scientists of renown, and he regretted that the champion of all this eccentric knowledge was this clumsy, buffoonish little man. He imagined that he could give the project the veneer of credibility that was lacking from Symmes's sideshow routine. Yes, Reynolds said to himself as he contemplated the drawings, perhaps the Hollow Earth theory was true after all.

"Not forgetting the numerous allusions in ancient myths to places in the Earth's interior," the captain added, studying the young man's response. "Surely you have heard of Atlantis or the Kingdom of Agartha, my boy."

Reynolds nodded absentmindedly: he had found Trevor Glynn's drawings. He studied the annotations and intricate calculations jotted in the margins. They gave such an accurate account of the distances between the various deposits, the different access routes, the approximate quantities of minerals, and the geological and topographical data that it was easy to picture Glynn himself having charted the territory, strolling through those hidden caverns wielding a pencil. And Reynolds understood in a flash that this was not about believing or not, but simply about taking a chance or not. He decided there and then to take a chance on the Hollow Earth theory. He would believe in it in the same childish way he believed in God: if God turned out not to be true, the consequences of having believed in Him would no doubt be less terrible than if God did exist and Reynolds had declared himself an atheist. Even so, it was easier for Reynolds to believe in the Hollow Earth theory, for if he believed in anything at all, he believed in destiny, and it was destiny that had made him walk into the lecture hall that afternoon. He reflected about all of this, trying to blot out Symmes's droning voice. If there was a world to discover, he was not going to waste time arguing over its existence. He would leave that to others; he had decided to take a chance on the Hollow Earth, and he would simply go to look for it. After all, the only thing he had to lose was his detestable life. And so it could be said that when he walked into a crowded lecture hall that afternoon, Reynolds discovered the hitherto elusive meaning of his life. And he had no choice but to embrace it with open arms.

Symmes's voice interrupted his meditations.

"However," he said, unsure whether this stranger deserved to be the beneficiary of his wisdom, of all the things he did not share with his audiences, "those are not the main reasons why I am sure the Earth is hollow."

"Really?"

"No, it is purely a matter of thrift, my boy," Symmes replied smugly. "Just as our bones are hollow, the idea of making the Earth hollow in order to save on materials cannot have escaped the attention of our Creator."

Reynolds managed to conceal his scorn at such a stupid argument and instead put on the face of someone confronted with the indisputable proof that an entire civilization inhabited the center of the planet, an expression that, naturally enough, satisfied the ex–army officer's expectations. The young man gave him a sidelong glance, which was not without compassion. He realized that, at least for the moment, if he wanted to carry out his plan, he would have to humor this ridiculous little man. Reynolds knew next to nothing about the Hollow Earth and could certainly benefit from Symmes's knowledge and contacts, although he had already begun to sense the likely hazards of any association with him. At any rate, it was too soon to be thinking about that now. If later on it became necessary to rid himself of Symmes, he did not imagine it would be all that difficult.

And so, the very next day, Reynolds sold his shares in the *Spectator,* the Wilmington newspaper of which he was editor, and, free as a bird, joined Symmes in his crusade, adopting the ex–army man's dream as though it were his own. They spent almost a year traveling around the country like a pair of evangelists heralding a weird and wonderful world that lay undiscovered, although, thanks to Reynolds's skillful improvements, their arguments were far better thought out and more engaging. However, time after time Symmes's ravings and eccentricities thwarted Reynolds's efforts to make their project credible, for he was incapable of sticking to the agreed formula, or, in any case, of keeping his mouth shut. Even so, the would-be explorer tried not to give in to his despair and concentrated on carrying out the alternative plan he had elaborated behind his companion's back. He soon knew everything there was to know about the various Hollow Earth theories and was able to distinguish which ones the public would find most appealing and easy to digest and which would interest the powerful officials whom he was intent on seducing. Encouraged by his progress, Reynolds busied himself furiously for several months, sending missives to his fellow journalists, arranging meetings with politicians, calling in every favor owed him, leaving no stone unturned in his search for funding. Gradually he succeeded in making people in different circles begin to speak of the Hollow Earth as a scientific theory, perhaps one whose inconsistencies still raised a few eyebrows, but which was certainly respectable enough not to be greeted with the usual hoots of laughter. Provided Symmes did not turn up and ruin everything, naturally.

One evening, while Symmes was celebrating what he considered his latest triumph, and Reynolds his latest act of sabotage, Reynolds finally accepted that the ex–army officer had a serious problem with alcohol. As usual, they had spent the day revealing the mysteries of the Hollow Earth to anyone who cared to listen, and now, with several beers in front of them, it was time to show each other the far simpler workings of their minds. Or at least that is what Symmes liked to engage in at the end of their evening repast, while his companion listened with a mixture of compassion and exasperation. For the past few nights, as the drink loosened Symmes's tongue, Reynolds had watched him become more and more bogged down in the miasma of his own illusions, which he soon labeled delusions. Symmes appeared to him increasingly pathetic, but also an increasing threat to Reynolds's plans. Symmes had imagined the subterranean world in the minutest detail, and the result was a kind of utopian sanctuary where happiness was in the very air and there were none of the torments that plagued men on the Earth's surface. In short, a world where it was impossible not to be happy, whose marvels Symmes described to him night after night with the feverish look of a man about to die, with his gaze already fixed on the joys of Heaven.

However, the night in question, which started out like any other, took a turn that allowed Reynolds to understand the full extent of his companion's insanity. Leaning sideways precariously in his chair, tankard in hand, his speech slurred, Symmes admitted that the reason he was able to imagine so clearly what the subterranean world looked like, and why he was so adamant that what was beneath their feet was exactly as he had described it and not otherwise, was because he had been there himself. The ex–army officer's sudden revelation naturally took Reynolds by surprise, and he listened in astonishment to Symmes's fantastical account of how he had traveled to the center of the Earth.

Unfortunately, to tell it in the same amount of detail as Symmes did would distract from our main story, so I shall limit myself to stating briefly that the alleged event took place in 1814 during the war against the British. The regiment under Symmes's command had been ambushed, and it soon became clear to officers and men alike that there was no sense in giving or obeying orders, that it was each man for himself. Pursued by two British soldiers, Symmes hid in a cave he came across. After wandering deep inside it for hours, he discovered a small staircase that appeared to lead to the center of the Earth. Descending it, he had found a beautiful domed city straight out of *The Thousand and One Nights,* as was the story he was now telling the stunned Reynolds. This included a romance with a beautiful princess of the realm, a palace mutiny, a revolution, and finally a hasty escape that left behind the aforementioned princess dying of love. And as Symmes ended his story, weeping bitter tears for the loss of his beloved Litina, princess of the subterranean kingdom of Milmor, Reynolds felt a sickening shiver run down his spine: he realized he had to get rid of the little fellow as soon as possible or he would never be able to achieve his goal. But that was easier said than done, for Symmes, despite his pathetic behavior, also had sudden flashes of inspiration, and during one of these had made them both sign a declaration that they would travel together to the center of the Earth, prohibiting either of them from embarking upon such a venture alone, unless one party predeceased the other. Now that he knew how difficult the little man was to handle, Reynolds could not help kicking himself for having signed it.

In the days that followed, not a moment went by when he did not wonder how he might get rid of Symmes. His companion was steadily drinking more, even during the day, and particularly before the lectures, as though he thought it would improve his oratory. And Reynolds was in a continual state of anxiety, fearful that Symmes would choose one of their meetings or lectures to reveal his idiotic personal story to the world, turning them into the laughingstock of the country. The only solution Reynolds could think of, since doing away with Symmes personally was out of the question, even for an amoral being such as he, was to limit the damage as much as possible. He began to arrange meetings behind Symmes's back and even encouraged him to drink more during the day, in order to keep him in a state of compliant semiconsciousness. This enabled him to go alone to the lectures, leaving Symmes asleep in his hotel room.

And then, one day, the opportunity he had been waiting for finally arrived. Reynolds was in the middle of a meeting with two senators in his hotel room when Symmes suddenly turned up in his underwear, drunk as a lord, and, kneeling before the two illustrious gentlemen, begged them to sponsor the project, to give his friend and him some money. He explained that at that very moment beneath their feet was a beautiful lovesick princess, whose sighs they could hear if they put their ears to the carpet, and what in life was worth fighting for more than true love? Thereupon, he collapsed at their feet and began snoring peacefully. Reynolds watched him with a look of disgust. He apologized cursorily and bade farewell to the two senators, who were still stunned by the grotesque apparition. Once alone in the room with Symmes, Reynolds studied him closely for a few moments, his look of revulsion giving way to a sinister smile. Did he have the guts to do it? If he allowed this opportunity to slip away, he might never have another one, he concluded. And so, avoiding thinking about the real significance of his actions, he went round opening all the windows with the diligence of a servant airing the room. They were in Boston, in the middle of a particularly harsh winter. An icy wind began to whip the curtains, while a torrent of dancing snowflakes invaded the room, flecking the carpet and the rest of the floor with white patches. After making sure everything was going according to plan, Reynolds left Symmes sprawled half naked on the floor, exposed to the raging storm, and, after telling reception he was not to be disturbed on any account, he went to sleep in Symmes's room. And it has to be said that Reynolds had no trouble falling asleep, undisturbed by the possible consequences of his actions. The following morning he returned to his room and found Symmes still unconscious, although a few yards from where he had left him, as though at some point during the night he had woken up and tried to drag himself over to the bed in search of shelter. His face had turned a bluish purple, his skin was burning, and he had difficulty breathing, emitting a noise like a death rattle or the sound of a trombone muted with damp cloths. Reynolds quickly carried Symmes back to his own room, where he laid him out on the bed. Then he called the doctor, who took one look at him and diagnosed pneumonia.

The patient never fully regained consciousness. For four days he perspired, writhed around on the bed wracked with fever, and called loudly for Litina. On the eve of his final day on Earth, which had subjected him to so many humiliations, Symmes opened his eyes and found Reynolds, who had not strayed from his bedside for a moment. The ex–army officer managed a hoarse whisper. All my efforts have been in vain, he told Reynolds. Litina will never know I was the victim of a conspiracy, that I truly loved her and have gone on loving her ever since I fled her world. Reynolds watched him, his heart brimming with a compassion that was as remarkable as it was profound for a life that could have ended with dignity had it not been cut short by madness. Almost instinctively, he clasped the dying man's hand and vowed to him, in that room reeking of medicines and mortality, that he would reach the center of the Earth if it was the last thing he did and pass on Symmes's message to Litina. As a final gesture, Symmes was able to muster a smile of gratitude; moments later his eyes glazed over, and his mouth opened in a desperate attempt to breathe in air that was no longer his. Reynolds discovered that the saddest thing in the world is to see a man die wearing the forlorn expression of someone who has failed to fulfill his dreams.

Ridding himself of Symmes in this way left a bitter aftertaste, yet there was no point in tormenting himself about it for the rest of his days, as a more sensitive soul would doubtless have done. And so the explorer decided to consign it to the place in his memory where he stored all his other shameful deeds and to carry on with his plan, as if the ex–army officer's death would have happened even without his intervention. And so, unencumbered at last, Reynolds resumed giving lectures up and down the East Coast, papering the walls with illustrations by Halley, Euler, and others, just as he had done when Symmes was still alive. Given that his private expositions appeared to have failed, out of desperation Reynolds began to charge a fifty-cent admission fee for his public talks in an attempt to drum up funds for the expedition Symmes had never made. But he soon realized the gesture was more idealistic than practical and decided it was time to set his sights higher. He went from city to city proselytizing, knocked on office doors with redoubled vigor, but received only rejections. Then it occurred to him to turn America's inferiority complex with regard to its European fellow nations to his advantage: he attempted to sell his polar expedition as the most important patriotic exploit ever undertaken. Thanks to what he instantly considered as a well-earned stroke of luck, his strategy caught the attention of John Frampton Watson, a wealthy businessman who was willing to fulfill Reynolds's dreams. Watson's money attracted a host of other powerful backers, who between them formed an intricate network of interests. Overnight Reynolds found himself scrutinized from behind the scenes by an alliance of powerful forces that were poised to celebrate his success—or to pounce on him if he failed. And so, amid wild cheers, the

Annawan set sail from New York Harbor in search of the polar entrance to the inner Earth, while the press hailed the dream that had poisoned Symmes's life as the Great American Expedition.

AND YET, HERE THEY were now in a place that did not seem to belong to the world, where the crowds' wild cheers no longer rang out, surrounded by a silence akin to oblivion. And as if that were not enough, something completely unexpected had happened, the consequences of which Reynolds was still unable to fathom. They had arrived in the Antarctic with the aim of finding the passage to the center of the Earth and had instead chanced upon a monster from the stars. Although at that moment fear blurred everything, Reynolds could not help beginning to play with the not entirely implausible idea that this accidental discovery might also crown him with glory and bury him under a pile of money. Did not the majority of important discoveries happen by chance? Did Columbus not stumble upon the New World when he was searching for a sea route to the East Indies? Indeed, the fate of great men seemed to be ordained by forces as powerful as they were mysterious. All of this could not be mere coincidence, he told himself. He was destined for glory, to go down in History, and he was determined to succeed come what may.

Reynolds tried to stay calm. Now more than ever he needed to study every possibility open to him. This much was obvious: if they managed to capture the demon and take him back to New York, it would cause a stir the like of which had never been seen before. The implications for humanity of the existence of other beings in outer space were incalculable. If the creature and its machine really came from there, as Peters claimed, they gave Man the opportunity to reconsider his place in nature and might even change his idea about the meaning of life. Like it or not, Man, that arrogant ruler of the universe, would have to acknowledge that Earth was just another planet in the vast firmament. In short, he would be forced to realize how terribly insignificant he was. Unquestionably, the monster from the stars would be an earth-shattering discovery, although, of course, they had to capture him first. But was that possible? All of a sudden another idea occurred to Reynolds: what if the monster from the stars was not an evil being, as everyone assumed, but had traveled to Earth on a peaceful mission? Would it be possible to communicate with him? Reynolds had no idea, but perhaps he ought to try, for it would be a far greater achievement than simply taking his head back to New York. The first ever communication with intelligent life from another world! What marvels a creature like that might reveal to the human race! And how Reynolds would be remembered for centuries as the instigator of such a miracle! The explorer had to stop his imagination from running away with him. All of this remained to be seen. First they had to find a way home, for what use would there be in freezing to death with the knowledge that other worlds existed, even if they had taken tea with a creature from one of them?

Two figures standing out against the horizon interrupted his meditations. Reynolds took the spyglass out of the pocket of his oilskin and trained it on a pair of dark shapes advancing toward the ship. Although he could not make out their faces at that distance, it had to be Carson and Ringwald. So they had not been eaten alive by the monster. And from the way they were walking they did not seem to be injured either. Then Reynolds noticed the sled they were pulling between them, on top of which was a large mound draped in a tarpaulin. Reynolds's jaw dropped in astonishment. This could only mean one thing: Carson and Ringwald had captured the monster from the stars.

V

*T*HE ARRIVAL OF THE MEN THEY HAD GIVEN UP for dead created the same stir among the crew of the *Annawan* as if they had seen a ghost. Reynolds, Captain MacReady, Doctor Walker, the boatswain Fisk, and some of the sailors, among them Peters, Allan, and Griffin, clambered down the makeshift ramp to welcome their lost companions, although most of them seemed more excited by the prospect of the two men having captured the monster from space. They came to a halt in front of the sled, plunged into a reverential silence.

"Did you find the demon?" MacReady asked, still unwilling to show any admiration for the two sailors whom he considered the most inept on the ship, while pointing at the mound upon which all eyes were focused.

"No, Captain," Ringwald replied, "but we found this."

The sailor gestured to his companion, and each tugged at a corner of the tarpaulin, revealing what was on the sled. The sight drew a murmur from the crew, for it was no less shocking than if it had been a demon from the stars. What Ringwald and Carson had brought from their search was the head of a gigantic elephant seal. The neck of the animal had been ripped apart, its huge skull crushed. The animal's wounds were so extreme that no one dared to imagine what might have caused them. While the astonished group were examining the carcass, Ringwald explained that when they had found it, the animal's innards were still steaming, which meant it could not have been long dead. The thick fog made it impossible for them to continue, so they had decided to open up the animal's abdomen even further and to take turns sheltering inside its still-warm interior. In this way, they had avoided freezing to death, although both had lost all feeling in their toes. Hearing their story, the others tried not to retch when they saw the thick, foul-smelling film covering the sailors' oilskins. They could not help imagining the two of them curled up inside the bloody cocoon, brandishing their muskets at the fogbound air. Leaning over the animal, Reynolds saw near its mouth what appeared to be shreds of strange reddish skin.

"Well, perhaps we still don't know what the monster looks like, but at least we know its skin is a bright crimson," he said, standing up straight. "It will be easy enough to spot in the snow."

"Crimson, sir?" one of the sailors said in surprise as he studied the shreds of skin. "It looks yellow to me."

"In that case, Wallace, you need your eyes tested," another sailor named Kendricks chimed in. "It's obviously blue."

Wallace insisted it was as yellow as straw, at which the other sailors leaned over to see which color the monster's skin was. Each appeared to see a different color.

"Stop arguing, damn it!" roared the captain, tired of this absurd debate. "Can't you see it doesn't matter what color the creature is? For God's sake, look at what it's capable of!"

Suddenly ashamed, the sailors fell silent. For his part, Reynolds felt a degree of disappointment as well as horror as he contemplated the carcass.

At that moment, Captain MacReady stepped back from the remains, scanning the horizon through narrowed eyes while the others looked on apprehensively.

"Listen carefully," he said, turning to them at last. "From now on, no one leaves the ship without my permission. We'll take shelter inside and take turns on watch. If that thing did this to an enormous elephant seal over sixteen feet long, I don't need to tell you what it could do to any of us."

An anxious murmur spread through the crew.

"As for the head of the seal," he added, "take it on board. At least we'll have something to eat while we wait for that thing to come after us, which it will do sooner or later."

The crew nodded as one and trudged back to the ship, trying to come to terms with the state of siege into which they had suddenly been plunged, although their apparent composure probably owed more to the fact that there was no one to gripe at. As if freezing to death on that accursed lump of ice were not enough, now they had to contend with a monster that could tear an elephant seal to ribbons. Reynolds, who had taken up the rear of the gloomy procession, noticed that Allan was still standing next to the sled, gazing thoughtfully into the distance. Finally, the young gunner turned around and followed the group, head bowed, a grim look in his eyes.

"We are alone . . . ," he said, as he drew level with Reynolds. "Alone with the creature."

His words made Reynolds's blood run cold. All of a sudden, that vast space seemed to him terribly small.

TWO DAYS LATER, EVERYTHING was still calm. It was a tense calm, filled with furtive glances and fearful faces, where the slightest noise made everyone jump, and the more sensitive souls spilled half their broth, while muskets sat alongside spoons at the table. A wary, strained composure where tempers frayed easily and arguments were generally resolved by one party drawing a knife or by the intervention of Captain MacReady. In short, the kind of nail-biting stillness that made them all secretly wish the monster from the stars would attack once and for all, so that they could see if they could defeat it—or, on the contrary, find out if all resistance was useless, as in the case of the seal, whose flesh was now sating their hunger in broths.

So that the monster's arrival would not take them by surprise, Mac-Ready had posted four lookouts on deck, one at each compass point of the ship, and had ordered the men to take two-hour watches. Despite having been exempted from lookout duty, whether because of his status as leader of the expedition or because of his wounded hand, Reynolds would occasionally come up on deck to take the air and escape the long hours of confinement that made his already cramped cabin seem even narrower. However, on this occasion it was not to escape his cabin, but rather because his room was too close to the infirmary in the ship's prow, and he had just learned that Doctor Walker, who had been so merciful toward his scalded hand, was intent upon amputating Carson's right foot before it became gangrenous. Having been subjected a few moments earlier to the hellish screams of Ringwald, who had only lost three fingers, Reynolds preferred to be freezing on deck than to face such brutal evidence of the cruel conditions endured by members of polar expeditions, such as the one he had so merrily organized.

Judging from the intense cold that hit him as he stepped outside, the temperature that afternoon must have been forty degrees below zero. A fierce wind roared above the stunted masts and up the ramp, blowing the snow hither and thither. Reynolds wrapped himself in his oilskin and glanced about. He was pleased to see that Allan was one of the lookouts. The gunner's figure, which seemed to be made up of long, slender limbs like those of a spindly bird, was unmistakable even beneath several layers of clothing. The sergeant was scanning the horizon attentively, cradling his musket in his poet's hands. After watching him for a few moments, Reynolds decided to engage him in conversation. After all, the youth from Baltimore was the only man in the crew whose impressions of what was happening might interest him.

As he had done with Griffin when they were walking over to the flying machine, Reynolds had first approached Allan to discover why someone who had so little in common with the others had signed up for his expedition. Allan stood out among those loutish men, with their vulgar tales and simple vices. From the very beginning, Allan had proved a brilliant conversationalist so that the explorer contrived to bump into him whenever possible, in order to lift his spirits. As the days went by and Allan also seemed at ease in his company, Reynolds had decided to invite him to his cabin to help him make inroads into the store of brandy he had brought from America. As a result, Reynolds had been able to witness the devastating effects of drink on poor Allan: if the first sip turned him into an eloquent speaker, the second made him ramble, losing himself in his own discourse, and the third left him sprawled across the table, semiconscious, a nearly full glass in front of him. Reynolds had never met anyone with less tolerance for alcohol than the gunner.

Those erratic, exalted discussions had allowed the explorer to form a clear enough picture of Allan's life. He discovered that the poet had joined the crew of the *Annawan* for no other reason than to escape his atrocious relationship with his stepfather. After years of discord, and even threats from both sides, which had rendered the atmosphere in the family home intolerable, the exhausted Allan had devised a way of placating the obdurate tyrant who had become his guardian following his parents' demise: he would offer to enroll at West Point. As Allan had anticipated, his stepfather accepted, relieved that the tiresome youth had at last found the path that would deliver him from idleness. However, as the day of his enrollment dawned, Allan realized there was nothing he would like less than to go to West Point. All he wanted was to disappear, for the earth to swallow him up or, if not, to find a place where time would stop miraculously and he would be able to think, gather his strength, decide what he wanted to do with his life, perhaps to write the new poem he could feel emerging in his mind, without having to worry about where his next meal was coming from. Was there such a place apart from prison? He realized there was when he heard about the expedition of the *Annawan,* which gave no guarantee of return but offered plenty of adventure.

And so, thought Reynolds, that motley crew consisted of men who were running away from something. In fact, neither Allan, nor Griffin, nor any of the crew on the *Annawan* gave a damn if the Earth was hollow. They were simply a group of desperate men fleeing their demons. And yet, in their flight to nowhere, the crew members' destinies had converged, and now they faced a real live demon, and probably a death worse than that of being relegated to oblivion.

Reynolds shook his head at his own thoughts. He was taking too much for granted, he told himself, as he approached Allan with a look of resignation on his face. How could he be sure the object's origins were not earthly? Did he trust the suspicions of an Indian who could not even follow a trail? His intuition told him the creature *was* from another world, but since that was what he was hoping for, his intuition was surely biased. And as for the creature's intentions, well, it was best not to dwell on them. Despite his desire to establish contact with the monster, Reynolds had been infected with the same fear as the rest of the men and had started going to bed with his pistol under his pillow, scarcely able to sleep as he imagined the monster outside, circling the ship.

Reynolds positioned himself alongside Allan, greeting him genially. For some minutes they maintained the respectful silence of two people sharing a box at the theater, admiring the spectacle of the white, icy terrain stretching out before them. The wind rocked the lanterns nailed to the posts forming a cordon around the ship, lending the scene a magical air, as though hidden in the snowy distance a ring of fairies were dancing. Were they being watched at that very moment? Reynolds wondered uneasily. Finally he cleared his throat and asked the gunner the question he had been longing to put to him from the very beginning.

"What do you suppose that thing is, Allan?"

The swaddled lump that was the sergeant's head went on gazing at the ice for a few moments.

"I don't know," he replied at last, with a shrug.

Not satisfied with his answer, Reynolds tried to formulate the question in a different way. "Do you think it comes from . . . the stars?"

This time the gunner responded instantly: "I do, my friend, probably from Mars."

The young man's precision took Reynolds aback. "Why Mars?"

The gunner nodded and turned round, staring at him with his huge eyes, those grey eyes Reynolds always avoided looking at for fear they would suck him in like a whirlpool.

"It is the simplest explanation," said Allan, almost apologetically. "And the simplest explanations are almost always the truest."

"Why?" the explorer asked, without clarifying whether he was questioning Allan's first or second statement, or both.

"Because Mars is the planet that has most in common with ours," Allan explained, his gaze wandering back to the ice. "Have you read the Royal Society's reports based on studies carried out by William Herschel, the astronomer royal, with his telescope?" Reynolds shook his head, inviting to Allan to go on, which he did immediately: "They maintain that Mars has a thick atmosphere, similar in many ways to ours, which means it is probably inhabited."

"I see you haven't considered the possibility that the creature and its machine could be part of a military experiment carried out by some foreign power, for example."

"Of course I have. However, it seems inconceivable that a foreign power could possess scientific knowledge so disproportionately superior to our own," said Allan, "and that they could have managed to keep it quiet until now, don't you agree? Therefore I am dismissing the idea that the creature comes from Earth, which only leaves outer space. And if we accept that premise, we may not be far wrong in supposing that our visitor comes from Mars, the planet that is both nearest to ours and most able to support life out of all those around us." Allan shot him a glance. "Of course, I could be mistaken, and I may even be distorting the facts to fit my theory, a common tendency in deductive reasoning. But until someone disproves it, this seems to me the simplest and therefore the most logical explanation," he concluded emphatically.

Allan raised his penetrating gaze toward the sky, appearing to look in a specific direction, perhaps toward the red planet itself. Shivering with cold at his side, Reynolds watched him with a mixture of disquiet and fascination, struck dumb by his analysis of the creature's origins. The extent of the gunner's knowledge never ceased to amaze Reynolds. He had not met anyone so seemingly informed in such a variety of subjects, or who was capable of such categorical and exhaustive analysis. Not for nothing had the gunner enrolled in the prestigious University of Virginia at the age of seventeen. Although, according to what he had told

Reynolds during one of his drunken rants, he had immediately incurred impossibly high gambling debts, and with no one willing to pay them off for him, he had been summarily expelled, but not before setting fire to every stick of furniture in his room. Another message that his step-father, whom Allan reproached for having educated him as a rich boy without giving him any money, had failed to interpret.

"Do you know something, Reynolds? I have always thought it was only a matter of time before they paid us a visit," the gunner suddenly added with an air of somber reflection, as he continued to gaze up at the star-studded sky.

"A Martian," Reynolds repeated, still incredulous.

The sergeant's words had made him feel elated and terrified at the same time. The man beside him, whose intellect was as keen as his own, believed, as he did, that the creature came from outer space. Over-whelmed once more by all the ramifications of this, Reynolds felt his head start to spin. A Martian had fallen out of the sky . . . And they would be the first humans to establish contact with it, the brave crew of the *Annawan,* the members of the Great American Expedition organized by the famous explorer Jeremiah Reynolds. The first man to communi-cate with a being from the stars, the man who would possibly never be appointed viceroy of the subterranean world, but who might go down in History as Earth's ambassador to outer space.

"Yes, a Martian," reiterated the gunner, who was by now looking at Reynolds, eyes shining, as if the brightness of the stars he had been contemplating were glinting in them. "And his existence changes every-thing, don't you think? How could Man go on believing in God now, for example?"

"Well," replied Reynolds, "I wouldn't be so sure. According to Gen-esis, God is the Creator of all things, of Heaven and Earth, of all that is visible and invisible: of everything, Allan, including the Martian. I think God will appear even more powerful to us for having been able to invent beings beyond Man's imagining."

"And what makes you so sure?" Allan gently replied. "Consider the

Annawan for a moment. She is a relatively modern vessel, and yet after almost four hundred years, the main thing that differentiates her from a simple galleon is that she is powered by coal as well as wind. And only a few miles away from her is a machine from another world, something so incredibly advanced it is beyond the grasp of our most brilliant minds. Try to imagine what kind of civilization could have created such a thing and what other marvels a society like that might reveal to us. A vaccine against aging? A cure for our most terrible afflictions? Creatures made in our image that could carry out the most backbreaking or the simplest chores for us? Immortality perhaps? Tell me, Reynolds, who will believers look to after this? I am afraid that when it all comes to light, no one will care what God and His Heaven have to offer," declared the sergeant.

Reynolds did not know how to challenge him, above all because he agreed with everything Allan had said. If Reynolds had played the devil's advocate, it was only because, unlike him, the gunner had given no thought to how he might benefit personally from all this. No, Allan had focused on the significance the Martian's arrival might have for humanity, making Reynolds feel small-minded, selfish, and grasping. Both men fell silent, watching the lights dancing on the surface of the ice. In any event, thought Reynolds, he was not going to waste time arguing, since it made no difference to him whether in fifty years' time Man still believed in God or had begun worshipping skunks. What he really wanted to ask Allan was whether, despite the revolutionary nature of their discovery, it was right that Man should welcome his supposed guest with a hail of bullets. If Allan agreed with him that this was a mistake, he might join him in trying to dissuade the captain from pursuing this course of action.

However, Reynolds did not get the chance to pose any more questions, for a sudden uproar inside the hold obliged them to cut short their conversation. The two men turned as one, and, after listening intently for a few moments, deduced that the sounds were coming from the infirmary. What the devil was going on in there? It seemed a little unreasonable of Carson to make such a fuss over losing a foot, Reynolds reflected. Like the rest of the lookouts, Allan did not dare to abandon his post, and so, after taking his leave with a shrug, the explorer was the only one who broke the icy silence on deck as he scrambled over to the nearest hatch to see what was going on. He clambered down to the lower deck and made his way to the infirmary. A group of sailors stood crowded outside, a look of terror in their eyes. Reynolds barged through them and into the infirmary. The grisly scene he encountered left him speechless, as it had Captain MacReady, who stood ashen-faced in the center of the room.

The cause of the captain's horror was none other than the dismembered corpse of Doctor Walker. The surgeon lay on the floor like a broken doll. Someone, or perhaps it would be more exact to say *some thing,* had torn him limb from limb with shocking meticulousness. His right arm had been wrenched from its socket, both legs hacked off, and his throat sliced right through so that his spinal vertebrae were exposed. His thorax had also been slit down the middle, and a medley of organs, entrails, and splinters of rib cage were strewn about the floor. The walls were covered with gruesome splatters of blood and viscous blobs, and wherever Reynolds looked his eye alighted on a fresh lump of flesh or organ. His face turned pale as he surveyed the carnage. It seemed unbelievable that if all these different bits were reassembled, they would form Doctor Walker, the same sentient being who only a few hours earlier had smiled at him and inquired about his hand when they had met in the gangway. And in the midst of all this destruction, trembling from head to toe as he crouched on the cot as though he had just witnessed all the horrors of the world, was Carson. It did not take long for Reynolds to conclude that the author of that bloodbath was the demon from the sky—or the Martian, if he was to believe Allan. The thought that in the monster's eyes a man deserved no more respect than a seal, and that apparently it could enter the ship undetected, made Reynolds's blood run cold, obliterating any trace of euphoria he might have felt when, only a few moments before, he and Allan had speculated about the creature and its origins. What he felt now had another name: fear. Fear unlike any he had ever known, fear that showed him how fragile, insignificant, and pitifully vulnerable he was, and above all the pathetic presumptuousness of his aspirations to grandeur.

"Good God . . . ," Captain MacReady murmured, unable to take his eyes off the surgeon's ravaged corpse.

When he managed to regain his composure, he walked over to Carson and questioned him about what had happened, but the sailor was in a state of shock. MacReady shook him a couple of times, then began frantically slapping him, but Carson seemed unable to respond. At last the captain realized he was wasting his time, and, thrusting Reynolds aside, he addressed his men.

"Listen, everyone. The thing that did this to Doctor Walker is probably still inside the ship," he said. "Go to the weapons store, take as many guns as you can carry, and search the vessel from top to bottom."

All at once Reynolds found himself lying on the infirmary floor, while in the distance he heard the captain barking orders to his men, organizing a sweep of the ship. Trying not to retch, he glanced once more at the gruesome remains of the surgeon's dismembered body. Then he looked at Carson and wondered whether he was shaking because he knew they were all going to die, because his stupefied mind had grasped that the demon from the stars was so terrifying that no human being stood a chance against it and they might as well give themselves up for dead. The creature would finish them off one by one, on that distant lump of ice, while God looked the other way.

VI

OLLOWING MacReady's orders, the sailors scoured every inch of the ship. Muskets at the ready, they inspected the coal bunkers and the powder store, where the gunpowder and munitions slept their uneasy sleep. They even peered inside the boilers in the engine room and laundry. The demon from the stars was nowhere to be found. After hacking the surgeon to pieces, the monster had apparently vanished into thin air. There was no trace either of any damage to the ship's hull, no hole through which the Martian, or whatever it was, could have slipped aboard the *Annawan*. Incredible though it might seem, the creature had found a way to enter and leave without being seen. Unnerved, MacReady's only answer was to double the number of lookouts. He even posted a few men outside on the ice, forming a ring around the ship.

But, regrettably, his strategy did nothing to wipe the fear from the eyes of the sailors, who went on obsessively searching the ship and grilling Carson about what he had seen. They needed to know what the monster looked like. But Carson's account was only sketchy. The sailor had been stretched out on one of the cots in the infirmary, semiconscious from the laudanum, so that he felt the teeth of the saw as little more than a pleasant, harmless tickle, even though the surgeon was about to take off his right foot at the ankle, when a huge shadow entered the room and hurled itself at the unwitting Doctor Walker. In a matter of seconds, the apparition had torn the surgeon to shreds, pieces of him flying about the room in a hail of bloody lumps of flesh and broken bone. Unsure if this was a hallucination caused by the laudanum, or, however insane it seemed, if it was really happening, the horrified Carson prepared himself to meet the same fate, wondering whether he would feel anything more than a pleasant tickle when the creature began to dismember him. But luckily for Carson, his fellow sailors' movements had alerted the demon, and it had fled the room. Carson could only offer a vague and incomplete description of the monster that added nothing new to the information Peters had gleaned from its footprints. The Martian, indeed, did have claws, not hooves, and was terrifying to behold, but they could get no more information out of Carson, not even about the color of its skin. Carson was a man of few words who knew when to unfurl a sail to make the most of the wind but whose vocabulary was too limited to describe a creature that probably resembled nothing he had ever seen before. When Carson had recovered from the shock, they dressed the tiny incision on his foot made by the saw, although none of them dared finish the amputation the doctor had started. They left him in the infirmary, hoping for a miracle or that a game of cards would decide who would wield the saw and put an end to Carson's suffering.

The following morning, they buried the remains of Doctor Francis Walker in a coffin expressly built by the carpenters, although what they placed inside it was little more than a smattering of fragments. They dug a grave in the ice with shovels and pickaxes, and they lowered the box into it, draped in a flag. Marking his final resting place was a simple plank of wood, with the following inscription:

In memory of Doctor Francis T. Walker, who departed this life
on 4 March 1830 on board the Annawan,
at the age of thirty-four years.

Peters took upon himself the task of driving the wooden plank into the ice with an enormous mallet. They performed the ceremony close to the ship, and although it was meant to be a solemn affair they could not help carrying it out as quickly as possible, since no one wanted to spend too long exposed to that bitter cold, especially when the monster responsible for what happened to the doctor was still at large.

AFTER THE BURIAL, REYNOLDS retired to his cabin and, lying on his bunk with his eyes closed, mulled over recent events. After seeing the doctor's fragmented body it was logical to assume the monster had no interest in fraternizing with them but rather seemed hell-bent on death and the annihilation of all forms of life, whether elephant seals or skilled surgeons. Still, Reynolds had not given up his idea of conversing peaceably with it. Must he rule out that option simply because the monster had not shown Doctor Walker the proper respect? Perhaps it had felt threatened by the frail-looking surgeon. Or perhaps it had still not grasped that they, too, were intelligent beings, and that it could therefore communicate with them if it so wished. Perhaps to the monster they were simple cockroaches, so that it had no moral scruples about crushing them. Reynolds abandoned that line of reasoning when he realized he was simply trying to find a way of justifying the monster's violent behavior, whereas perhaps what he ought to be doing was accepting the fact that, for whatever reason, the demon was intent on destroying them, giving them no choice but to kill it before it killed them. Although he could not be sure of that either. They lacked information, and staying posted around the ship, ready to blast away anything on the snow that moved, whatever its size or shape, was clearly not the best way to get any. The explorer sighed and sat upright in his bunk. Something prevented him from giving up hope of communicating with a being from another planet. Perhaps they would succeed if they dealt with the situation a little more calmly instead of giving way to panic. They had the opportunity to establish diplomatic, peaceful relations with another world! They should not rule out that possibility simply because they did not yet know what they were up against, he told himself. Reynolds stood up and, brimming with resolve, made his way to Captain MacReady's cabin to discuss the matter with him.

MacReady greeted him with his usual lack of interest. The captain's cabin was almost four times bigger than the explorer's, spanning the breadth of the ship's stern. It boasted a substantial library and an enormous food store crammed with hams, cheeses, pots of marmalade, sacks of tea, bottles of excellent brandy, and other delicacies paid for out of the captain's own pocket. But more significantly, it was fitted with its own privy, where MacReady could relieve himself away from the stresses and strains of his command. Reynolds envied him this tiny closet on the starboard side, which he considered a great luxury, a slice of civilization as comforting as it was incongruous. The captain offered him a glass of brandy and gestured wearily toward a chair.

"Well, Reynolds, to what do I owe the honor of your visit?" he said sardonically as soon as his visitor had sat down.

The explorer gazed pityingly at this giant of a man who, despite being aware he was defeated, utterly overwhelmed by circumstances, insisted on exerting his authority with a kind of crude malevolence. For perhaps the ship becoming icebound was a foreseeable event, a setback that years of experience had prepared the captain to face with professional equanimity, imagining perchance that the arrival of summer would bring the long-awaited miracle: the thaw that would liberate them. Yes, the accursed icepack would eventually break up, and the *Annawan,* less damaged than they had feared, would be free to sail away from there, down the channels that would widen with their passage, in a genuine apotheosis of human will, but above all in a celebration of life, shared by petrels and skuas flocking gaily overhead, as well as shoals of cod and herring and even Arctic whales, which would escort them home in a majestic convoy. Reynolds took a sip of brandy and went straight to the point.

"Captain, I think we need to talk about the strategy we should follow in the current circumstances."

"The strategy we should follow?" MacReady repeated in astonishment, looking Reynolds up and down as if he had just walked in wearing a clown's outfit. "What the hell are you talking about?"

"It is very simple, Captain. As organizer of this expedition, I am the one in charge of any discoveries we might make along the way, and although we are clearly no closer to finding the passage to the Hollow Earth than we were when we left New York, we are nevertheless on the brink of one of the most significant discoveries in the History of Mankind, one that I believe requires us to establish a plan of action and a set of criteria."

MacReady carried on gaping at the explorer for a few moments before throwing his head back and letting out a loud guffaw. Spluttering, he dried his eyes with his chubby fingers and, regaining his composure, declared, "For Heaven's sake, Reynolds: you never cease to amaze me! So you want us to discuss criteria . . . Well, mine are very simple. As soon as that thing, whatever it is, shows its ugly face around here, my men and I will shove a musket up its backside, cut its head off as a memento, and providing its flesh isn't too disgusting, we'll feed it to the dogs. That's my plan of action in the *current circumstances*. In the meantime, if you wish to carry on playing explorer, be my guest, only kindly do it in the confines of your cabin so that you don't get in the way."

Reynolds had to make a supreme effort to keep calm. He knew the captain would not make it easy for him, but he had gone there with a clear purpose, and he refused to allow MacReady's continual provocation to deflect him. He took another sip of brandy and waited for a few moments before responding, resorting this time to flattery.

"Captain," he said, "you are not a simple drunken sailor, like the rest of the crew. You are a gentleman, an experienced ship's captain, and intelligent enough I am sure to grasp the magnitude of what is going on. I have been speaking with Sergeant Allan, who as you know is a man of letters, well versed in, er, astronomy, and he agrees with me that the creature doubtless comes from Mars. Do you realize what this thing is we are fighting? A Martian, Captain! A being from another planet! I refuse to believe you do not appreciate the enormous significance of such a discovery and how reckless it would be of us not to consider carefully every possible alternative. Allow me to give you an example: if we kill the creature before communicating with it, how will we know where it comes from? And more importantly, if all we take with us to New York is a strange animal's head, how will we prove the thing really is from another planet? It won't give scientists much to go on, will it, Captain? And this leads to my next request. I would like you to organize another expedition to the flying machine."

"Are you out of your mind?" said MacReady, genuinely taken aback. "I've no intention of sending my men out there with that thing lurking in the snow. I would be sending them to their death. Besides, that machine is impossible to open, we can't even touch it, or perhaps you've forgotten what happened to you." MacReady tilted his chin toward the explorer's still-bandaged hand. "And anyway, why the devil would we want to do that?"

"Primarily because if we manage to get inside the machine we will probably find some information about the creature that is attacking us," Reynolds explained patiently. "This could prove essential if on the one hand the creature's intentions are peaceful and we simply need to learn how to communicate with it, and on the other if they are not, because we may find some clue as to how to destroy it, a weapon even." Seeing that the captain was still staring blankly at him, Reynolds realized he must take a different approach, and so he tried enticement. "Supposing that were the case—I mean, supposing we had no choice but to kill the creature, and, assuming we succeeded, and then the ice thawed and we sailed home, don't you think we would be entitled to some compensation for all we had been through? For I assure you, if we arrive in New York with the Martian's head, together with some proof from the machine that this is indeed a being from another planet, we will be showered with more money and recognition than you can imagine."

"I still don't know if you are a visionary, a complete idiot, or both, Reynolds," MacReady said. "To begin with, I don't understand how you can go on doubting the creature's intentions after the *courteousness* he showed poor Doctor Walker. I assure you I need no further proof. I know exactly how we should *communicate* with that thing. As for the flying machine, how the devil do you intend to get inside it? Through sheer brain power?"

"I don't know, Captain," Reynolds confessed, irritated by the officer's mocking tone. "We could try blowing it up with dynamite . . ."

The captain shook his head, as though he were conversing with a lunatic, and a sullen silence descended on the two men. Reynolds tried to think. He was running out of ideas.

"I've never understood men like you, Reynolds," MacReady suddenly murmured, gently swirling his brandy. "What is it you want? To be remembered by History? Of what use is that to a God-fearing Christian once the maggots have finished with him? I told you the other day, Reynolds: I don't give a fig about your Hollow Earth. The same goes for that creature's origins. It could come from Mars or Jupiter or any other planet for all I care. My job is to bring this ship and her crew safely back to New York, and I'll be well paid if I do. That's all I care about, Reynolds: saving my skin and getting my money."

"I refuse to believe you have no other desires in life," Reynolds hissed, with as much contempt as he could muster.

"Why, of course I do. I dream of a cottage in the country, with a garden full of tulips."

"Tulips?" the explorer asked in astonishment.

"Yes, tulips," the captain repeated, defensively. "My mother was Dutch, and I still remember her planting them in our garden when I was a child. I hope to have saved enough by the time I retire to live a quiet life and devote myself to growing tulips. And I assure you, I won't give up until I have grown the most beautiful tulip on our side of the Atlantic. I shall name it after my mother and enter it in all the flower shows. That's all I want, Reynolds: a beautiful tulip garden and a sitting room with a fireplace, above which I shall hang the head of the monster you are so intent on communicating with."

Reynolds gazed at him in silence for a while, trying to thrust aside the alarming image of the captain, a pair of pruning shears in one hand and a basket of tulips in the other. Could a brute like MacReady hold a tulip without crushing it? And if his tulip failed to win, would he take the loss with a smile, or would he shoot the judges? The explorer leaned back in his chair, trying to gather his thoughts while taking another sip from his glass. He had to admit that whereas he had failed to win over the captain with his arguments, MacReady had almost succeeded in convincing him with his. What did he hope to find inside the flying machine? Perhaps it would be best if he took the captain's advice and saved his skin so he could return to Baltimore and carry on with his dreary, pedestrian life. Compared to what he was going through on that vast expanse of ice it did not seem half so bad, and maybe if he took up gardening it would be easier to bear. He set his glass down on the table, surprised that part of him longed to surrender to that life. But the other part, the part that had poisoned him with dreams of glory and had brought him there, sank its fangs into him once more. What the devil was he thinking? He had not come all this way for nothing!

"Tell me, Captain, has it not occurred to you that the creature may be unaware that it is behaving in a malevolent fashion?" he blurted out, in a tone of bitterness born of despair. "Perhaps the monster's thought patterns are so different from ours that it sees what it has been doing as comparable to crushing a spider underfoot or pulling up weeds." He paused to allow MacReady to digest his words, then added, "Can you really not see what I am driving at, Captain? Whether we intend to communicate with the creature or to kill it, clearly we must first understand it. Moreover, I am sure any one of the sailors will readily accompany me to the machine when I explain it's our only hope of survival."

MacReady stared at him coolly.

"Have you quite finished?" he asked, addressing the explorer with unnerving slowness. "Good! Now listen to me, Reynolds. I shall ignore your veiled threat of mutiny, for which I could have you locked up in the ship's hold until you rot. But, although you don't deserve it, I shall be lenient and simply inform you that the circumstances of the expedition have changed radically. We are now in a state of emergency, which gives me complete control over this vessel, whether you like it or not. You no longer have any say in the matter. From now on, I decide what action we take against the ruthless enemy that is attacking us. We shall wait for it to come after us, that is what we shall do. If you disagree and want to return to the flying machine, I shan't try to stop you. Take as many weapons from the armory as you can carry, but don't count on the support of any of my men. They will stay on the ship with me, waiting for that thing."

At first, Reynolds had no idea how to respond. With obvious satisfaction, MacReady had relieved him of his authority, thereby leaving him with only one possible line of attack.

"I can assure you that when we reach New York," he said, "I intend to hold you fully responsible for the failure of this expedition: I shall accuse you of causing the ship to become icebound through your inept navigation, of refusing to explore the area in search of the passage to the center of the Earth, and, above all, Captain, I shall hold you to account for every death that occurs from now on, including that of the first visitor from space ever to set foot on our planet."

Reynolds fell silent, glowering at the captain. He bitterly regretted having to resort to threats, but that stubborn, arrogant devil had proved immune to every other approach. It seemed, however, that even this outburst did not have the slightest effect on MacReady, who simply sighed wearily.

"Reynolds, you are the stupidest man I have ever met," he said. "And I have nothing more to say to you. This conversation has already gone on too long, and we have both made our positions clear. With all due respect, I shan't deny that your wild fantasies have been a source of great amusement to certain gentlemen and myself. But this is no time for laughter, and the last thing I need on board now is a buffoon."

Reynolds stared at the captain openmouthed.

"If that is all, Reynolds," said MacReady, standing up and turning his back on the explorer, "kindly allow me to carry on with my duties. Go ahead with your plan if you want, but don't even think about approaching my men."

Speechless, Reynolds contemplated the captain's broad back. There was no point insisting. He let out a grunt of frustration and rose to his feet.

"As you wish, Captain. But you can forget about ever naming a tulip after your mother," he retorted.

And he walked out of the cabin, slamming the door behind him.

VII

ON THE WAY BACK TO HIS OWN CABIN, REYNOLDS thought of dozens of far wittier, more stinging rejoinders than the one he had muttered behind the captain's back. Too late now. Like it or not, MacReady had come out on top, forcing Reynolds to withdraw from his quarters like a sulky child. He heaved a sigh as he opened the door to his cabin. In the end, what he most regretted about his dramatic exit was having abandoned the excellent brandy the captain had offered him. Now more than ever he longed to feel the liquor slide down his throat like a tongue of red-hot lava, calming his anger even as it warmed his insides. What he wanted, in fact, was to drink himself into oblivion without the slightest feeling of remorse. No impartial bystander could deny that his situation more than justified opening one of the bottles that had survived his discussions with Allan and polishing the whole thing off.

He grabbed the nearest one and ensconced himself in the leather armchair he had brought with him, not so much because he thought it might bring him luck, but because it belonged to a world he would not see again for a long time. This piece of furniture would become the guiding light that prevented him from losing sight of his real life, the memory of which would no doubt fade as his days at sea multiplied. It spoke to him of a more rational and comfortable world, where there were no threatening monsters and where the worst thing that could happen was to cut himself shaving.

He drank lengthily from the bottle, nearly choking a couple of times.

What had MacReady meant by insisting he had been a figure of fun? he wondered. He did not know whether this was bluster on the captain's part or whether he knew something Reynolds didn't. Was the expedition no more than a giant smoke screen concealing interests about which he knew nothing? He took another swig of the brandy. In any event, Reynolds reasoned, if he was indeed the victim of some ruse, if those who were watching him from the shadows had arranged everything so that he would embark on this adventure for some obscure reason they had refrained from telling him about, there was clearly one thing they had been unable to plan in advance: the appearance of the creature. And now the monster from the stars was providing Reynolds with the opportunity to refuse the role of buffoon his sponsors had reserved for him and to return triumphantly to New York, holding the key to the universe. If he succeeded, the whole world would have to bow at his feet. Whatever the case, he had to do something. If they were plotting behind his back, he had to cover himself. But how? MacReady had authorized him to return to the flying machine with as many weapons as he could carry, perhaps because deep down he was convinced Reynolds would not go, that he would cower in his cabin, where MacReady would go to look for him when it was all over, a broad grin on his face, brandishing the monster's head.

But MacReady was mistaken, Reynolds told himself, taking another swig from the bottle. He did not plan to sit there twiddling his thumbs! Far from it! If the captain refused to give him the men he had asked for, he would go alone to the Martian's machine, blow it up, and return to the ship with the information they needed to successfully confront the demon from the sky. He was more of a man than any tulip lover could ever be! He swallowed another mouthful. And what exactly did he expect to find in the flying machine that might help them? He was not sure. A weapon, perhaps, something more sophisticated and powerful than the simple musket Man used to wage his petty wars in the privacy of his own planet. He raised the bottle to his lips once more. He actually hoped to find something quite different, something that would help him establish contact with the creature when it finally showed itself. Of course the monster would not be expecting that. Reynolds would prove to the creature that they, too, were rational beings. Or perhaps he would find some kind of sacred text revealing the history of the creature's race, a manuscript that explained their conception of the universe and whether they viewed Earthlings as more than a mere hindrance or simple fodder.

He greedily downed the remains of the bottle and sat for a moment staring into space, lulled pleasantly by the effects of the drink, while he began to fancy that the notion of going off alone to the place where the flying machine had crashed was a less reckless endeavor than he had at first thought. Why shouldn't he go? What the devil was stopping him? A surge of optimism gave him an uncanny sense of his own strength, as if he might crush the creature with his bare hands if it crossed his path or dissuade it from its present course of action with stirring perorations on interplanetary harmony. Reynolds rose from his armchair, determined to prove to MacReady he was no naïve fool, but rather someone capable of rising to the occasion in an extreme situation like the one in which they found themselves. Yes, by Jove, he would revisit the machine and return triumphant, saving them all from certain death, even though they did not deserve it! He pulled on his oilskin, wound his neckerchief around his head, and lurched toward the armory.

Once there, he began enthusiastically equipping himself with weapons. He thrust two pistols into his belt and, seeing he still had space for more, grabbed a third. He slung three muskets over his shoulder, stuffed two machetes down his front, and, to top it all off, crammed his pockets with sticks of dynamite. Although tempted by one of the famous harpoons, he decided it was too heavy and contented himself with his present haul. It was only when he tried to move that he realized all that weaponry prevented him from walking normally. Undeterred, he staggered over to the ladder leading to one of hatches, ignoring the uncomfortable sensation produced by one of the gun muzzles digging into his right testicle each time he took a step. He crossed the deck, reeling helplessly, partly owing to his unwieldy load, partly due to the brandy. Such was his light-headedness that he imagined he saw Carson on watch on the poop deck. But that was impossible, unless the man's foot had miraculously recovered from frostbite. He shook his head to rid himself of the absurd notion and moved on laboriously, pausing now and then to retrieve a stick of dynamite that had fallen out of his pocket or to adjust one of the irksome pistols. At last, he came to the snow ramp, where he had to take care not to slip. Too late: rather than sliding he was dragged down by the sheer weight of his load and ended up sprawled on the ice, half throttled by the gun straps that had become tangled as he rolled down the ramp. For some minutes he lay on the ground trying to catch his breath, glad not to have been ludicrously strangled to death at the foot of the vessel. When he recovered, he clambered to his feet, then set off toward the mountains scarcely visible in the distance, enveloped in ribbons of mist.

After walking some twenty yards, Reynolds realized he would not have the strength to carry his arsenal all the way to where the flying object had crashed, and when one of the pistols slipped from his belt for a third time, he decided to leave it where it lay. Next he dropped one of the muskets, and thus, gradually shedding his weapons, he began closing the distance, straining not to lose sight of the mountains as the fog thickened. Much to Reynolds's despair, they soon vanished altogether in the accursed mist, as did the rest of the landscape. He suddenly realized in bewilderment that he could not see anything around him. Through his drunken haze, he dimly perceived that what he was doing was complete madness and doomed to failure. Not only had he lost sight of his objective in the dense fog but he could no longer see his way back to the ship. With a weary gesture, he flung the last musket to the ground. There was no need to play the hero anymore. But what was he to do? He needed to think, to weigh up the situation. Clearly he could not stay where he was, out on the ice, exposed to that merciless cold. Unfortunately, his head was spinning and his thoughts were muddled as he flailed around desperately in search of a solution. He was forced to accept that he was stuck in the middle of nowhere and too drunk to think straight. Not only that, but he must not forget the monster from the stars, which was doubtless lurking out there, perhaps even spying on him at that very moment from behind the wall of fog, smacking its lips at the sight of his vulnerability. Suddenly aware that he was at the creature's mercy, Reynolds was seized with the same terror he had felt when he saw Doctor Walker's dismembered body. He grabbed one of the two remaining pistols and aimed it frantically in all directions. The monster could pounce on him from any side, he realized with horror. He thought he glimpsed a shadow in the fog but could not tell whether it was real or a figment of his overwrought imagination. His fear reached an intolerable pitch, causing his arm to twitch uncontrollably, and all of a sudden he found himself running helter-skelter through the fog, he did not know where or why, feeling the monster's breath on his neck, aware that his panic would spur him on as far as his legs would carry him.

It was then he tripped over something and landed flat on his face on the ice. Half dazed, he got to his knees and felt his way nervously in the fog, trying to discover whatever had made him stumble. What the devil could it be out there in the middle of the snow? Then his hands touched a boot, which seemed to rise from the snow like a grotesque mushroom. Mystified, the explorer clutched it for a few moments, as though warming it, unsure of what to do next. Then, as his shock subsided, he slowly began to dig in the snow. He soon managed to excavate the calf that was attached to the boot and, a few handfuls of snow later, the thigh that was joined to the calf. He went on digging, gradually exposing an entire corpse buried under the snow. Finally out of the white grave a reddened face loomed, still blurry beneath a thin layer of ice that covered it like a widow's veil. Gingerly, he brushed the ice off with one of his gloves. And, gazing at him from his snowy grave and from the great beyond with the astonished look of someone receiving an unexpected visitor, was Carson. Reynolds's jaw dropped; he was unable to comprehend what he was seeing. Then his eye fell upon the horribly familiar wound to Carson's abdomen, which had been sliced open. Bewildered, the explorer tried to fathom what the devil Carson was doing there. It must have been him on watch on the poop deck, and when he saw Reynolds leave the ship in that drunken state on his way to God only knew where, he had followed him, unluckily as it turned out, for the monster had found Carson first.

When he realized this, Reynolds leapt to his feet and cast a horrified glance about him. The demon was out there watching him. He knew that now; he could sense its presence. It had ripped Carson's guts out, and it was only a matter of time before it tore Reynolds limb from limb, because that was what the monster did, that was its way of communicating with them. Yes, was it not clear enough to him now that there was apparently no guarantee that a superior being would show any kindness or consideration toward the poor, inferior races in the Cosmos? Beset by panic, Reynolds did the only thing he could do in his situation: he ran. He ran in any direction, on and on through the fog. He ran as he had never run in his life. He ran with the unnerving sensation of not knowing whether he was running away from the monster or straight into its clutches.

VIII

WHEN REYNOLDS GLIMPSED THE DARK OUT-line of the *Annawan* in the distance, faintly illumi-nated by the dozen lanterns, his one thought was that the Creator's hand had guided him there. How else could his frenzied path through the fog, now running, now walking exhausted, have led him to exactly where he wanted to be? He hurried toward the ship, turning constantly to look over his shoulder, afraid the creature would materialize at any moment. Once he reached the vessel, Reynolds dragged himself, on the point of collapse, up the ramp. Griffin, who was on watch on the starboard side, observed his labored ascent with compassion, and when Reynolds passed close by, Griffin kindly held out his hand to help him.

"Carson is dead!" Reynolds managed to gasp, struggling for breath. "The monster has torn him to pieces!"

Far from responding with shock to the terrible news, as Reynolds had expected, Griffin stared at him blankly.

"Did you hear what I said, Griffin?" Reynolds repeated, more loudly this time. "Carson is dead, I tell you!"

"Calm yourself, sir," the sailor responded at last. "I heard you per-fectly well, only I think you are mistaken: Carson is over there."

The explorer looked toward where Griffin had pointed, and saw the lookout standing some twenty yards from them, on the poop deck.

"Is that Carson?" he asked, confused, peering at the dark figure with its back turned, busily keeping watch.

Griffin nodded.

"Are you sure?"

The sailor gazed at the distant shape almost ruefully.

"Yes, sir, absolutely certain," he replied. "It's Carson."

Reynolds went on staring at the figure, incredulous.

"Are you all right, sir?" he heard the sailor say again.

"Yes, Griffin, quite all right, do not fret . . . ," Reynolds murmured slowly. "I must have had too much to drink, that's all."

"I understand, sir," Griffin replied sympathetically. "This situation is intolerable for everyone."

Reynolds nodded absentmindedly as he walked away from Griffin as if in a trance, indifferent to what the man might think of him. Indeed, he was scarcely aware of the sailor, whose eyes remained fixed on his back, contemplating him with something more than simple curiosity as he crossed the deck of the *Annawan*. Ironically, despite what he had said to Griffin, Reynolds had never been more sober. The long trek through the snow had cleared his head, and he felt oddly lucid as he walked with measured steps toward the dark figure of the other lookout. The closer he got, the more terrifying the man's imposing stillness became. Griffin had assured Reynolds this was Carson, but the explorer knew that was impossible: he had just found Carson's body in the snow. He only had to close his eyes and he could see Carson's contorted face, that look of terror preserved for all eternity. He strained to make out the figure he was approaching but found it difficult in the pale half-light and due to all the layers of clothing they were obliged to don before venturing out. The easiest figures to recognize from a distance were no doubt those of Peters, the giant Indian, and Allan, whose painful thinness rendered him almost wraithlike. But that formless blob, scanning the white plain, unaware that Reynolds was watching it, could have been anyone, from the ship's cook to George IV to President Jackson. And Reynolds would have been less surprised to encounter any of those three than the sailor who lay with his guts torn out in the snow.

But what if that figure really was Carson, as Griffin claimed? Reynolds pondered as he moved toward it slowly and deliberately, as though carrying a pitcher on his head. Ought he then to doubt what he had seen out there in the snow? Surely doubting his senses was the most logical thing to do. After all, there could not possibly be two Carsons, one up there on watch and the other lying in the snow, his innards spilled to the air! And he must not forget that he had been drunk. The dead sailor had looked to him like Carson, but it could have been another sailor who resembled Carson. Could he remember the face of every sailor on board? Good Lord, no, he had not given most of them a second glance! When Reynolds was close enough to glimpse the lookout's vaporous breath rising from his padded head, a sudden thought struck him like a stone, causing him to stop dead in his tracks a few yards from the figure. He had been forced to dig the body out from under a thick blanket of snow! And, on further reflection, it must have been lying in the snow a lot longer than an hour, for even the raging winds and subzero temperatures could not freeze a body solid in such a short time. Reynolds's theory that Carson had followed him off the ship suddenly seemed completely absurd. Why had he not realized this when he was digging him out? The body might have been there for a day or two.

Reynolds remained motionless on deck, a few yards from the lookout, scouring his memory. The last time he saw Carson was in the infirmary, where he had been reduced to a catatonic stupor after witnessing the surgeon's brutal murder. Several of Carson's fellow sailors had gone to see him there, keen to find out more about the monster. But since then Reynolds had seen nothing more of him. True, when he had left the armory he had thought he recognized Carson on watch, but now he was not so sure. He must have mixed him up with someone else, as no doubt had Griffin. Carson had probably left the infirmary and slipped off the ship without anyone noticing, God only knew for what reason. Perhaps he had fled in a moment of delirium brought on by the fever, or because he could no longer bear the apprehension of waiting. It did not really matter why. Had he, Reynolds, not committed the same act of folly? Whatever the case, the poor wretch had stumbled on the creature, which had given him the same treatment as it had the surgeon. And Reynolds had found his body scarcely an hour ago, while everyone thought Carson was still on board ship. But he *could not* have been, he said to himself, contemplating the shadowy shape standing out against the mist, almost within reach.

His heart knocking in his chest, Reynolds cursed that idiot Griffin for making him so absurdly anxious. Clearly that bright spark had been mistaken, and doubtless once he had covered the four or five paces between himself and the lookout, and had placed his hand on the man's shoulder, he would feel a wave of relief as he saw Kendricks, Wallace, or even George IV staring back at him. Then, after suggesting to Griffin he purchase a pair of spectacles at the first opportunity, he would go straight to Captain MacReady to inform him of the sad news. Having resolved to get to the bottom of the mystery, Reynolds took a deep breath and stepped forward once more. But before he was able to move, the dark figure, alerted to his arrival by the creaking boards, began slowly to turn around. Forgetting to breathe, Reynolds watched the man's hazy profile emerge from behind the earflaps of his hat, growing ever more distinct as the sailor turned with exasperating slowness, until the two men stood face to face. On the *Annawan*'s deck, Reynolds and the sailor who lay dead out in the snow stared at each other in silence. Reynolds's face registered surprise and disbelief, while that of Carson had a slightly lost look, as though the explorer had woken him abruptly from a deep sleep. And yet it was Carson who broke the silence enveloping the two men.

"Can I help you, sir?" he asked.

Reynolds thought his voice sounded a little hoarse, like someone who has not used it for a long time. He had to make a supreme effort to overcome his astonishment and utter a reply.

"No, thank you, Carson . . . I just came to say how glad I am to see you have recovered."

"Very kind, sir, I'm sure," the other man said amiably.

Reynolds could not help comparing his face with the one he had dug out of the snow—that bruised countenance, contorted by fear, identical to the one before him now, which had been etched on his memory forever. Carson's face. But if that was Carson's body . . . Reynolds's heart missed a beat as a terrifying question formed in his mind: who was he talking to now? Yes, who the devil was he?

"Sir . . . can I help you?" the sailor repeated.

The explorer shook his head slowly, unable to speak. There was definitely something strange about the sailor's voice. It belonged to Carson all right, yet it was subtly different. Perhaps all this was pure imagination on his part, thought Reynolds, and yet he sensed something was not quite right about the man. His gestures, his way of speaking, of looking . . . It was as if he were watching someone forcing himself to play a role. What are you? Reynolds said to himself, mesmerized by Carson's small, unremarkable eyes, which seemed to peer back at him in an overly guarded manner, with a look of mistrust uncharacteristic of the sailor.

Just then, a bulky figure that could only be Peters emerged on deck, interrupting the two men's mutual scrutiny. Peters descended the ramp agilely and, hunched against the cold, made his way over to the dogs' cages, which he usually kept covered with a tarpaulin for a few hours during the day to enable the animals, unsettled by the continual half-light, to fall asleep. Carson and Reynolds watched the Indian go about his business in silence, grateful for the respite afforded by his sudden appearance—especially the explorer, who desperately needed time to order his thoughts. However, no sooner had Peters drawn back the tarpaulin than the dogs began to stir, visibly uneasy, scenting the air. All at once, as though following a choreographed gesture, the dogs turned as one toward where Reynolds and Carson were standing and almost immediately broke into a frenzy of barking, pressing themselves against the bars, lunging at the cage door. Reynolds was taken aback at the dogs' sudden outburst of aggression, those wild barks and growls directed at them. Peters did his best to calm them, but the animals appeared possessed. Then the explorer looked at Carson, who stared back at him blankly.

"The dogs seem on edge," Reynolds remarked, holding Carson's gaze with difficulty.

Carson simply shrugged. But the explorer thought he glimpsed a flash of anger behind his tiny eyes. Then a mad thought occurred to Reynolds, swift as a bolt of lightning streaking across the sky; beneath all his layers of clothing he broke into a cold sweat. He swallowed hard, cleared his throat, and with the complete calm of a suicide, who, hours before taking his own life, already feels he is dead, addressed the sailor once more.

"When you have finished your watch, Carson, come to my cabin. I'd like to offer you a glass of brandy. I think you've earned it."

"That's kind of you, sir," said the sailor, looking straight at him with alarming intensity, "only I don't drink."

The look on Carson's face, together with the disturbing tone of his reply, made Reynolds shudder. Or perhaps it was simply Carson's thick Irish brogue that made his voice sound menacing, Reynolds reflected, trying to reassure himself.

"Think about it," he forced himself to say, feeling a knot in his stomach. "A brandy like the one I'm offering you is not something to be passed up."

Carson contemplated him in silence for a few moments.

"Very well, sir," he replied at last, still fixing him with that disconcerting gaze. "I'll go to your cabin when I've finished my watch."

"Marvelous, Carson," the explorer declared with as much enthusiasm as he could muster, his heart in his throat. "I shall be expecting you."

With this, Reynolds turned around and walked casually toward the nearest hatch, unable to avoid feeling the dead sailor's eyes boring into the back of his head. The die was cast, he told himself with a shudder. He had decided on that course of action almost on impulse, and now it was too late to change his mind. Like it or not, he had no choice but to carry it through to the end. However, he would need assistance, and there was only one person on the *Annawan* who could help him. Feigning nonchalance, he made his way toward Allan's cabin, leaving the sound of the dogs' frenzied barking behind him.

• • •

THE GUNNERY SERGEANT WAS in the middle of composing a poem when Reynolds burst into his cramped quarters. The explorer was visibly agitated and breathed uneasily, yet the young poet scarcely looked up at him before returning to his labors, as though inspiration were like a handful of sand that would slip through his fingers if he slackened his grasp. And despite having little time to spare, the explorer bit his tongue rather than interrupt. Allan had explained to him that many years earlier, after one of his countless arguments with his stepfather, he had set sail for Boston to try his luck there and had succeeded in publishing his first book of poetry, although sadly he did not sell enough copies to save him from poverty. Desperate, and without a penny to his name, he had enlisted in the army as a foot soldier and had even risen to the rank of sergeant major before fleeing that rough environment, scarcely appropriate for someone wishing to pursue his vocation as a poet. He had been forced to return, tail between his legs, to his benefactor's home. This had happened prior to Allan's strategy of enrolling at West Point, and Reynolds could see how vital it was to him to try to make his living from writing. So he sat down on his bunk and waited for Allan to finish, taking the opportunity to catch his breath and gather his thoughts. The trance into which Allan was plunged, however, ended up diverting Reynolds. The pale young man sat hunched over his table, a cascade of dark hair falling down over his eyes. He seemed more fragile than usual, his body wracked by an almost imperceptible spasm, as though he were distilling on paper the dark essence of his soul.

Reynolds nodded to himself. He had done the right thing in coming there, he reflected, his eyes still fixed on the gunner. Only a mind like Allan's could grasp what Reynolds was about to tell him, only a soul as devoid of worldliness as his could join him in the venture he was about to propose. Most important of all, only a man possessed by the demon of creativity would agree to remain discreetly in the shadows when it came to reaping the rewards of earthly fame, for Reynolds suspected Allan was only interested in the glory he might obtain through his writings. Yes, the sergeant was undoubtedly the ideal person to assist him in the foolhardy plan he had elaborated whilst speaking with Carson up on deck, a plan he could never hope to carry out alone. Now all Reynolds needed to do was tell the gunner about it without seeming as though he had completely lost his mind. When Allan finally set aside his quill and turned to Reynolds, his eyes glowing faintly like the embers of a fire, the explorer still did not know where to begin.

"An unusual theory has occurred to me regarding the Martian, Allan," he said, for he had to begin somewhere, "so unusual that were I to make it known, no one on this ship would take me seriously."

"Are you in need of someone who does?" Allan grinned, gathering up his writing implements as a pathologist might carefully tidy away his instruments.

Reynolds nodded with brooding solemnity.

"I am, and I believe you are the only one capable of it. Therefore, I am going to share it with you, in the hope you may shed some light on this madness, for I fear if you do not, we shall all perish even sooner than we thought."

Allan shook his head in amusement, raising his slender harpist's hands in a theatrical gesture.

"We have seen a Martian come down from the sky in a flying machine, Reynolds. How could my poor wits refuse to believe anything now?"

"I hope you are right, for I think I know how the monster got on board." He let his words hang in the air and settle like specks of dust on the surface of Allan's mind before resuming. "And, more importantly, I believe it is still among us."

"Do you know where it is now?" the young man asked, sitting bolt upright in his seat.

"If I'm not mistaken," the explorer murmured gloomily, "it is up on deck, finishing its watch. And in ten minutes' time, it will be in my cabin having a drink with me."

Reynolds contemplated Allan as he digested those words in silence.

He had been unable to resist giving that cryptic reply, but he knew Allan needed no further explanation. Such were the gunner's extraordinary powers of mind that sometimes Reynolds could not help thinking he viewed the world around him not necessarily from above but at one remove, and that from his watchtower, wherever that was, all of mankind's victories, advances, and triumphs over his environment and over himself must appear little more than a quaint child's game. And yet, over time, Reynolds had also noticed, not without some regret, that Allan's tumultuous, fragile mind was too fanciful for its own good.

"Do you mean to say that . . . it has changed into one of us?" the gunner said at last.

Hearing Allan voice his own suspicions, Reynolds felt a shiver run down his spine as though he had stepped barefoot onto cold marble. Spoken aloud, the idea sounded at once insane and terrifying. Reynolds nodded and smiled feebly. The young man had not disappointed him, and, judging from his inquiring expression, as a reward he wanted more details. Reynolds cleared his throat, ready to provide them, although he decided to leave out a few in order to save face in front of the only ally he had on the ship.

"A few hours ago I left the ship with the aim of going back to the flying machine, but I lost my way in the fog. For a while, I walked around in circles, fearful the monster would pounce on me at any moment . . . until I stumbled on Carson's body. It had been ripped open just like the elephant seal and poor Doctor Walker, and lay half buried in the snow. It was frozen solid and must have been there for at least a day or two. I ran back to the ship as fast as I could to raise the alarm, but when I arrived I was surprised to find Carson on watch on deck, his entrails intact." He paused for breath and gave a wry smile before going on: "I was bewildered at first, as you can imagine, but then I had a mad idea, which, the more I think about it, seems like the only possibility: what if the sailor who came back with the seal was not the real Carson, but something that had—"

"Taken on his appearance," Allan concluded.

"Yes, let's suppose for a minute that while the others were searching the area around the flying machine, Carson and Ringwald lost each other in the fog, and the creature took the opportunity to kill Carson and, well . . . to step into his shoes."

"And now, according to you, that thing, whatever it is, is on watch up on deck."

"Precisely. And God only knows what its intentions are," Reynolds replied, smiling awkwardly at the gunner, as though apologizing for making him listen to such ravings. "What do you think, Allan? Does the idea strike you as completely insane?"

The gunner stared silently into space for what seemed to Reynolds like an eternity.

"The question is not, I think, whether the idea is insane," he spoke at last. "The mere fact of being alive has for a long time seemed to me an unfathomable riddle. What we should be asking ourselves is whether there is any other possible explanation, one that allows us to rule out this apparent madness. For example, are you sure the body you found out there belonged to Carson? You said yourself the fog was thick and it was half buried in the snow. In addition"—Allan coughed uneasily—"I don't wish to seem impolite, but I confess I can smell the alcohol on your breath from here."

Reynolds let out a sigh of despair.

"I don't deny I've been drinking, Allan, but I assure you I have never felt more sober. And I would like nothing more than to tell you I was too drunk, and terrified, to know what I saw. It would save me having to defend a position that no one in his right mind would willingly accept. Why, I myself would question the sanity of anyone who told me such a story. But I'm afraid I know perfectly well what I saw, Allan. It's Carson's body lying out there in the snow."

"I see . . . ," murmured the gunner.

"At all events, Allan, if the body was not Carson's, then whose was it? No one else has disappeared from the ship. It would be equally absurd, if not more so, to think that the body belonged to someone who did not travel here with us, don't you agree?" Reynolds paused for a moment before adding: "But there is something more, Allan, something that makes me believe my theory is right. The Carson I spoke with up on deck seemed . . . How can I explain it? . . . He seemed odd, different. And when the dogs caught a whiff of him they began barking like mad. Doesn't that strike you as strange?"

The gunner rose from his chair and began pacing the narrow cabin, visibly on edge.

"Assuming you are right, how could that thing change into Carson? Do you know how complex our bodies are? It would have to duplicate each one of our organs, not to mention language, consciousness, knowledge . . . the psyche, Reynolds, memory! Carson was not a hollow shell, a suit of clothing anyone could put on. Carson was a man, a masterpiece of creation . . . How could it possibly imitate the Creator's exquisite work, and without anyone noticing, to boot!"

"Come, come, Allan, I understand the difficulty of replicating a man from his nose down to his accursed penis, but you know as well as I do that Carson's mind would scarcely present much of a challenge. That yokel was not exactly the most shining example of our species. We both know he was a man of few words and unusually limited intelligence. And I don't suppose Carson being quieter than usual would have aroused the rest of the crew's suspicions. But besides the dogs, there is further evidence to back up my theory. Don't you find it odd that despite his frostbitten foot Carson is able to carry out his watch without the slightest difficulty? Can a human being recover from frostbite as if by magic?"

"Yes, I have to admit that is rather odd," the gunner agreed, musingly. "Still, I find it hard to believe that—"

Reynolds lost his patience. "For the love of God, Allan! Didn't you try to convince me the creature must come from Mars because the simplest answer is always the most logical? Well, now we have two Carsons in the Antarctic, one lying dead in the snow, and the other up on deck, bewildered but very much alive. I don't know about you, but it seems to me the simplest explanation for this extraordinary phenomenon is that the Martian has changed itself into the sailor. Having ripped his guts out first, naturally."

Allan made no reply. He gazed at the wall for a long while, as though at any moment he expected the answers he was searching for to spell themselves out there.

"Very well, Reynolds," he finally murmured somewhat grudgingly. "Let's say that the Martian is able to transform itself into one of us, and that it has taken on the appearance of Carson. For what reason? What are its intentions? Why did it attack Doctor Walker and not us? What is it waiting for?"

"I've no idea," confessed the explorer. "That's why I have invited it to my cabin, to try to understand it, to converse with it, because I'm beginning to suspect the creature does not wish to kill us. Otherwise it would have done so by now, don't you think? Disguised as Carson, it could easily move unhindered about the ship, picking us off one by one. This leads me to think that Doctor Walker's death was an accident. The Martian must have killed him in self-defense, as it were, when the good doctor tried to saw off its foot."

"That is possible," murmured Allan.

"We have no idea how the creature sees us," Reynolds went on. "Perhaps it is more afraid than we are and is simply struggling to survive in what it considers a hostile environment. All we know is that its responses can be extremely violent, and we must therefore approach it with the utmost caution. I believe this is the only chance we have of communicating with the Martian. And if there is one man on this ship I can count on to help me do that, it is you, Allan."

"I understand your motives, Reynolds, but why not tell Captain MacReady about this? Why do you want us to do this alone?"

"You know how *highly* the captain thinks of me, Allan," the explorer said forthrightly. "It's obvious he would not believe me unless he saw Carson's dead body with his own eyes, and I doubt I could guide him

back there. If I told you that only a few hours ago he and I had an . . .
exchange of views in his cabin, after which he suggested I lock myself in
mine for the rest of the voyage and even threatened to have me locked
up in the hold if I insisted on pestering him with my *crazy ideas,* perhaps
you'll understand why I have not hurried to tell him that the Martian
has taken on the form of one of his men. Even if MacReady did believe
me, he would no doubt be hell-bent on killing the creature, thereby destroying any possibility of communicating with it. And that is exactly
what I intend to do: to communicate with it. Not simply because I think
it is our only way of saving ourselves, but because of what it signifies.
If we are right and there is a Martian on board ship, don't you see how
incredible it would be to make contact with it? To converse with a being
from another planet, Allan!"

The gunner nodded understandingly, although he seemed less en-
thusiastic about the idea than Reynolds, who felt obliged to continue ha-
ranguing him.

"This could be the biggest step forward in the History of Mankind,
Allan! If we are right, we are about to discover something of immeasurable significance. Do you really want us to leave it all in the hands of a
bunch of fools? We are the only two men on the ship capable of doing
what needs to be done. The others are only interested in saving their
skins. We owe it to humanity and to future generations to take the lead
in this matter. Fate has brought us here to prevent the arrival on Earth of
the first visitor from space from turning into a vulgar bloodbath."

The gunner nodded and heaved a sigh, which Reynolds hoped was
a sign of determination rather than weariness. Then he sat down once
more and stared absentmindedly into space.

"Perhaps the creature's machine crashed before it was able to reach
its destination, wherever that may be," Allan surmised, unable to help
feeling a thrill at the idea of a Martian being on board, "and now it finds
itself in the wrong place, trapped on an expanse of ice with no hope of
escape."

FÉLIX J. PALMA

"I think you're right," Reynolds conceded. "Perhaps the creature sees us as the solution to its dilemma and has infiltrated the ship because it thinks we know how to get out of here."

"I'm afraid it will be disappointed in us as an intelligent species." The gunner grinned, and then, as though suddenly aware that allowing himself to joke about the situation might cost him dear, he put on a solemn face. "Very well, Reynolds, you can count on me. Now, what is your plan?"

Reynolds glanced at him uneasily. His plan? Yes, of course, Allan wanted to know his plan. Something he would have liked to know himself.

"Well, I have to confess, I've not thought much about how I will conduct the meeting," he admitted. "I expect I will improvise depending on the creature's reactions."

"And what if its intentions are indeed destructive?" the gunner asked. "What will you do if it tries to attack you?"

"Of course I have considered the possibility that the Martian may refuse to converse with me, preferring to rip my guts out. That is why I want you there, Allan. As my guarantee, my life insurance," replied Reynolds.

"But won't the thing be surprised to find me in your cabin?" the gunner protested, clearly preferring to wait in his cabin until the encounter was over.

"The creature won't see you, Allan. You will be hiding in the cupboard, and if things get ugly, you will jump out and shoot it before it has a chance to attack me."

"Ah, I see . . . ," Allan breathed, white as a sheet.

"Can I count on you, then?" Reynolds said in an almost plaintive voice.

The gunner narrowed his eyes and remained silent. For what seemed like an eternity the only sound they could hear was the groaning the ice made as it slowly tightened its stranglehold on the ship.

"Of course you can, Reynolds, why do you even ask?" he said at

· · 114 · ·

last, hesitating slightly, as though he himself were unsure how to respond. "Besides, I am the only sailor on the ship who could fit into your cupboard."

"Thank you, Allan." Reynolds smiled, genuinely moved by the gunner's gesture, and he believed he was being sincere when he added, "The last thing I expected to find in this hellhole was a friend."

"I hope you remember that when you no longer have need of me," murmured Allan. "Incidentally, do you have any brandy left? If I am to shoot at a being from another planet, I think I could do with a glass or two."

"Why not wait and drink a toast with the Martian?" Reynolds hurriedly suggested, wondering how to remove the brandy from his cupboard before the gunner hid inside.

IX

REYNOLDS CAST A CRITICAL EYE OVER HIS tiny cabin, like a theater director assessing the stage props. He had emptied the cupboard he used as a pantry, taking care to conceal the two or three unopened brandy bottles from view. Allan, a gun in his poet's hand, was now hiding in its narrow interior. Reynolds had placed one of the bottles and two glasses on the table in the middle of the cabin and, adding a sinister touch to this everyday scene, to the right he had placed a freshly loaded pistol. Reynolds preferred to display the weapon openly as opposed to concealing it in his pocket, where he had stuffed the tamping rod and the gunpowder. He thought this would arouse less suspicion, given that everyone had been armed since the state of siege began. On one side of the table was a chair, and facing it the comfortable, reassuring armchair he had brought from his other life. All that was missing was one of the actors, who, if his theory was correct, would come in disguise.

In a state of nerves, the explorer caressed his bandaged hand, trying to calm himself. Carson would be arriving any minute, and he had still not decided how to open the conversation. What was the most polite way of greeting a being from another planet? A few moments earlier, despite their differences of opinion on the matter, he and Allan had managed to agree on how to conduct the interview. They had ruled out broaching the subject directly, in favor of a more subtle approach. Reynolds would begin with a few stock remarks in order to create a relaxed atmosphere and, when the creature's guard was down, would fire a series of cleverly aimed questions designed to corner it and force it to tear away its mask. Yes, that was what they had agreed. No direct questions or threatening tones. They must first reassure the monster, so that when the time came to reveal that they knew the truth, they could still offer it the chance of a dialogue. Reynolds was not entirely satisfied with this overly cautious approach, which had been Allan's idea. The explorer had advocated getting straight to the point, but Allan had objected, on the grounds that the Martian might respond aggressively the moment it felt harried. Thus Reynolds's unmasking of the monster should be as graceful and restrained as possible, little less than a master class in manipulation, in order to demonstrate to the creature "the exquisite wisdom of the human species," the poet had concluded somewhat pompously, before installing himself in the pantry with the dignity of a pharaoh trying out his new sarcophagus, leaving Reynolds even more confused about what strategy to follow. The only thing the explorer knew for sure was that at some point during the conversation he and the creature would both be forced to show their hands. And the question that really tormented him was whether the Martian would attack or be willing to converse once it discovered it had been found out. In fact, much depended on the way he conducted the interview: his own life, for one, as well as that of everyone on board ship, but also the place his name would occupy in History, and even History itself.

Reynolds repositioned the glasses on the table for the umpteenth time and looked up at the clock, wondering whether Allan could hear his heart pounding in his chest from inside the cupboard. The mixture of dread and exhilaration that overwhelmed him was understandable: he was about to speak with a creature from outer space. Two intelligent life-forms originating on two different planets in the universe were about to listen to each other, have a conversation, perform a small miracle unbeknownst to the world. Realizing this, Reynolds felt strangely light-headed. Then he remembered the flash of anger he had glimpsed in Carson's eyes when the dogs began to bark, and he wondered whether, exposed to his scrutiny for a longer time, their owner would be able to hide the memory of what they had seen, for that creature from the stars had traveled through space in a flying machine on its way to Earth and must have seen a host of meteorites, shooting stars, and all manner of things the Creator had been pleased to place out of Man's sight.

At that moment, there was a gentle knock at the cabin door. Reynolds started. Casting a meaningful glance at the cupboard, where he knew Allan could see him through the latticework, he nodded, as though signaling to the audience that the show was about to begin, and went to open the cabin door, doing his best to keep his knees from knocking. Carson entered, greeting him timidly as he unraveled the kerchief wound around his head and took off his mittens. Reynolds was struck by Carson's rather clumsy way of walking, which despite the sailor's attempts to conceal it, looked unnatural, as though he were wearing his shoes on the wrong foot. Doing his best not to give in to panic at the thought that this hideous little man might be no man at all, but a monster from outer space capable of pulverizing him in a second, Reynolds offered Carson a seat before quickly ensconcing himself in his armchair, where he felt instantly cocooned by its leather and wood. Once they were seated, Reynolds poured two glasses of brandy as calmly as he could. The sailor watched him in silence with a blank expression. The explorer fancied he had never seen a face less fitted to registering any form of emotion. It looked like the work of a Creator already weary of inventing men. When he had finished pouring their drinks, he picked up his glass and quickly raised it in the air, as though thrusting with a rapier, before downing it in one. Reynolds had been unable to avoid taking advantage of this point in the pantomime to steel himself. Carson looked on impassively, his glass untouched before him.

"Go ahead, Carson, try it," Reynolds urged, doing his best to steady his voice. "You will see I wasn't exaggerating when I said it was an excellent brandy."

The sailor picked up his glass gingerly, as though fearful he might break it if he gripped it too tightly, raised it to his lips, and took a small mouthful. He contrived a grimace of pleasure that replaced the bovine look stuck to his face when it had nothing to express, then set his glass down again on the table, as though with that birdlike sip he had observed the customary courtesies required of him.

"I imagine you have still not recovered from the shock of what you saw," Reynolds remarked, trying to recall whether he had ever seen the real Carson drink, or whether he was in fact in the presence of the only teetotaler in the entire crew and was jumping to conclusions. "Although I have to confess, your description of the creature has not been much help in understanding what we are up against."

As he spoke, Reynolds fancied he glimpsed that strange flash in Carson's eyes once more. He instinctively drew back slightly from the table as he imagined the creature observing him with suspicion from inside the sailor.

"I'm sorry, sir, it all happened so quickly," Carson said at last, as if he had suddenly noticed Reynolds was waiting for him to reply.

"There's no need to apologize, Carson. It's normal you should not want to speak of the matter. I imagine you are afraid." The explorer waved a reassuring hand. Then he stared fixedly at him. "I am right in thinking that you are afraid, am I not . . . *Carson?*"

Reynolds uttered the sailor's name with deliberate irony, wondering whether Allan would find that subtle or downright crude.

"I suppose I am, sir," replied the sailor.

"Of course you are, of course you are, we all are," the explorer went on, his smile broadening. "There is no need to be ashamed. However, you must understand that a more detailed description of the creature would be invaluable. It is quite conceivable that we appear as hideous and threatening to the monster as it does to us, perhaps even more so. I am only interested in knowing as much about it as possible because I wish to acquaint myself with it, to try to communicate with it," Reynolds said, staring intently at the sailor. "I am convinced we may be able to understand each other. Do you see what I am saying . . . *Carson?*"

"I think so, but I'm afraid I can't help you," the sailor said apologetically. "I remember nothing of what I saw. Only the sound of my own screams. Although in my humble opinion the creature wasn't afraid when it tore the doctor limb from limb, at least no more than I was . . . *sir.*"

Reynolds forced himself to nod sympathetically.

"So you don't think the creature was afraid," Reynolds went on, willing himself to produce one of his most dazzling smiles. "Isn't that a very bold statement, Carson? After all, who could possibly understand the feelings of a creature so different from us? Surely only the creature itself. We could only discover what it felt if we asked it directly, don't you think?"

"Possibly, sir," the sailor acknowledged, somewhat intimidated by Reynolds's words.

"For example, you and I are human beings and therefore recognize each other's expressions. You see me smile and you know I am happy."

"I'm very glad to hear it, sir," Carson said, visibly bewildered.

"No, no . . . I do not mean I am happy this very minute," Reynolds explained, "only that if I were, you would have no difficulty knowing it, because we share the same codes. By the same token, I could read your face like a book and name any emotion reflected on it. Such as fear, for example, or despair—emotions I, too, am familiar with, and have even experienced at times in my life. Do you follow me?"

"I think so, sir," the sailor replied, his face devoid of any expression.

"Good. Now reflect on this," Reynolds requested. "The differences between the creature and ourselves are no doubt so great that we are sending each other the wrong messages. Our mutual attempts at communication, such as they are, must have gone unnoticed by the other. Rather like someone raising a white flag before an army of blind men."

Carson remained silent.

"What is your view on the matter?" Reynolds was obliged to ask.

The sailor gave him a faintly startled look.

"That only an army of fools would surrender to an army of blind men, sir," he replied at length.

Reynolds observed him silently for a few moments.

"Indeed, that would be so if this were not a metaphor, Carson. What I am trying to explain is the idea that a peaceful gesture would not be interpreted as such by the other," he said. "Now do you understand?"

Carson gave no sign of having done so.

"Very well, we shall forget that example," Reynolds said, visibly impatient. "Something else concerns me, Carson. We found no hole in the ship's hull through which the creature could enter or leave. Are you not concerned the creature might still be among us?"

Hearing this, Carson gave a look of terror, which Reynolds found somewhat exaggerated.

"God forbid, sir," replied Carson, trembling. "If that's true, then you can take it from me we're all doomed."

The sailor's reply sent a shiver down Reynolds's spine. Saints alive, he told himself, that gave every appearance of being a threat. Was the creature warning him to let the matter drop, telling him how dangerous it would be to upset the seeming calm on board?

Reynolds tried not to become agitated. He must not let fear cloud his thinking. Not now when it was imperative he hold his nerve if he wanted to bring the conversation to a successful conclusion. He cast a furtive glance toward the cupboard. At that moment, he would have given anything to know what Allan thought of Carson's words.

"You may be right. But what concerns me most now is to find out how the creature came aboard the ship," Reynolds went on pensively, avoiding as best he could the presumed threat. "What do you reckon, Carson?"

"I don't know, sir."

"Have you no theories on the matter? I find that hard to believe. Why, the thing almost killed you in the infirmary. And its appearance terrified you so much that it left you in a state of shock for almost an entire day. I am sure you see it each time you close your eyes, or am I mistaken?"

"No, sir, you aren't mistaken," the sailor conceded.

"Good. In that case I am sure the question of how it got onto the ship has been bothering you as much as it has me. What have you concluded?"

"I'm afraid I haven't concluded anything, sir," the other man replied with a puzzled grin.

Once more, the sailor's manner sowed a seed of doubt in Reynolds's mind. Was the creature mocking him or was he unconsciously imbuing the little man's words with a sinister tone they did not have? He could not be sure. All he knew was that he was getting nowhere and there was no longer any point in beating about the bush. The time had come to try a different, more perilous approach. He shot a glance at the cupboard, hoping Allan would know how to interpret it.

"On the other hand, I do have a theory. Would you like to hear it, Carson?" he asked, smiling through clenched teeth, as though he had an invisible pipe in his mouth.

Carson shrugged, clearly beginning to tire of the conversation. The explorer gave a slight cough before continuing.

"I believe it came up the ice ramp the same way as the rest of us."

"But what about the lookouts?" the sailor declared, astonished. "None of them saw it, did they?"

Reynolds smiled at him with amused benevolence.

"D'you know that something curious happened to me a few hours ago?" he said, ignoring Carson's question, his hand moving surreptitiously closer to the pistol lying on the table. "I went for a walk in the snow and stumbled upon a dead body."

He paused so that he could study Carson's response. The sailor held his gaze. He was no longer smiling, and when his face showed no emotion it had the same stupid expression. And yet, once again, Reynolds fancied he saw something flicker deep inside the eyes, alert and uneasy.

"And do you know whose it was?" Reynolds asked.

The sailor contemplated him rather cagily. "No."

"It was Carson's," Reynolds declared, staring straight at him. He let his revelation hang in the air for a few moments before adding, "I assumed you had followed me when you saw me leave the ship, and that you had been unfortunate enough to cross the path of the monster from the stars. Yet when I returned, I found you on deck. And now here you are sitting opposite me, alive and well, even though only hours ago I saw you dead in the snow, your chest sliced open. What conclusion would you draw from all this?"

Carson's habitual dumb expression intensified.

"Since I am here, sir, I'd think you were mistaken," he replied, bewildered. "Perhaps it was another sailor you mistook for me."

"Hmm . . . possibly," Reynolds acknowledged, "except that I checked and no one else is missing from the ship. Moreover, I know what I saw. The body I found in the snow had your features, Harry Carson's features." He paused for a moment to make his voice sound more harsh, his heart beating with such force he thought it might burst through his chest. "Now imagine for a moment that I am convinced of what I saw. What conclusion do you think I reached? I shall tell you: I believe poor Carson was killed during the first expedition, that the monster assumed his appearance, and that is how it slipped on board. That explains why we found no hole in the ship's hull, and how it was able to kill the surgeon and then vanish."

The sailor stared at him blankly for a moment. Suddenly, he burst into fits of laughter. Reynolds observed his charade with a frown.

"I'm sorry, sir, but that is the most ridiculous thing I ever heard," Carson said when he had finished laughing. Then he shook his head slowly, gazing at Reynolds with sudden curiosity. "What does Captain MacReady think of all this?"

Reynolds did not reply.

"Oh, I see. You haven't dared tell him," the sailor concluded with a sad look the explorer found grotesque. "I understand, sir. It must be difficult to find someone who would believe such a load of nonsense. That means you are the only who knows about it, doesn't it? And now me, of course."

Reynolds felt every sinew in his body tighten. He glanced anew at the cupboard, wondering whether the gunner was also alert, ready to leap out as soon as the Martian confirmed that threat. Beads of cold sweat broke out on Reynolds's brow and trickled down his temples. He wiped them away with a trembling hand, while Carson watched him impassively, with the blank expression of a simpleton. If at that moment, Reynolds reflected, someone was asked to judge their guilt based on appearances, he would certainly be the one condemned. He gave a grunt of irritation and decided the time had come to end the charade by addressing the monster directly.

"At all events, you disappoint me," said he, making no attempt to hide his vexation. "Can't you see I am giving you the chance to talk before exposing you?"

Carson went on staring at him in silence.

"We humans are not an inferior race. You and I can communicate as equals!" Reynolds declared, but the sailor showed no sign of being interested in his offer. Reynolds gave a resigned sigh. "I assume from your behavior that you disagree. I truly regret it. I honestly believed our two races could learn a great deal from each other."

Carson sniggered unpleasantly, as if to say the human race had nothing to teach him. Although, of course, it could also have been interpreted as the desperate laughter of a sailor who did not know how to respond to the ravings of his superior. When he stopped, he resumed staring stupidly at Reynolds. The explorer settled back in his armchair and contemplated him in silence for a long time, wondering how to resume their discussion. It was obvious he had been unable to conduct it with the skill and discernment he had promised Allan, and he imagined the gunner shaking his head disapprovingly inside the cupboard. Somehow he had lost control of the conversation, and now it was at an impasse. How could he revive it? Should he continue goading the Martian until it revealed itself simply to stop him from talking? But nothing prevented Carson from walking out of the cabin and going to complain to the captain. Reynolds had no doubt that this would provide MacReady with the perfect opportunity to accuse him of mutiny or some other trumped-up charge and throw him in the hold. He looked beseechingly at the cupboard. What more could he do, for the love of God? He rested his elbows on the table and looked straight at Carson.

"You may be surprised to know that our species is a lot more intelligent than you think," he said, a hint of desperation in his voice. "And I can assure you my intentions are entirely honorable and well meaning. My only wish is to talk to you, to reach an understanding. However, if you persist with this attitude, I shall have no choice but to expose you."

"Sir, I—"

"Confound it, Carson, stop playing games!"

The sailor sighed and leaned back in his chair. Reynolds shook his head, disappointed and disgusted by his stubbornness.

"And you're mistaken if you think I am the only one who knows your secret. I took the precaution of covering myself before revealing my discovery to you. So, if anything happens to me, someone will raise the alarm, and I can assure you there will be nowhere, and no body, left for you to hide in on this ship. We outnumber you, and once the others know your secret they will waste no time in cornering you. Only by then I will no longer be there to offer to speak with you. Believe me, they will shoot you down. And despite having seen what you can do to an elephant seal, I am afraid you won't be able to slaughter an entire ship's crew before they slaughter you," he said, aware of how ridiculous he felt addressing those words to the diminutive man in front of him.

"Oh, of course I couldn't, sir!" the sailor exclaimed, shaking his head in despair. Then he added in hushed tones: "Only the monster from the stars could do that . . ."

"Are you threatening me again, Carson?" Reynolds said, more annoyed than afraid. "Yes, of course. The monster could do it. But not you, because you are a simple sailor, aren't you?" Reynolds looked straight at him, and added: "A simple sailor who came back with his foot so badly frostbitten that the doctor recommended amputation, and who is now miraculously able to walk around. Do you suppose a simple sailor could cure himself in that way?"

"Doctor Walker, may God rest his soul, obviously made a mistake in his diagnosis," said Carson with a shrug.

"I very much doubt it: Doctor Walker was no novice. He had been practicing for years."

"But all men make mistakes, sir," the sailor said, smiling timidly. "And Doctor Walker was only human, like you or me. As fragile, mortal, and prone to making mistakes as all humans are."

Exhausted and annoyed, Reynolds fell silent once more. Clearly his words, whether friendly or aggressive, were having no effect. Perhaps his fate was not to attain glory, but to carry on that conversation until the thaw came, or until Judgment Day, although he did not think the creature's patience would last that long. In fact, it seemed to be playing cat and mouse with him, waiting for the moment when it would tire of the game and gobble him up. That was when Reynolds understood there was only one thing left for him to do. Of course it would change everything irreversibly, as well as ending that interplanetary dialogue between species he had so longed for: a longing that in the light of events seemed as ludicrous as it was childish. Surely a being that wished to communicate would have embraced his offer? He was forced to admit that MacReady had been right all along. Faced with a creature that had more than proven its hostility, the most intelligent solution was to shoot it down the moment it came within range. However, Reynolds had ruined that option by alerting the creature with his insistence on sitting down for a friendly chat. And the result spoke for itself: there he was in his cabin, the monster in front of him, all his cards on the table, frantic, humiliated, terrified, and only too aware that he had handled the situation like an arrogant fool. He glanced one last time in the direction of the cupboard, hoping Allan would understand that their fleeting moment of glory had arrived, and praying he was equal to the task.

He contemplated the creature with genuine disappointment. He would have liked to speak with it, to discover why it had landed on Earth, to know where it came from. Unfortunately, he would have to be content with shooting it. His hand darted to the pistol, and he aimed it between the sailor's eyes. And yet he did not pull the trigger. He remained with his arm outstretched, observing the sailor coldly.

"I'm sorry you do not wish to communicate, because you leave me with no choice."

"You're going to shoot me?" Carson asked, with a look of utter stupefaction. "Are you going to kill one of your men? They will convict you, arrest you, the—"

"Your concern is touching, Carson; however, I am sure that as soon as I shoot, you will change shape, and everyone will be able to see that I have killed the monster from the stars," Reynolds replied with a calm he did not possess. "I gave you the chance to resolve this in a civilized way, but you refused. You have until the count of three to change your mind, and then I will pull the trigger."

Carson stared at him, his face contorted in terror.

"One," said Reynolds.

The sailor squirmed in his chair, overcome with anguish, and immediately burst out crying, his hands clasped in prayer.

"I beg you, sir, don't shoot! You're mistaken; the body you found in the snow can't be mine. For the love of God, you are about to commit a folly!" he wailed, tears streaming down his cheeks and into his mouth.

A moment of terrible doubt flashed through Reynolds's mind, and he had to force himself to steady the hand holding the gun. What in the name of God was he going to do now? Kill the sailor in cold blood? What if he was mistaken and the body in the snow was not Carson? Was he prepared to shoot an innocent man? Yet he was sure it was Carson! And the sailor cringing in front of him could not also be Carson. No, he was the Martian. That was the simplest explanation, and Allan had told him that, however crazy, the simplest explanation was always the— But all of that depended on his being certain that the body in the snow was Carson, and he was not completely certain. Or was he?

"Please, sir, I beg you," sobbed the sailor.

"Two," Reynolds went on, doing his best not to let the terrible inner conflict he was suffering show in his voice.

The sailor sank his head on his chest in an attitude of surrender, his body wracked with sobs. Overcome by doubt and indecision, Reynolds, who was also shaking, observed Carson for a few moments. Finally, he dropped the pistol on the table. He could not kill him without being completely sure. He was no murderer. Or at least he was incapable of killing a possibly innocent man in cold blood, someone who had never done him any harm and was not standing in the way of his plans, as Symmes had been.

"Three."

At first, Reynolds did not know where the voice had come from that had finished the count. He glanced uneasily toward the cupboard, thinking it might have been Allan urging him to shoot, to be resolute, to believe what he had seen in the snow, but the cupboard door remained closed. Then he turned his gaze once more to the sailor, and his heart froze when he discovered Carson staring at him, with no sign of any tears, a twisted smile suffusing his face with evil. Reynolds reached for the pistol, but before he could seize it, the sailor's mouth opened in a grotesque fashion, as if he were dislocating his own jaw, and a greenish tentacle shot out, cracking in the air like a whip before darting the short distance across the table and coiling itself around the explorer's neck. Taken aback as much by the abrupt appearance of the slippery snake as by the sudden pain gripping his throat, Reynolds let out a cry of panic, which was instantly stifled by a lack of air. Terrified, he gripped with both hands the tentacle attempting to choke him and struggled to free himself, but he could gain no purchase on the slippery loop. Before he knew it, the tentacle had snatched him from his armchair and was lifting him high above the table, until he was almost touching the skylight. All of a sudden, he found himself thrashing about ridiculously in midair, held aloft by that muscular snake, while out of the corner of his eye he could see Carson sitting rigid in his chair, oblivious to the nightmarish member sprouting from his mouth and writhing above his head, with Reynolds dangling from one end. But he also saw Allan burst from his hiding place, pale with fear at the ghastly scene unfolding in the cabin, and aim his gun at the sailor's throat. Looking down, Reynolds saw Carson turn abruptly, reaching for Allan's pistol with his left hand. As it moved closer to the weapon, it turned into a monstrous claw. Allan cried out in pain as the razor-sharp talon slashed his hand open, but he managed to fire the pistol before the monster could snatch it from him. The two men heard what sounded like a loud yelp. The bullet hit the sailor in the left shoulder, and the impact sent him reeling backward. Reynolds felt the tentacle's hold on him slacken, and the next thing he knew, he had fallen onto the table. Half dazed and gasping for breath like a fish on dry land, he saw Allan standing in front of him, gazing with horror toward where the creature had collapsed.

Reynolds could not see from his position but was able to deduce from the look on the gunner's face that the monster was recovering. Being shot at close range must have caused the creature enough pain for it to cast off its disguise, so that no doubt poor Allan was now confronted with whatever its true appearance might be. Or perhaps the Martian was simply trying to raise itself up off the floor in order to renew the attack, still only half transformed, still looking like Carson, but with one of the monster's claws, as though the sailor had been surprised while dressing up for carnival. But what rose from the floor was neither of these things. Reynolds could not help his mouth opening in a grimace of horror as he found himself contemplating two Allans. Two Allans facing each other, with the mirror that should have stood between them missing, as though someone had smashed it. Two identical men, differentiated only by their wounds. The hand in which the real Allan was holding the pistol was bleeding, and the shoulder of the Allan whose appearance the creature was using as a disguise was oozing a gelatinous green liquid. But there was one other difference: the false Allan was smiling calmly at his real double, who was trembling as he attempted to aim at him.

"Are you going to fire at yourself, Allan?" he heard the creature say.

Allan hesitated, and the creature's smile widened into a sinister leer as it stepped forward.

"Of course not," the creature concluded. "No one can fire at himself, no matter how much despair darkens his soul."

A second later, the false Allan's chest received the full force of the bullet, which knocked it back to the floor. The real Allan turned toward where the shot had come from and saw Reynolds holding a smoking gun.

"Thank you, Reynolds," he murmured, trembling.

"You needn't thank me. I was merely showing the creature the exquisite wisdom of the human species, as you requested," Reynolds replied, a smile flickering on his lips. Then, looking down at the creature, which had begun groaning, he commanded Allan: "Shoot! Shoot before it gets up again!"

Before the gunner had time to reload his pistol, the creature had scuttled under the table. Reynolds watched with a mixture of horror and disgust as the bundle of tentacles darted across the room toward the door, scurrying like a kind of spider the size of a large dog and sweeping aside everything in its path, which, given Reynolds's scant possessions, amounted to his armchair. The explorer watched in dismay as it flew through the air, smashing to pieces against the nearest wall. Just then, Griffin opened the cabin door, pistol at the ready. But before he had a chance to shoot, the creature knocked him over and fled down the passage.

"Son of a bitch," muttered Reynolds, surveying his wrecked armchair, at last finding the perfect excuse to vent all the fear and hatred that had built up inside him over the past few hours. "You won't escape this time."

X

HE WAS STILL ALIVE.

He had exposed the Martian and was still alive.
And that made him absurdly, deliriously happy, despite his plan having
turned into a complete fiasco. He had failed to persuade the creature,
peaceably or by any other means, and as a result his dream of a glorious future as Earth's ambassador to outer space was in tatters; indeed,
following that debacle he doubted they would allow him to manage an
interplanetary telegraph office. Moreover, he had failed to kill or capture the Martian. On the contrary, he had so enraged the creature that
in all likelihood Fate had already decreed the death warrant of the entire ship's crew. But that did not matter. For the moment, he was still
alive: breathing, running, feeling life flowing through his veins like a
raging river. Whereas before he had considered his life dull, mediocre,
and despicable, now it seemed to him like an invaluable gift. He was
alive, damn it! he said to himself, as he sprinted down the passage on
the lower deck brandishing a pistol, followed closely by Allan, who was
groaning bad-temperedly, and the skinny sailor Griffin, who was running behind him, lips pursed, silent and tense. Reynolds had been struck
by how swiftly Griffin had come to their aid. Almost as though he had
been listening at the door. Perhaps Reynolds's peculiar behavior up on
deck, insisting to Griffin that Carson was dead, then blaming it on a
drunken hallucination, had puzzled him, but Reynolds was in too much
of a hurry to reflect about that now; he was content that the mysterious,
dogged fellow was following him with a loaded weapon.

When their pursuit of the creature took them to the crew's quarters, the explorer had to hold his breath as they were hit by a stench of lamp oil, soiled clothes, buckets of urine, and even fear, if, as some people claim, fear can be smelled. The creature had left a trail of greenish blood, as well as a row of sailors quaking against the walls, unable to believe the aberration they had just seen scuttle past them. Reynolds instantly realized that the gunshots had brought the whole crew running, from the lookouts up on deck to the carpenters and the kitchen boys. Right at the back, he could make out Captain MacReady, roaring above the noise, trying to get someone to explain to him what the devil was going on.

"The monster is on the ship, Captain," he heard someone cry out amid the uproar. "It's gone into the hold."

"On the ship?" MacReady said, drawing his pistol. "That's impossible! How in damnation did it get on board?"

No one except Reynolds could answer that. Buffeted like a leaf in the wind, the explorer forced his way through the crowd of anxious sailors until he reached the captain.

"The monster can change into a human being, Captain," he explained, going into less detail than he had with Allan. "It changed into Carson, which is how it was able to kill Doctor Walker."

"It changed into Carson? What nonsense are you talking, Reynolds?" said MacReady, his eyes fixed on the trapdoor leading to the hold as he cocked his rifle and began descending the ladder.

"I am telling you the creature can make itself look like any one of us," the explorer said, out of breath, clambering down after him. "You must warn your men!"

"Keep your crazy ideas to yourself, Reynolds," the captain muttered when he reached the bottom. "I will tell my men nothing of the sort."

Reynolds felt his frustration boil over into fury, and without thinking, he tucked his pistol into his belt, grabbed the captain by his lapels, and pushed him against the wall. Taken aback, MacReady stared at the explorer in astonishment.

"Listen to me for once, damn it," Reynolds said without loosening his grip. "I am telling you that thing can change into a human being, and if you refuse to inform your men we will all perish!"

MacReady listened yet made no attempt to wriggle free, perhaps because he was trying to make sense of Reynolds's unexpected response, at odds with the crude idea the captain had of him.

"Very well," he said coldly. "You have said your piece, now unhand me."

Reynolds let him go, surprised and slightly ashamed at his own behavior. The captain slowly straightened his lapels and gazed contemptuously at the explorer. Reynolds was about to apologize when he suddenly found himself pressed up against the wall, MacReady's pistol digging into his left temple.

"Listen carefully, Reynolds, because I'm not going to say this twice," the captain growled in a hoarse voice. "If you ever, ever grab me by the lapels again, you'll live to regret it."

The two men stared at each other in silence for a few moments.

Reynolds's voice seemed to ooze through his clenched teeth. "Captain, if you refuse to do as I say, neither of us will live long enough to regret anything. A few moments ago, Carson was in my cabin, and before my very eyes, and those of Gunner Allan, he changed into the monster from the stars and then tried to kill us both. We managed to shoot at the creature and it escaped, but not before changing into Allan, and then into a kind of gigantic spider. Do you understand what I am saying? That thing can change into anything it likes, including into one of us!"

"Do you expect me to believe that Carson burst into your cabin to treat you to a preposterous fancy dress parade?" MacReady said, beside himself.

"I invited him there because I was suspicious of him," the explorer explained. "I had stumbled upon the real Carson's body a few hours earlier while I was looking for the flying machine."

"What? You found Carson's body? Why the devil didn't you inform me?"

"I didn't consider it necessary," Reynolds replied, shrugging as much as he dared with MacReady's gun to his head.

"You didn't consider it necessary!" roared MacReady. "Who do you think you are? I've no more patience with you, Reynolds!"

"Would you have believed me, Captain? You yourself ordered me not to bother you again, nor any of your men," Reynolds reminded him, with more irony than bitterness.

"Gentlemen," declared Allan, who had climbed down after them, "I don't think this is the time to—"

"I'm the captain, Reynolds! It was your duty to inform me of the incident," bellowed MacReady. "Do you realize that your heroics have put us all in danger?"

"On the contrary, Captain. Thanks to my discovery our lives might yet be saved. Without knowing what the creature is capable of, we would be lost."

"And if the creature didn't know that we knew, we would be at an advantage!" MacReady hissed. "God damn you, Reynolds, why didn't you tell me so that we could capture the thing? What in Heaven's name did you hope to gain by inviting it to your cabin?"

"I wanted to make contact with it," Reynolds acknowledged reluctantly, with some embarrassment. "I thought that—"

"To make contact with it?" the captain roared, spraying Reynolds's face with saliva. "You invited it to take tea, as if you were a couple of young ladies?"

"Captain . . . ," Allan ventured timidly, "don't you think that—"

"Hold your tongue, Sergeant!" MacReady snapped. "I thought you had more brains than this idiot. I swear to you, Reynolds, when all this is over, I'll have you put behind bars for mutiny. I'm tempted to put a bullet in your head right now." The captain contemplated Reynolds in silence, carefully weighing up his own proposition. "In fact, maybe I should do exactly that. Didn't you say the monster could change into any one of us? How do I know it hasn't taken on your appearance?" he said, stroking the trigger of his pistol.

"I can vouch for Mr. Reynolds, Captain," a voice chimed out behind MacReady. "I was with him when the creature fled before us. I saw it with my own eyes. Lower your weapon, I beg you."

MacReady glanced sideways at the barrel of the gun aimed at his left temple, and at the skinny arm of the sailor called Griffin, who was clasping it firmly.

"And if I may say so, Captain, I agree with Allan: this conversation could take place some other time," he suggested, still brandishing his pistol.

MacReady contemplated the three men in turn, his face apoplectic with rage. Eventually he lowered his gun with a sigh and, pushing past Griffin, strode angrily toward the cargo hold, the others following close behind. A group of anxious sailors encircled the door, awaiting their orders.

"Are you sure the monster is in there?"

"Yes, Captain," Wallace confirmed. "I saw it go in. It looked like a huge ant . . . Well, not exactly; in fact, it was as big as a pig, though it didn't look like a pig either. It was more like a—"

"Spare me the descriptions, Wallace," snapped MacReady.

The captain fell silent, while the crew huddled round the narrow door to the cargo hold watched him expectantly.

"Pay attention," he said, emerging finally from his deliberations and looking disdainfully at Reynolds. "Incredible though it may sound, that son of a bitch is capable of taking on a human appearance—that is, it can change into any one of us."

MacReady's words unleashed a murmur of incredulity among the sailors, yet none dared offer an opinion. Reynolds, surprised by the captain's reaction, could not help heaving a sigh of relief. At least now there was some hope of salvation. The explorer nodded his thanks to MacReady, who signaled toward the crew, inviting the explorer to address the handful of brave men clustered before him. Reynolds stood beside the captain and cleared his throat before speaking.

"I know it sounds crazy, but what the captain says is true: the creature can make itself look like any one of us. Do not ask me how, but it can. It killed Carson, then came aboard looking like him. So, if you meet Carson in there, do not hesitate to shoot; the real Carson is lying out in the snow with his guts ripped out."

He paused, waiting for the sailors to digest his words.

"How do we know it isn't one of us?" ventured Kendricks, voicing the common fear.

"We don't. It could be anyone . . . even me," Reynolds said, glancing at the captain. "That's why we need to be doubly vigilant."

"I think it will be safer if we split up into pairs," MacReady suggested, taking the floor again. "Whatever happens, each of us should try not to lose sight of our partner even for a second. That is the only way we can be sure the monster doesn't change into one of us."

"And if you notice anything odd about your partner," Reynolds warned, "whether a strange glint in his eye, or a change in his voice—"

"Or a hideous tentacle extruding from his mouth," Allan added, almost inaudibly.

"—don't hesitate to warn the others immediately," Reynolds concluded.

"Good. You heard what he said, lads," growled MacReady, eager for the hunt to begin.

He divided part of the crew into five pairs and told Shepard to distribute the lanterns hanging from the hooks. When the sailor had placed the last of them in the captain's hands, MacReady spoke to his men once more.

"That son of a bitch couldn't have chosen a better place to hide. We may have a hard time finding it, but we have one advantage: this is the only exit. Lieutenant Blair, you and Ringwald stay here and watch the door. If that thing tries to get out, shoot it dead, understood? You others," he said, addressing the carpenters and the rest of the maintenance crew, "I suggest you go back up to the lower deck and wait there, armed with whatever you can lay your hands on."

"What about me, Captain?" asked Reynolds, who was not prepared to wait outside the hold.

"Reynolds, you come with me."

The explorer was so astonished he could barely nod his agreement. He drew his pistol and positioned himself next to MacReady, feigning a resolve he was far from feeling. Pairing up with the captain was the last thing in the world Reynolds wanted to do, in particular because he had no idea whether MacReady had chosen him because of his expertise about the monster or because he considered him a liability who would get in the way of any sailor unfortunate enough to be saddled with him. Or perhaps he was intending to shoot him in the back the moment they were alone, thus ridding himself of the explorer's irksome presence once and for all. Whatever the case, Reynolds said to himself, he must show he was equal to the task if he wanted that fool MacReady to know that he, Jeremiah Reynolds, deserved every bit of the respect and admiration the captain begrudged him.

"All right, let's get the bastard," the captain commanded.

WEAPONS AT THE READY, the group entered the hold, lanterns aloft, infiltrating the dense blackness like a swarm of fireflies. The icy space seemed at least thirty degrees colder. And despite the large space, Reynolds soon realized it was almost impossible to move around freely, for beyond the pale glow of the lantern he could make out an intricate maze of passageways formed by mounds of crates, coal sacks, water tanks, baskets, barrels, bales, and dozens of mysterious bundles covered with tarpaulins piled right up to the ceiling. At a sign from MacReady, Reynolds watched the other men slip like silent shadows into the narrow spaces, muskets sniffing the air. Peters brandished an enormous machete the length of his forearm as he moved forward, scrutinizing the darkness, his face set in a cruel grimace, in defiance of whatever was lurking in there. Griffin, incredibly small and frail by comparison, ventured into the enveloping blackness with calm self-assurance. Out of all the sailors, only Allan seemed as convinced as he was that they were all going to die in there.

MacReady and Reynolds took the central aisle. The captain went first, moving very slowly, pistol cocked, lantern held high. Reynolds, his weapon also loaded and ready to fire as soon as he perceived the slightest suspicious movement, tried to follow at what he considered a prudent distance: not close enough to appear fearful, not too far away for them to defend each other in case the monster ambushed them. Reynolds was convinced the Martian would attack him before any of the others. It was a reasonable supposition, for he was the one who had exposed the creature. He was to blame for them hunting it down now.

Suddenly they saw an enormous figure pass a few yards in front of them. Without delay, MacReady raised his pistol in the air and ran toward where the creature had vanished. Reynolds, on the contrary, remained motionless, horrified by the monster's new shape, as the darkness fell on him like a shroud. He had scarcely glimpsed the Martian as it darted across the passageway, but he had seen enough to know that the monster had reached another stage in its metamorphosis. What he had seen was a vaguely humanoid creature, more like one of the demons that had so terrified him as a child than like a spider. And although it appeared slightly hunched as it ran, he thought it looked bigger than Peters. That was all he could say about it. The darkness in the hold had made it impossible even to make out its color. A couple of loud reports interrupted the explorer's reverie. He deduced from their proximity that the shots had come from MacReady's gun. Reynolds swallowed hard, trying to overcome the fear that had seeped into his bones, and a few seconds later he found himself running in the same direction as the captain. When Reynolds reached his side, bathed in sweat and panting, he found MacReady peering furiously into the inky blackness stretching beyond the lantern's glow.

"That bastard is fast," he said.

"Did you hit it?" said Reynolds, trying to catch his breath.

"I think so, but I'm not sure. Did you see it, Reynolds? It looks like a goddamned orang-utan, but with a kind of forked tail—"

Before MacReady was able to go on, they heard the fire of muskets, followed by a din of shouts and crates crashing to the floor. When the rumpus ended, Reynolds could hear several sailors exclaiming excitedly that they had shot the creature, although their voices appeared to emanate from different areas of the hold. MacReady shook his head ruefully.

"Regroup at the door!" he yelled, the lantern light illuminating his vaporous breath.

With a nod of his head, he ordered Reynolds to follow him. They hurried back to the meeting place and found several of the men already there. The others arrived seconds later, and they were relieved to see that no one was missing. The men huddled near the narrow entrance to one of the passageways, and while the captain tried to form an idea of what had happened from their jumbled accounts, Reynolds leaned against what seemed like a solid pile of crates and observed the scene with a strange ambivalence: the creature he had glimpsed was far more powerful and terrifying than he had imagined in his worst nightmares, and his earlier euphoria at having escaped from his cabin alive was beginning to be eclipsed by the notion that all their attempts at survival would be in vain. But he must banish these morbid thoughts, he told himself; he had to carry on believing there was some hope of survival, however slight.

"I think I hit it," Ringwald assured them excitedly.

Reynolds looked at him askance, as did the others, because they were all claiming the same thing. Suddenly, a drop of blood appeared on Ringwald's brow, followed by another, and soon a small trickle was running down his face into the corner of his mouth. Ringwald touched his fingers to his forehead, puzzled, and, verifying that the blood was not coming from him but from above, he peered up at the ceiling. The others did likewise. On top of a very tall pile of crates they were able to make out what looked like a dead body, although all they could see was one leg sticking out at an impossible angle.

"Good God," muttered Lieutenant Blair.

"Why did the monster put him up there?" Kendricks wondered, equally horrified.

They went on gawping at the leg, dangling like a question mark in the air, until a wave of comprehension began to wash over them. Then, the sea of heads swathed in scarves began bobbing this way and that as, with a growing sense of horror, the sailors confirmed over and over again that no one in the group was missing. Some even instinctively moved away from the man next to them.

"Damnation!" roared MacReady, enraged that the Martian refused to let itself be hunted like any other wild beast. "Who lost sight of his partner?"

The men shrugged as one and exchanged suspicious glances. Apparently no one. But someone must have, Reynolds thought. Then he remembered with a shudder that he had. He had lost sight of MacReady briefly, just after they glimpsed the creature. As though his gesture were a continuation of that thought, Reynolds turned and aimed his pistol at the captain, but MacReady must have reached the same conclusion, for Reynolds found himself staring down the barrel of a gun. The sailors looked on in horror at the two men pointing their weapons at each other. For a few moments there was silence.

"If I were the monster, Reynolds," MacReady said, cocking his gun, "I would take on your appearance so as not to arouse suspicion."

The explorer twisted his mouth in disgust.

"I don't intend to waste my breath talking to you this time, whatever you are," he replied. "Three."

The shot from Reynolds's pistol knocked MacReady's head back. When it flopped forward again, he stared at Reynolds with a puzzled expression, as though unable to believe he had shot him. Finally, the captain's legs crumpled and he fell to the floor, where he lay stretched out at their feet. Reynolds gazed at him, amazed at the ease with which he had dispatched the creature.

"Good God, he's killed the captain!" Lieutenant Blair exclaimed.

Reynolds turned to the others, reassuring them with a wave of his hand.

"Keep calm. This is the monster, not the captain. I lost sight of Mac-Ready for several minutes. Long enough for the creature to kill him and adopt his appearance," he explained in a steady voice. Then he looked once more at the captain, who was lying faceup in the middle of the circle they had formed. "Pay attention and you will see how the creature's true form reemerges."

Their objections silenced, the sailors keenly contemplated Mac-Ready's body. He had a bullet hole right in the middle of his broad forehead, and death had finally erased his look of permanent irritation, replacing it with a surprisingly affable, almost kindly, expression, far more suited to entering the afterworld without arousing fear or loathing in his fellow spirits. But the minutes went by and the captain's face failed to undergo any change whatsoever. Perhaps the monster preserved its disguise after death, Reynolds reflected, as the sailors' anticipation quickly turned to disbelief, and he began to feel uncomfortable under their increasingly mistrustful gaze. He turned to them, shrugging foolishly.

"Well, we may have to wait a little longer," he apologized.

Allan gave a timid cough.

"Don't forget that when it changed shape in the cabin it was only wounded," he reminded him.

"Yes, perhaps that's it." Reynolds smiled reassuringly at the men. "Perhaps it cannot change once it is dead."

"In that case, how can we be sure it isn't still among us?" Lieutenant Blair asked nervously.

"Because I am the only one who lost sight of his companion," Reynolds explained.

"And Captain MacReady lost sight of you." The gigantic Peters stepped forward, his huge machete swinging alarmingly at the end of his arm, his voice booming among the crates like distant thunder.

Reynolds looked uneasily at the suspicious, even angry faces staring back at him.

"Surely you don't think . . . Oh, God, no," Reynolds gulped with horror. "I am not the creature, for pity's sake! Allan, please, tell them . . ."

The gunner gave him a beleaguered look, overwhelmed by the pace and madness of events.

Allan finally spoke in a muffled voice. "Listen, please. This man is Reynolds, believe me. I saw the creature change itself, first into Carson and then into me, and although the likeness is exact, I can assure you there is something that distinguishes it from the original!"

"And what is that, Sergeant?" Lieutenant Blair demanded, looking askance at Reynolds.

"I can't say exactly . . . ," the gunner replied apologetically, his hushed voice all but drowned out by the sailors' anxious murmurs.

"Listen! There is a far easier way of resolving this." Griffin's voice pierced the darkness like a tiny ray of light. "We can take down the body and see who it is."

For a few moments everyone remained silent, amazed that there should be such a simple solution.

"All right!" roared Peters, pointing his machete at the other sailors. "Two of you men see to that, but for the love of God, let it be two of you who know they didn't lose sight of each other. In the meantime, we will watch Mr. Reynolds. I'm sorry, sir," he apologized, waving his blade at the explorer's throat, "but right now you are the other half of the only pair that became separated."

Shepard and Wallace stepped forward as one.

"We'll see to it," said Shepard. "We're sure we didn't become separated, aren't we, Wallace?"

"That's right, Shepard. We were together all the time," Wallace said, staring straight ahead with an alarmingly fixed gaze.

"Like Siamese twins we were," Shepard joked in a peculiar voice that sounded like his but was slightly distorted, as though his tongue were too big for his mouth. Then, to everyone's astonishment, that same hideous voice chimed up once more, only this time in the mouth of Wallace. "You said it, Shepard. Closer than a wedded couple: together even in the afterlife."

Bewildered, Reynolds looked from one sailor to the other, until he noticed with horror the mesh of slimy fibers joining Shepard's right boot to Wallace's left one. At that moment, he knew he had killed MacReady pointlessly. And from some vague part of his body, perhaps from the base of his spinal cord, he felt a wave of pure terror coursing through him, through every nerve ending, every ganglion, threatening to paralyze him, to drain all his energy or whatever it was that enabled him to move. The other men looked equally startled.

What happened next is hard to describe. Perhaps a more seasoned narrator would have no difficulty—I am thinking of Wilde or Dumas—but unfortunately it falls to me. Having said that, I shall be as precise as possible in my choice of words so as not to confuse you even more. What happened was that, all of a sudden, before anyone had time to react, the bodies of Shepard and Wallace began to dissolve until they slowly melded into one, their deformed features floating in a glutinous substance like chunks in broth, a hideous fusion of eyes, mouths, and hair. Terrified, Reynolds could not help watching the creature's metamorphosis with fascination, and increasing alarm, as the issue of that gelatinous substance grew ever larger and more monstrous. And suddenly, like yeast bread in an oven, the slimy creature began to solidify, becoming more compact, its elongated body endowed with powerful muscles and covered in a reddish skin, as though draped in seaweed. When the transformation had finished, the explorer could see that its arms and legs did indeed end in long, razor-sharp talons. He also noticed that what he took to be its head, for no other reason than because it was sitting between its shoulders, had formed into a nightmarish countenance that looked like the result of an unnatural coupling between a wolf and a lamb: it had a pointed snout and a pair of spiral-shaped horns on either side of its massive skull. Then the thing appeared to smile, drawing back its lips like a dog, to reveal a row of small pointed teeth. Without delay, it turned to Foster, the unfortunate sailor standing on its left, and with a rapid movement sank one of its claws into his stomach, only to pull it out a moment later trailing a slew of organs that spilled onto the floor with a dull plop. Allan's face turned pale as he watched the jumble of entrails land at his feet, but he was scarcely able to retch politely before the monster wrapped its talons round his throat and lifted him off the floor like a doll. Luckily, Peters roused himself from the state of shock paralyzing all the men and moved toward the creature, swinging his machete. He plunged it forcefully into the creature's shoulder. The blade sank into its flesh with astonishing ease, and it let out a loud high-pitched wail that echoed among the crates. It automatically released its grip on Allan, who fell to the floor, coughing and spluttering as Peters wrenched out the machete, splattering a greenish spray in all directions, and raised it to strike a second blow. But this time the monster reacted more quickly. It stopped the Indian's arm by grabbing his wrist and bent it double as easily as a child snapping a twig. The color drained from Peters's face at the sight of his arm, twisted at an impossible angle, the bone poking out at the elbow, but his suffering was brief, for with another incredibly swift movement, the creature decapitated him with one of its claws. Peters's head hit one of the boxes with a dull thud before rolling across the floor, a look of bewilderment on his face at having met such a sudden death. Then the monster turned toward the rest of the men, but Griffin, with a composure that startled Reynolds, raised his musket, took aim, and fired straight at the creature's chest. The impact at such close range propelled the Martian backward. This brought the struggle to a halt for a moment, and those still standing watched the monster writhing on the floor, desperately trying to change shape.

"Finish it off, Kendricks!" Lieutenant Blair ordered the sailor closest to the Martian.

But Kendricks, crouched beside the crates, face splattered with greenish blood, was slow to react. By the time he began moving toward the monster, it had changed itself back into the spiderlike creature that had fled Reynolds's cabin and was scuttling toward the hold door, where it quickly vanished into the darkness.

"Where do you think you're going, you demon from Hell?" Kendricks cried, giving chase.

Lieutenant Blair, Griffin, and the others followed him, and Reynolds suddenly found himself in the hold, once more having survived, while the bodies of his fallen companions lay around him. By the light of the only lantern that had not been snuffed out during the commotion, he made sure there was nothing he could do for any of them, except for the young gunner, who was sitting propped against the wall of crates, a glazed look in his eyes, unaware of what was going on. Reynolds's first impulse was to flee the hold and look for a safe hiding place, abandoning Allan to his fate. And yet something held him back. Only moments before, when everyone believed he was the creature and were preparing to kill him in cold blood, the gunner had stepped in to defend him against the entire crew. Nor could he forget that Allan had also agreed to hide in his cupboard. But was that display of loyalty reason enough for him to risk his life for the gunner? Since when was he moved by such considerations? He no longer needed Allan, so he could leave him there. Taking him along in his present state would make them both an easy target for the Martian. Just then the gunner raised his head, and Reynolds thought he had at least partially recovered his senses, because Allan managed to look straight at him and whisper his name.

"Reynolds, Reynolds . . ."

The explorer knelt at his side.

"I am here, friend," he said, placing his arm around Allan's shoulder, ready to help him up.

"Where is everyone?" Allan inquired in the faintest of voices.

"Well, having seen what is in the hold, the Martian has decided to inspect the rest of the ship. I think it wants to make sure we are seaworthy," Reynolds jested, managing to elicit a weak smile from the gunner. "Do you think you can stand?"

Allan nodded feebly, but as he tried to rise to his feet, his ankle gave way, and he fell to the floor with a grimace of pain.

"Damnation, I think I've sprained it. I am not sure if I can walk, Reynolds," he said in a strangled voice. "What the devil are we going to do?"

"I don't know, Allan," the explorer replied, slumping beside him. He pushed Peters's head to one side with the toe of his boot. "Perhaps we should stay here and wait if you can't walk—this is as good a place as any. Maybe the others will manage to kill the monster. And if it comes back, we have more than enough weapons," he concluded, signaling the pistols that Foster and the captain were still clasping.

"No, Reynolds. You go and help the others," the gunner croaked. "There is no need to stay here with me."

But before the explorer was able to reply, they heard Kendricks's voice in the distance.

"I've found him, Lieutenant!" he cried. "That son of a devil is hiding in the powder store!"

"Be careful, Kendricks!" the lieutenant warned him. "Don't open fire in there!"

Then Reynolds and Allan heard several musket shots.

"For God's sake, Kendricks, I told you not to—"

A blast cut the lieutenant short, and almost immediately afterward Reynolds and Allan felt the ship shudder violently. The pile of crates they were leaning against began to wobble, and Reynolds hurriedly pushed the gunner to one side, then rolled on top of him as several crates containing whole sides of lamb toppled over and crashed to the floor, right where they had been sitting.

"Damn you, Kendricks," cursed Reynolds, standing up and hauling the gunner to his feet. Allan clung to him, stifling a cry of pain as he tried to rest on his injured foot. "Come on, Allan," Reynolds encouraged him. "We're leaving. I don't think it is such a good idea for us to stay here."

The echo from the first blast was still reverberating when they heard another, followed by a fresh convulsion. Reynolds realized that Kendricks had set off a chain reaction in the powder store, and it would not be long before the boxes of ammunition and barrels of gunpowder exploded, blowing the ship sky high. They had to get off the *Annawan* as quickly as possible. He dragged the gunner over to the trapdoor leading up to the deck where the officers' and crew's quarters were. Clouds of thick black smoke were billowing down the passage between the powder store and the hold, making it almost impossible to see. Reynolds assumed the sailors who had chased after the creature were dead and even dared hope the creature was too. Not wishing to suffer the same fate, he wasted no time praying for their poor souls, but urged Allan to climb the steps. Once they had managed to get to the lower deck, where there was not a sailor in sight, the explorer tried to think what to do next, but he scarcely had time to give Allan any instructions when they were startled by a third, even bigger explosion. The blast raised some of the floorboards, splintering the wood, and hurled the two men into the air, together with a handful of equipment and a few barrels. The explorer was flung against one of the walls and rolled along the floor for a few yards. Half dazed, he lay amid the debris; a dark fog began to cloud his consciousness.

"Reynolds . . ."

Allan's voice roused him from his stupor. He blinked several times, coughed, and was surprised to find himself still alive. His whole body ached, but no bones appeared to be broken. He half sat up and tried to locate the gunner amid the thick clouds of smoke obscuring everything. The blast had torn some of the lanterns from their hooks, and here and there tiny fires had broken out, which would soon spread, kindled by the tinder-dry wood from which the polar frost had wrung every drop of moisture. But before Reynolds could find Allan, he made out a figure at the far end of the deck, trotting calmly toward the armory, like a sinner so used to being in Hell that he feels completely at ease there. He realized it was Griffin, that curious sailor, who apparently had not followed the others into the powder store, thus escaping with his life, and who, instead of leaving the ship, which seemed the most sensible thing to do, was arming himself, as though he did not consider the battle with the creature to be over. Reynolds shrugged. That lunatic could do what he wanted with his own life; he had no intention of trying to stop him.

"Reynolds . . . ," he heard Allan wailing from somewhere.

Then the explorer saw him, trapped under a heap of shattered beams. He was still alive but would not be for much longer if Reynolds did not dig him out and help him to abandon ship. This time, Reynolds surprised himself by not even entertaining the option of leaving Allan there. He rose unsteadily to his feet and ran over to help him. When he arrived, he noticed a deep gash in Allan's forehead, which was bleeding profusely. He was still half conscious, yet beneath his matted hair, his bright eyes were flickering like two candle flames before an open window. Reynolds managed to pull him out from under the fallen beams, help him to his feet, and drag him over to the nearest hatch. Hauling him up the ladder proved grueling. When they finally emerged on the *Annawan*'s upper deck, Reynolds felt the cold like a rejuvenating balm. But they were not yet out of harm's way. Reynolds quickly collected himself and located the ice ramp. He pushed Allan toward it, and, placing his arms around the gunner's waist, they hurled themselves over the side, as behind them another violent blast shook the vessel.

Once they were on the snow, Reynolds heaved Allan up off the ground and dragged him to what he thought was a safe distance from the *Annawan*. The two men collapsed close to the cage where the dogs were barking wildly. As they tried to catch their breath, they gazed in fascination at the slow, relentless destruction of the ship, as though it were a prearranged spectacle. The blasts followed one another at irregular intervals, and, according to how powerful they were, either blew a hole in the hull or gently rocked the boat on its plinth of ice. Meanwhile, the fire, greedy and unstoppable, had spread to the bridge. Huge tongues of fire leapt from the forecastle and coiled themselves like flaming serpents around the wooden masts, in a disturbingly beautiful display that was undiminished by the awful sight of sailors hurling themselves from the top deck, some of them in flames. The poor wretches must have been hiding from the monster somewhere on the ship and been unable to escape when the blasts began. Fortunately, Reynolds and Allan were far enough away not to hear the crack their bones must have made as they hit the ice. Then Reynolds saw a dense mass of smoke, like a thundercloud, rise from the bridge, a sinister overture to the violent explosion that followed, scattering a hail of splintered wood, metal, and human limbs in all directions. Reynolds threw himself facedown in the snow and covered his head with his arms, while Allan remained sitting beside him, admiring the deadly shower of debris with the fascination of a child enjoying a firework display. The thunderous noise resounded off the icy hillocks, and the air itself seemed to shatter into a thousand pieces. When the echo died away, only the din of the dogs barking and leaping around in their cage prevented the two men from being engulfed in a tomblike silence.

Reynolds sat up slowly, relieved to see that none of the debris had fallen on Allan, who remained sitting on the snow as though at a picnic. He studied the devastation around him and in spite of everything felt a wave of joy wash over him as he realized the Martian must have perished at some moment during that orgy of destruction. The nightmare was over. After the final explosion, the ship had been reduced to a pile of timber and twisted metal, from which a plume of smoke arose, while the snow around it was strewn with an assortment of variously burnt and mutilated bodies. By pure chance, Reynolds's gaze rested on one of them, which was smoldering faintly, like a torch about to go out, and he was seized once more by an absurd and irrepressible euphoria. He knew he would only be able to enjoy his salvaged life for a few more hours, before cold and hunger finally snatched it from him forever, but that did not stop him from smiling to himself in the middle of that white immensity, simply because he was still alive.

It was then that the dead body he had been watching idly slowly began to stir. Reynolds contemplated it with fascination, wondering how anyone could possibly have survived that devastation. But suddenly, he realized that the figure that had begun to pick itself up from the snow was too big to be a man. With a mixture of panic and helplessness, he saw the Martian stand up, huge, unscathed, and indestructible. The skin on its shoulders was smoldering, but the monster did not appear bothered. Once it was on its feet, it sniffed the air, glancing about until it spotted them, twenty or so yards away, slumped in the snow, insultingly alive. The Martian began loping toward them over the ice. Reynolds glanced at Allan. The gunner had also seen the monster and, with a contorted expression that was beyond fear, was watching it approach.

"May God have mercy on our wretched souls," Reynolds heard him murmur.

The explorer looked back at the creature, which at the pace it was going would soon reach them. But he calculated that he had time to make one last attempt to kill it. He stood up, leaving Allan where he was, and ran toward the cage where the dogs were barking frantically, flinging themselves at the bars. He broke the padlock with the butt of his gun, released the door, and stood aside, praying the dogs were barking out of anger and not fear. He felt immensely grateful when he saw that, once released, the team of twelve or more snarling dogs made straight for the Martian. Reynolds's tactic took the creature by surprise, and it stopped in its tracks, watching the dogs hurtling toward it. The lead dog flung itself at the Martian, unleashing all the fury that had been fermenting since Carson first came aboard the ship. But, with an almost effortless movement of its claw, the monster sliced the dog in two in midair. Fortunately, the rest of the pack was undaunted, for it did not enter their brains that they might suffer the same fate. Or if it did, then they did not care, for they leapt at the monster with the same primitive ferocity, like brave soldiers doing their duty, perhaps because they could not help making that final gesture for Man, their master. They attacked the monster with their powerful jaws, but within seconds it had pulled them off, hurling them in the air or decapitating them with its talons, and Reynolds soon realized that the dogs' spirited attack would detain the Martian for only a matter of seconds. Knowing they must keep running, the explorer hurried back to Allan and pulled him to his feet. Then he took off in the opposite direction, practically dragging the gunner, while behind them he could hear the dogs yelping as they were torn limb from limb. A couple of them, reduced to bloody shreds, even went sailing over the two men's heads before landing with a dull thud on the snow.

Suddenly, Reynolds felt he had no more strength to go on running and came to a halt, exhausted. Without Reynolds to hold him up, Allan slid to the ground on his knees and gazed up at the explorer with a weary face. What was the point in trying to flee? he seemed to be asking. Would it not be better to surrender to the creature, to let it kill them without further ado, so that they could at last be allowed to rest in peace? Reynolds stared at the vast expanse of ice stretching in front of them, which had seemed so claustrophobic, and realized it made no sense to keep running, that it would only prolong their end. He took a deep breath and turned to face the monster, which was making its way slowly toward them over the snow, a pair of dogs still clamped to its body like some macabre adornment. Reynolds drew the pistol from his belt and gazed at it for a few seconds, as though weighing up the possibility of using it once more, before throwing it onto the snow. There was no longer any need for heroic or desperate deeds, because no one was watching. From the very first scene, the drama had taken place without an audience, in the intimacy of that godforsaken stretch of ice.

The monster came to a halt ten or twelve yards away, contemplated them, its head tilted to one side, and let out a noise resembling an animal screeching. Now that the creature was no longer using a man's vocal cords, what they heard was its real voice, a kind of cawing sound, like a domesticated raven attempting to speak. Naturally, Reynolds could not understand it, but he fancied the tone was triumphant. He prepared to die hacked to pieces. He lowered his head and let his arms flop to his sides in an attitude of surrender, or simple exhaustion, or possibly of indifference to his fate. Then his eyes fell on the pistol he had so casually cast aside a few moments earlier, and an idea formed in his head. Why succumb to a slow and gruesome death at the hands of that creature when he could take his own life? A bullet in the head and it would all be over quickly and cleanly. That would be a far more merciful end than the one the Martian no doubt had in store for him. He glanced at Allan, who was lying flat, his cheek resting on the ice, his gaze focused on horizons that only he could see. In the meantime, the monster continued edging toward them, as though savoring the fear of its quarry. Even so, Reynolds doubted he would have time to shoot Allan, take out the gunpowder and tamping rod, reload his pistol, and then shoot himself in the head before it reached him. No, he would only have time to kill himself. In any event, the gunner seemed to have found refuge somewhere beyond consciousness or reason, and he prayed with all his might that his friend could remain in that place until the very last moment, so that he could escape in some way the torment that would be the end of his life.

"Forgive me, Allan," he whispered, hurriedly reaching for the pistol and cocking it. "I fear that even in the final moments, I will not attain the greatness I so yearned for."

Yet that no longer mattered. A last heroic, altruistic act would have changed nothing. He aimed the pistol at his temple, gently, almost affectionately, caressing the trigger. Then he looked at the Martian, which, as though sensing that Reynolds was about to deprive it of its satisfaction, had quickened its pace and was ominously spreading its claws. Reynolds smiled. However fast it ran, the Martian wouldn't make it, he said to himself, as he caught a whiff of rotten flesh and chrysanthemums. The creature's smell. A smell that also vanished when it changed itself into a human.

"I shall see you in Hell, son of a bitch," he whispered, preparing to pull the trigger and spill all his dreams onto the snow.

Suddenly the Martian stopped dead in its tracks, raised its misshapen head to the sky, and let out a bloodcurdling cry. An instant later the tip of a harpoon burst violently through its chest. The creature looked at it with the same puzzlement as Reynolds. It grabbed the harpoon with its claws, and the explorer, lowering his pistol uneasily, watched the creature grappling vainly to pull it out, writhing in agony, as its features began dissolving once more. First it was Wallace trying to wrench himself free, then Shepard, then Peters, then the young gunner, even though the real one was lying at Reynolds's feet. The appearance of Carson, howling, mouth contorted, eyes popping out of his head, ended the sequence of transformations, the chain of agonized corpses. It was then that Reynolds noticed that whoever had fired the harpoon had also taken the trouble to tie a couple of sticks of dynamite to it. Without a second thought, he threw himself on top of Allan, shielding him with his body. A second later, a thunderous roar rang out and the Martian exploded into a thousand pieces that scattered in all directions. When silence returned to the ice field, Reynolds ventured to look up, half dazed, his ears ringing. And through the smoke that had begun to clear, he made out the calm figure of Griffin silhouetted against the polar twilight.

XI

I IMAGINE THOSE OF YOU WHO HAVE BEEN FOL-
lowing my tale at all closely will have realized that despite
my precautions I have made a mistake in my choice of where to begin.
Obviously, if the sailor called Griffin destroys the Martian, as he has
just done in so startling a manner, no expedition will be able to find it
years later entombed in the ice, nor take it back to the Natural History
Museum, where Wells will stumble upon it. I fear that when going back
in time I must have chosen the beginning of another story similar to this
one, but with a very different ending. I cannot apologize enough! However, permit me to try to make amends for my clumsiness.

How can I make this story fit with the prologue I have already narrated? Clearly there is only one possible way: by having Griffin not kill
the demon from the stars. Let us imagine, then, that this curious sailor
did not make an opportune appearance. Furthermore, let us imagine, to
be on the safe side, that he never boarded the *Annawan* at all. You will
agree that the story would have evolved very differently if we had dis-
pensed with any of the other crew members, although not all of them
would have had such a dramatic effect on the course of events. Say, for
example, we had omitted the cook, an ugly, potbellied brute who answers to the resonant name of Dunn; there would be no change to the
main events, beyond those relating to the crew's daily meals, or how
much rum the aforesaid individual filched from the store cupboard each
day, something I have not referred to until now, for, unless it is absolutely necessary, I prefer not to sully the image of the human race by

describing the dissoluteness of some of its members. Nor would it have produced any substantial change in the story had Potter and Granger boarded the *Annawan* and not Wallace and Ringwald; the former pair arrived when the crew was complete and signed up on another vessel, where Potter ended up stabbing Granger over a game of cards. For Potter and Granger would have behaved in exactly the same way as their predecessors, of that I am sure, because, as I have already told you, I am able to see all the other possibilities beyond the veil of our universe, the flowers that grow in the neighboring garden. However, in the tale that concerns us, Griffin's appearance could not have been more relevant. Would the Martian have ended up frozen in the snow if the sailor had not turned up and skewered it with his harpoon? Would Reynolds really have had the guts to shoot himself in the head, or would he have scraped the bottom of the barrel of life, despite knowing it would condemn him to a horrific end? Would they have been saved thanks to some other unforeseen miracle not of their making or, on the contrary, would a blaze of inspiration have allowed one of them to perform a checkmate *in extremis* on that chessboard made of ice?

Let us discover the answers to those questions by making the sailor in our story disappear, as one might remove a cuckoo's egg from the nest, thus restoring the natural course of things. Imagine that, as we have decided, Griffin never joined the crew of the *Annawan* and that the ship therefore set sail on her deadly mission with one less sailor on board. This did not simply mean that Dunn had to prepare one less meal a day, or that the waste bucket needed emptying less frequently. Without Griffin, for example, no one would have noticed that the object that hurtled through the sky and crashed into the mountain was being steered; Reynolds would have had no one to talk to on the way over to the flying machine; another sailor would have helped him back on board the *Annawan* after he stumbled on Carson's body; and no one would have intervened when Captain MacReady placed a pistol to Reynolds's head and threatened to kill him because he might be the creature. But first and foremost, and this is what should most concern us, no one would have harpooned the Martian just as it was about to end the lives of poor Reynolds and Allan. What would have happened then? How would the hunt have continued had Griffin never boarded the *Annawan* to escape a woman's clutches, only to end up confronting the demon from the stars?

Ignore my mistake, which is almost certainly due to my failings as a narrator, and travel back with me a few moments in time, to when the monster has fought off the dogs and is lurching toward Reynolds and Allan, spreading its claws, and let us see how things turn out.

The explorer, pressing the pistol to his head, watched the powerful, inhuman, enormous creature approaching and noticed that a strange calm had come over him. He no longer felt fear, euphoria, or defeat. He felt nothing. He had used up his supply of emotions during the drama of the past few hours. Now he was empty, save for a flicker of terrible indifference about his own fate. None of this seemed to be happening to him. It was as if he were watching it from a great distance, as might a bird sailing overhead, only vaguely interested in the strange goings-on below, where usually nothing much happened. The explorer stroked the trigger, pressing it lightly. He looked up at the Martian, which, as though sensing that Reynolds was about to deprive it of its satisfaction, had quickened its pace. The explorer smiled, watching the creature approach, its gaze fixed on him. He wanted to keep his own eyes open until the moment he pulled the trigger, so that he could take with him to the afterlife the look of defeat that would no doubt register on the Martian's face when it realized he had escaped its claws by taking the shortcut of suicide. Reynolds tried to swallow the lump in his throat. Would it hurt, or would he feel nothing when the bullet made his brain burst into a spray of thoughts, scattering his dreams over the snow? How easy it is to destroy a man and all he brings with him! Reynolds thought. And how naïve of them to imagine they could destroy with their pathetic weapons that powerful being, whose superiority far outstripped Man's wildest dreams! That creature was Evil incarnate, indestructible and eternal. It had survived repeated shootings, as well as the explosion. The cold did not affect it. He knew now that even the bullet encrusted in MacReady's skull would not have killed it. Everything had failed. All that was left to him was the pyrrhic victory of taking his own life.

"Burn in Hell, demon," he said, contemplating the creature's colossal build, its gigantic proportions and powerful musculature, with a scientist's detachment.

He wondered idly how many tons a creature like that would weigh. Would it be heavier than an ox? Lighter than a baby elephant? And then, to his astonishment, a crazy idea struck him like a bolt from the blue. He withdrew his finger from the trigger. What if . . . ? Would it be worth a gamble? He glanced at Allan, who was stretched out on the snow, mesmerized by the monster's advance, like a lamb waiting for slaughter. The change of plan Reynolds had in mind would upset the gunner, but he might forgive him if in the process he was spared dying at the hands of the creature, even if it only meant dying from starvation or exposure instead.

With a swift movement, Reynolds turned the gun away from his head and pointed it at the Martian, who gazed at him, surprised by this unexpected gesture. Reynolds shot the monster in the head without remorse or pleasure, as one carrying out a routine task. The blow knocked the monster to the ground, and although Reynolds knew he had not killed it, he hoped this would give him time enough to carry out his plan. Quick as a flash, he wrenched Allan to his feet once more and forced him to run, circling round the monster this time and heading for the wrecked ship.

"Run, run for your life!" he urged the gunner, who had begun a flailing sprint with what appeared to be the last of his energy.

Reynolds ran beside him, trying to keep the young man on the right track, all the while glancing back over his shoulder at the monster. Once it had recovered from the gun blast, the Martian had stood up, still a little dazed, and resumed its pursuit, although for the moment it did not seem in too much of a hurry, like a predator that knows its victim has no chance of escape. All the better, Reynolds thought, reaching the destroyed vessel on the point of collapse. He made the gunner stop next to a pile of debris so they could catch their breath. When he managed to tear his eyes from MacReady's privy, which was perched incongruously on top of a pile of timber, the explorer glanced once more over his shoulder. He saw the Martian still coming toward them, taking ever greater leaps across the ice, perhaps because it was suddenly in a hurry to end that stupid chase. Smiling to himself, Reynolds skirted round the ship and pushed Allan ahead of him out onto the ice on the port side, where the unfortunate MacReady had forbade the men from walking. Allan looked at him with alarm as the ice creaked under their weight, threatening to break up like pastry crust. But instantly, a flash of comprehension crossed his dark face. Reynolds urged him on, and the gunner obeyed, filled with renewed energy, even as the ice began to crack more and more with every step. They soon had the alarming feeling of walking on a moving sea.

When they considered they had ventured a sufficient distance onto the flimsy surface, they stopped and turned toward the wreck of the *Annawan,* just as the Martian was rounding it. The creature took a spectacular leap, unaware it was falling into the improvised trap Reynolds had laid, and landed some five yards from where they had come to a halt. To the amazed relief of the supposed victims, the ice gave way under the monster's incredible weight, and they watched it go down, arms thrashing about in a sea as dark as wine, as the ice closed up again. The impact, similar to a blast of dynamite, caused a skein of cracks to spread out in all directions, splintering the ice within a twenty-yard radius. The sudden tremor knocked Reynolds and Allan to the ice, and they clung to each other so as not to be separated as the ice broke into fragments around them. They listened in terror as the Martian struggled to punch its way through the thick frozen layer above its head, but it only succeeded in cracking, not piercing the ice. Gradually the frantic thudding grew fainter, until it was no more than a sinister tapping sound, ever more distant, leading them to conclude that some timely coastal current was dragging the monster away. When the tapping finally stopped, Reynolds prayed aloud to the Creator, or rather he demanded imperiously that He entomb the monster in that frozen sea. Yes, even if the Martian proved as immune to drowning and freezing as it was to bullets and fire, he prayed it would in one form or another meet its end there, for indestructible though it might seem, as far as he knew, the Creator had never shown the slightest interest in blessing any of His creatures with immortality.

After he had finished praying, Reynolds slumped down next to the gunner on the improvised raft that was floating down one of the channels the fractured ice had created. The two men were so exhausted and breathless they could scarcely speak. Even so, Reynolds heard the soft flutter of Allan's voice.

"Thank you for saving my life, Reynolds. The last thing I expected to find in this hellhole was a friend."

The explorer smiled. "I hope you remember that when you have no more need of me," he replied between gasps. "Assuming such a moment ever arrives."

The gunner gave a chuckle, which died away no sooner than it touched the air. Then there was silence. Reynolds half dragged himself up and saw that Allan had spent his last reserves of energy laughing at his jest, for the gunner lay unconscious beside him. Reynolds smiled wearily and fell back onto the ice, close to collapse, reflecting about what he had just said to Allan. Why had he carted the gunner back and forth, never even considering leaving him to his fate? It wasn't like him. And yet he had, for he was incapable of ignoring the spell the poet's voice cast on him each time he called out his name, with the blind trust of a child calling to its mother in the dark. Answering that desperate appeal had made him feel something profound and alien, something he had never felt before, he realized in the haze of his fatigue: for the first time in his life, someone had placed his trust in him, someone had needed him. Allan, the gunner who dreamed of being a poet, had called his name in the hold, up on deck, on the ice, and he had gone to his aid instantly. He sensed that by saving Allan, he would in some way also be saving his own selfish soul. Yes, that is what had motivated him. And who could tell—perhaps that last-minute gesture would redeem him from Hell and redirect him to Heaven. For one thing was certain: unless some miracle occurred, the merciless cold would kill them within a matter of hours.

Oddly content at the thought of the long-awaited rest this would bring, Reynolds let himself be transported on that icy carriage as it drifted between the icebergs, a wind gently blowing them wherever it wished to take them. The crushing fatigue and emotional drain of the last few hours soon plunged him into a kind of daze, from which only the stabbing cold or the relentless booming of the ice would rouse him. And in that dreamlike state, Reynolds passed the time gazing at the sky, fascinated by the dark tufts of cloud and the jagged gorges they passed through on their uncharted journey, relieved that it was no longer up to them whether they lived or died, that there was nothing they could do but lie there until someone, possibly the Creator Himself, decided on their behalf. He soon lost track of how long they had been drifting, waiting to die, and yet when he came around a little, he was surprised to find his heart still beating. He reached out and touched Allan's body, which, despite being covered with a film of ice, appeared to contain a tiny glimmer of life that might miraculously be awakened if they could only find shelter. Or perhaps it would fade silently and imperceptibly there on the ice. After all, what did their lives matter? What essential ingredient would they have added to the great stew of life? Yet they must have contributed something, he concluded when, some time after the monster's disappearance, the raft floated into a much broader channel, which he fancied was the open ocean. Seasick and blue with cold, he thought he detected signs of civilization on the coastline.

Drifting in and out of consciousness, he let himself be hauled up by strong hands, warmed beside the gentle glow of a stove, and revived with warm broth that slipped into every crevice of his throat. And he felt life begin to stir inside him, slowly and cautiously, until one day, he did not know how or when, he woke up and found himself in a warm, cozy cabin next to a simple cot where Allan lay, breathing tenaciously. Despite being delirious with fever, he too had survived. When the captain of the whaler, a huge fellow capable of ripping a kraken's head off with his bare hands, asked their names, Reynolds had to reply for them both.

"Jeremiah Reynolds," he said, "and my companion is Sergeant Major Edgar Allan Poe. We are crew members on the *Annawan,* which set sail from New York on the fifteenth of October for the South Pole, in search of the entrance to the center of the Earth."

XII

*A*ND YET, NEITHER THEN NOR IN THE DAYS
that followed did Reynolds mention the monster that
had come from the stars, nor the slaughter they had survived. At that
moment, he did not think there were any words that would accurately
describe that horror, any words with which to explain to their rescuers
that Hell, whilst unarguably inhabited by demons, did not lie beneath
their feet or above their heads. And in the days that followed, when
Allan's fever finally abated and he awoke with the melancholic look
of one who has walked with death, both men agreed it was best never
to tell their secret to anyone. What good would it do to reveal to the
world a truth for which it was doubtless unprepared? Besides, they had
no way of proving what had happened. If the Creator had answered
Reynolds's prayer, the monster would be lying buried somewhere in
the Antarctic ice and, thanks to the interminable snow blizzards, so
would its flying machine, long before any other expedition managed to
reach that accursed place. And perhaps the only thing they would find
when they did get there would be the charred wreck of the *Annawan*
surrounded by the remains of her brutally murdered crew. This might
turn out to be worse, of course, for as the only survivors they would no
doubt become prime suspects in that mysterious orgy of destruction.
And yet there would always be a handful of visionaries who would not
only believe them but would go to great lengths to prove that their
story about the first Martian to visit Earth was true. However, a far

greater number would make them out to be madmen, or impostors, or both. And neither Reynolds nor Allan wished to spend their lives explaining, proving, and denying: in short, defending their sanity, or their honor.

No. That was not why they had struggled to survive. In common with many who escape the jaws of death, both men felt that life was an unexpected gift, and each made a secret promise to himself to be worthy of that second chance, to renounce what he considered his previous inertia and numbness and to live passionately, to do everything it was possible to do with a life. Allan had decided to persist in his dream of becoming a writer with renewed vigor. He wished to do this single-mindedly, without being reminded of his sojourn in Hell. So he made a firm decision to put those days behind him, never consciously to think of them again. And if necessary he could always exorcise that horror by writing a story. The gunner could not think of a better way of ridding himself of the things that bedeviled his soul than by imprisoning them forever on paper. As for Reynolds, after coming so close to tasting the glory of the great adventurers, he had learned to love life in all its simple splendor. His only desire was to live in peace, celebrating each beat of his heart, each molecule of air he breathed, while doing his best to purge his soul of anything that might prevent those who had known him from saying after his death: there lies an honorable man. The last thing he intended to do was to turn his life into a sideshow with himself as the main attraction, ridiculed and pitied by the public. Those days had ended with Symmes. Reynolds intended to live a different life now, secretly knowing things others would never know, content to become one of a handful of simple, honest men who accepted their place in the world uncomplainingly. Neither Allan nor Reynolds considered they had vanquished the monster from the stars to live in the shadow of that event. It was best to say nothing.

And so, there in the modest cabin of the ship ferrying them back to America, they shook hands on what neither ventured to describe as a gentlemen's agreement, for theirs was clearly a pact between cowards. Both men realized that keeping such a transcendental truth from the world might be considered a shameful betrayal of the human race, and yet both believed they could easily live with that on their conscience. And so they agreed to lie. And if as he watched over the gunner, Reynolds evaded their rescuers' questions by supplying the occasional snippet of their ordeal, and when Allan awoke he added all that was necessary in order to elaborate a tale as fantastical as it was plausible. They spent entire evenings embellishing it with further details, most of them the product of Allan's prodigious imagination, smoothing out any contradictions until they had produced such a solid, incontrovertible truth they ended up believing it themselves.

However, during the voyage, surrounded by the expansive silence of the ocean, Reynolds and Allan did more than invent the story that would protect their lives: they also resumed the intimate discussions they had begun on the *Annawan,* sealing the friendship with which Fate had chosen to bind them together. Without knowing why, they talked until the early hours, each eager to reveal the innermost parts of his soul to the other, perhaps because each had saved the other's life. And, as though he considered the gunner had earned the right to know everything about him, one night Reynolds even confessed the secret he should have taken with him to his grave. This was tantamount to placing his fate in the gunner's hands, yet the explorer knew that if there was one man in the world incapable of betraying him, it was Allan. Thus, in the same fearful whisper with which his mother used to tell him tales of graveyards filled with ghosts and goblins, Reynolds told the gunner his darkest secret: Captain MacReady was not the first man he had killed; he had already killed someone else before he joined the *Annawan.* But not with a gun. No. That time he had simply opened a window. When Reynolds had finished telling him how he had ended Symmes's life, Allan's gaze wandered for a moment. Reynolds wondered whether his somber eyes were envisaging that unknown hotel room in Boston, in which a wretched man lay abandoned on the floor while the snow wove an icy blanket over him. Then he looked straight at Reynolds with that half grin of his, which made him look at once younger and older, and said, "My dear friend, if one day you are judged for this in Heaven, I only hope I can be there to help you invent a good excuse."

Reynolds beamed, pleased that Allan had not condemned his act. No man was a complete saint or a complete sinner, the gunner must have thought, and however much Reynolds tried to convince himself that what had happened in the Antarctic had made a new man of him, that he had emerged from that savage catharsis an honest, upright individual, no one changed completely, except in bad novels. To think that would be as absurd as to believe he had come through the experience knowing how to play the violin.

For his part, Allan seemed equally forthcoming, and as Reynolds looked on affectionately, the gunner poured out every detail of his young life with the same jubilant despair with which he spilled his soul onto paper. He traced a portrait in which he himself tried to decipher what kind of man he had been in those distant days when he had encountered terror only as a product of his ghoulish imaginings. The explorer listened spellbound, admiring the gunner's ability to conjure up images whose vividness made his own memories seem pale by comparison. Thus Reynolds could picture him swimming with his sleek, amphibian body six miles up the James River to emulate his hero Byron; becoming enamored of Mrs. Stanard, the frail mother of a friend, whom he converted into his muse, until she was swallowed up by the murky waters of insanity; crying with rage after every argument with his stepfather, who was determined that he become a lawyer, no matter that each night by the light of a candle he struggled to compose the verses that would turn him into a poet; writing love letters to the young Sarah Elmira Royster, which, he would later discover to his fury, her father had intercepted before they could set her heart aflame with their declarations of ardent love. It was the portrait of a rebellious youth, to whom his parents had left nothing save the corrupt blood of a consumptive; an avid reader and a brilliant student burdened with a troubled soul; someone left intoxicated by a single sip of alcohol; a poet who had just finished a lengthy ballad called *Al Aaraaf* when the Martian had descended from the stars to plague their nights with bad dreams, and in passing—for every cloud has a silver lining—to inspire a novel he had already begun to forge in his mind, which, he was certain, would turn him into a writer. Why else had he escaped from Hell? Why else indeed, Reynolds concurred.

And so the two men came to know each other better even than they knew themselves, and in that friendship they found a refuge from the loneliness that invaded them after discovering that Man was not the only inhabitant of Creation. However, as they drew closer to their destination, the two men ceased talking about the monster from the stars. To begin with they did this out of caution, to avoid any slipups when they reached America, and then later on because they became so used to the story they had invented that they accepted it is as true. Reynolds did so consciously, relieved that those fearful memories had begun to fade; but the unhealthy zeal with which Allan appeared to devote himself to keeping up the farce began to worry Reynolds. He even began to fear for the gunner's sanity when in the middle of a conversation at which no one else was present he alluded to that apocryphal story as though it were the true one. As the days went by, Allan seemed more and more nervous, distant, transparent even, as though his mind were wearing imperceptibly thin, like a hallway carpet. It worried Reynolds, who had still not made up his mind to confront the gunner about it, for fear of making things worse. Be that as it may, on reaching America, both men were able to relate their story unflinchingly to the army of journalists awaiting the arrival of the only surviving members of the Great American Expedition to the South Pole. For long hours, in slow, strained voices (as if remembering what had happened still reverberated in their souls), they described all they had experienced since the day they sailed from New York Harbor in search of the passage to the center of the Earth.

And the world appeared to believe them.

• • •

FOLLOWING AN ENDLESS ROUND of interviews that left them worn out, they traveled at last to Virginia, where Reynolds was relieved to see that the air appeared to agree with Allan. Within a few days he had completely recovered, emerging intact from his feverish chrysalis, or at least as intact as he must have been before Reynolds knew him. Even so, the explorer could glimpse in his eyes the vestige of horror left in his soul, and he was unsure whether Allan recalled what had actually happened in the Antarctic or whether he had buried the memory beneath that mound of lies. A week after their arrival, unable to assuage his doubts, Reynolds decided to ask him straight out. Allan stared at him, slightly astonished.

"Why, of course I remember what happened to us there, my friend. Each night I force myself to remember, so that the horror feeds my nightmares, and each morning I force myself to forget, so that I can set them down on paper with a steady hand," he confessed, smiling gently. "Don't worry about me, Reynolds. I am an artist. And an artist is simply a man who is pulled along by a river: on one side sanity lies, and on the other madness, yet he will find no peace on either, as the current of his art drags him away from the everyday life on its banks, where others watch, unable to help him, until he reaches the immensity of the ocean."

Reynolds nodded, although he did not fully grasp Allan's convoluted metaphor. He had understood the first part of what he said and that was enough: Allan remembered everything. He was perfectly well aware they had been attacked by a Martian. He could tell the difference between reality and fantasy. He had not lost his mind, as the explorer had feared. And, content with Allan's reply, he spoke no more of the matter. Since setting foot on America's blessed soil, Reynolds had, metaphorically speaking, cast off his dreamer's garb and thrown it onto the equally metaphorical fire, to embrace instead his true, pragmatic nature. And so, once the gunner's mental and physical health appeared to be out of danger, he busied himself with his own affairs, considering he had more than fulfilled his duties as a friend.

The first thing he did was visit his fiancée, Josephine, with the intention of jilting her, as he had decided during the expedition. But, to his surprise, he left her house having agreed on a wedding date. At the outset, Reynolds had studied her with inscrutable intensity, expecting to feel something akin to repulsion welling up inside him, for, having discovered a renewed and boundless lust for life, he did not wish to spend another day in the company of someone who was able to breathe without being moved to joy by such a miracle. There was a time when he might have resigned himself to that, but now he no longer needed money, respect, glory, or social status. He needed something more; to experience love, to fall passionately, everlastingly in love. He did not want to die without having tasted what suddenly struck him as the most sublime of all emotions.

Reynolds was certain Josephine was not the woman to stir such feelings in him. Yet, when he saw her sitting there, wearing the appropriate dress for that time of afternoon and listening to his exploits with demure politeness, but without the slightest interest in a world which for her had no validity or substance simply because it was not the one she lived in, Reynolds came to doubt the existence of another world at the Earth's core or in the depths of outer space. Perhaps it would be more precise to say that he preferred not to know, because, for the very first time, the self-evident world before him, filled with things that not only could he touch but that were devoid of all mystery, such as the porcelain teapot on the table or the young woman's choker, was enough for him. And Josephine, the empress of that falsely true reality inhabited by the uncurious, seemed to him to offer the perfect refuge from the horror pulsating beneath the surface. All at once, he realized that the only escape from being overwhelmed by fear or madness was to become as ordinary as she was, to shelter behind the ignorance and apathy of singularly uncomplicated souls. As he contemplated the young woman, he told himself it was up to him to find her more beautiful and interesting than she really was. And so he set himself to the task, helped by his relentless pragmatism, and after half an hour of sparkling conversation he managed to make Josephine forget the desultory manner in which he had previously courted her and to surrender her heart to the surprisingly ardent lover whom the frozen wastes had delivered back to her. What better way to secure his place in this innocuous world that Man had constructed than to apply himself to making sure it ran smoothly? thought Reynolds. Having planted his first heartfelt kiss on Josephine's lips, he threw his belongings into a trunk, bade Allan farewell, and set off for New York to study the law.

However, despite taking shelter behind the façade of an ordinary life, each time Reynolds lowered his guard he was plagued by memories of his experiences in the Antarctic. For that to happen he need only examine the tiny burn mark on the palm of his right hand, the letter or symbol whose meaning he would never know, which was a constant reminder of the hidden mysteries that lay beyond the visible world. Some nights, this thought would keep the explorer awake, and he would gaze out of the window at the star-speckled sky, wondering what had become of the Martian. Had they really managed to kill it, or had it survived and contrived to follow him to America? Was it keeping watch on him, having usurped the appearance of one of his fellow students? He realized this was unlikely, but it did not stop him from feeling a stab of fear whenever he noticed one of his classmates staring at him more intently than usual. He had even stopped speaking to a certain Jensen, who had invited him to his room for a brandy. Reynolds realized he was being overly cautious, yet he could not help such fears affecting his life. He felt alone, gripped by a strange, absurd sense of his own isolation. Only Allan's letters managed to dispel his unease, as the gunner was the sole person who could understand him.

Since Reynolds had left for New York, his friend would send him long missives keeping him abreast of his news, although it was obvious that his true reason for writing was to relate the sorry state of his soul. And so the explorer was able to observe the life of his only friend begin to change shape. In his first letter, Allan told of his expulsion from West Point. This had caused a fresh altercation with his stepfather, of such violence that Allan had decided to seek refuge at the home of his aunt, Maria Clemm, in Baltimore. He made up his mind to devote himself to writing short stories, since he had been greatly discouraged by his relative lack of success with the publication of *Al Aaaraf,* the long poem he had written during his sojourn on the *Annawan.* However, Reynolds soon realized that those bland details were merely a polite preamble, and what Allan really wanted to share with him were the sinister nightmares his brain engendered in the dark. He told him of dreams filled with immeasurable horrors: ships crewed by dead men, ladies with dazzling teeth that, prey to some mysterious malady, rotted away in front of his eyes. He even saw himself tortured by the Spanish Inquisition or putting out the eyes of a cat with a quill pen, only to hang the creature without remorse. Such was his state of anxiety that sometimes when he ventured out of the house he thought he saw himself. *These monsters, which have with such subtlety infiltrated my dreams,* he wrote disconsolately, *cause me to awake in the middle of the night in a fit of anguish, my heart beating wildly, bathed in an icy sweat, although I confess I have never written as much as at present. Nor would I wish to banish these nightmares, for I fear they are the only way I have of diminishing the horror that fills my wretched soul, a horror which I have at last understood how to convey to paper, as authentically as if I were writing in my own blood.*

Reynolds had smiled wistfully as he put away this letter from Allan. The Martian had cast an ominous shadow over their souls, and yet Reynolds could not help feeling glad that at least in Allan's case this had fallen on astonishingly fertile ground. For his part, it merely prevented him from gazing innocently at the stars and caused him to be irrationally suspicious of anyone who looked at him with curiosity. It made Reynolds happy to imagine his friend in Baltimore, doted on by his aunt and intent upon making a name for himself as an author whilst trying to keep hardship from his door.

Two years later, when his own fears had all but faded, Allan wrote to him at last with some good news: *My dear friend, I am pleased to be able to tell you that one of my stories has won a literary prize. It seems that hard work does indeed pay off, something I had begun to doubt. Although in this instance, the prize has only filled me with a feeling of joy and confidence without delivering me from poverty, in whose grip I am now firmly held, for you should know that my stepfather has passed away and left me none of his money. And so, no inheritance will save me from the eternal shipwreck that is my existence. But do not concern yourself on my behalf, my friend, for although I do not even possess a suit in which to go out to eat, life has not beaten me yet. You, better than anyone, know that I am a survivor, and in a few days from now, I shall have found refuge in the best sanctuary possible: my cousin Virginia. Yes, my dear friend, I want you to be the first to know: Virginia and I are to be married, swiftly and in secret.*

Reynolds was not surprised by the blow that Allan's stepfather had dealt from the grave, yet he would never have guessed that the gunner would decide to marry his cousin Virginia, a girl scarcely thirteen years of age. However, such an extraordinary marriage seemed to bring Allan luck, for not long afterward he moved to Richmond, where he took up a post offered him on the magazine the *Southern Literary Messenger*. Even so, Reynolds soon learned that it was becoming increasingly common to see his friend stumbling drunk out of the seediest taverns, and his aunt and Virginia were finally forced to move to Richmond to keep him from the demon drink. Thanks to their loving ministrations, Allan appeared to return to normal.

It was then Reynolds received a letter in which the gunner announced that in view of the growing popularity of maritime adventure stories, he had begun writing a novel inspired by their experiences in the South Pole. The novel, which was called *The Narrative of Arthur Gordon Pym of Nantucket,* was serialized a few weeks later in the *Southern Literary Messenger*. Reynolds read each fresh installment with a heavy heart, for those pages obliged him to dredge up memories of their days in the Antarctic. And yet they no longer inspired fear in him, only a strange regret, for he realized that the exhilaration of that horror was something he would never have experienced in the comfortable mediocrity of his life as a journalist: he had conversed with a Martian, chased it, fled from it, trapped it in the ice, not to mention killing a man and saving another one's life. Those were not things people often did. And yet he, Reynolds, had done them, however dreamlike it seemed to him now, and although when the time came he would be buried as a simple lawyer, his body would face eternity with a mysterious Martian symbol engraved on the palm of its hand.

Allan's tale began with the voyage of a whaler, the *Grampus,* to the South Seas. In addition to certain rhythmic similarity between the author's name and that of his eponymous hero, there were other autobiographical elements in the story, some of which clearly referred to their journey: part of the action took place in a hold as suffocating as the one the monster from the stars had chosen as its hiding place, and one of the characters was an Indian named Peters. However, all comparisons between the novel and their failed expedition ended there, for in the second installment, which described their journey to the Antarctic Circle, Allan had let himself be guided solely by his imagination, perhaps fearing he would lose impetus were he to recollect the truth: after several lurid, violent passages, in which the ship avoided icebergs and various crew members showed symptoms of scurvy, they managed to reach an island where they encountered a tribe that tried to take them captive. The finale to that grisly show had the crew sailing south on a milk-white ocean beneath a fine shower of ash, and just before plummeting over a gigantic waterfall, they glimpsed a mysterious, dazzlingly white figure, larger than any creature living on Earth.

Reynolds wrote to Allan at length, telling him how much he had enjoyed his novel, and tried as subtly as he could to find out the meaning of that strange, allusive ending. But, to his astonishment, the writer himself did not seem to have the slightest idea what awaited his characters on the edge of that waterfall. *My novel's abrupt ending has given rise to all manner of speculation, my dear friend,* he wrote. *Some critics maintain I did not know how to end it, and so I gave up at the climax, possibly owing to indolence, or because the wellspring of my impoverished imagination had dried up, or because the story itself somehow obliged me to end it there. Let them speculate, poor wretches. The truth is, even I do not know the answer, for I wrote those final pages in what can only be described as a state of intense delirium, while being assailed by terrible nightmares in which a hideous creature invariably appeared, of which I remembered nothing upon waking but the horrific impression it had caused me. But do not worry yourself on my account. I know you well enough to suppose you are afraid your friend is losing his mind. Rest assured, that is not yet the case. Although I will not deceive you of all people: in some strange way I sense I am drifting ever closer to insanity. My nightmares have invaded even my waking hours. There are times when I ask myself: Am I sick? What will become of me? And I know you are the only one who can guess at the answer.*

Reynolds read Allan's last words with a sense of foreboding, as he revisited the doubts he had had about his friend's mental health during the journey back to America. Perhaps the gunner's brilliant, fragile, complex mind had been unable to cope with a life built upon a conscious act of forgetting. Such a life had posed no problem for Reynolds. Perhaps he had succeeded in forgetting because the workings of his mind were far simpler than those of the gunner, Reynolds thought unashamedly. Had he not managed to forget that he had murdered Symmes? In contrast, Allan was incapable of expunging those memories voluntarily and had been forced to wall them up behind a carefully constructed barricade, even though he had been unable to stop them seeping through the masonry and spilling onto the endless white expanse of the blank sheets he placed on his desk each day. Yes, that was where Allan had exiled all the monsters he wished to banish from his life. And yet, Reynolds feared his friend was finding it increasingly difficult to distinguish between real life and his imaginings. Despite these disturbing conclusions, Reynolds filled his reply with clichéd words of comfort: he knew there was little else he could do to help his friend except to pray to God (in whom his belief was steadily waning) that the huge white figure awaiting Allan on the edge of the waterfall was not the specter of total madness.

Allan's next letter was sent from Philadelphia, where the gunner had gone to try his luck after his continuous drinking had irreparably damaged his situation at work. *Yet like a faithful dog poverty has followed us here, too,* he wrote, *and I have been forced to employ my pen in more mundane activities than I would have wished. I was even commissioned to write a textbook on conchology, and you can imagine how little pleasure that afforded me. Although happily I still have time to write tales, tales so dark and menacing that I myself am horrified by them. Yet, I know they could not be otherwise, my friend, for they are fashioned from the sinister stuff of my nightmares. Not even the Auguste Dupin stories, which I strive to make less baleful, escape from the inevitable horror that envelops them all, like a dank moss. Only my beloved Virginia is able to cast a little light into my dark soul, when each day upon my return from work she greets me with a spray of freshly picked flowers.*

Unhappily, that light proved as fragile as a candle flame, for it was soon extinguished. Allan's next letter was terrible and harrowing, penned by a man who had lost all belief in life. *My dear friend,* it began, *I write to you on the brink of the deepest abyss of despair, for I am at last convinced that my miserable soul is the plaything of Fate. Virginia, my delicate nymph, is gravely ill. A few days ago, while she was entertaining me with some of my favorite songs, accompanying herself on the harp, her voice broke on a high note, and in a gruesome spectacle arranged by the Devil himself, blood began to pour from her sweet mouth. It is consumption, my dear friend. Yes, that vile harpy has come to snatch her from me in two years' time, or less, according to the doctors, mindless of the fact that no one can take her place. What will become of me when she is no more, Reynolds? What will I do when she begins to fade, when her gentle beauty starts to lose its bloom, like so many petals falling into my clumsy hands as I vainly try to reconstruct the flower of her youth?*

Deeply moved by the illness of the young woman he had not even met, and the terrible suffering it caused his friend, Reynolds resolved to do whatever was in his power to help. He offered them the solace of a farm in Bloomingdale, on the northern outskirts of New York, a rustic paradise where the fresh air and soft grassy meadows could breathe new life into Virginia's slowly deteriorating lungs. The couple apparently enjoyed a brief respite and even managed to squeeze a little happiness out of life, until the fierce winter forced them back to the city.

Shortly after his return, Allan threw the literary world into a stir with the publication of "The Raven," a poem he had been working on for some time, and which their peaceful sojourn in the country had enabled him to finish. The explorer was told that people came in droves to listen to him recite those dark verses, which struck fear into their hearts. Intrigued, Reynolds attended one of those performances and was able to see for himself the effect Allan's reading had on the audience, particularly on the impressionable ladies, as he sat stiffly in his chair, his face luminously pale. When the function was over, Reynolds invited him to dine at a nearby restaurant, where, after clumsily dissecting his meat pie, the gunner broke down and confessed that the continual veering between hope and despair caused by Virginia's illness was having a worse effect on his soul than if she had died outright. And the only relief he could find was in alcohol and laudanum. Naturally, they no longer spoke of the distant days spent together in the Antarctic fighting against the terrible creature from outer space intent on killing them. All that seemed unreal now, perhaps imaginary, and of no consequence. As they gave each other a warm farewell embrace, it no longer mattered to Reynolds whether or not Allan had lost his mind. The love of his life was dying, Virginia was slowly being taken from him, and there was nothing anyone could do. Somewhere someone had decided at random that those two good, generous souls would suffer for no apparent reason. This and this alone was what made the world a truly terrifying place.

Reynolds did not need to open the gunner's next letter, sent from one of the places to which his peripatetic wanderings took him, to know that it contained painful news. The next he heard of Allan was that he had returned to Richmond. There he had discovered that Sarah, the childhood sweetheart who had never received his letters, was now a respectable widow, and he had looked her up immediately, as though needing to close the circle. Sarah had accepted his courtship, and within weeks they were engaged. It was then that Reynolds received Allan's last letter, informing him that he planned to stop off in Baltimore on his way to Philadelphia to fetch his aunt for the wedding. Reynolds replied instantly, offering to pick Allan up when his boat docked and to stay with him until he caught his train. However, Reynolds was needlessly held up by various matters, so trivial in nature he could only remember them later with bitter rage, and by the time he reached the port, Allan was gone.

XIII

*O*N THE MORNING OF SEPTEMBER 29, 1849, BAL-timore awoke in the grip of an icy cold. It was Election Day, and in the doorways of the taverns, which had been turned into polling stations, the citizens had lit fires to combat the freezing temperatures. Failing to find Allan, Reynolds remembered with a start that it was the habitual practice of election gangs to drag any poor wretch they could find from tavern to tavern, inebriating him along the way, and getting him to vote several times for the same candidate. He suddenly feared that his friend might have fallen prey to one of these gangs, and so he began scouring the taverns of Baltimore asking for the gunner. And had anyone been able to observe Reynolds's trajectory from above, they would have noticed sadly how on more than one occasion he might have chanced upon Allan if he had not at the last moment turned down one street and not another.

Thus, without bumping into Reynolds once, Allan wandered from tavern to tavern, stinking drunk, jostled by a gang of heartless rogues who had pounced on him the moment he arrived at the port. He went from tavern to tavern, arms wrapped round himself to ward off the cold penetrating the threadbare clothes they had dressed him in as a disguise, while everything around him became increasingly blurred. Finally he fell to his knees, exhausted, outside one of the taverns. Unable to drag him back to his feet, the gang left him to his fate. Gasping for breath and seized by violent fits of trembling, Allan tried to fix his gaze on the fire blazing in the tavern doorway to provide him with an anchor in that heaving world. But his head was spinning so much that the flames took on the proportions of a conflagration, and the merciless cold combined with the dancing flames to stir his memory.

Terrified, Allan felt a tiny dam burst inside his head, and the memories it was holding back flooded into his consciousness with such blinding clarity he thought he was living them anew: he could see the *Annawan* enveloped by the roaring blaze, the sailors in flames hurling themselves onto the ice from the top deck, the monster from the stars loping toward them, its claws dripping with blood and a trail of headless dogs in its wake. He could hear Reynolds's voice ordering him to get up, telling him they must run if they wanted to live even a few more minutes. Allan began flailing his arms desperately, convinced he was running, oblivious to the fact that he was scraping the skin of his knees raw as they rubbed against the hard ground. The gunner ran across the snow, urged on by Reynolds, fleeing the monster that dwelled in his nightmares and was coming for him once more, a monster that had landed on Earth from Mars, or some other planet in the universe, for the universe was inhabited by creatures so horrifying that they were beyond the scope of Man's paltry imagination, a monster that was going to tear him limb from limb because he could not run any farther, he was exhausted, and all he wanted was to lie down on the ice and let that be the end, but no, his friend kept urging him on, run, Allan, run! And so he ran, he ran round in circles, on his knees, in front of the blaze, while a white void stretched out before his fevered eyes, and he heard the creature's roars behind him and his own voice calling out to the explorer, begging him for help over and over:

"Reynolds, Reynolds, Reynolds!"

He was still calling his friend's name at the Washington College Hospital, where Reynolds finally found him after going to every hospital in the city.

They had installed the delirious Allan in one of the private rooms at the hospital, an imposing five-story building with arched gothic windows situated at one of the higher points of Baltimore. The hospital was renowned for being spacious, well ventilated, and run by an experienced medical team. According to the nurse who took him to Allan's floor, through wards filled with beggars suffering from varying degrees of exposure, the gunner had not stopped calling his name since he was brought in. When they finally reached the room where his friend lay dying, Reynolds could scarcely make out his shuddering body through the crowd around his bed: gawping medical students, nurses, and other members of staff, who must have recognized the celebrated author.

"I am the man he is calling for," Reynolds announced in a solemn voice.

The group turned as one toward the door, surprised. A young doctor came over to him.

"Thank Heaven! We didn't know where to find you. I am Doctor Moran." Reynolds shook his hand warily. "I was the one who attended Mr. Poe when he was brought in . . . For it is Mr. Poe, is it not? Despite his beggar's garb."

Reynolds gazed mournfully at the stinking clothes the doctor was pointing to, draped across a chair with a care unworthy of such rags. He could not help wondering what must have happened to his friend to have ended up dressed in those garments. Then he contemplated Allan's skinny body, barely covered by a sheet drenched in sweat.

"Yes," Reynolds confirmed, "it's him."

"I thought as much. I have read many of his stories," the doctor said, gazing at his illustrious patient with compassion. Then he turned to Reynolds. "Mr. Poe arrived at the hospital in a complete daze, unaware of who carried him here. Since then he has not stopped calling your name and insisting he is being pursued by a monster."

Reynolds nodded, smiling wistfully, as though accustomed to his friend's ravings.

"Did he say anything else?" he asked without looking at the doctor.

"No, he simply repeats the same thing over and over."

As though confirming what the doctor had said, the gunner cried out once more: "It's coming for us, Reynolds. The monster is coming for us . . ."

The explorer gave a troubled sigh, then looked at the people gathered around Allan's bed.

"Could you leave me alone with him, gentlemen?" he ordered rather than asked. But then, seeing the doctor's reluctance, he added, "It will only take a moment, Doctor. I would like to say good-bye to my friend in private."

"The patient hasn't much longer to live," protested the doctor.

"In that case let's not waste any more time," Reynolds replied brusquely, looking straight at him.

The young doctor nodded resignedly and asked the others to follow him.

"We shall wait outside. Don't be long."

When he was alone, Reynolds finally approached Allan's bed.

"I'm here, Allan," he said, taking his hand.

The gunner tried hard to focus, staring at him with glassy eyes.

"It's coming for us, Reynolds!" he cried once more. "It's going to kill us . . . Oh dear God . . . It has come from Mars to kill us all!"

"No, Allan, it's over now," Reynolds assured him in an anguished voice, casting a sidelong glance at the door. "We killed it. Don't you remember? We did it, we defeated the monster."

Allan gazed about him distractedly, and Reynolds realized the gunner was not seeing the room in the hospital.

"Where am I? I'm cold, Reynolds, so awfully cold . . ."

Reynolds took off his coat and draped it over Allan's frame, which was still lying on the ice, in temperatures of forty degrees below zero.

"You're going to get well, Allan, have no fear. You'll get better and they will send you home. And you will be able to carry on writing. You will write many books, Allan, just wait and see."

"But I'm so cold, Reynolds . . . ," the gunner murmured, a little calmer. "In fact I've always been cold. It comes from my soul, my friend." The explorer nodded, tears in his eyes. The gunner seemed to have regained his sanity for a moment: his mind had somehow come back from the icy wastes and once more occupied that body shivering on a hospital bed. Allan's increasing serenity made Reynolds uneasy. "I think that's why I joined that accursed ship, just to find out whether anywhere in the world was colder than inside me." The gunner gave a feeble laugh that turned into a dreadful coughing fit. Reynolds watched him convulsing on the bed, fearing the violent jolts would shatter his fragile bones. When they finally abated, Allan lay, mouth open, gulping for air that seemed to get stuck in some narrow duct in his body before it could reach his lungs.

"Allan!" Reynolds cried, shaking him gently, as though afraid he might break. "Allan, please . . ."

"I'm leaving you, my friend. I'm going to the place where the monsters dwell . . . ," the gunner murmured in a faint whisper.

Desperate, Reynolds watched Allan's neck tense and his nose seem to grow horribly sharp. His lips were turning a dark shade of purple. He understood his friend was dying. Allan choked with a bitter sob, but managed to croak, "May God have mercy on my wretched soul . . ."

"Have no fear, Allan. We killed it," Reynolds repeated, stroking his friend's brow with the tenderness of a mother trying to convince her child there are no monsters lurking in the dark. He realized that these would be the last words his friend ever heard. "There are no monsters where you are going. Not anymore."

Allan gave a feeble smile. Then he looked away, fixing his gaze somewhere on the ceiling, and left his tortured existence with a gentle sigh, almost of relief. Reynolds was surprised at how discreet death was: he had expected to see the gunner's soul rise up from his body like a dove taking to the air. More out of bewilderment than politeness, he remained beside the bed for a few moments, still holding the gunner's pale hand in his. Finally he laid it on Allan's chest with the utmost care.

"I hope you are at last able to rest in peace, my friend," he said.

He covered Allan's face and left the room.

"He's dead," he murmured as he walked past Doctor Moran and his students, who were standing outside the door. "But his work will be immortal."

As he found his way out of the hospital, Reynolds could not help wondering whether Edgar Allan Poe's work would have been different had he not encountered the monster. No one could know, he said to himself with a shrug. On the steps of the hospital, the explorer stared at the radiant morning before him, the carriages jolting over the cobblestones, the hawkers' cries, the people strolling up and down the pavements, all of them making up the vibrant symphony of life, and he let out a sigh. In the end, the monster from the stars had killed his friend. He had to acknowledge it had beaten them. Yet rather than filling him with hatred or fear, it merely served to strengthen his terrible feeling of loneliness. He was now the sole survivor of the *Annawan,* the only person who knew what had really happened in the Antarctic. Could he remain the sole guardian of that secret? Of course he could, he told himself, because he had no choice. Besides, what solace could it bring him now to share that secret with anyone else? And with whom could he share it? With his practical, adorable Josephine? Whom would it profit to know they were not the sole inhabitants of the universe? The coachman, the flower seller on the corner, the innkeeper unloading barrels on the far side of the street? No, none of them would be better off knowing that from the depths of the universe, intelligences greater than theirs were observing the Earth with greedy eyes, perhaps even now planning how to conquer it. As he had discovered, such information was worthless and only brought suffering to those who possessed it. Whatever had to happen would happen, he concluded with his relentless pragmatism, putting on his hat and descending the steps. He would not be the one to deprive the world of its innocent enjoyment of the astonishing beauty of a starry sky.

But for the next nine years at least, the length of time in which Reynolds was able to check the news, the Martians did not revisit the Earth. Afterward, of course, Reynolds could not know what might happen.

Perhaps his children or his grandchildren would see those strange flying machines descend from the sky. But that would no longer be his responsibility, nor that of Allan, MacReady, the brave Peters, or any of the shipmates who had lost their lives in the Antarctic attempting to kill the demon from the stars. It would fall to others to fight them. He and his companions had played their part. After his death, there would be no man left alive who, while his wife gazed up at the night sky straining to make out the constellations, would look down surreptitiously at the strange burn mark on his hand, afraid that if he stared into the abyss of space, something would stare back at him from the other side.

What Reynolds could not know was that more than twenty years after his death, another expedition to the South Pole would stumble upon the burnt-out hull of the missing *Annawan*. They would find its charred remains ominously surrounded by skeletons, and at the foot of an enormous range of icebergs they would discover an amazing flying machine entombed in the snow. But the most astonishing discovery of all would be a strange creature buried in the ice, a creature unlike any they had ever seen on Earth, and which in their eagerness to examine they would transport back to London in the greatest secrecy, where Wells would discover it. For let us not forget that in this tale no mysterious sailor by the name of Griffin ever boarded the *Annawan*. And therefore, no one blasted the Martian to smithereens. The monster from the stars simply sank into the Antarctic ice, on a remote isle, which, after Jeremiah Reynolds's marriage, would appear on the maps as Josephine Island.

PART TWO

*I*S THERE STILL A SMILE ON YOUR FACE,
INTREPID READER, OR HAVE THE HORRORS
OF THE FROZEN ANTARCTIC LEFT YOU
QUAKING IN YOUR COMFORTABLE CHAIR?

IF YOU YEARN FOR FURTHER ADVENTURES,
I INVITE YOU TO PLUNGE WITH YOUR
CUSTOMARY FEARLESSNESS INTO THE PAGES
THAT FOLLOW, WHERE YOU WILL WITNESS
A GENUINE MARTIAN INVASION. THIS TIME,
I SHALL NOT ALERT YOU TO THE TERRIFYING
EVENTS AWAITING YOU. BUT THIS MUCH I WILL
SAY: IF YOU PAY ATTENTION YOU WILL GLIMPSE
THE VERY BEST AND WORST OF HUMANITY.

THOSE OF A SENSITIVE NATURE MAY PREFER A
LESS DISTURBING KIND OF READING MATTER.

"It's ludicrous of you to suspect me of having some connection to the Martians simply because I wrote a novel announcing their invasion!" Wells suddenly declared, as if to himself.

The author's outburst made the inspector jump.

"As ludicrous as someone re-creating a Martian invasion to win a woman's heart?" he retorted with a grin.

XIV

Emma Harlow would have liked the Moon to be inhabited so that she could stroke the silky manes of the unicorns grazing in its meadows, contemplate the two-legged beavers building their dams, or be borne aloft by a man with bat's wings, and gaze down upon the lunar surface dotted with thick forests, oceans, and purple quartz pyramids. However, on that radiant spring morning in 1898, Emma, like all her contemporaries, already knew that the Moon was uninhabited, thanks to a new generation of powerful telescopes, which, together with numerous other scientific inventions, had robbed the world of the magic it had once possessed. And yet, only sixty years before, fantastical creatures beyond Man's wildest dreams had inhabited the Moon.

In the summer of 1835, long before Emma had been born, a man had looked at the Moon and thought it might make a good repository for the magic that human beings needed to make life bearable, the magic that was being slowly but surely eroded by progress. Since no one could examine it and therefore prove otherwise, the Moon seemed like the perfect place for dreams, that powerful restorative of humanity. And who was this champion of dreams? He was Richard Adams Locke, an English gentleman who, after graduating from Cambridge, had moved to New York, where he became chief editor of the *New York Sun*. As regards his appearance, he had a pockmarked face, which scarcely deterred the ladies, who were attracted by his willowy, noble bearing. In addition, his eyes gave off a calm luminosity, a serene sparkle characteristic of those lofty spirits who invariably act as a guiding light to others. However, nothing could have been further from the truth. For Locke was not the sort of person whose eyes were windows onto his soul: concealed beneath the English gentleman's benign, almost priestly appearance was a truly mischievous spirit. What did Locke see when he cast his majestically solemn gaze over the world? He saw Man's folly, his astonishing inability to learn from his mistakes, the grotesque world he had built up around him, and, above all, his excessive zeal to imbue the most preposterous things in life with a transcendent meaning. And although Locke secretly delighted in all that, such collective madness also made his blood boil when he realized it was not very flattering to the species of which, unhappily, he was a member.

He had left England for America convinced that after a difficult birth and a few faltering first steps, the United States had produced a nation guided by the light of reason and universal freedom. He had hoped it would represent the ultimate flowering of everything that the old, tired Europe had failed to achieve, even after the auspicious rupture brought about by the Enlightenment and the French Revolution. However, to his astonishment, he had found a country infected with religiosity, where the customary European superstitions flourished side by side with a host of newfangled ones. Was America discovered merely so that it could be turned into a pale imitation of England? Locke wondered, greatly troubled. For the new society seemed as convinced as the old one that everything visible to the naked eye bore the mark of God's Creation. The imminent arrival of Halley's comet was no exception: who but the Creator could organize a fireworks display of that magnitude in the September skies? And so, numerous telescopes had been set up in parks throughout New York, to enable everyone to admire God's pyrotechnic manifestation of His own existence, to the delight of His faithful followers. Contradictory as it might sound, that faith lived side by side with a blind belief in progress and in scientists, with the result that anyone proposing the first crazy idea that came into his head was liable to be taken seriously. Such was the case with the Reverend Thomas Dick, whose works enjoyed great popularity in the United States around the time Locke first arrived there. In one of his most successful books, the Reverend had calculated that there were 21,891,974,404,480 inhabitants in the solar system, a number that may appear somewhat exaggerated, although perhaps less so if we take into account that according to the same calculation, the Moon alone had a population of 4,200 million. Those and other foolishnesses convinced Locke that the Americans were a people in dire need of being taught a lesson. And who was better placed to do that than he? Thus, Locke's initial intention was less to care for the dreams of humanity than to teach his new neighbors a lesson, and to amuse himself as much as possible in the process. He decided to invent a sensational story, which would poke fun at this and the many other outrageous astronomical theories that had hitherto been published, thus obliging the American public to reflect upon the flimsiness of its beliefs. It would also boost sales of the *Sun,* the best platform for his scheme he could have hoped for, as the newspaper boasted a mass circulation, distributed as it was not through subscription but by an army of children who in exchange for a miserable cent went round the streets advertising its lurid headlines at the tops of their voices.

And what might that story be? Locke was aware that a scientist by the name of John Herschel, son of William Herschel, the famous astronomer royal to the court of King George, was in South Africa that August carrying out astronomical observations. Two years earlier, he had set sail from England to the Cape of Good Hope with a battery of optical instruments, in order to set up an observatory and catalog the stars, nebulae, and other objects of the southern skies, in the hope of completing the survey of the northern heavens undertaken by his father. But there had been no news of the astronomer in two years, and from where he was now, communication with New York took at least two weeks. This would give Locke more than enough time to bombard the American public with a series of articles listing Herschel's numerous alleged discoveries, without the astronomer knowing or being able to refute them.

Locke immediately set to work, his usually solemn face wearing a playful grin, and on August 21 his first report appeared under the heading "Important Astronomical Discoveries." The article announced that during a visit to New York, an erudite Scotsman had provided the *Sun* with a copy of the *Edinburgh Journal of Science,* which contained a fragment of the travel diary of Doctor Andrew Grant, a fictitious collaborator of Herschel's. The first section of Locke's article was taken up with a description of the wondrous telescope built by the astronomer, with its massive lens that could capture objects as small as eighteen inches on the Moon's surface and project them onto the observatory wall. Thanks to Herschel's brilliant invention, he and other astronomers had been able to study every planet in the solar system, and many others in adjacent ones. It had also enabled them to elaborate a convincing theory about comets and to solve almost every problem of mathematical astronomy. Having laid the groundwork, the subject of Locke's second article was the Moon itself. On careful examination of its surface, the astronomers had been able to make out an area of dark green rock and what looked like a field of rose-colored poppies. While exploring Riccioli's Mare Nubium, they had discovered beautiful white sandy beaches dotted with strange trees and purple quartz pyramids more than sixty feet tall. And then, as they continued peering through that extraordinary lens, they had noticed strange stirrings of life. Astonished, they glimpsed the first animals. Herds of creatures resembling bison filled the Moon's plains, and crowning its gentle hills, like watery blue etchings, were a few graceful unicorns. In his third article, taking the hoax to an extreme, Locke continued his zoological classification of lunar species. He described Herschel and Grant's mixture of shock and fascination as they contemplated a dwarf reindeer, a horned bear, and even some charming two-legged beavers busily building wooden huts with plumes of smoke billowing from their tall chimneys.

Thanks to Locke's articles, sales of the *Sun* superseded those of the *Times* of London. However, he was not done yet. His fourth article contained the most surprising revelation of all: the astronomers had seen the Moon's inhabitants, whom they named *Homo vespertilio,* or bat man. According to their description, these creatures were about three feet tall, covered in a coppery coat of fur, and equipped with membranous wings that reached from their shoulders to their knees. With their wings folded, they had the same elegant bearing as humans, and with them spread, they soared through the air like graceful ballerinas. Their faces were like those of the orangutan, except more intelligent looking, and their prominent lips moved as if they were speaking. The telescope showed them lazing happily in the grass, albeit in a manner that on Earth might have been deemed somewhat improper. And after that fabulous disclosure, which left readers of the *Sun* reeling, Locke prepared to deliver the final blow. In his last article, he described how, in the midst of that primitive Eden, Herschel had glimpsed what was unquestionably an enormous religious temple of polished sapphire with a roof of golden metal. What god did those creatures worship? But just as readers' interest had reached its peak, the paper reported that owing to an unfortunate oversight on the part of the astronomers, what had come to be known as the Telescope of Marvels had been left pointing toward the Sun, and its rays, intensified by the enormous lens, had burnt a twenty-foot-wide hole in the floor of the observatory, rendering it useless.

After the stir the story caused in the United States, it had appeared in almost every newspaper around the world, many of which claimed to have had access to the original articles in the *Edinburgh Journal of Science.* Consequently, a committee of scientists from Yale University was encouraged to pay a visit to the *Sun*'s offices, with the innocent intention of seeing the documents for themselves. However, despite being deceived by the newspaper's employees, who sent them on a wild goose chase for several days, and never actually seeing the articles, the scientists returned to New Haven without suspecting that these antics concealed an elaborate hoax. Other newspapers were more skeptical and accused the *Sun* of hoodwinking its readers. The *Herald* even claimed that the *Edinburgh Journal of Science* had gone out of print several years earlier. A few days later, the *Sun*'s editors hurriedly published an article considering the possibility that the story was a hoax, while asserting they could not be sure until the English press corroborated it.

Locke never publicly admitted that the whole thing had been a practical joke. He was surprised it had taken on such proportions. He had only intended to show the American people the fragility of the foundations underlying all religions. However, the majority of readers had failed to notice the irony and continued to believe that the Moon was actually inhabited by those ludicrous creatures, that it was an imitation Eden or a playground for the characters in fairy tales. A few members of the clergy considered the possibility of printing Bibles for the bat men, while a group of Baptists even began a collection to fund a mission to the Moon aimed at saving the souls of the planet's depraved inhabitants. And even though with the passage of time such sophisticated telescopes as that of John Draper produced daguerreotypes showing a pristine, uninhabited Moon, where there was no sign of Locke's fanciful creatures, many New Yorkers stubbornly believed that science would one day confirm the veracity of Grant's descriptions. In case any of you are wondering what Herschel's response to all this was, the astronomer did not in fact find out about the hoax implicating him for some time, because, as the articles stated, he was indeed in Cape Town carrying out astronomical observations. When the story finally reached Herschel's ears, he took it in good humor, perhaps because he was aware that his own observations would never be as astonishing. However, when steadfast believers began bombarding him with questions about obscure details such as the sexual habits of *Homo vespertilio*, the smile soon vanished from his face.

Such were the unforeseen effects on American society of Locke's hoax. And after recovering from his own disbelief, Locke himself learned a lesson from it all: Man needed to dream. Yes, he needed to believe in illusions, to aspire to something more than the miserable, hostile life that suffocated him. And he, Locke, had been clever enough to invent a perfect fantasy for that disenchanted dreamer. At first, this unexpected success had helped Locke weather the storm of criticisms and insults from his rivals, but as the years went by and things gradually returned to normal, and his practical joke became an amusing anecdote, Locke began to feel more and more proud of his achievement. He had given people a paradise about which they could dream, where they could take refuge from their earthly woes, and he had done so without robbing them of their free will, or forcing them to comply with absurd rules, or threatening them with hellfire and brimstone. Making others dream should not be the domain solely of religion or of artists, he told himself. No, governments the world over should create ministries devoted to helping people dream of a better world. As he entertained these thoughts, Locke began to feel more and more pleased with what he had achieved, although at the same time he was frustrated that no one else appreciated it. He had discovered that creating illusions on a grand scale had its problems, and however much he liked to think of humanity as a little child clamoring for a bedtime story, he realized not everyone was the same. Many preferred to accept the world the way it was, without the adornment of imagination. Others simply could not tolerate the idea of a power superior to the one they liked to flaunt. And all those different opinions were too much for one man to fight against. All Locke could do was share the magic potion he had stumbled upon by chance with those who really deserved it. A door-to-door effort, as it were. However, although he considered humanity as a whole worthy of the remedy, no single member of it seemed to him particularly deserving.

YET THE DAY HE held his first child in his arms, and she gazed up at him with that intense, probing look newborn babies have, Locke knew he had at last found someone who deserved the gift of a more beautiful world by rights. And so, on Eleanor's tenth birthday, he made her a very special present. He gave her the power to dream, the physical expression of which consisted of a scroll of paper tied with a bright red ribbon. When she unfurled it, the girl saw a map of the universe drawn by Locke himself. He could no longer populate the Moon with magical creatures (the scientists had seen to that), but the universe had yet to be discovered. With each passing decade, telescopes would gradually reveal its mysteries, and men would even be able to soar through it in winged machines heavier than air. But it would be a long time before that happened, centuries perhaps. For the time being, the universe could be exactly as Locke had depicted it on that scroll of paper.

And of course, his daughter, Eleanor, never doubted for a moment that it was any different, for she was as much of a dreamer as her father. But that was not her only quality. From an early age she showed signs of being an impulsive spirit, one of those souls from whom laughter and tears suddenly flow with equal exuberance. A delicate ray of sunshine appearing after a storm could fill her with the wildest joy, just as a wilting flower might cause her to cry inconsolably, although to everyone's surprise, her father's gift of the Map of the Sky proved the best remedy for her tears on such occasions. Sometimes opening it and running her little hands over the marvels shown there was enough to make her face light up once more. Fortunately, the map always managed to soothe her, whether she was upset because the runt in a litter of puppies was born dead or irritated by one of her suitors greeting her in a way that obviously betrayed his waning interest. No matter what the drama of the day was, Eleanor only needed to step into the garden and look up at the night sky to become instantly aware of a distant melody, like the clamor of a fairground with its promise of unimaginable delights, which for her was the real sound of the universe pulsating behind that shadowy veil, a universe no telescope could penetrate, and of whose existence only she and her father were aware.

The day her own daughter, Catherine, turned ten, she could think of no better gift than the Map of the Sky. Sadly, Catherine had not inherited what appeared to be the family talent for dreaming. Nor was she susceptible to the stormy passions that had dominated her mother's life: Eleanor found it incredible that she had given birth to a child in whom she recognized nothing of herself. Catherine was too matter-of-fact to want to complicate life, and Eleanor, who believed that to live intensely one must overcome torment and unhappiness, immediately considered this a defect. As she never tired of reminding her husband—that suitor whose aloofness she had so often reproached—the serene smile their daughter wore on her lips, far from being a mark of a happy disposition, betrayed a complete lack of comprehension of the meaning of happiness. However, contrary to what her mother thought, Catherine did not grow up viewing the world with indifference. Rather, it seemed to her ideal, flawless, and beyond question. Nothing appeared sufficiently awful to disturb the tranquillity of her soul or fascinating enough to make her tremble with joy. If, for example, a suitor failed to pay her the attention she thought she deserved, rather than torment herself pointlessly she simply struck him off her list without the slightest sense of resentment. You will have no difficulty understanding, then, that for Catherine her grandfather's map was never a port in a storm or a magic charm that restored her joie de vivre. It simply confirmed that she did indeed live in the best of all possible worlds, where even the strange universe was a friendly place filled with peace and harmony.

Confident as she was, she never suspected that this feared lack of harmony would issue from her own belly. And yet it did. From the moment Emma was born, she made clear her dissatisfaction with the world and its inhabitants, for if one of them leaned over her cradle to contemplate the innocence concentrated in that tiny creature, he or she was surprised to find a pair of fiery eyes threatening to scorch them. Her face purple with rage, the girl would cry if her food was colder or hotter than usual, if she was left alone for too long, or if she was cradled half-heartedly. There seemed to be no pleasing her. And on the few occasions when she did not cry, it was even worse, for she would gaze about her with unnerving solemnity. Emma relaxed only when she fell asleep, and during that brief respite her mother would watch over her, admiring the delicate, exotic beauty of a daughter who had become the first inconvenience in her life she could not turn her back on.

When Emma was ten, Catherine passed the Map of the Sky down to her daughter, as her own mother had done before her. She secretly hoped the drawing would have some effect upon Emma, preferably reconciling her to the world she lived in. Clearly nothing around her, nothing she could see or possess, was capable of satisfying her, but perhaps that map with its wonders and miracles would show her that the universe was far more perfect and beautiful than her disappointing surroundings might suggest. And the fact is, at first it seemed to work, for Emma would not only spend hours gazing excitedly at the map but would not be parted from it either: she would put it on the table at mealtimes, take it with her when she went to the park with her governess, hide it under her pillow when she went to sleep.

As Emma grew older, she began to understand the hushed conversations for which she had hitherto assumed adults used a special language. She was just twelve when she found out about Great-Grandfather Locke's hoax. One evening, when a headache prevented her from sleeping, she wandered down to the sitting room and through a crack in the door overheard her mother reminiscing about it to her father. She almost fainted with shock and had to prop herself up against the wall as she listened to the tale of how the tall, distinguished gentleman whose portrait stood at the top of the stairs had deceived a whole country with his invention of a Moon inhabited by unicorns, beavers, bison, and even bat men soaring majestically through its skies, a Moon that had proved completely false in the face of the disappointing reality. When the conversation was over, Emma returned to her room, where she picked up the map and, giving it one last bitter glance, eyes brimming with tears, buried it at the bottom of a drawer. She knew now that the map was false, that the universe was no more idyllic than the Moon had been. It was all a lie, another fabrication by her great-grandfather. Through her affection for him as the author of the map, Emma had become aware of a hint of mischief in his eyes that belied his apparent severity, but now she had discovered he was laughing at her, just as he had at her mother and her grandmother and at the whole country. She curled up in bed like a gazelle pierced by an arrow. She could expect nothing more from life now apart from disappointment. The world around her was so dreadfully dull, crude, and imperfect, and there was nothing beyond that could redeem it.

As time went by, she began to look upon New York as a dirty, noisy city full of injustices and ugliness. It was too hot in summer, and its harsh winters were unbearable. She despised the poor, crammed together in their tiny hovels, brutalized by hardship, yet she also hated her own class, their lives constricted by silly, rigid social customs. She found artists vain and selfish, and intellectuals bored her. She had no female friends worthy of that name, for she could not tolerate tedious discussions about dresses, balls, and suitors, and she thought men were the simplest, easiest to manipulate creatures on the planet. She was bored with staying at home and bored with strolling in Central Park. She despised hypocrisy, could not stand sentimentality, and felt constricted by her corsets. Nothing was to her liking. Her life was an absurd pretense. Still, a person can grow accustomed to anything, and Emma was no exception. And as the years passed, she gradually resigned herself to this humdrum reality, and like a fairy-tale princess in her lofty tower, she awaited some extraordinary miracle that would at last bring joy to her lifeless soul, or simply someone who would make her laugh. In the meantime, oblivious to her woes, nature took its course, and the promise of her youthful beauty flowered dramatically, undiminished by the permanent grimace of distaste on her lips. However, it will scarcely surprise you that by the age of twenty-one, when many of her peers were either betrothed or wed, Emma had still not met the man capable of convincing her that the Creator's mind was not on other things during the six days it took Him to make the world. And there were times when she could not help remembering with sadness the years when the Map of the Sky had given her a comforting glimmer of hope. That was no longer possible since she had discovered her great-grandfather's hoax. Still, to her surprise, Emma was unable to think badly of him. On the contrary, as she grew older her admiration for him increased, with the predictable result that during the tumultuous years of her adolescence, Great-

Grandfather Locke became the only type of man for whom she could feel anything at all. Someone audacious, imaginative, and intelligent, who was so superior to all others he could dupe them, and enjoy himself in the process. Encouraged by the inexorable optimism of youth, Emma would imagine her great-grandfather's stern face dissolving into laughter each time one of his hilarious reports shook the world, and that thought would in turn soften her demeanor by making her smile. However, the fact is Emma did not know any man equal to him, and as the dust of the years settled over her heart, the Map of the Sky lay discarded at the bottom of a drawer.

ON THE MORNING THAT concerns us, while searching for something in her desk, Emma came across the roll of paper that had once inspired her many childish fancies. She thought of putting it away again but instead held it in her hand and gazed at it with great affection. The bitterness toward her great-grandfather that had compelled her to bury the map at the bottom of that drawer nine years before had vanished, and although she was aware that it was only a silly drawing, it was still a thing of beauty, and so she untied the ribbon, smiling to herself as she recalled the absurd excitement she used to feel when doing so in the past. Then she stretched the roll out on the desk, contemplating it with that nostalgia adults feel for the things that made them happy as children, and it saddened her that time had made her immune to its effects.

The Map of the Sky, which it is perhaps time to describe, was an illustration of the universe framed by a border decorated with ornate arabesques. It showed a dark blue surface with light blue flecks, more like the ocean than the sky. At its center was the sun, a flaming ball with streaks of fire spurting from various places along its edge. Surrounding the golden orb was a spray of mushroom-shaped nebulae, celestial bodies that gave off silvery wisps of light, and stars that glinted as though made up of tiny diamonds. Several painted balloons, their baskets filled with people, floated amid the sprinkling of planets. The space travelers were dressed in very thick overcoats, and most wore scarves over their mouths and held on to their hats so as not to lose them to a cosmic gust of wind. Each basket was fitted with a tiny rudder and a telescope, and hanging from their sides, amid the trunks and suitcases, were cages of mice. The travelers would let these out whenever they landed on a planet to make sure the air there was breathable. Some of the balloons appeared to be fleeing from what looked like swarms of giant wasps; however, the drawing gave an overall impression of peaceful coexistence, as evinced in one of Emma's favorite scenes in the bottom right-hand corner. This depicted some passengers in one balloon doffing their hats to a small procession of creatures from another planet riding on what looked like orange-colored herons. But for their pointed ears and long forked tails, the creatures were not so different from men.

As she studied the map, Emma could not help comparing the magical feeling of excitement she had experienced as a child to her present sensations, dampened by disappointment, which in her case had preempted reason. For magic had been torn from her life in too abrupt and untimely a manner, instead of slowly fading with the years. And yet, she said to herself in a sudden flash of insight, wasn't that what growing up was all about? A progressive blindness to the evidence of magic dotted about the world, which only children and dreamers are able to glimpse.

With a wistful smile, Emma rolled up the map and placed it back in the desk drawer. She could not throw it away, for she had to hand it down to her own daughter when she reached the appropriate age. So dictated the absurd family tradition, which Emma had sworn to respect even though for her it was an empty gesture, for she was convinced she would never have any offspring: she was not and never would be in love, and therefore a man could scarcely inseminate her unless, like spores, his seed was carried to her on the wind.

XV

HIS IS THE LAST DAY YOU SERVE IN THIS HOUSE, Emma thought, as her latest maid tugged violently on the laces of her bodice. How could such a scrawny girl possess the strength of an ox? She had not been there long enough for Emma to learn her name, but that did not matter now. She would ask her mother to dismiss whatever her name was without further ado. When the maid had finished dressing her, Emma thanked her with a smile, ordered her to make the bed, and went down to breakfast. Her mother was already waiting for her on the porch, where breakfast had been laid out that morning owing to the clement weather. A light breeze, gentle as a puppy, teased the shutters, the flowers on the table, and her mother's hair, which she had still not gathered into her usual bun.

"I want you to dismiss the new maid," Emma said.

"What, again, child?" her mother protested. "Give her a chance. She came highly recommended by the Kunises."

"Even so, she has the manners of a heathen; she almost suffocated me lacing up my bodice!" Emma declared, sitting down at the table.

"I'm sure you're exaggerating," her mother exclaimed. "I expect that once you get used to her—"

"I never wish to see her again!" Emma cut in.

"Very well, my child," her mother conceded with a sigh. "I shall dismiss Daisy."

"Daisy, what a name for that brute," muttered Emma, sipping her orange juice.

During breakfast, the maids paraded in front of Emma the custom-ary array of gifts sent by her suitors every morning: Robert Cullen's offering was an exquisite emerald choker; Gilbert Hardy's, a beautiful cameo brooch made of sculpted pearl; Ayrton Coleman had bought her two tickets to the theater and a dozen cream doughnuts; and Walter Musgrove had bade her good morning with his usual bouquet of wild irises. Emma's mother watched her nod halfheartedly as she was shown each gift; her daughter already had all those things, she thought. The only child of one of New York's wealthiest families, she was not easily impressed with gifts. Her suitors were therefore forced to use their in-genuity. Yet none seemed able to please this young woman, who lived in one of the few town houses in New York that boasted a ballroom, pre-ceded by an endless series of elegant rooms filled with artworks.

"Oh, Emma," sighed her mother. "What does a man have to do to win your heart? I really wish I knew, so that I could instruct some of them. You know how much I'd love to have a granddaughter."

"Yes, Mother," Emma replied wearily, "you've been saying the same thing every single day since I turned twenty."

Her mother fell silent for a few moments and gazed sadly up at the sky.

"A little girl running about would bring the place alive, don't you agree, darling?" she said presently, renewing her attack wistfully.

Emma snorted.

"Why are you so sure it would be a little girl?" she asked.

"I'm not, Emma. How could I be?" her mother parried. "I simply wish for a girl. Naturally, it is for God to decide the sex of his creatures."

"If you say so . . ."

Emma understood perfectly well why her mother had said this. Hitherto, only women had inherited the Map of the Sky: first Grandma Eleanor, then Emma's mother, Catherine, and after her, Emma. It was as if the selfsame drawing had mysteriously inclined the embryo that would receive it toward the female sex. So that if one day Emma were to fall in love, an event she considered very unlikely, she would naturally give birth to a girl. After which her womb would mysteriously dry up, as had happened to her grandmother and her mother, who following the birth of their first child and notwithstanding their respective husbands' vigorous efforts, had been unable to repeat the miracle.

"And on her tenth birthday I would give her the Map of the Sky, I suppose," she remarked sarcastically.

Her mother's face lit up.

"Yes, indeed," she said dreamily, "and it will be as magical a moment for her as it was for you, Emma. Why, I can still see the look of excitement on your little face when I unrolled your great-grandfather's drawing."

Emma sighed. Her mother was impervious to irony. It simply did not occur to her that anyone might say something for any other reason than to please her, and if she suspected otherwise, she would stop listening. Nothing and no one could ruffle Catherine Harlow, thought Emma. However, she refused to give up trying, she told herself, frowning as she saw one of the maids approaching the porch from the house carrying the mail on a small tray. After the dull procession of gifts came the string of invitations to dinners, balls, and sundry events that coming week. She hoped there would be nothing she could not wriggle out of by professing some passing ailment. She was fed up with attending parties and dinners where everyone engaged in slandering those absent whilst observing perfect table manners. Happily, this time only one sealed envelope lay on the tray. Emma opened it with her usual apathy and read the neat, elegant writing on the note inside:

My dear Miss Harlow: I do not know your heart's desire, but I
assure you I am the man who can satisfy it, impossible though it
may be.

Montgomery Gilmore

Emma tucked the note wearily back into its envelope. As if she hadn't enough suitors, now Gilmore seemed to be renewing the assault. The latest in a long line of admirers, each as wealthy as he was insipid, Mont-gomery Gilmore was an impossibly tall man, with a soft, round face, like a snowman when it begins to melt. He repelled Emma as much as if not more than the others, for not only did he lack the saving grace of good looks but also she found him far more conceited than his rivals. Or perhaps it would be more correct to say that he was less adept at reining in his natural boastfulness. The others were, in the main, consummate charmers, and those who lacked experience appeared to have swallowed whole the guide to being a model suitor, which included how to dissim-ulate their arrogance beneath an elegant cloak of modesty. This, on the other hand, seemed to be Gilmore's first encounter with that universe known as womankind, and he behaved toward her with the same vigor-ous spontaneity with which he no doubt conducted himself in the world of business, which had been ruled over since time immemorial by men as exuberant as he. However, Emma was not a piece of property to be acquired, nor a contract to be argued over; she was someone who, while considering gallantry a tedious if necessary ritual, could at least appre-ciate when it was performed with a measure of skill. Accordingly, she demanded some minimum requirements of her suitors, which Gilmore insisted on ignoring.

Two meetings with the man had sufficed for Emma to realize that, although she might in time feel a lukewarm affection toward one or two of her other suitors, Gilmore could only provoke a growing revulsion in her. Both meetings had taken place at her house in the presence of her mother, as was customary with any serious courtship. During the first of these, Gilmore had simply introduced himself, vaunting his posses-sions and investments in order to leave Catherine Harlow in no doubt that the man courting her daughter was one of the wealthiest in New York. In other respects, he had proved a person of ordinary tastes, who held more or less conventional views on politics and other social affairs about which Emma's mother had questioned him in order to test his integrity. And, yes, he had shown an indefatigable, brazen, almost exas-perating self-confidence. This he had kept up during their second meeting, to which, to Emma's astonishment, her mother brought along her father, who was not in the habit of deigning to meet his daughter's suitors. Yet, when her parents had allowed the two of them to take a romantic stroll together in Central Park, the staggering self-assurance Gilmore had shown when describing his tiny empire suddenly crumbled, and he replied to her questions in a clumsy, stumbling manner. Then, in what seemed to Emma a desperate bid to prove once more that he was a worthy representative of a supposedly intelligent race, Gilmore fell into pride and arrogance. At no time did he make use of that amorous language most men employ when alone with the woman they love. Emma did not know whether Gilmore's clumsiness in matters of the heart was due to his inability to treat love as anything other than a business transaction, or whether he suffered from a kind of crippling shyness that prevented him from enjoying intimate conversations with women. Whatever the case, it made no difference, for Emma did not feel the slightest attraction for that man who was by turns painfully shy and infuriatingly smug, and she was certain she never would. And so, as they were traversing one of the overpasses on their way out of the park, Emma demanded Gilmore abandon his futile wooing of her. To her surprise, he did not turn a hair. He simply shook his big head and grinned to himself, as though her opinion on the matter was of no consequence. Then, amused at his own ingenuity, he said, *If I stop courting you, Miss Harlow, it will be the first time in my life I don't achieve what I want.* At those words, Emma had left him high and dry in the park, incensed by the impudence of that brute, who hadn't the first idea how to treat a lady, and, what is more, appeared proud of it. The following week, Emma heard nothing from Gilmore. She concluded that upon reflection he had decided to give up courting her, a pursuit that required a great deal of effort for very little reward. No doubt he would be better off devoting himself to the more straightforward matter of business.

However, she was mistaken, as attested to by that untimely missive promising her the impossible in neat handwriting. Apparently, Gilmore had decided to continue wooing her in an even clumsier fashion. He had been too lazy to send her flowers or jewelry and had concealed the fact beneath unpleasant bluster that irritated her even more. Gilmore deserved a rebuke more than any of the others, one that would put him in his place and, with any luck, finally dissuade him from wooing her. There was no lack of marriageable young ladies in New York, and Gilmore could devote himself to annoying someone more long-suffering than she.

After four o'clock tea, Emma went up to her room to devote the afternoon to the tedious task of writing thank-you notes to her suitors for the gifts they had regaled her with that morning. For the choker, she thanked young Robert, whose father was grooming him for the family business with the same rigor he used in training his mastiff dogs. And for the cameo, she thanked Gilbert, a wealthy young man who liked to vex her with his forwardness, and yet who became intimidated when she pretended to want to go further. For the theater tickets and sweets she thanked Mr. Coleman, an extremely sophisticated gentleman who was intent upon dragging her to the city's theaters and galleries with the aim of improving her already charming mind by exposing her to the arts. And for the flowers she thanked Walter, the brilliant lawyer who bored her with his political ambitions, his social gossip, and his plans of their shared future, which Emma envisaged as a display case filled with luxury items where a special place had been reserved for her. She was very careful to show equal politeness and lukewarm affection to all, as she was aware that many of them would compare letters in the hope of discovering some sign that they were favored. A similarly thankless task occupied her maids' afternoon as they ran hither and thither delivering envelopes. She left until last her reply to Gilmore, who besides saving himself the trouble of speculating about her preferences, had the audacity to challenge her by inviting her to ask him for something he could not possibly give her. Emma thought for a few moments, her latest-model fountain pen poised over the crisp white notepaper. No doubt he was expecting her to ask for something he would spend a fortune on. But Emma had no intention of stooping so low. At last, she wrote:

You are too kind, Mr. Gilmore. But my heart's desire is something
no one could ever give me. And I am afraid anything you might
be able to give me I would not want.

Her reply satisfied her, for not only did it show off her skills at word-
play, but it portrayed her as a young woman who desired something beyond material possessions. It would make Gilmore realize she had no
interest in playing his game and, more importantly, that she disdained
anything he might have to offer. The message was perfectly clear; Gilmore could not possibly misinterpret or ignore it. Emma placed the note
in an envelope and handed it to the last of her army of maids whom
she had yet to send out into the city: the uncouth Daisy, whom Emma's
mother had still not gotten around to dismissing.

The maid walked off hurriedly toward Gilmore's house, where she
was received by his footman, a stiff, haughty youth who condescend-
ingly instructed her to wait at the door while he carried the note to his
master's study on a silver tray.

Gilmore picked up the note absentmindedly, but as soon as he saw it
was from Emma, he tensed in his chair. Emma, his Emma, had deigned
to reply! He held his breath as he read the note, as if he were underwater. Emma, it seemed, had a fortunate talent for irony, which, even
though he was the brunt of it, pleased him. There was every indication
that when at last she agreed to join her life to his, he would never be
bored. Moreover, while Gilmore was not versed in the art of gallantry,
he had overheard many a gentleman in his club declare that for some
unknown reason women were capricious creatures, capable of expressing themselves only by means of complex riddles, which men had to
waste their time and energy deciphering. Faced with men's undisguised
simplicity, women, perhaps because they wished to feel superior, liked to
hide their true desires behind a veil of irony. And Emma's letter exuded
irony, so Gilmore could only conclude that while the true meaning of
her message unfortunately eluded him, one thing was clear: her words
could mean anything except what they actually said. He reread the note

twice, hoping its true meaning would leap out at him, but no such miracle occurred. Then he placed it very carefully on his desk, as though any
brisk movement might dislodge the letters, rendering her words permanently illegible. Now then, he said to himself, contemplating the note,
how would he reply to her? He decided to play safe and take up the challenge clearly laid down in the second sentence. He picked up a card and,
taking advantage of the chance to pay her a compliment he would never
have been bold enough to say outright in the middle of Central Park, he
wrote:

> Miss Harlow, do not make something impossible simply in order
> to deny me the opportunity to make it possible. I assure you I can
> make any wish of yours come true, unless you desire to be more
> beautiful than you already are.

Contented, he handed it to Elmer, his young footman, who passed
it on to Daisy, who stood idling in the doorway. In less than a quarter
of an hour, the maid was back at her mistress's residence. Emma opened
the small envelope, convinced that at last she would find Gilmore's polite surrender inside. She gave a sigh of frustration when she saw that
this was not the case. What must she do to put him off? Any other
gentleman, realizing that not only was she not interested in him, but
that his wooing was beginning to annoy her, would have given up. But
not Gilmore. He insisted on throwing down the gauntlet. This was no
courtship; it was a battle of wills. And not content with that, Gilmore
accompanied his challenge with a compliment as inappropriate as it was
absurd. Emma took out another sheet of notepaper, and, biting her lip so
as not to shock the maid by letting out a string of oaths, wrote:

> I am sorry to disappoint you, Mr. Gilmore, but that is not my
> desire. My beauty would make you happier than it would me, for
> beauty never makes the person who possesses it happy, but rather
> the one who loves and worships it. I wish you better success with

your compliments in conquering some other young woman, for anyone can see that in your case I am an unassailable fortress.

That would put an end to things. She had tried to go about it in a ladylike way, but Gilmore had been incapable of taking a hint, leaving her no other choice but to resort to rudeness. Satisfied with her message, she handed the envelope to Daisy, who, twenty minutes later, placed it once more on Elmer's silver tray. The footman, noticing the maid's pink cheeks, commanded in the tone of a kindly but firm general that she be served a glass of water downstairs in the kitchen. Then, after glancing at the young girl in what she thought was a somewhat forward manner, he went up to deliver the envelope to his master, who snatched it off the tray with uncharacteristic urgency.

Emma's new message pleased Gilmore, for she was continuing to play with him. She referred to herself now as an unassailable fortress, which in the mysterious language of women must have translated as something like . . . an open garden, or a fountain from which he could drink after a long journey. He couldn't be sure, but he knew it must refer to a place where he would be welcome. Excellent, his strategy was working. Now it was his turn. He took another card and for a few moments stared off into space, pondering his reply. Should he also hide behind a veil of ambiguity? No, as a man he must reveal himself as he was, expose himself fearlessly, cut straight to the chase. What did he want out of this exchange? he asked himself. He wanted to see her again. Yes, to tell her how he felt about her, but not with arrogant pronouncements or stuttering speech. However, for that to happen he must be sure the meeting took place under the most favorable conditions. And there was only one place where he might conceivably appear calm. He picked up his fountain pen and wrote, as though her annoyance were genuine:

Forgive me for offending you, Emma. Allow me to make amends by inviting you to take tea with me tomorrow at my house, at the time of your choice. Then I shall be able to look into your eyes and see how fervently you desire the thing no one can offer you. I am sure your desire will give me the strength to lay it at your feet, even if in order to do so I must go to Hell and back.

He blew on the ink and reread the message. It seemed a little risky. What if Emma were to say no? If she refused his invitation, there would be little point in going on. Although, truth be told, that prospect did not worry him unduly, for nothing would deter him from his mission, which would only end when one of them expired.

Elmer handed the message to Emma's maid, and twenty-eight minutes later, just as Emma was beginning to think she had finally rid herself of Gilmore for good, another envelope sealed with an ornate "G" appeared under her charming nose. She opened it and read the message in disgust. "What a persistent egomaniac that man is!" she exclaimed after she had finished reading. Much to her annoyance, Gilmore had not only ignored her last message, but he was growing emboldened in his wooing, calling her by her Christian name and inviting her to his house. Had no one taught him anything about courtship? The game was over, his king had been toppled, why couldn't he accept defeat? Any relationship, amorous or not, required a rhythm, a measured pace, and a series of rituals, but above all it must obey certain rules, of which Gilmore seemed unaware. Such ineptitude was exasperating. She took another sheet of paper and toyed with her pen as she mulled over her response. Clearly Gilmore had no intention of giving up the fight, however hard she tried to discourage him. As he himself had said, he was used to getting what he wanted, and his arrogance merited his being taught a lesson, a lesson he had never learned in the business world. She would not achieve this with words, unless she resorted to insults. And although quite a few came to mind, she would never use any of them, for she was perfectly aware that insults bring more shame on the deliverer than on the receiver. Thus she must think of a way more befitting her upbringing and intelligence in order to humiliate that insufferable swell-head, so that not only did he remove himself from her life but from the city itself.

Emma gently gnawed one of the knuckles of her left hand as she tapped her little foot on the floor. So Gilmore thought he could attain anything she wanted, did he? Well, that remained to be seen, she said to herself, as she began to envisage a possible solution to the problem. What if she asked him for the unattainable? In that case, he would have two choices: he could surrender and hang his head in shame or make a complete fool of himself trying to attain it. It followed that her request must provide some hope of success so that his failure would be even more humiliating. Yes, she concluded, that was the only way; she must play along by accepting the challenge. Only then would she succeed in ridding herself of that oaf. She would go to his house and demand something no one could possibly attain! She seized her pen and wrote:

> Very well, Mr. Gilmore. Does five o'clock seem like a good time
> for you to learn that you cannot get everything you want?

Daisy set off with the question to Gilmore's house. She halted at the front door and straightened her little hat. Then she rang the door chime, which summoned the footman with a pleasing trill. As he opened the door, Elmer gave her a knowing grin, which she liked, for it wiped away his ordinarily stern expression. After depositing the envelope on the tray with a theatrical gesture, Elmer vanished upstairs, though not before inviting her to some muffins he had ordered to be left on a pedestal table.

Gilmore held the envelope for a moment before opening it. Perhaps it wasn't a refusal, he thought optimistically. He inhaled sharply and took out the note. He read it again and again to make sure he wasn't dreaming: Emma had accepted his invitation! Yes, she had accepted that desperate invitation. A joyous smile spread over his face. He had guessed right, he had known how to read between the lines: Emma wanted to see him again. He was sure she had liked him calling her by her Christian name. His challenge had in fact been a pretext, a pleasurable, amusing game designed to conceal his true intention. And Emma, skilled in the art of flirtation, had gamely pretended to accept it in a spirit of competition. What a truly adorable creature she was! Gilmore conceded, feeling that his devotion to her was boundless. He reached for another card and let out a sigh of love. It was his turn once more, but there was no longer any need for pretense; all he had to do was play along with Emma. He wondered whether there was anything in the world he could not attain, and decided there wasn't. He sat hunched over the card and, feigning the requisite smugness, wrote:

I fear you will be the one who discovers that you lack the nec-essary imagination to conquer a man in love, Emma. And five o'clock seems an ideal time. Only death will prevent me from being here to receive you tomorrow.

He slid the card into its envelope and handed it to Elmer, who hur-ried downstairs almost at a trot. Waiting for him in the hallway was the grateful Daisy, who was still savoring the delicious muffins. They were almost as good as the blueberry jam beignets she bought as a treat on payday from Grazer's bakery. Thirty minutes later, a few crumbs the wind hadn't dislodged still sprinkled around the neck of her dress, Daisy delivered the note to her mistress.

Emma tore open the envelope and read Gilmore's reply, her lips pursed as she stifled a cry of rage. How dare he question the power of her imagination or the ambitiousness of her desires! Although the mes-sage didn't require answering, Emma could not resist responding. There was no sense in wasting any more ink discussing a contest she knew she would win the following day as soon as she revealed what she wanted. It was best to be humorous:

In that case, Mr. Gilmore, I advise you not to practice any danger-ous sports until tomorrow.

She placed the card in the envelope and gave it to her maid. Daisy dragged herself over to Gilmore's house, only to find a plate of blueberry beignets awaiting her. Before she could recover from her surprise, Elmer held out the little tray with an affectionate smile, and she placed the envelope on its polished surface, stunned yet touched. How could he have had time to go Grazer's bakery and back? she thought; it was some distance away. That diligent, thoughtful young man must be quick on his feet. With a pompous bow, Elmer took his leave of her momentarily and went up to his master's study, while she waited below overwhelmed by a feeling of gratitude verging on love.

When he saw the footman enter, Gilmore snatched the envelope from him and tore it open eagerly. Emma had refused to be provoked by his first sentence and, under the guise of her usual irony, now appeared concerned about his health. Gilmore grinned and shuddered with delight. Could she be any more adorable? He took up another card and wrote:

Have no fear, Emma, besides wooing you, dangerous sports have no appeal for me.

Ah, if only he was as witty when he was in her presence! Elmer hurtled down the stairs and handed the envelope to Daisy, boldly brushing his fingers against hers and causing the girl's face to flush with confusion. Trying not to swoon from the sudden rush to her head, the maid thanked Elmer for the beignets, and, as a way of breaking the awkward silence that had descended between them, she told him how amazed she was that he had produced them so swiftly. Elmer gave a little cough and, like a child reciting Shakespeare from memory, said in a monotone, "I can make any wish of yours come true, unless you desire my beauty to be more than it is." Daisy stared at him bewildered, unclear why he thought she would find his looks wanting. Elmer gave another cough and, turning his back to her, consulted the words scrawled on the palm of his hand. Then he turned around again, and, in the same dispassionate tone, said, "I can make any wish of yours come true, unless you desire to be more beautiful than you already are." Daisy instantly turned bright pink, stammered a farewell, and walked back to her mistress's house floating on air, wishing she knew how to write so that she could tell the increasingly attractive footman how she felt at that moment, unaware that he had already seen it in her eyes.

Some forty minutes later, she delivered the card to Emma, who realized despondently that Gilmore also had to have the last word. She tore open the envelope. How could anyone be so brazen? she thought after reading his reply. Did Gilmore have no limits? Emma took a deep breath, exhaling slowly to try to calm herself. She would have liked to reply, but the maid was fidgeting impatiently, as if she had sore feet, and sending her to Gilmore's house yet again seemed too cruel a gesture, even for Emma. She comforted herself with the thought that, as Oscar Wilde had said, better than having the last word was the prospect of having the first.

XVI

ONTGOMERY GILMORE LIVED IN A PARISIAN-style town house near Central Park. In Emma's mother's day, the area had been a wasteland, where the few houses belonging to wealthy residents floated like luxurious islands in a sea of mud. But now those splendid mansions were squeezed between new dwellings and stores of strained elegance. Emma rang the door chime at ten minutes past five—ten being considered in polite society the proper number of minutes to arrive late for an engagement. Accompanying her was her maid Daisy, whose dismissal had been revoked in return for her keeping quiet about the meeting. It was utterly unthinkable for a young woman of Emma's social class to call at a bachelor's residence without a chaperone. And so, much to her regret, Emma had been forced to lie to her mother and to offer that deal to her maid, whose joyful acceptance, as you will have guessed, was not entirely due to her regaining employment. Shortly after Emma rang the bell, she heard someone striding jauntily toward the door. Instinctively, she straightened her hat, which matched her crimson dress, and noticed with surprise that Daisy did the same. After admonishing the maid with a gesture, she waited for the door to open and put on her most insincere smile.

The owner of the sprightly footsteps was a slim young footman, who bobbed his head in greeting, then led them to the library the long way round, no doubt at the behest of Gilmore, who wasn't going to waste any opportunity to impress his guest. Emma followed the footman with an air of indifference, trying hard not to show the slightest expression of awe at the wealth of exotic, lavish objects. When at length they reached the library, lined with dark walnut shelves and exquisite cabinets filled with ancient volumes, Emma saw that the room gave onto a cool and shady patio, like a cloister, where the tea table had been laid. Shaded by an enormous oak tree, whose leafy branches scattered the afternoon light, the place struck Emma as a delightful sanctuary, which she would have liked to explore further had Gilmore not suddenly made an appearance. Dressed in an elegant dark brown suit, he was accompanied by a dog, which, after giving the two women a cursory sniff, slumped down in a corner and gazed at them wearily.

"Sir, Miss Harlow has arrived!" the footman announced quite unnecessarily, causing his master to jump.

"Thank you, Elmer, you may go now. I shall pour the tea myself," Gilmore replied, glancing anxiously at the maid.

Without taking her eyes off her host, who was now staring at his shoes, Emma said, "Daisy, go with Elmer to the servants' quarters and wait for me there until I call you."

"Yes, miss," Daisy whispered awkwardly.

Once both servants had withdrawn, the host, still visibly ill at ease, looked up from his shoes and went over to greet Emma.

"Thank you for accepting my invitation, Miss Harlow," said Gilmore, who apparently dared not call her by her first name except at a distance.

Out of politeness, Emma offered her hand to the millionaire, who leaned forward awkwardly and planted a hesitant kiss on it. Then, unsettled by her proximity, he asked if she would have a seat.

Once she had done so, Emma gave him a polite but defiant smile and declared, "Surely you didn't imagine your presumptuous proposal would frighten me off?"

"Of course not," he exclaimed, pausing briefly before adding with a mischievous grin, "even though it can mean only one thing: that you don't consider me a danger."

Emma did not acknowledge the jest but silently contemplated the awkward suitor Fate had decided to impose on her, trying her best to find something attractive about him. But she could find nothing: his cheeks were too chubby and rosy, his nose too small in proportion to his eyes and ears, while the sparse tufts of his blond whiskers and beard seemed to her a ridiculous adornment.

"There's another possibility that you have overlooked, Mr. Gilmore," she replied coldly.

"And what might that be?" he said with interest, trying to steady his hand as he poured her cup of tea.

"That I'm quite able to defend myself against anything that might happen between these walls."

Gilmore set the teapot down on the table with an amused grin, pleased by the astuteness of her remark.

"I don't doubt it, Miss Harlow, I don't doubt it. But have no fear, for as you can see we are all perfectly harmless in this house." At which he gestured toward his dog, asleep in the corner beneath a stream of light filtering in through the window. "My dog is too old and, far from being fierce, responds to everything with complete indifference." Then he gestured toward the door through which the footman and the maid had left the room moments before. "And what can I say of my faithful footman, Elmer? He takes his mission in life far too seriously to deviate from the proper behavior expected of a manservant." Finally, after pausing for effect, Gilmore looked straight at Emma and said, "Besides, I am in love with you and could never do anything to harm you."

Emma had to mask her astonishment at Gilmore's verbal acrobatics, which ended in such a passionate and startling declaration. Had he been rehearsing all this time? He, on the other hand, was incapable of concealing his excitement, and during the awkward silence that followed, he watched her expectantly, hoping for a response. Emma took a sip of tea to buy some time.

"So, you would never do anything to harm me," she repeated in an amused voice. "Not even if I were to tell you I could never return your love?"

He gazed at her in amazement.

"How would you respond then, Mr. Gilmore?" Emma went on. "Aren't crimes of passion committed for that very reason, because one is unable to win another's heart and decides no one else should have it?"

"I guess so . . . ," Gilmore admitted, at a loss.

"Consequently, you could quite easily hurl yourself at me right now and try to throttle me with those strong hands of yours," she said with a dreamy voluptuousness, "and I would have nothing but my poor little parasol with which to defend myself."

Emma had scarcely finished her sentence when she chided herself for her attempt at flirtation. Why torment the poor man like that when she had gone there with the intention of freeing herself from him? She felt a pang of compassion as she saw Gilmore's bewildered face darken. Despite his apparently relaxed demeanor, it was obvious he was stifling a desperate urge to leap up and satisfy his desire without wasting any more time talking. She imagined him clasping her in his thick arms and, in keeping with his outlandish wooing methods, covering her arms with kisses like an eager puppy.

"Oh no, Miss Harlow," Gilmore replied, his voice faintly shrill, "I assure you I would never behave in such a manner."

His unease made Emma vaguely uncomfortable, but she had not gone there to be overwhelmed by pity.

"I see: you are not the reckless type driven by passion like a leaf borne on the wind," she persisted. "I suppose that if I rejected your love, you would prefer to think of me with the fatalistic indifference of the romantic hero. And, having overcome your brief sorrow, you would transfer your affections to some other young woman."

Gilmore looked at her, suddenly solemn.

"You are wrong, Emma," he said with ridiculous earnestness. "I would go on loving you for the rest of my life in the hope that one day you might change your mind."

Emma pretended not to notice he had called her by her Christian name.

"You would sacrifice your life for such a slender hope?" she said, unsure whether to feel flattered or appalled. "Would you never marry, for example?"

"No, I wouldn't," he replied in the same solemn tone. "I would simply wait, removing any obstacle in my life that might stand in the way of my love for you, should you one day return. I would do no more than stay alive."

"But why?" Emma asked, trying to conceal the strange agitation Gilmore's words were beginning to cause her. "New York is full of young women every bit as beautiful as I, if not more so. Any one of them might—"

"I could spend the rest of eternity traveling the world," Gilmore interrupted, "admiring all the paintings and sculptures in the great museums, and nature's most magnificent landscapes, but I would never find a greater beauty, or anyone who could move me as much as you, Emma."

Emma remained silent, taken aback by Gilmore's reply. That didn't sound like an experienced ladies' man making a calculated speech, but like someone saying what he truly believed. A man, in short, who has fallen in love for the first time and is incapable of expressing his overwhelming emotions in anything other than grandiloquent, ridiculous, and naïve phrases. Gilmore had not used such language during their two other meetings. However, the man in front of Emma now had nothing in common with the clumsy, boastful companion whom she had left in Central Park. Her host possessed a quality she could not comprehend, for she had never encountered it in any of her other young suitors. Gilmore looked at her with passionate sincerity. He wanted to lay at her feet a love so generous that he would give his life for her without expecting anything in return, except the hope that she might one day love him. But was she painting a true picture of Gilmore, or was she in the presence of an inveterate charlatan? And why should she care either way, since she could never love him?

"I confess you have a way with words, Mr. Gilmore," she said. "You could convince anyone of anything."

He smiled modestly.

"You exaggerate, Emma: I can't convince you to marry me, for example."

"That's because I'm not seduced by words that dissolve in the air as soon as they are uttered," she retorted. "The way to win my heart is through action."

Because actions do not lie, she almost added, but halted herself. Gilmore played with his teaspoon for a few moments, before venturing:

"And what if I fulfilled your wish; would you marry me then?"

Emma pondered her response. She wouldn't marry a man like Gilmore for all the tea in China, but what she intended to ask him for even he was incapable of achieving.

"Yes," she replied, with absolute conviction.

"Do you give me your word?"

"Yes, Mr. Gilmore," said Emma. "I give you my word."

"Mmm . . . that can mean only one of two things: either you are certain I cannot possibly achieve what you want, or you want it so badly you are willing to pay any price, however high," Gilmore reflected with an amused grin. "Or is there a third possibility I have overlooked?"

"No, this time there is no other possibility," Emma replied coldly.

"Good," said Gilmore impatiently, "then let us unveil the mystery once and for all: what is this wish I cannot fulfill?"

Emma cleared her throat. It was time for her to put the man in his place. Gilmore was expecting her to ask him for some priceless jewel, a horse that never lost a race, or a house that could float on a river, or in the air, held aloft by a flock of birds. But she wasn't going to ask him for anything like that. She was going to ask him for something he could not possibly do. Something only one exceptional man had achieved, a man whose blood also ran in her veins. She was going to ask him to make the whole world dream. And Gilmore could not even make her dream.

"Sixty-three years ago, in 1835," she began, "an editor on the *Sun* convinced everyone that the Moon was inhabited by unicorns, beavers, and bat men. Did you ever hear about that?"

"Of course. Who hasn't heard about one of the biggest journalistic hoaxes of the century?" Gilmore replied, intrigued.

"Well, that man was Richard Locke, and he was my great-grandfather."

"Your great-grandfather?" Gilmore said, startled.

Emma nodded.

"Then you will also know that even after the whole thing had been proved a fraud, many people went on believing his descriptions were genuine."

"That doesn't surprise me, Miss Harlow; people have a desperate need to believe in something," said Gilmore. "But surely you're not asking me to repeat that stunt? Now we know for a fact that the Moon is uninhabited; no one would believe the contrary. Today's telescopes—"

"Of course no one would, Mr. Gilmore," Emma said, cutting him short. "But many people believe there is life on Mars."

"On Mars?"

"Yes, on Mars. Have you heard about the canals? Some scientists believe they prove there is intelligent life on our neighboring planet."

"I have read something about it, yes," said Gilmore, visibly ill at ease. "In that case, you want me to . . . ?"

Emma interrupted him once more, sliding across the table a volume that looked familiar to him.

"Do you know this, Mr. Gilmore?" she asked, gesturing toward the book she had placed next to the teacups. It was a novel with a light brown cover, published by Heinemann.

Gilmore took it gingerly in his huge hands and read aloud the title: "*The War of the Worlds* . . . H. G. Wells."

"A well-known English author wrote it," Emma said. "It's a story about Martians invading the Earth."

"H. G. Wells . . . ," Gilmore said under his breath.

"The Martians land on our planet in giant cylinders fired from Mars. The first of them appears one morning on Horsell Common, not far from London. In the crater made by the impact, the Martians build a flying machine in the shape of a stingray, in which they then advance on the nearby capital. In less than a fortnight, the Martians conquer London." She paused, then chuckled. "I want you to reproduce that invasion."

Gilmore raised his eyes from the book and looked at her, openmouthed.

"What are you saying?"

"You heard me: I want you to make everyone believe that Martians are invading the Earth."

"Have you gone mad?" Gilmore exclaimed.

"You don't have to reproduce the whole invasion, of course," she explained. "The first stage would suffice."

"The first stage? But, Miss Harlow, that's—"

"Impossible?"

"That isn't w-what I was going to say . . . ," Gilmore stammered.

"Just as well, Mr. Gilmore; then you will have no problem carrying it out. If you succeed in making an alien cylinder appear on Horsell Common and have a Martian emerge from it and if the following day every newspaper in the world runs a headline about an invasion by our interplanetary neighbors, then I shall agree to become your wife."

"A Martian invasion . . . ," Gilmore spluttered, "you're asking me to re-create a Martian invasion . . ."

"Yes, that's what I desire," confirmed Emma. "Think of it as a tribute to my great-grandfather, who made everyone believe the Moon was inhabited by unicorns and bat men."

Gilmore sat back in his chair and contemplated the book for a few moments, shaking his head in disbelief.

"If you think you aren't up to it, Mr. Gilmore, then I suggest you accept defeat," said Emma. "And please, stop sending me those ridiculous messages assuring me you can attain the impossible."

Gilmore gazed at her and laughed defiantly.

"The Martians will come to Horsell, Miss Harlow, I can promise you that," Gilmore said, in the solemn tone of someone declaring his love. "They will come all the way from Mars so that I can marry you."

"When?" she declared boldly.

Gilmore appeared to reflect.

"When? Mmm . . . let me see. It is May now. I could arrange to leave for England in a week's time, and the journey would take the better part of a fortnight. After that I would need at least a couple of months to carry out your request . . . that will take us up to August. Yes, that should give me enough time . . . All right, Miss Harlow, do you think August first is a good day for the Martians to invade Earth?"

Emma nodded, smiling. "Perfect, Mr. Gilmore. And I promise to be on Horsell Common to see it," she said, rising to her feet and stretching out her hand. "Until then, Mr. Gilmore."

Surprised by her sudden departure, Gilmore leapt to his feet, hurriedly pulling the service bell before kissing her hand.

"Until then, Miss Harlow," he repeated.

Emma nodded politely, then headed for the library door. As the footman escorted her once more to the main entrance, she reflected about how well the meeting had gone.

But let us leave the endless succession of rooms and return to the little patio. For our true concern is not what Emma might be thinking at that moment, still less the footman or for that matter the maid Daisy, who was waiting in the spacious hallway for her mistress to appear. Our true concern is what was going on inside the head of Montgomery Gilmore, who was completely baffled. Having said good-bye to Miss Harlow, he was seated once more, caressing the volume she had left behind, a pensive expression on his face. He ran his plump fingers over the author's name in embossed letters below the title and shook his head in amused disbelief at life's strange twists and turns.

"A Martian invasion . . . ," he muttered. Heaving a deep sigh of resignation, he gazed tenderly at his dog and declared: "Can you believe it, Eternal?"

The golden retriever stared back at him with what his master liked to think was equal skepticism.

XVII

$\mathcal{M}$ONTGOMERY GILMORE WENT BACK TO England two years after his death.

His first port of call after arriving in London was a certain square in Soho, at the center of which stood a bronze effigy of the man who had gone down in the annals of History as the Master of Time. Not everyone had the privilege of contemplating his own memorial statue. Montgomery Gilmore, the man once known as Gilliam Murray, carefully compared the figure to himself, as though he were looking in a mirror. Yet the fact was that after the changes he had imposed on his own body, he bore only a vague resemblance to his own statue. He had once weighed more than two hundred and fifty pounds; he'd had to lose quite a bit in order to achieve a complete transformation. However, to be on the safe side, Murray had also grown whiskers and a beard, cut his hair, and even learned to dress less ostentatiously. He was pleased with the result. He grinned, amused at the conjuring gesture his supposed double was tracing in the air with one hand, like a perfect charlatan. He also appreciated the likeness the sculptor had achieved of his faithful dog, Eternal, whom on reflection he had left behind in New York in Elmer's care, fearing that to bring him along might ruin his disguise.

He grimaced as a pigeon's dropping landed on the effigy's head. Having indulged his desire to go and see the sculpture, he had no wish to linger and witness firsthand the humiliations it would suffer before someone finally ordered its removal: the slow but steady erosion by time and the elements, the desecration and acts of vandalism, the relentless shelling by countless generations of those delightful pigeons. Yes, that indignity was enough of a taste of things to come. Murray gave the statue a complicit smile and set off slowly toward Greek Street, greeting any passersby with a friendly nod. He grinned complacently when he realized that no one recognized him, despite his being immortalized only a few blocks away. Although in truth he was not unduly worried, for given the susceptibility of the English to spiritualism, anyone recognizing him would undoubtedly take him for Gilliam Murray's ghost, an explanation that was more easily acceptable than someone successfully staging his own death.

When he reached Greek Street, he came to a halt in front of his former business premises, for which he had sacrificed his life. It was a disused theater, which Murray himself had remodeled, adorning its façade with a variety of ornamentation alluding to time, such as a frieze of carved hourglasses and an entablature depicting Chronos spinning the wheel of the zodiac, a sinister expression on his face. Between the carving of the god of time and the lintel, in flamboyant sculpted pink marble letters were the words MURRAY'S TIME TRAVEL. Murray ascended the steps and gazed wistfully at the poster beside the entrance inviting passersby to visit the year 2000. Murray waited until the street was clear before taking the key from his pocket and stealing into the building. The inside reeked of the past, of neglect, of faded memories. Murray paused in the vast foyer and listened to the silence—the only sound emanating now from the legions of clocks, which two years before had disrupted the place with their incessant ticking. The sculpture that took up the central area, and symbolized the passing of time with its gigantic hourglass turned over by a pair of jointed arms, had also ground to a halt and was shrouded in cobwebs. The same dust that jammed its mechanism had settled on the levers and cogs of the display of antique timepieces along one side of the vestibule and on the casings of the innumerable clocks lining its walls. Murray walked straight past the stairs leading up to his former office and made his way to the vast warehouse, where the *Cronotilus* stood like a tired old beast shivering from neglect. The vehicle had been adapted for venturing into dangerous territories, which was what had happened, for the *Cronotilus* had traveled to the future through the fourth dimension, where Murray had met his end.

Murray had made millions from becoming the Master of Time. And when he decided he had amassed enough of a fortune, he could think of no other way to close down Murray's Time Travel than by staging his own death. In fact, he had had no choice; no one would have accepted him closing down his business without good reason, thus denying the public the chance to travel in time, and it was impossible for him to sell it as one might a china shop or a tavern. His demise provided a horribly simple solution, and his legacy would retain a wonderfully tragic quality. And die was precisely what Murray had done: he had invented a grisly but perfect end for himself that had shaken the whole of society, which in his honor had erected a bronze statue of him in the middle of a square. Yes, Gilliam Murray had died as only heroes do, on a grand scale, and he had taken the secret of time travel with him to his grave. And while everyone resigned themselves to being once more hopelessly trapped in the present, Murray had sailed across the Atlantic Ocean, his pockets lined with money, to begin a new life in the modern city of New York, under the name Montgomery Gilmore.

His arrival had caused a small tidal wave in the otherwise tranquil sea of stuffy New York society. He soon realized he had fled to a place no less ambiguous and elusive than the one he had just left. For even as life appeared to flow like a serene river over its immaculate surface, kept from bursting its banks by a set of archaic rules, beneath there lay a world of passion and human frailty, meticulously documented by the spokespeople of that strange realm of appearances. Murray observed all that inherent hypocrisy from the outside. The way in which at every dinner someone would bring to the table a fresh snippet of gossip, an illicit affair, or the union through marriage of two well-to-do families. Disgusted by it all, and once the novelty of his presence had worn off, Murray showed his face little in society. Indeed, he would only attend very important business lunches, and his discreet, almost monastic existence ended up protecting him from those rumormongers, who soon grew tired of rummaging for scandal in what they must have considered his tedious life, beyond all earthly temptation. Murray finally blended into the wealthy New York landscape as a mysterious misanthropic magnate who posed no threat to the delicate fabric of its traditions.

And yet the life he led, which he was the first to consider pathetic, was not so much voluntary as inescapable. Even if he had wanted to live in a different way, it would have been impossible: the city's plethora of shows and exhibitions bored him, and rather than help refine his mind, that flurry of aesthetic emotions simply highlighted his unfortunate awkwardness in society, as did the dinners and dances and sundry entertainments he agreed to attend. Unable to enjoy the pleasures his wealth could afford, and not knowing what to do with his life after he had achieved his main goal, which had been the creation of his time travel company, Murray the millionaire cast a sorrowful eye over his vast dominion and felt that being forced to live was a harsh punishment. What was there in life that could excite him, fascinate him, free him from the deadly solitude that assailed him, and which even the monthly parcel of books from England failed to alleviate? He seemed to derive no pleasure or comfort from life, and so the simplest thing was to accept it, to face the facts, and to do absolutely nothing. Indeed, his only important task was to preserve his wealth, which he achieved every day without the slightest effort, but also without the slightest enthusiasm, meeting with businessmen, investing in this and that, for if Murray had one good quality it was his enviable sixth sense for discovering successful investments in mining, shipping, hotels, and even the fledgling subway system. In order that his wealthy neighbors should not suspect he was a dreamer, he even collected antiques, which his representatives acquired at auction houses and junk shops throughout Europe, and with which he crammed every room in his house, much to the despair of Elmer, who had a natural antipathy toward dust traps. Yet however many ruses he invented to pull the wool over others' eyes, the truth was that Murray's life was tedious, unproductive, and depressing.

And so it would have gone on, had not a freak gust of wind quite literally changed everything. Until then, Murray, like most people, thought that wind was the result of masses of air moving in the atmosphere. However, after what occurred on that certain Sunday morning, Murray fancied it was something else, something far deeper, more decisive, transcendental, perhaps the very breath of the Creator Himself. The day was so luminous that to remain indoors would have been criminal, and the whole of New York seemed resolved to savor it. Even Murray could not help leaving his shell and enjoying a walk with his dog in Central Park.

The moment he walked through the entrance, he could see the park was teeming with people who had had the same idea as he. Many were strolling in couples or in groups, reading on benches, or enjoying improvised picnics on the grass or teaching their children how to fly kites, and as Murray walked stiffly among them, as though to an altogether different tune, unable to blend in with his happy, lively surroundings, Eternal frolicked gaily up and down, jumping around eagerly. To Murray's surprise, just like a normal dog Eternal seemed willing to fetch anything Murray threw for him, even things he had not thrown. And so it was that after retrieving a stick and then a stone, the dog dropped a pretty red sun hat at his master's feet. Murray looked up, searching for the owner of the elegant bonnet he was now clasping. In the distance, he made out a group of young women sitting on the grass, near an artificial lake. At that precise moment, one of them had stood up and was gesturing to him to come over. As she was the only one not wearing a hat, Murray easily deduced that a gust of wind had sent hers rolling across the grass, providing an irresistible temptation for Eternal. And now the hat was in his possession. He cursed. Because of that evil conspiracy between the wind and his dog, he would now be obliged to go over and give it back, and no doubt strike up a conversation with that woman, something that, given his limited experience of talking to ladies, filled him with dread. He walked nervously over to the unknown woman, clearing his throat and practicing a few polite phrases that would smooth the progress of the unavoidable conversation.

Moving with deliberate slowness over the grass, accompanied by his dog, Murray began to realize that the girl who his faltering steps were bringing into focus was lovely, although he did not appreciate how much so until he was much closer. As the gap between them closed, Murray took the opportunity to study her beguiling features. Taken one by one, they were not conventionally beautiful: her nose seemed too big, her eyes too narrow, her skin a peculiar color, and yet together they created an effect that left anyone who saw her speechless. And then something happened to him that he had never believed could: he fell in love. Or at any rate he experienced, one by one, all the symptoms of love at first sight, descriptions of which he had so often read in novels, causing him invariably to stop reading in irritation, convinced that something so absurd and impulsive could only take place in the exaggerated world of romantic fiction. And yet now he was feeling every symptom! His heart throbbed painfully, as though straining inside his constricted chest like a trapped animal; he felt lighter, as though he were floating across the grass; the colors around him had taken on a dazzling intensity; even the breeze seemed to rumple his hair almost with tenderness. And by the time he had closed the distance between them, Murray was certain there was no other woman in the world more exquisite than the owner of that hat, and he knew it without any need for the rest of womankind to parade before him in all their finery. He came to a halt in front of her and stood, completely spellbound, while the young lady arched her eyebrows daintily, waiting for the gigantic fellow into whose hands her hat had found its way to say something. However, Murray had forgotten that what differentiated Man from the animals was his gift of speech. At that moment, Murray was only capable of one thing: contemplating that girl with adoration.

Whoever had fashioned her appeared to know Murray's tastes better than he did himself. Everything that appealed to him in a woman, and everything he did not know appealed to him, converged

harmoniously in the young woman before him. Her delicate bone structure was enclosed in silky skin, which instead of the customary paleness
seemed to have been sprinkled with cinnamon. From her face, framed
by long dark locks grazing her brow, shone two intriguing eyes, which,
besides surveying her surroundings, appeared to enfold them in a pleasant glow, as if they had been exposed to the winter sun. And as a finishing touch, Mother Nature in her infinite wisdom had added a mole to
the only place where it would not look like a blemish: above the corner
of her top lip, as though marking it out for a kiss. Yet for Murray none
of that would have had more than a purely aesthetic meaning, had he
not also been captivated by the soul that brought it all to life, making her
move in a delightful series of gestures.

However, as he was admiring her, a frown had appeared on that
adorable brow, instantly awakening Murray from his reverie. The hat, he
remembered with a jolt; he had gone over there to give back the hat. He
swiftly handed it to her, only to realize what he was giving her was nothing more than a soiled, chewed-up bit of rag. Due to his embarrassment,
their ensuing exchange was as brief as it was insipid, to the point where
he could not even remember it.

Even so, on his way home, Eternal walking meekly by his side, Murray found himself imagining a happy scene: he sitting with a book beside
a glowing hearth, she sitting at a piano, sprinkling the room with lively
notes, while upstairs, the nanny was putting to bed the fruit of their
love, two, possibly three, why not four beautiful cherubs. He felt complete, buoyant, as though with a run and a jump he might soar above the
street. He did not know whether that feeling was love, for he had never
experienced anything like it before, but he certainly felt a new sense of
purpose. For the very first time he was no longer the focus of his own
world, because now, to his surprise, everything centered on that extraordinary, unknown woman. What was his life like before their encounter
in the park? He could no longer remember. His only desire was to see
her again, to make that his sole purpose in life. But he also needed to
find out who she really was, what tea she preferred, her most painful

childhood memory, her most ardent desire. In short, he needed to see inside her soul and discover how she became who she was. Could that young woman be the missing piece that would make him whole, the person destined to know him better than he knew himself, his guiding light, and all the other clichés used to describe the one we love? Murray had no idea, yet he knew he would never give up until he had found out. He, Gilliam Murray, would conquer that mysterious territory the same way he had conquered the fourth dimension. He had never wanted anything so passionately. Never. And so, when he arrived home, he ordered Elmer to go to the park and follow the only hatless girl there to her house and find out her name. The following day, he sent an array of hats to the address his footman had given him, together with a card on which he wrote the message he had ruminated over all night:

Dear Miss Harlow,

As I have no idea which hat you would choose, I am sending you the shop's entire stock. And I take the opportunity to declare that you would make me the happiest man in the world if you allowed me to get to know you well enough to send you a single hat next time.

> Montgomery Gilmore,
> the blameless owner of a churlish hound

The same afternoon she sent a card in return, thanking him for his gifts:

I am most grateful for the thirty-seven hats, Mr. Gilmore. I must confess it is a very effective way of making me unafraid of another dog eating my hat in future. My mother and I would both be delighted to have the opportunity to thank you in person if you would kindly accept our invitation to tea tomorrow afternoon.

> Emma Harlow

The girl's drily humorous tone pleased Murray even more than her invitation. True, there was nothing spontaneous in the message that might indicate her desire: Emma had simply observed the rules of etiquette, no doubt at the instigation of her mother, who would not wish her daughter's name to appear in the little black book of civilized New York society as the girl who did not know how to express her thanks for a gift. Murray called at their house at teatime, prepared to make the most of the situation. Although he knew nothing about wooing young ladies, he assumed it was similar to clinching a good deal. He turned the mother's head with the sheer size of his fortune and investments, to the point where the good lady must have fancied he owned the planet as well as part of the universe, so that before they had finished off the cakes, she had already given him permission, if he so wished, to pursue her daughter. Emma's mother's approval made Murray deliriously happy, until he discovered that in order to woo Emma he must join a long list of other suitors. That band of lithe, self-assured contenders made him miserable. For a moment he even considered throwing in the towel but then thought better of it. Giving up was not in his nature; he would challenge those whelps and win, by Jove he would. He could hire someone to bump them off one by one. But, while swift and easy, such a method would arouse suspicion sooner or later and could end up incriminating him, the only one of her suitors left alive. The police were no fools, although they might seem so at times. Besides, he preferred to beat them in a fair fight. It was really a question of using his ingenuity, which he possessed in abundance.

Thus, Murray arrived at their second meeting brimming with optimism, although unfortunately that did not prevent it from turning into a disaster. He was able to charm Emma's mother, and even Mr. Harlow, who, despite showing no interest in meeting his contrary daughter's suitors, turned up in the drawing room for tea that afternoon, intrigued by his wife's rapturous descriptions of Murray. Indeed, he was so captivated by Murray's conversation and investments that he even arrived late for shooting practice for the first time in his life. In short, Murray enchanted Emma's parents, but as soon as he was alone with Emma, he became tongue-tied. During the stroll in Central Park that Emma's mother had suggested they take to round off the visit, he remained silent most of the time, simply giving her adoring sidelong glances as she walked beside him with dainty steps, shading herself with her parasol. The more he observed her, the more he discovered her hidden charms. He saw that her eyes contained a flush of innocence combined with a glint of cruelty, as though she had some panther in her, and he fancied that beneath her arrogance a stream of kindness flowed, as from an underground spring. Her supercilious exterior no doubt owed itself to that faintly exotic beauty that set her so apart from the other young girls. Yet while Murray was observing all that, absorbed in his own euphoria, he failed to notice how tedious their stroll must seem for Emma. She made him aware of it by giving a yawn as exaggerated as it was contrived before posing a question, the reply to which was undoubtedly of no great interest to her.

"So, Mr. Gilmore," he heard her say, in a resolutely disdainful tone. "How do you like America? I imagine that, accustomed as you are to the old country, you must consider us little better than savages."

"Indeed," Murray replied hastily.

Emma gazed at him in surprise.

The millionaire tried to correct himself: "No, I didn't mean that . . . What I mean is that I like America. I like it very much. America is a great nation! And of course I don't consider Americans savages, least of all you."

"Am I to understand, then, that you think my mother more of a savage than I?" the girl chided him gently as she twirled her parasol, the shadows playing on her face.

"Oh, certainly not, Miss Harlow. Nor are you more of one than she . . . I mean to say . . ." Murray became flustered, stumbling over his words, perfectly aware the girl was mocking him. "Neither you nor your mother deserve such an epithet. That of savages, I mean. Nor does any member of your illustrious family, naturally . . . nor any of your neighbors or friends . . ."

Murray's convoluted explanation caused a fresh silence to fall between them. Fearful lest it prove fatally long, he tried to think up another topic of conversation, one her many other suitors would broach with ease. But once more it was Emma who broke the silence.

"I imagine that a busy man like you, who spends his time carrying out mergers that increase his wealth, must have little time for ordinary amusements . . . You probably consider them frivolous, or even beneath you. I'm sure this very instant you are far away, lost in thoughts of your innumerable business deals, while trying to hide the fact that you consider this stroll an obvious waste of time."

"If my clumsy silence has caused you to harbor such thoughts, then pray accept my heartfelt apologies, Miss Harlow," the increasingly bewildered Murray apologized hurriedly. "I assure you I had no intention of giving you such a wrong impression."

"I see. Am I to understand that I am mistaken, then, and that you simply prefer to enjoy the healthy exercise of walking without any other activity to distract you from the difficult task of placing one foot in front of the other?"

"I . . . well, yes, it is true, I greatly enjoy taking exercise. I'm not a man who likes to be inactive, Miss Harlow. I find walking . . . er, invigorating. And I believe that, as you pointed out . . . it is good for one's health."

"Very well, now I know what it is you want, let us continue our stroll plunged into a healthy, invigorating silence."

Murray opened his mouth as if to speak, then instantly closed it again, unsure of how to respond to her remark. He heaved a sigh, as the dreaded silence descended upon them once more. And so they walked on, Murray still struggling to find a way to initiate a conversation while Emma twirled her parasol in a desultory fashion, aiming an occasional kick at one of the stones strewn across the path, making no attempt to conceal her increasing irritation. Murray made a last desperate attempt.

"May I ask what your hobbies are, Miss Harlow?" he said rather diffidently, fearing the possible consequences of such an innocent question.

"Clearly you aren't accustomed to speaking to refined young ladies, Mr. Gilmore, or you would have no need to ask. Like any self-respecting young lady, I play music, sing and dance to perfection, and in order to improve my mind and enrich my education I read widely, in my own language as well as in French, which I speak fluently, *mon cher petit imbécile*. I also regularly attend the theater, the ballet, and the opera, and every day I try to . . . *invigorate* myself by walking in Central Park. As you see, a life of pure enjoyment."

"Is that so? I beg your pardon, but you don't seem to enjoy your life very much, Miss Harlow," Murray could not help remarking.

"Really?" The girl gave him a puzzled look. "What makes you say that?"

"W-well . . . ," Murray stammered somewhat nervously. "I still haven't had the pleasure of hearing . . . your wonderful laugh."

"Ah, now I understand! In that case, forgive me, dear Mr. Gilmore, for not having made more of an effort to laugh like an idiot for no reason at all, thus depriving you of that pleasure. But don't confuse not hearing my laugh with my not having one. The fact is, the things that amuse me don't usually amuse others, and so I am in the habit of laughing by myself or to myself."

"A lonely sort of laughter . . . ," Murray murmured.

"Do you really think so?" the girl snapped. "I daresay you're right. But when the stupidity of others is the only thing that amuses one, then it is only good manners to laugh to oneself, don't you agree?"

"Am I to infer that you have been laughing to yourself during our entire walk?" Murray jested by way of making peace.

"My good manners prevent me from answering that, Mr. Gilmore, and my principles from telling a lie. Draw your own conclusions."

"I already have, Miss Harlow," Murray said in a tone of resignation. "And I'm proud to have been the cause of your amusement. But don't you ever laugh at anything other than human stupidity? Haven't you ever laughed for a different reason, or for no reason at all? Simply because it is a lovely day, or the cook has made your favorite dessert—"

"Of course not," the girl cut across. "I fail to see why everything working out perfectly should be grounds for rejoicing."

"—or because you have fallen in love."

Emma raised her eyebrows, astounded.

"Is love a source of hilarity for you?"

"No, but it is a reason to rejoice," the millionaire parried. "Have you never been in love, Miss Harlow? Have you never felt so alive, so intensely alive that you have to laugh out loud to stop yourself from bursting with joy?"

"I'm afraid your question is too forward, Mr. Gilmore."

"That could be the reply of a demure young lady, but also of someone afraid to admit she is incapable of falling in love," replied Murray.

"Are you insinuating that I'm incapable of falling in love simply because I don't prostrate myself at your feet?" Emma cried.

"My good manners prevent me from answering that, Miss Harlow, and my principles from telling a lie. Draw your own conclusions." Murray smiled.

"Mr. Gilmore, you can't woo a refined young lady with such impudent remarks. No self-respecting lady would allow—"

"I don't care what others would do!" Murray exclaimed, with such passionate vehemence that the young woman could not help pausing, disconcerted, in the middle of the little bridge they were crossing. "I don't care what is proper and what isn't. I'm tired of this game! The only thing I care about, Miss Harlow, is knowing what it takes to make you happy. Tell me, what makes you happy? It's a very simple question that only requires a simple answer."

"What makes me happy?" Emma almost stammered. "But, I already told you . . ."

"No, you didn't tell me, Miss Harlow. And more than anything, I need to know what it is you desire," Murray insisted, with the same determination he displayed when negotiating a contract, tired of this ritual whose absurd rules were alien to him.

Emma looked straight at him, disturbed and upset by his sudden change of tone. And then, something happened: it was as though a fissure had opened in the young woman's dark pupils, and, like peering through a hole in a wall, Murray glimpsed through the flutter of eyelids a small girl gazing back at him with pleading eyes. That angry, sad girl had black ringlets, wore a yellow dress, and was clutching a strange scroll of paper tied with a red ribbon. Startled, the millionaire wondered who this was. Was he seeing Emma as a child? But how could that be? Or was he simply imagining her as a little girl? But if so then how could he conjure her up in such vivid, precise detail? Her hair, her dress, the strange scroll . . . Murray had no idea, yet he sensed he was in communion with Emma's soul, that some form of miracle or magic was occurring between them, making the impossible happen, allowing him to see her as she really was. The illusion vanished as quickly as sea foam left by the waves. Yet, before the little girl sank back into the shadows, before the fissure in the eyes staring at him closed up once more, Murray was able to know everything about her: he knew that she was not happy, that she could not remember ever having been happy, and that, in truth, she was not sure she ever would be happy. And above all he knew that that little girl was afraid, terribly afraid, because the woman in whose body she was trapped was slowly smothering her, and that soon there would be nothing left of her. That glimpse lasted only an instant, but it was more valuable to Murray than a lifetime's acquaintance. When the little girl vanished, and Emma's pupils recaptured their intense arrogance, Murray averted his gaze, shaken to the roots of his being. That little girl had been pleading for help, and he knew, with absolute certainty, that he must save her. That only he could prevent her from disappearing forever.

"Well, Mr. Gilmore," he heard Emma say, as though speaking to him from a dim, distant place, "since you are so keen to know what I want, I shall tell you in plain English, and hope that you mean it when you say you only desire my happiness."

Murray looked up slowly, still overwhelmed by that peculiar, unexpected communion he had experienced with the girl from whom Emma appeared so estranged. He must make the glimpsed girl smile so that the woman whom she was trapped inside could also smile. He had to show her how wonderful the world was, the myriad reasons it contained for making its inhabitants happy, even though he himself had doubted this. Yet what did the real world matter when he had enough money and imagination to create any world she desired, a world where everything was perfect, and whose laws she alone would decree.

"I want you to stop courting me," Emma said brusquely. "That's what I want. I shall never reciprocate any of your sentiments, and I'm afraid that, unlike many women, I wouldn't be capable of pretending something I don't feel. So, you may keep your precious time, Mr. Gilmore, and I suggest you put it to some better use than trying to attain something that, although your pride prevents you from recognizing it, is beyond you."

Murray smiled at her and shook his head gently.

"If I stop courting you, Miss Harlow, it will be the first time in my life I don't achieve what I want. And *depuis notre rencontre, vous êtes mon seul désir,*" he concluded.

Emma looked at him, incensed by his rudeness. With a sigh of frustration, she turned and strode off, leaving him standing alone on the bridge. Murray watched her walk away, still smiling despite her response. It was true that he had always achieved what he wanted, yet the thing he desired now, for the first time in his life, had nothing to do with his own happiness, but with hers. Consequently, all of a sudden, he no longer felt any urgency, no burning, selfish need to fulfill his desire. And that was his advantage over Emma's other suitors: he could spend his life waiting for her, because his life was no longer his own. He belonged to her. And Emma would be his because he had all the time in the world to wait for her to accept him. His whole life. He would love her for as long as necessary, ceaselessly, and with the same intensity. He would love her from afar, without any need to touch her, as one might admire a star or the stained glass windows in a cathedral. He would love her as they grew old, watching her live out her life from a distant shore, like a thousand-year-old tree that time had given up on, in the hope that she would at last turn toward him and open her arms, whether because she was disillusioned, curious, widowed, cuckolded, fickle, or for any other reason, and then he would show that lost little girl what happiness was.

MURRAY REALIZED AT LAST that Emma had gone there with the sole purpose of beating him at his own game, of ridding herself of him in a manner as polite as it was refined: by asking him for something he could not possibly achieve.

Emma's visit to his house for tea had made it clear to him that she only valued actions, that in order to marry her he had to reproduce the Martian invasion in H. G. Wells's novel.

Him, again. The man he hated more than anyone in the world.

And now, strolling around the abandoned warehouse, he wondered whether he could re-create the Martian invasion. But he was a past master at such challenges, he told himself. Gazing at the time tram with which he had penetrated the future, he was filled with an almost aching happiness. For on August 1, Emma Harlow, the most beautiful woman on the planet, would agree to become his wife. And then she would fall in love with him. Yes, of that he was certain. For he was Gilliam Murray, Master of Time.

And he could achieve the impossible.

XVIII

A FORTNIGHT HAD SUFFICED, HOWEVER, TO transform a happy man into a desperate one. Murray had arrived in London at the beginning of June and had immediately set to work, only to discover that reproducing a Martian invasion was not as easy as he had imagined. On the morning of June fifteenth, Murray was on his way to his offices to attend another rehearsal, even though he was sure it would be no more satisfactory than the previous ones. He had been unable to assemble the same team from two years before when he had transported his contemporaries to the year 2000, and although Martin had sworn blind that the new men were every bit as competent, all Murray had been able to conclude from his employee's assertion was that he was given to making wild claims.

Reaching Greek Street, Murray slipped unnoticed into the old theater. Martin, a burly redhead almost as big as Murray, came out to the lobby to greet him.

"Everything's ready, Mr. Murray," he announced.

"I told you to call me Mr. Gilmore, Martin. Poor Mr. Murray passed away two years ago."

"Sorry, Mr. Gilmore, it's just habit."

Murray nodded absentmindedly.

"Well, no matter," he said anxiously. "Let's see what you've come up with this time."

Martin guided him into the warehouse, where the performance

would take place. Banished to a corner of the vast hangar, the only surviving witness to his glorious past, stood the *Cronotilus*. Murray glanced fondly at it before his gaze alighted on the Martian cylinder, now taking up the center of the warehouse. As before, he stood at a distance of about five to six yards, which according to his estimations was as close to it as the alarmed onlookers would dare approach. As for the cylinder, Murray had to confess that Martin's team had done a splendid job, for it was exactly as Wells had described it. In the novel, which Murray was using as a guide, the Martian device traveled through the 40 million miles separating it from Earth, broke through the atmosphere, hurtled through the sky until it was over Winchester, and finally crashed onto Horsell Common, creating a giant crater where it came to rest, surrounded by a ring of charred grass and gravel. Needless to say, Murray was not capable of creating all that and would have to be content with dismantling the cylinder and transporting it to Horsell under cover of darkness, then reassembling it on the common and singeing a few surrounding tufts of grass, so that in the morning everyone would believe it had flown through space and landed at that precise spot.

However, the machine by itself was regrettably not enough. A Martian had to emerge from it, too. Murray sighed and motioned with his hand toward Martin, who yelled at the cylinder:

"All right, lads, let the show begin!"

With a muffled sound, the top of the cylinder slowly began to unscrew. In Wells's novel, the capsule took almost a whole day to unscrew itself, so that when the top fell to the ground, dusk was beginning to fall. By that time, an anxious crowd of onlookers and journalists had gathered around the cylinder. Murray realized that he must tell the men inside to take equally long to open the top, so that news of the Martians' arrival had time to reach the rest of the country, and most importantly to be reported in the newspapers. He might need to bore a few discreet air holes in the casing if he did not want to lose any men during the performance. And he also had to find a way of heating up the cylinder's surface, less to make it seem as though it had flown through space than to deter inquisitive souls from coming too close to it. Murray's ruminations were interrupted when he noticed that nearly a foot and a half of the shiny metal screw was now sticking out. A moment later, the top fell to the floor with an almighty clatter. Murray held his breath, as had the numerous witnesses in Wells's novel, curious to see what was inside. They had all expected to see a man come out, perhaps with some slight physical differences, but a man all the same. A man from Mars. However, the thing stirring in the darkness did not appear human. Wells's alarmed crowd glimpsed something grey and sinuous, and two luminous disks that could only be eyes, before a pair of tentacles shot out from inside, uncoiling in the air and clasping the sides of the cylinder, unleashing a deluge of horrified screams. Then, slowly and painfully, owing to the greater gravitational pull of the Earth, a greyish rounded bulk emerged from the artifact. According to Wells's description, the creature's body glistened and its face exuded a thick, nasty slime. A few seconds later, the Martian appeared to fling itself deliberately into the crater, where it would produce the flying machine in the shape of a stingray, which it would use to attack Earth's cities. But prior to that, a kind of mast with a parabolic mirror on the end of it would appear from its improvised lair. This would vibrate ominously for a few seconds, and then a heat ray would burst forth from its polished surface sweeping the area and savagely burning to a crisp anything in its path, whether trees, bushes, or people. Murray obviously had no intention of killing the civilians gathered around his cylinder, among whom would figure Emma Harlow. But he needed to scare them, and for that he was depending entirely on the emergence of the Martian. It had to be convincing enough to create the headlines that would win Emma's heart, or at least that would permit him to marry her.

Murray breathed in sharply and waited for the replica of the Martian his men had made to emerge from the cylinder. He braced himself, ready to face all the horror the universe had to offer, and was instantly overwhelmed by the most terrible dread. Not for the reasons he had expected, for, whichever way Murray looked at it, what emerged from the cylinder would not have scared even a child. It was a kind of rag doll, to which the men had sewn on a few painted cardboard tentacles, with two electric lamps for eyes poking out above the hole that was its mouth, from which oozed what looked like mushy peas mixed with another revolting, lumpier substance. For a few moments, the would-be Martian swayed ridiculously from side to side, pretending to respond to the Earth's gravity, and finally a pair of hands hurled it from the cylinder. It landed on the ground with a dull thud. The performance over, Martin burst into applause. He looked expectantly at his boss.

"Well, what did you think?"

"Get out and leave me alone," Murray ordered.

"What?" replied Martin.

"Get out!"

Alarmed, Martin rapped on the cylinder. A tiny hidden hatch opened on its side, and the two men operating the puppet crawled out.

"Did you like it this time, Martin?" one of the men asked eagerly.

"The boss needs to be on his own to reflect, Paul," Martin said, gesturing to them to leave the hangar.

When Murray was at last alone, he gave a forlorn sigh that echoed through the warehouse. Things were going from bad to worse. On their first attempt, one of the men had chosen to dress up as the Martian, but the disguise made of painted cardboard and wool gave the impression of a sheep sheared by a blind man rather than a creature from another planet. Displeased with the result, Murray had engaged two employees from Madame Tussauds to make a wax effigy of a Martian, but the outcome, while more convincing than his men's disguise, had the jolly air of a snowman and was of course unable to move, which to Murray's mind inevitably made it less terrifying. And the thing he had just seen emerge from the cylinder was even more dismal. He approached the Martian rag doll, which lay on its side on the floor next to the machine. That dummy was all that stood between him and his marriage to Emma. Unable to help himself, he aimed a kick at it, sending it flying. Propelled by Murray's rage, the doll went tumbling across the floor, losing one of the Robertson bulbs that were its eyes in the process. Murray shook his head. He needed to think, to find a proper solution, and quickly, for his time was running out.

He left the warehouse and climbed the stairs to his office, where he poured himself a glass of brandy. Sitting back in his armchair, savoring the liquor calmly, he tried to compose himself. He did not wish to fall prey to one of his usual, futile fits of rage, which, since falling in love, he viewed as a thing of the past. He would do better to reflect serenely upon the matter. All was not lost. He still had time. Murray picked up a piece of card containing a sketch of Wells's Martian he had done to give his men something to go on. If only the author had thought up something simpler . . . But no, that kind of overdeveloped octopus was impossible to replicate. He had come to London believing Emma's request would be easy to fulfill, a mere formality he had to see to before enfolding her in his arms forever. But creating a Martian was proving complicated. It might have been easier to fly to Mars and hunt one down. He had to concede that his imagination, which he had always depended upon, had let him down this time. He, who had taken the whole of England to the year 2000, was incapable of reenacting a stupid Martian invasion. He was guilty of hubris. He had truly believed he was the Great Murray who could conjure the impossible. And reality had just demonstrated that he was only Monty G., a sad puppet master. His rage got the better of him, and he tore up the drawing and threw it into the wastepaper basket.

"Why?" he bellowed, rising from his chair and turning his distraught face to the ceiling, as though demanding an answer. "Why are you making things so difficult for me now of all times, damn it! I don't intend to gain money or fame from this! All I want is to win a woman's heart!"

As had been his custom since time immemorial, the Creator was unforthcoming. In response to His antediluvian silence Murray gave a pitiful howl, like a wolf with its leg caught in a trap, and, unable to find a more sophisticated way of venting his frustration, he swept off the objects on his desk, sending a cascade of papers and books crashing to the floor. Scarcely soothed by this feeble release, he took a deep breath and clucked in dismay: he had only managed to come up with a pathetic dummy, and it was clear that in the six remaining weeks he could produce nothing better. He desperately needed help. But from whom? Who on earth could help him? With a gesture of despair, he looked out of the window and discovered the same sunny day he had been walking in scarcely an hour before. He imagined if he stared at it long enough he would infect it with his gloom, the sky would fill with leaden clouds, and a storm would erupt.

Then he saw him. And for a few moments he could scarcely believe his eyes. Was it him, was it really him? Yes, without a doubt! Murray said to himself, after carefully scrutinizing the fellow. Before his astonished eyes, standing on the pavement opposite, staring up at the building with discernible bitterness, was H. G. Wells. Although doubtless Wells could not see him due to the sun reflecting on the windowpanes, Murray swiftly hid behind the curtain and observed him with interest. What the devil was Wells doing there? He was looking at the building, yes, but why? Obviously he could not have guessed that Murray was inside. He no doubt imagined him in some other part of the world, happily spending his fortune under an assumed name, which indeed had been the case. But clearly the author still saw the old theater as the embodiment of Gilliam Murray's hateful fantasy, for the expression on his birdlike face suggested that of a man visiting his worst enemy's grave and lamenting not having killed him himself. But why had he come there at that precise moment? Why had he organized his day, his life so as to be standing at the exact spot where Murray had directed his gaze? Such synchronism could not be simple coincidence. Could it be a sign from the Creator, who was so fond of communicating with His creatures through such subtle gestures? For a few moments, Wells appeared deep in thought; then, after consulting his watch, he gave the theater a parting glance and walked down Charing Cross Road and into the Strand. He seemed in a hurry, as though he were keeping someone waiting somewhere.

Murray sat down once more at his desk, took out a sheet of paper, and paused for a moment. Did he have the nerve to do it? No. Yes. Of course he did; he had no choice. He was a man who knew how to read the signs. But above all he was a man at the end of his tether. And such men are capable of anything. Hunched over the blank page, Murray began writing the most humiliating letter of his life:

Dear George,

I imagine it will come as no surprise to you to receive a letter from a dead man, for we are both aware that you are the only man in all England who knows I am still alive. What will doubtless surprise you is the reason for my writing, and that is none other than to request your help. Yes, that is right, I am sending you this letter because I need your help.

Let me begin by not wasting time dissembling. We both know that our hatred of each other is unmitigated. Consequently, you will understand the humiliation I feel at having to write you this letter. However, I am willing to endure that humiliation if it means obtaining your help, which gives you some clue as to how desperate I am. Imagine me kneeling and begging at your feet, if it pleases you. It is of no consequence to me. I do not value my dignity enough not to sacrifice it. I realize the absurdity of asking for help from one's enemy, and yet is it not also a sign of respect, a way of admitting one's inferiority? And I fully recognize my own: as you know, I have always prided myself on my imagination. But now I need help from someone with a greater imagination than

my own. And I know of none comparable to yours, George. It is
as simple as that. If you help me, I will happily stop hating you,
even though I don't suppose that is much of an incentive. Bear in
mind I will also owe you a favor, and, as you know, I am a millionaire now. That might be more of an incentive. If you help me,
George, you may name your price. Any price. <u>You have my word,
George</u>.

And why do I need your help? you must be wondering. Well,
at the risk of rekindling your hatred of me, the matter relates to
another of your novels, this time *The War of the Worlds*. As your
brilliant mind has no doubt already deduced, I have to re-create
a Martian invasion. However, this time I assure you I am not attempting to prove anything to you, nor do I intend to profit from
it. You must believe me. I no longer need either of those things.
This time I am driven by something I need more than anything
in the world, and without which I shall die: love, George, the love
of the most beautiful woman I have ever seen. If you have been
in love you will understand what I am referring to. I daresay you
will find it hard, perhaps impossible, to believe that a man like me
can fall in love, yet if you met her it would seem strange to you
if I had not. Ah, George, I was unable to resist her charms, and I
assure you her immense fortune is not one of them, for as I told
you, I have enough money to last several lifetimes. No, George,
I am referring to her charming smile, her golden skin, the savage
sweetness of her eyes, even the adorable way she twirls her parasol
when she is nervous . . . No man could be immune to her beauty,
even you.

But in order to have her, I must arrange for a cylinder to land
on Horsell Common on August 1, and for a Martian to emerge
from it, just like in your novel, George. And I don't know how!
I have tried everything, but as I told you, my imagination has its
limits. I need yours, George. Help me, please. If I pull it off, that
woman will be my wife. And if that happens, I promise I shall no

longer be your enemy, for Gilliam Murray will be finally laid to rest. Please, I beg you, I implore you, assist this lovesick soul.

Yours,

G.M.

Murray sank back in his chair and gazed at the humiliating letter, at the flowing lines of fresh ink covering the white page. Would his words achieve anything? He reflected that it might be wiser to threaten Wells, to warn him that Jane could be the victim of a cycling accident, for instance, but he instantly rejected the idea. He would have stooped that low once, but now that he was in love he dared not consider it. The thought was abhorrent to him. He could not bear the idea of Emma being hurt and so could therefore easily understand what Wells would feel if he received such a threat. Besides, he had no need to resort to his old thuggish ways, for he was convinced Wells would help him, for the simple reason that he believed himself superior to Murray and was eager to prove it. That kind of ploy always worked with people of integrity, which, rightly or wrongly, is what Wells undoubtedly considered himself. And he, Murray, had only sacrificed his dignity, which was no great loss. From now on, with Emma by his side, he would remodel himself, he would be reborn as a better person, a new man, uncorrupted, redeemed by love. He blew on the ink, placed the sheet of paper in an envelope, and sealed it.

The following day he posted the letter. And he waited.

And waited.

And waited.

Until at last he realized that Wells would never reply. Apparently, the author had no intention of helping him. Wells's hatred was stronger than he had imagined; it clouded his mind, poisoned his thoughts. For a few days, Murray toyed with the idea of sending Wells a second, more servile letter, or even of calling on him, hurling himself at the author's feet and clutching his skinny knees until Wells had no choice but to help him if he wanted to carry on with his life. But Murray soon dismissed those ideas as futile; a shrewd businessman such as he knew when someone was impervious to civilized methods of persuasion. Clearly, Wells would never help him. And so, if he wanted to produce a convincing Martian, he would have to do it without Wells's help. And sooner rather than later; otherwise, on August 1 Emma would be smiling triumphantly as she contemplated the grass gently swaying in the summer breeze on Horsell Common, whose delicious earthly peace was undisturbed by any alien presence.

XIX

$\mathcal{I}$N A COTTAGE ON THE OUTSKIRTS OF LONDON, IN Worcester Park, on the exact day Murray had chosen for the Martians to arrive, Herbert George Wells was sleeping soundly in the belief that the day awaiting him beyond the rising curtain of dawn would be the same as any other. He slipped out of bed carefully, so as not to rouse Jane, who was still sleeping beside him, her breath imitating the ebb and flow of the surf. He left the bedroom, had a strip wash, and began his habitual pilgrimage through the house, which was plunged into a dense silence at that time of the morning. Wells liked to get up before dawn, when the world had not yet arisen, and, free of any obligations, creep around the house like an intruder before his working day began. Like a field marshal strutting proudly over the battleground strewn with his enemy's remains, he surveyed each room, making sure no one had invaded the territory he had struggled so hard to conquer. Everything appeared in order: the furniture was in its proper place, the dawn light was streaming in through the windows at the correct angle, the wallpaper was the same color. The Wellses' house was far from luxurious, but was bigger than the one they had in Woking and infinitely bigger than the warren they had inhabited in Mornington Crescent. For Wells the steady increase in the size of his sanctums reflected better than anything else the measure of his success. Ranged on a special shelf in the sitting room were his five published novels to date, the palpable fruit of his imagination. The renown those few works had won him in England had recently spread to America. He plucked from the end of the row the copy of *The War of the Worlds,* recently published by Heinemann, and cupped it gingerly in his hands, as he might a batch of eggs. "*The War of the Worlds,*" he murmured solemnly in the gloom of the sitting room, "by H. G. Wells." He liked to whisper the titles of his books, as though somehow that brought them to life. Then he noticed a letter sticking out from between its pages. He grasped it between his thumb and forefinger, as though with revulsion. The letter had arrived well over a month before and was from Gilliam Murray, the person he most hated in the whole world. Yes, he bore that man a deep and abiding grudge, which in Wells's case was quite an achievement, because from the earliest age he had shown an unerring inability to sustain any emotion, even hatred.

Wells remembered the shiver that had run up his spine when he discovered Murray's letter in his mailbox, a reminder of the old days when he was plagued by Murray's invitations to travel to the future. Wells had torn it open with trembling fingers, unable to stop his mind from inventing a hundred reasons why Murray might have written to him, each more alarming than the last, before his eyes finally absorbed its contents. When he had finished reading, he gave a sigh of relief, and his fear gave way to loathing. Murray had apparently emerged from his lair and returned to London, where he had the nerve to ask for Wells's help for nothing less than to re-create the Martian invasion the author had depicted in his novel. Murray had no qualms in his letter about acknowledging the limits of his imagination, and he hinted at a reward if Wells agreed to help him and even appealed to Wells's sentiments by confessing that his motives this time were far from pecuniary, and that he was driven by the noblest feeling of all: love. If he was able to make a Martian cylinder appear on Horsell Common on August 1, the woman he loved would agree marry him. Why would anyone devise such an outlandish test? Wells wondered. Had the mysterious woman whom Murray loved set him a challenge she knew he could not meet? But more importantly: did such a woman even exist, or was this all a cunning ruse to secure his aid? Whether Murray's story was true or not, Wells had decided to refuse his request. He had slipped Murray's letter between the pages of his novel and thought no more of it until that morning. He loathed Murray too deeply to want to help him, regardless of how much in love the man was or pretended to be. Placing the book back on the shelf, Wells realized that if his story turned out to be true, then the deadline was this very day. Had Murray pulled it off? he wondered with vague curiosity. Had he actually managed to make a Martian cylinder land on Horsell Common? He doubted it. Even for a man like Murray, who could apparently achieve anything, it was an impossible feat.

Wells went into the kitchen to make his morning cup of coffee, assailed by a tormenting thought: had he refused to help Murray simply because he was his enemy? Perhaps it was time he answered the question. No, he reflected, assembling the percolator. Of course not; there had been other equally important reasons. Such as the fact that for the past six weeks he had been a different man. A bewildered, terrified man. A man forced every day to convince himself he had not taken leave of his senses, for, ever since he had entered the Chamber of Marvels in the basement of the Natural History Museum, where the unimaginable was stored, where he had beheld wonders no one knew existed, extraordinary things that made the world a miraculous place, Wells had wondered how he was to live. For days afterward, he had been plunged into a state of confusion similar to the incomprehension he had felt when, as a child, he discovered that the world extended beyond the British Isles, the only focus of the geography class at school. It seemed incredible, but the world did not end at the coast. Beyond it loomed the Colosseum, the Taj Mahal, the Pyramids. Thus Wells had gained a notion of the Earth's size, just as a visit to the Dinosaur Court at the Crystal Palace to see the plaster reconstructions of, among others, the megatherium, had enabled him to establish its age, the beginning of time, before which existence was a mere euphemism. Thus, from an early age, Wells had believed he lived in the world that was, and always had been, a world whose coordinates in time and space had been carefully mapped out by science. Yet he knew now that those coordinates were wrong, that there was a world beyond the fictitious boundaries that their rulers, who determined what they ought to know about and what not, were intent on drawing up. On leaving the museum, Serviss had told Wells it was up to him whether or not he believed in the authenticity of the wonders in the Chamber of Marvels. And Wells had decided to accept as true the existence of the supernatural, because logic told him there was no other reason why it should be kept under lock and key. As a result he felt surrounded by the miraculous, besieged by magic. He was aware now that one fine day he would go into the garden to prune the roses and stumble on a group of fairies dancing in a circle. It was as though a tear had appeared in every book on the planet, and the fantasy had begun seeping out, engulfing the world, making it impossible to tell fact from fiction.

However, as the days went by, Wells had managed to overcome his bewilderment, since in the long run knowing that miracles existed changed nothing, for perhaps the fairies only danced in his garden while he was asleep. Life went on as before, and he had no choice but to continue existing within the confines of the tangible world, the dull, quantifiable, inhospitable world. The rest was fantasy, fables, and old wives' tales. Even so, Wells could not help feeling a tinge of resentment, the uncomfortable impression of being in a farce on a miniature stage designed by those in power who determined which props remained in the wings. What right did those men have to limit the world? Like him, they were mere specks of dust in the universe, a moment in time. But as the museum's head curator had explained to Serviss, there were boundaries not all men were ready to cross. And Wells had paid the price, for he was clear about one thing: he would never write another fantasy novel. How could he, now that he knew there were more impossible things in the world than any writer could ever imagine? He had written a book speculating about the existence of Martians because he had never touched one before with his own hands. But that had changed: now he had, he had touched the arm of a genuine Martian, a Martian that had hurtled through space in a flying saucer, and that looked more like a moth than an octopus. With that in mind, what sense was there in helping Murray to re-create a Martian invasion as preposterous as the one he himself had described?

He poured himself a cup of coffee and sat at the kitchen table in front of the picture window overlooking the garden. On the other side of the glass, a soft orange light was slowly tracing the outline of things. Wells gazed with quiet sadness at the vista appearing before him, knowing this was merely the tip of the iceberg, the rest of which was submerged, hidden from the vast majority of mankind. He sipped his coffee and sighed. That was enough. If he wanted to stay sane he should forget everything he had seen in the Chamber of Marvels, he told himself. And he tried to concentrate on resolving the problems he was having with the plot of *Love and Mr. Lewisham,* the realist novel he was planning to write.

It was then that something blinded him. A flash coming from outside. Wells stood up and narrowed his eyes, trying to see what had dazzled him, perhaps secretly hoping to glimpse at last one of the fairies he had seen in the photographs in the Chamber of Marvels. But, to his astonishment, he saw a metallic hand grappling with the latch on his gate. He watched, disconcerted. The prosthesis belonged to a slender young man in an elegant, sober three-piece suit. When at last he managed to open the gate with the aid of his left hand, Wells watched the young man walk up the stone path leading to the front door. Wells could tell from the air of frustration on his face that the man was annoyed at the clumsy artificial hand poking out of his right sleeve. Perhaps he had wanted to practice using it to open the gate, with disastrous results. What could such a fellow want with him? Wells hurried to open the door before the bell rang, so as not to wake Jane.

"Are you H. G. Wells, the author?" the stranger asked.

"I am," Wells replied warily. "How can I help you?"

"I am Inspector Cornelius Clayton from the Special Branch at Scotland Yard," the young man said, waving a credential in Wells's face, "and I'm here to request that you accompany me to Woking."

Wells remained silent, gazing at the stranger, who in turn gazed back at him without a word. The young man had a long, resolute-looking face, crowned by a mop of wavy hair that fell over his brow in a cascade of dark curls. Bushy eyebrows accentuated his narrow, intense eyes, and his full lips were set in a faint grimace, as though he were constantly aware of some nauseating stench. Lastly, his body was so angular it was not difficult to imagine him thrust down the barrel of a cannon waiting to be shot out in a circus ring.

"What for?" Wells asked at last, although he already knew the answer.

The inspector stared at him ominously before replying:

"A Martian cylinder appeared on Horsell Common tonight, exactly as you described in your novel."

XX

*N*O MATTER HOW HARD THE INSPECTOR'S driver urged on the horses, it was impossible to make the journey from Worcester Park to Woking in less than three hours, Wells reflected, doing his best to give the impression that he was oblivious to the irksome jolting of the carriage. He was sitting bolt upright, hands folded neatly in his lap, having allowed his gaze to wander across the fields racing by outside as he tried to assimilate the absurd, exasperating situation in which the affairs of the heart had landed him. Another man's heart this time, his own being so dull as to scarcely cause him any problem. For it appeared that Murray had succeeded. And without his help. Wells had no idea how, but the millionaire had contrived to adorn Horsell Common with a replica of the cylinder he had described in his novel. And it must have been quite a convincing one for Scotland Yard to send Inspector Clayton to ferry him to the scene. The young man had explained to Wells that although he had not yet seen the artifact in question, the description he had been given corresponded in every particular with the one in Wells's novel, not to mention that it had turned up in exactly the same place. How could he possibly have known what the Martians were going to do a year in advance? he had inquired rather casually, even as he looked at the author askance. As far as the head of Special Branch, who had sent Clayton, was concerned, this was a logical question, especially if he believed in Martians, and on that matter Wells was in no doubt, for he had noticed a familiar-looking key decorated with a pair of angel's wings round the young man's neck. Even so,

Wells could not help feeling a flash of anger at the hint of accusation in the inspector's plainly rhetorical question. Wasn't it more logical to think that someone might be trying to emulate his novel? Wells had replied, making no effort to conceal his irritation. And he was still waiting for an answer. He turned his gaze toward the inspector, who was silently absorbed in Murray's letter, which Wells had produced to back up his argument. That letter cleared him of any accusation the inspector might make, however wild. The author awaited his reaction, trying to appear calm.

"So, the Master of Time isn't dead after all . . . ," Clayton muttered to himself, without looking up from the letter he was cradling in his hands, as he might a dove.

"Evidently not," Wells replied disdainfully.

Clayton folded Murray's letter, and, instead of giving it back to Wells, he slipped it inside his jacket pocket, a gesture that for Wells transformed it into an incontrovertible piece of evidence that absolved him of all guilt.

"Naturally this letter provides us with another possible explanation to consider," said Clayton, in an amiable yet guarded manner.

Another! Wells bridled. How many more could there be? "Forgive me, Inspector," he said, "but I am at a loss as to how any other explanation could be as simple and logical as the conclusive evidence of that letter."

The young man smiled. "Quite so, Mr. Wells. However, I was trained to consider every avenue, without being restricted by logic or simplicity, concepts which are, moreover, subjective and overrated. My job is not to whittle down the possibilities, but rather to increase them. And that is why I refuse to ascribe the adjective 'conclusive' to any fact. The letter's existence opens in my mind a host of fresh alternatives: you may have written it yourself, for example, to hamper the investigation and point the finger at a dead man."

"B-but then," stammered the astonished Wells, "am I to understand that the preposterous notion that I predicted a Martian invasion one year in advance, down to the very last detail, is in your view still worthy of consideration? Do you think I have some connection to the Martians, that my novel was a kind of premonition rather than a product of my imagination? Do you think I am their typist, or their messenger?"

"Calm down, Mr. Wells, there is no need to upset yourself," the inspector insisted. "Nobody is accusing you of anything. We are simply two gentlemen having an informal discussion, are we not? And during the course of this interesting conversation I am communicating to you my tedious working methods. That is all."

"The fact that you feel it necessary to reassure me about this hypothetical accusation only strengthens my anxiety, I can assure you."

Clayton chuckled softly.

"All the same, allow me to insist that you have no reason to worry. I am not taking you in for questioning, much less arresting you. Not for the moment, anyway," he added, gazing at Wells with an intensity that belied for an instant his mild, friendly manner. "I have simply requested that you accompany me to Woking in the hope that your presence there might help shed light on a mystery, which, for the time being, implicates you because of a connection to your novel. And you have been kind enough to accept, for which I am infinitely grateful."

"Everything you say is true, Inspector; however, I feel I must emphasize that *I have already been of assistance* by handing over to you a letter that, in my opinion, clears up any mystery surrounding this tiresome affair," Wells reiterated, unable to prevent a tone of sarcasm from entering his voice.

"Let us hope you are right, Mr. Wells. If so, we shall both be home in time for supper, and you will have an amusing story with which to regale your charming wife."

With those words, Clayton became absorbed in contemplating the scenery, bringing the conversation to a close. Wells gave a sigh of resignation and did the same. For a few moments both men pretended they had an inordinate interest in studying the monotonous English countryside filing past the windows, until the silence became unbearable for Wells.

"Tell me, Inspector Clayton, what cases does Special Branch at Scotland Yard deal with?"

"I'm afraid I can't give you any details about that, Mr. Wells," the young man replied respectfully, his eyes still glued to the landscape outside.

"Oh, don't get me wrong, Inspector. I'm not suggesting you disclose the contents of any secret files or anything. In fact, I know more than you think about the kind of information our country's rulers conceal from their citizens," Wells said, unable to resist showering the inspector with some of the mounting indignation he had been feeling since his visit to the Chamber of Marvels.

As though prey to a sudden spasm, the inspector turned his eyes from the window and fixed them on Wells.

"What are you trying to insinuate, Mr. Wells?"

"Nothing, Inspector," Wells replied, backing down, daunted by the young man's penetrating gaze. "I am merely curious about the kinds of cases your division deals with. As a writer I am in the habit of gathering information for future novels. It is something I do almost automatically."

"I see," the other man replied skeptically.

"Good, then can you not even tell me what kind of cases you investigate? Murders, political crime, espionage? The comings and goings of Martians on our planet?" Wells said with a forced smile.

The inspector reflected for a few moments, gazing back at the scenery. Then he turned to Wells, his lips set in that distinctive scowl conveying an impression of smugness, which whether deliberate or not, was beginning to get on the author's nerves.

"Let's say we deal with cases that at first sight defy any rational explanation, as it were," the inspector finally conceded. "Everything that Man, and consequently Scotland Yard, cannot explain using reason, is passed on to Special Branch. You could say, Mr. Wells, that we are the dumping ground for all things inconceivable."

The author shook his head, feigning surprise. Was it true, then? he wondered. Was everything he had seen in the Chamber of Marvels real?

"But," the inspector added, "our work usually produces more evidence of the criminal imagination than of the unexpected. Almost every mystery has a simple explanation that would disappoint you as much as discovering the rabbit hidden in the lining of a conjurer's hat."

"So," concluded Wells, "your job is to sift through the world's illusions, to separate fact from fantasy."

The inspector smiled. "That is an elegant way of describing it, worthy of a writer of your stature."

"But what of the other cases?" Wells asked, brushing aside the compliment. "Those that continue to defy logical explanation after being analyzed by your *remarkable* minds?"

Clayton leaned back in his seat and observed with compassion the author's attempt to reach the heart of the matter.

"Well . . ." The inspector paused for a few moments before continuing. "Let's say such cases force us to accept the impossible, to believe that magic really exists."

"And yet such cases never leak out to the public, do they? No one ever finds out about them, they go unreported," Wells said, biting his tongue in order not to divulge what he knew, even as he tried to stifle the intense irritation he always felt when anyone underestimated his intelligence, or his knowledge.

"Understand that the majority of cases are never closed, Mr. Wells. Future generations will continue to investigate them long after you and I have become fodder for the worms. And I am convinced they will find logical and natural explanations to many of those that appear to us, shall we say . . . supernatural. Have you never thought of magic as a branch of science we have yet to discover or understand? I have. So, why alarm people with fears of the unknown, when many of these mysteries will be solved by the knowledge that lies beyond the mists of time?"

"I can see that you regard the public as a child to be protected at all costs from the monsters lurking in the darkness, in the hope that he will grow up and stop believing in them," Wells responded irately.

"Or in the hope that a light we don't yet possess will illuminate the darkness concealing those potential horrors, which if he knew about them would undoubtedly terrify him," said Clayton, "by way of extending your excellent metaphor, Mr. Wells."

"Perhaps you should stop treating people like children and recognize that there are those of us who would like to decide for ourselves what we wish and do not wish to know, Inspector Clayton!" Wells declared angrily, fed up with the young man's tone.

"Mmmmm. That would make an interesting subject for debate, Mr. Wells," Clayton replied calmly. "However, allow me to remind you that I am a humble inspector following orders, and naturally I take no part in my division's or the government's policy decisions regarding the information they make public. My job is to investigate cases, and in this one in particular, I intend to find out what is behind the appearance of a cylinder, which you described one year ago as coming from Mars. That is all."

"Am I mistaken, then, in thinking that you have some proof of the existence of Martians, and that this isn't the first time they have visited our planet?" Wells pounced, feeling a twinge of satisfaction when he saw that his remark had ruffled the inspector for the first time.

"What makes you think that?" said Clayton, looking at Wells mistrustfully.

"Simple logic, Inspector Clayton," the author replied, emulating the young man's smug grin. "Something must have happened to prove the existence of Martians, otherwise the discovery of a cylinder like the one in my novel, planted in exactly the same place I described, would have been viewed as no more than a childish prank, and not a reason to call in your division. Am I right?"

Clayton let out an amused chuckle, as though relieved by the author's reply.

"Without doubt you'd make an excellent detective, Mr. Wells. If I weren't such a fan of your novels, I would go so far as to suggest you'd chosen the wrong vocation." He smiled. "But I fear there is no need for the kind of event you are suggesting. I'm sure that as the author of *The War of the Worlds* you understand better than anyone how conceited as well as illogical it would be to assume that we are the sole inhabitants of this vast universe, isn't that so?"

Wells nodded resentfully. Clearly he would get no more information out of that insolent young man without admitting he had been inside the Chamber of Marvels and had therefore seen, and even touched, the Martian they had hidden in there, as well as the machine in which it had apparently flown through the blackness of space. But that was something he preferred to keep quiet about for the time being, lest he provide the inspector with a reason to arrest him: he had trespassed on private property, not to mention breaking a supposedly valuable object belonging to the museum, or to the government or to Scotland Yard, or whoever owned that astonishing assortment of miracles—or were they forgeries? Wells no longer knew what to think. Making an enemy of the inspector was not the most intelligent thing to do, Wells told himself. He had no idea what nonsense Murray had dreamed up, and how it might affect him, so it was better to have the law on his side just in case.

"Forgive me for prying, Inspector, it was unforgivably rude of me," he apologized. "I understand perfectly that you aren't at liberty to discuss your work, let alone with a stranger. I can only defend myself by saying that the reason for my curiosity is that I find your occupation fascinating. Even though I fear it is a dangerous one," Wells said, gesturing toward the inspector's artificial hand. "Or did you lose it carving the turkey?"

Clayton gave a rueful smile as he gazed down at the metal appendage poking out of his sleeve.

"You are right, Mr. Wells," the inspector avowed. "I lost it on a . . . mission."

"I hope it was worth it," Wells commiserated.

"Let's say it was decisive," the inspector replied, reluctant to expand.

Wells nodded, signaling that he was not going to interrogate him any further on the subject.

"It seems an exquisite piece of equipment," he limited himself to responding.

"Yes, it is." Clayton smiled, with visible pride, moving it toward Wells so he could inspect it more closely. "The work of a surgeon and a French master gunsmith."

Feigning a greater interest than he in fact had, Wells cradled the prosthesis in his hands, as he might a holy relic. The young man acquiesced and explained to Wells that it could be unscrewed, allowing him to attach an assortment of gadgets whose functions ranged from eating through to killing. Wells recalled his uncle Williams, who had lost his right arm and would attach a hook to his stump, happily using it in place of a fork at mealtimes. But Clayton's elaborate prosthesis made his uncle's seem like the handiwork of a schoolboy. When Wells had finished his desultory inspection, he pulled his hands away, and silence descended once more in the carriage as the two men resumed their contemplation of the scenery.

"It's ludicrous of you to suspect me of having some connection to the Martians simply because I wrote a novel announcing their invasion!" Wells suddenly declared, as if to himself.

The author's outburst made the inspector jump.

"As ludicrous as someone re-creating a Martian invasion to win a woman's heart?" he retorted with a grin.

"Well, we shall soon find out," Wells murmured, shrugging.

Clayton nodded and went back to gazing at the landscape, bringing the conversation to a close. But presently, he gave a little cough, and to Wells's astonishment, declared, "Incidentally, did I tell you I am a huge fan of your work? I've read all your novels with great pleasure."

Wells nodded coldly. He was in no mood just then to be forced into polite acknowledgments of his admirer's praise.

"I dabble a little myself, you know," Clayton went on to say, with the overweening modesty of the beginner. He gave another little cough before adding: "Might I send you one of my manuscripts so that you can give me your opinion? It would mean a lot to me."

"Certainly, Inspector Clayton, I'd be delighted. Send it to my residence on Mars," Wells replied, focusing his gaze on the landscape framed by the window.

XXI

FTER A FEW MORE MILES SPENT IN SILENCE, the carriage reached Horsell Common. Once they had crossed the bridge at Ottershaw that led to the sand quarries, they had begun to encounter groups of curious folk who had come from Woking or Chertsey to see the same thing. However, once they reached the Martian cylinder's supposed landing site, that trickle of people turned into a tidal wave. Peeking through the window, Wells could see for himself that it was complete mayhem out there. The common was teeming with people, and here and there, lads were vending newspapers hot off the press, announcing with shrill cries a host of headlines voicing Man's doubts and speculations about the object that had appeared on Horsell Common: "Are we under invasion from Mars? Strange machines in Woking. Fantasy becomes fact. We are not alone! Is H. G. Wells a Martian?" They came to a halt next to a dozen other coaches and cabriolets parked at the edge of the common, among which Wells could not help noticing an exceptionally fine-looking carriage. He and Clayton stepped out of the vehicle and made their way through the throng of cyclists, apple barrows, and ginger beer stands, toward a plume of smoke that denoted the cylinder's position. As they drew near, Wells and Clayton could see that the machine was half buried in the sand. The impact of the missile had made a vast crater in the ground, flinging sand and gravel in every direction and setting alight the adjacent heather, which was still smoldering and sending wispy threads of smoke into the midday sky. They elbowed their way through the sea of spectators until they reached the front, where Wells was able to confirm that Murray had indeed done an excellent job. The so-called Martian cylinder was nearly identical to the one he had described in *The War of the Worlds*. A few boys near the edge of the pit were tossing stones at it. People had reacted just as he had predicted, creating a picnic atmosphere around the lethal machine. Some were having their photograph taken with the cylinder in the background like a monument.

As though reading Wells's mind, Clayton gestured toward the scene, arms outspread, and said, "You will agree that it is like being in your novel."

"Indeed, it is a perfect reconstruction," Wells avowed with admiration. "Murray is the world's greatest charlatan."

"Doubtless he is, Mr. Wells, doubtless he is. Why, he even managed to conjure up identical weather: warm and without any breeze," Clayton declared sarcastically. Then he took out his pocket watch and added, with mock disappointment, "He hasn't managed to make our watches stop, though, and I seem to recall in your novel they did, and that all the compasses pointed to where the cylinder had landed."

"I would take that part out if I could write it again . . . ," Wells murmured absentmindedly.

His gaze had been drawn to a well-dressed young woman, who was observing the cylinder at one remove from the crowd. Like a widow's veil, the frill on her parasol obscured part of her face, yet as she appeared to be the only wealthy-looking young lady there, Wells assumed she must be the woman Murray loved, who had probably traveled there in the luxurious carriage he had seen earlier. His suspicions were confirmed when he saw her begin nervously twirling her parasol. So, she really did exist. Murray had not made her up, however idealized Wells considered Murray's portrait of her in his letter. Wells watched her closely while she gazed at the cylinder, her solemn expression in stark contrast to the relaxed gaiety of the others gathered there. And he could not help pitying her, for the girl would have to marry the millionaire if Murray succeeded in making a Martian emerge from the iron cylinder he had dragged there. That meant Murray must be there, Wells thought, perhaps mingling with the crowd, delighting in all the excitement he had created with his toy. Clayton went over to talk to the chief of police, who was trying to prevent the onlookers from getting too close to the pit. Wells took the opportunity to glance fleetingly at the noisy crowd, but Murray was nowhere to be seen. Might he have drastically changed his appearance so as not to be recognized? Wells wondered.

He took out his pocket watch and looked at the time. At that very moment, Jane was probably boarding the train to London, where she would be lunching with the Garfields. Before the inspector took him off, Wells had left a note for her in the kitchen, in which he explained briefly the situation but urged her not to change her plans, because his whole morning would doubtless be taken up with the affair. In all likelihood, she would arrive back from London at about the same time as he, for it would not be long before Murray executed his next move: making a Martian jump out of the cylinder, or whatever his plan was, and at last everyone would see that the whole thing had been a practical joke. Clayton would apologize for his preposterous suspicions, and Wells would be free to go back to Worcester Park and carry on with his life, at least until Murray attempted a reenactment of his novel *The Invisible Man*.

After speaking with the police chief, Clayton elbowed his way impatiently through the crowd to rejoin Wells.

"Several companies of soldiers are on their way, Mr. Wells," he informed the author. "In less than an hour they will have surrounded the cylinder. The Royal Welch Fusiliers are being deployed from Aldershot. And another company will take charge of evacuating Horsell, just to be on the safe side. They are also expecting some Maxim guns. As you see, your novel serves as an excellent source for staying ahead of events."

Wells gave a weary sigh. "I don't think it is necessary in this case to call in the army," he retorted.

Clayton looked at him, amused.

"You still think this is Gilliam Murray's doing, don't you."

"Naturally, Inspector."

"Then he must have spent a small fortune on his wooing, for Captain Weisser has heard rumors of other cylinders falling on a golf course in Byfleet, and in the vicinity of Sevenoaks."

"Falling, you say? Does he know of any sightings of them falling from the sky? Don't you think the observatories would have noticed a thing like that?" Wells asked disdainfully.

"He didn't mention any." Clayton scowled.

"In that case, someone could have placed them there, as one might a chess piece, don't you think?"

The inspector was about to respond when something caught his eye.

"What the devil is that?" he exclaimed, staring over Wells's shoulder.

The author turned toward the cylinder and glimpsed the reason for the inspector's surprise. A sort of metal tentacle had emerged from inside and was swaying in the air, rising up like a cobra. Attached to the end of it was a strange object resembling a periscope, but which might also have been some kind of weapon. Clayton reacted without hesitation.

"Help me make these fools move back! Apparently none of them have read your novel."

Wells shook his head.

"Calm down, Clayton!" he insisted, grabbing the inspector's arm. "I assure you nothing is going to happen. Believe me, this is all a sham. Murray is simply trying to frighten us. And if he succeeds . . ."

Clayton did not reply. His gaze was fixed on the tentacle's mesmeric movement.

"The whole thing is a sham, do you hear!" Wells repeated, shaking the inspector. "That thing isn't going to fire any heat rays."

At that moment, the tentacle wobbled slightly, as though taking aim, and a moment later a heat ray burst forth from its tip with a deafening hiss. Then, what looked like a jet of molten lava struck the band of on-lookers gathered round the pit, hitting four or five them, who burst into flames before they knew what was happening. The deflagration lasted only a few seconds. Then someone seemed to pull back the blanket of fire covering them, to reveal a handful of distorted, charred figures that instantly crumbled, scattering gently over the grass. Fear struck; the crowd observed the horrific scene and then in unison turned toward the tentacle, which was preparing to take aim anew. The response was instantaneous. People began fleeing from the pit in all directions.

Unable to comprehend how Murray could possibly have given the order to fire on innocent bystanders, Wells ran for cover toward a patch of trees a few hundred yards away. Clayton, who was running beside him, shouted to him to run in a zigzag so as not to make an easy target for the tentacle. Jostled on all sides by the terror-stricken crowd, Wells tried to do as the inspector suggested, even as he felt fear seeping into his entrails like ice-cold water. Then came another hiss, and immediately afterward a second ray hit the ground five yards to his left, hurling several people into the air. Before Wells could shield himself, a clod of earth struck him in the face, dazing him enough to make him almost lose his footing. He was forced to stop his frantic dash and glance about, trying to orient himself. When the smoke had cleared, he contemplated with horror the string of cindered corpses sprawled across the grass a few yards away. Behind them he glimpsed the woman whom he had identified as Murray's beloved. The ray had narrowly missed her, but the accompanying blast had knocked her to the ground, and she was kneeling on the grass, too shaken to give her legs the order to stand up. The tentacle swayed once more in the air, choosing a fresh target, and Wells took the opportunity of the moment's calm between blasts to hurry to the young woman's aid. Avoiding the burnt remains and the hollows in the ground, he managed to reach her side and grabbed her by the arms so as to lift her to her feet. The girl allowed this without putting up any resistance.

"I didn't want . . . I told him it was enough to . . . ," she gasped, seized by a fit of panic.

"I know, miss," Wells reassured her. "But what matters now is to get away from here."

As they stumbled toward the trees, the sound of the tentacle firing indiscriminately at the terrified crowd resounded in their ears. Wells could not resist looking back over his shoulder. He watched with horror as several rays cut through the air, striking the parked carriages at the edge of the common, creating a vision of Hell from which a pair of horses emerged, enveloped in flames. The condemned animals, wreathed with golden streamers by death, careened wildly over the grass, imbuing the nightmarish scene with an eerie poetry. Just as in his novel, the ray swept over the countryside swiftly and brutally, doling out death, destroying everything in its path with a cold disregard. He saw trees burnt to a crisp, smoldering gashes in the earth, women and men fleeing terrified, and upturned carts, and he understood that the much-heralded Day of Judgment had arrived. How could Murray . . . ? But his mind was unable to finish forming the question, for a few yards to their right a ray landed suddenly, sending them flying across the grass. Stunned, his ears ringing and his skin burning as though he had been scorched by a dragon's breath, Wells looked around for the girl and was relieved to find her sprawled beside him. Her eyes were shut tight, though she was apparently uninjured. But the longer they stayed on the ground, the more likely they were to be hit by another ray or crushed by the panic-stricken crowd. He took a deep breath and was steeling himself to get up and resume their desperate flight when he heard the inspector's voice.

"The ray has wiped out all the carriages!" Clayton shouted as he approached. "We must make our way across the fields. Come!"

Wells helped the girl to her feet, and the two of them followed the inspector. Yet Clayton did not seem to know where to take cover either, given that nowhere was safe from the rays. After pushing their way with difficulty through the terrified crowd, Clayton decided to halt for a moment to assess the situation. They had managed to break away from the mass of onlookers but were still trapped inside the rectangle marked out by flames where the slaughter was taking place. One side of that improvised cage of fire was formed by the houses stretching toward Woking Station, which were now blazing like a funeral pyre, and another by the row of trees bordering the road, which had also been transformed into a glowing curtain. The only way out was straight ahead, over the neighboring fields toward Maybury, but that would make them a tempting target for the tentacle. Before they had time to make up their minds, they saw emerging from behind the trees a luxurious carriage with an ornate "G" painted on the door. They watched in disbelief as the carriage hurtled toward them, wondering who but a madman would drive toward that carnage. Astonished, they saw a huge man stretch his out hand to the girl.

"Come with me, if you want to live!" the man cried.

But the girl stood motionless, unable to comprehend what was happening. Without thinking, Clayton shoved her into the carriage then clambered in after her. Wells followed, flinging himself inside just as the crash of another heat ray resounded behind them. A fountain of stones and sand sprayed the carriage, shattering its windows. Wells, who was the last to get in, had served as an involuntarily parapet, his back sprayed with broken glass. When the effects of the blast had died away, the author struggled to get up as best he could, disentangling himself from the heap his companions had formed on the floor. They, too, had begun hauling themselves up, wondering perhaps whether they were alive or dead. Through what remained of the window, Wells could make out the hole the ray had made in the ground, alarmingly close to the carriage, which at that very instant began racing off once more. Wells, like the others, slumped back onto the seat, relieved the driver had not been hit by any flying debris. He could hear the whip cracking furiously across the horses' flanks, straining to get them out of there. It was then that he recognized the man who had rescued them, who was sitting right opposite him. Wells gazed at him dumbfounded. He was remarkably slimmer, but there was no mistaking him. The Master of Time himself.

"George," Murray said, bobbing his head slightly and giving the forced smile of someone who has bumped into his enemy at a party.

"You damned son of a bitch!" Wells cried, hurling himself at the millionaire and attempting to throttle him. "How dare you!"

"It wasn't me, George," Murray said, defending himself. "This is not my doing!"

"What the devil is this about?" Clayton cried, trying to come between the two men.

"Don't you recognize him?" the author declared, breathless. "It's Gilliam Murray!"

"Gilliam Murray?" stammered the girl, who was looking on in horror at the impromptu brawl from a corner of the carriage.

"I can explain, Emma," Murray blurted out apologetically.

"You have a great many things to explain, you damned fool!" Wells growled, struggling to free himself from Clayton's grip.

"Calm down, Mr. Wells," the inspector commanded, removing his pistol from his belt and trying to point it at the author, who, owing to the lack of room inside the carriage, found himself with a gun inches from his nose. "And be so good as to return to your seat."

Reluctantly, Wells obeyed.

"Good, now let's all stay calm," said Clayton, who also sat down and tried to keep control of the situation by speaking in a measured voice. "I am Inspector Cornelius Clayton of Scotland Yard." He turned to Murray and gave him a polite smile. "And you, I assume, are Gilliam Murray, the Master of Time. Although you have been officially dead for two years."

"Yes, I am he," Murray replied, irate. "As you can see, I've risen from the grave."

"Well, we can discuss that another time," Clayton remarked coldly, trying to sit up straight despite being thrown about by the swaying carriage. "There's a more pressing question that needs answering now. Tell me: are you behind all this?"

"Of course not!" the millionaire replied. "I'm no murderer!"

"Good, good. Yet it so happens that I am in possession of a letter from you addressed to Mr. Wells, here on my left, where you explain to him that you have to re-create the Martian invasion in his novel, today no less, in order to win the heart of the woman you love, whom I assume must be you, Miss . . ."

"Harlow," the girl replied in a faint voice. "My name is Emma Harlow."

"Pleased to meet you, Miss Harlow," said Clayton, smiling graciously and doffing his hat before readdressing the millionaire. "Well, Mr. Murray, are you the author of that letter?"

"Yes, damn it!" Murray confessed. "And everything in it is true. I asked for Mr. Wells's help, but he refused to reply, as he himself will confirm. I persisted in trying to re-create the invasion on my own, but after failing to come up with anything credible, I gave up. I only came here today because I read in the newspaper that someone else had pulled it off."

"Do you really expect us to believe that people have nothing better to do than try to reenact the invasion in my novel!" Wells interrupted angrily.

"Please be quiet, Mr. Wells," Clayton said. "Or I shall have no choice but to knock you unconscious."

Wells stared at the inspector in amazement.

"How could I do anything that would put Miss Harlow's life in danger?" Murray exclaimed.

"So that you could come to her rescue, I imagine, as you just did," Wells retorted. "Who knows what a warped mind such as yours is capable of thinking up."

"I would never put Miss Harlow's life in danger!" Murray declared angrily.

Clayton appealed for calm once more, raising his artificial hand.

"Quite so," he said, "but in the meantime, until we discover what is in that cylinder, I'm afraid, Mr. Murray, you are under arrest. And that goes for you too, Mr. Wells."

"What!" protested the author.

"I'm sorry, gentlemen, but the situation is as follows: A strange machine is killing dozens of people just as you described in your novel a year ago, Mr. Wells. And you, Mr. Murray, are the author of a letter professing that you intend to reenact the invasion described by Mr. Wells. Regardless of what is actually going on, one or other of you has some explaining to do." He paused, giving the two men time to assimilate what he had just said. "Now, Mr. Murray, order your driver to take us to Woking Station, please. I need to send a telegram to my superiors."

Reluctantly, Murray drew back the hatch in the roof and gave the command.

"Excellent," declared Clayton. "I shall inform them as soon as we arrive that I have detained the two main suspects. And I am sure the young lady will wish to telegraph her family to assure them she is safe and sound. And that she could not be in better hands," Clayton added, giving Emma what was meant to be a winning smile, but which to the others appeared more sinister than anything else. No one broke the silence that descended on the carriage as it passed alongside the Maybury viaduct, then left behind the row of houses known as Oriental Terrace as it clattered toward Woking Station, while only a few miles away, Martians were preparing their invasion of the planet.

XXII

When they reached Woking Station,
Wells and his companions were astonished to discover everything carrying on as normal in the station. People came and went, apparently unflustered, while the trains were shunted around like beasts of burden. Fascinated, they watched how a train arrived from the north, emptied its passengers onto the platform, and then picked up others and continued on its way, as though nothing untoward was happening nearby. Only a faint red glow lit up the horizon, and a thin veil of smoke shrouded the sky. It was the horror of war, which from a distance gave the impression of an exquisitely decorative display. If news of the slaughter they had survived had reached Woking, no one there seemed unduly alarmed by it. No doubt they believed in the might of the British army, which was advancing toward the cylinders with great military strides, ready to defeat the Martians, or whatever they were, in a matter of hours, the same way they had always done when an enemy dared threaten the Empire.

"So far, the panic doesn't seem to have spread here," Clayton observed, glancing about. "Just as well: that means we need only concern ourselves with our plan."

Pointing his pistol discreetly at Wells and Murray, Clayton ushered them to the stationmaster's office, where he introduced himself, gave the stationmaster a prompt and in no way alarming account of the situation, and persuaded the man to let him lock the suspects up in one of the station's storerooms.

"Try to behave like gentlemen," Clayton appealed to Wells and Murray before shutting them in and leaving with Miss Harlow to telegraph his superiors.

The two men were obliged to remain on their feet in the center of the tiny room crammed with boxes, provisions, and tools, but which contained nothing they could sit on while they waited. In the moments that followed, they were content to simply eye each other in mistrust.

"I'm not responsible for the invasion, George," Murray said at last, in an almost pleading tone. Wells was not sure whether this was an attempt to strike up a conversation or he'd spoken because it tormented him not to be able to prove his innocence.

Whatever the reason, the author continued to glare at Murray, exasperated that circumstances obliged him to communicate with the man. Although Wells had dreamed that Fate would provide him with an opportunity to unleash his anger on Murray, time had dampened his anger, burying it beneath a layer of contempt, with the result that it had lost some of its urgency. It was too late to rake it all up now, especially considering the alarming situation they found themselves in, which demanded they put aside personal grievances. And so Wells set himself to focus on the present, to discover who was behind it all.

"Are you suggesting we believe that this is a genuine Martian invasion?" he inquired coldly.

Murray gave a worried groan.

"I've no idea what we should believe, George," exclaimed the millionaire, who in his agitated state tried to pace round in circles, something the confined space would not allow. "This can't be happening!"

"Well, Gilliam, *it is happening*. The invasion I described in my novel is taking place exactly as you intended. Let me remind you there is a letter signed by you, in which you plead with me to help you carry it out," Wells retorted, not pulling any punches.

"But in that letter did I say anything about killing hundreds of people?" the millionaire groaned. "Of course not, George! All I wanted was to build a cylinder from which that accursed overdeveloped octopus of yours would emerge and make headlines to win the heart of the most beautiful woman in the world! You must believe me, George! I would never do anything to hurt Emma! Never!" And with that, Murray brought his fist crashing down on one of the boxes, causing the wood to splinter in various places and making Wells wonder whether provoking Murray was the best approach at that moment. Fortunately, venting his frustration appeared to calm the millionaire, who placed both hands on the shattered box, sank his head to his chest, and whispered, "I love her, George, I love her more than my own life."

Wells shifted awkwardly on his feet, to the extent a room as narrow as a coffin would allow. Here he was, locked in this room with Murray, listening to him speak about love in such childish terms, while outside someone, or something, was killing innocent people, using his novel as a blueprint. And then, contemplating with faint embarrassment the bleating millionaire's ridiculous ode to love, Wells realized he could not go on denying the obvious: much as his hatred of the man compelled Wells to hold him responsible, Murray had nothing to do with the invasion. The fact that the tentacle had fired so nonchalantly on the onlookers, and particularly on the girl he intended to marry, almost incontrovertibly proved his innocence. And to Wells's astonishment, a wave of pity swept over him, something he would have never believed he could feel toward the man he had diligently devoted himself to loathing for the past two years. Pity! And for Gilliam Murray! For the giant fellow next to him, struggling not to burst into tears, who must not only defend himself against a false accusation but who would at some point have to admit to the woman he adored that he had failed, that he was unworthy of her love. And as if that were not dreadful enough, Emma almost certainly held him entirely to blame for the fact that she was fleeing for her life, far from home, along with a smart-aleck investigator and an author of fantasy novels, who it so happened had written *The War of the Worlds*. Yes, it was only logical he should feel pity for Murray. But also for the girl, he thought. And even for himself. But more than anything because he was unable to feel more than a conventional concern for Jane's well-being.

Jane, his Jane. Was she in danger? He had no idea, and for the time being he preferred to imagine her safe and sound in London with the Garfields, who, if news of events in Horsell had reached the city, were undoubtedly cheering her up at that very moment, assuring her that he was all right. He gave a sigh. He must not torment himself with these thoughts. His life was in peril, and if anything he must focus his efforts on discovering what the devil was going on and on finding a way to stay alive as long as possible, at least until it became clear whether the entire human race was going to perish and surviving would be the worst thing that could happen to him.

"Very well, Gilliam," he said, carefully adopting a gentle tone. "Let's accept that the invasion has nothing to do with you. Who is behind it, then? Germany?"

The millionaire gazed at him in astonishment.

"Germany? Possibly . . . ," he said at last, trying to collect his thoughts and give his voice a firm sound. "Although I think it unlikely that any country has a sophisticated enough technology to produce the lethal ray that almost killed us."

"Really? I don't see why such a thing couldn't have been carried out in secret," Wells proposed.

"Perhaps you're right," replied the millionaire, who appeared to have regained some of his composure. "What is certain, George, is that those behind the attack are copying your novel."

Yes, that much was certain, the author acknowledged to himself. The location of the cylinders, their appearance, the heat ray . . . Everything was happening almost exactly as he had described. Accordingly, the next phase would be the construction of flying machines shaped like stingrays that soared across the counties on their way to London, ready to raze it to the ground. Perhaps at that very moment, in the deserted meadows of Horsell Common, strewn with charred corpses and smoldering trees, the relentless hammering sound of their construction was echoing in the silence. But, in the meantime, there was no way of knowing who was behind all this. And given that as yet no Martian had popped its gelatinous head out of the cylinder, the only thing they could be sure of was that these machines were deadly, and that anyone could be operating them, or no one, he thought, wondering whether they might be activated from a distance, via some kind of signal. Anything was possible. Wells then realized with surprise that he felt no fear, although he suspected his sudden display of pluck was because he still did not know exactly what it was they ought to be afraid of. The test would be if he managed to stay calm when the attackers made their next move and things began to make sense; only then would he discover whether at heart he was a hero or a coward.

Just then, the two men heard a loud clamor outside. They looked up toward the tiny storeroom window, straining to determine the cause of the row, but were unable to make out what the voices were saying. They could only conclude that some unrest had now broken out in the station, hitherto immersed in an unnerving calm. People seemed to be running hither and thither, and, although their cries did not yet sound panic-stricken, something strange was definitely going on. Wells and Murray exchanged solemn glances. During the next few minutes, the din appeared to intensify: they heard doors slamming, objects crashing to the floor, bundles being dragged along the ground, and occasionally someone barking an unintelligible order or uttering a frantic oath. The two men were starting to get nervous when the door to their temporary cell swung open and in walked Inspector Clayton and Miss Harlow with looks of unease on their faces, which did not bode well.

"I'm glad to see you are both still in one piece, gentlemen," the inspector said with a sardonic grin as he closed the door hurriedly behind him. "Well then, I bring both good and bad news."

The two men looked at him expectantly.

"The good news is that whoever is doing this isn't as keen on your novel as we had thought, Mr. Wells," Clayton announced, scrutinizing Wells with exaggerated curiosity. "It seems the Martians haven't built flying machines shaped like stingrays with which to attack us from the skies. I recall that in your novel they were propelled by magnetic currents that affected the Earth's surface . . ."

"Yes, yes, please go on," Wells said.

"Well, it was an ingenious idea in any case, truly ingenious," the inspector mumbled as if to himself before resuming in a matter-of-fact voice: "But apparently as yet unrealized, for the would-be Martians are traveling on foot."

"On foot?" said the author, perplexed.

"That's right. According to my information, the accursed things have sprouted legs. Yes, spindly birdlike legs about twenty yards long. And as they move along crushing pine trees, barns, anything in their path, they keep on firing lethal rays at the terror-struck crowds." The inspector punctuated his speech with exasperating pauses that left them all on tenterhooks. Wells realized that while he was informing them, Clayton was also attempting to assimilate his own words. "Perhaps the similarities between the beginning of your novel and the initial invasion are a coincidence, I don't know." He paused abruptly once more, his lips twitching as though keeping time with his thoughts, then went on: "The fact is, things have begun happening differently than in your novel, Mr. Wells, and that casts some doubt on your involvement."

"I'm pleased to hear it, Inspector Clayton," Wells replied curtly.

"And the same goes for you, Mr. Murray," the inspector began, addressing the millionaire. "As I said, we have a proper invasion on our hands. There are tripods everywhere, and however wealthy you may be, I imagine such a thing is beyond even your means, not that winning Miss Harlow wouldn't be worth every penny," he said, beaming at Emma. "In any event, what I think doesn't count, and so for the moment I'm sorry to say you are still under arrest. My superiors are the ones giving the orders and they like to explore every avenue. All I can—"

"What about the bad news?" snapped Murray, who could not have cared less about Clayton's apologetic soliloquy.

The inspector looked at him inquiringly.

"The bad news? Ah, yes! The bad news is that the tripod from Horsell is coming toward us, wreaking havoc along the way," he said.

Wells and Murray exchanged anxious looks.

"And what are we to do?" inquired the millionaire.

The inspector raised his head suddenly, as though surfacing from underwater, and said, "Right. We'll go to London, to Scotland Yard headquarters. And not simply because I have to interrogate you there, but because, things being as they are, in a few hours' time London will undoubtedly be the safest place in England. My superiors have informed me that the army is cordoning off the city in readiness to fend off the invader. We have to reach London before they block all access. Staying outside the perimeter would be the most perilous thing we could do at present: several battalions are marching on the cylinders, and if we stay here we'll soon find ourselves caught in the crossfire."

"That sounds sensible," Wells said, suddenly remembering Jane.

"Sensible?" protested Murray. "You call heading toward the place the Martians intend to obliterate sensible, George?"

"Yes, Gilliam," replied the author. "If we head in the other direction, we'll probably—"

"I wasn't inviting you to debate the plan, gentlemen," Clayton interjected. "I was simply telling you what we're going to do, whether you like it or not."

"Well, I don't like it," Murray complained. "And neither I nor Miss Harlow is prepared to—"

A thunderous bolt rang out in the distance, causing the tiny storeroom to shudder.

"What the devil was that?" Murray exclaimed nervously.

"It was the heat ray," Wells said grimly, "and it sounded very close."

"My God!" cried the girl, shifting uneasily.

"Calm down, all of you," Clayton demanded. "As I already told Miss Harlow, you are in the best possible hands. I am Inspector Cornelius Lewis Clayton of Special Branch at Scotland Yard, and I'm trained to deal with this kind of situation."

"With a— Martian invasion?" the girl stammered.

"Strange though it may sound, yes," Clayton replied, without looking her in the eye. "An invasion of our planet by Martians or other extraterrestrials was always a possibility, and consequently my division is prepared for it."

The inspector's speech was punctuated by a fresh explosion, a deafening bang whose echo went on for several seconds before dying out. They looked at one another in alarm. It was even closer this time.

"Are you sure, Inspector?" the millionaire asked, a sardonic smile on his face.

"Certainly, Mr. Murray," Clayton replied solemnly.

"Aren't we perhaps jumping to conclusions when we refer to them as Martians?" Wells chimed in. "They could be machines designed by Germans, for example."

Ignoring Wells's remark, Clayton drifted off into another of those brooding daydreams to which he seemed so partial, this time studying the ceiling of the tiny storeroom.

A few seconds later, the inspector emerged from his meditations. "Here's what we'll do. We'll take the carriage and drive to London as swiftly and safely as possible. We'll do our best to travel inconspicuously and avoid any cylinders along the way—in the unlikely event we encounter any. We may need to camouflage the carriage, but we can see about that as we go along. An invasion takes longer than a few hours . . . yes, indeed," he said suddenly, as if to himself, and nodded vigorously. "It takes time to wipe out a planet. I wonder if the same thing is happening everywhere? Is this the destruction of our civilization? I expect we'll find out soon enough . . . In the meantime, they are here, in our country. The Martians have clearly understood the strategic importance of the British Isles. But we're ready for them, of course!" He turned to the others, giving a reassuring smile. "We mustn't give way to panic. The whole thing will be over before we even realize it. At this very moment our defense plan is being put into place in London. This area is outside my division's jurisdiction, but while you are with me you have absolutely nothing to fear. I shall get you to London safe and sound. You have my word."

And with that, the inspector rolled his eyes and collapsed in a heap on the floor. Startled, his three companions stared at one another, and then finally gazed with interest at Inspector Clayton's body curled up in a ball on the floor, wondering whether this was part of his plan.

"What the devil?" Murray exclaimed when he realized the inspector was out cold.

Murray made as if to give him a kick, but Wells preempted him, kneeling beside the inspector.

"He's alive," he told them, attempting to take Clayton's pulse.

"Then what's the matter with him?" the millionaire asked, bewildered. "Has he fallen asleep?"

"Clearly he has suffered some kind of fainting fit," Wells replied, remembering vaguely what Serviss had told him. "Perhaps he suffers from low blood pressure, or diabetes, although I'll wager—"

"In the best possible hands!" Murray cut across, raising his eyes to Heaven in despair. "For God's sake, one of them is made of metal!"

Wells stood up and looked with an air of disappointment at the inspector lying on the floor at their feet.

"What are we going to do now?" the girl asked Wells in a faint voice.

"I think we should stick to the plan of going to London," Wells proposed, eager to get there as soon as possible to look for Jane.

"I'm not taking Miss Harlow to London, George," the millionaire protested.

"If it's all the same to you, Mr. Gilmore, or Murray, or whatever your name is, I shall decide for myself where I want to go," the girl intervened coldly. "And I do want to go to London."

"What! But why, Emma?" Murray became frantic. "We may as well walk straight toward the gates of Hell!"

"Because things can only be done in the proper manner," Emma retorted. Apparently she had recovered the conceited self-assurance she displayed at home, and Murray found this unacceptable, given their current predicament, which seemed to have completely slipped the girl's mind. He was about to object, but Emma silenced him with an angry stare. "And for your information, Mr. Murray, seeing as you haven't deigned to ask, I happen to be staying in London—at my aunt Dorothy's house in Southwark, to be exact. And I left there this morning without telling a soul, because my intention was to witness your pathetic spectacle, to settle the tiresome and humiliating episode of your defeat, and arrive back in time for lunch without anyone having noticed my absence. However, that wasn't to be . . . ," she murmured, glancing about the storeroom with the bewildered look of someone having just woken from a deep sleep. But she instantly took hold of herself, continuing in a resolute voice. "If news of the invasion has reached London, my poor aunt, who must have realized by this time that I'm not in my room, will be in a dreadful flap, and so I must go put her mind at rest. And besides, my things are there, all my trunks containing my dresses, not to mention the two maids I brought with me from New York, whose well-being is my responsibility. Are you suggesting I flee with you to goodness knows where, with nothing more than the clothes on my back, and forget about everything else?"

"Listen to me, Emma," Murray said with undisguised exasperation, as though trying to drum sense into the head of a spoiled little girl, "we are being invaded by an army of alien machines intent upon killing us, and I'm afraid no one will care very much what you are wearing when they aim their heat rays at you. Don't you think that in a situation like this your baggage should be the least of your worries?"

"I am not *only* worried about my baggage! Did you hear a word I said, Mr. Murray?" Emma exclaimed, clenching her teeth angrily. "You are the most insufferable man I have ever met! I've just told you I have relatives here in London, and I wish to join them as soon as possible. Besides, my parents' reply to my telegram will be sent to my aunt's house, and they will want to know we are together and out of harm's way. I have *responsibilities,* don't you see? No, of course you don't. What can someone who stages his own death know of responsibilities, someone who by his actions deprives the world of what is undoubtedly the greatest discovery in the History of Mankind, the possibility of traveling to the future, out of pure selfishness, no doubt because he has enriched himself enough and wishes to enjoy his wealth in peace? And a man such as he, who thinks only of himself, dares to criticize me for worrying about my clothes? Do you really think I would place myself in your hands, Mr. Murray? Why, you are to blame for my being stuck in the middle of this chaos in the first place!"

"I am to blame?" the millionaire protested. "Let me remind you that you challenged me to re-create the Martian invasion in Mr. Wells's novel as a condition for marrying me, despite not loving me. Yet I love you, Emma. And I promise you that if I'd known something like this was going to happen, I would never have allowed you to travel to London. I only took up your challenge because it was a chance to make you happy, while your sole intention was to humiliate me! Which of us is more selfish?"

"I forbid you from calling me by my Christian name again, *Mr. Murray*!" the girl cried. Then she took several deep breaths to try to calm herself before adding in a serene but stinging voice: "And I'd like to make one thing perfectly clear before leaving for London, which is where I intend to go, given that both Mr. Wells and Inspector Clayton consider it the most sensible thing to do: not only are you the last person on Earth I would ever marry, you are also the last person with whom I would want to survive the destruction of this planet."

The young woman's words seemed to knock the wind out of Murray. His face grew dark, and for a moment he looked as if he might explode, but then he lowered his head, too abject to hold the angry gaze of the girl, whose eyes appeared capable of blasting him with a heat ray more powerful than any Martian machine.

"I understand, Miss Harlow," he murmured. "Then I suppose there is nothing more to say."

In spite of himself, Wells could not help giving the millionaire a pitying smile.

"Come on, Gilliam. Be sensible," he heard himself say cheerily. "Where else would we go, for the love of God?"

Still staring at his feet, Murray gave a sigh of resignation.

"Very well," he murmured. "We'll go to London."

Just then, a fresh explosion, closer than the previous ones, made the walls shudder, and a shower of plaster fell on them from the ceiling.

"Whatever our destination, the quicker we leave the station the better, don't you agree?" said the author, once the echo from the blast had died away.

"Yes, let's get out of here as quickly as possible," Murray concurred.

He made as if to leave, but the girl's voice stopped him in his tracks.

"What do we do with him?" he heard her say, pointing at the inspector's inert body.

"For Heaven's sake!" Murray exclaimed, at the end of his tether. "What do you expect us to do with him, Miss Harlow?"

"We can't leave him here," Wells interposed. "If that machine destroys the station, he'll be buried alive. We must take him with us."

"What?" the millionaire protested. "Have you lost your senses, George? He was planning to arrest us the moment we reached London."

"Do you want us to abandon him to his fate?" the author cried.

"Oh, no, Mr. Wells. Naturally Mr. Murray wouldn't dream of leaving him here. He isn't that selfish. Are you, Mr. Murray?"

The millionaire did not know how to respond and simply looked at her dumbfounded.

"I didn't think so," Wells jested, and, hoisting the inspector up by his armpits, he said to Murray: "Come on, Gilliam, don't sulk, take his feet and help me get him out of here."

IN THE STATION, THE peace that had reigned when they arrived had turned to violent chaos. As they had gleaned from the noises and shouts reaching them in their cell, people were rushing back and forth, or clustered together in bewildered groups into which a gradual panic was creeping. "The Martians are coming!" many of them cried, dragging their luggage from place to place, as if suddenly no refuge felt secure enough in the face of such a threat. The Martians are coming! They watched as a desperate tide of people tried to clamber aboard the only train standing in the station, clogging its doorways so that many could only get on by smashing the windows. Some tried to force their way through, brutally thrusting aside anyone blocking their way, even women and children, some of whom fell onto the tracks. Looked at from the calm of the platform, that chaos offered a spectacle at once shocking and fascinating, a display of barbarism that illustrated perfectly how fear can destroy people's reason, reducing them to simple animals driven only by a selfish will to survive.

"Let's get to my carriage," said Murray urgently.

They pushed their way through the crowd as best they could, the two men carrying the inspector's limp body and Emma clearing the way with her parasol when necessary, until they managed to leave the station. But once they reached the area reserved for waiting vehicles, they came across the same mayhem as inside. Murray's carriage, like all the others, was surrounded by a surging crowd that was struggling to commandeer it. They had just managed to knock the driver from his perch and were enthusiastically beating the poor wretch as he dragged himself across the ground. Wells took the opportunity of leaving Clayton in Murray's care a few yards from the carriage and helping the girl to climb aboard through the door farthest from the skirmish. But scarcely had Emma placed a foot on the running board when a man grabbed her arm and flung her callously to the ground. Without thinking, Wells seized hold of her aggressor's jacket, before realizing with unease that the man was much bigger than he.

"That's no way to treat a—"

A fist striking his face prevented him from finishing his sentence. Wells staggered and fell backward, landing close to the right-hand wheel. Half dazed by the blow, his mouth filled with blood, Wells watched from the ground as two burly men planted themselves in front of the carriage door, while the girl, scarcely a yard away, struggled to pull herself up.

Wells noticed that the two brutes, both the one who had knocked him down with a right hook and his companion, were wearing the uniform of station porters. Until only an hour ago, he reflected, the two men had been obsequiously carrying the luggage of customers like him, in the hope of receiving a tip that would pay for their supper. But the Martians had created a new order in which blunt force prevailed. If the invasion flourished, it would be men like these who would flaunt their power and possibly even decide the fate of others. With no clear idea how to help the girl or make off with the carriage, Wells spat out a gob of blood and leaned on the wheel to hoist himself up, much to the amusement of the fellow who had knocked him down.

"Haven't you had enough?" he yelled, turning toward Wells and raising his fist in a threatening gesture. "Do you want some more?"

Naturally, Wells did not. However, he clenched both fists, squaring up ridiculously, prepared to return the blows as best he could. He could not back down now. Scarcely had he time to raise his fists when a shot rang out, startling the crowd encircling the carriage. All turned in the direction of the noise. Wells saw Murray, pointing Clayton's pistol into the air. The inspector was curled up next to the splayed-out legs of the millionaire, who, with an imperturbable smile, fired a second shot, which prompted the mob to step back from the carriage. Wells wondered what would become of the bullet, where it would land once the speed that propelled it skyward died out and it fell back to earth. After firing the shot, Murray slowly lowered his arm, like a snow-covered branch bowing under its load, and took aim at the crowd.

"That carriage belongs to me, gentlemen, and if any of you get near it, it'll be the last thing you do," he shouted, edging nimbly toward the band of men led by the two porters.

When he reached them, he offered the girl his hand, still brandishing the gun.

"Miss Harlow, allow me to help you," he said gallantly.

The girl appeared to hesitate, then finally stood up, leaning her weight on his hand. She stood behind Murray, shaking the mud from her dress as she glanced about in a dazed fashion. Still pointing the gun at the porters, Murray gestured to Wells and Miss Harlow to climb aboard.

"Hey, Gilliam . . . ," Wells whispered behind his back.

"What is it, George?"

"I think you've forgotten Inspector Clayton."

Without lowering his weapon, Murray glanced over his shoulder and saw the inspector's body lying on the ground where he had left it. He blurted out an oath between gritted teeth and turned his attention back to the group of thugs, who leered at him, and then once more to his companions, his gaze resting tentatively on the girl, who was still standing beside him, a bewildered expression on her face.

"Very well," he said, making a decision. Then, handing Emma the gun, he said softly, "Miss Harlow, would you be so kind as to hold these gentlemen at bay while Mr. Wells and I lift the inspector into the carriage? Forgive me for asking, but do you believe you can manage that?"

Emma gazed with puzzlement at the weapon Murray was holding out, and then peered at him. Murray gave her a smile as warm as it was encouraging. This instantly roused the girl's anger once more.

"Manage? Why of course, Mr. Murray," she snapped, grabbing the weapon with her slender hands. "I don't think it will be too difficult. You should try wearing a corset sometime."

As the weapon changed hands, the porter who had attacked the girl let out a howl of laughter and took a step forward. As the girl aimed the revolver at him he stopped in his tracks.

"I'm warning you, my friend, one more step and I'll do more than knock you to the ground," she declared fiercely.

"Oh, I'm quaking in my shoes," the porter mocked, turning to his band of men. "The little lady wants us to believe she can—"

However, he was unable to finish his sentence because Emma, with a sudden movement, lowered the gun and shot him in the foot. The bullet pierced the toe of his boot, a jet of blood spurting out. The porter fell to his knees cradling his foot, his face contorted with pain.

"You damned bitch!" he cried.

"Right," the girl said, addressing the others. "Next time I'll aim for the head."

Fascinated, Murray gazed at the girl, astonished at her pluck. Wells was obliged to tap him on the shoulder to remind him about Clayton. Between the two men, they heaved the inspector into the carriage. Then the millionaire approached the girl and asked her for the gun, with an admiring smile.

"Nice job, Miss Harlow," he congratulated her. "I hope you can forgive me for putting you in such a perilous situation."

"You're very kind, Mr. Murray," she replied sarcastically as she handed him the pistol. "However, I should point out that you were the one taking the risk by entrusting the weapon to me. I'm sure you believed those ruffians might wrest it from me."

"Oh, not for a moment." The millionaire grinned. "Remember, I've taken tea with you."

"Ahem . . ." Wells gave a little cough from inside the carriage. "Forgive me for interrupting, but remember that the Martians are heading this way."

"Quite so, quite so," Murray said, helping the girl into the coach. Then he turned to the mob, gave a little bow, and said, "Thank you, gentlemen, you've all been most kind. Unfortunately, this carriage is too grand to accommodate your lowly posteriors."

With these words, Murray climbed in a leisurely manner onto the driver's seat and, once installed, gave a crack of the whip.

"The insufferable bighead," Wells muttered.

"I agree. He's the most conceited man in the world. But thanks to him we recovered the coach," the girl acknowledged grudgingly.

She was right about that, Wells reflected, as the carriage moved away and through the window he watched the band of aggressors grow smaller in the distance. If Murray had not kept his calm, he himself would almost certainly have taken a beating, and they would be the ones left behind at the station watching those brutes make off with Murray's coach.

They took the Chertsey road to London almost at a gallop, causing Clayton, whom they had propped up in front of them, to slump sideways on the seat. The violent jolting of the carriage made his arms jump about, and his head flopped from side to side, like a man in the throes of drunkenness. Wells and Emma tried not to look at him, ashamed to witness an intimate moment in the inspector's life that few would ever see.

As he gazed out of the window, Wells realized night had fallen. A large part of the landscape outside the window was now plunged into darkness. On the horizon he could make out a cherry-red glare and a plume of smoke rising lazily up into the starry sky. From the distant woods of Addlestone came the disturbing boom of cannons, muted and sporadic, which made him think that the army was doing battle with the tripods somewhere.

"Oh my God!" exclaimed Emma.

The girl's gaze was fixed on something happening outside the window. Alarmed by the look of horror on her face, Wells leaned over her shoulder and peered into the night. At first he saw nothing, only a pine forest immersed in blackness, but then he glimpsed, slipping through the dense shadows, the vision that was terrifying her. A huge bulk was moving swiftly down the slope parallel with the carriage. When he managed to make it out against the darkness, Wells could see that it was a gigantic machine held up by three slender, jointed legs, advancing in great strides like some monstrous insect. Giving off a deafening metallic grinding sound, and swaying ominously, the shiny metal machine moved clumsily yet resolutely through the pine forest, casually crushing the trees underfoot as it went. Wells could see that the uppermost part of the device closely resembled the Martian cylinder he had described, but that the rest of its structure was very different—more like a vast round box covered with a complex mesh of plates, which reminded him of a hermit crab's shell. He also glimpsed a cluster of jointed tentacles, slender and supple, which moved as though they had a life of their own. Taller than several houses, the moonlight glinting on its metal surface, the thing was marching implacably toward London, opening a pathway through the stand of trees.

The machine suddenly tilted its hood slightly toward the carriage, and Wells had the uneasy feeling that it was watching them. His suspicions were confirmed when a second later the device deviated slightly from its path and began approaching the road. From the sudden jerk of the carriage, Wells deduced that Murray had seen it, too, and was trying to gain some distance by urging the horses on even more forcefully. Wells swallowed hard and, like Emma, gripped the seat to keep himself from being thrown into the air by the coach's violent shaking. Through the rear window he could see how one of the legs of the tripod emerged from the ditch and planted itself on the road. Then, dragging a clump of splintered pine trees, the other two also appeared. As soon as it was steady on its three legs, the thing set off in pursuit of the carriage. Its huge strides echoed in the night like booming thunderclaps, as the mechanical monster gained on them. His heart beating furiously in his chest, Wells watched as at the top of the machine the strange apparatus that launched the heat ray began its familiar cobralike movement as it took aim.

"That thing's going to shoot at us," he shouted, grabbing Emma and forcing her to the floor of the carriage. "Get down!"

There was a loud explosion a few yards to their right. The blast shook the carriage so violently that for a few instants its wheels left the ground, and when it landed again the shock threatened to shatter it to pieces. Surprised to find he was still alive, Wells struggled up as best he could and tried to glance out of the rear window again. Steadying himself against the wild sway of the carriage, he wondered whether Murray was still up on the driver's seat or had fallen off at some moment during the chase so that they were now speeding on in a driverless carriage. Through the window, Wells saw the small crater the blast had left in the roadside. Behind him, the tripod was still bearing down on them with ominous leaps and bounds, rapidly reducing the twenty yards or so that separated it from the carriage. His heart leapt into his mouth as he saw the tentacle that spat out the ray snaking through the air in preparation for a new strike. It was obvious that sooner or later it would hit them. At that moment, the coach shuddered to a halt, throwing him forward onto the crumpled body of Inspector Clayton. Wells rose and helped the girl up from the floor before returning to his seat. He felt the carriage start moving again. Through the window he could see they were turning. Startled, he poked his head out of the left-hand window and found that Murray had swung round to face the tripod, which continued its ungainly advance toward them.

"What the devil are you doing?" he shouted.

The reply was a whiplash, urging the horses on. The coach rattled forward to meet the tripod.

"You've gone mad, Murray!" he cried.

"I'm sure that thing can't turn as quickly as we can," he heard the millionaire cry above the wheels' infernal screeching.

As the coach began hurtling toward the tripod, Wells realized in astonished disbelief that Murray was hoping to pass beneath the colossus as if it were a bridge.

"Good God . . . the man is insane," he muttered, seeing how the tripod had halted to take aim at them.

He fell back into the coach and held the girl as tightly as he could.

"He's going to pass under its legs," he explained in a voice choked by fear.

"W-what?" she stammered.

"He's crazy . . ."

Emma clung to him desperately, trembling. Wells could feel her fragility, her warmth, her perfume, her womanly shape pressing itself into the hollows of his body. He could not help but lament the fact that the only chance a man like him would have to hold a woman like her was when they were fleeing a Martian invasion together, even though this was a fleeting notion that had no place at a moment like this, when both of them were being thrown at high speed against this metal monster, which in a few seconds would reduce them to ashes with its heat ray. But while waiting for death, in those few seconds when their lives extended beyond any reason, Wells had time to realize that the quandary in which they found themselves could not only make one a hero or a coward but also drive one insane.

XXIII

*A*ND WHILE THE REAL WELLS'S HEART WAS racing fearfully, that of the other Wells, of whose existence he was completely unaware, was beating calmly, like a gentle melody on a xylophone. For the invasion he was heading was going according to plan. In a couple of hours, the tripods would arrive at the gates of London, where the brave and admirable British army waited behind their Maxim guns, unaware they were about to be slaughtered. Studying the map of the planet pinned to the wall of his headquarters, the other Wells smiled as he imagined the coming massacre.

I hope that despite the time that has elapsed, you will not have forgotten about the creature that adopted Wells's appearance and that, like the conductor of an orchestra, is currently directing the attack from his hiding place. How did he get there? you will ask. Let us go back a few weeks, to the point where we left our story to travel to the Antarctic wastes, and peer inside the copper-riveted sarcophagus lying forgotten in the basement of the Natural History Museum. There, amid the industrious sounds of shifting flesh and bone, a being from another planet is rearranging its physiognomy by taking on that of the author H. G. Wells. Wells has just been steered out of the chamber by another, less brilliant author named Garrett P. Serviss. Both authors left the building unaware of the fatal consequences of their actions, in particular Wells's fleeting stroke of the extraterrestrial's arm. That gesture of timid admiration deposited on the creature's skin was the greatest gift Wells could ever have given it: a minuscule and insignificant drop of his blood, which nevertheless contained everything he was. And everything the creature needed in order to come back to life.

And so, in the seclusion of its coffin, like a caterpillar in a chrysalis, the being from outer space slowly took on a human appearance, nurtured and guided by Wells's blood. The creature's spine had shrunk to the length imprinted in Wells's blood, and while its skull was reforming at one end, at the other a narrow pelvis was sprouting two rather short femurs, brittle as twigs, which were instantly attached to two tibias and fibulas by a pair of knee joints. Gradually the creature fabricated the framework of a skeleton, cloaking it in a mantle of flesh, nerves, and tendons. Once the sternum and ribs were in place, the spongy lungs appeared, emitting through the narrow conduit of the newly installed trachea a puff of vapor that filled the urn with the moist novelty of breath. The liver and intestines were formed, while the deltoids, triceps, biceps, and other muscles threaded themselves around the bony frame, like armor plating. Through the intricate calligraphy of veins and arteries a furtive current of blood now flowed, fed by the heart, which was already pulsing in the chest cavity. From a blurry mass of skin on the thing's face emerged the birdlike countenance of the author, an exact replica of Wells upon the carbon paper onto which the hazy features of a few sailors from the *Annawan,* and even those of another author, Edgar Allan Poe, had previously been imprinted. A freshly formed mouth gave an almost triumphant, fierce smile that betrayed a festering desire for revenge, decades old, while a slender pair of pale human hands clutched the chains binding it before snapping them with an otherworldly strength. Then the lid of the coffin lifted from inside with an ominous creak, shattering the surrounding silence. Yet had anyone happened to be in the room to witness the miraculous resurrection, they would not have seen a sinister creature of the Cosmos rising from its tomb, but rather H.G. waking up following a drunken spree that, God only knew how, had ended with him in that coffin. However, despite its ordinary appearance, what emerged from that box was a deadly creature, a fearful being, or, if you prefer, Evil incarnate. Evil in all its glory, bursting once more into the world of rational man, as it had done before in the form of Franken-stein's monster, or of Count Dracula, or any of the monsters with which Man had disguised the intangible horror that haunted him from birth; that unnerving darkness that began poisoning his wretched soul from the moment his nanny blew out the candle shielding his cradle.

Like a blind man suddenly able to see, the false Wells studied the place he found himself in, crammed with bric-a-brac that meant noth-ing to him, relics of a fantasy world that belonged only to Earthlings. He felt an enormous relief as he glimpsed something familiar amid the plethora of nonsensical artifacts: his vehicle, raised on a plinth, consid-ered as miraculous as the other objects in the room. The machine ap-peared intact, exactly as he had left it in the snow when he infiltrated the Earthlings' ship, though it was still no doubt out of action: it did not take much intelligence to see that the humans had not even managed to open it. He walked over to the machine, halting a few yards from the plinth, and he narrowed his eyes in concentration. A chink slowly appeared in the machine's domed lid. The bogus Wells climbed inside. Seconds later, he emerged carrying an ivory-colored cylindrical box, smooth and shiny save for the tiny symbols on its lid that gave off a coppery glow. In the box was what had forced him to fly through space to Earth, that faraway planet almost 30,000 light-years from the center of the galaxy, which the Council had chosen as the new home of its race. And although he had taken longer to get there than predicted, at last he was able to continue his mission.

He opened the door of the chamber and left the museum like any other human, mingling with the late-afternoon crowd of visitors. Once outside, he took a deep breath and glanced around him, testing his newly acquired senses even as he tried to ignore the thrum produced by the mind of the man whose body he had replicated. The din of the real Wells's thoughts surprised him, as it was far more intense than that emitted by any of the men he had replicated in the Antarctic. But he had no time to enter into that mind and rummage among its quaint ponder-ings, and so he tried to ignore them and to focus instead on perceiving the world through his own senses, not the rudimentary ones of the Earthling he was inhabiting. And then, all of a sudden, he was filled with an intense feeling of well-being, a serene and tender melancholy such as a man might feel when evoking scenes of his childhood. He had discovered that he was in the place where the colony had been established. Yes, his last memory was the ice closing over his head like the lid of a coffin, and now, after floating in limbo for many years, outwitting death by lowering his energy requirements to enable his body to enter a state of hibernation, he had awoken in London, exactly where he had been headed when his vehicle came down in the Antarctic. He did not know whom he should thank, but, unluckily for the human race, someone had clearly rescued him from the ice and brought him here.

He climbed one of the turrets of the Natural History Museum and from that vantage point narrowed his eyes and sent out another signal. And that call, inaudible to any human, soared across the late-afternoon sky, riding on the warm breeze to spread through the city. Almost instantaneously, in a rowdy Soho tavern, Jacob Halsey stopped washing up glasses, raised his head to the ceiling, and for a few moments remained motionless, heedless of his customers' requests, until, all of a sudden, tears began to slowly trickle down his face. The same happened to a watchman, Bruce Laird, who for no apparent reason stopped in the middle of a corridor in Guy's Hospital, as though he had suddenly forgotten where he was going, and wept with joy. A baker in Holborn by the name of Sam Delaney repeated the gesture, as did Thomas Cobb, the owner of a clothier's shop near Westminster Abbey; a nanny watching over some children playing in a Mayfair park; an old man hobbling down a street in Bloomsbury; Mr. and Mrs. Connell, a couple strolling in Hyde Park feeding the squirrels; and a moneylender who had a shop on Kingly Street. They all looked up at the sky in silent rapture, as though listening to a tune no one else could hear, before stopping what they were doing, eyes brimming with tears, leaving glasses in the sink, business premises unlocked, young charges unprotected, and walking out of their houses and places of work to march slowly through the streets like a trail of ants. Gradually swelling in number, their ranks were joined by teachers, shop assistants, librarians, stevedores, secretaries, members of Parliament, chimney sweeps, civil servants, prostitutes, blacksmiths, coalmen, retired soldiers, cab drivers, and policemen, all moving in an orderly fashion toward the place to which the voice that had interrupted their thoughts was summoning them. It was a long-awaited call, heralding what their parents and their parents' parents had yearned for: the arrival of the long-awaited one, the Envoy.

FATHER NATHANIEL WRAYBURN, MINISTER of a small parish church in Marylebone, contemplated himself solemnly in the looking glass in the sacristy. He had carefully shaved and slicked back his unruly hair, put on his collar and brushed his cassock, all with slow, ceremonious gestures as if he were performing a service—not because he was required to, but because of the solemnity of the occasion. He sighed with relief when he saw that the wrinkles furrowing his desiccated face gave him an air of dignity rather than decrepitude, and that while the body he had usurped was worn out and emaciated, at least he was blessed with bright blue eyes, much revered by mankind and more particularly by womankind. The Heaven you speak of is reflected in your eyes, Father, a member of his flock had declared. She was unaware that the promised Heaven was inhabited by creatures none of which, unfortunately, enjoyed the status of divinity—however much Father Wrayburn liked to toy with the idea that his race embodied the gods whom human beings venerated. But if that were true, they would not be planning to exterminate them, he said to himself with a pained expression. No god would treat his worshippers like that. He finished smoothing down his hair and walked toward the door of the sacristy, hoping the Envoy would be pleased with his appearance.

"Good evening, Father Wrayburn. Or would you prefer, at last, to be called by the traditional name of your race?"

The voice came from the doorway, where the figure of a small, skinny man was watching him, hands plunged into his trouser pockets. The Envoy's chosen appearance startled him, not so much because it lacked manliness but because this was no anonymous individual, but rather someone whom any discerning reader would recognize.

"I must admit, sir, that after five generations, we descendants of the first colonizers use the Earthling language and Earthling names even amongst ourselves. I fear that when the long-awaited time comes, we will have trouble habituating ourselves once more to speaking in our old, much-loved tongue, despite having conscientiously passed it on to our children, together with the ancient wisdom and knowledge of our race," the priest replied.

Father Wrayburn uttered these words with head bowed and his hands composing a triangle above his head, a gesture that may seem absurd to us, but which for his race was a traditional mark of respect. He also spoke in his ancestral tongue, which to any human finding himself in the sacristy would have sounded like a muddled collection of grunts, whistles, and agonized wails, which for fear of wounding your sensibilities I have chosen not to reproduce.

"I appreciate how difficult it is for human vocal cords to reproduce our language, Father," the Envoy replied magnanimously. "If it is easier for you, let us communicate in the Earthlings' tongue, which I shall also use to give my welcoming speech to our brothers."

"I am grateful for your understanding, sir," the priest replied, trying to hide the catch in his voice, and still more his trepidation. He collected himself and approached the Envoy, hand outstretched, not without a hint of embarrassment at that strange and intimate way Earthlings had of greeting each other. "Welcome to Earth, sir."

"Thank you, Father," the Envoy said, abandoning his relaxed posture and walking toward the priest, whose hand he finally clasped in the gloom. "I'm afraid I am still not familiar with earthly customs. Not that it matters now, since there is no longer any reason to try to learn them, is there?"

The Envoy gazed intently into the priest's eyes, as though defying him to contradict this affirmation. When he finally let go of the priest's hand, Father Wrayburn, faintly alarmed by the Envoy's arrogance, cleared his throat a few times and tried to stick to his plan, in a British spirit of hospitality.

"Would you like a cup of tea?" he said. "They drink it a lot here, and I'm sure your host body will find it quite refreshing."

"Certainly, Father." The Envoy nodded with a grin. "I see no reason not to enjoy the native customs before wiping them out."

His words caused a shiver to run down the priest's spine. The Envoy seemed bent on reminding him continually that everything he knew, everything around him, would, in a matter of days, cease to exist. Yes, the being in front of him was charged with destroying the only world the priest treasured in his memory, and he even had the temerity to despise it without considering that its destruction might be worth lamenting.

"Follow me," the priest said, trying not to let his frustration show, since he knew that his role was to help the Envoy in his mission.

Father Wrayburn guided him to a small table he had placed beside the window overlooking the back courtyard of the church, where a tiny garden flourished thanks to his ministrations. The sun was sinking in the sky, and an orange glow spread over the few plants he had been able to nurture in his spare time. Carried on the evening breeze, their perfume floated into the sacristy. He felt a pang of sadness when he realized his little garden would perish along with the rest of the planet, and with it the sensation of peace he had whenever he worked there, with his gardening gloves and tools, wondering whether that feeling of well-being was the same one humans experienced when they were engaged in the futile activity they referred to as leisure. Attempting to conceal the wave of sorrow sweeping over him, he poured the tea with a deferential smile, while the clock in the corridor chimed merrily.

"You are right, it is a delicious beverage," the Envoy said after taking a sip and placing the cup gingerly back on its saucer. "But I'm not sure whether that is due to the drink itself or to the collection of organs the Earthlings possess in order to savor it: nose, tongue, and throat. Now, for instance, I can still feel the warmth it has left as it goes down, and the way it slows as it reaches the intestine."

The priest smiled as he watched the Envoy rubbing his stomach with wondrous delight, like a child discovering a new toy. The excessive care with which he handled the cup, as though it were a test tube, and dabbed his mouth with the napkin betrayed how unpracticed the Envoy was at operating the body he had replicated, an affected daintiness that would only fade with years of experience.

"They are good bodies," said the priest, sincere in his praise. "Limited in their perception of the world due to their rudimentary senses, and yet able to enjoy intensely the small amount of pleasure they derive from it. And Ceylon tea is delicious. Moreover, it can be drunk safely now. Up until a few years ago, when the sewage still flowed directly into the Thames, one of these innocent-looking teacups could carry typhus, hepatitis, or cholera. It is quite unpleasant, I assure you, when the body we inhabit falls ill."

The Envoy nodded absentmindedly and glanced slowly about the room, contemplating its chalices and missals and the wardrobe with its chasubles and cassocks.

"Notwithstanding your sufferings, you have certainly managed to occupy a respectable position in earthly society," he concluded after his scrutiny, gesturing vaguely at the tiny sacristy. "You are the minister of an Anglican church and that is the official religion of England and Wales, or is the information stored in my host's head incorrect?"

"Indeed, sir, it is not," the priest confirmed, unsure whether the Envoy's remark was disapproving or congratulatory.

Then he remembered the day of his "human" birth, as told to him by his parents, who had lived under the guise of lowly shopkeepers in Marylebone. A week after his mother gave birth (with the aid of a midwife as nonhuman as they, who informed the neighbors the child was stillborn), his father heard that a young priest had arrived at the neighborhood church. He instantly decided that this was the ideal host body for the newborn larva hidden away in their attic bedroom. He contrived to lure the priest to his house under the pretext that his mother was dying. "What do you think, my love? He is young and strong and holds a position in society that would suit us very well," he asked his wife, much to the alarm of the priest who asked to what they were referring. "Nothing you need to worry about," she had told him, urging him to follow her up to the bedroom, where her mother-in-law was allegedly dying. But of course, the person waiting for the priest there was he himself, in his original larval form, eager to meet the body he would reside in during his time on Earth. The young priest scarcely had time to raise his eyebrows at the unexpected and terrifying spectacle before he felt the knife plunged to the hilt in his back. After putting his blood to good use, they buried him in the garden, and less than an hour later, once he had familiarized himself with the workings of his new body, the newborn Father Wrayburn took up his post in the church. He supplied the extraterrestrial colony with a fresh meeting place, as his father had requested, but without neglecting his duties as a priest. He was particularly proud of that, for it was not an easy job, and he resolved to convey as much to the Envoy, taking advantage of one of his pregnant silences.

"However, I confess the situation has become complicated of late," he explained in a cautionary tone as he poured the Envoy another cup of tea. "Our biggest challenge derives from a crisis of faith: the Bible, the book of their beliefs, is becoming increasingly difficult to interpret literally due to its lack of historical rigor."

"Is that so?" The Envoy smiled with an air of tedium as he raised his cup to his lips.

"Yes. The Bible claims the world is scarcely six thousand years old, something any geologist is able to disprove. However, it is the theory of evolution elaborated by a human named Darwin that has undermined the very heart of the Christian doctrine by secularizing the act of Creation."

The Envoy gazed at him in silence, a supercilious smile playing over his lips. After a moment's hesitation, the priest continued. "The theologians in our church try to appear more receptive to scientific advances, and some even demand the reinterpretation of biblical texts, but it is no good: the harm has already been done. The increasing secularization of society is a reality we must accept. Each day, new forms of leisure entice our flocks. Do you know what a bicycle is? Well, even that ridiculous object has become our adversary. On Sundays, people prefer taking a ride into the country to coming to hear my sermons."

The Envoy placed his cup on the saucer as though it weighed a ton and tilted his head, amused at the priest's consternation.

"You feel as strongly about it as a real priest would," he remarked, with a look of studied surprise.

"Isn't that what I am?" replied the other man, immediately regretting his boldness. "What I mean is . . . Well, this is the only world I know, sir. Except for the fact that my ancestors weren't born on this planet, I could consider myself an Earthling." His smile froze when he noticed the Envoy's stern expression. He took a moment to choose his next words judiciously, while his palms started to sweat. When he finally spoke, it was in a tone close to reverence. "Perhaps it is hard for you to appreciate our situation, sir, but we have endured a terrible, agonizing wait that has forced us to mingle with them to the point where we have difficulty continuing to be . . . extraterrestrials."

"Extraterrestrials . . ." The Envoy smiled.

"That is how they refer to us . . ." the priest began explaining politely.

"I am aware of that." The Envoy's irritated tone banished any trace of indulgence he might have previously shown, as though the idiotic vicissitudes of humans had suddenly ceased to amuse him, together with anything else the priest might have to say about them. "And I must confess the arrogance of this race never ceases to amaze me."

At this, the Envoy's eyes narrowed, as though he were preparing to pray. Father Wrayburn realized that he was aware of the colony beginning to gather inside the church.

"Our brothers are arriving," he pointed out unnecessarily.

"Yes, I can sense the excited thrum of their minds, Father."

"And with good reason," explained the priest, who hastened to defend his brothers, despite his unease at the Envoy's attitude. "We have been waiting too long for the Envoy to come. Since the sixteenth century in Earth time, to be precise, when our ancestors first arrived on Earth."

"And you consider that a long time?" the Envoy inquired.

The priest could not tell from his expression whether the Envoy's words concealed true interest or a veiled threat, though he feared it was the latter. In any event, he was unable to stop himself from continuing his reproaches, even though he was careful to voice them in a tone of extreme deference.

"I do, sir. We are the fifth generation, as I said before," he declared solemnly. "And as I'm sure you will easily appreciate, our ancestors' planet is almost mythical to us. My father died without his life on Earth ever having made sense, as did my grandfather before him . . . However, we are blessed," he hastened to add, "for we are going to achieve their dream of meeting the Envoy and welcoming our true race."

The Envoy simply smiled disdainfully, as though the colony's sufferings and joys were a matter of indifference to him. At this, the priest threw all caution to the winds.

"My ancestor killed and adopted the appearance of a man who wore a ruff!" he exclaimed, as though that accessory humans draped around their necks in olden times illustrated better than anything their lengthy wait. "Since then, we have infiltrated their world, procreating discreetly amongst ourselves in order to survive, and above all watching over the war machines our ancestors buried underground."

"Father Wrayburn," the Envoy interjected in a conciliatory tone, "I assure you there is no need for you to continue listing all your grievances. I am well aware of the excellent job you have been doing in our colony here on Earth, as I have personally been in charge of evaluating the various reports on the conditions of the planet, which you have sent us so punctually. And rest assured," he added, fixing the priest with a menacing gaze, "had I not been satisfied with your work, I would have recommended to the Council that we exterminate the colony and send new explorers."

"Yes, yes, of course," the priest was quick to reply, alarmed by the Envoy's last words. "We always gather here in my church at the appointed time, joining our minds to send our transmission through the Cosmos. It is our duty, sir, and so it has been done." He paused, as though considering whether it was opportune or even wise to go on. Finally, after fingering his teacup nervously, he added, "However, I confess we nurtured a secret hope that a response from our mother planet might one day be forthcoming. Yet it never was. Still, we continued to do our duty, sending reports about the planet we were monitoring to a world that, regardless of its silence, we were forced to assume still existed and was receiving the bottles we launched as requested into the ocean of the universe. Surely you will agree that is an act of faith."

"As you know, explorers are volunteers. They accept their lot, with all its consequences, for the good of the race," the Envoy retorted, attempting to dampen the priest's bitterness. "And it is their responsibility to raise the awareness of their descendants to prevent them from building up the resentment I perceive so clearly in you, but which I shall overlook, given that, as you point out, you belong to the fifth generation."

"I appreciate your indulgence," the priest replied submissively, deciding he had gone far enough, both with his complaints and in revealing so clearly his feelings toward the humans. It would be very dangerous to continue irritating the Envoy, and through him the Council and the emperor. Who was he, after all? A mere fifth-generation volunteer, a nobody. And so, he resumed in the humblest of voices: "I did not mean to give that impression, sir. But in our most recent messages we also informed you of our delicate situation. We are perishing, as you must know. It is difficult for us to procreate, and we die younger and younger. Something in the air on this planet affects us, yet we can't find out what that is because, as you understand, we lack the necessary expertise."

"I appreciate your frustration," the Envoy cut in with a weary gesture that made it clear he intended to end the discussion there. "But it is naïve of you to imagine that the difficulties experienced by a colony would concern our mother planet. What do a few lives matter compared to the fate of an entire race? Besides, you know that a process of selection dictates where we go. The most favorable planets have preference, and Earth was never among them."

"Then the situation must be terrible if Earth is now considered the best option," the priest reflected bitterly. "Are there really no other more favorable planets to which our race can move?"

"I'm afraid not," the Envoy acknowledged somewhat ruefully. "We have exhausted their resources at an increasingly rapid pace. Our continual evolution makes that almost inevitable."

"Well, even so, the important thing is that you have arrived in the nick of time," the priest said in a conciliatory tone. "And I do not refer only to saving our colony. Earthling science is progressing by leaps and bounds. A few hundred years more, and conquering this planet would have been much more difficult."

"You exaggerate, Father. From what I have seen, the Earthlings' so-called Industrial Revolution is lamentable. I have no doubt we will crush them with ease," the Envoy declared emphatically. "In any case, my arrival was delayed, as you are probably aware."

"Yes, our colony received your signal sixty-eight years ago," the priest confirmed, "when I was only a few months old. But then suddenly it vanished. No one ever knew why. We were surprised when we picked it up again, and in London."

"I am to blame. However, my journey was eventful, to say the least," explained the Envoy. "As I entered the Earth's atmosphere, one of my engines failed, and I was forced to make an emergency landing in the Antarctic. There, I attempted to sneak on board a ship in the hope of reaching civilization, but an accursed human called Reynolds foiled my plans, and I ended up trapped in the ice: that's why you stopped hearing my signal."

"Your cry for help was the last thing that was heard of you," the priest said, secretly impressed that a human had succeeded in putting the Envoy out of action, at least for several decades.

"It was a cry of rage, Father," the Envoy retorted. "That arrogant Earthling Reynolds was hoping to communicate with me. He didn't realize it would take several thousand more years of evolution before they could understand our minds. Can you imagine them conversing with their cockroaches before crushing them underfoot? Of course not!" the Envoy roared, slapping the table. Then he let out a sigh and controlled himself. "But let us talk no more of that unpleasant experience. Other humans must have rescued me and brought me here, together with my machine. That's why I was able to salvage this."

He took the ivory cylinder out of his jacket pocket, placed it on the table, and caressed it gently with his mind. The inscribed lid lifted, revealing something resembling a cluster of small bluish-green gemstones.

"Are these what activate the combat machines?"

The Envoy nodded with theatrical fatalism.

"So, in a few days' time the devastation will be complete," the priest murmured with an air of foreboding.

"It will, Father, it will."

They stared at each other, plunged into an awkward silence.

"Something intrigues me, Father," the Envoy said at last. The priest's deference had renewed his desire to continue their conversation. "Do Earthlings believe in other forms of life in the universe, or are they one of those races blinded by their own megalomania?"

The priest paused briefly before replying.

"That is a question I have followed with great interest, in view of our situation. And I can assure you Man has believed in life on other planets since ancient times, even though his desire to explore the universe is, shall we say, a more recent phenomenon. Until a few centuries ago, he was content to dream about it. However, thanks to the advances of science, he now sees it as a tangible possibility. This is reflected in the increasing number of scientific romances produced by Earthlings, which, as you will appreciate, I find irresistible." He stood up, walked over to the cabinet lined with books, which the Envoy had mistaken for missals, and selected a handful, depositing them on the table. "This is one of the first books to speak of their interest in space. It's a story about the building of a giant cannon that shoots a manned missile onto the Moon."

The Envoy took the book the priest was holding out to him and contemplated it without much interest.

"*From the Earth to the Moon,* by Jules Verne," he read aloud.

The priest nodded, gesturing toward the pile of books on the table.

"As you can see, I like to gauge the pulse of the Earthlings' desires, and above all to keep abreast of their notions about us. I'm sure you would find many of these books extremely amusing."

"Possibly," the Envoy said, unconvinced.

"And you might be interested to know that our invasion will come as no surprise to them," the priest said, regarding the Envoy pensively. "I suppose you already know."

"And why would you suppose that?"

The priest gazed at him in surprise.

"Because many people have considered the possibility of being invaded thanks to a man whose name must be familiar to you," he said, handing him another book from the pile.

"*The War of the Worlds,* by H. G. Wells," the Envoy read aloud, unaware of what the priest was referring to.

"Don't you recognize the book? The author is the man whose form you have taken on!" the priest explained.

"I wrote this book?"

"The human you are impersonating did. H. G. Wells, a well-known and highly respected man here in England. But don't you have that information in his head?"

"I confess that the brain of this human makes me extremely . . . uneasy," the Envoy avowed, somewhat embarrassed. "It's a peculiar feeling I didn't experience with the other minds I reproduced. And to be honest,

I try not to delve more than is necessary into his memories, which are of little interest to me anyway," he added disdainfully.

"Strange indeed. Although I have heard of cases of our brothers finding some bodies incompatible and even having to change host. Unusual, but it does happen," the priest reassured him. "Then you will also be unaware that you are impersonating the first Earthling who dared turn the accepted scenario on its head."

"What are you talking about?"

"Unlike in the majority of the novels by his colleagues, in Wells's *The War of the Worlds* Earthlings don't conquer other planets inhabited by primitive people unable to confront technology. Instead, Earth itself is invaded by the inhabitants of its neighboring planet, Mars."

"Mars?" The Envoy chortled. "But Mars is uninhabited."

"They don't know that," the priest replied. "Their primitive telescopes have recently discovered strange marks on its surface, which they have elevated to canals. And many astronomers believe the Martians are a dying race that uses these canals to channel water from the poles to the arid equator."

"Don't they know that the average temperature of the planet is too low to stop water from freezing?" the Envoy asked with astonishment.

The priest simply shrugged. The Envoy shook his head with a mixture of amusement and disappointment.

"And how does Wells depict us? Does he come even close to understanding our nature?"

"Oh no, of course not," the priest replied, before adding rather ashamedly, "In fact, he portrays us as monsters similar to one of Earth's sea creatures."

"Do you think they see us as we really are when we aren't projecting their appearance?" the Envoy asked the priest.

"I doubt it. Remember, we are completely alien to them. We aren't animal, vegetable, or mineral. Not even a mixture of those. We are quite simply beyond the bounds of their comprehension."

"But they must perceive us in some way, don't you think? We have a shape, we make sounds and give off odors," the Envoy surmised.

"I assume that in order to stay sane, their minds compare us to what we most resemble," the priest reflected. "And since we are the unknown, I imagine what they see is not exactly flattering. They undoubtedly portray us as monsters with claws, tentacles, and fangs, a hideous amalgamation of all their fears. It is even conceivable they all see us differently, according to their own innermost fears. You'd be surprised to what extent men's hearts are ruled by fears: some are afraid of spiders, others of reptiles, still others of dragons. They can even develop a phobia of peas if they are forced to eat them when they are small. That is the way their minds work."

"The possibilities are endless," the Envoy murmured, "but always monstrous."

"Exactly. That's why our scientists enabled us to project the appearance of any one of them by using the information stored in his or her blood."

The Envoy seemed to find it comical that the Earthlings would envisage them as the most hideous thing they could imagine, for he found the current inhabitants of that planet just as repulsive, with their conceited vulgarity.

"And do they succeed, Father? Do the Martians in his novel conquer the Earth?" he said, indicating Wells's book.

"Yes," the priest replied. "Their technology is far superior to that of the humans, and they conquer the Earth in a matter of days."

"Then this Wells fellow is the most sensible Earthling I have met so far." The Envoy nodded approvingly. "It is fitting I should have adopted his appearance."

"That isn't all, sir. Wells also guessed where our machines are buried," the priest revealed. "Imagine what I felt when I read the novel and discovered that an Earthling had guessed where the majority of them are located."

"Well, Father, you better than anyone ought to know that the Earth-lings still haven't learned how to make full use of their minds. They still only utilize an infinitesimal part of their brains. But I suspect this doesn't prevent a few of the more developed human minds from per-ceiving, in a completely unconscious way of course, some aspects of the universal energy we have been tapping into for thousands of years. How else would we be able to converse across unfathomable space or create mental projections in order to assume different shapes before their eyes? Humans are oblivious to all that, even though some may occasionally be able to perceive the odd energy wave, in a way they are unable to define."

"Are you suggesting they might be able to intercept our messages?" the priest said in astonishment.

"It's possible. But in a completely random way, and they would inter-pret them differently, as premonitions, obsessions, fantasies. It could be that their so-called inspiration simply consists of these accidental thefts."

"Yes, perhaps . . . ," the priest replied, unable to stifle the overwhelm-ing enthusiasm he always felt when discussing certain phenomena and eccentricities he had observed in his beloved humans. "It is curious, for instance, that a philosophical idea, or a literary trend, or even a piece of scientific investigation often crops up simultaneously in different parts of the planet without there having been any prior contact between their human authors. To take an obvious example, the great American inven-tor Thomas Edison once said, when lauded for his discoveries, that the air is full of ideas, which came to him from a higher source, and if he hadn't had them someone else would have. *The air is full of ideas.* Doesn't that strike you as a poetic way of describing the energy of the universe?"

"Possibly, and yet our dear Mr. Wells doesn't seem to think Edison deserves to be liked," the Envoy remarked ponderously, oblivious to the priest's enthusiasm. "I am inhabiting the body of a decidedly peculiar mind. Wells obviously intercepted some of our communications, and that is where the idea for his novel sprang from."

"Really? I don't believe Wells is simply a medium. He's an intelligent man with a talent for—"

"In any case," the Envoy cut in, "you wouldn't need to be a genius to discover where we concealed our machines. All it proves is that Wells is a good strategist. Where else would we place them if not in a circle around the largest city of the planet, which we propose to conquer?"

"I daresay you are right," the priest conceded.

"I hope he will not determine the whereabouts of our headquarters, Father, which I presume has been completed."

"Naturally, sir," the priest replied hurriedly. "We have had ample time."

"Excellent, Father. I shall oversee the attack from there. And then we will rebuild London from the rubble in our own image and likeness, a London that will be the center of a new empire. A magnificent London that will await the arrival of our emperor."

The priest nodded sadly. He fell silent for a few moments before asking, with feigned indifference, "Did you kill him?"

"Who?"

"Wells. Did you kill Wells?"

"Ah, no, I couldn't," the Envoy responded, waving away the question. "I received his blood by accident."

"I'm glad," the priest said, relieved. "As you yourself mentioned, he possesses one of the most . . . exceptional minds on the planet."

"Yes, but not in the way you imagine," the Envoy acknowledged enigmatically.

"What do you mean?"

"I'm not sure how to explain it . . ." The Envoy stroked his whiskers pensively. "His mind contains something peculiar, an additional feature lacking in the brains of the other bodies I usurped. A button he hasn't yet pressed. And I've no idea what it's for. Yet it makes me feel uneasy and stops me from venturing into the furrows of his mind as I should like. If it weren't for the fact that no human can pose a threat to us, I'd even go so far as to say that it feels menacing."

The priest looked at him quizzically, unsure how to respond. "Well, tomorrow even that won't matter," he concluded, rising to his feet and gathering up his books. "Despite his mysterious mind, Wells will no doubt perish during the invasion, together with most of the rest of humanity."

The Envoy felt a twinge of pity as he watched the priest place the books back in the cabinet. He could not help giving him a warm smile when he returned to his seat.

"I recommend you look at things in a different light, Father," he said. "Remember, it is the survival instinct of an entire race that drives us."

"I hadn't forgotten," the priest grunted.

The Envoy gave a solemn nod. "Besides, we shall also prevent the Earthlings from spreading through the Cosmos like a harmful virus." He grinned.

The priest suppressed a bitter laugh. "I suppose that's how they would see us if they knew we existed," he said, "like a dormant virus in their organism."

"I believe you have become too fond of the Earthlings," the Envoy snapped.

"It is inevitable," the priest murmured, shrugging his shoulders. "We were born and raised among them. And despite their limitations they are truly . . . unique. They are my flock."

"From what I've observed, they certainly are resilient," the Envoy resumed, ignoring the priest's words. "They will make superb slaves. And their minds are abuzz with energy. They will be of more use to us than even they could imagine. Don't weep for them, Father. How long before they drain all their natural resources and make themselves extinct: three, perhaps four hundred years? What is that in comparison to the age of the universe?"

"From that point of view, perhaps only the blink of an eye," the priest persisted, "but from their position it is whole lives, generations, History."

"They could only survive by fleeing to other planets, like we do," the Envoy replied, trying to conceal his frustration. "Do you think their science will be sufficiently advanced by then to allow them to travel into space? And if it were, what do you think they would find? Only remnants, depleted planets, worlds squeezed dry. Scraps from the banquet table. As you know, all the other races in the universe are doing the same as us. In fact, the matter is very simple: it is them or us. There is no God to decide who deserves to prevail. You may not believe it, but we are alone. Cast adrift. No one knows what we should do, what game of chess we are playing, or for whom."

The Envoy peered curiously at the priest before adding, "Could it be that you consider them a model of civilization, an irreparable loss?"

The priest gazed at him for a few moments in silence. "No," he replied, with an air of regret. "They wage war on one another, they commit atrocities, they kill in the name of absurd ideologies and invent vengeful gods to soothe the pain of their loneliness."

"Good," the Envoy said contentedly, rising to his feet. "I wouldn't like to think you were siding with them. You know that in any case we will conquer the Earth. And afterward you will have a good position, providing I don't send any negative reports about you. Don't forget that."

"So, let's slaughter them," the priest said at last, with an air of resignation, lowering his head and clasping his hands reverentially above his head.

"No, Father," the Envoy replied almost with affection, turning his back on the priest and walking slowly toward the arched doorway leading to the church. Then he paused, closing his eyes once more and listening. When he spoke again, his voice sounded distant and faint, as though floating on the breeze. "Remember, this will only be a slaughter from their point of view. The Cosmos cares nothing for the Earthlings' absurd morality."

The priest lowered his hands with a downcast air. A solemn silence descended on the sacristy, a silence undisturbed even by the clamor of the minds of the colony. The Envoy remained with his eyes closed, listening, as a wistful smile played over his borrowed lips.

"They are all here, sir," the priest announced timidly. "They are eager to greet you."

The Envoy nodded and, turning toward the priest, he opened his eyes.

"Then let us not keep them any longer," he said, buttoning his jacket. "They have waited long enough, don't you think?"

The priest smiled wearily back at him. He stood up from the table and led the Envoy toward the church, trying hard to appear excited about what was happening, which was nothing less than the event they had all been waiting for since their ancestors first arrived on Earth. The priest motioned to his guest to go before him. The Envoy lifted his head as he stepped through the curtain separating the sacristy from the church and walked forward with as much grace as his human form allowed. He was aware of a murmur of expectancy, this time from the hundreds of throats in the church. A varied sample of humanity filled the benches and aisles, a range of social classes, of men and women, all very different, yet all with the same awed expression. The Envoy raised his hand slowly in a gesture of greeting, which the reddish glow filtering through the stained glass windows imbued with solemnity. Then he walked ceremoniously over to the pulpit, planted his hand on it, and spoke to the colony.

"First of all, please accept my apologies for the sixty-eight-year delay, brothers and sisters. My journey here has not been easy, but I have arrived at last. And it is you who will fulfill your ancestors' dream, for tomorrow we shall conquer London."

XXIV

*L*ET US NOW RETURN TO THE REAL WELLS, whom we left clasping Miss Harlow inside a luxurious carriage with an ornate "G" emblazoned on one of its doors, which at that moment was hurtling toward the Martian tripod in an insane bid to pass beneath its legs. I hope you will forgive me for having left our hero in such a delicate situation; think of it as my homage to the serialized novels of the time. As the jolting carriage careered across the dozen or so yards separating it from the lethal machine, Wells gritted his teeth, expecting the heat ray to vaporize them at any moment. However, the author was still able to wonder whether the flames would consume their bodies so swiftly that they wouldn't have time to feel any pain. But death's caress was slow to arrive. Astonished that the machine had still not fired at them, Wells opened his eyes and turned toward the window, convinced these would be his last gestures. As he did so, he saw one of the tripod's legs pass so close to the carriage that it sheared off a lantern on the left side. A second later, he heard a deafening blast from behind, which shook the coach violently once again. Then Murray gave a cry of triumph. Looking over his shoulder through the rear window, Wells could see the vast hole the ray had bored in the road. With a mixture of relief and joy, he realized the tentacle had waited too long before firing at them. The speed at which the millionaire had driven the horses had confused the machine, and it had not had time to take proper aim. And as the tripod grew smaller in the rear window, so the likelihood of it firing at them again diminished, for as Murray had realized, the machine could not turn as quickly as they. The author watched as it tried to swivel round in the middle of the road like a clumsy ballerina, realizing that by the time it did so, their carriage would be out of sight. He turned once more in his seat, breathless with anxiety, and gently lifted the girl's head, which was still pressed against his chest.

"We made it, Miss Harlow, we made it," he stammered between gasps.

The girl sat up straight, a look of shock on her face. Gazing through the window, she saw that indeed they had succeeded in passing under the machine, which had given up pursuit and was moving in the opposite direction toward Woking.

"Are you all right in there?" they heard Murray ask.

"Yes, you bloody lunatic, we're all right!" Wells shouted, unsure whether to explode with rage or give in to the hysterical laughter threatening to rise from his throat.

Instead, he simply fell back in his seat, his heart still pounding, and tried to calm himself. They had been on the point of dying, he said to himself, yet they were alive. This was a reason to rejoice. Or it ought to have been. He looked over at Inspector Clayton, who was still sprawled on the seat opposite wearing the peaceful expression of someone having a pleasant dream, oblivious to the vicissitudes suffered by his body. Wells sighed and gazed at the girl, who, like he, was attempting to recover from the shock. They remained like this for a few moments, silent, and grateful, as though they had just been reunited with their souls, which had almost escaped from their chests like scared birds. The carriage continued on its way, much more slowly now that it was no longer being pursued by the machine.

Yet before either of them could break the silence they were struck dumb by the devastation that began to emerge around them. With a mixture of horror and fascination, they contemplated a patchwork of pine forests reduced to ashes and half-burnt woods still smoldering in places, with tiny fires scattered throughout, filling the air with a resinous odor. Plumes of smoke rose from a succession of collapsed houses along the roadside. Among them, an occasional dwelling, surprisingly intact, stood out, spared from destruction by a mysterious whim of the tripod. After several minutes of utter devastation, they came across a derailed locomotive, which looked like a gigantic fiery snake stretched out across the grass. Around it were several smoking craters, and even in the dimness they could make out the bodies of passengers mown down as they tried to flee.

Scarcely had they left this sinister spectacle behind when they heard distant cannons firing at regular intervals, and they assumed the tripod that had been pursuing them had encountered an artillery battalion. Wells wondered which side had the advantage as he looked out of the window at the ruins that bore witness to the cruelty or indifference this enemy from outer space showed toward the human race.

They circled Chobham and headed once more toward London as the pale dawn began to unveil the contours of the world. There was no evidence of any destruction along this part of the route, Wells realized in relief, for it meant that for the time being London was safe. Presently, when they glimpsed a farmhouse on the road to Addlestone, Murray suggested they make a stop to give the horses a rest before they ended up collapsing unexpectedly on the road. They all needed some sleep, and the farmhouse seemed like a good place for it. The others agreed, and so the millionaire pulled up outside the house. They realized the owners had fled when they discovered two abandoned, horseless carts next to a small barn and at the entrance to the farmhouse a trail of utensils and personal effects: shoes, teaspoons, a wall clock, and a couple of flattened hats that suggested a hasty departure. Leaving Emma to watch over Clayton's inopportune slumber, Wells and Murray went inside to explore the farmhouse. It was a modest two-floor dwelling, poorly furnished, and with three upstairs bedrooms. They inspected each room and found no signs of life. This spared them the onerous task of asking to stay and even rubbing elbows with the family living there, who would doubtless be eager to exchange stories about the invasion or share their fears, a prospect that daunted the exhausted Wells. After the inspection, they gave the horses water and carried Clayton into the main bedroom, where they laid him on the double bed. It was decided that Wells would sleep beside the inspector in case he suddenly woke up, while Emma and Murray would occupy the other two rooms. Once they had deposited the inspector, they went down to the kitchen to satisfy the hunger that had begun to assail them. Sadly, the fleeing family had also plundered the pantry, and after an exhaustive search all they could find was a stale crust of bread and some moldy cheese, which none of them deigned to taste, for it would have meant accepting that the situation they were in was totally desperate. Following this disappointment, each retired to his or her improvised bedroom to try to rest for at least a couple of hours before resuming their journey.

Wells went into his allotted chamber, took Clayton's pulse to make sure he was still alive, and then lay down beside him. He had forgotten to take the precaution of drawing the curtains, and a dim light filtered through the windows. He was too exhausted to get up again and so resigned himself to sleeping in the bothersome glare that was beginning to illuminate every corner of the modest room. As he waited for sleep to come, he studied the meager possessions the house's owners had been forced to leave behind: the rickety wardrobe, the small chest of drawers, the shabby mirror, the small lamp and candles beside the bed. Those forlorn objects had so little in common with those of his own world that he was surprised they were able to offer comfort to anyone. And yet there were those who lived with such possessions, who journeyed toward death surrounded by objects emanating ugliness. Wells kept to his side of the mattress, arms tightly by his sides, not wishing to touch the sheets any more than he could help it, for he was convinced that if he came into contact with them, or with any of the other hastily abandoned objects, his fingers would break out in an unpleasant rash. As he lay there, besieged by that respectable poverty, the author was forced to acknowledge that it was one thing to imagine the privations of the lower classes in a general, almost abstract way, but quite another to witness at first hand the hideous drabness surrounding their lives, which was something he had never alluded to in the few articles he had written in support of their rights.

Then his eye fell on a photograph atop the chest of drawers. It showed a couple and their two sons wearing the suspicious expression of those who still believe the devil has a hand in the workings of the camera. The couple, with their coarse features and simple clothes, had placed their hands on their sons' shoulders, as if showing off the prize fruits of their orchard. Those poor lads could have been born anywhere, but the roulette wheel of life had decided it would be to that family, condemned to toil in the same fields as their parents before them. They would accept their fate as a matter of course, and their souls would never burn with a curiosity that would force them to question the order of things. But, looking on the bright side, Wells said to himself, their lack of imagination was an excellent insurance against life's many disappointments, which happily they would never experience. If they were content with their lot, they would have no urge to migrate to the city, where they would doubtless have a much harder life, for at least in the countryside the air was pure and the sun was warm. In the city they would have been crammed together with others like them in a rented room in some filthy East End backstreet, easy prey to tuberculosis, bronchitis, and typhus. And the healthy, robust glow they brought with them from the countryside would fade in some factory, as would their will to live, all for a miserable wage that would afford them no greater happiness than a drunken spree in a seedy tavern. Luckily for them, those two able-bodied lads had got the best of a bad deal, for surely it was they who had occupied the two other bedrooms. Wells looked away from the photograph, wondering what had made the family abandon their house, which was certainly their only home. Had they been scared by the rumors they had heard, perhaps encouraged by their neighbors? And how would their simple minds have reacted to the news that the enemies attacking their country came from outer space, from that starry sky they had never seen as anything but a decorative backdrop? Now though, regardless of the fate to which each had been allotted or the possessions they had managed to accumulate, all the inhabitants of the Earth were reduced to the same level: that of fleeing rats.

Wells fell asleep thinking of Jane.

WHEN HE AWOKE, HE sat up slowly, his muscles aching, and glanced at his pocket watch. He had been asleep for nearly three hours, although he did not feel as rested as he had hoped, no doubt because he had not managed to drift into a pleasant slumber but rather a kind of half sleep that he could only describe as fitful. His recent experiences had seeped into his dreams, turning them into a merry-go-round of disturbing images. He could not recall any of them, and yet his mind was still darkened by a terrifying, familiar sensation of falling. One thing he did remember hearing was Inspector Clayton's voice, urging him to wake up. This was why he found it so odd that the young man was still asleep alongside him. He looked at Clayton with a mixture of pity and annoyance, wondering whether they would have to cart him around for much longer. He even considered forcibly waking him up but then decided this was unwise. If the inspector's sleeping fits were an illness, it might not be a good idea to interfere. He left Clayton on the bed, smoothed down his unruly locks in front of the grimy mirror, and walked out into the corridor.

The doors to the other rooms were open, so that Wells could see they were empty. He went downstairs in search of his companions, but they were not in the sitting room either. Embarrassed about having slept the longest, something that gossips like Murray might attribute to his lack of concern about the grave events unfurling around them, Wells approached the kitchen, which was also deserted. Suddenly, it occurred to him that the damned millionaire might have managed to persuade the girl to leave him and Clayton behind. But this fear was soon erased from his suggestible mind when he glimpsed Murray's carriage through the window, standing exactly where they had left it. Unless they had decided to travel on foot, his companions must still be around somewhere. Wells reproached himself for his suspicions: though the millionaire was petty-minded and untrustworthy, he appeared willing to set aside their differences given the circumstances. They were a team, now, whether he liked it or not. Baffled as to their whereabouts, the author left the house and surveyed the balmy morning that had spread over the world. The day was as calm as any other, save for the distant rumble of cannon fire from the southeast, telling him that somewhere the British artillery was doing battle with a tripod. In the other direction, a thick plume of smoke was rising beyond the distant hills that hid Epsom from view. Wells wondered how many tripods were positioned around London. Clayton had told him that other cylinders besides the one at Horsell had appeared on a golf course in Byfleet and near to Sevenoaks. However, if this was a proper invasion, there would certainly be more.

Suddenly, Wells heard his companions' voices coming from the barn. As he headed for the door, Wells heard Emma exclaim in a frustrated voice, "This is much harder than I thought!"

"I believe rhythm is the key, Miss Harlow," Murray replied to her calmly. "Try using short, sharp movements."

Wells stopped in his tracks, disconcerted by the conversation.

"Are you sure?" Emma asked. "Won't it hurt?"

"Such delicate hands as yours would be incapable of causing any pain, Miss Harlow," was the millionaire's reply.

"Very well, I shall try doing as you say," the girl said resolutely.

A silence followed lasting several seconds, during which Wells stood motionless.

"Well?" he heard Murray ask.

"That doesn't seem to work either," the girl replied, somewhat dismayed.

"Maybe you're pulling too hard," Murray hazarded.

"Is that so?" Emma bridled. "Why don't you do it yourself, then, instead of telling me what to do!"

"I didn't mean to, Miss Harlow, I was merely suggesting—" Murray began apologizing, stopping in midsentence, as though the remaining words had stuck in his throat.

A fresh silence followed. Wells stood rooted to the spot, wondering whether or not to go in. They couldn't possibly be . . .

"Perhaps we ought to tell Mr. Wells?" he heard Emma suggest. "He might be more experienced than us."

Hearing his name, Wells blushed. Tell him?

"I doubt it somehow, Miss Harlow," Murray replied hurriedly.

It piqued Wells that the millionaire should be so convinced of his lack of experience, even though he was unsure in what.

"Why not try placing your hand farther up," he heard Murray propose.

"That's it, I've had enough!" Emma flared. "Do it yourself!"

"All right, all right." Murray tried to calm her. "But please don't be upset, Miss Harlow. I only let you do it because I thought you liked trying new things."

There followed another, lengthier silence. Wells resolved once and for all to go into the barn as he had originally planned. Uncertain what he might stumble upon, he approached the half-open door almost on tiptoe. When he reached it, he peeped inside apprehensively. The scene taking place inside came as a great relief. His two companions had their backs to the door and so were unaware of his presence. Murray was sitting on a milking stool, hunched forward, while a very large cow grudgingly allowed him to grope its teats with his big paws. The girl stood beside him, arms folded, viewing with a critical eye his feeble attempts to squeeze a few drops of milk from the creature.

"Well, Mr. Murray?" the author heard her say in a sarcastic voice. "Are you getting anywhere? Perhaps you should try using short, sharp movements?"

Wells grinned, and deciding that by barging in he would certainly spoil the scene, he was content to wait noiselessly beside the door, observing the millionaire's laughable attempts to show the woman he loved that he could tackle even the most unexpected situations life threw at him.

"Cows are supremely generous creatures, Miss Harlow," Wells heard him pontificate. "This animal, for example, is only too willing to quench our thirst with her milk, and this is where skill comes in, for we must treat her udders with care and respect—"

As he spoke, the millionaire must have done something amiss, for the creature swung round so abruptly that it knocked him clean off the stool, causing him to utter a curse. Emma gave the prettiest laugh Wells had ever heard.

"Well, I've discovered another thing I do as badly as reenacting a Martian invasion," the millionaire murmured, standing up with an embarrassed grin.

The air rippled once more with the sound of Emma's mirth. Murray, too, began to laugh, and for a moment, which to Wells seemed magical, the two of them appeared to forget they were fleeing death, doubtless protected by that enveloping joy that had arisen from nowhere. Before one of them had time to turn round, the author moved quietly away from the door, walking back the way he had come. This was a shared moment that was exclusively theirs, and he did not want them to know he had witnessed it. As he walked back into the house, Wells felt envious of the millionaire, for he knew that making a girl laugh was the surest way to gain her affections.

Once in the kitchen, Wells was content to wait patiently for them to return, watching the barn door through the window. He was astonished to see two strange men walk past. They were shabbily dressed and were heading toward the barn in the same stealthy way that he himself had only moments before, but with far less innocent intentions, for both were armed with what looked like sharp blades. After his momentary incredulity, Wells bolted up and took a few hesitant steps. Were they the owners of the house? he wondered, then instantly ruled out the idea, because the men's clothes were not those of country but of town folk. They could only be marauders, the kind of opportunists who use any type of social unrest to their own ends. And it was clear they were planning to surprise his companions, unaware that he in turn was watching them. This gave him an advantage over them, which any man more determined and brave would exploit. But Wells was not such a man. He was incapable of calming his nerves sufficiently to confront the situation, to grab anything he could use as a weapon and attack from behind, knocking out the intruders with a pair of swift blows. His heart began thumping wildly, and, seized with panic, he found himself hurtling out of the house recklessly, noisily even, with the aim of yelling to alert his companions and thereby get himself off the hook. However, before he was able to make a sound, he felt a cold, sharp object pressing against his throat.

"Calm down, my friend," a gruff voice whispered in his ear. "You wouldn't want to spoil the surprise for your companions."

XXV

*T*HERE WERE NOT TWO, BUT THREE OF THEM,
Wells realized with irritation, as the men herded them all
into the house like an unruly flock of sheep. And regrettably their faces
were more familiar than he would have liked. The two men who had
taken his companions prisoner in the barn (one had emerged with his
arm around the girl's dainty neck while the other pushed the millionaire
forward contemptuously) had looked vaguely familiar to him, but it had
only dawned on him who they were when his attacker had pushed him
into the corner of the sitting room, thus enabling Wells to see his face. It
was coarse and stubbled, with small piggy eyes that flashed with a crude
animal rage. But what allowed Wells to identify him was the makeshift
bandage that was wound around his left foot, a soiled rag stained with
various reddish hues. After one of his henchmen, an apelike, restless
creature, handed him the pistol he had wrested off Murray, the lame
man glowered at them ominously. For a few moments he said nothing,
letting the situation sink in, giving them time to realize that the tables
had turned since their skirmish at the station, which had left him with
the indelible souvenir of a bullet in his foot. He grinned at them menacingly, relishing the opportunity fate had given him to smile that way
at those he usually served. Wells shot a sidelong glance at Murray, who
remained alert, jaw clenched, a faint expression of disdain on his lips,
as though the possibility of dying bothered him less than having been
overpowered by these louts. It was clear from his posture that he was
more concerned for Emma's safety than his own, for he was standing

as close to her as possible, as if preparing to shield her at the first sign of danger.

The limping man spoke at last. "Well, well. What a pleasant surprise, eh? There's nothing I like more when traveling than to bump into old friends who I can share a pleasant moment with, don't you agree, lads?"

The two henchmen guffawed loudly, drawing out their laughter until it sounded like forced braying. Murray clenched his jaw even more tightly and edged closer to Emma.

"Yes, life's full of little surprises," the lame man continued to reflect aloud. "Didn't I say, lads: 'If we take the Chobham road, we'll catch up with our good friends.' And so we have. Although, if we hadn't seen that carriage with the big 'G' on it, we would have gone straight past, and wouldn't that have been a shame?" he said to his comrades in mock regret. "But no, our friends were thoughtful enough to leave the carriage in full view, which shows they wanted to see us again. Am I right, miss? Of course you did! All the ladies who bump into good old Roy Bowen want a bit more of him. They can't get enough. And good old Roy doesn't like to disappoint a lady, no sir. I should warn you, though, your manners leave a lot to be desired, and if you want good old Roy Bowen to give you a good time, first you'll have to learn how to behave."

As he said these last words, he gazed fixedly at the young woman, who was no doubt having regrets for shooting him in the foot. Now they were all going to pay for her bravado, reflected Wells, who despite his fear could not help observing with anthropological interest the simple soul, whose desire for revenge had driven him to pursue them regardless of the fact that the world was falling down around them. His henchmen seemed not to care either: the man with the apelike face and the one who had helped him defend the carriage in the station, a bulky redheaded individual who revealed a row of blackened teeth when he smiled.

"Now let's see how we can resolve this unpleasant situation," the lame man resumed with menacing calm, his eyes still fixed on Emma.

"I pushed you to the ground, and in return you shot my foot off. Good. What should my response be now, miss?" The porter ogled the girl's body with intentional crudeness. "Mmm . . . I think I know. And I'm sure your two friends here will have no trouble guessing what I have in mind either, because we men understand each other, don't we, gents?" He smiled sardonically at Murray and Wells before turning his predatory gaze back to Emma. "If you come upstairs with me willingly, without a fight, I assure you it will be much more pleasurable for us both."

"If you touch one hair on the lady's head, I'll kill you," Murray interrupted icily.

The millionaire's voice made Wells think this was not an empty boast. Unfortunately, given the circumstances, there would be few opportunities for him to carry out his threat.

"Ha, ha," the lame man cackled. "You, kill me? I'm afraid you haven't got the picture, big guts. Who's got the gun now?"

"That changes nothing, Roy," Murray replied coolly, confusing the porter by uttering his name, an effective way of showing that he inspired neither fear nor respect. "Go ahead: kill me, then I'll kill you."

"Really? And how do you propose to do that? Can you stop a bullet?" The lame man turned to his companions, looking for support. The two men let out appropriate guffaws. "It looks like we've got a genuine hero on our hands, lads." The porter turned back to Murray, this time with a grimace of pity. "So, you'll kill me if I touch a hair on the young lady's head, will you?"

The millionaire smiled serenely. "That's right, Roy," he said, in the same tone he might use with a not very intelligent child.

"We'll soon see," the lame man hissed defiantly, "because I'm going to do much more than that."

At that he fell silent, observing Murray with a mixture of anger and curiosity. Suddenly, he knitted his brow, as if he were doing calculations.

"Hold on," he said. "Where's the other fellow?"

"There was no one else in the shed, Roy," the apelike fellow obligingly replied. "Only the lovebirds."

The lame man shook his head slowly, as though not satisfied with the reply.

"These two were lugging round a drunk fellow, don't you remember? Go upstairs and have a look, Joss," he ordered the redhead, gesturing at the ceiling with his chin.

With doglike obedience, the man called Joss began walking toward the staircase. Wells felt his heart begin to knock. He watched the man mount the stairs warily, trying without much success not to make them creak under his considerable bulk, his knife firmly clasped at waist level, ready to be thrust into the guts of any drunkard who might pounce on him. When, after what seemed like an age, he finally managed to reach the top, he vanished down the corridor, stealthy as a cat. Their eyes fixed on the top of the staircase, the others waited eagerly for the redhead's verdict so that they could resume the matter at hand. Wells waited anxiously for the fellow to announce he had found Inspector Clayton, who in all probability was still fast asleep on the bed. But a few minutes later, they observed Joss skipping blithely down the stairs.

"There's no one there, Roy."

The lame man expressed surprise at these words, and Wells gritted his teeth, trying hard not to let his own surprise show. Clayton had woken up, and apparently in time to hide! All was not lost, then. An inspector with Scotland Yard, trained to act resolutely in situations such as this, was hiding somewhere upstairs, no doubt elaborating a rescue plan. Wells did his best to conceal his joy, while the lame man questioned the redhead warily.

"Are you sure, Joss? Did you check every room?"

"Yes, and they were all empty."

The lame man appeared to meditate, shaking his head mistrustfully. All of a sudden he turned to Murray.

"Where's the other man?" he demanded.

"He was a nuisance," the millionaire replied nonchalantly. "He kept getting drunk, so we decided to leave him behind in a ditch. No doubt he's still there sleeping it off."

The lout eyed the millionaire suspiciously, while Wells tried his best to control his nerves, thankful that he himself had not been asked, for he doubted he would have been able to tell a lie with the same composure as Murray. After what seemed like an age, the lame man guffawed.

"That's not a very nice way to treat your friends," he remarked after he had finished laughing. "But that's enough chitchat. Now, where were we? Oh, yes: the young lady and I have unfinished business. A little matter of revenge, if I remember right."

Still fixing them with his malevolent gaze, the lame man passed the pistol to his apelike companion, with the relaxed gesture of one handing gloves to his butler.

"Be a good lad, Mike, and watch over the lady's companions while she and I repair upstairs, will you?" he said louchely.

Mike nodded, solemn as a child whose sole desire in life is to make his father proud. He took charge of the weapon and glared at the prisoners. Without further ado, the lame man took a step toward the pale and tremulous Emma, offering her his hand and giving a grotesque bow.

"Please, miss, would you permit me the pleasure of a private dance in my chambers?"

He had scarcely finished speaking when Murray made as if to stand between them, but Mike, who had been watching the millionaire like a hawk, pulled him up short by placing the gun barrel to his temple.

"Stay where you are, fat face," he barked. "Don't make me waste a bullet."

The millionaire sized him up for a few seconds, during which Wells's heart leapt into his throat, but finally obeyed and stepped back, realizing if he was dead he could not help Emma. The lame man grinned at his submissiveness and yanked the girl toward him.

"Very good, gentlemen, that's what I like to see," he gloated, brandishing his knife an inch from Emma's neck. Then he spoke directly to Murray: "Would you like me to leave the door open so you can hear her groans of pleasure?"

Murray said nothing. He simply gazed at the man with an aston-

ishingly calm, even condescending expression on his face, as though he
considered the whole thing a tedious game. Yet the look of icy determination in his eyes did not escape Wells's notice. It was the look of a man
who has understood that the meaning of his life had suddenly changed,
that all his past actions and future plans no longer mattered because his
only aim in life was vengeance. And Wells realized that, exactly as he had
promised, the millionaire would kill the lame man, that even if Murray
met his death, he would return from the afterlife to do so. The hatred
that had begun to possess his soul would form a bridge between the two
worlds, allowing him to come back.

At that moment, through the window next to the staircase, Wells saw
a dark shadow drop to the ground then stand up and vanish to one side.
He felt a pang as he realized this could only be Clayton. Fortunately
their captors had their backs to the window, which meant the inspector
still had surprise on his side. Wells glanced at Murray to see whether
he had also seen Clayton jump, but the millionaire's eyes were fixed on
the lame man as he dragged the terrified girl up the stairs. When he
saw them disappear down the corridor, he lowered his eyes in despair, as
though he were about to pray, preparing himself to hear the woman he
loved cry out with pain and rage as she was violated by the station porter,
who, through some cruel twist of fate, had become the person in the
whole world who could most harm her.

"Now, now, don't look so sad, gentlemen," he heard Mike say sarcastically. "What shall we do to pass the time and forget what's going on
upstairs?"

"Why not make them dance, Mike?" the redhead suggested with a
grin, displaying a row of decaying teeth. "You know, we could shoot at
their feet."

The other man looked at him contemptuously.

"How many bullets do you think are in the gun, Joss?"

"I don't know, Mike."

"Six, six bloody bullets. Are you suggesting we waste them on that?"

Six bullets. Until that moment, it had not occurred to Wells that the gun might be empty, but he quickly worked out they would have no such luck: three shots had been fired during the skirmish at the station, two into the air and one into the porter's foot, which unfortunately meant there were three left, enough to kill them with. At that moment, a noise came from the kitchen. Wells realized Clayton must have climbed in through the window and was attracting their captors' attention as part of his rescue plan. Or so he hoped. The two henchmen turned toward the kitchen. So did Wells, also tensing his body, ready to act if necessary. Only Murray appeared oblivious to the scene, his eyes glued to the top of the stairs.

"What was that?" Mike said, still pointing the gun at them. "Go and have a look, Joss."

"Why me?" the redhead protested.

"Because I've got to stay here and watch these two idiots!"

Joss opened his big mouth to protest once more, but his companion's stern gaze dissuaded him. He gave a disgruntled sigh and walked cautiously toward the kitchen door, waving his knife. He surveyed the room carefully from the doorway but did not seem to notice anything untoward. Wells wondered whether Inspector Clayton would be able to overpower such a bulky individual, who although clearly none too intelligent, doubtless had a record of street fights as long as his arm. For a few moments nothing happened. The redhead's companion, who was not exactly a paragon of patience, was about to call out when, suddenly, they heard a series of dull thuds, stifled grunts, and pans clattering to the floor.

"What's going on, Joss?" Mike shouted.

When no reply was forthcoming, the fellow with the apelike face, without lowering the pistol, began edging slowly backward in the direction of the kitchen door to find out what was happening. Wells swallowed hard, his body tense as a spring. It occurred to him that he and the man called Mike had more or less the same build, and that if he jumped on him unawares, he might manage to wrestle the weapon from him. No sooner had he formulated the idea than it seemed completely mad, given he had never had a fight in his life. But Clayton would almost certainly need some assistance, however feeble, and the millionaire, whose eyes were still fixed on the staircase, was clearly in no state to offer him any. If they were to have any chance of reversing the situation, Wells would definitely need to intervene. And so the author took a deep breath and got ready to spring. Just then, two entwined bodies burst from the kitchen and crashed to the floor, rolling a few yards before coming to a halt beside Mike's feet. Wells could see that one of the men was Clayton. As the inspector began pulling himself up off the ground, a carving knife plunged up to the hilt in his adversary's chest became visible. Wells saw immediately that Clayton would not have time to get up and confront the other man, for Mike had instantly turned the gun on him. Wells realized his best chance was now, while Mike's attention was on Clayton, since if Mike shot the inspector he would be obliged to kill them, too. Although Wells had no background in fighting, his rugby experience at school had taught him how to tackle. In a flash he lunged at Mike, just as the man was preparing to shoot Clayton. The impact of the bullet knocked the inspector backward: his head hit the floor with a dull thud. However, as Wells had calculated, the fellow could not wheel around quickly enough to shoot at him. Wells managed to land on him before he had time to react, using the force of his leap to hurl him against the wall. The collision caused the pistol to fly out of his hand. They both watched it glide over the floorboards and come to a halt in the middle of the room, out of their reach but close to Murray, who gazed at it in bewilderment, as though he had just awoken from a deep sleep. Wells felt Mike twisting violently beneath him, trying to get his hands round Wells's throat. He saw Murray slowly rouse himself and pick the gun up off the floor, as though not quite realizing what it was. Murray glanced at the staircase and after a moment's hesitation bounded upstairs, a look of grim resolve on his face.

"Gilliam, help me, damn it!" Wells cried, struggling to keep Mike from throttling him.

But Murray had already disappeared up the steps, making the whole house shudder with his hulking gait. He reached the room, breathless, his eyes burning with rage and impotence. But the scene he came across was not the one he had anticipated. The lame man was kneeling on the ground groaning, his hands at his groin and his face twisted with pain. On the far side of the room stood Emma, the neck of her dress torn, fiercely clutching the knife she must have forced from him. When she saw Murray come in, she seemed to breathe more easily.

"Hello, Mr. Murray," she said in a voice that was almost cheerful, trying her best not to show how afraid she must have been before managing to overpower the porter. "As you can see, the situation is under control. He scarcely had time to rip my dress. There's nothing like trembling a little to make a man lower his guard."

Murray gazed at her in disbelief, relieved to find that she was surprisingly untouched. Here she was before him, a woman with a slight tear in the collar of her dress, which could have come from snagging it on a branch. A woman with no more than a spot of blood on her lip.

"And that blood?" he asked her gently.

"Oh, that," Emma said dismissively. "Well, he was able to slap me before I could—"

Murray wheeled round to face the lame man, who had stopped sobbing and was crouched in a corner, watching them through terrified eyes.

"Did you hit her, Roy?" Murray demanded.

"No sir, I never hit her, of course I didn't," the lame man gabbled.

Murray stared at him in disgust.

"You aren't calling the young lady a liar, are you, Roy?"

The lame man said nothing, wondering whether it was better to carry on lying or to tell the truth. In the end he shrugged, suggesting he had neither the desire nor the energy to undergo an interrogation.

"So, you hit the young lady," the millionaire said, pointing the pistol at him.

The lame man raised his head, alarmed. "What are you doing!" he exclaimed, the blood draining from his face. "You aren't going to shoot an unarmed man, are you?"

"I can assure you, Roy, that in other circumstances I would never do such a thing," the millionaire replied in a calm voice that even contained a hint of theatrical remorse. "But I gave you my word, do you remember? I told you I'd kill you if you touched a hair on the young lady's head. And the word of a gentleman is his bond."

Emma turned away as the shot rang out. When she looked again, the lame man was sprawled on the floor, with what seemed to her an excessively small hole in his forehead, from which blood was beginning to seep. This was the first dead person she had ever seen, and she found it hugely disappointing.

"Forgive me, Miss Harlow," said Murray ashamedly, "but I couldn't live in the same world as a man who hit you."

Emma gazed at him in silence. Murray looked back at her with a hangdog expression that almost caused her to laugh; he seemed like a child waiting to see whether he would be punished or pardoned for his latest act of mischief. Emma bit her bottom lip, and as she glanced once more at the body sprawled on the floor, she was aware of the metallic, salty taste of her own blood. That thug had slapped her, she remembered, her gorge rising. And although she had managed to fight him off and gain the upper hand, who knew what might have happened if Murray had not appeared. She gazed back at the millionaire, who was standing in the middle of the room, waiting for a word, a look, a smile, anything that would give him an inkling of what was going through her mind. Yet she herself did not know what to think. And this confused her. Normally she was able to assess any situation, for she had very clear opinions of what was right and what was wrong, and when classifying actions and people her standards brooked no modification. But now that had changed. The world seemed stripped of all sense, and she had no idea what to think about revenge killings, or about love at first sight, much less about that giant of a man, for whom only days before she had felt a contempt she was now unable to reproduce. However, to her astonishment she found that this confusion, which had turned her beliefs and principles on their head, was far from disagreeable; indeed, she found it liberating. Murray had lowered his head, pretending to examine the pistol carefully, but the sidelong glances he kept giving her to gauge her response were so obvious that Emma could feel the rage and anguish that had choked her moments before begin to dissolve, and a smile played over her lips.

"I must confess you have a very original way of wooing a lady, Mr. Murray. But I did warn you that I don't become enamored easily," she said, watching with amusement as the millionaire swallowed hard, waiting for her verdict. "You'll have to make more of an effort."

Murray grinned, waves of joy coursing through him like sweet liquor.

"I'm honored that you allow me to keep trying, Miss Harlow," he replied gratefully.

"I think it's time you called me Emma, without worrying you might provoke one of my annoying temper tantrums, don't you think?"

The millionaire nodded and heaved a sigh of relief, then immediately protested: "Oh, but Miss Harlow, I mean Emma, your temper tantrums don't bother me in the slightest. I assure you—"

"Are the others all right?" Emma interrupted, alarmed by the sounds of a struggle coming from downstairs.

"The others?" Murray replied absentmindedly, as though he hadn't a clue what she was talking about, then suddenly he exclaimed: "Damnation, Wells!"

Remembering the precarious situation in which he had left the author, Murray led Emma downstairs, where the girl was startled to find Wells grappling with one of their aggressors on the sitting-room floor. But she could see immediately that, owing to their matched strength and their apparently flagging energy, the fight looked more like a scrap between two boys: the man called Mike was rather clumsily attempting to throttle Wells, who was defending himself as best he could, hitting his opponent haphazardly in the face, twisting his ears, and pulling his hair. What horrified her was the sight of the redhead sprawled on the floor next to them, a cleaver buried in his chest. And beside him, she recognized with alarm Inspector Clayton. She wondered first how he had got there, and then whether he was dead. Judging from his position (which was oddly contorted, his nose squashed against the floor as if he were sniffing the wood), she thought the latter was the most likely answer. He must have received the bullet she had heard fired from upstairs, which had distracted the lame man long enough for her to knee him in the groin.

"I was forced to shoot Roy, George," Murray confessed, giving Wells a knowing smile. "He was about to stab Miss Harlow with his knife."

Hearing Murray's voice, Wells and Mike stopped grappling with each other, and, as though they had been caught doing something shameful, they scrambled to their feet, only to find the millionaire and the girl standing next to them. Wells noticed the torn collar of Emma's dress.

"Miss Harlow . . . That man . . . ? I mean . . . are you all right?" he asked, blushing slightly.

"Perfectly all right, Mr. Wells," the girl declared blithely. "In fact, it was unkind of you all not to warn that wretched man about the feisty nature of New York women."

"Good, I . . . you can't imagine how glad I am," said Wells in relief, then turning suddenly to the millionaire, he added, "You're a complete blackguard, Gilliam! This fellow might have strangled me." He spat, gesturing toward the man with the apelike face.

"I thought the young lady was more in need of assistance than you, George," Murray said, grinning contritely.

"Even so, you must confess I was managing quite well before you arrived, Mr. Murray," Emma declared, smoothing out the creases in her dress.

"Oh, no. Definitely not, Miss Harlow. Whilst I praise your pluck, ahem, I have to confess that when I entered the room, well . . . let us say the situation was such that I was . . . *obliged* to shoot that rogue in order to defend your honor."

"Oh, yes, of course," the girl hurriedly agreed, glancing furtively at the astonished Wells. "Your intervention was *absolutely necessary,* Mr. Murray. If you hadn't appeared when you did, I couldn't have held that brute at bay a moment longer."

"My dear Miss Harlow, that is something we shall never know. And I don't mean to imply that you couldn't have managed without me. If I decided to intervene it was simply because I didn't think it was *appropriate* to wait and see . . . ," Murray replied politely. He glanced out of the corner of his eye at Wells, who was by now contemplating them suspiciously. Then, still wearing the vapid smile of an opium eater, Murray turned to the man called Mike. "But let us not quarrel in front of our guest, Miss Harlow. Whatever will he think of us?"

"I—I . . . ," the man with the apelike face stammered.

The millionaire smiled at him amiably.

"Well, Mike, I am the one with the pistol now. Interesting the way a weapon confers power, isn't it? But you know all about that, don't you?" he added in a friendly tone, weighing the pistol in his hand. "I believe this is a Webley double-action revolver, no less. I daresay that while you were holding it you felt capable of playing with our lives, didn't you, Mike? You even wanted us to dance for you."

"Is this necessary, Gilliam?" Wells intervened.

"Don't you think Mike should at least learn something from all this, George?" the millionaire asked.

Wells gave a sigh.

"Go ahead, carry on playing the tough," he said.

The millionaire smiled at him good-naturedly, then looked back at the man with the apelike face.

"Well, Mike," he said, "how shall we amuse ourselves?"

"I don't know, I—I . . . ," the other man stammered. "I swear I didn't want to go after you, it was Roy who forced Joss and me to—"

Murray interrupted suddenly, as though he'd had a flash of inspiration. "Can you milk a cow?"

"Yes . . . ," Mike replied, bewildered.

"Wonderful, isn't it, Miss Harlow?" the millionaire declared, apparently unable to contain his joy at having the girl beside him, unharmed. "Let's go to the barn and find out!"

"What the . . . ?" Wells murmured.

But no one paid him any mind, for Murray, the girl, and the man called Mike were already headed for the barn. Wells shook his head in disbelief. Unsure what to do next, he glanced about the room, contemplating the two bodies on the floor, then gazed toward the top of the stairs leading to the bedroom where the other dead man lay. He tried to absorb everything that had just happened: only moments before, they were about to be killed or roughed up at least by those thugs, hideously mutilated perhaps, although this would have been nothing in comparison to the girl's fate, and now, here they were, alive and well thanks to the actions of poor Inspector Clayton. Wells congratulated himself on his own crucial intervention and wondered whether they should take the inspector to London or give him a Christian burial there. He sighed deeply: clearly he would have to decide this alone, since Murray was too busy milking cows. Just then, Clayton raised his head, startling the author.

"You're alive!" Wells exclaimed, once he had recovered from the shock.

"Considering what this hand cost me, the least it can do is to save my life," the inspector explained, showing Wells the deplorable state of his prosthesis after it had taken a direct hit. The inspector stood up, slowly rubbing his neck, then added, as though to himself, "I must have been knocked unconscious when I hit the floor."

"I'm glad one of us is capable of stopping a bullet," Wells remarked.

"Anything is possible in this life, Mr. Wells, as you will soon discover."

Although the inspector's pompous reply nettled Wells, he was relieved that Clayton was alive. Not just because the inspector had risked his life for them, or because he no longer needed to decide whether to bury him or take him to London, but also because it meant he was spared the tedious task of having to urge the others to resume their journey.

"What is the situation?" Clayton asked Wells, as if reading his mind, surprised there was only one dead body in the sitting room.

"Er, you might say we handled things rather well, Inspector," the author told him. "The lame man is upstairs . . . dead, I believe."

"Good. What about the fellow who shot me?" he inquired.

"Well . . ." The author paused, unsure how to respond to that question. "He's in the barn milking a cow."

Clayton looked at him, perplexed.

"I'm quite serious, Inspector, I assure you," the author replied, irritated. "Murray has taken him prisoner and . . . well, you had better come with me."

The pair left the house and made their way over to the barn, gazing up at the magnificent spring sky unfurling above them, an unlikely backdrop for a Martian invasion.

"I thought that for those on the side of the law killing was a last resort," Wells remarked, recalling the redhead's demise.

"And so it is," Clayton replied with a somber expression that made it clear he had been forced to use the cleaver.

"I see," murmured the author, who was beginning to feel at a definite disadvantage for not having killed anyone during the fight.

They arrived at the barn to discover that the milking had been successfully completed. Apparently the man with the apelike face had not been boasting simply to save his skin, and now, his task completed, he stood expectantly, hardly daring to interrupt the millionaire and the girl, who were gorging themselves on the fruits of his labor, to inquire about his fate.

"You're alive!" Murray and Emma declared as one to the inspector.

"Yes, indeed," Clayton affirmed unnecessarily, and, after studying the duo with a contented smile, he added, "I'm glad you two are safe, particularly you, Miss Harlow."

"Miss Harlow is in the best of health," Murray said coldly, offering him a bowl of milk. "Here, drink some of this. You must be thirsty."

"Thank you," the inspector said, raising the bowl to his lips. Passing it on to Wells, he said, to no one in particular, "I suppose I must have fainted at the station."

"Just so," Murray confirmed with a smirk. "But as you see, despite being in your custody, we didn't abandon you there."

"And thanks to that we are all still alive," Emma intervened, flashing the millionaire a disapproving look.

Murray shrugged, declining to add another comment. Clayton then went over to where a snarl of ropes lay amid a pile of tools by the door. He plucked one out and, after dismissing the possibility of accomplishing his task alone, held it out to the author.

"Would you mind, Mr. Wells?"

The author took it from him grudgingly and began tying up the prisoner, who meekly offered no resistance.

"Can someone tell me where we are?" Clayton said.

"At an abandoned farmhouse on the Addlestone road," the prisoner himself politely informed the inspector.

"Good," said Clayton, and then, holding his hand out to the millionaire, he ventured: "Would you be so kind as to return my gun, Mr. Murray?"

"I don't see why I should," the millionaire began to protest.

"Gilliam . . ." Emma cautioned him with the dreamy indulgence of a mother.

"Of course, Inspector," the millionaire replied, handing the revolver over with a vexed expression.

Once he had it in his hands, Clayton examined the chamber.

"Hmm . . . only one bullet left. I hope we won't need to shoot anyone else on our way to London, because, if you are all sufficiently rested, I suggest we continue our journey at once."

XXVI

HE ROAD TO ADDLESTONE GAVE OFF A CERTAIN disquieting calm. There was no sign of any destruction, from which the group deduced that the tripods had not yet organized themselves for their advance on London. It probably would not take them long, but in the meantime it was easy to forget about them, for not only had the sporadic cannon fire ceased, but the air was filled with the smell of fresh hay. And so the passengers might easily have been mistaken for a party of friends enjoying an outing in the country. Except for the fact that instead of a picnic hamper, they had brought along a man bound with rope.

Wells glared sullenly at the fellow whose finger marks were on his neck, sitting opposite him and the inspector. Clayton's pistol was resting on his lap like some sinister cat, but it offered Wells little reassurance; they all knew the gun contained a single bullet, which for the moment had no name on it. It bothered Wells that the inspector had, as the hours went by, stopped pointing it at the prisoner, even though the man called Mike appeared to have no intention of trying to escape. Why would he, seeing as the carriage was headed for the only place where he might be safe? Better to travel by coach than on foot, he must have thought. And now the oaf was gazing out the window at the scenery, a mournful expression on his face. Perhaps he was ruing what he had been obliged to do during the past few hours, spurred on by the hapless lame man, or perhaps he was simply afraid of impending death. He had told the others that after their failed attempt to seize the millionaire's carriage, they had succeeded in making off with another, moments before the tripod demolished Woking Station. None of them had glimpsed the machine, but from a nearby rise they had seen the flaming pile of rubble to which within a few minutes it had reduced the station where they had fetched and carried so many suitcases and trunks. This story had been his sole contribution to the conversation, after which he had lapsed into the anguished state of a Romantic martyr that so irked Wells. What was the meaning of such an attitude? Why was this oaf behaving as though his death were a great loss to humanity when he had only been born to make up the numbers, because someone had to perish during invasions to provide excitement? Deep down, it bothered Wells that they were both forced to flee death, that the invaders made no distinction between their enemies and did not notice they were firing indiscriminately at those who had been born to endure life and those who had been born to create it. He closed his eyes, tired of looking at that apelike face with its ridiculously wounded expression.

Wells became aware, above the clatter of the coach, of Murray and the girl chattering excitedly up on the driver's seat. He could not hear their exact words, but they sounded so happy he had to admit that, amazingly enough in this anomalous situation, the millionaire was managing to make the girl see him as an attractive man, far more so, no doubt, than had he wooed her in the usual fashion. Wells no longer doubted the millionaire's feelings: how could he, when he had seen how ready Murray was to protect her. Under the pretext of being too tired to give it any thought, the author avoided asking himself whether he would have done as much for Jane, or whether his love was a mere show, a tender yet feeble emotion, which she had nevertheless considered significant enough for her to marry him, accepting, perhaps from their first conversation, that the romantic love of novels would never inflame such a pragmatic soul.

Wells was immersed in these thoughts when they arrived in Weybridge, only to find that twenty or so cavalrymen were evacuating the town. On foot or on horseback, the soldiers were busy urging the locals to pack up their most prized possessions and leave the area at once. They had to make their way through a confusion of carriages, carts, cabriolets, and other improvised means of transport, in the midst of which men in plus fours or boaters and their well-groomed wives voiced their displeasure at this absurd evacuation. Whilst everyone appeared willing to collaborate with the army, even bundling their belongings onto an omnibus commandeered for the occasion, Wells noticed that most of them seemed oblivious to the seriousness of their situation.

It took them a long time to get across the town. When they got beyond Sunbury, they ran into a lengthy procession of vehicles and pedestrians, which, like a biblical exodus, was slowly wending its way toward London. With haunted faces, its members carried trunks and suitcases, pushed carts or even prams piled high with their belongings. Only the children appeared to be enjoying the novel situation, laughing gaily atop the piles of rolled-up mattresses and small bits of furniture, like the unwitting lookouts for disaster. In spite of everything, no one doubted that the powerful British army would trounce the so-called invaders in a matter of days, putting an end to this unexpected war that was causing everyone so much trouble. *They're only tin pots on stilts!* they heard one elderly gentleman cry out as he wheeled his cart brimming with useless sticks of furniture, unaware of the Hell that was being unleashed on Earth. And as the carriage with the emblazoned "G" weaved its way through the crowd, Wells took in each detail of what was happening around them. He cursed himself for not having a notebook handy. In his novel the Martians had constructed airships that they flew directly to London in order to attack, so it had not been necessary for him to describe terrible mass exoduses of this sort. Now that he had realized their dramatic potential, however, he told himself that if he ever had the chance to rewrite his novel, he would replace the ferocious flying machines shaped like stingrays (which he had only invented to make the vessel Robur flew in Verne's novel seem like a toy) with tripods such as these, which with their spiderlike advance across the countryside fueled the spread of rumors among the inhabitants of those areas. This created a far more intimate kind of horror, because instead of merely flying far above people's heads they were trampling over their gardens.

Having managed to skirt around the terrified lines of fugitives, they reached Hampton Court, which was shrouded in a peculiarly noiseless calm. They drove around the perimeter of Bushy Park, with its deer cavorting beneath the chestnut trees as carefree as ever, then crossed the river and took the Richmond road. At last, in the distance, they were able to make out the hills around London. They sighed with relief at the sight, because this was where the inspector had told them the lines of defense had been established.

"Dozens of cannons will be waiting for the enemy," Clayton had assured them. "The tripods will have trouble crossing our lines."

"Do you still think they are Martians, Inspector?" Wells asked. "Murray doesn't believe they might be Germans either, but I—"

"For the love of God, Wells, what do you have against Germans?" Clayton interrupted. "I assure you they aren't to blame for all the world's ills. Besides, I don't think we should waste our time on fruitless speculation about who the enemy might be. In a few miles we'll find out, as soon as our cannons defeat the first tripod."

"I hope you're right," the author said glumly.

"Have confidence in our army, Mr. Wells," was the young man's arrogant reply.

"Remember that you haven't seen a tripod, Clayton, and we have. We passed under its legs while you were sound asleep."

"Ah, Mr. Wells, the most terrifying thing is sometimes not what we see, but rather what we are forced to imagine," the inspector retorted.

Wells gave an exasperated grunt, momentarily wondering whether it might not have been a good idea to leave that ceaseless fount of wisdom in a ditch.

"I assure you, Inspector Clayton, it was no puppet show," the author replied rather tetchily. "And, needless to say, the tripods bear no resemblance to tin pots on stilts, like that old fellow said."

The inspector gave a patronizing smirk. "I confess I'm most interested to see one of these monsters. How then would you describe them? I'm sure that with your talent you can produce a far more accurate simile."

"Well . . . ," the author murmured, vexed at having to respond to the inspector's absurd challenge. "I'd say they look like—"

"Like a milking stool?" the prisoner suddenly inquired.

"Yes, you could say that," Wells conceded, irritated by this interruption from the apelike man.

"With something dangling from the top like a . . . tentacle?" the oaf inquired again.

"Yes, from which it shoots its deadly ray," Wells snapped.

"In that case, we have a problem," Mike said, motioning with his chin toward the window.

Wells and the inspector turned as one and saw behind them a tripod approaching along the road. Although it was still far off, the three men realized in horror that with its huge strides it would soon overtake them.

"Good God!" said Clayton.

For a moment, the inspector appeared mesmerized by the terrifying vision before his eyes.

"I don't think your pistol will be of much use now," remarked the man with the ape face.

Ignoring his comment, Clayton slid open the hatch and yelled, "Have you seen what's coming after us, Murray? Drive the horses on! Make them fly, damn it!"

A few moments later, they felt a violent jolt and gripped their seats for dear life. The millionaire was urging on the horses hard now, trying to whip into them the power of flight. The lovers' jaunt was at an end. This was a desperate race to reach the safety of the hills before the tripod hunted them down. Boxed in between Clayton and the prisoner, Wells could not help letting out a cry of anguish as through the rear window he saw the machine gaining on them, kicking up fountains of sand and gravel each time its powerful legs sank into the ground.

"Faster, Murray, faster!" Clayton shouted.

With a fresh leap that made the earth shudder, the tripod came to within twenty yards of the carriage. Wells could see the tentacle sway in the air, and a feeling of dense, viscous panic clogged his veins: he knew what that familiar rocking movement meant. And this time there would be no escape. As the tentacle took aim, he resigned himself to perish in the coming moments, together with the prisoner and the smuggest inspector in Scotland Yard. Just then, they heard a deafening blast. But to their amazement, it was the tripod that received the hit. Its monstrous head shook violently, and one corner shattered into a dozen metal shards that scattered to the ground like a deadly shower of pollen. A splinter hit the tail end of the carriage, causing it to veer momentarily from its path, but Murray swiftly regained control. They heard a second blast coming from a different direction than the first, and the tripod shook once more, but this time the shot glanced off its left side. Wells saw the tentacle turn away from them, seeking out its aggressors—no doubt the cannons Clayton had told them about. These must have been positioned among the stands of trees toward which the carriage was rattling, now managing to outstrip its monstrous pursuer. The tentacle fired, and with a disquieting hiss the powerful heat ray spat out a shaft of fire to its left, blasting a dozen trees into the air. Wells had the impression that it was firing blindly, rousing his hopes that the duel might have a favorable outcome. Just then, the carriage must have crossed the line of defense, for all of a sudden they found themselves in the middle of a bewildering battle scene: dotted all around were various munition carts, dozens of heavy cannons, behind which gunners were hard at work, and a multitude of soldiers camouflaged behind trees and hillocks. The scene was one of total chaos, in which Wells hoped some order existed. With a violent jerk, Murray halted the carriage as they passed the last group of cannons. With surprising agility, he leapt from the driver's seat and helped the girl down.

"Is everyone all right?" he bawled, in order for those inside to hear him above the deafening cannon fire.

Wells, Clayton, and the prisoner all nodded, though none of them stepped out of the carriage, preferring to follow the progress of the battle through the rear window. From what felt like a relatively safe distance, they watched the tentacle launch another shot, much more accurate this time. The heat ray sent half a dozen heavy cannons flying into the air, along with their respective gunners, many of whom, reduced to charred lumps, thudded into the trees. A dense odor of seared flesh floated over the battleground. The tripod, it appeared, was not willing to lay down its arms. Then, all of a sudden, whoever was in command, or perhaps an inspired gunner, fired at the legs of the machine, striking one of them and shattering it instantly. The tripod's colossal head appeared to bob before lurching forward slowly and crashing to the ground a few yards away from a battalion of terrified soldiers.

"My God, they've shot it down," Wells murmured, exhilarated by the brutal heroism of the confrontation, but most of all by its outcome.

"If the Creator had considered it wise to put a three-legged creature on this Earth He would have done so, but obviously the design is flawed," Clayton remarked with his habitual pomposity.

After the felling of the tripod, the roar of cannons halted abruptly, and a dense silence descended, which all were too abashed to break. Then, somewhere amid the smoking ruin of the tripod's head, what looked like a hatch opened, and from it emerged the pilot.

Gilliam Murray's first impression was of a giant cockroach made of thick pea soup. But as his eyes grew accustomed to what he was seeing, the thing took on the appearance of a giant maggot, whose segmented body moved with suppleness, almost undulating across the ground, suggesting it had no bones or any kind of frame inside holding it up. The thing was roughly the size of a rhinoceros, and its outer layer put Murray in mind of the skin on certain poisonous toadstools. Somewhere on that amorphous body he thought he glimpsed a cluster of orifices and slits, which he assumed must be its head. Dotted over its pliant body he also thought he saw clusters of fine tentacles that seemed to give off a bluish glow and an occasional spark, like an electrical charge. After moving a few yards, the lump came to a halt, keeling over on one side, and seconds later the flesh stopped rippling, and it remained chillingly still. In its own way, the thing had perished before their eyes.

"As I told you, George," the millionaire muttered, recalling with horror the nauseating green pap his governess used to shovel into his mouth as a child, "these are no Germans."

"No, no they aren't," Wells agreed, staring with horror at the body sprawled beside the machine, its sinister appearance striking him as familiar.

"I realize it's a fascinating sight," said Clayton, "but if you look up you'll see something even more startling."

Wells and Murray raised their heads and witnessed, outlined against the smoke from the blasts, more than a dozen tripods approaching in great strides toward the shattered line of defense.

"My God!" cried Wells. "Murray, get us out of here!"

The millionaire obeyed immediately, seizing the reins and spurring on the horses. Seconds later, the carriage was hurtling toward Sheen, leaving the detachment of soldiers to their fate. On their way through Putney, they heard the roar of cannons start up again, revealing that the tripods had reached the hills. Moments later, the disquieting hiss of the Martian ray fired back. Night was beginning to fall as they crossed Putney Bridge and took the King's Road toward Scotland Yard. Filled with dread at what they had just seen, they rode in grim silence through the darkened streets of a city that still harbored the naïve hope of defeating the invaders.

XXVII

*A*ll London seemed to be holding its breath. In Fulham as in Chelsea the carriage with the ornate "G" had to force its way through clusters of people clogging the streets. Londoners stood on corners, chatting idly or smoking their pipes as they gazed expectantly at the gradually darkening sky. No one wanted to miss any part of the invasion they might glimpse from there. Even those who had followed police instructions and stayed indoors kept leaning out of their windows, waiting for the battle on the outskirts of the city to be over at last so they could resume their lives. From the carriage, the group caught sight of a few solemnly concerned faces, but human nature being unpredictable, they also saw people drinking, singing, or playing cards in taverns, unwilling to let the situation upset their routine. Needless to say, no one there had seen a tripod. The few who had, and had lived to tell the tale, had not yet reached the city. Nor had the news that the invaders were Martians, which meant this flood of people almost certainly had no idea what was attacking the all-powerful British Empire. People had been advised to stay inside the protected area of the city, and to judge by their calm attitude, no one appeared to believe they were in any real danger. Their cocksureness struck Wells as pitiable. But what could he do about it? Tell them about the terrifying destruction his group had witnessed? No, that would only cause panic to spread like wildfire through the restless crowd. They had no choice but to do as Clayton had ordered: head for Scotland Yard, where they would deliver the prisoner and pool their information, fully aware they were only pretending to carry on as usual.

On their way they stopped off in a side street close to where Westminster Cathedral was being built. It was the house of the friends Jane had been visiting the day before, and Wells thanked Clayton for allowing him to look for his wife, slightly uncomfortable because Emma would have to wait to do the same with her relatives, as Southwark was quite far out of their way. He descended from the coach, entered the building, and raced up the stairs to the Garfields' flat, praying Jane would still be there. But before he could even knock, he found a message addressed to him pinned to the door. Recognizing Jane's handwriting, Wells tore the note off. In it his wife informed him she was fine, but that they were leaving the house to try to find out what was going on outside the city, as not much information was coming through, and she was worried about him. She also told him she hoped he reached London safely and found her note, and ended by saying that, come what may, she would be waiting for him on Primrose Hill the following morning at dawn. Wells stuffed the note in his pocket and aimed an angry kick at the door, cursing the fact that she had left the house to try to find out whether he was still alive. Where could they have gone? He had no idea where to start looking, and wandering the streets calling her name seemed to him as pointless as it was impractical. He returned to the carriage disgruntled and relayed what was in the message to the others.

"Very well," said Clayton, "in that case we'll carry on with our plan until your meeting tomorrow. And don't worry, Mr. Wells, I'm sure the tripods won't manage to enter the city before dawn tomorrow. Your wife will be all right."

Wells nodded. He hoped the inspector was correct, since it was plain that this calm would last only until the tripods succeeded in breaking through the lines of defense. When that happened, no one would be safe. He was about to thank Clayton for his reassurances, but the inspector had already turned away and was watching with interest a group of four or five men who were breaking into a bicycle shop at the end of the street. This was the first disturbance they had witnessed, and doubtless it would not be the last. However, what had attracted Clayton's attention wasn't this minor act of looting, but rather the three policemen watching the scene from the opposite corner without intervening. The only one not in uniform was a young inspector, a pale, skinny fellow whom Clayton appeared to recognize. He told the others to wait a moment and approached the trio, intrigued.

"Inspector Garrett?"

The young man swung round and looked at Clayton, surprised. For a few moments he simply gazed at him in silence, as he would a stranger.

"Inspector Clayton," he whispered at last, as though he had plucked his name from a distant hazy memory, despite the fact that they regularly bumped into each other at Scotland Yard.

Garrett fell silent again, staring fixedly at Clayton with a startling coldness that made the latter shudder. Clayton had imagined exchanging excited impressions about what was going on, or discussing the possibility of joining forces and devising a plan together: anything but this unnerving indifference. A few steps away, the two uniformed police constables contemplated Clayton with the same cold expectancy. Not knowing what to say, Clayton motioned with his chin toward the robbery taking place on the other side of the street.

"Do you need some assistance, Inspector?" said Clayton, pointing his chin at the looters.

Garrett gazed nonchalantly toward the looters.

"Oh, no, we have the situation under control," he assured Clayton.

"Good . . . ," Clayton said skeptically, as Garrett turned back to look at him with the same disconcerting indifference. "Then I'll continue on to Scotland Yard."

"Why are you going there?" the young man inquired abruptly.

"I have a prisoner to deliver," Clayton replied, thrown by this sudden show of interest.

Garrett nodded slowly, his lips pursed in a grimace of regret, and then, breaking off the conversation, he gestured to his men, and the three of them sauntered over to the bicycle shop. Seeing them approach, the thieves abandoned what they were doing and, after a brief exchange, ran off down the street. At this, Inspector Garrett glanced over his shoulder to see whether Clayton was still there and found the other man watching him. Clayton wheeled round uneasily to return to the carriage, but not before taking one last look to make sure the two policemen were picking up the bicycles and replacing them in the shop. As he moved away, Clayton puzzled over the policemen's strange behavior, in particular that of the young inspector. Garrett was a mere acquaintance, yet Clayton knew he was one of the Yard's finest brains. His ability to solve cases, apparently without stepping out of his office, was legendary, as was his squeamishness about blood. Perhaps this detachment was the only way a sensitive mind such as his could respond to the invasion, Clayton told himself. The situation had undoubtedly overwhelmed him, turning the flawless logic with which he solved everyday crimes on its head and leaving him all at sea, incapable of responding or giving orders to his men.

Clayton shrugged and climbed aboard the coach. They were soon heading toward Scotland Yard, threading their way through streets filled with the same leisurely crowds. Leaving the carriage in front of the building on Great George Street, they marched into police headquarters. Clayton headed the motley band, pulling along the man with the ape face with his good hand while the other dangled, shattered, from his right sleeve; then came Wells, haggard and cross and worrying about Jane, while Murray and Emma brought up the rear, exchanging joyous glances and engaging in lively banter, like a couple out choosing wedding presents. To the group's surprise, they found the entire place deserted. There was no one in the main entrance or the adjacent offices, and the pervading silence made them think they would probably not find a soul in the whole building. Startled, they walked warily around the entrance hall, here and there discovering disturbing signs of violence: an occasional upturned table, a smashed typewriter that had been thrown against the wall, a dented filing cabinet. But the most eerie things of all were the splashes of blood on the walls and floor. Hundreds of stains everywhere, like macabre symbols no one dared decipher.

"What the devil happened here?" Murray declared at last, puzzled by the enormous stain in the shape of Australia that covered one of the walls.

"I don't know," murmured Clayton.

"What's that smell?" Emma asked.

"Yes," Wells remarked, sniffing the air, "what a stench."

"It seems to be coming from upstairs," Clayton observed, gesturing toward the staircase leading to the upper floor housing the inspectors' offices.

The group glanced nervously at one another, realizing they had no choice but to go up there. Handing the prisoner over to Murray, Clayton took out his pistol and led the hesitant procession as they climbed the stairs. With each step, the evil smell grew more intense. When they reached the floor above, which was equally deserted, it became unbearable. Grimacing with revulsion, Clayton led the others down the corridor where Scotland Yard's inspectors and other high-ranking officers had their offices. By chance, the nauseating odor guided him to the end room, which belonged to Inspector Colin Garrett. The coincidence baffled Clayton. The office door was closed, but the stink was clearly coming from within. Clayton swallowed hard, placed his metal hand on the doorknob, and gave the others a solemn look, as though warning them to be prepared for anything. The others nodded, equally solemn, and watched as he tried to open the door with his fake hand while brandishing his firearm with the other. For a few moments, Clayton struggled feebly, testing his companions' patience, until finally he succeeded in prising open the door. The putrid odor wafted from the room, turning their stomachs. Gritting their teeth, they ventured into the office, trying hard not to retch. But the bloody vision they found inside was more appalling than any of them could have expected.

The room seemed to have been turned into a kind of makeshift abattoir. In the center, piled on top of one another like sacks of flour, lay more than a dozen half-dismembered bodies. Besuited inspectors, uniformed policemen, and even a few high-ranking officers in full dress lay in a ghastly jumble, faces twisted, guts ripped out, blood dripping from their multiple injuries, red rivulets slowly merging as they trickled down the pile, pooling on the floor below. All of them had met a grisly end, throats slit, bones snapped, stomachs brutally sliced open, slain by a killer with no notion of pity. Limbs torn from sockets and various organs lay strewn about the macabre monument, giving the impression that whatever had done this had slaughtered its victims all over the building and then hidden them there, gathering up every piece down to the last morsel of lung.

"Good God . . . ," Clayton muttered. "Who could have done this?"

Wells stifled the urge to vomit.

Stepping gingerly over a piece of liver lying on the floor, Clayton leaned over and examined a wound on one of the victims' faces: three deep cuts from the forehead down to the chin. It looked like the work of a fierce set of claws, which had not only flayed the skin but had gouged out one eye and sliced off half a nose. The inspector shook his head slowly as he surveyed the baleful scene. Wells was stooping over the pile of bodies, observing some of the wounds with clinical interest. Murray had dragged the girl out into the corridor, opening a window so the evening breeze would revive her, while the prisoner stood in the doorway, white as a sheet. Then Clayton noticed the dead man slumped in Garrett's chair, his head turned toward the wall at an impossible angle, as though the killer had broken his neck by twisting it round a hundred and eighty degrees. His stomach had been ripped open and his intestines lay in a heap on his lap. And yet instead of throwing him on the pile like the others, his killer had clearly taken the trouble to sit him in the chair. Curious as to the identity of the policeman who had been singled out for this special treatment, Clayton turned the dead man's head around.

"What on earth?" he cried, startled out of his wits.

The others looked at him in alarm.

"What's going on?" Wells asked, walking over to the inspector and trying not to slip on the entrails strewn over the floor.

"It's Colin Garrett," Clayton explained, bewildered. "The young inspector I was talking to not five minutes ago outside the bicycle shop."

He went out into the corridor, overcome in equal measure by the nauseous smell and his own bewilderment. Wells followed.

"Are you sure it's the same man?" asked Murray. Clayton was about to nod when a spine-chilling voice echoed along the corridor.

"Didn't they teach you to respect the dead, Clayton?"

As one, the group turned toward the direction the icy voice was coming from, only to discover a dim figure observing them from the end of the passageway. As the intruder moved toward them, stepping into a halo of lamplight, they made out the features of the same pale, skinny young man whose broken neck and torn face they had just seen inside the room. They stared at one another in disbelief at the sight of this disquieting double.

"This is not possible," Clayton whispered.

"I thought you believed anything was possible, Clayton," the false Garrett retorted, his voice devoid of all humanity.

Clayton responded to the provocation by stepping forward away from the others and raising his revolver.

"Stop! Don't move another inch, whatever you are," he commanded in an unnecessarily theatrical voice.

The false Garrett contemplated him for a few seconds with the air of a sleepwalker, then replied almost indifferently, "I wasn't intending to, Clayton."

At this, his mouth opened grotesquely, and what looked like an incredibly long, reddish tongue like a toad's or a chameleon's darted along the corridor toward Clayton. The inspector felt the hideous appendage coil itself round his arm, and his gun went off without him even realizing he had pulled the trigger. Even though he had not had time to aim, Clayton saw the bullet hit the head of the false Inspector Garrett.

As Garrett dropped to the floor, his monstrous tongue uncoiled, furling back into his mouth like a ball of flesh. Before anyone had time to react, Garrett's body began to writhe hideously in the middle of the corridor.

Agent Cornelius Clayton of the Special Branch at Scotland Yard, who was standing between the convulsing form and his companions, saw how the same monster he had seen emerging from the tripod shot down on the outskirts of London—that reptilelike biped that had dragged itself moribund along the ground for a few moments before expiring in front of them—began to worm its way out of Garrett's body. The head of the hapless Garrett began to contract as though it had been crushed in a vise. His jaw stretched until it resembled a crocodile's maw. At the same time, his hands began to taper into hideous talons, joined by a kind of membrane, while his skin grew greenish scales and his body swelled up to monstrous proportions. And then, before the ghastly transformation was complete, the monster, which still bore a faint resemblance to Inspector Garrett, sprang to its feet and once more shot out its slimy tongue at Clayton, who was still aiming his now empty gun at the creature. Diving to the floor, Clayton managed to avoid the viscous coil. He watched helplessly as it struck the prisoner's chest, knocking him to the floor. Then it raised the poor wretch up off the ground and began drawing him toward its enormous fangs. Struggling desperately, the prisoner managed to grasp hold of the open window. This halted his advance for a moment and even managed to confuse the creature as its laborious metamorphosis continued. Overwhelmed with pure terror, the apelike porter managed to plunge out of the window, grabbing hold of the windowsill from the outside. He stubbornly clung on in midair, while the hideous tongue tried to jerk him back into the corridor. Clayton stood up, placing himself once more between the creature and the terrified group. Not knowing what to do, he simply watched Garrett's continuing metamorphosis into what looked more and more like a two-legged reptile, shredding the hapless inspector's skin. Just then, with a swift movement that surprised everyone, Murray leapt away from the group toward the window, where with savage determination he began pounding the hands of the unfortunate Mike, who, unable to cling on, gave a muffled yell as he plunged downward. The rest of them looked on as the monster's tongue tensed and the weight of its victim dragged it, helpless, toward the window. The startled creature made a desperate lunge for Murray, who managed to tear himself free with a cry of pain, then it clasped hold of the window frame. Fortunately, the monster's claws were not yet properly formed, and it was powerless to stop itself from plummeting to the street, attached to the prisoner by what looked like a grotesque umbilical cord.

After Murray's astonishing intervention, thanks to which they found themselves alone once more in the corridor, safe from attack by any hideous creature, the group gradually recovered their composure. Everything had happened incredibly quickly; moments before they had been in mortal danger, and now, suddenly, they were not.

"I'm sorry I had to sacrifice him," Murray lamented a few seconds later, "but it was his life or ours."

"Don't apologize, Mr. Murray," Emma replied, trying to stop her voice from shaking and to appear as resolute as possible. "If that creature had completed its transformation, it would have killed us all."

"Quite, Gilliam, you needn't apologize," said Wells, still a little pale, although unable to prevent a hint of sarcasm creeping into his voice. "And you needn't make excuses for him either, Miss Harlow. Not on this occasion."

They all shuffled over to the open window and found themselves gazing down at an alleyway piled with refuse. The man named Mike lay in a crumpled heap on the ground. Next to him, still attached by its monstrous tongue, the thing was sprawled in a pool of greenish blood.

The group raced downstairs and into the alley where the bizarre creature had fallen. But when they arrived, they found only the body of their former prisoner. All that remained of the creature was a big patch of greenish liquid on the ground.

"Curses! Where the devil is it hiding?" Murray declared, rubbing his shoulder, which had a small scratch, visible through the rent in his jacket.

"I don't know. The alleyway appears to have no other exit," Clayton replied, pacing around the group in circles. "But it was here only a moment ago!"

In his irritation, he kicked at the greenish puddle, causing the revolting substance to splatter in all directions. With a martyred look, Wells noticed that some of it had landed on his trousers.

"Do you think it had time to reach the main street?" asked the millionaire.

"It's possible," Clayton replied pensively.

"I doubt it," remarked Wells. "There's no trace of blood, or whatever it is the creature exudes, leading to the—"

He broke off as Clayton, oblivious to what he was saying, ran toward the street, swinging his head from side to side like a street sweeper's broom. Suddenly, he stopped in his tracks, then, retracing his steps, he stood dramatically, arms akimbo, tut-tutting mechanically as he eagerly examined the fronts of the buildings facing the alley. Wells gave a sigh. He could not decide which irritated him more: the inspector's supercilious attitude in moments of calm or the theatrical gestures with which he accompanied his deductions in tense situations.

"Do you think the creature can climb, or . . . fly?" Wells heard him ask.

"If he could fly, he would have done so before hitting the ground, don't you think?" the author retorted.

"Perhaps the prisoner's weight made that impossible," Clayton surmised.

"Surely you aren't serious?" Wells said scornfully. "That thing must weigh twice as much as—"

"Do be quiet!" cried Emma. Until then, although pale and trembling, the girl had managed to control her nerves, but now she seemed on the point of collapse. Murray gallantly offered her his arm, and the girl leaned on him like a delicate bird. "My God, didn't you see that . . . thing? Garrett was turning into a . . . Oh, my God, it looked like a . . ."

Her voice gave way suddenly, and Murray had to seize her to stop her from falling to the floor.

"Emma . . . ," he whispered, holding her in both arms. "Emma, look at me. You can't give in now, do you hear? Not now."

"But what are we to do, Gilliam? What is that thing?" she said, gasping for breath.

"Calm yourself, Emma," whispered Murray. "I won't let anything happen to you, do you see? I swear on my life."

The young woman looked at him in silence for a few moments. She gulped hard several times before replying in a faint voice.

"But Gilliam . . . How can I believe someone who swears on their life and yet has been dead for two years?" she replied, in an attempt to revive her beleaguered sense of humor.

"Emma . . . ," Murray breathed, transforming her name into a vault in which the tumult of his feelings could scarcely be contained.

"Ahem . . ." Clayton cleared his throat awkwardly. "Clearly we shall gain nothing if we give way to panic. We must keep our heads and try to look on the bright side," he suggested. "The fact is we are better informed now. We know the Martians can change into any one of us. And I'm sure knowing that will give us an enormous advantage over them."

"We also know they aren't merely out there, trying to invade London," Wells said. "They've already infiltrated and are here among us. And who knows since when," the author added, and, remembering the cadaver that had been lying in the basement of the Natural History Museum for the last twenty years, he glanced meaningfully at the inspector, who of course did not take the hint.

"Well," concluded Clayton, "let's not waste time speculating. We know what the situation is—or at least part of it. We must go to a safe place where we can consider what to do. We need to pool our information and devise a plan."

"Didn't you say your department was prepared for this kind of contingency?" the author asked dryly. "I thought you already had a plan."

"My aunt!" Emma remembered suddenly. "She's an old lady . . . We must rescue her! And my maids! My God, we must tell them they can't trust anyone!"

"Calm yourself, Miss Harlow," the inspector hastened to reassure her, ignoring Wells's comments. "Naturally, the very first thing we will do is to send for your venerable aunt and your beloved maids. After that . . . But let's not waste time chattering, I shall inform you on the way. Now let's be going!" he cried, clapping loudly and marching ahead, even as he shot Wells an annoyed glance. "Man has a thousand plans, Heaven but one," he murmured.

Murray and Wells followed behind resignedly. When they reached the main street, they perceived a reddish glow and plumes of smoke rising above the rooftops down toward Chelsea. And as if that were not enough to make plain what was going on, the evening breeze brought the familiar hiss of the Martian rays. Emma clutched Murray's arm, and he squeezed her hand tight.

"It looks as if they've already entered London," Wells declared solemnly, trying to conceal the fear he felt for Jane's safety.

XXVIII

*E*MMA WAITED FOR A FEW MOMENTS, MAKING SURE her face betrayed none of the shame she felt. When she had composed herself sufficiently, she turned toward the three men, who were standing behind her in the middle of the opulent drawing room they had just entered, and gave them a nonchalant smile.

"Well, clearly the house is empty!" she declared with a shrug. "We've searched every inch of it, from the servants' quarters down to the last sitting room. Evidently my aunt Dorothy and her staff, and my maids, have vanished, no doubt to find somewhere more secure." She pretended to smooth down the cuffs of her dress, struggling to contain her growing anger. "And it seems they've done so without any thought of me. Without even leaving so much as a note telling me where they've gone."

"You mustn't think that, Emma," Murray hastened to console her. "Perhaps they had to leave in a hurry. Imagine how terrified your aunt must have felt when she learned of the invasion, a frail old lady like her."

"My aunt is no more a frail old lady than you are a missionary," the girl objected, finally venting her fury. "She's a selfish old spinster who has never cared a bit for anything or anyone, least of all her only niece, as you can see." Emma smiled ruefully as she stared at the three men, then gave a bitter laugh. "Do you know what my mother used to threaten me with when I spurned another of my suitors? 'You'll end up like your aunt, old, alone, and embittered!' she would say. But the prospect never scared me. On the contrary, my mother would despair when I told her I couldn't imagine a more agreeable fate. Only now . . . now . . ." The girl was surprised to feel her eyes suddenly brim at the memory of her mother. She could picture her sitting in the small sunny music room, peering at her daughter over her gold-rimmed spectacles with her usual look of concern, and it seemed so far away and dreamlike now, that world without Martians, where the worst she could expect was to end up like Aunt Dorothy. "I'd give anything now to take back all the times I made my mother angry," she said at last, turning her grief-stricken face toward the large drawing room window, through which Southwark Cathedral loomed.

"Don't fret, Emma," Murray implored, taking a few hesitant steps toward her. "I promise you will live to infuriate your mother many more times. And even your father. I don't know how yet, but you will return to New York safe and sound."

Wells glanced sideways at Clayton, who was rolling his eyes to Heaven, a gesture that only added to the author's dislike of the young man. Who the devil did that prig take himself for? Much as it pained Wells to admit it, Murray had so far proved himself a much more invaluable companion than the conceited inspector from Scotland Yard's Special Branch. Indeed, apart from his timely intervention at the farm, Wells had yet to see what they had gained from having ferried the insufferable young man back and forth. Fortunately, the two others did not notice Clayton's rude gesture, for they were too involved in their own drama.

"Would you care to ask your aunt's neighbors as to her whereabouts, Miss Harlow?" Wells suggested, taking advantage of the sudden silence. "Perhaps they might know something."

"We have no time for that, Mr. Wells." Clayton frowned, his limited patience wearing thin. "Can't you hear the gunfire coming from Lambeth? I'm sure the tripods are invading London from that side, too. We must leave immediately, or else . . ."

As though to illustrate the inspector's argument, a couple of blasts in quick succession lit up the horizon through the drawing-room window. They sounded much closer.

"I have no intention of traipsing around London in search of my aunt, gentlemen. I believe I've already fulfilled my duty as her niece," Emma announced boldly. "However, if it's all the same to you, Inspector Clayton, I'd like to go up to my rooms and change into something more comfortable. I have a riding outfit that is much better suited to fleeing Martians. I'll only take a few minutes."

"Go ahead, Miss Harlow," Clayton conceded, "but I implore you to hurry."

The girl gave Clayton a little nod and swept out of the room followed by her huge, faithful guardian.

"May I go with you, Miss Harlow?" Murray asked. "Only as far as the door, of course."

"Oh please do," replied the girl. "That way, if a Martian leaps unexpectedly out of my trunk, you can rush in and hurl us both out of the window."

"I'd never do such a thing, miss. Perhaps to Wells or the inspector, but not to you."

The millionaire's reply scarcely reached Wells's and the inspector's ears, coming as it did after a series of loud creaks on the stairs. Clayton clapped Wells so hard on the back that he gave a start.

"Good! Now help me find something to write with, Mr. Wells," the inspector ordered, pulling open drawers and rummaging around as though he were intending to steal the old woman's jewelry. "Let's use the time to work out the safest route from here to where we want to go. We'll try to anticipate the path the tripods will take, even if we have to do so following the logic of Earthlings' military advances. We'll take the alleyways and backstreets leading away from the line of— Hells bells! Doesn't anyone in this house use a pen? Perhaps in the library . . . Incidentally, Mr. Wells, are you familiar with this area?"

"Do I look like a cabby?" said Wells, visibly irritated, as he walked over to an elegant escritoire in a corner of the drawing room, where of course he found what he was looking for. "Here's your ink and paper, Inspector. There's no need to dig holes in the walls or lift up the flooring."

"Good, there, that's something," Clayton replied, snatching them from Wells. He walked toward the table in the center of the room and without a second thought swept a pair of candlesticks from it with his arm. "However, since neither of us is familiar with the area, we'll have to draw the route from memory. Let's see, if the cathedral is here and Waterloo Bridge is over there . . ."

"Clayton," Wells interrupted solemnly. "You don't believe we're going to get out of this alive, do you?"

The inspector looked at him in astonishment.

"What makes you think that? I'm sure that with a little luck . . ."

"You can't fool me, Inspector. I saw the face you made when Murray told Miss Harlow he would take her back to New York safe and sound."

"Don't be mistaken, my friend." Clayton smiled. "I wasn't expressing disbelief at the possibility of getting out of London alive, but rather at the probability that New York is still a safe place to go."

For a moment, Wells looked at him, demoralized.

"Do you mean to say . . . Good God . . . The Martians might be invading New York . . . and perhaps other cities, too?"

"It's a possibility," replied Clayton, turning his attention to the sheet of paper on the table, flattened beneath his battered prosthesis. "And as such, we ought to take it into consideration . . . No, the bridge is farther up . . ."

"But, in that case . . . ," Wells murmured, ignoring the inspector's lack of interest in the conversation, for he had to express this horror in words. "If the whole planet is being invaded, what is the use of fleeing?"

Clayton looked up from the sheet of paper. He gazed intently at Wells, his narrow eyes glinting.

"Staying alive for a single second is worthwhile, Mr. Wells. And each second we stay alive multiplies our chances of surviving the next one. I suggest you think of nothing else," he said gravely, and then focused once more on his map. "Now, where's Waterloo Bridge?"

WHILE MURRAY STOOD GUARD outside the door, Emma began changing out of her clothes. Exasperated at the difficulty of undoing all the fastenings of her dress without a maid, she took a small pair of silver scissors and simply cut the dress open, then tossed it under the bed. She slipped into her riding outfit, a Parisian ensemble consisting of a light-weight jacket, a pair of culottes, and a pale green belt. She tied her hair back in a low bun and, with the air of a delicate youth, gazed at herself in the mirror, unable to help wondering what Murray would think of her in that apparel. She was about to leave the room when something poking out of one of her trunks caught her eye.

She recognized it immediately, yet hesitated for a moment, her hand on the door, before flinging herself at the trunk and seizing the object, as if she feared it might dissolve in the air. Still kneeling on the floor, she clasped it to her for a few moments before untying the red ribbon around it and carefully unrolling it. The Map of the Sky, which her great-grandfather had drawn for his daughter Eleanor, opened out ef-fortlessly, with a melodious crackle, like a fire in the hearth. Apparently it did not resent her having locked it away for so many years. Emma recalled the moment, seemingly ages ago, when she had decided to take it with her on her trip to London to see her aged aunt. What use could she possibly have had for it on such a voyage, the sole purpose of which was to humiliate the most insufferable of men? Yet now she was glad she had brought it with her, to be able to admire it once more, for perhaps the last time.

Spreading it out on the floor, Emma ran her hand over the familiar picture, just as she had done when she was a child. Her fingers moved fleetingly over the dark blue sky, a gigantic nebula, a cluster of stars, and several balloons filled with passengers before coming to rest at one cor-ner of the map. There, funny little men with pointed ears and forked tails were flying through space astride a flock of orange herons, head-ing for the edge of the drawing, beyond which their home undoubtedly lay. Their home . . . Emma remained kneeling like that, motionless. She wanted to roll up the map, to stand up, but something forced her to remain there hovering in time. And then, very slowly, a heavy sorrow began to well up inside her. With great intakes of breath she attempted to swallow all the pain floating in the air around her, all the frustration, fear, and futility of life. When she thought she would burst from sorrow and despair, her body began shaking, and a wave of inconsolable sobs rose from her throat, carrying her far from there, tearing her away from herself.

Just then the door swung open, and a distressed Murray, poised to confront any possible horror, burst into the room.

"What the devil's going on? Are you all right, Emma?" he demanded, pale with worry, eyes darting about the room in search of some enemy to hurl from the window.

Realizing there was no one there, Murray approached the girl, kneeling beside her and gingerly placing his great paw on her shaking back. Emma went on crying, but gradually calmed down, as though lulled by the sound of her own sobbing. Murray sat her up gently, leaning her head on his shoulder, and put a sturdy arm around her. His eyes were drawn to the map spread out before them.

"What is this, Emma?" Murray asked at last with infinite tenderness.

"It's the Map of the Sky," she said in a whisper. "A picture of the universe by my great-grandfather Richard Adams Locke. He gave it to my grandmother, who gave it to my mother, who gave it to me. All the women in our family have grown up believing this was what the universe looked like."

"Is that why you were crying?" Murray asked, then added, "Well, it's beautiful to dream."

Emma raised her head and peered into his eyes. Their faces were so close now that Murray could smell her tears.

"Yes, I realize that now. Isn't it awful, Gilliam? Now . . . ," the girl said, and Murray caught a whiff of sweet, faintly sour breath, like that of a little girl who has just woken up, a smell unknown to him and that melted his heart. "I wasn't crying for the days when I dreamed the universe looked like that, or because in the last few hours dreaming has been obliterated from the face of the Earth forever. I was weeping over my own silly irresponsibility. Had I known dreaming would one day become impossible, I would never have stopped doing it. I would have done things differently. And now I don't know how to recover that lost time. That's why I was crying. For lost time, and lost dreams. Where do undreamt dreams go, Gilliam? Is there a special place for them in the universe?"

Murray noticed the girl's eyes were not completely black, as they had looked from farther away. A few honey-colored flecks, and other finer ones, seeped from her pupils like filaments of gold floating in the unfathomable darkness of space.

"They don't go anywhere. I think they stay inside us," he replied. Then he gave a sigh and smiled at her gently before adding, "I saw you, Emma. I saw you as a little girl."

"What do you mean?"

"I saw you. Don't ask me how, Emma, because I couldn't tell you. But I did," he insisted, shrugging his shoulders. "I know it sounds crazy, but the day of our second meeting, in Central Park, just before you walked off in a huff leaving me alone in the middle of that little bridge, there was a moment when I looked into your eyes . . . and I saw you. You must have been about ten or eleven. You were wearing a yellow dress—"

"I don't think I ever had a yellow dress."

"And ringlets—"

"My God, Gilliam, my hair was never—"

"And you were clutching this rolled-up map to your chest," Murray said finally, pointing to Locke's drawing.

Emma remained silent and looked straight at the millionaire, trying to discover whether he was deceiving her. Yet she knew he was telling the truth. Gilliam had seen her. He had penetrated her eyes, entered her soul, and seen the little girl who dwelt there.

"I saw you, Emma, that was you. Inside you. Clutching your dreams," Murray said, experiencing the same astonishment that was overwhelming her.

And then, if falling upward were possible, if gravity could stop working for a moment, stop pinning us to the floor like a paperweight, it happened to Emma. She felt she was falling upward, toward the sky. Emma slid toward Murray's face, and such was the overpowering seriousness, the smoldering intensity of his gaze, that she imagined she was spinning into the sun and would burn up at the first touch of his lips. However, neither of them was able to test their skin's flammability, because at that moment they heard Wells's voice echoing down the corridor.

"Miss Harlow, Gilliam! Where the devil are you?"

"We're in here! At the end of the corridor!" the girl's voice rang out. She leapt to her feet, drying her tears, while Murray remained kneeling in front of her, as though waiting to be knighted. "Come on, Gilliam, get up," Emma whispered.

Wells came in, followed by Clayton. The two men remained in the doorway, taken aback by the odd tableau before their eyes: Emma standing, dressed like a boy, her eyes red and puffy, Murray at her feet, genuflecting theatrically.

"But, what . . . did you trip over, Murray?" Clayton asked in astonishment.

"Don't be absurd, Inspector," the millionaire muttered, rising to his feet.

"Don't you realize what's happening?" Clayton said, exasperated. "Look out of the window. See those flames in the distance? The tripods are rampaging through Lambeth. We must leave at once!"

Murray gazed calmly out of the window, as though none of this concerned him. The inspector sighed.

"Well, let's go. I'm taking you to a safe place where we can spend the night, and at dawn we shall join Mr. Wells on Primrose Hill," he informed them sharply.

"Just a moment, Inspector! I have no intention of moving Miss Harlow from here until you tell us where we are going," Murray protested angrily. "Is anywhere safe in London? You're not taking us to a church, I hope. You don't imagine God can protect us, do you?"

"I suspect God is too busy today to concern Himself with us,

Mr. Murray. We are going to a place outside His jurisdiction," he said, striding down the corridor.

Wells trotted after him, shaking his head. Murray found himself imitating the author's gesture, and he stepped aside for Emma, who, before leaving the room, glanced over her shoulder at the Map of the Sky.

"Don't you want to take it with you? Are you going to leave it here?" the millionaire asked her uneasily. "We could roll it up and—"

"There's no need," she interrupted, smiling. "I carry it inside me. You saw, remember?"

Murray nodded, closing the door quietly behind them, as though out of respect for the map lying asleep on the floor, depicting a benevolent but evidently erroneous universe.

XXIX

"*I*S THIS YOUR IDEA OF A SAFE PLACE?" MURRAY asked, casting a dejected glance at his surroundings. "I think you overrate your home, Clayton."

The inspector's house was a modest dwelling on the Euston Road. It comprised a sitting room and a study on the ground floor and several bedrooms on the upper floors, each smaller than the last, so that the house diminished in size as it ascended. Wells knew those cramped houses that lined the streets of Bloomsbury better than he would have liked, for he had lived in one as a student, and they had always struck him as perfect examples of the criminal lack of planning that was endemic throughout London. They had traveled via Blackfriars Bridge, the Victoria Embankment, Covent Garden, and Bloomsbury, and had driven down the narrowest streets, only emerging when absolutely necessary into the main thoroughfares, where an ever-thickening multitude of panic-stricken people were running hither and thither as the explosions came gradually closer. Clearly, Londoners had finally realized the city was not the impregnable fortress they had been led to believe, even though none had yet seen the tripods. As he watched them scatter in all directions, Wells reflected that those poor wretches were fleeing the terrors created by their own imaginations, encouraged by the deafening explosions. As the carriage with the ornate "G" made its way through the human tide flooding the streets, and the author scanned the crowd in the hope of glimpsing Jane, they could hear snippets of conversation confirming their fears. They heard, for example, that Queen Victoria had been assassinated, that someone had broken into Windsor Castle, brutally murdering her guard and servants, leaving not a single person alive in the building. A similar thing had happened at the London Fire Brigade's headquarters, the Houses of Parliament, the Royal Hospital Chelsea, and others of the city's institutions. They also heard that some-one had let out all the prisoners in Pentonville and Newgate prisons. Ev-eryone was at a loss as to how others could use the situation to commit seemingly gratuitous acts of violence, how anyone could do something so insane as to release criminals and slay ministers. The four in the car-riage knew, of course. They knew these brutal attacks were not arbi-trary, much less human. Creatures like the one they had come across at Scotland Yard were perpetrating them, following a plan to destabilize the city's defenses from within that had probably been elaborated over years. In fact, the tripods were simply assault troops, the heralds of destruction, crude symbols of a campaign that also had a more calculating side.

There, in Clayton's house, the deafening blasts of the tripods seemed to reach them from several directions at once. The noise was coming from Chelsea, Islington, and Lambeth, and even from the other side of Regent's Park, toward Kilburn. As they had suspected, not only had the invaders from space broken through the line of defense at Richmond, they were also breaching the army's blockade elsewhere and were at that very moment overrunning the city from different, if not all directions. The whole of London would soon be at the mercy of the Martians, and there would be nowhere for them to hide, in any case not in Clayton's house, which seemed to them flimsy at best. However, the inspector ap-parently did not share this view. He simply smiled enigmatically at the millionaire's remark and asked them to follow him. He led them to the basement, a poorly lit, airless part of the house where the kitchen and the coal cellar were located. Still smiling, he began rooting around in the oven.

"What are you doing?" Murray asked angrily. "Are you going to offer us a cup of tea? It's very kind of you, Clayton, but I doubt we will be able to relax sufficiently to enjoy it with the sound of those accursed tripods closing in on us—"

The millionaire was unable to finish his sentence, for at that moment Clayton pulled a lever inside the oven, and, thanks to some hidden mechanism, the kitchen wall began to move. They all looked on in astonishment as it parted like a stage curtain, revealing a space no bigger than a closet, with a trapdoor set in the floor. With a polite grin, Clayton ushered them through, and once they were all packed inside, he waited for the wall to slide back to its original position. Then he opened the trapdoor and began walking down a narrow flight of steps into the gloom below.

"Follow me," he commanded. "And would the last one down please close the trapdoor."

To everyone's surprise, the stairs led to a vast stone chamber, furnished in a luxurious and exotic fashion, as though it were the refuge of a king. Clayton was already lighting the small lamps scattered about the luxurious room, while the others studied the refuge with a mixture of admiration and disbelief. Shelves of books with embossed bindings lined the walls, the floor was covered in silk Persian rugs, Chinese vases stood in every corner, a set of Venetian glasses glistened in a cabinet, and armchairs and couches of varying styles had been arranged throughout the room. There was even a magnificent marble hearth, whose chimney must have climbed through the house above, or twisted through the rock, spewing out its smoke God knew where. The chamber appeared to contain everything necessary to spend a reasonable amount of time there, for next to the vast room was a tiny pantry, seemingly stocked with all manner of provisions and useful objects.

"As you can see, we'll be safe here until dawn," Clayton said, after he had finished lighting the lamps.

"One could even spend one's holidays here," Murray quipped, examining the exquisite Louis XIV clock, which, from its wooden mantelpiece, was filling the room with its gentle ticktock.

The inspector chortled smugly.

"I didn't build the house myself," he explained. "It was confiscated from its owner, a man I apprehended in one of my most famous cases. The department was kind enough to award it to me for services rendered."

"Who was the owner?" asked the author, surprised that jobs existed that could be rewarded with this species of villain's hideaway.

"Oh, I'm afraid that I'm not at liberty to say, Mr. Wells."

Wells had expected as much and nodded resignedly. Whoever had built the inviting chamber, they could certainly relax there safely, but he doubted he could sleep a wink knowing that Jane might be out there even now running through the streets amid the panic-stricken crowd. However, since for the moment there was nothing he could do for her, it was best if he took this opportunity to rest and have something to eat. Yes, they must recover their strength to confront whatever the day ahead might bring. The girl, for example, was already raiding the pantry, driven on by the forced starvation they had endured since the invasion began. But much to his disappointment, when she came back into the room, she was carrying only a small first-aid kit, apparently containing everything necessary to dress a wound in the millionaire's shoulder made by the creature's claw, which Wells had not even noticed. She asked the inspector's permission to use it.

"Of course, Miss Harlow. Please, make yourselves comfortable," Clayton replied, motioning to the armchairs. Then he looked at the author and said, "As for you, Mr. Wells, follow me. I want to show you something I think will interest you greatly."

Wells followed him reluctantly, vexed because not only would he now be forced to conceal a need as pedestrian as hunger from those lofty souls, but because he was going to be obliged to endure another ordeal before he could rest his weary bones in one of those sumptuous armchairs. Clayton led him along a passageway flanked by doors on either side, until they reached a small padlocked iron gate. The inspector began fumbling with the padlock, clutching it in his battered metal hand, but

Wells was in no mood to wait until he had succeeded in inserting the tiny key, and so he snatched it from him impatiently and opened the lock himself. Then he stood aside and ushered Clayton in with the theatrical gesture of a hotel porter. Slightly put out, the inspector stepped into the gloomy interior.

Once the two men had finally disappeared, Murray could not help feeling secretly pleased to be alone with the girl in these relaxed surroundings. Emma asked him to sit down on one of the chairs, which he did eagerly. They needed a moment alone together, in a place they did not have to flee from at any second. As he watched her open the kit and lay out bandages, dressings, and scissors on the nearby small table, Murray smiled indulgently, feigning a lordly indifference to the wound on his shoulder.

"You needn't concern yourself, Emma, really," he said affably. "I can scarcely feel it."

"Well, it looks like a nasty wound," she replied.

"How nasty?" Murray said, alarmed.

Emma grinned.

"Don't worry, it's only a scratch," she assured him. "It won't kill you."

"I'm glad to hear it," the millionaire replied, a mischievous smile on his lips.

"Or, should I say," Emma corrected, suddenly serious as she began disinfecting the wound, "it won't kill you a second time."

The millionaire bit his lower lip and cursed under his breath.

"I suppose I owe you an explanation," he acknowledged, sorry not to be able to spend this peaceful interlude discussing more intimate matters.

"Yes, that would be nice," she said with a hint of sadness as she dressed the wound. "Then at least I won't die with so many unanswered questions."

"You aren't going to die, Emma, not if I can help it," Murray blurted out. "You have my word."

"Don't waste time trying to reassure me, Gilliam." The girl gave a resigned smile. "We don't have much left."

"What do you mean, Emma? We have all the time in the world! Good God, I'm the Master of Time!" Murray objected fervently. "Besides, you and I are only just getting to know each other. We have our whole lives ahead of us!"

"Gilliam, the Martians are invading the Earth at this very moment, remember?" she said, amused by his naïveté. "Hasn't it occurred to you that this might interfere with our plans a little?"

"I suppose it might, yes," Murray admitted, vexed. "Now of all times, damn it."

Murray was of course fully aware of the situation they were in. He knew the Martians were invading the planet, and yet it was as if, until this moment, that had not mattered. He was so overjoyed at their blossoming relationship that the Martians seemed like an annoying hindrance he would be able to deal with later. The importance Emma gave to the invasion bothered him. He realized then that if she had accepted his promises of salvation earlier, it was not because she believed in them, but rather because she wanted to please him, and this thought excited and distressed him in equal measure. But in the end he had to admit Emma was right: the invasion had thwarted everyone's plans, including his, and he knew full well it would be difficult for them to come out of it alive.

"Yes, it's a nuisance, isn't it?" he heard Emma say, and then, gazing at him gently, the way a mother might her disappointed child, she added playfully, "You won't have time to make me fall in love with you."

Murray grinned.

"I wouldn't be so sure," he said. "How long do you think I need?"

She shrugged.

"I don't know. I wish I could tell you, but I've never fallen in love," she lamented. "And I'm afraid I'll die without ever having done so."

At this, she fell silent, surprised at her own candor. This was the first time she had shown her vulnerability to a man. In fact, it was the first time she had shown her vulnerability to anyone. As vulnerable as a little girl. And she didn't care. On the contrary, it gave her a pleasant feeling of relief. In the current situation, there was no point in continuing to pretend, but if she had taken off the mask she wore to protect herself from the world, it was not only because it was meaningless to do so in a world that was about to be destroyed. It was also because this giant of a man before her had shown he loved her, her and only her, in spite of who she was. Yes, this man who treated others with contempt and even cruelty, and yet spoke to her so gently, this man who had even tried to milk a cow in order to quench her thirst, had won that privilege. She did not want to go on pretending to him. She was probably going to die a gruesome death quite soon, and she did not want to meet her end pretending to be someone she was not. If she was going to die, she wanted at least one man on the planet to know who she really was. A vulnerable little girl, who would have liked the world to be the way her great-grandfather had described it, and who would have liked to fall in love just once. This was the real Emma Catherine Harlow.

And this man, the man destined to see her as no one else had ever seen her, opened his mouth to tell her once more that he would not let her die, but then stopped himself. No, he thought, I must not lie to her. What good would it do when it was obvious they were all going to die? And just then, as though confirming this, a loud explosion resounded above their heads. They both looked up at the ceiling, terrified. The blast had sounded very close, which could only mean the tripods were in Bloomsbury. They might even be coming down the Euston Road at that very moment, marching victoriously on three legs, firing randomly at buildings, wreaking destruction as they advanced, ruthlessly mowing down everyone, without considering for a moment that these humans falling beneath their ray were more than just cockroaches, they were beings with dreams and desires, and he himself had one desire in particular: to go on living in order to make the woman he loved fall in love with him.

"Tell me what I can do to make you fall in love with me," Murray asked gently, once the echo of the blast had died away. "I might have time to make it happen before we die."

Emma smiled, grateful to Murray for not having lied to her one last time by assuring her they would come out of this alive, or something of that sort, as anyone else would have done. And she liked the fact that this great bear of a man also differed from the others in that way.

"Well, I already know you're capable of killing for me, even of hurling a monster through a window on my behalf," she said, grinning. "That might be enough for any other woman, but I need something more, even though I can't tell you what that is. In any event, there isn't time for you to do much more." She gazed at him with a mixture of tenderness and resignation even as she clasped his hands in hers. Murray acquiesced with a downcast look that made Emma sigh. Suddenly, her eyes lit up. "You'll have to make me fall in love with you because of something you've already done! Yes, that's it! What have you done in your life that could make me fall in love with you, Gilliam?"

Murray sighed. He loved hearing her say his name. In her mouth it sounded like a slice of cake or a segment of orange.

"Nothing, I'm afraid," he replied with bitterness. "If I'd known I would have to make you love me by my actions, my life would have been very different, believe me. But I never thought I'd have to impress a lady that way, not a lady like you, at any rate."

He leaned back in his chair and looked at her despondently. He loved her, and perhaps for that reason he knew her while scarcely knowing her. And he would go on loving her, even if she told him she had robbed or killed someone in the past, because he loved her and nothing she did would ever make him see her in a bad light. His love for her was so intense and irrational it even prevented him from judging her. He loved her for what she was, regardless of what she did or did not do. He loved her for her beauty, even though that would be a feeble way of putting it. Perhaps it was truer to say that he loved her way of being in the world, he loved her eyes, her smile, her mannerisms, the gentle way she would have robbed or killed. In contrast, she did not love him for who he was. How could she? he told himself, glancing at the reflection of the lumbering giant in the mirror opposite. His way of being in the world was worse than that of a cactus. She could only love what he was inside, what he was capable of doing, or perhaps what he had done, but unfortunately there was not much more he could do now, nor was there in his stockpile of memories any noble gesture of which he could be proud, no selfless act that he could now use to his advantage to conquer this woman's heart.

"What must a man do to make you fall in love with him?" he asked, more out of curiosity than anything else, for he assumed that, whatever it might be, he could not have done it, even unintentionally. "Has any man ever done anything that made you feel you could fall in love with him?"

Emma's eyes narrowed, her face expressing a quiet intensity, which made the millionaire wish he had mastered the difficult art of painting in order to be able to capture it on canvas. But since his skill with a paintbrush was, to put it politely, practically nonexistent, he could only memorize each detail of her face, carefully storing them away among his other memories.

"My great-grandfather," the girl pronounced at last.

"Richard Locke . . . the hoaxter?" Murray was surprised.

"Don't call him that!" Emma protested. "I know he pulled the wool over everyone's eyes, including mine." She paused, smiling absentmindedly. "You know, it used to amuse me that he had outwitted everyone. Yes, I was proud to be related to someone who was superior to the stupid, gullible majority. But that's only one way of seeing it. I see things differently now. Now I believe I could love someone who did what he did . . . simply because all he did was to make the world dream."

For a few moments, Murray stared at her in silence. And then, very slowly, a smile began to spread over his features. To make the world dream . . . Yes, why not? As the girl had said, everything could be seen in a different light. It was all a question of perception.

"In that case, Emma, I'm going to tell you a story. Something nobody knows. And then you'll have no choice but to fall in love with me."

"Really?" said the girl, with a mixture of amusement and surprise.

Murray nodded. "What do you know about Murray's Time Travel?"

"Well, only what was in the newspapers," she replied, intrigued. "And that it closed down just when I'd managed to convince my mother to go with me to London and join the third expedition to the year 2000. They said the closure was due to your demise."

"Well, then, you're in for a surprise . . . ," Gilliam began.

FORGIVE ME FOR BREAKING off at such a tantalizing moment, but although the conversation is taking a fascinating turn, I, like you, am very curious to know what is happening at this very moment inside the little room where Wells and Clayton went a few minutes earlier. "I want to show you something I think will interest you greatly," the inspector had said to Wells. Was this simply an excuse to leave the lovebirds alone? Knowing the inspector's perceptiveness in such matters, I doubt it. Perhaps it was a subtle way of taking Wells aside without offending the others? More likely.

The room turned out to be smaller than the chamber but bigger than the pantry, and at first sight, Wells was unable to make out whether Clayton used it as an armory, a laboratory, or a simple junk room, for it was filled with an assortment of strange machines, weapons, and objects pertaining to the occult, witchcraft, necromancy, and other dark arts, which the author had always viewed as pure superstition.

Clayton walked over to a glass cabinet standing in a corner of the room, where Wells could make out a neat display of at least a dozen artificial hands. They were made of diverse materials, mostly wood or metal, and while some attempted to reproduce as realistically as possible the inspector's missing appendage (these were the ones he would no doubt wear when he went to a gala dinner or similar event, where he would need to use cutlery, or hold a cigarette, or, if he was lucky, a woman's hand), others looked like lethal weapons: one had razor-sharp stiletto-like fingers, one looked like a hand crossed with a pepper-box revolver, and a couple resembled outlandish devices the purpose of which Wells was unable to fathom. Clayton unscrewed his smashed prosthesis and laid it carefully to one side. Then he pored at length over his collection of artificial hands, which, resting on their fingers, gave the impression of hairless tarantulas. He pondered which one best suited the predicament they found themselves in.

While he was deciding, Wells took a desultory stroll around the inspector's eccentric emporium. Next to a medieval bestiary with fabulous illustrations of griffins, harpies, basilisks, dragons, and other magical creatures, in whose margins Clayton had made several minute annotations, on one of the tables he came across a Ouija board.

"I didn't know you practiced spiritualism, Inspector," he remarked, fingering the alphabet fashioned into the exquisite wooden board.

"It shouldn't come as such a surprise," Clayton replied without turning round. "Ghosts are a policeman's best informer: they see everything, and they don't charge anything, even though they occasionally ask you to carry out some absurd task they never got around to completing when they were alive."

"I see . . . ," Wells said cagily, unsure whether or not Clayton was pulling his leg.

Then he examined the half-dozen or so other peculiar artifacts next to the table. His attention was particularly drawn to a strange object that looked like a cross between a gramophone and a typewriter. The anomaly, bristling with rods and levers that stuck out like cactus spines, was endowed with four wheels and crowned by a species of copper-plated cornucopia.

"What is this?"

"Oh, that; it's a metaphone," the inspector said, giving it a cursory glance.

Wells waited for an explanation, but since none was forthcoming, he was obliged to ask, "And what the devil is it for?"

"In theory for recording voices and sounds from other dimensions, but in view of its poor results you could say it is completely useless." Clayton continued examining his collection of fake hands, dithering. "I'm using it to try to find a boy called Owen Spurling, who went missing late last winter in a village in Staffordshire. His mother sent him out to the well to fetch water, and he never came back. When they went looking for him, they were astonished to find that his footsteps came to an abrupt halt in the snow a few yards from the well, as though an eagle or other bird of prey had carried him off. They combed the area but found no trace of him. No one could understand what had happened to him, especially since his mother had been watching him through the window and had only looked away for a few seconds. The boy literally vanished into thin air. The most likely explanation is that he has crossed into another dimension and can't get back. The metaphone might enable me to hear him and give him instructions, assuming I manage to record anything other than the chirp of Staffordshire birds."

"And why bring him back? Maybe this Owen is happier in that other world frolicking with five-legged dogs," the author jested.

The inspector ignored his remark, deciding at last on one of the more real-looking fake hands, which did not appear to have been converted into a weapon, although Wells noticed some kind of screw or spring mechanism attached to the wrist.

"Perhaps the time has come to give you a first outing, my friend," the inspector murmured with a wistful smile, cradling the prosthesis.

He screwed it on carefully and turned toward the author, slowly bobbing his head.

"I understand your reluctance to believe in such things, Mr. Wells," he said. "Countless times I would find myself staring into the same skeptical face in the mirror, until gradually that face disappeared. Believe me, Mr. Wells, one can get used to anything. And once you have accepted that there are things in this world that have no explanation, you will be able to believe that the impossible is possible. Indeed, you will be able to believe in magic."

"If you say so," murmured Wells.

For a few moments, Clayton fell silent, gazing benevolently at the author, and then he said, "Let me tell you about when I was like you, when I was not yet Inspector Cornelius Clayton. Perhaps it will help. More than a decade ago, I was an ordinary man. Yes, a man who thought the world was what it was. I had the same impoverished, narrow idea of it you have now, except that then I had no difficulty picking up peas with a fork, because both my hands were made of flesh and bone."

The inspector uttered these last words in a tone of joviality, but Wells fancied his voice contained an underlying air of melancholy like the rustle of dead leaves in autumn. He seemed reluctant to weigh up what he had lost, for fear the balance might go against the decision he had made, so long ago now that he could no longer see himself in that youth who had casually chosen his fate.

"My father was a policeman, and following in his footsteps I joined Scotland Yard to fight against crime. My dedication, together with the advice and training I received from my father, soon yielded an excellent reputation, which, added to my extreme youth, quickly won me the admiration of my superiors, who would frequently and unreservedly congratulate me. One of these, Superintendent Thomas Arnold, called me to his office when I had scarcely been two years with the force. He told me someone was keen to meet me and, there and then, introduced me to the oddest-looking fellow I had ever seen in my life, until that moment at least.

"He was about fifty years old, stout, but with a lively manner, and he wore a peculiar-looking patch over his right eye. At first I wasn't sure whether he had lost the real one or whether it was still intact beneath the artificial one now occupying its socket. This was a kind of globular lens with a carved edge, held on by a strap that went over his forehead. Inside the globe, which appeared to move, was a smaller circle that gave off a faint reddish glow. Unflustered by my bewilderment, he stretched out a chubby yet vigorous hand laden with rings with strange symbols on them and introduced himself as Angus Sinclair, captain of a division inside the police force that I had no knowledge of. The superintendent beat a swift retreat, leaving me alone with this eccentric fellow, who immediately ensconced himself in the superintendent's chair, gesturing with a wave of his hand for me to sit opposite him. Once I had done so, he beamed at me, browsing with a satisfied expression through the papers in front of him, which I soon discovered was my curriculum vitae.

"'You have a brilliant record, Inspector Clayton, I congratulate you,' he said in a solemn tone.

"'Thank you, sir,' I replied, noticing the strange badge on the left-hand lapel of his black three-piece suit: a tiny winged dragon.

"'Mmm . . . with your youth and intelligence, I imagine you'll go far. Yes, indeed, very far. In time, you will doubtless achieve the rank of colonel. And when you reach seventy or eighty years old, you'll die a happy man, stout like me, and with a shock of white hair, content, no doubt, to look back on what could only be seen as a happy life and a career built on solving crimes and sending wrongdoers to prison, and so forth.'

"'Thank you for the exercise in fortune-telling,' I replied, vexed by the provocative tone with which he had belittled not only my achievements thus far, but also my future achievements.

"The captain grinned, amused at my display of youthful insolence.

"'Oh, they are admirable achievements, of which anyone could be proud. However, I am sure you aspire to more, much more than this.' He stared at me fixedly for a few moments. His mechanical eye glowed intensely, and I fancied I even heard a strange buzzing noise coming from behind the lens. 'The problem is you have no idea what this more entails, or am I mistaken?'

"He wasn't mistaken, but I preferred not to admit it. I simply remained silent, curious to know what this fellow wanted from me.

"'Yes, thanks to your intelligence and commitment you'll make the grade of colonel, or whatever it is you aspire to. Yet you will know nothing of the world, my boy. Absolutely nothing, however much you might think you know everything.' He leaned over the desk and gave me a challenging smile. 'That is your future. But I am offering you a far more exciting one.'

"'What are you talking about, sir?' I asked, startled by the eccentric fellow's fervent tone.

"'I am inviting you to use your talents to solve other kinds of cases. Special cases,' he explained. 'This is what we do in my division, Inspector Clayton, we solve special cases. However, it is not enough to have a brilliant record. You must possess a certain, shall I say . . . temperament.'

"'I don't understand, sir.'

"'You need an open mind, Inspector Clayton. Do you possess such a thing?'

"I hesitated for a moment, unsure how to respond. Then I nodded vigorously; I had never stopped to think about it, but until someone told me otherwise, I had an open mind. Captain Sinclair nodded with satisfaction.

"'Let's see if it is true!' he declared with theatrical enthusiasm, even as he extracted a newspaper clipping from his file and placed it before me on the table. 'Read this carefully and tell me what conclusions you draw from it, no matter how far-fetched. What do you think the man died of?'

"The clipping dated from two years before and announced the death of a vagrant. His body had been discovered in a heap on the outskirts of the city, his face half chewed off by stray dogs, but the causes of his death were a mystery: the autopsy had revealed nothing. The journalist writing the article must have been a timid soul, for he ended by stating that the crime had been committed on the night of a full moon, and that in the sand around the body, the victim had desperately traced several crosses, as though trying to ward off the devil. After carefully rereading it several times, I relayed to the captain the various causes of death that had occurred to me. Considering that no one with enough strength to chase a dog away would allow himself to be killed by it, I told him, and since dogs rarely attack living humans, the man had probably been poisoned then dragged there, and his murderer had for some reason traced those crosses before fleeing the scene. I also suggested it might have been an accidental death that someone was trying to cover up, and a few other explanations of a similar nature that occurred to me.'

"'Is that all?' asked Captain Sinclair, exaggerating his disappointment. 'I asked for all the possibilities, no matter how far-fetched.'

"I grinned impishly and replied, 'I also think it could have been a werewolf that killed and mauled the vagrant at the refuse heap, not the dogs. It happened during a full moon, which is when they change. And while the creature was stalking him like a two-legged wolf, the victim drew crosses around himself in an attempt to send the creature back to the Hell from whence it came.'

"Captain Sinclair asked once more, in the same disappointed tone, 'Is that all?'

"'No, that's not all,' I replied with a grin. 'It could have been the work of a vampire, given the crime was committed at night, and this would also explain why the victim drew the crosses in the sand. Or perhaps it was a vampire imitating a werewolf, pointing the finger at his age-old adversary, with whom from time immemorial he has been vying to take over the planet. That is all, Captain. Did I get it right?'

"'You aren't ready to know yet.' He leaned back in his chair and studied me with cold curiosity. 'But tell me: are you interested in joining a division where these could be the answers, where the impossible is sometimes the only solution? Those in my division place no limits on our imagination; we carry on searching beyond the point where normal minds would give up.'

"I looked at him, not knowing what to say, and was relieved when Sinclair told me I could have a few days to think about it, also warning me that everything we had discussed in that office must be considered top secret, and that if my answer was no, I would do well to forget that the conversation had ever taken place. That was the first warning he gave me, but not the last, nor was it the most astonishing. He then handed me a note containing the address of the Special Branch, where I was to report the following week if I decided to accept his offer. I left and went home. But I only needed one sleepless night to realize that however hard

I tried I would never be able to forget our conversation. In fact, from the moment I stepped through that office door, I was doomed. I was young, ambitious, and full of myself, and now I was aware that others had access to information to which the rest of us mortals were not privy. I couldn't go on living without wanting to know it, too. I didn't wait a week. The following morning, I went to the address printed on the note and asked to be shown to Captain Sinclair's office, where apparently he was expecting me. And there I sealed my fate forever."

Clayton concluded his tale with a pained smile and waited for Wells to respond.

"Congratulations on believing in werewolves and vampires," the author said in an almost pitying voice.

"Oh, no, Mr. Wells, you're wrong: I didn't believe in them. I merely told the captain what he wanted to hear. No, the young man I was then didn't believe in vampires or in werewolves. But that fellow headed a group of special inspectors, the cream of the Scotland Yard crop. Whatever they did, I wanted to be part of it, for the thought of continuing to solve murders and apprehend common criminals no longer appealed to me. I would have told him the vagrant was killed by an elf, if necessary." Clayton gave a bitter smile. "But that was twelve years ago, Mr. Wells, twelve years. And now I can only affirm that I believe in more things than I would like."

"Oh, really? Do vampires exist, for instance?" Wells took the opportunity to ask.

Clayton gazed at him with a smile on his lips, like an adult enjoying a child's curiosity.

"This house belonged to one," Clayton avowed, watching with amusement as Wells raised his eyebrows. Then he added with a grin, "Or so the man in question believed. His name was Lord Railsberg, and he suffered from a pigmentation disease that made his skin turn red when exposed to the sun. He was also allergic to garlic and even had an enlarged sacrum, all known traits of the vampire, according to fables and novels. As you well know, the works of Polidori, Preskett Prest, Sheridan Le Fanu, and in particular Stoker's best-selling novel popularized the vampire myth to the point where anyone possessing these traits can think he is one. Lord Railsberg built this house and lived here with a group of acolytes who, like him, fled the light. They ventured aboveground only to abduct women, whom they callously slaughtered so they could drink and even bathe in their blood, as the Hungarian countess Elisabeth Báthory was rumored to have done. When we tracked down his lair, the place was piled with corpses and people sleeping in coffins, but I assure you none of the so-called vampires was able to escape prison by changing into a bat. So I can't affirm the existence of vampires, but if they do exist, I expect they have more in common with the abject beasts of Slavic legend than the suave aristocrats portrayed by novelists."

"I see," Wells said, not taking the remark personally.

"But, naturally, we don't only deal with madmen," Clayton added. "As I already told you, occasionally we also discover the impossible."

With these words, Clayton glanced mournfully at a portrait hanging on one of the walls. Wells followed the direction of his gaze and discovered a painting of a beautiful, wealthy-looking lady in a finely carved mahogany frame. The young woman looked down on the world with a mixture of melancholy and pride. Her dark eyes glittered rapaciously, and an inscrutable smile, which Wells thought betrayed a hint of cruelty, played on her lips like a dewdrop on a rose petal.

"Who is she?" he asked.

"Countess Valerie Bompard," the young man replied, trying unsuccessfully to disguise the catch in his voice as he uttered her name.

"A beautiful woman," the author commented, unsure whether this was the word best suited to her.

"Yes, Valerie always had that effect on men: she made all who met her believe they were in the presence of the most beautiful woman in the world," Clayton confirmed, in an oddly faint and weary voice, as though he were sedated.

"Did she die?" Wells asked, noticing that the inspector had referred to her in the past tense.

"I killed her," Clayton replied in a cheerless voice.

Wells gazed at him in astonishment.

"It was my first case," the inspector added. "The only one I solved with both my hands."

Clayton let his gaze wander back to the portrait, as did Wells, vaguely disturbed by the inspector's words. Had that woman been responsible for his losing his hand? Wells studied her more closely, and again he felt "beautiful" was not the best way to describe her. She was undeniably very striking, and yet her eyes gave off a kind of somber, animal glow that unsettled him. It was as though her pupils contained something greater than she, something elusive. Undoubtedly, thought Wells, if he had met her he would have found it hard to behave naturally in her presence. Much less woo her, he reflected. He had no idea what had gone on between this woman and the policeman, but whatever it was, the event had marked Clayton so deeply he had still not recovered from it, and doubtless never would. Wells toyed briefly with the idea of questioning him about it, because he thought Clayton might expect it. Perhaps he was longing to tell someone what had happened between him and the woman whose portrait he kept hidden in the cellar, especially since the world was about to end, and this was his clumsy way of saying so. However, Wells finally decided against it, because he did not want to risk the inspector humiliating him again by telling him there were things in the world he was not yet ready to know. This thought riled Wells somewhat, and he recalled how in the carriage on the way to Horsell, he had refrained from mentioning to Clayton his visit to the Chamber of Marvels, for fear he might be accused of trespassing. But things had changed so much since that distant morning, and all of a sudden it occurred to him that divulging this information was the perfect antidote to Clayton's irritating qualms, the only way he could think of that would put them on an equal footing and enable them to conduct a balanced conversation.

"Yes, we live in a world full of mysteries," he declared, smiling at the portrait, "but, then, you know them all, don't you, Clayton? You even knew what Martians looked like before we stumbled on one at Scotland Yard, didn't you?"

Clayton turned from the portrait, and as though emerging from a deep sleep, he gazed at Wells, slightly bewildered.

"I don't know what you mean," he said at last, coldly.

"Come now, Inspector, don't treat me like a fool. I know perfectly well what you open with that little key round your neck."

"Do you?" the inspector said, taken aback, instinctively touching it.

"Of course," Wells affirmed, looking straight at him. "I've been in there."

Clayton looked at him in amazement, then gave an amused smile.

"You truly are an intriguing man, Mr. Wells. So, you've seen the Martian and his spacecraft."

"And all the other marvels hidden away from the world," the author went on bitterly.

"Before you become so enraged that you hurl yourself at me, ruining our little chat, allow me to remind you what I told you the day we met: all that *fantasy* is in quarantine, so to speak. There's no sense in announcing these marvels to the world when the majority will undoubtedly turn out to be fraudulent."

"Really? Well, Inspector, the Martian and his spacecraft seemed real enough to me."

"In that particular instance," Clayton began to explain, "the government deemed it too dangerous to reveal to the world—"

"Well, perhaps if they had, this invasion would not have taken us quite so unawares," Wells interjected.

"I'm not so sure . . . I've no idea how you managed to get into the Chamber of Marvels, Wells; what I do know is that you must have done so several days before I went to your house, otherwise you wouldn't have seen the Martian, because it was stolen two days before the start of the invasion."

"Stolen?"

"That's right, Mr. Wells. In fact, the reason I went to your house in the first place was because I thought you might have taken it."

"For God's sake, Clayton! What the devil would I want with a dead Martian?"

"Who knows, Mr. Wells. It is my job to suspect everyone." The inspector grinned. "It also occurred to me that Murray might have stolen it to make it emerge from his cylinder."

"If he'd known there was a real Martian in the museum basement, you can be sure he would have done so," Wells could not resist commenting.

"But it's clear neither of you took it. Still, I'm convinced there is a connection between the theft of the Martian and the invasion. I can't believe it's a coincidence."

"I congratulate you on having reached that conclusion, Inspector. Perhaps if you'd confided in me sooner, I might have helped you to reflect about this, but your infuriating obsession for keeping things to yourself—"

"Apparently I'm not the only one with bad habits, Mr. Wells. If you'd been open with me about your visit to the Chamber of Marvels . . . Let's not waste time quarreling. There's a far more pressing matter we need to discuss, and I confess that your having been in there will make it a lot easier for you to comprehend what I'm about to tell you."

"Another mystery, Inspector?" the author remarked dryly. "Haven't we had enough for one day?"

"This one concerns you, Mr. Wells. And I suggest you calm down and listen to what I have to say. We're on the same side now, in case you hadn't realized it."

Wells shrugged but remained silent.

"Good," said the inspector. "You must be wondering, Mr. Wells, why I'm showing you all this, and even revealing aspects of my work to you, which my code of ethics prohibits me from discussing with anyone. And yet I've made an exception in your case. Have you any idea why?"

"If we assume it has nothing to do with my irresistible charm," Wells said sarcastically, "all I can think of is that nothing matters to you now we are about to die."

The author's quip elicited a loud guffaw from Clayton.

When he had finished laughing, he said, "I assure you, even that would not induce me to breach the rules. We are only authorized to do so when in the presence of a magical being."

With this, he fell silent, simply observing Wells, who quickly lost his temper.

"What are you getting at, Inspector?" he exclaimed. "Are you suggesting I'm a vampire? I assure you my sacrum is perfectly normal. Don't make me undress in order to prove it to you."

"I need no such proof," the inspector said, without returning his smile. "I saw your reflection in the mirror in the chamber."

"Good. Well, what am I, then?"

"You are a time traveler," Clayton declared solemnly.

Wells looked at him uneasily, then burst out laughing.

"What the devil makes you think that? Is it because I wrote *The Time Machine*? You've been reading too many of my novels, Inspector."

Clayton gave a chilly smile.

"As I told you, in my work I come across the impossible," he retorted.

"And have you come across people who travel from the future in machines like the one I invented?" Wells chortled.

"Yes and no," Clayton said enigmatically. "I've come across a few time travelers. Except that they prefer traveling by other means. The machine you described may be quite plausible, but I'm afraid all future scientific attempts to travel in time will fail," he avowed. "In the future people will travel in time using their minds."

"Their minds?"

"Yes. And I have had what we might call . . . contact with some of these future time travelers, enough at any rate to discover that in the future the human brain will be found to possess a kind of button, which when pressed, enables movement in any direction along the time spectrum, although, unfortunately, it is not possible to choose a destination."

The author gazed at him in silent disbelief.

"Naturally, I've given you a very simplified explanation," Clayton added. "But that is what it boils down to."

"Assuming what you say is true," Wells said, "what makes you think I can do it?"

"Because I saw you, Mr. Wells," the young man replied.

"This isn't funny, Inspector Clayton!" The author was becoming incensed. "I'm getting fed up with—"

The inspector interrupted him. "Do you remember our eventful stay at the farm?"

"Of course," Wells muttered. "I shan't forget that in a hurry."

"Good. As you know, I woke up at a crucial time for all concerned. However, what you don't know is that while I was up in the bedroom trying to listen in to what was happening below, you materialized asleep on the bed, despite being a captive of the intruders downstairs. That's to say, you were in two places at once."

"W-what . . . ?" Wells stammered.

"You can imagine how startled I was," Clayton explained. "And from the way you tossed and turned on the bed, it was clear you were having a nightmare. It took me several minutes to realize what was happening, that you were traveling in time before my very eyes! I went over to the bed and tried to wake you by calling your name. But at that moment, you disappeared. And then there was only one Wells in the house."

"I don't understand," the author said, shaking his head.

"I appreciate your confusion, Mr. Wells, but it is quite simple. As far as I know, time travelers can accidentally activate the button I referred to during moments of extreme tension. This is the usual way most people discover their, er . . . peculiar gift. I assume that while you were asleep on the bed next to me you must have had a disturbing nightmare, which caused you to press that button and travel at least four hours forward in time. That would explain why you appeared in the room while I was glued to the door, giving me the fright of my life because at that moment your future self was downstairs. Then you must have accidentally activated the mechanism once more, this time propelling yourself back into the past, back to the bed where I was still lying unconscious, probably only a few minutes after you had left it. There you went on sleeping, and when you woke up you had no memory of traveling in time, because it had happened while you were asleep, as I said, probably due to tension. Of course, the future time travelers I have come across don't need to experience tension in order to travel in time: they have perfected their technique and are able to travel at will. The government of the future has set up a training program to help time travelers develop their skill. Unfortunately, you have no one to help you master yours. In fact, you're the oldest time traveler I've ever met. But in the end, of course, that is logical . . ."

The author opened his mouth to blurt out the hundred questions that had formulated in his head, but this meant accepting that what Clayton said was true: that time travelers existed, and he was one of them. And in the first instance this was something he was not prepared to believe.

"I don't believe you," he said.

"Very well." Clayton shrugged, as though what Wells chose to believe was of no consequence to him. "There's no reason why you should. I've done my duty, which was to inform you. Confidentially."

With this, the inspector left the room and headed back toward the chamber. Wells followed him, on the one hand perturbed by Clayton's revelation (which had reduced his own confession about the Chamber of Marvels to a mere sensational turn), and on the other annoyed at his arrogant indifference. But suddenly he remembered the bad dream he had had when he dozed off at the farm. When he awoke, Wells had remembered nothing of the dream. His only recollection was Clayton's voice whispering to him, "Wake up, Mr. Wells, wake up." But Clayton had not come round until at least four hours later, so how could he have possibly heard Clayton's voice? Wells remembered the words of Clayton's superior, Captain Sinclair: "Read this carefully and tell me what conclusions you draw from it, no matter how far-fetched." Wells sighed; he had to acknowledge that, impossible though it seemed, this could be an explanation, perhaps the only explanation. And what was the other thing Sinclair had told Clayton? "The impossible is sometimes the only solution." Wells massaged the bridge of his nose, trying to dispel the headache growing behind his eyes. For the love of God, how could he possibly believe such a thing! Especially coming from that crank? He had written *The Time Machine* and then discovered he was a time traveler? He had written *The War of the Worlds* only to find himself fleeing from Martians? Would he become invisible next?

Fortunately, these thoughts that threatened to unhinge him subsided as they reached the chamber. There he beheld a scene for which he was unprepared. Had Captain Sinclair been present, Wells might have cited this as a far-fetched possibility. Yet love, too, was a magical sphere in which the impossible could happen. Ensconced in an armchair, a bandage round his wounded shoulder, Murray's face was tilted toward the girl, who, her eyes gently closed, was perched on another seat waiting for their lips to touch.

Murray sat up abruptly in his chair, cleared his throat, and greeted Wells and Clayton in an irritated manner, trying to hide his embarrassment, while Emma did the same. Was Wells bent on foiling his every attempt to kiss the girl? Was this his way of getting back at Murray, by preserving his bachelorhood, making sure he remained chaste?

Oblivious to the romantic tableau he had just interrupted, the inspector glanced at his watch and announced, "It's almost dawn. Mr. Wells and I will make our way to Primrose Hill in search of his wife. I think it's best if we go through Regent's Park."

"Ahem . . . there's no need for you to come with me, Clayton," Wells said, unused to involving others in his private life.

"Are you joking?" the inspector declared. "God only knows what's waiting out there. I don't intend to let you go alone."

"We'll all go with you, George," said Murray, rising to his feet. "Isn't that so, Emma?"

"Of course, Mr. Wells," said the girl. "We'll all help you find your beloved."

Wells gazed at them in astonishment. Very seldom in his life had he been on the receiving end of such a touching and selfless display of friendship, and it must be said he had not practiced it much himself either. So, was it true that the worst situations brought out the best in people? No, this sentiment couldn't be genuine, he told himself. If he delved a little deeper, he would discover the real reason why each of them was willing to risk his or her life to accompany him. And there had to be another reason, he reflected, otherwise it made no sense, for it was inconceivable to Wells that someone could be capable of such an unselfish act, above all because he himself could never do so. But what if he was mistaken? What if they truly wanted to help him? Wells considered them one by one. He contemplated the arrogant Inspector Cornelius Clayton, who was willing to protect his makeshift flock with his life. He looked at Emma Harlow, who was confronting the situation with admirable fortitude: her eyes seemed to sparkle with a special intensity, like those dewdrops that sit patiently on leaves, waiting for the sun to make them glisten. Finally he contemplated Gilliam Murray, the Master of Time, the person he despised most in the world, whom a woman's love had changed so utterly that even that man was now prepared to help him. Or perhaps he was right, he reflected. Perhaps none of them really cared whether he found Jane or not, but was it not wonderful to think they might?

"T-thank you," he stammered, a catch in his voice.

At that moment, Cornelius Clayton collapsed on the floor. They all looked with irritation at the crumpled figure lying at their feet.

"I hate it when he does that," said Murray.

XXX

AWN MATERIALIZED WITH EXASPERATING SLOW-
ness. And beneath its fitful light, London awoke confused
and in pain, like a dog after its first beating. The tripods had marched
down the Euston Road, demolishing buildings as they went, including
Clayton's house, although happily the debris had not buried the trapdoor. Around them, all was devastation: many of the buildings had
been reduced to mounds of smoking rubble, and all over the place lay
half-crushed or upturned carriages. The only one that seemed to have
survived miraculously intact was Murray's, his horses standing obligingly where he had left them, planted amid this orgy of destruction. But
what convinced them this was the beginning of the end were the bodies strewn about, cinder dolls that looked vaguely human, gradually dispersed by the breeze. They were forced to step around them on their
way to the carriage with the ornate "G" as they carried the unconscious
Clayton, whom they had scarcely managed to get through the trapdoor.

The decision as to what to do with the inspector had been hastened
by the approaching dawn. It seemed most practical to leave him behind
in the safety of his lair, comfortably stretched out on a couch, with a
note beside him explaining that he had fainted and promising to return
for him once they had resolved the matter of Wells's potential widower-
hood. But the few hours they had spent together, each moment of which
seemed to conceal an unexpected turn of events that changed the course
of their lives, had made nonsense of their ideas about what was practical.
They had no notion what might become of them during their excursion

to Primrose Hill, and whether or not they would be able to return to Clayton's cellar, and so they finally resolved to take the inspector with them. It was perfectly clear to them: they were in this together. And so, eschewing the common sense with which most of them had led their lives until the arrival of the Martians, they hauled the inspector from his refuge, even remembering to bring his hat.

Although the tripods had already passed through, and a strange calm had settled over the street, they could still hear shots and blasts coming from the surrounding neighborhoods, which made them realize the invasion was far from over. With Murray once more grasping the reins, they set off for Regent's Park. Wells gave an anguished sigh. In a few moments—the time it took to cross the park—they would find out whether or not Jane had survived the invasion. Whenever their eyes met, Emma, who had the air of a weary, worldly Madonna as she sat opposite Wells cradling the inspector's head in her lap, gave him a reassuring look. But it was obvious she knew as well as he did that the likelihood of Jane still being alive was slight. Jane could have been dead for hours, Wells told himself, she could be lying under a mound of rubble or have been transformed into one of those baleful cinder figures strewn up and down the Euston Road, and he had not yet shed a single tear for her. Yes, perhaps she was dead and he still believed her alive. But could that have happened without his somehow knowing it? How could she have died without his sensing it physically, or without the universe having made him aware of it? And shouldn't sacred love be like a spider's web that not only encircled them but, with a tremor of its threads, informed each of them when the other had abandoned the web? The author took a deep breath and closed his eyes, trying to ignore the rattle of the coach in order to concentrate on the inner music of his being, lest with a discordant note it had been trying to inform him for hours that Jane was dead. Yet his body did not appear to feel her death, and perhaps that was the strongest proof that she was still alive, for it was inconceivable to Wells that the person he most loved in the world had stopped existing without his perceiving it, or that he had not, out of solidarity, died seconds later from a heart attack, with a synchronicity more sophisticated than that evinced between twins. From the moment he found the note pinned to the Garfields' door, Wells feared Jane might have been killed or fatally injured in the invasion, but he had forced himself not to think about it. And he must continue that strategy, sealing off the wellspring of pain until he had actually confirmed her death.

The uneasy veneer of calm that lay over the Euston Road had spread to Regent's Park. There was no one around, and in the park itself, everything appeared in order. Every tree, stone, and blade of grass was unharmed, doggedly clinging to the planet. If a tripod had passed that way, it must have been sufficiently moved by this oasis of vegetation in the heart of London to spare it. The only reminder that they were in the throes of a Martian invasion was a dog, which crossed in front of the coach carrying a severed arm in its mouth. At least someone was benefiting from this, Wells reflected, while Emma averted her gaze with a look of revulsion. But besides this macabre detail, the journey proceeded uneventfully until they glimpsed the contours of Primrose Hill.

They came to a halt at the foot of the rise and then, not daring to abandon Clayton in the carriage, carried him to the top of the hill, where they propped him against a tree. From there, they were able to get a more precise idea of the total and utter destruction that was spreading across the city. London was expiring before them, wounded and in flames. To the north, the houses of Kilburn and Hampstead had been reduced to jagged heaps of rubble among which three or four tripods moved languidly. To the south, beyond the green waves of Regent's Park, Soho was in flames, and through its streets, moving with the ungainly elegance of herons, a handful of tripods opened fire from time to time. Far off in the distance, they could make out what had once been the magnificent mansions of the Brompton Road, almost all razed to the ground. Westminster Abbey was reduced to a ruin. Farther off, through a veil of smoke, St. Paul's Cathedral was still standing, although a Martian ray had perforated its dome. Wells contemplated the devastation before him with a feeling of humiliation more than of fear. It had taken so much time to build this vast city, this anthill where millions of souls lived out their lives without realizing they meant nothing to the universe, and only a single day to reduce it to ashes.

A woman's sudden cry broke the desolate silence.

"Bertie!"

Wells wheeled round toward where the voice was coming from. And then he saw her running across the hill toward him, flushed, bedraggled, hysterical, and alive, above all, alive. Jane had survived all this destruction, she had defied death, and even though she might soon perish, now she was alive, like him, she was still alive. Seeing her running toward him, Wells thought of doing the same to fuse in a passionate embrace, yielding to the sentimentality that the scene required. His pragmatism had always made him resist such gestures. Particularly when Jane had insisted on them in their daily life, where he felt these actions so characteristic of romantic literature were silly, out of tune with the everyday routine of domesticity. But now appeared to be the only moment in his life when such a gesture would be completely appropriate, de rigueur even, not to mention that he also found himself before an audience that would be let down if the scene ended any other way. And so, wary of disappointing everyone, Wells began trotting stiffly toward Jane, his wife, the person who meant more to him than anyone in the world. Jane gave a shriek of joy as the distance between them narrowed and flew across the grass, delighted to find him alive, for his wife had also been forced to endure the anguish of imagining her husband dead while she was still breathing. And this, the author reflected, was true love, this selfless, irrepressible joy, the perplexing knowledge that one meant more to someone than one's own life, and the acceptance that someone else meant more to one than oneself. Wells and Jane, husband and wife, writer and muse, embraced amid all this cruel destruction, this planet on its knees awaiting the final death blow.

"Bertie, you're alive! You're alive!" Jane cried between sobs.

"Yes, Jane," he said. "We're alive."

"Melvin and Norah are dead, Bertie," she told him between gasps. "It was horrible."

And Wells realized that Jane, too, had suffered. That, like him, she had her own tale to tell, an exciting adventure he would listen to with a tender smile, in the calm knowledge that, although at times it had seemed impossible, these perilous events had ended happily, in each other's arms. Next to them, Murray and Emma beamed, moved by this miraculous reunion. The sun shone on the grass with the sweetness of dawn, and everything was so unequivocally beautiful that all of a sudden Wells felt euphoric, immortal, invincible, capable of kicking the Martians out all on his own. Yet one glance at the devastated city told him they were doomed: it was only a matter of time before the Martians gave the last knife thrust to this brick dragon and went around on foot killing anyone who had escaped the tripods. Yes, his euphoria was simply the final splendor of the wilting rose before it disintegrated in a shower of petals on the grass. But what the devil did it matter. He felt it and was happy, happier than ever before.

Just then, someone began to applaud. Startled, the group turned as one toward the sound of the clapping. A few yards away, propped against a tree, they discovered a young man, apparently moved by the tender scene.

"I'm beginning to think love is man's greatest invention," he said, doffing his hat. "Don't you remember me? I'm Charles Winslow."

Wells recognized him instantly. Winslow was the young dandy who had burst into his house brandishing a pistol in the belief that he possessed a time machine like the one he wrote about in his novel. And despite the young man's present dishevelment (his hair was tousled and his jacket soiled and torn), the author had to admit he had not lost his stunning good looks.

"Of course, Mr. Winslow," he said, going over to shake Charles's hand.

After greeting Wells, the young man noticed the millionaire and suddenly turned pale.

"Mr. Winslow, you look as if you've seen a ghost," chuckled Murray.

"Perhaps I have," Charles said hesitantly.

"Shake my hand and you'll see you're mistaken," the millionaire said, stretching out his great paw. The two men shook hands warmly. "But we can discuss my resurrection another time. Allow me to introduce you to Miss Harlow."

"Pleased to meet you, Miss Harlow," Charles said, kissing her hand and dazzling her with his mischievously angelic smile. "Under other circumstances I would have asked you to dine with me, but I'm afraid there are no restaurants open in London. Or at least none that are worthy of you."

"I'm glad to find you in such good spirits despite the invasion," said the author, stepping in before Murray had a chance to fly off the handle.

"Well, I don't think we need worry too much, Mr. Wells," the young man replied, signaling the surrounding destruction with a wave of his hand. "Clearly we're going to survive."

"Do you really think so?" the author said, not trying to conceal his disbelief.

"Of course," Charles assured him. "We already know that in the year 2000 our problem will be the automatons, not the Martians. This situation will clearly resolve itself."

"I see." Wells gave a resigned sigh. "And what are we supposed to do?"

"Leave it to the heroes, of course," the young man replied.

"To the heroes?" Murray chortled. "You mean you?"

"Oh, no, Mr. Murray. You flatter me, but I wasn't referring to myself. I was referring to a real hero," said Charles, beckoning to a man standing a few yards from the group. "To someone who has come from the future to save us."

The young man approached timidly and gave them a smile that was meant to be reassuring.

"Ladies and gentlemen, allow me to introduce the brave Captain Shackleton."

PART THREE

*D*EAR READER, OUR EXCITING
ADVENTURE IS DRAWING TO A CLOSE.

CAN OUR HEROES DEFEAT THE MARTIANS,
OR DOES THIS TASK SEEM AS IMPOSSIBLE TO
YOU AS WINNING A PROUD LADY'S HEART?
I TRUST YOU HAVE ENJOYED OUR CURIOUS
TALE, THOUGH IT IS FILLED WITH INCIDENTS
SO ALIEN TO OUR HUMAN EXPERIENCE THAT
IT MAY HAVE OBLIGED YOU ON MORE THAN
ONE OCCASION TO RAISE AN EYEBROW. I DO
NOT BLAME YOU, ALTHOUGH I FEAR THAT WITH
THE PASSAGE OF TIME THESE EVENTS WILL,
ALAS, BE ROBBED OF THEIR STRANGENESS.

SHACKLETON CAUGHT ME LOOKING AT HIM, AND, ARCHING HIS EYEBROWS SKEPTICALLY, HE SPREAD HIS ARMS TO ENCOMPASS ALL THIS DESTRUCTION.

"AS YOU SEE, MR. WINSLOW, WE CAN'T POSSIBLY TRAVEL TO THE YEAR 2000."

I SHRUGGED, AMUSED BY WHAT WAS UNDOUBTEDLY NOTHING MORE THAN A MINOR SETBACK.

"IN THAT CASE, I'M AFRAID WE'LL JUST HAVE TO DEFEAT THE MARTIANS ON OUR OWN, CAPTAIN," I REPLIED, GRINNING.

XXXI

CHARLES WINSLOW WOULD HAVE LIKED TIME TO BE A river whose banks offered a quiet haven in an unchanging landscape of stately, chiseled mountains, of lakes where the evening would descend softly, of undulating hills, or something similar. Its actual makeup did not concern him so much as its permanency. For this landscape had to stay the same not only when he paused to contemplate it, but also when he decided to leave, rowing upstream in his little boat or letting himself drift downstream. No matter what he did, it must remain unchanged, a place of tranquil repose, tied with unbreakable threads to the banks of the river.

But, apparently, time did not resemble a river at all, and it was a mistake to think that if one went away everything stayed the same. Thanks to Murray's Time Travel, Charles had traveled to the year 2000, had witnessed the bloody war of the future where mankind did battle with the evil automatons for control of the planet, and had subsequently returned to the year 1898, when automatons were still considered mere toys. But that present had carried within it, like a latent disease, the seeds of the future. And two years later, events had so substantially altered the present that it could no longer lead to the future Charles had once considered immutable. The world he lived in now in 1900 had taken a different path and was no longer headed for the year 2000 as shown to them by Murray. Charles did not know where it was headed, but certainly not there, he said to himself, as he stood up from his straw pallet and stumbled jerkily toward the cell door. From there, he peered despondently at the outside world and gave a sigh: another morning and he had still not awoken from the nightmare in which he seemed to be living. As if to remind himself of this fact, he ran his fingers despairingly over the iron collar around his neck.

Dawn had not yet broken, but night was beginning to fade on the horizon, and a dim, faintly coppery light was slowly spreading over the plain where the gigantic metal construction built by the Martians stood. By now, everyone was aware the invaders did not come from Mars, but since their true origin was unknown, most people went on calling them that, possibly because they believed it was insulting to the invaders. Charles contemplated the tower with a rage deadened somewhat by the profound exhaustion that had seeped into his bones until it became part of his being. It was rumored that the pyramid was a machine that, once finished, would convert the Earth's atmosphere into an element less harmful to the invaders. This transformation was one of many the Martians were carrying out on the planet in preparation for the long-awaited arrival of their emperor, who would be accompanied by the other members of their race, crossing space in a convoy of vast airships, their whole world packed into its holds. The handful of invaders that had conquered the Earth with such ease had in fact been no more than a small advance guard.

Farther away, close to the ruins of what until two years ago had been the greatest city in the world, stood the Martian camp, a jumble of randomly positioned globular tin shacks that housed the tiny task force in charge of the work camp where Charles was a prisoner. He had no idea where the extraterrestrials that had led the invasion lived, but he knew there were camps all over England and throughout the rest of the world, because now, two years after the invasion had begun, it could be said that the conquest of Earth was complete. After reducing London to rubble, the invaders had attacked other British cities, as their counterparts had done in Europe and on other continents, encountering nothing more than the token resistance offered by the mighty British Empire. And so Paris, Barcelona, Rome, Athens had all fallen. The entire planet had been subjugated, millions of humans had perished during the great war, and the few who had survived, among whom Charles had the dubious fortune to be counted, had been turned into slaves, into a labor force that the invaders had no qualms about working to death.

How could this possibly have happened? Charles asked himself again and again as the familiar feelings of despair and disbelief stirred within him. He had seen the future, a future that was clearly no longer going to happen. And there was something strange, something not quite right about all of it. No one else seemed to think so, not even Captain Shackleton, who was in the same camp, and whose cell Charles would visit as often as he could, perhaps because he hoped Shackleton might be able to answer all these questions. Most of the time, the captain would simply shrug or look at Charles with sympathy when he brought the subject up, when he insisted this *couldn't* be happening. Well, it had been happening for two years, damn it! Shackleton would occasionally exclaim angrily when Winslow's ceaseless questions tried his patience. The conversation would usually end there.

Charles shook his head, trying to chase away these thoughts. Why go on tormenting himself by insisting he was living a mistaken life, today of all days, when he needed every precious moment left to him? As soon as it was light, the Martians would drag them all from their cells, and they would have to return to work, to the draining task of building the purification machine. Charles had only a few hours until then, so he walked over to the small table in a corner of his cell, sat down, and took out the pen and notebook for which he had bartered five of his least rotten teeth. He had no idea what Ashton, his fellow prisoner who could procure anything, wanted them for, but he knew he himself would soon have no use for them. He had asked Ashton for these writing tools because he planned to put something down on paper, something he supposed could be described as a diary, although he did not intend to record his day-to-day life (which could be summed up in a few lines) but rather the events leading up to his present predicament. The one thing clear to him was that he had to write it before he died, which would be soon now. As if to confirm his fears, Charles was racked by another of the coughing fits that had been assailing him increasingly in the past few weeks. After it had passed, throat parched and lungs aching, Charles tried to loosen his iron collar with the same gesture he had once used on his bow tie. Then he knitted his brow, remaining silent for a few moments, gathering his thoughts before he began to write:

DIARY OF CHARLES WINSLOW

12 February, 1900

My name is Charles Leonard Winslow; I am twenty-nine years old and a prisoner at the Martian work camp in Lewisham. But I shan't waste the little time I have left writing about myself. Suffice it to say that before the invasion I wanted for nothing: I enjoyed a privileged position in society, a charming wife, and the perfect combination of cynicism and robust health necessary to be able to take full advantage of the daily pleasures life offered me. As things stand, I have been stripped of everything, both materially and spiritually, even my belief in myself. I have nothing left except the certainty that within a week I shall be dead. For that reason I am writing this diary, so that everything I have learned about the invaders will not die with me. For I know things about them that not everyone is aware of, and while this can no longer help me, it may yet prove of some use to others. I am conscious, however, of how unlikely it is that any human will ever read these pages. I need only look around me to realize this. And yet, something inside me makes me cling to the thought that one day, sooner or later, we will overcome the Martians. And if that happens, the information in these pages might play a part in it. Even if I am mistaken and my intuition is no more than the foolish longing of a madman, this diary might still provide the only evidence that Earth was not always ruled over by Martians or whatever they may be. No, over vast stretches of time, Earth belonged to Man, who came to believe he was lord and master of the universe.

Only a few exceptional minds, such as that of the author H. G. Wells, to whose memory I dedicate these pages, were able to observe the Cosmos with a clarity that helped them understand that not only were we not its only inhabitants, we were also probably not the most powerful. Wells announced this to the world in his novel *The War of the Worlds,* which, with their habitual arrogance, his fellow men read as if it were a simple work of fiction. No one believed anything like that could really come to pass. No one. And, I confess, neither did I, not because I believed we were alone and powerful, but because I had seen the future that awaited my grandchildren. Yes, I had seen the year 2000, and in it there was no trace of any Martians.

For that reason, on the day of the invasion, I found myself at Madame M——'s brothel, the exquisite sanctuary I frequented at least once a week. I seem to recall that the appearance of strange machines on Horsell Common, Byfleet golf course, and at Sevenoaks, Enfield, and Bexley, had already been announced in successive editions of the *St. James's Gazette.* It gradually became clear that the machines were hostile, for some of them had opened fire on the bystanders, who had gathered around them as if they were a fairground attraction. Apparently, they made their way toward London on legs that looked like stilts, destroying everything in their path with their terrible heat ray. However, the newspaper assured its readers that there was no need for alarm, for, in an unprecedented display of military strength, the great British army was waiting for them on the outskirts of London and had created a cordon around the city. Rather than spread fear among the population, all of this caused a buzz of interest and anticipation. Keen to see their army defeat the invaders, which some claimed were Martians from outer space, many Londoners had traveled to the outskirts to witness the spectacular confrontation as advertised. However, this crowd of would-be onlookers had been swiftly turned back by the troops, foiled in their desire to see our soldiers give the enemy a drubbing. For reasons of security, nobody was permitted to leave London, and even the train stations had been closed down by order of the government. It was only possible to enter the city, and many of those fleeing Molesey, Walton, Weybridge, and adjacent towns were doing so in droves, flooding the streets with their vehicles crammed with luggage and valuables. According to these fugitives, the devastation in the outlying towns was terrible, and yet no one believed for a moment that we might lose the imminent battle. The final edition of the *St. James's Gazette* announced the breakdown of telegraph communications, and with no more news coming through, we all waited to see what happened.

As one might imagine, this created some unease among the population, but no undue panic. And in my own case, I must confess it scarcely caused me any concern. Why should it, when I was convinced our powerful army would destroy these bizarre machines before they managed to march into London? There was no question in my mind that we would defeat the Martians, or whatever they were. It couldn't be any other way, and not because their machines were marching toward us on ridiculous stilts, instead of soaring through the air with unquestionable superiority, as Wells had described them in his novel. No, we would defeat them because the future said we would. However much they terrified us, and however powerful they seemed, I was already sure of the outcome and therefore incapable of worrying about it. I only felt condescension for those who, incapable of putting two and two together, were afraid for their lives. And so, free from fear, I resolved to go about my daily life as usual. Alas, Victoria, my wife, did not share my peace of mind, despite also having traveled to the year 2000 and seen no sign of any Martian invasion. Much to my annoyance, she insisted on sitting out the battle with my cousin Andrew and his wife—her sister—and a few of our friends at my uncle's mansion in Queen's Gate. None of them seemed able to understand that there was nothing to fear.

Unable to take refuge with this group of startled children without feeling ridiculous, I left the house in the opposite direction. People had crowded into the streets and taverns and formed restless clusters in the squares, but they appeared curious rather than alarmed about what might be happening on the city's outskirts. Strolling aimlessly, I noticed a knot of people eager for information surround one of the fugitives' carts, their faces aghast as its owner related in a garbled manner the destruction from which he had miraculously escaped. These simple folk had not traveled to the year 2000, and so their fear, whilst grotesque, was in some sense justified. I, on the other hand, had been there, and so I resolved to make my way to Madame M——'s brothel as I already mentioned—one of my favorites owing to its exotic merchandise. I couldn't think of any better place to amuse myself while the invasion was being quelled. After that, I would return to Queen's Gate to fetch Victoria and with a smirk on my face try to resist the temptation to point out her lack of judgment with a cutting remark. I might even take her out to dinner to make up for the anxiety she had suffered unnecessarily.

Inside the brothel, I crossed the spacious, rococo hall with its caricature of *The Birth of Venus,* far less sublime and more brazenly sensual than that of Botticelli, on the back wall. The room, perfumed and intimate, was strangely empty. Almost no one occupied the chairs and tables where the whores would usually converse, engage in banter, or smoke their long-stemmed opium pipes with the clientele. Nor did I glimpse any movement behind the drapes, through which it was customary to see some bigwig floating on a sea of fluffy cushions. The women weren't even shimmying around the room, flaunting their contours swathed in diaphanous gauze. Most were seated in gloomy silence, giving the impression of being at a wake, regardless of their plumed headdresses. The bleakness enveloping the brothel discouraged me; even so, I resolved to cheer myself by taking advantage of the lull in proceedings to enjoy two of the most sought-after girls, who were amazed I could muster an erection in such a situation. What better way to die than in your arms, I told them. After pleasuring myself, I took an apple from the fruit bowl beside the bed, although I couldn't help biting into it with a degree of annoyance. I had enjoyed myself, yet I had sensed the girls' minds were elsewhere. Even these poor wretches were concerned about the invasion.

It was then I heard the first blast, far away in the direction of Chelsea. The girls gave a start and hurriedly began dressing. There was a second blast. These explosions were too close to be coming from the outskirts, which could only mean that the tripods had broken through the line of defense and were entering London. A third blast, even closer now, made the building shake and confirmed my suspicions. I poked my head out of the window amid a gaggle of hysterical girls. There were people running, panic-stricken, through the streets, but I could see nothing above the rooftops, save for a few peculiar reddish flashes coloring the evening sky. I pulled on my clothes and left the brothel, together with a small number of fellow customers, just as what sounded like all the church bells in London began to ring out. In the street, I heard some men shouting that these were Martians and one had been shot down in Richmond. I smiled at the news. But, apparently, following this heroic action, our mighty army had been wiped out. From the garbled rumors circulating among the crowd, I learned that the Martians had broken through the line of defense at Kingston and Richmond. And, if the increasing number of blasts resounding in the distance was anything to go by, they would soon do the same elsewhere, if they hadn't already. But this couldn't be happening! I said to myself, dumbfounded, even as I narrowly escaped being run over by a cartload of refugees.

As I puzzled over why things weren't turning out as they should, I found myself being jostled this way and that by the nervous crowd.

Finally I found my way into a square, where, more shaken and anxious than I cared to admit, I sat down on a bench. I needed time to think. It was impossible to know exactly what was going on, although clearly the terrible explosions were occurring more frequently and coming ever closer. It was always the same: first there was a loud hissing noise, then the roar of the blast, and finally the air would shake as a building crashed to the ground. The worst thing was that this gruesome symphony was apparently being played all over London, from Ealing to East Ham.

In a bid to calm my nerves, I plucked a cigarette from my cigarette case and smoked it with the icy composure of a suicide, while those rushing by gazed at me in astonishment. I returned their gaze defiantly, even though the panic I was stifling had started to give the tobacco a bitter, metallic taste. I exhaled the smoke slowly and tried to assess the situation: why hadn't whatever had been destined to prevent the invasion already snuffed it out? The inspired command of a minister, a powerful secret weapon, an unexpected natural phenomenon, a detachment of soldiers specially trained to deal with this type of situation, or perhaps a lone individual who by some random action would restore the order of things. I did not know how, but I was convinced something had to halt the invasion. I surveyed the crowd fleeing before me: innkeepers in their aprons, maids in uniform, children dragged by their mothers, vagrants and bankers running side by side, now and then a solitary rider. Their confusion and terror were so overwhelming it seemed clear that none of these wretched souls could save London, much less the planet. Even our own army appeared incapable of doing that, according to the snatches of conversation I was able to overhear, and which were immediately corroborated by the growing proximity of the blasts. Yet I knew someone *had* to do something, and quickly. What if that was my role? I wondered suddenly. What if I was the one who had to intervene and put events back on the right track? But the thought seemed as pompous as it was absurd. What could I possibly do to set things straight?

Suddenly, there was a fearful explosion a few streets away, followed by a deafening crash. The noise made me leap up from the bench with a start, my whole body trembling. From the street opposite, accompanied by that peculiar hissing noise, there emerged what I can only describe as a bolt of lightning tamed by a god, which, instead of zigzagging through the air, sliced through it in a straight line, parallel to the ground, like the beam from a lighthouse. The strange ray shot across the square, igniting the treetops in its path before thudding into one of the buildings on the far side, blowing it to smithereens, and ruthlessly scattering a handful of coaches and their passengers.

Those of us in the square became aware of an increasingly loud clanging of metal behind us. The ground began to quake, and, terrified, everyone turned toward the street from which the ray had emanated, certain that what was approaching us could only be one of the tripods the fugitives had told us about. Sure enough, through the thick cloud of dust from the falling rubble, we glimpsed the gigantic spidery outline of a tripod. Seconds later, it emerged from the dust cloud and planted its three powerful feet firmly in front of us. Many people scattered in terror, but others, myself included, remained motionless in the center of the square, transfixed by this apparition. This was the first tripod I had seen, and to this very day the memory of it makes me shudder. It looked more powerful than any machine Man had ever built or could ever build. It must have been about a hundred feet tall, possibly taller, and swaying on top of slender, jointed legs like the ribs of an umbrella was something resembling the baskets attached to hot-air balloons, only bigger and sealed like an impregnable carapace. From the front dangled a kind of tentacle, probably made from the same shiny material as the machine, only more pliable. This twitched slowly in the air, like a fly's proboscis. Attached to it was a strange artifact that looked like a weapon. Just then, as if to confirm my suspicions, it spat out a second ray, which smashed to the ground close to its feet. However, as the machine raised its tentacle, the ray began to slice diagonally through the square as if it were a wedding cake, reducing everything and everyone in its path to cinders. The terrible shaft of heat ended its trajectory by cleaving the corner building in two. The house exploded in a shower of debris.

Even though I was fifty feet away, I could feel the heat from the ray prick my skin painfully, and it goaded me to react. I realized my life was in danger, that I could die at any moment. However impossible it might seem to me, the invasion was taking place. And regardless of whether or not it was successful, I was a mere bit player who could die in any number of ways: roasted by a heat ray, crushed by falling debris, mown down by a runaway carriage. I became more aware than ever of how dreadfully vulnerable I was. I could be killed this instant; I could already have been killed. All of a sudden, just as the machine was preparing to resume firing at the buildings, I thought of Victoria, and my cousin and his wife, who could also be killed when the tripods reached Queen's Gate. Like me, they were frail and mortal. I had to do something, get away from there, I had to reach them at once!

The demolished building formed a smoldering barricade preventing entry to the main streets that led to Queen's Gate, and so, partly out of choice and partly swept along by the frenzied crowd, I began running down a side street, away from the tripod that had burst into the square and from another one that had just joined it. I then found myself carried along a maze of alleyways, unsure of where I was going, perceiving the explosions in the square and trying not to fall over for fear of being trampled, like many others. As I ran, I saw the sky above my head tinged with reddish flashes, I smelled smoke from the fires, and I heard an almighty crash mixed with screams from the crowd, the roar of cannons, and the relentless hiss of the tripods that seemed to be coming from all sides. Only when I emerged onto the Chelsea Embankment did I realize I had been running away from South Kensington, the direction I wanted to go. Instead, I had ended up at the river, panting and wheezing, crushed amid dozens of others, whose faces, like mine, were covered in white dust from the fallen debris. Suddenly overcome by dizziness, I was forced to lean over, my hands on my knees, and remained like that for a few moments, examining the toes of my shoes while I tried to stop myself from being sick. The last thing I wanted was for the crowd to see me as a cowardly young man. When I was finally able to raise my eyes, I noticed a cluster of launches at the foot of the jetty, their passengers hesitating over whether they should cross the river or climb back onto dry land. Then, straightening myself up, I discovered the reason for their indecision.

The glittering river Thames stretched before me, adorned with bridges, the nearest of which was the magnificent Albert Bridge resting on its four cast iron piers. This structure, which I had always considered a perfect example of Man's ingenuity, now looked pitifully fragile faced with the sinister tripods that were advancing on the far side of the river. The ghastly horde stood out against the blazing buildings they had left behind in Battersea and were clearly approaching the Thames with the aim of crossing it on their gangling stilts to wreak havoc on the other side. But before any of them could reach the water, a destroyer appeared at the scene. Gliding up the river like a fearless Leviathan, it positioned itself between the tripods and the swarming crowd on the quayside, of which I was a part. Craning my neck above the mass of bobbing heads, I could see that similar scenes were occurring the length of the Thames. The river was dotted with warships attempting to keep at bay the hordes of tripods that had penetrated London from the south and had razed Lambeth and the outlying neighborhoods. Judging from the blasts coming from that direction, some of the destroyers had already opened fire on them.

With a vague feeling of security, like people watching from their theater boxes as the stage is destroyed by fire and wondering uneasily whether the flames will reach them, we all waited, pressed together on the quayside, to see the duel about to take place before our eyes, for at that moment the destroyer in front of us began firing furiously at the Martians, hitting a few buildings on the opposite bank, which crumpled like paper, but none of the tripods, which succeeded in dodging the shots with a slow rolling motion. They did not return fire but simply continued their terrifying and relentless advance toward the river. Then a cannon hit one of them, shattering its shell. The tripod reeled like a drunken giant before toppling over onto a building. Filled with excitement, we celebrated the strike with loud hurrahs, but our euphoria was short-lived, for we instantly perceived the brutal response of the other tripods. At least three of them closest to the riverbank fired their powerful heat rays straight at the destroyer, which rocked violently in the water. For a few moments, a thick cloud of smoke and steam obscured the combat from us, but we all heard the ferocity of the ensuing blasts and even saw a shower of metal shards and part of a funnel emerge from the vapor. Then the firing came to an abrupt halt.

A few moments later the smoke lifted to reveal the smoking wreck of the destroyer floating on the water like a dead bird. A pair of tripods fired at Albert Bridge, slicing through it with their swords of fire and spilling the handful of people fleeing toward Chelsea into the water, together with a shower of flaming debris. The rubble from the bridge formed a kind of barricade, isolating us from the bloody battle being waged up and down the river. We watched as the tripods waded into the roiling waters of the Thames, tottering like ghostly old men. It was clear to us that however precarious their foothold on the riverbed, they would soon be upon us, and no warship would be able to stop them. The most impatient among them began aiming at our side of the river. The first shot ripped into the quay not forty feet from me, reducing the onlookers who had been standing there to cinders and forcing the rest of us to make a mad dash toward the nearby side streets. Once more, I found myself being dragged along by the crowd. A few yards in front of me,

I saw a little girl fall, only to be trampled by the unseeing mass of people, and then, powerless to stop myself running, I felt her little bones crack beneath my feet. This incident persuaded me to make a supreme effort to separate myself from the human tide of which I unwillingly formed a part. Eager to regain my autonomy, I flattened myself against a wall, letting the crazed mob surge past me, until the street was almost empty except for a few battered corpses. Then I resolved to find my bearings, and once I had done this, I set off at a trot toward South Kensington, doing my best not to give in to dread. Stopping every now and then to listen for the direction of the blasts, I managed to steer clear of the tripods, as well as of the fleeing crowds, and, sticking to the deserted alleyways whenever I could, I made my way cautiously across the city until I reached the Cromwell Road. I don't know how long it took me to get there, but it felt like an eternity. At last I arrived, exhausted and trembling, and was relieved to find that all was calm in Queen's Gate, and its splendid stuccoed mansions remained untouched.

I hurried toward my uncle's house and burst through the door, breathless from running. Surprised to find the first floor deserted, I ran up the marble staircase to the second floor, discovering no one there either. Before going back downstairs, I could not help pausing to look at the terrifying panorama afforded by the picture windows. Columns of black smoke were billowing up to the sky from various neighborhoods, while far away, on the other side of the Thames, a rippling curtain of flame was visible. The tripods were spreading across the city like an unstoppable plague. In no time at all they would be here, and these lofty mansions would be razed.

I returned to the ground floor, shouting at the top of my lungs to announce my presence. But my voice was scarcely audible above the strident blasts and the clanging bells. Pausing, I glimpsed a chance reflection thrown back at me from one of the mirrors in my uncle's drawing room and was startled at the sight of this grimy, frantic Charles with a haunted look in his eyes. I had lost my hat, my hair was disheveled, my jacket caked with dust and torn at the shoulder. I turned away from the mirror and paced the ground floor, wondering where my cousin and his guests could be. Had they left the house, driven by fear or curiosity?

Suddenly, I realized I hadn't looked in what was undoubtedly the safest place in the house in the case of a catastrophe: the servants' quarters in the basement. Alarmed by the explosions, everyone had no doubt decided to take shelter below. In all my visits to the house, my uncle had never invited me below, but I knew the way through a small, unobtrusive door next to the kitchen. I descended the stairs like an interloper, wondering whether I was mistaken, but instantly heard a voice emanating from one of the rooms. Letting the sound guide me through those bare passageways, soon I could make out what it was saying. The voice belonged to an older man, who spoke calmly and politely, as though he was accustomed to addressing people in a tone of scrupulous respect. I assumed this must be Harold, my uncle's faithful coachman.

"And then I realized that if I was going to scare away the ferret, I needed to find the rake, but that was no easy feat, for as I already explained, I was trouserless," Harold was saying.

Howls of laughter followed, from which I deduced that the coachman was telling his story to an audience as numerous as it was attentive, probably the rest of the domestic servants and the guests. And I was not mistaken, as I discovered when I pushed open the door behind which the gale of laughter had erupted. I stepped into what must have been the servants' parlor. The chairs had been placed in a semicircle, at the center of which was the coachman, hands raised like a magician surprised in the middle of a conjuring trick. I was relieved to see my wife Victoria, her sister Madeleine and her husband, my cousin Andrew, sitting amongst the servants. They were the only members of the family in the house at the time, as my uncle and aunt were vacationing in Greece with my parents when the invasion began. But I also spotted their esteemed guests, who were none other than my wife's and her sister's two best friends: the former Misses Lucy Nelson and Claire Haggerty. Lucy's husband, an inspector at Scotland Yard by the name of Garrett, was not there (it was reasonable to assume he was on duty, bringing order to the streets, if such a thing was possible), but Claire had brought her husband, John Peachey, whom I had yet to have the pleasure of meeting. I noticed they all had a brandy in their hands, and the faraway smiles on some of their faces suggested they were on their second glass. In order to enliven proceedings, a gramophone in the corner was filling the room with a merry tune, muffling the explosions. Victoria seemed happy that I was still alive, although her irritation prevented her from responding with anything more than a triumphant smile: my lamentable appearance was proof of the fact that the invasion was indeed making inroads, regardless of what the future held, as she had reasoned during our discussion. For my part, despite what I had witnessed, I continued to believe this meant nothing, that before long in some way or another the Martians would be defeated. Adamant in our opposing views, neither of us made the slightest move to embrace each other, as we would have liked, for, as everyone knows, wounded pride is a great destroyer of affection. It was my cousin Andrew who rose to greet me, breaking the harmonious tableau they formed.

"Thank God you're here, Charles!" he exclaimed, delighted to see I was unscathed. "We didn't know what was going on out there, and we feared for your safety."

"I'm fine, Andrew, don't worry," I replied, noticing with dismay that a couple of the maids were remarking to each other on the sorry state of my clothes.

"All we heard were explosions, and it was making us terribly nervous, so we came down here," my cousin explained, raising his brandy glass to indicate the room. "Harold had even begun telling us a funny story to take our minds off what's happening outside."

The coachman played down my interruption with a brief wave of his hand.

"Nothing I can't finish some other time, sir," he said.

With an obsequious gesture, the butler hurriedly passed me a glass of brandy from a tray on a small table.

"Here, sir. You look as if you could do with a pick-me-up."

I thanked him absentmindedly, trying to reconcile this cheerful atmosphere with the terrifying scenes I had witnessed outside.

"What's going on, Charles?" Andrew asked, as soon as I had taken a sip of brandy. "Is this . . . an invasion?"

Everyone gazed at me expectantly.

"I'm afraid so. The Martians have marched into London and . . ." I paused, unsure how best to describe the devastation I had seen, but there was no way of telling them gently. "Well . . . they're destroying the city. Our army has been routed, and there's no one left to protect us, we are entirely at their mercy."

There was a murmur of consternation all round the room. A couple of the maids began to weep. My wife and her sister clutched each other, while Mr. Peachey put his arm around his wife, who nestled her head on his chest like a scared child. Next to me, my cousin gave a sudden sigh.

Apparently, until then, Andrew had refused to believe there was an invasion, despite the series of blasts resounding in the distance, which could still be heard downstairs despite the cheery music. Seeing my cousin's unease, I realized that deep down he wanted me to be right in thinking the invasion wouldn't happen; he seemed more let down than afraid, as if I had somehow failed him by being mistaken in my predictions. I contemplated the others in the room; my words seemed to be the command they had been waiting for to begin trembling. "My God," several of the servants murmured in tremulous unison, exchanging looks of despair.

"There's nothing to fear," I reassured them, even though I, too, had difficulty believing this after what I'd seen aboveground. "Everything will be all right, I'm sure of it."

Victoria shook her head, and her lips set in a fold of sorrow and ridicule. When would I admit defeat?

"What makes you say that, Mr. Winslow?" Claire asked expectantly, raising her head from her husband's chest.

I took a deep breath before replying. I knew I'd have difficulty convincing my impromptu audience, and indeed, after the latest events, even I was beginning to consider the possibility that my logic was flawed. Still, I tried to put my argument across as clearly as I could, ignoring my wife's disapproving looks.

"As you know, Mrs. Peachey, some of those here, including yourself, have traveled to the year 2000 and have taken a stroll through a future where the only threat to the human race was the automatons. Clearly that means the invasion to which we are being subjected cannot flourish. I'm convinced something will happen soon to put an end to it, although I still don't know what. The future tells us this."

"I wouldn't take much notice of the future if I were you, for as the word suggests, it's something that hasn't happened yet," her husband interjected.

Annoyed by his interruption, I looked at him with curiosity, raising my eyebrows exaggeratedly, and Claire hastily introduced us.

"Charles, this is my husband, John Peachey," she said.

Hearing my name, the man promptly offered his hand, as though fearing he might break some rule of etiquette were he to delay for a few seconds. But that didn't prevent me from shaking it with a bored expression. I must confess that my first impressions of this Peachey fellow were less than favorable, and not only because he had the nerve to contradict me. I've always felt an uncontrollable dislike of men who underestimate their own potential, and who squander it as a result, and Peachey was most definitely one of those men. He was a strapping youth, whose perfectly proportioned face was endowed with a pair of fiery eyes and a noble chin, and yet he appeared to devote his morning ablutions to sabotaging these attributes, obtaining through his meticulous efforts a dull, pusillanimous individual whose lacquered hair was combed down over his brow, and who wore a pair of enormous spectacles. It was as if he lacked the personality to go with his physique, the determination needed to make full use of his formidable appearance. Everything about him was insipid, self-effacing, contrary to his nature. Although I had never met him, I knew Peachey was an honorary director of Barclay & Company, where Claire's father was a major shareholder. One look at the man told me it was not due to his assiduous, aggressive business acumen that he was occupying that coveted office in Lombard Street.

"Good, now that we have finally been introduced, Mr. Peachey, may I ask what you were insinuating just now with your naïve comment?" I said with thinly veiled rudeness.

"I was saying that the future hasn't happened yet, Mr. Winslow," he hastened to reply. "It doesn't exist yet, it isn't tangible. And so, basing one's suppositions on something that hasn't happened yet would seem to me very—"

"Ah, you appear to know a great deal about the future, Mr. Peachey!" I interjected, with that perfect mixture of sarcasm and civility that only a man of breeding knows how to carry off. "Have you ever visited the year 2000? I have, and I assure you it all seemed very tangible to me. But I don't recall seeing you there. Which expedition did you go on?"

Peachey looked at me for a few moments in silence, as though unsure how to respond to my exquisite ambiguity.

"No . . . I've never visited the future . . . ," he confessed awkwardly.

"Never? Oh, what a shame, my dear Mr. Peachey. Then I suppose you'll agree with me when I say that he who pronounces on what he has not seen runs the risk, far too costly in my view, of making a blunder and looking foolish in front of others," I said, smiling amiably at him. "Consequently, before you continue down that path, allow me to inform you, and Claire will doubtless back me up, that the future does exist. Yes, somewhere in time that future is happening at this very moment, and it is no less real than this instant in which we are conversing. And, unlike you, I can vouch for this, for I *have* been to the year 2000. A year in which the human race finds itself on the verge of extinction due to the evil automatons, not the Martians, even if thanks to a man named Derek Shackleton we will succeed in defeating them."

"I wish Captain Shackleton were here now," Harold murmured behind me.

Peachey glanced at him with sudden interest.

"I don't think one man could do much," he said dryly, shrugging his shoulders.

The banker's second comment nettled me even more than his first. Not only did this man appear impervious to my disdain, choosing to ignore my last remark and responding to that of the vulgar coachman instead, he also dared to comment on what Shackleton could or could not do.

"Captain Shackleton isn't just anyone, Mr. Peachey," I said, trying not to show my annoyance. "Captain Shackleton is a hero. A hero, do you understand?"

"Even so, I doubt very much whether in this situation he could—"

"I'm afraid, Mr. Peachey, I couldn't disagree with you more," I interrupted him once again, with deliberate contempt. "However, this is no time to become embroiled in what has the makings of a fascinating discussion, and which under other circumstances would have given me great pleasure, for there is nothing I like more than an exchange of opinions as clever as they are frivolous. I shall simply point out to you that if you had traveled to the future, you would know what a true hero is and what he can achieve." After smiling at him politely, I could not help offering a final barbed remark: "How rude of me, Mr. Peachey; why, I've only just realized that, not having enjoyed as comfortable a position two years ago as you do now, the price of a ticket was doubtless beyond your means."

I watched Peachey purse his lips to stop himself from saying something that might have spoiled his outward show of refinement. Then, having stifled this urge, he tilted his head to one side, searching his mind for a more appropriate but equally stinging retort, and I realized that without meaning to we had entered into a verbal sparring match. While the banker was busy trying to think up a reply, I took the opportunity to glance quickly about the room. Everyone had stopped talking and was looking at us: the servants had taken a backseat, no doubt incapable of following the discussion, excepting Harold, who was sitting closer to Lucy, Madeleine, and my wife. They had risen from their chairs, alarmed by the dangerous direction our conversation was taking, while a step away from us, tense as the strings on a violin, stood Claire and Andrew. I grinned at Peachey, my excitement doubled by having such a large audience. The gramophone's lively melody cut through the silence.

"What do you know about my life two years ago?" my adversary said at last, barely able to contain his agitation.

I shook my head slowly, disappointed at Peachey's response. He had made the classic beginner's error: even a child knows that answering with a question forcibly exposes one to the wit of the person who must respond to it.

"As much as I need to know, Mr. Peachey," I retorted calmly, swirling my glass. "That you appeared quite literally out of nowhere, with no name and no money, only to marry the daughter of one of the wealthiest men in London."

"What are you insinuating, Charles?" Claire chimed in.

I turned toward her with a movement as theatrical as it was graceful.

"Insinuating? Oh, God forbid I should insinuate anything,

Claire!" I said, giving her my most dazzling smile. "Insinuations rarely satisfy the one who makes them, for they force those who are blameless to defend themselves, whilst the guilty can simply ignore them without arousing anyone's suspicions. That's why I have always preferred being labeled impudent rather than a hypocrite, my dear, not because I care about other people's opinion of me, but because I like everyone to know mine."

"Oh we all know perfectly well how you love giving your opinion, Charles. But allow me to remind you that in this instance you are referring to someone about whom you know nothing," Claire retorted, visibly upset. "And as you yourself warned John a few moments ago, he who pronounces on things he knows nothing about runs the risk, far too costly in your view, of looking foolish in front of others."

I positively beamed.

"But I'm the first to admit my ignorance, Claire!" I exclaimed, spreading my arms and glancing around me with a look of innocence. "And I'd like nothing more than to remedy it. My dear Claire, speculating about where your mysterious husband sprang from has been the favorite pastime of all London for the past two years! I'm not exaggerating when I say that since the tragic death of Mr. Murray it has been the most popular topic of discussion in the clubs and salons."

"Charles, I think everyone here will agree that there is a fine line between impudence and downright ill manners, and tonight you seem intent on stepping over that line," I heard my wife say. Clearly, whilst considering our argument too important to dispel with a tender embrace, she did not mind breaking our silence with a reproach.

"My dear, it is impossible not to take an interest in another person's life without being ill-mannered. If not, one risks falling into mendacity," I said, turning to her. "You better than anyone ought to know that, or do you intend to put me in the awkward position of reminding you in front of everyone that yours was one of the sharpest tongues when commenting on the matter behind your dear friend's back?"

I admit that my comment was too much of a poisoned dart, but one cannot always judge these things properly. Victoria bit her lip, suppressing her rage, and I confess I felt a pang of remorse, even though in those days I was convinced that remorse was a luxury I could ill afford.

"You pride yourself on your exquisite manners, Mr. Winslow," Peachey intervened, at last forgoing his wife's protection and stepping valiantly into the fray, "yet you don't seem to know how to treat your wife, much less to make her happy, as I do mine."

I wheeled round, ready to fend off his attack, but the accuracy of his blow caught me off guard, and, just as even the finest swordsman can make a false move, I mistakenly answered him with a question.

"And how did your sharp mind arrive at that conclusion, Mr. Peachey?"

Peachey used my slip to better advantage than I could have imagined, mirroring my smirk to perfection.

"Because, as we all noticed, you left her here alone, while you went out to attend to apparently more pressing matters."

I had to clench my fists so as not to reveal the pain his answer caused me, and I confess, when I replied, I was hard put to maintain my habitual composure.

"I don't think you are best placed to judge the urgency of my affairs, Mr. Peachey. But at least I decide what I do or don't do in the light of the affection I feel for my wife, and not for fear of upsetting the person to whom I owe my position."

Peachey pursed his lips once more.

"Do you dare question my love for Mrs. Peachey?" he demanded, no longer bothering to conceal his anger.

I grinned: the time had come to administer the killer punch.

"My dear Mr. Peachey, I couldn't possibly do such a thing without belittling one of society's most beautiful and interesting young ladies. But, make no mistake, if I were to dare to question your love for our adorable Claire, attributing it to something other than her myriad qualities, what I would actually be calling into question would be your manhood."

Peachey clenched his jaw, trying hard to contain his rage. This he managed by snorting a little, the way some animals do.

"Charles, you don't know what you're talking about," Claire protested behind me.

"My dear Claire, you women are very good at believing whatever suits you," I replied, turning toward her, while out of the corner of my eye I observed Peachey remove his spectacles, close them, and place them in his jacket pocket very carefully, like someone officiating at a church service.

"Don't speak to my wife like that, Mr. Winslow," he said calmly, making sure his spectacles were properly protected.

The fact that he did not deign to look at me enraged me more than what he said.

"Is that an order, John?" I said, grinning at his veiled threat and spreading my arms in front of him, as if to convey my bewilderment.

"I trust I expressed myself clearly enough for you to be in no doubt, my dear, ill-mannered fellow," he retorted.

And what followed happened so quickly I'm unable to describe it as precisely as I'd like. All I remember is Peachey grabbing my wrist with an impossibly swift movement and finding myself with my right arm twisted behind my back. Then, a foot kicked my leg out from under me, and before I knew what had hit me, the room tilted sideways, and, like a listing vessel, I ended up with my face pressed into the carpet. Peachey was on top of me, effectively immobilizing me under the weight of one of his legs. Each time I tried to move, I felt a pain shoot down my arm, almost preventing me from breathing.

"That's enough, John," I heard Claire say in a clear, steady voice.

Like a panther suddenly pacified by a maiden's dulcet tones, Peachey released his quarry. I felt him stand up, while I remained where I was, my face half buried in the carpet, hiding a humiliating grimace of pain caused by the ache in my arm.

"Charles . . ." Claire spoke to me once more in a gentle, almost motherly tone. "I'm going to agree with you about one of the things you said: Captain Shackleton is indeed a hero, an exceptional man who is capable of saving our planet from the automatons—"

"Claire, please . . . ," I heard her husband implore, while he shifted awkwardly on his feet, inches from my face.

"No, John," his wife interrupted, "Mr. Winslow is an old friend and must be made aware of his mistakes so that he has the opportunity to apologize, as I have no doubt his honor as a gentleman will dictate."

"But . . . ," her husband replied timidly.

"However, Charles," I heard Claire resume. I still didn't turn around, keeping my face pressed to the floor, sensing that no matter what she said, there was nothing I could say to redeem myself. "There's something else you should know about Captain Shackleton. Derek Shackleton isn't just a great hero. He is also a man who is capable of renouncing glory for the woman he loves, of traveling back in time to be by her side, even if this means having to conceal his true identity behind the guise of a simple bank director."

I raised my head from the carpet with as much dignity as I could muster, and managed to address her feet. "What the devil are you trying to say, Claire?"

Her voice floated down to me as gently as a feather. "That you are in the presence of your beloved Captain Shackleton."

"W-what?" I stammered, completely bewildered.

My gaze moved slowly up the banker's powerful legs, at the sides of which hung his enormous paws, over his waist and his broad chest, settling at last on his face, from which, unhindered by spectacles, his large, intense eyes were now flashing. For what seemed like an eternity, I contemplated with amazement the calm, indomitable countenance, which from below had the air of an Olympian god. Then, like a reflection in a steamed-up mirror, my memory of the brave Captain Shackleton, savior of the human race, was superimposed on the man who, moments before, I had sought to humiliate. No one had ever seen Shackleton's face, because his helmet had covered all except his chin, but I had to confess Peachey's chin had a similarly noble air. Could it be true, then? Was this spineless, timid banker really Captain Shackleton? Peachey stretched out the same hand with which moments before he had forced me to the ground and offered to help me up. I accepted, still unable to believe this was Shackleton, and he hauled me, half dazed, to my feet.

"You're pulling my leg," I said, still refusing to believe it. "You can't be Captain Shackleton."

"Of course he is, Charles." Claire was adamant. Then she looked at me with a dreamy smile. "Derek and I met two years ago . . . although, strictly speaking, our first meeting hasn't happened yet, because it took place in the year 2000. But the fact is, it all began during one of Murray's Time Travel's expeditions to the future, although he had to travel to our time for—"

"Hold on, Claire, hold on . . ." I tried to interrupt, completely flummoxed.

"Well, all that isn't important now. I can explain another time," she said, ignoring my protest. "The fact is, Charles, we fell in love. And Derek decided to leave everything and stay in the present with me, the woman he loved."

"But . . . that's impossible, Claire," I said, incapable of reacting.

"No it isn't, Charles. That's what happened. Why would we lie to you?" she said, genuinely touched by my bewilderment. "My husband is Captain Derek Shackleton, the savior of the human race."

I looked at Peachey, who smiled at me diffidently. Could he really be Captain Shackleton? I carried out a quick piece of mental arithmetic and calculated that Peachey had appeared from nowhere in London society exactly when Murray's business closed down, which was certainly a strange coincidence. Moreover, even the most consummate gossips in London had been unable to dig up anything about his past, despite devoting many months of their leisure to the task. Was this the explanation? Did Peachey have no past simply because his past belonged to our future? Bemused, I looked at Claire, who stared back at me with such sincerity that any doubts I might still have harbored were swept away. This man was Captain Shackleton himself, hero of the year 2000. Incredible though it seemed, Shackleton was here in the present, standing before me. And he had come here out of love.

"My God . . . Forgive my rudeness, Captain, I . . . your disguise was so . . . ," I stammered, breaking off to clear my throat, then giving a ridiculous bow before resuming. "It's a pleasure to meet you, Captain Shackleton. Allow me to thank you on behalf of the entire human race for saving our planet from the evil automatons."

"Thank you, Mr. Winslow," Shackleton said unassumingly. "But anyone in my place would have done the same."

"Oh, you know that isn't true." I smiled, amused at his modesty. "I wouldn't, for example."

I contemplated him in awe for a few moments longer, while behind me there arose a growing murmur of confused voices. I think I even heard Andrew address me, but I didn't pay him any attention because I remained focused on the captain. I still had difficulty believing he was Shackleton and that he'd been living among us in the present for two years, concealed behind the identity of an ordinary man, who every morning went to the trouble of hiding the fact that he was the savior of the human race, of pretending he hadn't seen what awaited us in the future. He had traveled back from a time that for us had yet to happen, all thanks to his love for Claire Haggerty. But whatever his reason for coming, the important thing was that he was here now, I told myself suddenly, in a city facing an invasion that mustn't have any consequences, an invasion someone had to bring to an end. And that someone could only be Shackleton. Suddenly, all the pieces fell into place so precisely and conclusively that I felt giddy with excitement.

"Then, the fact that you are here, in our time," I said, filled with elation, "can only mean you are the one who will save us, who will stop the invasion. Yes, there can be no other possible explanation. This is why you are here."

Peachey shook his head, amused by my pronouncement.

"No, Charles, Derek came here because of his love for me," Claire interjected.

When a man has once loved a woman he will do anything for her except continue to love her, Oscar Wilde had written for posterity. This was something any man who had enjoyed his fair share of love affairs knew only too well. No, Shackleton hadn't come here because of that fickle emotion, but because of something far more powerful. He was here because it was his destiny. Yes, Shackleton was the missing part of my equation, the hero we had all been waiting for. There was no question about it: he was renowned for his bravery and intelligence. Not for nothing had he already saved the planet once, even though chronologically speaking that hadn't yet happened. He alone could defeat the Martians, just as he had already defeated the automatons.

"Of course, Claire, of course he came here for love of you," I said. "But we mustn't forget that Captain Shackleton is a hero, and now more than ever a hero is what we need."

"I'm grateful for your belief in me, Mr. Winslow, but as I already said, one man alone can do nothing in this situation," said Shackleton.

"But you aren't just any man, Captain," I countered. "You're a hero!"

Shackleton sighed and shook his head. His modesty surprised

me. I looked around at the others for the support I was sure they would give but was disappointed to find that Shackleton's reason for being here was apparently not as clear to the others as it was to me. The servants gaped at me, visibly overwhelmed by the rapid sequence of impossible events: the Martian invasion, the defeat of the mighty empire, the presence in their parlor of a hero from the future, who according to our calendar had not yet even been born. They were dumbfounded by it all, but then I had expected nothing more from these simple minds. I felt much more let down by my wife Victoria, who wore an expression of weary resignation, as if to say that even a Martian invasion was less bothersome than having to put up with her husband's eccentricities. And what about my cousin Andrew and his charming wife Madeleine? They looked utterly bewildered, incapable of backing me up in any way. Was there no one in that room who could see what I saw? I turned to Shackleton once more, in despair.

"Captain, I've seen you fight a duel with the king of the automatons and win," I insisted. "You're the savior of the human race. And I can think of only one reason why you're here: you have to save us once more."

"I'm sorry, but I'm afraid I can't," Shackleton protested, as though he found it difficult to take off his disguise and was still playing the part of a bank manager refusing one of his customers a loan.

"Of course you can!" I exclaimed. I turned to my cousin for support. "Can you honestly say I'm wrong, Andrew? We both saw him kill Solomon. And now he's here among us, exactly when we need him most. Do you honestly believe that's a coincidence, Andrew? Say something, damn it!"

"I . . . ," my cousin replied, confused, "I don't quite understand what it is you're asking of Mr. Peachey . . . I mean Captain Shackleton . . ."

"Your cousin is right, Mr. Winslow," the captain said. "I wasn't alone when I defeated Solomon. I had my men with me. I had powerful weapons, I had—"

"Well, then, we'll travel to the year 2000 and get them," I proposed. "Yes, that's it, we'll travel to the future and bring back your weapons and your men. They'll fight with you to the death, and we'll destroy these accursed Martians—"

"How?" Shackleton asked, breaking off my harangue in midstream. "How do you expect us to travel to the future?"

I looked at him, bewildered.

"I don't know . . . ," I admitted, "I assumed . . . How did you get here, Captain?"

"That's the problem, Charles," Claire intervened. "Derek came here in a machine that was later destroyed."

I was surprised. I didn't know any other time machine existed apart from the *Cronotilus,* although I should have realized that such a thing was highly likely in the future from which Captain Shackleton hailed. In any event, if what Claire said was true, and his machine had been destroyed, we would not be able to use it. That left only one way for us to get there.

"We'll go to Murray's Time Travel and take the *Cronotilus* to the year 2000," I explained triumphantly.

"But Murray's Time Travel closed two years ago, Mr. Winslow, after Gilliam Murray's death," Shackleton reminded me.

"Yes, I'm aware of that," I replied, "but what do you think happened to the hole leading to the fourth dimension and the year 2000? Is it still open?"

"I doubt it," Shackleton said with a conviction that took me by surprise.

I gazed at the captain fixedly, wondering how to get around his objections.

"Well, I think it is. And I'm convinced we will be able to use it to travel to the future. Don't you see it has to be this way? There is no trace of the Martians in your future, which must mean that at some point, somehow, we will defeat them. Otherwise none of us here would have been able to glimpse that future." I glanced around me once more and thought I saw a flash of comprehension on my cousin's face, and that of Madeleine, and even of Harold and a few of the other servants. I felt encouraged to speak even more heatedly. "We'll go to Murray's Time Travel, travel to the future, and defeat the Martians. And do you know why? Because we've already done it!"

"But we can't be sure my intervention will be what stops the invasion," Shackleton replied stubbornly. "It could be one of our allies coming to our aid, or anything."

The captain looked around, seeking the approval of his audience, but his words died in the growing buzz of admiration. My heartening speech and my simple explanation of the complicated matter had stirred them more than the captain's shilly-shallying. A few of the servants approached him, mesmerized: standing in their parlor was the man who would save the human race from extinction after first defeating the Martians and destroying the powerful machines that were razing the city of their birth.

"Perhaps he's right, Derek," Claire addressed her husband. "Perhaps it wasn't only your love for me that brought you here. Perhaps there is another reason?"

"But Claire . . . ," Shackleton protested.

Claire placed her hand on her husband's arm with the utmost tenderness.

"I think you should at least try, Derek," she insisted, giving him a pleading look.

Shackleton remained silent, gazing into her eyes, while we all awaited his decision anxiously.

"Very well, Claire, I'll try," he said.

"Excellent!" I exclaimed, overjoyed at his decision, while everyone began applauding, overcome with emotion. "We're going to the year 2000!"

I watched Harold the coachman surreptitiously wipe a tear from his cheek, while the other servants exchanged hugs and pats on the back. Only my wife remained frosty, refusing to join in the general merriment.

"I'll go with you," my cousin declared, overcome with emotion.

"No, Andrew," I said, smiling. "Only the captain and I will go. It's dangerous out there. Remember, Captain Shackleton plays a crucial role in this situation: he must stop the invasion, and the future tells us he will, which means he won't die at least until then. However, there's no guarantee that those who go with him will also be spared, so you must stay here, Andrew, and take care of the women. I'm sure the charming Keller sisters could not endure being widowed at the same time," I joked. My cousin made as if to protest, but I cut him short with a gesture. "Harold, prepare the carriage."

The coachman shot a glance at Andrew, who nodded.

"The carriage will be ready in five minutes, Mr. Winslow," he said.

"Make that two." I grinned.

After he had gone, Shackleton and I began saying our good-byes to those staying behind in the refuge. Claire implored Shackleton to be careful, and I told Andrew once again to look after the women as best he could. Victoria did not approach me: she simply shook her head in dismay, and I gave a shrug. That silent exchange of reproaches constituted our farewell. She didn't know I was trying to save the planet, and I didn't know I would never see her again. And even if we had known, would we have behaved any differently?

XXXII

CHARLES BLEW GENTLY ON THE LAST PARAGRAPH until the ink was dry. He closed the notebook, placing the pen diagonally across it, and stared at it blankly. Two years had passed since he last saw his wife, and now it pained him deeply, as few things ever had in his life, that he had refused to swallow his pride and bid her farewell with a loving kiss, or failing that, if modesty prevented him, with a more or less affectionate, more or less heartfelt embrace.

Just then, he became aware of the rodent-like squeak coming from his neck shackle. Almost immediately, he felt the familiar tickling sensation that seemed to originate from the spot where the shackle was implanted in his back through a web of thin tentacles, roughly at the level of his fourth vertebra. Within seconds, the tingling sensation spread like a stream of molten lava down his back, searing his spinal cord, before subsiding as it reached his feet in a series of painful spasms. Clenching his teeth, Charles waited for the torment to pass, leaving him, as it did every morning, with a knot in his stomach, his body limp, his legs shaking. Fortunately the pain did not last long, a few seconds, and as time went on he had almost become accustomed to it. At first, he thought this sword of fire scorching his back would melt his spinal cord, or possibly his insides, but the only lasting harm had been a couple of cracked teeth and a sense of shame that would haunt him for the rest of his days, for more than once he had lost control of his bowels and been forced to attend the work camp carrying a humiliating load in his ragged trousers.

With this unnecessary fanfare, the buzz of the shackle was telling him it was time to leave his cell. When the spasms in his feet had subsided, Charles got up and placed the notebook under his pallet, pleased at having finished the entry just in time. He left his cell sleepily, pretending he had just woken up. His cell was one of the topmost cubicles in the vast metal barracks where the prisoners lived, and from the narrow walkway, along which his fellow prisoners were now dragging their weary bodies, he had a view of the entire Martian camp. Charles decided to stop for a moment and survey the place where he would die, the panorama that seemed stranger to him each day, for it was changing imperceptibly.

Although not yet complete, the huge pyramid being built at the center already dominated the camp. Just then, as the rising sun peeped out from behind one side of the pyramid, casting an orange glow over its chromed surface, Charles even thought it looked beautiful. Yet he knew this vast edifice was in fact monstrous. For the past few months, greenish sparks that emitted a peculiar buzzing noise had begun running horizontally around the lower levels of the pyramid, closest to the ground. The pyramid's perimeter was so vast that these sparks took hours to travel round it, and if Charles happened to be working in the vicinity of the structure when the strange flashes passed, he felt a sharp pain in his lungs, which instantly sparked a fit of coughing. Whatever effect that colossal pyramid was supposed to have on the Earth's atmosphere, it had already started.

Beyond the pyramid stood a cluster of unsightly Martian huts, like pale pink bubbles. Poking through the top of them were rubbery glass tubes that drooped gracelessly down the outside, giving them the appearance of giant upturned jellyfish. The tubes trailed down to the ground and, at a distance from the huts, disappeared underground in the direction of the pyramid. To the left of the camp, quite close to the huts, was a huge, funnel-shaped hole in the ground where they threw the dead human bodies, which would revolve in slow circles before sliding down and being sucked into the hole in the center. But not only dead bodies went into the grisly orifice. If the Martians thought a prisoner deserved to be punished, or if one fell ill and was too weak to work, his neck shackle would give off a high-pitched wail, and the wretched man would start walking helplessly toward the funnel, like a puppet guided by invisible threads, and hurl himself into it, spinning faster and faster as he descended, until with a howl of terror he disappeared into the central maw.

Charles gave a shudder and averted his gaze from the funnel. Not a day went by when the accursed hole didn't gobble one of them up, dead or alive, and, as he did every morning, Charles wondered whether at some point during the day, the shackle would take control of his legs and he would find himself walking toward the funnel in what might seem like a perfectly natural way, were it not for the grimace of horror that would appear on his face. His eyes wandered toward the horizon. Although the camp appeared to have no perimeter fence, so that any prisoner might feel tempted to flee across country, it was in fact surrounded by an invisible wall of death. No one knew the exact location of the deadly demarcation line, but if a prisoner strayed a few yards too far from the camp's center, his neck shackle would instantly begin to choke him, and he would be forced to retrace his steps if he wanted to be able to breathe again. This of course did not prevent some prisoners, in moments of deep despair, from forgetting about the invisible fence, or simply from thinking they could run faster than the time it took the shackle to choke them. But during those two long years, Charles had never seen anyone succeed. He, in contrast, had made no attempt to flee since they had brought him there. Where would he go, given the whole world was one big prison camp? As far as he knew, there was no sign anywhere of his longed-for human resistance. And one look at his fellow prisoners filing down the stairs to the camp was enough to convince him that no hidden seed of rebellion would flourish there either.

Charles descended the steps, mingling with the other prisoners as they left the barracks, which from the ground looked like a huge metal box turned on its side. As he did every morning, Charles headed for the food dispensers, situated around the rim of the funnel; in fact, they appeared to grow out of it, so it would have been naïve to imagine their positioning was entirely coincidental. But Charles had long since chosen not to consider what horrors this implied. With a little imagination, the dispensers could be described as giant mushrooms, ten feet high. They were crowned by a kind of cap made of shiny scales, and their stem was a long cylinder, narrow enough for a man to wrap his arms around it. To complete their similarity with the Earth's flora, they were equipped with metal roots, some of which plunged into the sand a few inches from the edge of the funnel, while at least a dozen others clung to the stem like metal ivy. These wires contained hundreds of tiny filaments that quivered in the air at waist level, each ending in a kind of serrated mouth. When the prisoners held their bowls close to these hideous faucets that resembled carnivorous plants, the mouth undulated gently before regurgitating a green pap, the prisoners' only source of nourishment.

After queuing for several minutes, Charles succeeded in filling his bowl and went to sit on a solitary rock. There he began shoveling the contents into his mouth, trying not to taste it. This was the only method he had discovered of not throwing up the putrid Martian concoction. And the only reason why he was still eating it was because he did not want death to take him before he had finished writing his diary. While he was forcing himself to eat the nauseating puree, Charles cast a weary glance at the small clusters of prisoners, but he could not see Shackleton among them, nor was he sitting alone over his breakfast. This meant the captain had probably been taken that morning to the women's camp, to empty his still potent seed into one of them. They were only given a few minutes to eat before the Martians made them resume building the purification machine, and so Charles scraped the bottom of his bowl and tossed it on the pile. As he headed toward the pyramid, he observed with tired resentment the dozen or so guards watching their every move. Although partially obscured by colorful copper masks strapped to their heads, which covered their mouths and nasal passages and were designed to filter the Earth's atmosphere, the Martians in the camp generally took on a human form. To begin with, Charles had considered this a thoughtful gesture on their part, until someone told him it was not to avoid terrifying the prisoners, but to make sure they understood the Martians' commands and insults.

Charles spent the day on one of the upper floors of the tower, transporting the heavy iron girders with a dozen other prisoners. He worked without taking a break, except when a fit of coughing forced him to step away from the group in order to deposit a blob of green phlegm onto the floor. When this happened, the other prisoners would give him a look of sympathy or indifference, although he could not help feeling anything but deep contempt for them. Charles considered himself different from the others, but not because he belonged to a higher social class. Two years had sufficed to reduce rich and poor to the same level, changing them into a downtrodden, evil-smelling throng that could only be told apart by their manners, and sometimes not even then. As time went on, conversation had been replaced by silence, monosyllables, and grunts, such was the weight of their crushing fatigue. If Charles still felt he was different, this was because he had not been captured whilst fleeing through the streets, like most of the others, and imprisoned there without knowing anything more about what was going on than vague rumors they picked up in the camp. No, before being taken prisoner, Charles had formed part of a group of valiant heroes led by the brave Captain Shackleton, which had been on the point of killing the Martian leader of the invasion, even though all this seemed like a dream to him now. It took a supreme effort of concentration for him to dredge up those events from the depths of his memory.

This was what he had to do when he returned to his cell after an exhausting day. He scarcely had an hour before the sun went down, and so despite the dizziness and fatigue overwhelming him, he took the diary out from under his pallet and resumed where he had left off, unraveling the knot of memories hidden in the farthest recesses of his mind.

Diary of Charles Winslow

13 February, 1900

When the carriage emerged into Queen's Gate, it was still quiet, as was Exhibition Road. I was greatly relieved to see that the tripods hadn't made an appearance there yet, not simply because it lessened the time our loved ones would have to endure them, but because I had no desire to bump into another sinister Martian machine, even if I was in the company of the brave Captain Shackleton. I quietly observed the captain, who appeared lost in thought, frowning. The man beside me was the same timid individual whom I had taken such a dislike to only minutes before, and yet now that I knew he was none other than Captain Shackleton, I could not help seeing him as a brave, intrepid hero, whose calmness would inspire anyone to follow him to the very gates of Hell. I was sitting next to a legend, but a legend who was armed, because before leaving the house, I had taken the precaution of purloining three revolvers from my uncle's collection: a Colt for Shackleton, a Remington for Harold, and a Smith & Wesson for myself, so that all three of us were traveling to our destination with a weapon in our laps and several boxes of ammunition stuffed in our jacket pockets. I was aware that my role in this momentous endeavor was that of humble shield bearer, but despite my fear, I could not help feeling a wave of confidence sweep over me: my meeting with Shackleton had been providential, for if I had not convinced him, he would never have accepted that it was he who must defeat the Martians. And since this could not be determined by a series of mere coincidences, I realized we were following our destiny, that everything we were apparently doing spontaneously and of our own free will had in fact been decided by the Creator long before we were born.

The carriage traveled at a leisurely, discreet pace past Hyde Park and down Piccadilly toward Soho. I was happy to discover that, for the moment, all was quiet. We could hear a barrage of explosions in the distance, masked by the relentless clanging of bells, but apparently the tripods had still not reached this area. Londoners had taken refuge in their houses, and the streets were deserted. However, soon after turning into Shaftesbury Avenue, which was still intact, we began to encounter people running panic-stricken toward us. It was the same motley crowd that had carried me down to the Thames during my flight: scruffy vagrants side by side with wealthy gentlemen, all wearing the same look of terror on their faces. Through the carriage windows, we noticed that some of those dodging the carts and other vehicles fleeing in the same direction had bloodstains on their clothes. Clearly we were traveling into the oncoming path of a tripod. I muttered a curse and scanned the street for a side alley we might slip into, but every exit seemed to be blocked by rubble, or clusters of bewildered people. We had no choice but to continue up Shaftesbury Avenue, in the direction of the tripod. Harold appeared undaunted and urged on the horses, weaving with difficulty through the torrent of carriages hurtling in our direction. I saw Shackleton begin to brace himself as the din grew steadily louder, and I, too, sat up in my seat, gripping the revolver tightly. Unlike the other two, I doubted we would come out alive.

Then, in the middle of the street, with its three legs planted firmly on the ground, we saw the tripod that had caused this stampede. It was swaying gently, confident and commanding, while behind it we glimpsed a row of half-collapsed buildings, like a set of rotten teeth. Shackleton seemed startled by the size of the Martian machine. Just then, the tripod spat a ray of fire from its tentacle, which enveloped the handful of panic-stricken people fleeing before it, instantly transforming them into grotesque cinder dolls.

"Good God . . . ," Shackleton breathed.

After seeing what the Martians were able to do to us, Harold appeared to lose his nerve. He swiftly turned the carriage about-face, ready to flee in the opposite direction, but a knot of vehicles had formed behind us, blocking the street. Coaches and cabriolets were hopelessly attempting to escape from the bottleneck they had created in their panic-stricken flight, and we quickly realized that before they could disentangle themselves the tripod would be upon us. We were trapped between the tangle of coaches and the Martian monster and would presently be reduced to a pile of ashes on the paving stones. Harold surrendered to the impossibility of the situation and stepped down from the driver's seat, unsure what to do next. Shackleton and I did likewise. Just then, the tripod took a step toward this ludicrous blockage, causing the ground beneath our feet to bulge and break up like the hackles on a cat. I made as if to cock my revolver but immediately decided against it. What was the use of shooting at that thing?

"We must leave the carriage here and flee on foot!" I shouted to Shackleton, who was staring intently at the machine's slow advance.

The captain shook his head, and Harold and I looked on in disbelief as Shackleton made a dash in the other direction. Astonished, I watched as he sprinted toward the tripod, which failed to notice that from among the fleeing multitude, a single individual was heading the other way. Only when the crowd dispersed was the Martian able to see the captain. I tried from a distance to make out what the devil he was attempting. Just one thing occurred to me: he planned to pass through the Martian's legs and flee in the opposite direction, leaving us behind. But what kind of hero would do such a thing? I thought to myself: what kind of hero would try to save his own skin without a thought for his companions? Then, all of a sudden, just as he was about to pass beneath the tripod, he appeared to change his mind, and instead of running between its legs, he tried to go round it to the right. Ignoring the others, the tentacle swayed in the air as it followed the captain's bewildering trajectory.

From where I was standing, struggling not to be trampled by the swarm of people fighting their way past the barricade of coaches, I could see the Martian machine trap Shackleton against a massive edifice, no doubt an administrative building, with a splendid neoclassical frontage and half a dozen elegant pillared archways. Together with the handful of onlookers who had stopped in their tracks to observe the apparently suicidal actions of a madman, I saw the captain contemplate the tentacle's cobralike dance, seemingly paralyzed with fear. The limb stopped moving a few yards from Shackleton, dangling in the air, before it aimed at him. The captain was a dead man, I thought, but suddenly Shackleton overcame his paralysis, hurling himself to one side, so that the ray struck the pillar behind him, producing a shower of lethal debris that scattered in all directions. The destruction of the pillar caused the front of the building to rock and a maze of cracks to spread across its façade. Through a veil of dust I saw the captain scramble to his feet, but the Martian at the controls of the machine wasn't ready to give up. Steadying itself on its long legs, the tripod launched another tongue of fire, forcing the captain to fling himself to the ground once more. The ray struck a second pillar, throwing up another fountain of debris.

Quick as a flash, Shackleton was again on his feet, and I saw him running as far away as he could from the tripod. The tentacle tried again to strike Shackleton with its ray, slicing through the remaining columns of the building like a scythe felling weeds, but still failed to hit its elusive prey. Having lost several of its sustaining columns, the building began to crumple forward with a deafening crack. Shackleton came to a halt beneath the last archway but could scarcely do more than watch as the huge building collapsed on top of him. Before the tripod had time to realize what was going on, an avalanche of rubble fell on top of it, jolting it violently. The tentacle thrashed around in the air, its heat ray sweeping the street and slicing through the fronts of the adjoining buildings.

This sudden, random destruction sent down a torrent of stones, bricks, and every imaginable type of architectural ornamentation, which landed on us from every direction. Not all of us were able to shield ourselves from the onslaught. Harold and I managed to take shelter behind our carriage, which only shook violently, but some of the nearby vehicles were not so lucky: we looked on appalled as a massive gargoyle plummeted from the sky onto the roof of one of them, crushing its occupants, a terrified couple who scarcely had time to grasp each other's hand. The cascade was brutal but short-lived, and when it was over, a sudden deathly hush descended, broken only by the relentless bells.

Spluttering, I peered through the thick cloud of dust filling the street. As it cleared, the few of us who had survived discovered with relief that our lives were no longer threatened by the Martian: the tripod had vanished beneath a pile of rubble, but alas so had Captain Shackleton. Alarmed, I contemplated the immense dusty tomb from which two of the tripod's legs were poking out. There lies the future savior of the human race, I said to myself, with a mixture of sadness and bewilderment, unsure what to think of this unexpected occurrence, which had once again confounded my thinking. As tolling bells and distant explosions shook the sky above our heads, someone suggested a prayer, but most of us were too shocked to respond. Suddenly, we heard the scraping sound of a stone being dislodged at the top of the mound. We all stared in bewilderment as the rubble began to stir, terrified the tripod was trying to raise itself up, but the two legs remained motionless. After the first stone, two more tumbled down, then several in quick succession, until a small avalanche of rubble began sliding down one side of the mound. Then a hand pushed a huge stone aside, sending it rolling slowly to the ground. After that, an arm appeared, and finally, as though emerging with difficulty from a stony womb, we saw Shackleton climb out, miraculously unscathed. I gazed at him with a mixture of joy and disbelief. God be praised . . . this was impossible. He was alive! After a few moments of stunned silence, the small crowd of onlookers began cheering, and several of us approached the mound. When I looked beneath the surface of the debris, I saw immediately what had saved the captain from certain death: the archway had formed a kind of shell around him. There, protected like a baby bird in a nest, he had withstood the building's collapse.

Shackleton greeted us awkwardly from atop the pile of rubble, then he clambered down timidly, brushing the dust off his suit.

He walked somewhat unsteadily toward the carriage, followed by a group of admirers who insisted on shaking his hand and even clapping him enthusiastically on the back. When he finally reached the coach, he climbed aboard, bade farewell to his admirers with a dusty wave of his hand, and sat down stiffly in his seat, ready to resume our journey. I sat beside him, brimming with admiration, if slightly ashamed of myself for what I had thought of him. How could I have considered for a moment that he would leave us to our fate? Nothing could have been further from the truth. While we were all desperately running away, Shackleton had judged the situation with his mind of the future: he had grasped the tripod's vulnerability; he had surveyed the street; he had analyzed the surrounding buildings with a cursory glance and had positioned himself in front of one resting on half a dozen arches, which if destroyed by the heat ray would cause the building to collapse; and finally, he had considered the possibility of sheltering beneath one of those arches. He had the courage necessary to carry out a daring plan he had elaborated in a matter of seconds, a plan that demanded he risk his life to save ours, without a moment's hesitation, displaying great mental as well as physical agility, for what I had initially thought was a clumsy way of rolling on the ground, I now realized were the deliberate movements of a panther.

"Stop staring at me like that, Mr. Winslow," Shackleton said with a certain irritation, which I instantly attributed to the tenseness of the situation.

"Captain, what you just did was the most extraordinary thing I've ever seen. What a strategist, and what presence of mind. Captain, you're a true hero," I replied, in raptures.

"I was lucky, nothing more . . . ," he said brusquely, shrugging aside my comments.

I shook my head, amused at Shackleton's modesty, and ordered Harold to turn the carriage around. I told him we were continuing our journey to Soho, confident that nothing bad could happen to us while we were with this exceptional fellow. Although he himself had seen what the brave Captain Shackleton had done, the coachman looked at me doubtfully, as if the captain's exploits had not impressed him in the slightest. Nonetheless, he climbed onto the driver's perch and drove the horses on without demur.

After skirting the funeral rubble beneath which the tripod was buried, we entered the stretch of road it had just passed through and saw the havoc it had wreaked. We came across numerous fallen buildings, but the real horror, the Martians' boundless contempt for our race, was illustrated by the scores of dead bodies strewn all over the place, and more than anything, the survivors: a woman weeping on her knees before the trampled body of a child of three or four, a man wandering in a daze, cradling a severed head, another crying in vain for help, half trapped beneath his horse. As we contemplated this parade of horrors, even the captain was shocked, despite hailing from a future where London had also been reduced to rubble. He was no doubt thinking how meaningless all our efforts were, because even if we did succeed in halting the invasion and rebuilding the city, another equally horrific devastation awaited it just around the corner. In the same vague way we had learned of their tragedy thanks to Murray's Time Travel, future generations would learn of ours through commemorative crosses and monuments. Only the brave Captain Shackleton would see the greatest city in the world twice razed to the ground.

We spent most of the journey plunged in a gloomy silence, until, as we entered Soho, Harold brought the carriage to an abrupt halt. Peering out of the windows to try to discover the reason, Shackleton and I glimpsed through the veil of mist some fifty yards ahead of us a half-dozen tripods leaving the area where we were heading, walking side by side like an eerie herd. We stayed motionless, pretending we were one of the many carriages abandoned in the streets, and only when they had disappeared toward the Strand did Harold urge the horses on once more.

Soho was unrecognizable. The column of tripods had reduced it to a smoky wasteland where scarcely a building was left standing to serve as a landmark. Faced with this horrific devastation, I realized no force as destructive as that of the Martians had ever existed on Earth. Wandering among the ruins, like castaways who have lost their minds, groups of the wounded were helping one another, or turning over the dead bodies in search of their loved ones. I gazed at them for a while as if under hypnosis, aware that even if we won this war, for many it was already lost. The carriage rolled to a halt, and we heard Harold's voice speaking to us from the driver's seat.

"I think this is number twelve, Greek Street," he said, pointing at nothing.

Shackleton and I stepped down from the coach and made our way, dazed, through the wreckage to the place where Murray's Time Travel had once stood. Harold followed a few paces behind. Somewhere amid that sea of rubble we came across the *Cronotilus,* brutally crushed beneath a heavy layer of girders and sections of roof. How would we travel to the future now? I wondered, pondering the battered time tram. Besides, even if it had been intact, there was no sign of any hole in time, and the fact was I had no idea what the opening into the year 2000 looked like. I felt a creeping sense of failure. Had I been wrong all along? Would we play no part in saving the world? It was then I stumbled on the poster announcing the expedition to the year 2000, to the day of the final battle that would decide the fate of the planet. It had always hung next to the entrance, like an unreal yet captivating lure, in the days when Murray's Time Travel was still open for business. In it Captain Shackleton was pictured raising his sword against the king of the automatons, whom Shackleton had defeated in a fabulous duel, which, thanks to Murray's magic, I myself had witnessed. I cast my eyes around for the hero himself, who at that moment happened to be talking to Harold while pointing to the top of a section of wall. With arm outstretched, each leg planted on a huge rock, and his noble chin jutting out in a gesture of unquestionable authority, Shackleton looked as if he were doing his best to replicate the warrior-like pose in the poster I was holding. I felt a surge of optimism as I looked again from the poster to the brave Captain Shackleton, who was here, in our time, and moments before had single-handedly destroyed one of the Martian machines. The fact that the tripods had ruined the *Cronotilus* only meant we weren't going to save the world by traveling to the future. We would do it some other way, but we would do it. Shackleton caught me looking at him, and, raising his eyebrows skeptically, he spread his arms to encompass all this destruction.

"As you see, Mr. Winslow, we can't possibly travel to the year 2000."

I shrugged, amused by what was undoubtedly a minor setback.

"In that case, I'm afraid we'll just have to defeat the Martians by ourselves, Captain," I replied, grinning.

XXXIII

*I*N THE PRISON CAMP THE FOLLOWING DAY, Charles at last spotted Shackleton at breakfast. He glimpsed him in the distance, sitting on a rock eating his puree. As he had anticipated, the captain had returned from the breeding camp wearing the same gloomy expression he had probably left with. And this could only mean one thing. Charles approached, greeting him with a worried look, and sat down beside him, swamped by the enormous overcoat he had been given when the last lot of clothing had been doled out. Judging by the second-rate workmanship and rough material, the item had probably belonged to a tradesman, not that Charles hadn't long since ceased caring about something as insignificant as wearing the clothes of a lowly commoner. He gazed silently at Shackleton, hoping his friend would feel the need to speak to him.

Once a week, the Martians would march a handful of the healthiest-looking male specimens to a nearby camp where they kept the youngest, most fertile women. Every member of this procession was forced to couple with one of the women, under the watchful eye of the Martians, and was then brought back, without knowing whether his seed had taken root. This way the Martians were sure to have a plentiful supply of slaves to carry out the arduous task of conditioning the planet. During the first few months of his internment, when he still looked like a specimen worth perpetuating, Charles had been regularly chosen, but hard labor and malnutrition had ruined his looks to the point where no Martian deemed his seed could produce anything satisfactory. Shackleton, on the other hand, was chosen almost every week, because the captain had contrived to keep his robust shape by eating everything he could lay his hands on (more than once Charles had surprised him scraping the bowls in the pile) and even exercising at night alone in his cell. At first, Charles hadn't been able to comprehend Shackleton's dogged refusal to waste away, to let his body become a dried-up husk like his own. Later he understood his reasoning: if Shackleton stayed in shape, he was more likely to be taken to the women's camp, and consequently more likely to be able to find Claire, whom he had not laid eyes on since the day Charles persuaded him to leave the basement of the house in Queen's Gate to fulfill a destiny that was subsequently shown to be mistaken.

They sat facing each other, eating their breakfast in silence. Charles knew without having to ask that the captain had not spotted Claire among the other women this time either. And as always, he felt guilty for having made Shackleton leave his uncle's basement. Charles had had plenty of time over the past few years to regret many things he had done in his life, but there was nothing he regretted so much as having separated Derek from his wife. In the first few months of their captivity, the captain had nurtured exaggerated hopes of an uprising. But those were the early days, when Shackleton still believed his wife was safe in the basement at Queen's Gate, and he could think of nothing else but returning to her side, the days when he was still incapable of imagining how the invasion would turn out, much less envisaging life without the woman for whom he had traveled back in time. However, thanks to Charles's disastrous intervention, that is what had happened, and during the first few months in the prison camp, Shackleton had spent all his time thinking up ways of escaping in order to find Claire. He had elaborated plan after plan, which would have raised Charles's hopes, too, had not each of his ideas appeared wilder and more desperate than the one before: he wanted to sew all the bedsheets in the camp together and leap from the top of the pyramid and glide through the air; he wanted to escape through the funnel, to organize an uprising in the women's camp. These madcap escape plans, which he would convey in a garbled fashion to a few randomly chosen prisoners, only showed how much he longed to find Claire. He devoted all his thoughts, all his energy to that. And when Charles protested that she could be anywhere (he never had the heart to suggest she might be dead), that she might have left England, the captain always replied that he had traveled even farther the first time to be with her.

Gradually he had begun to speak less and less about his harebrained schemes. Shackleton's hopes of escape, of forming a resistance group out of the ravaged prisoners, of attacking camp after camp, of visiting every destroyed city in which groups of fugitives were hiding out, of crossing the whole planet if necessary to find his wife were reduced to weary comments, spoken without conviction, which petered out as the months went by. Never again did Shackleton mention the word "escape." All he did now was await the new batches of females with which they replenished the women's prison camps, clinging to the hope that one day he would recognize Claire among the women filling the breeding pavilions, whose pointed rooftops could be seen on sunny days glittering in the distance like a sea of bristles. But why? Charles thought; what was the point of finding her in this situation, in these dark days where they could have no hope, only the pain of knowing they were still alive and suffering?

One day, also during breakfast, the captain's irrepressible, absurd optimism had brought out the old cynic in Charles. He had immediately asked Shackleton cruelly, *And what would you say to her, Derek, if you did eventually find her?* The captain had looked at him in surprise, remaining silent for a long time, before dredging up a reply from the deep well of sorrow that was his soul: *I would beg her forgiveness,* he had said. *I would say to her: forgive me for having lied to you, Claire.* When Charles heard this he had tried to cheer Shackleton up, insisting that Claire could not possibly blame him for having wanted to stop the invasion. On the contrary, Charles had said, she would be proud of you for trying, for keeping the promise you made to her in the basement at Queen's Gate, and . . . But the captain had dismissed Charles's clumsy attempts to console him with a wave of his hand. *You don't understand, Charles,* he had said, shaking his head in dismay. *You couldn't possibly understand.*

But whatever the case, whether to beg her forgiveness, or for some other reason, the captain had never stopped waiting. He rose each morning because every day could be the day when he might see her again. And he went on eating, breathing, and keeping in shape because it helped him to get up each morning. Charles felt sorry for Shackleton. Here, mechanically wolfing down his revolting puree unfit for a pig, was the greatest hero the world had ever known, the savior of humanity, reduced to a nameless prisoner, hunched and filthy among thousands of others. But no, Shackleton wasn't like the others. Shackleton clung to his hope. And no one, not even a monster from outer space, could take that away from him.

"I didn't see Victoria, either," the captain blurted out suddenly.

Charles said nothing. He felt an overwhelming sorrow upon realizing that the captain assumed he was just as anguished not to have received any news of his wife. But it wasn't true, Charles acknowledged bitterly; he cared no more about Victoria's fate than his own. Attempting to change the subject, Charles pointed to the purification machine glowing in the distance.

"If only Mr. Wells could see this," he said, "I'm sure one glance and he would know exactly what it does."

Shackleton made a noise that Charles wasn't sure whether to interpret as a laugh of approval or a grunt of disapproval.

It began to rain, one of those strange showers that had become more and more frequent of late. Every two or three days, tiny green crystals would fall from the sky, as though it were raining gemstones. Within seconds the ground was carpeted in a slithery green film, as though the skin of some bizarre insect or reptile had grown over the Earth's surface. After a while, these bizarre crystals began to melt, giving off poisonous fumes that stained the mist an emerald green, while the greenish liquid they released mixed with the mud to produce a kind of malodorous green moss, from which strange plants grew, spreading over every surface with extraordinary tenaciousness, like some repulsive web. None of the prisoners had ever seen anything like these vile weeds, which had slowly begun to invade the camp, covering the rocks and trees in a dark green shroud. These putrid plants had also grown up along the borders of the camp, where the crystals created stagnant pools, creeping steadily toward the Earthling trees, adorning them with their sinister drapes, turning them into dark, menacing forests, which in fairy tales lead to witches' lairs. At first, Charles and Shackleton had spent hours discussing these curious changes to the climate and vegetation: the crystals were simply the colorful culmination of the disturbing coppery hues that so often stained the sky, the sudden tornados that rattled their cells, or the dead birds that had rained from the sky in the first few months, blanketing the fields at dawn. They were convinced this was caused by the pyramids, like the one they were helping to build, which were springing up all over the planet, and they often discussed whether such changes would be reversible when the long-awaited uprising took place and those monstrosities were destroyed along with all the rest. But gradually they had become resigned to the changes, as though things had always been that way, as though from the beginning of time on Earth the skies had always turned the color of rusty copper, and showers of green crystals had always filled the fields. In fact, for months now, they barely spoke about anything much.

Charles and Shackleton stood up, protecting themselves from the hail of crystals, and joined the group of prisoners whom the Martians had begun assigning their daily tasks. Charles was sent to work on one of the upper levels of the tower. As always, his day was grueling, and yet he was almost glad of all the physical exertion, because besides exhausting him, it also stopped him from thinking. Back in his cell, Charles took out the diary and resumed his story where he had left off.

DIARY OF CHARLES WINSLOW

14 February, 1900

With our plans to bring reinforcements from the future frustrated, Shackleton resumed his pessimistic tune, insisting again and again that he was no hero, that he could do nothing without his weapons and his men, while I reminded him again and again that only moments before he had destroyed one of the tripods single-handed, using only his formidable gifts as a strategist. And besides, why this need to travel to the year 2000? Hadn't he formed his brave army of the future out of a few exhausted survivors? Then we would do the same: we would comb the ruins and assemble a group of proud, able-bodied men, whom he could mold into the resistance fighters we needed, an elite band of soldiers devoted to the cause. I was convinced that once they knew who Shackleton was, they were sure to follow him, as his warriors of the future had done. After a few long arguments in which I harangued the captain as a general would his troops, I succeeded in coaxing him out of his despair, and he showed some willingness to fight. However, before proceeding with any plan, he insisted on going back to Queen's Gate to make sure our wives and friends were still safe and sound.

When I saw how concerned he was for Claire, I understood why great heroes are nearly always loners. Love makes them vulnerable. I knew almost nothing about Captain Shackleton's private life in the year 2000, only the brief biography Mr. Murray had given the pas-sengers before they climbed aboard the *Cronotilus*. Yet I thought it likely that in his time, the captain had been a sullen, solitary fellow, whose heart was filled with loathing and the desire to destroy, and who would have forsaken love and a female companion with whom to share the terrible burden of defending the human race. However, the Shackleton before me now, the Shackleton who lived among us, was a man in love and apparently unwilling to put anything before his beloved Claire, even the whole of the human race. Obviously I couldn't ask him, as I would have liked, if he could damn well for-get about his wife for once, much less argue that a hero should be prohibited from falling in love while on duty. And so I agreed to go back to my uncle's house, but not before convincing him to find some elevated spot with a good view over London, where we could get a clearer idea of the progress and extent of the invasion. This would help us to reach Queen's Gate without any mishaps and to plan our next moves. We decided to go to Primrose Hill, that natural balcony overlooking the city, where Londoners spent their Sundays, and to this end we crossed the Euston Road. It was the luckiest decision we could have made, for there we bumped into another group of people who had survived that terrible night. What they had endured, together with the view from Primrose Hill of a London brought to its knees, had discouraged them to the point where what they needed most was a hero. And I had brought with me the greatest hero of all.

The group was made up of the author H. G. Wells and his wife Jane, whom I had had the pleasure of meeting a few years before because of something that has no relevance here, and whom I greeted with genuine affection and pleasure; a beautiful young American woman by the name of Emma Harlow; a young drunkard propped up against a tree, who would later be introduced to us as Inspector Cornelius Clayton of Scotland Yard; and a phantom: Mr. Gilliam Murray. After I had recovered from the shock of discovering he was still alive, I greeted Murray with enthusiasm, which was not entirely due to my admiration for the Master of Time, but also because I was certain this coincidence could only be another sign that we were indeed on our true destined path. Was it not striking that we should by chance bump into the man responsible for Captain Shackleton meeting Claire, and therefore for his presence among us now? However, I should first point out that, as I already mentioned, the group seemed extremely disheartened by the situation, which was understandable, as from the hill we could see that the tripods had overrun the city and were destroying it with the slow tenacity of the termite. The majority of the city's districts had been reduced to smoldering ruins, and here and there fires had broken out, giving off dense clouds of smoke, while crowds of panic-stricken Londoners attempted, amid a throng of vehicles of all types, to flee the city to the north and east, toward the distant fields, where there apparently were no Martians. And so, with the aim of lifting their spirits, I instantly, and in an admittedly unnecessarily theatrical manner, revealed to them the identity of my mysterious companion. And, as if Shackleton's credentials did not speak for themselves, I described how I had just seen him annihilate a tripod before my very eyes. Unfortunately, Shackleton's presence did not hearten them as much as I had expected. When I had finished relating his exploit, Murray looked askance at the captain, but finally stepped toward him, proffering his hand.

"Pleased to meet you, Captain Shackleton," he said.

I watched as they shook hands with grave solemnity for what seemed like an eternity. Unbeknownst to the captain, Gilliam had been spying on him through the keyhole of the future, letting us admire him from afar; consequently, the captain had traveled to a time where everyone knew of his exploits before he had even performed them. The two men could be said to have worked together without ever having met.

Murray finally released the captain's hand, much to the relief of the others, and then said, with an exaggerated smile, "What a surprise to find you here. I could never imagine you in our world."

"I'm sorry I can't say the same," Shackleton replied, in a tone that was surprisingly reserved in contrast, "but I'm sure you'll understand that it gives me no pleasure to meet the man who turned my duel with Solomon into a circus sideshow for the amusement of bored aristocrats."

Murray's mouth grew taut with displeasure, but with surprising adroitness he resolved it into a smile.

"Why deprive the English people of such an exciting duel? You're an extraordinarily accomplished swordsman, Captain. And one could even say I'm your most loyal admirer: I never tired of watching you fight Solomon. I confess that no matter how many times I witnessed your duel, I was always astonished that you defeated such a formidable adversary. If you don't mind my saying so, you're a difficult person to kill, Captain . . . it seems you're protected by mysterious forces."

"Perhaps my adversaries aren't as formidable as you think," Shackleton retorted coldly.

"Don't you think we might leave this vigorous exchange of opinions for another moment, gentlemen?" Wells interposed, gesturing toward the beleaguered city below. "I fear we have more pressing issues to attend to."

"You're quite right, Mr. Wells," Shackleton hurriedly agreed. "I, at least, have something much more important to do than to argue with Mr. Murray. My wife Claire, the woman for whom I left behind my time, is down there, in Queen's Gate, and I need to go to her immediately." He gave the author a meaningful look, which seemed to me disproportionate, and murmured, "She believes in me. And I won't let her down for anything in the world. Do you understand?"

"Of course, Captain. We all do," Wells replied solemnly, taking his own wife's hand, "and I think I speak for all of us if I suggest we make our way there without delay. However, afterward, things being as they are, I think we ought to leave the city as soon as possible, which is what everyone else appears to be doing. We might, for example, try to reach Folkestone and from there sail to France."

Needless to say, this new plan made me uneasy. How were we going to halt the invasion by fleeing London? Had Captain Shackleton traveled to our time only to run away from the Martians like a terrified maiden?

"I'm afraid I can't accept this plan, gentlemen," I protested. "Naturally, I'm grateful to you all for wanting to accompany us to

Queen's Gate, and I'm aware that, given the way the invasion seems to be going, leaving London is the most sensible course of action, but I don't think that's what we should do."

The author was surprised. "And why ever not?"

"Because in the year 2000 our problem is the automatons, not the Martians," I said for the hundredth time, feeling I was telling an unfunny joke. "Clearly, this can only mean the invasion will fail. Someone will find a way of defeating the Martians, and I think that person will be Captain Shackleton. I don't believe he came here by chance. I'm certain the greatest hero in the world will do something to turn the situation around, because the fact is, he already has."

Murray and Wells looked at each other doubtfully, then they observed the captain, who shrugged with annoyance, and finally they fixed their gaze on me, with a look of incredulity that exceeded even that of my own wife. This took me by surprise, because I was convinced my reasoning would appear obvious to someone with Wells's intelligence.

"Even if your theory is correct, Mr. Winslow," Wells replied, "and the year 2000 is immutable, because, as you so rightly say, in a sense it has already happened, the invasion could still be stopped in a thousand different ways without our involvement. Furthermore, if we're the ones destined to put a stop to it, then that will happen regardless of whether or not we stay in London. Consequently, I insist we go ahead with our plan to leave the city once we have been to Queen's Gate."

"What if leaving the city is precisely what we *shouldn't* do? What if by fleeing we change the future?" I looked imploringly at Shackleton. "What is your view, Captain? As a hero, isn't your main concern to save the human race?"

"I may be a hero, Mr. Winslow," Shackleton said, looking straight at Murray, "but first and foremost I'm a husband, whose duty it is to rescue his wife."

"I understand, Captain," I said, somewhat disgruntled by his stubbornness. "However, Claire and my wife will remain quite safe in my uncle's basement, I'm sure, while we—"

"I'm afraid Mr. Wells is quite right, Mr. Winslow," Murray cut in impatiently. "I don't think the captain can be of much help to us in this situation. Clearly he is out of his depth." Then he leered at the captain: "I trust you won't be offended, Captain, if, notwithstanding your celebrated victory over the automatons, we doubt your ability to defeat the Martians, but you see these machines of theirs are infinitely more powerful than a handful of toys with steam engines stuck to their backs."

"Of course I'm not offended, Mr. Murray," Shackleton replied, with his thinnest smile. "At least I saved the human race. All you've managed to do so far is to empty people's pockets."

Murray paled briefly, then gave a loud guffaw.

"I made them dream, Captain, I made them dream. And, as everyone knows, dreams have a price. I don't know how you traveled to our time, but I can assure you ferrying people across the fourth dimension to the empire of the future is expensive. But why not leave this agreeable discussion for another time, Captain, and concentrate on our predicament." Murray put his arm around Shackleton, steering him gently to face the vista afforded by the hill. "As you can see, the city is overrun by Martians. How would a hero like you reach Queen's Gate without running into the tripods?"

Shackleton observed bleakly how the tripods were mechanically, almost indifferently, destroying London.

"I thought as much," Murray responded to Shackleton's silence. "Even you can't do that." He moved away from the captain, shrugging at us to show his disappointment. Only I was aware of the smile that at that moment had appeared on the captain's face. "As you can see, some situations are insurmountable, even to the greatest heroes," Murray announced in a tone of mock regret. "However, I'm sure we'll find a way to—"

"You should have more faith in the heroes whose exploits line your pockets, Mr. Murray," the captain interrupted him, his gaze fixed on the Martians' progress. "We'll go underneath the tripods to Queen's Gate."

"Underneath them?" Murray said with astonishment, turning to Shackleton. "What the devil do you mean?"

"We'll use the sewers," the captain replied without looking at him.

"The sewers? Are you out of your mind, Captain? Are you suggesting these charming ladies should go down into the stinking sewers of London?" Murray declared, gesturing toward Emma and Jane. "I'll never let Emma—"

"Oh, take no notice of him, Captain," the American girl chimed in, stepping forward and placing her hand gently on Murray's arm. "Mr. Murray has the annoying habit of deciding where I should and shouldn't go and doesn't seem to realize that I have a tendency to do the opposite of what he says."

"But, Emma . . . ," Murray protested, in vain.

"Honestly, Gilliam, I think you should let Captain Shackleton explain his idea," the girl said, so sweetly I found her quite disarming.

If this beautiful girl was Murray's beloved, I told myself, clearly the oversized braggart I had met two years ago had made excellent use of his death and subsequent resurrection.

Murray gave an exasperated grunt but gestured to the captain to continue.

"It's the safest way," Shackleton said, addressing the others. "There are hundreds of miles of tunnels below this city, spacious enough for anyone to move about in. Not to mention the cellars and underground storehouses. There's a whole world down there."

"How do you know the sewers so well, Captain?" I asked, intrigued.

Shackleton paused for a few moments before replying.

"Er . . . because we hide in them in the future."

"So, you hid in the sewers, did you?" Murray scoffed. "Well, isn't the quality of British plumbing extraordinary! I'd never have thought they would last a whole century."

The American girl was about to call Murray to order when someone preempted her:

"You ought to have more faith in the empire, Mr. Murray."

We turned as one toward the owner of the sonorous voice, who was none other than the young man I had taken to be a drunkard when I first arrived on the hill.

"Captain Shackleton, I'm Inspector Clayton of Scotland Yard," he said, doffing his hat. "And from what I could gather while I was, er . . . recovering my strength, you think you can guide us through the sewers to Kensington, is that right?"

Shackleton nodded with grim determination, as only a hero can, accepting responsibility for our little flock. Then I stepped forward, somewhat nettled that this peculiar fellow, who saw fit in such a situation to doze off under a tree, was unaware of my presence. Clearing my throat noisily, I caught his attention and thrust out my hand.

"Inspector Clayton, I'm Charles Winslow, the . . ." I hesitated. To say "the man who discovered Captain Shackleton" suddenly seemed a trifle pompous, so eventually all I said was, "Well, let's just say I'm the captain's faithful shield bearer on this mission."

"Pleased to meet you, Mr. Winslow," the inspector said, pressing my hand perfunctorily before turning back to Shackleton. "Yes, Captain, you were saying—"

"Actually, while you were . . . taking a nap," I interrupted the inspector once more, "*I* was saying I didn't think we should leave London, because—"

"Mr. Winslow, we've already established that we all wish to leave London," Wells chimed in. "What we're now discussing is how to go first to—"

"Just so," Murray reiterated, frowning, "but *I* continue to insist that the captain's absurd idea of fleeing London through the sewers, as if we were rats, is not the most appropriate way."

"If you have a better idea, Mr. Murray, go ahead and share it with us," the captain retorted, his eyes flashing, "but I would point out that rats are usually the first to escape any catastrophe."

A moment later, we were all talking at once, caught up in a heated discussion. Until suddenly Inspector Clayton raised his voice above everyone else's.

"Ladies and gentlemen, please!" he cried. "I think we should trust Captain Shackleton and flee through the sewers this instant. Not only because of the captain's impeccable credentials, but because the pair of tripods coming toward us is not planning a romantic picnic on Primrose Hill."

We all looked with horror at the two tripods crossing Regent's Park toward us like a couple taking a leisurely stroll.

XXXIV

*W*HILE CHARLES RELAXED AFTER THE DAY'S hard toil, admiring from his cell the strange and unsettling sunset that had gradually supplanted the traditional earthly ones in the past few months, he reflected with deep sorrow that if anything around him indicated that Man had lost his home, it was without doubt the fact that the sun no longer set in the way it had in his childhood. With disgust he observed the dusky greens and purples congealing around the sun, giving it the appearance of a malignant growth. A sun stripped of its customary gold and orange haze, and that now, seen through the coppery veil of polluted air obscuring the sky, resembled one of those grimy, worn coins beggars would tap against the bar top to ask for a glass of ale.

Just then, Charles glimpsed three Martian airships taking off from the port outside the camp: three shiny flying saucers that rose a few yards into the air with a melodious purr before soaring at impossible speed through the turbulent ocean of greens and purples and vanishing into unfathomable space. Their airships so patently demonstrated the gulf between human science and that of their jailers: the Martians had far outstripped the Earthlings when it came to conquering their own skies, which they had scarcely penetrated with their puny air balloons. But from the indifference with which Charles watched them disappear, no one would have guessed that, in the first few months, their arrivals and departures had provided a spectacle for the prisoners as exciting as it was terrifying.

In addition, the airships usually brought Martian engineers, who unlike their fellow Martians were unable to replicate the appearance of humans and so moved about the camp in their normal state. The first time Charles saw them, he thought they were beautiful, a cross between men and herons. Although no one there explained anything to them, it wasn't hard to work out that the engineers' task was to design the tower and fill the camp, and doubtless the entire planet, with their technology. They would elegantly flutter about almost without stopping. Yet even more fascinating was watching them walk on extraordinarily slender, stiltlike legs, with multiple joints that allowed them to adopt the most extraordinary and varied postures, each more graceful than the last. Charles had tried to capture the beauty of their movements in his diary, comparing them to glass dragonflies or other equally beautiful and fragile objects, but had eventually given up: their extraordinary grace was impossible to put into words. The engineers remained in the camp for a while, fluttering hither and thither, until one day it seemed they had relayed all the instructions necessary to build the purification machine. After that, they would turn up every three to four months to supervise the works. Each time they left, for a few days Charles would be invaded by an absurd end-of-summer longing, the origins of which he never fully understood, though he suspected it had something to do with the comfort it gave him to contemplate those extraordinary creatures in a world where beauty had become a rarity.

And yet, although he tried not to dwell on the thought, Charles knew the scientists were not as he saw them. After their first visit, he had discussed their appearance with his fellow prisoners, only to find out to his astonishment that no two prisoners' descriptions of them coincided. Everyone had their own idea of what the creatures looked like, and each assumed the others must be joking when they described them. This had led to an argument that had ended in a stupid brawl, from which Charles had prudently retreated. Back in his cell, he had reflected long and hard and had come to a conclusion. He would have liked to discuss it with someone intelligent like Wells to find out whether his idea was half-baked or not, but unfortunately there weren't too many keen minds around him. The conclusion Charles had reached was that the Martians must be so different from anything Man knew that somehow mankind was unable to see them. Most of his fellow prisoners saw them as monstrous creatures, no doubt influenced by the hatred they felt toward the Martians. But Charles had always worshipped science, progress, and the marvels Jules Verne had described in his novels. Yes, Charles belonged to that brotherhood of visionaries who before the advent of the Martians had dreamed of ships that could sail the Atlantic in five days, of flying machines that could soar through the skies at great speed, of telephones without wires, of time travel. Perhaps this was why he saw the Martian engineers as beautiful long-legged angels, able to create miracles. And although he knew now that those miracles consisted in transforming his planet into a nightmarish world, he continued to see them as beautiful.

The sun finally disappeared, exhaling a burst of greenish rays into the sky and bathing in a ghoulish light the distant ruins of London, visible behind the dank forests that had slowly spread around the camp in a stealthy embrace of tangled branches. This planet belonged less and less to Man and more and more to the invaders. Before the invasion, when no one suspected the world as they knew it could change so suddenly, Charles would rail against it at the slightest opportunity, with wit or anger, depending on the weather. In his opinion, the empire was little less than a ship about to keel over due to the idiots at its helm, who were only versed in the arts of extravagance, inefficiency, and embezzlement. The useless and corrupt British government was responsible for more than 8 million subjects living and dying in the most shameful poverty. Charles, of course, did not share their miserable fate, and on the whole it could not be said of him that he worried unduly about those who did, but it was clear that human civilization, as such, had failed.

Charles gave a sigh and retrieved his diary from beneath the pallet, wondering once again what drove him to set down on paper those memories no one would ever read, why he didn't just lie down and die. But he simply could not accept another defeat. And so this man, who had already begun to forget what sunsets on his planet looked like, sat at his table, opened his notebook, and resumed writing.

DIARY OF CHARLES WINSLOW

15 February, 1900

Before the Martian invasion, London was the most powerful city in the world, but not necessarily the most salubrious. It pains me to admit this, as it did my father before me, but before the city's entrails were sliced open and installed with an artificial intestine in the form of a modern sewer system, Londoners stored their excrement in cesspits, which were cleaned out with a regularity that depended on the depth of the householder's pockets. In these pits, it was not uncommon to come across tiny skeletons, because the stinking holes were ideal places for women to rid themselves of the fruits of their illicit unions. Each morning at dawn, a trail of brimming carts would leave London with their foul-smelling cargo. When at last it was decided, as yet another sign of progress, that all cesspits should be sealed off and all drains be connected to a rudimentary sewer system that emptied out into the Thames, the result was an epidemic of cholera that killed almost fifteen thousand Londoners. This was followed by another, five years later, which carried off almost an equal number of lives. My father used to tell me that in the hot, dry summer of 1858 the smell was so appalling that the curtains in the Houses of Parliament had to be daubed with lime in a desperate attempt to ward off the foul odor wafting in from the river, which had become an open sewer for the excrement of nearly 2 million people. As a direct result, and notwithstanding the exorbitant cost, Parliament passed an act allowing the civil engineer Joseph Bazalgette to remodel London's entrails with his revolutionary new sewer system. I can still recall my father describing Bazalgette's great work to me as though he had built it himself: nearly a hundred miles of interceptor sewers made of brick and Portland cement that would carry human waste mixed with ordinary drainage water fifteen miles downstream from London Bridge. This explained why now, beneath our feet, following the course of the Thames, were six interceptor sewers fed by another four hundred and fifty miles of mains sewers: the intricate maze that in the year 2000 would have the privilege of sheltering the last surviving members of our race. No doubt my father would have been pleased to know that what he considered one of the greatest technological achievements would still be of use in the distant future.

We descended into London's sewers through one of the drain covers closest to Primrose Hill. We clambered down the rusty ladder attached to the wall and reached the ground without anyone slipping, which, given the almost total darkness, seemed nothing short of miraculous. Shackleton assumed the role of guide. After getting his bearings, he led us through a narrow, winding tunnel, where we were obliged almost to grope our way along. We came out into what, owing to its size, I deduced was one of the three main sewers to the north of the Thames. What first struck us was the shocking stench. Fortunately, this stretch of the tunnel was illuminated by tiny lamps hanging at intervals along the slimy brick walls. Their faint glow gave us some idea of the place where we would be walking for the next few hours, passing beneath the city to Queen's Gate. The sewer was an endless gallery with a vaulted roof, from which opened out other, narrower tunnels. I assumed the majority of these side tunnels carried the raw sewage into the main tunnels, while many others led to depositories or pumping stations. A canal ran through the middle of the sewer we were in. We tried not to look at it, for the congealed evil-smelling slime flowing through it, besides carrying every kind of filth, brought other surprises. I saw a dead cat drift past us with its glassy, unseeing eyes, being swept along on the water down one of those mysterious pipes. Luckily on either side of the canal there were two brick paths wide enough for us to walk along in single file, if we didn't mind sharing them with the rats, which would occasionally dart out to greet us, running alongside our feet before vanishing into the gloom. Nauseous from the insufferable stench, we set off in pairs, trying not to slip over on the layer of moss carpeting stretches of the walkway. The air was dank and cold, and the silence absolute, broken only by the sporadic rumble of the sewer's watery insides. I have to say I found these sounds almost relaxing. At any rate, they were preferable to the deafening blasts and relentless ringing of bells we had endured aboveground.

During our journey, as I brought up the rear with Inspector Clayton, I finally had a chance to reflect for a few moments on our plan. Despite what Wells had said, I was certain we should not leave London, convinced that Fate and not coincidence had brought our motley group together for a purpose. Glancing at the chain we formed, I pondered what part each link might play. Shackleton was at the front, untroubled by the foul smell, leading us through the maze of tunnels, a watchful expression on his face. I had no need to consider his role, for clearly it would be the most crucial of all. Behind him came Wells and his wife, who seemed relieved to be together again, yet despondent about the devastating speed of the invasion. I assumed that when it came time to defeat the Martians, it was natural for the only author who had described a Martian attack to be present. I had to admit that, despite our recent disagreement, I was relieved that Wells was part of our group, for even if his physical prowess didn't apparently amount to much, I considered him one of the most intelligent men I had ever met. Following them, holding an embroidered handkerchief to her face, was the American girl. Her role in our group was a complete mystery to me, unless it was to manage the otherwise unmanageable Gilliam Murray. Murray had been nicknamed the Master of Time for having miraculously succeeded in taking us all to the year 2000, but clearly he held the key not only to the fourth dimension, but to the afterlife as well, from whence he had apparently returned. I wondered what if any Murray's contribution to our group would be, apart from watching over Miss Harlow and attempting to belittle Shackleton. Behind him came the faithful coachman Harold, who was perhaps wondering why I had made him leave the basement in Queen's Gate only to return there a few hours later, endangering our lives on both occasions. I imagined that of all of us, he was the most dispensable. Perhaps he had no part to play, except for having driven Shackleton and me to Primrose Hill. And finally, striding imperiously beside me, a pompous look on his face, was Inspector Clayton, whose inclusion in the group anyone would readily understand. But there was one other person: me. What role was I to play if our group was called upon to put a stop to the invasion? Perhaps, I reflected with a shudder, I had merely served to bring Shackleton and the others together. Yes, perhaps without my knowing it, I had already carried out my task, and, like Harold, I was dispensable.

I had been immersed in these thoughts for some time when, all of a sudden, Wells's wife tripped over her flowing skirts and fell to the ground with a thud, almost dragging Wells with her. Murray and Emma rushed to her aid, while I made a mental note to tell all the women, once we reached Queen's Gate, to follow the American girl's example and change into something more suitable for escaping through the sewers. Fortunately, Jane got away with only twisting her left ankle. We had been walking for quite a while, and although Shackleton, who was clearly eager to be reunited with Claire, had insisted we press on, we decided to have a break so that Wells's wife could rest her ankle. We took this opportunity to fill one another in on the horrors we had endured on our way to Primrose Hill. I told them about the naval battle I had seen on the Thames, and Wells gave an abridged version of his group's perilous journey from Horsell Common with the tripods on their tail. Wells said he suspected the Martians had been living among us for a long time, possibly centuries, passing themselves off as human beings. I jested about having possibly rubbed elbows with them, for I could well imagine some of my more eccentric acquaintances hailing from other planets, but no one laughed.

When the conversation died away, I lit a cigarette and looked around for a place where I could smoke in peace. I needed a few moments alone to reflect about our situation. I noticed that to our right, amid a dizzying succession of identical archways, there was a tunnel that seemed to lead to the back of beyond, and I walked into it, not intending to stray far. Strolling absentmindedly, I came to a door, which was ajar. Intrigued, I pushed it open and discovered a tiny storeroom filled with tools and building materials. I glanced about, in case there was something in there we could use, but saw nothing, or rather everything in there looked useful, but I had no idea what our needs might be. In the end, I decided to sit down on a crate near the door and smoke my cigarette, imagining the startled look on Victoria's face when, instead of returning with the invincible army of the future, I showed up in the basement with that ragged bunch, only to inform her we planned to flee through the stinking sewers of London to God knows where. Just then, I heard voices and footsteps echoing in the tunnel. Apparently someone else had felt a similar need for solitude. I could make out the voices of Murray and the American girl.

"Gilliam," I heard Miss Harlow say, "you're being unfair to Captain Shackleton. Knowing what you do about him gives you no right to speak to him like that."

This admonishment surprised me. What had Emma meant? I wondered. What was it Murray knew about the captain?

"I don't think—" Murray protested.

"Your remarks are hurtful, Gilliam," she interrupted him, uninterested in his excuses. "But above all, unfair. Right now all of us need a reason, any reason, to carry on."

"I already have a reason to go on, Emma. You know that."

"Yes, I know," the girl said softly. "Not that you need one; after all, you're the great Gilliam Murray, the Master of Time—you don't have to believe in anything or anyone. But the others do need something to believe in. And I'm convinced that the only thing that keeps them going now is their belief in Shackleton." She paused before adding, "And it's all your fault."

"M-my fault?" Murray stammered. "I don't know what you mean."

"Oh, Gilliam, of course you do: you opened the doors to our world for him, taking him away from his world and the fate that awaited him. If he's with us today, it's because you paraded him to everyone as the savior of the human race. Do you think it's right to try to destroy him now, when everyone believes in him?"

"Yes, yes . . . ," Murray muttered. "Damn it, Emma, you're right! I don't know why I'm behaving like this. But the captain isn't the answer to their prayers!" he countered angrily, only to end in a controlled whisper. "And you know it. You and I both know it."

"But the fact that we have no hope doesn't give us the right to destroy theirs," she said in that stern but soft voice that invariably succeeded in calming Murray.

What the devil did it all mean? I wondered from my hiding place. Why shouldn't we put all our hopes on a hero of the future like Shackleton? What was it Emma and Gilliam knew about him? I had too many questions, which my unwitting confidants appeared unwilling to satisfy, because a moment later I heard the girl say, rather abruptly, "I think we should rejoin the others."

"Wait, Emma," Murray said, and I imagined I heard a rustle of fabric, which made me think Murray had probably grasped her arm. "We haven't had a chance to talk in private since we left Clayton's cellar, and I need to know what you think of what I told you. Since then you seem to be avoiding me. I've caught you looking at me a couple of times, and you immediately turn away."

Sensing the approach of a lover's tiff, I rose from the crate I'd been sitting on and crouched behind it as noiselessly as I could, stubbing my cigarette out on the sole of my shoe so the smoke wouldn't give me away and hoping that if Murray and Emma came into the storeroom in search of more privacy, they wouldn't find me curled up there like a hedgehog.

"Oh, for goodness' sake," the girl objected. "That isn't true."

"Just tell me one thing, Emma," Murray interrupted her accusingly. "I shouldn't have let you in on my secret, should I? Instead of winning your heart, I've managed to make you despise me."

"Of course I don't despise you, Gilliam. You always misunderstand what I—"

"Evidently my confession has had the opposite effect to what I intended," Murray reflected, oblivious to the girl's words, his own voice accompanied by the sound of footsteps, as if he had set off down the tunnel. "I suppose that the part of you who believes there is only one orderly way of doing things in a world as disorderly as this one despises me now."

"Gilliam . . ."

"Clearly you've had time to think about what I told you and, well, this is the result. I wanted you to love me, and yet I've become the most hateful person you've ever met."

"Hateful? Gilliam, I—"

"But, since all is lost, at least let me tell you how I feel about you, Emma," Murray said pathetically.

"Gilliam, if you'd give me a chance to speak, I could—"

"Emma Harlow!" Murray's voice boomed, with such authority that even I couldn't help jerking upright in my hiding place. "I want you to know that these have been the happiest few days of my selfish, absurd life. Being with you, consoling your tears, making you laugh, irritating you from time to time, or simply watching you looking at me . . ."

"They have been for me, too."

"And if a few Martians had to come from outer space and turn the planet into a slaughterhouse for it to happen, then so be it! I don't care if you think I'm being cruel, and even— Wait! Did you just say, *They've been for me, too?*"

For a moment the girl's laughter left me breathless. Good God, how could this aloof young woman have such an enchanting laugh?

"Oh, Gilliam, Gilliam. That's what I've been trying to tell you. These have been the happiest days of my life, too. Isn't it crazy? The world is being destroyed around us, and we . . ."

Their laughter intertwined, like fireflies crossing in the night sky.

"But it's crazy, crazy," Emma gasped delightfully, slowly beginning to calm down. I was relieved that one of them finally came to her senses. "Look around you, Gilliam. The Martians are destroying London, and we're talking about love as though we were at a ball. Oh, Gilliam." Her voice sounded suddenly sad. "Don't you see that if I were in love with you it would make no difference?"

"No, I don't. Be so good as to enlighten me. Remember I'm a *petit imbécile.*"

"For goodness' sake . . ." Emma sighed with feigned annoyance. "I hope I die before you. I can't think of a more exasperating man with whom to survive a Martian invasion."

"Is that so? Well, I can only think of one good reason why I'd want to be the only other survivor on the planet apart from such an arrogant, unfeeling, obstinate young woman as you!"

Emma must have been questioning him with her eyes as to what that reason was, perhaps afraid that her voice would betray the wave of emotions undoubtedly sweeping over her. Murray's words rang out.

"To be able to kiss you once and for all, without worrying about being interrupted by the distinguished author H. G. Wells or by Inspector Clayton."

After a few moments of tense silence, I heard the girl's laughter bubble over once more, so infectious that even I smiled, despite not having heard Murray's jest. Suddenly the delightful tinkle stopped. I didn't need to be a genius to know that Murray had decided to kiss the girl without waiting to be the last survivors on the planet, and despite the continued threat posed by Wells and Inspector Clayton. A few moments later, I heard the girl give a faint moan, almost a sigh, and the rustle of clothing when two bodies separate with voluptuous slowness.

"I love you, Gilliam," Emma said. "I'm in love with you, as I never thought I'd be with anyone."

How can I describe her tone of voice as she said this? How can my clumsy words convey what Murray must have felt when he heard them, what I myself felt in my gloomy hiding place? Emma uttered these words with a voice as sweet as it was solemn, conscious that she was saying them for the very first time. She had waited years to be able to say them, fearing that day would never come, and if it did, envisaging herself in a conservatory or a garden, surrounded by beautiful flowers, not in the stinking sewers of London with only the repulsive rats for company. But that didn't matter. She had uttered these words in the tone they merited, as though they were part of an ancient spell, as though her voice were magically emanating from her heart and not her throat. Her words were unadorned, the same words I had heard spoken hundreds of times by lovers, actors, friends, yet now they brimmed with an emotion so pure it stirred me to the depths. I reflected sadly that the girl had uttered them with full awareness that, the way things were going, she would not have many opportunities to repeat them in the future.

"I realized it when you confessed to me in Clayton's cellar," she went on, "yet since then I've done nothing but try to suppress it. I'm sorry, Gilliam, I'm sorry. But when I found out I'd fallen in love for the first time in my life, all I could feel was great sorrow. What good was this to me, a few hours before the end of the world?" There was a catch in the girl's voice. "I thought if I told you we would suffer much more. I don't want to see the man I love die, and I don't want to die so soon after I've found you! And so I refused to accept it. But it seems that it's impossible to refuse the Master of Time anything."

"You've just made me the happiest man in the world, a title I shall bear with great honor."

"But it's a world that is being demolished, don't you see?" Emma sighed. "It's too late, Gilliam . . ."

"Too late? No, Emma, no. At your aunt's house you told me you'd never stop dreaming again. You said you knew now that the Map of the Sky was part of you. And that map is the guardian of your dreams. Time doesn't exist in dreams, Emma. Time stops, as it did on the pink plains of the fourth dimension . . ."

And in the long silence that followed, suggesting another passionate embrace, I breathed as noiselessly as I could, trying to get rid of the lump in my throat. I had always insisted that other people's love was ridiculous to those outside it. In fact, I was convinced that love, as such, did not exist. I believed everyone confused it with a more or less elegant, overblown, or pompous sublimation of our fear of loneliness, boredom, or of roasting in the eternal hellfire of yearning. My feelings for my wife Victoria amounted to little more than mild affection, a vague tenderness that waxed and waned, which I was sure was no fault of hers, for I doubted I could love any other woman more. So, why had I married her? Simply because I wished to be married, to raise a family, to stop squandering my father's fortune on ephemeral pleasures and to enjoy the illusion of peace afforded by planning a future with someone else. As you can see, my wretched, selfish, misguided way of loving was very different from how Murray loved, and realizing this I felt overwhelmingly sorry for myself. I was going to leave this world without ever having loved anyone, and what was worse, having belittled the love of every woman who had ever loved me.

My clear inability to love had shaped my life. And it was still doing so now, because from the moment I left my uncle's house, my main concern had been to find a way of defeating the Martians in order to save the human race—a somewhat vague concept. Whom in particular did I want to save? No one, I told myself, with a sense of horror and deep regret, no one in particular. Naturally, I didn't want my wife to die, or my cousin Andrew or his wife, but not for their sake, rather for mine, because of the way their sudden disappearance would affect me. For this reason I took refuge in an idea as abstract as the human race. At that moment, I would have given anything for there to have been someone, somewhere on the planet whose death could truly matter to me, could cause me more pain than my own. But there was no one, I realized with bitterness; there was not a single person among the millions of inhabitants on Earth whom I loved selflessly. The tripods were slaughtering my fellows, yet I was incapable of grieving for any one of them on his or her own. None stood out among the rest as Claire did for Shackleton, or Emma for Murray. I could only grieve for the extinction of the whole of which they were a part: the human race. The race to which I did not deserve to belong.

My eyes still brim with tears when I recall that moment, despite only managing at the time to sneer at my new and unexpected sensitivity. And although my hand is trembling so much I am having difficulty writing, I wouldn't want to finish without telling the reader that if I have described these facts in such detail it is not because I wish to celebrate my discovery of the true meaning of what it is to love, but to leave a record of the noble, sublime sentiments that the finest specimens of our race are capable of generating. Perhaps love is a sentiment shared by other species in the universe. But the love that a human being can generate is exclusively his own and will die with him. After that the universe, despite its unfathomable vastness, its apparent infinity, will no longer be complete.

XXXV

*T*HE FOLLOWING DAY, FOR THE FIRST TIME, THE Martians sent Charles and a small group of other men to work deep inside the pyramid. Until then he had always worked on the outside, transporting and soldering the heavy girders that took it skyward with the slowness of a stalagmite. A few months before, he might have felt a thrill at the prospect of seeing inside the structure, but that morning, all Charles could feel was a vague unease about the effects that being exposed to the poisonous interior of the machine might have on his precarious health. Going in there would certainly accelerate the disease and perhaps prevent him from finishing his diary. Those working in the bowels of the pyramid usually died within a few days, and so, in order not to squander the workforce, the Martians would employ prisoners who already showed signs of carrying the disease. If his neck shackle, which apparently registered the state of prisoners' blood through the tendrils embedded in their flesh, considered him ready to work inside the machine, that meant he was doomed. This came as no surprise to Charles; he knew he had the mark of death on him the moment he coughed up onto the floor a clot of blood that gave off a greenish glow.

They entered the pyramid through circular hatches in the floor next to its base and climbed down ladders bolted into the wall. They emerged into a cramped tunnel, the walls of which glowed a phosphorescent green, and followed one of the Martians in an orderly file. Ashton, the prisoner who had obtained his precious notebook for him, was in front of Charles, and although he tried to walk with the deliberate swagger with which he had no doubt once paraded down his neighborhood streets in some filthy East End slum, Charles thought he saw beads of sweat trickling down Ashton's grimy neck. Behind Charles was young Garvin, a boy of about fourteen, still a child when the invasion began. Hearing his troubled breathing, Charles looked round to find Garvin's innocent little face, weirdly cadaverous in that ghostly light, eyes open wide with fright, cheeks moist with tears, as if he were the ghost of a boy wandering through the corridors of what had once been his home, unaware that he was already dead. Without so much as a smile or a word of encouragement, Charles turned back, staring ahead at Ashton's filthy neck. After all, what could he do to console the boy? Consolation was another of the many things the Martians had eradicated from the planet.

After walking for several minutes past rows of secondary passageways, the procession finally seemed to reach the end of the tunnel. In the distance, they could see an archway, and behind it a room that had the same phosphorescence emanating from its walls, only much more intensely. Charles tried to get his bearings, wondering how far they had come. Was the room they were approaching at the center of the pyramid? He couldn't tell, just as he couldn't tell whether they were still underground, or, as it had seemed at one point, if they had walked up a slight incline and were now on one of the higher levels. And yet, although his footsteps echoed as if the ground beneath him were hollow, he felt as if he were buried deep below the Earth's surface, breathing in a dense, acrid air that seemed thousands of years old. As they approached the archway linking the tunnel to the phosphorescent room, he had only one thought in his mind: what could be in there?

Yet, no matter what he had seen over the past two years, or how close to insanity he had come as he struggled to understand and accept the impossible, Charles realized none of it had prepared him to face what was inside that room. The prisoners crowded in the doorway, nervous and hesitant, pressing against one another as they held their hands up to shield their eyes from the green light, which was so intense they could almost hear and smell it. Once their eyes grew accustomed, they glanced about, blinking, half dazed. For a long while they were unable to grasp what it was they were seeing. It was as though their eyes were confronted with a dreadful conundrum, the horror of which would only become clear to them after they had spent centuries contemplating it.

The room was empty and cylindrical, no more than fifteen yards in diameter, with a ceiling that must have been as high as a cathedral, for they were unable to see the top. Lining its walls were rows of tanks made of a semitranslucent material, similar to glass, which ascended like organ pipes to the darkened ceiling. These transparent vats were filled with a syrupy green liquid, from which the dazzling light filling the room seemed to emanate. And inside these immense tanks, bobbing gently in the liquid, were bodies. Hundreds of tiny, soft baby bodies. Charles's face twisted in a horrified grimace. More than stupefied, he contemplated the flock of newborns submerged in the infernal fish tank, like pieces of fruit suspended in green jelly. They all still seemed to be attached to their umbilical cords, but on closer inspection, Charles realized these were not organic, but had been replaced with tubes made from some strange material, which emerged from their navels and disappeared down the drainlike holes covering the floor of the fish tank, making the little baby bodies look like buoys tethered to the floor of this gelatinous sea. The babies rocked gently, their tiny limbs twitching almost imperceptibly, as if they were dreaming about running. But the most macabre thing of all was to see that their skulls had been cut open, exposing their soft brains, which were pierced by a mass of fine threads floating around their heads like clumps of hair blown by a nonexistent breeze. At regular intervals, the tips of these snaking strands emitted flashes of gold-colored light that traveled upward through the unspeakable liquid, vanishing into the murky darkness above like shooting stars.

Faced with this vision, the prisoners began vomiting, watched impassively by the two guards, who waited patiently for them to empty the contents of their stomachs, as no doubt always happened with each fresh group. When the humans had finished soiling the floor, the Martians barked their orders. The prisoners' job was to bring in a large number of barrels from a nearby storage room, rolling them through the tunnels. They would then connect the barrels to a machine at one end of the tanks, which was apparently responsible for renewing the fluid the babies were floating in. Supervised by the Martians, the prisoners went about their task in stunned silence, only occasionally daring to exchange anxious or terrified looks. Every now and then, Charles would cast a furtive glance at the sinister glass cases in an attempt to grasp what he was seeing. Something told him he ought to understand what it all meant, and so, as he shifted the barrels mechanically from one place to the other, he struggled to draw some conclusions. Apparently, the babies weren't being bred to renew the workforce in the camps, as he had always assumed. It struck him as painfully obvious now that the pyramid would be finished long before these children would be old enough to do the kind of work he and his fellow prisoners did. No, the Martians were forcing them to procreate because they needed the babies to power the pyramids scattered around the world. Or was he misinterpreting this horror? Clearly the Martians were extracting something from the babies through the undulating threads inserted in their brains, something that floated upward with a faintly golden glow. But what? Their souls? Was the Martian pyramid powered by children's souls? Charles did not know what to think, yet clearly something was being sucked out of them. And whatever that was, the Martians could be refining it in another part of the pyramid and using it to run the machine. He remembered Mary Shelley's novel, in which Dr. Frankenstein uses a stroke of lightning to breathe life into a monster concocted from several dead bodies. Did the human body contain such a force, a force that could be extracted and used in a similar way, a force that could breathe life into an inanimate object? Apparently his soul, the abstract idea that embraced everything he was, all his thoughts, dreams, and desires, in short, everything death snatched from his body, could be used as fuel by the Martians.

A muffled noise broke his chain of thought. Glancing down the far end of the tunnel, he saw that Garvin had collapsed from sheer exhaustion, so that the barrel he was transporting had rolled over his poor legs. All of them heard the crunching sound of his bones breaking in several places. The guards exchanged glances, and a few moments later, the boy's shackle emitted a sound that was so familiar to all of them. The unconscious Garvin began rising grotesquely to his feet. Once he had stood up, his head swinging from side to side like a pendulum, he began marching on impossibly twisted legs toward the exit. Charles watched aghast as he left the pyramid, praying the boy would not regain consciousness before falling into the funnel.

That night, back in his cell, his diary open on the table, Charles could not help remembering the lithe, cheerful boy Garvin had been during his first months of imprisonment. He recalled how he had volunteered to form part of the resistance group Captain Shackleton was trying to assemble, for he was proud of having been the only survivor of a tripod attack on his building and was eager to avenge the death of his parents. He was convinced that, in time, he could even become the brave captain's right-hand man. But above all Charles recalled, with a rueful smile, the boy's laughter, that melodious experience they had been deprived of for so long in there, the uplifting sound of children's laughter. Yet Garvin's was not the only laughter he recalled.

DIARY OF CHARLES WINSLOW

16 February, 1900

We had been walking for a couple of hours in the sewers when, echoing down the dank tunnel, we heard the last sound we would have expected to hear in such a place: children's laughter. We walked on, glancing uneasily at one another as the ringing sounds filled the air. Their laughter echoed in the distance, awakening in us a familiar and forgotten sense of well-being. These children, with their happy, fragile laughter, had dared to defy the Martians, had refused to accept the end of the world. Increasingly excited, we quickened our pace, smiling at one another, guided by the laughter—so incongruous in our present situation—which, with the burble of the water, seemed to compose a delicate and magical symphony.

We soon saw them: there were at least a dozen aged between four and eight, busy playing on the narrow walkway, illuminated by the faint lamplight. Most of them wore modest, grubby garments, but three or four of them were neatly dressed, as though they had just left their nanny sitting on a park bench. And yet these differences didn't seem to bother them: they played together in the natural way children do, without making the distinctions we adults make, sometimes unconsciously. Bunched into small groups, they resembled characters in a diorama: a few of the younger children were holding hands and turning in a circle as they sang nursery rhymes; next to them, two older girls had chalked lines on the grimy floor and were playing hopscotch; farther away, a pair of girls turned a skipping rope while a third jumped, her long braids flapping in the air; three or four boys suddenly hurtled from the dark end of the tunnel chasing a hoop with a stick, charging past another group playing spinning tops.

They were so absorbed in their games that they didn't notice us until we were about a dozen yards away. Then they all stopped playing and gazed at us suspiciously, even with a hint of annoyance, as if we were nothing more than eight grown-ups who might threaten their enjoyment and who had appeared as if by magic in a place they had perhaps begun to think was exclusively their own, where the only rule was to take pleasure in the moment. Yet it was enough to look at them to see that once the novelty of their newfound freedom had worn off, they would be suddenly vulnerable, afraid to find themselves alone there, without any adult to watch over them. For a few moments the two groups stared at each other, visibly bewildered, each finding the other's presence there absurd. Then, like a pair of experienced nannies, Emma and Jane approached the children cautiously, as though afraid they might take off, stooping so they were at the same level. The children watched them mistrustfully.

"Hello, children," Wells's wife said, smiling at them amiably. "My name's Jane and this is my friend, Emma."

"Hello!" Emma said in a singsong voice. "Don't be afraid, we won't hurt you. We just want to say hello, that's all, isn't it, Jane?" she said to Wells's wife, who nodded enthusiastically, still smiling at the little ones.

The children stood motionless on the brick path staring at them unblinkingly. Then one of them moved suddenly, scratching his head vigorously so that the hoop propped against his leg rolled away slowly, spinning in a silvery spiral until it collapsed with a clatter at Jane and Emma's feet. Emma took the opportunity to pick it up gently and pretend to admire it.

"Goodness, what a pretty hoop," she said. "I had a wooden one when I was small, but this one's made of . . . iron, isn't it?"

"It's from a barrel, miss. They roll much better than the wooden ones, and they're sturdier," replied a skinny child, a mop of curls falling over his eyes, who looked like the eldest among them.

"Is that so?" Emma said. "Well, I didn't know that. And where did you get it from . . . er, what's your name, young man?"

"Curly," the boy murmured, somewhat reluctantly.

"Curtis?" Emma pretended not to have heard, while two of the smaller girls stifled a giggle.

"Curly, they call me Curly . . . on account of my hair, you see," the boy replied, shaking his ringlets and proffering his hand in a delightfully grown-up manner.

"Pleased to meet you, Curly," Emma replied, shaking his hand.

Jane repeated the gesture. "Pleased to meet you, Curly."

The other children clustered behind the eldest boy, eyeing us suspiciously.

"My name's Hobo," chirped the youngest, a small blond boy whom one of the older girls was holding by the hand.

The rest of us were huddled behind Emma and Jane, more due to our scant experience at dealing with children than because of the lack of room. We grinned at Hobo in a way that we intended to be friendly, but which he probably found disquieting.

"And I'm Mallory," said the girl with plaits who had been playing skipping rope.

The others felt encouraged and began tentatively introducing themselves. Emma and Jane beamed at each of them as they stammered their names. When they had finished, Emma and Jane began introducing us. The children nodded apathetically as they recited our names, except when Jane pronounced Wells's name. This elicited a few sniggers, which the author responded to by pulling a face. I assumed their reaction was due to the contrast between Wells and the other men in the group, all of whom were taller, more muscular, and, why not say it, more handsome than he.

"Good," Emma declared, once the introductions were over. "Now that we all know one another's names, and we're friends, tell me: what are you doing down here on your own?"

The boy called Curly stared at her in surprise.

"We were playing," he said, as though stating the obvious.

One of them gave a chortle, amused at Emma's ignorance.

"What about your parents? Are they up there?" Emma asked, voicing all our curiosity.

Curly shook his head emphatically.

"No? Where are they, then?"

"Near," the child said enigmatically.

"Near? You mean they're down here?"

Curly nodded, and Emma exchanged surprised looks with us.

"There are other people hiding down here . . . ," I heard Murray murmur beside me.

"It would seem so," I said eagerly.

"We must make contact, see how many there are," Clayton whispered to us, excited, I assumed, at the prospect of meeting up with other people to form a larger group and pool information about the invasion.

Clayton stepped away from us and approached the children, keeping his artificial hand out of view in his jacket pocket.

"That's wonderful, children, wonderful," he said, gently pushing Emma aside. "So, your parents are nearby. Can you take us to them?"

The children glanced at one another. Then Curly said, "We can."

Clayton turned to us, raising his eyebrows in amazement. "They can."

He turned back to the children with a satisfied smile; for a few moments everyone exchanged looks again in silence.

"Well, what arc we waiting for?" Clayton said at last in a tone of theatrical enthusiasm, as though nothing in the world could have given the children greater pleasure.

The children began conferring amongst themselves with surprising seriousness, until, with an imperceptible gesture, Curly motioned to them to start walking. They filed higgledy-piggledy into one of the side tunnels. He then invited us to follow them with a nod of his head, which Clayton replicated, like an image in a hall of mirrors. We all obeyed, and for several minutes we walked four or five yards behind the children, who were skipping and hopping and singing songs, as though being guides bored them so much they had to amuse themselves somehow. Their shrill voices ricocheted off the walls of the tunnel, producing a babble as incongruous as it was soothing, a kind of charm evoking the world from which the Martians had evicted us, a world of bustling streets teeming with carriages and parks full of children laughing. Our world. A world we never imagined anyone might covet from outer space, let alone fly across the Cosmos to snatch from us. I tried to cheer myself up with the thought that they hadn't succeeded yet, that there were many more of us hiding in the sewers, ready to defend ourselves, perhaps waiting for a man who could show us how to fight, and I looked at Shackleton, who was walking glumly beside me.

"Isn't it exciting, Captain?" I said, trying to cheer him up, too. "There are people hiding in the sewers, exactly as you did—I mean *will do* in the future."

Shackleton nodded unenthusiastically but said nothing, and I did not insist. We continued walking in silence until, suddenly, the children told us to stop beside the entrance to a small side tunnel in the wall. To our horror they began filing into it, and we had no choice but to follow, stooping so as not to bang our heads. It seemed like a disused pipe from the old sewer network and turned at right angles, as in a maze. At last, just when we were beginning to think it would never end, we came out in a large storeroom, filled with building materials. At the far end of it, concealed behind some bundles, was a vertical ladder descending into the darkness. The children began clambering down it fearlessly, giggling at their own jokes.

"Where the devil are they taking us?" I muttered, tired of the endless walking and beginning to feel increasingly sweaty and grimy.

But no one had the answer. Presently, we came to a dank, cold hall with a vaulted ceiling. The room was lit by a few lamps hanging from the walls and pillars, but they scarcely made a dent in the darkness, and it was difficult to see exactly how big it was.

"We're here," Curly announced.

We surveyed the gloomy catacomb uneasily. It appeared to be deserted.

"But . . . where are your parents?" I asked Curly.

"Here," the child said, pointing to our surroundings.

"But there isn't anyone else here, Curly, just us," Emma protested gently, gazing uneasily after the child's hand.

"They're here," Curly insisted stubbornly. "They've been here a long time."

Somewhat bewildered by Curly's insistence, we studied the vast chamber once more, peering into the shadows, but as far as we could see we were alone in there. I was about to ask Curly to explain himself when all of a sudden, Wells and Clayton, as though acting on a shared intuition, unhooked a pair of lanterns from the nearest column and edged their way cautiously toward the far wall. Intrigued, we all followed them, forming a kind of procession, while the children remained in the middle of the chamber. When the author and the inspector reached the wall, they each headed for a different corner. They raised their lanterns and began to examine it closely. As the lamplight shone onto the surface, we could see that it was divided into squares, like a checkerboard, each decorated with strange, vaguely oriental-looking symbols. Wells moved his lamp along the wall, revealing it to be covered in these chiseled boxes with their peculiar signs, which gave off a coppery glow, while Clayton did the same at the other end.

"Good God . . . ," gasped the author.

"Good Lord . . . ," Clayton's voice echoed.

"What is it?" I asked, unable to fathom what was going on.

Wells wheeled round to face us, then looked nervously at the children, who were clustered together in the center of the chamber.

"They've brought us to see their parents—only their parents are their ancestors," the author murmured in amazement.

"What do you mean, Mr. Wells?" I said, still puzzled.

"Look, Mr. Winslow." Clayton beckoned me over. "What do you think each of these squares is?"

"I've no idea," I avowed with irritation, in no mood to play guessing games.

"So you don't know," he replied disappointedly. Then he turned to the author. "But you know, don't you, Mr. Wells?"

Wells nodded solemnly. They were the same as the ones he had seen on the spaceship hidden in the Chamber of Marvels.

"They are Martian symbols," he said. "And these squares on the wall, Mr. Winslow, are tombs."

Tombs? Wells's words startled me, as they did the others. And as he spoke we wheeled around with a mixture of confusion and unease, taking in the rest of the walls in the vast chamber, which we could now see was a shimmering mosaic of tombstones, marking hundreds of niches dug into the rock.

"Are we in a Martian cemetery?" Murray asked.

"It looks like it, sir," Harold replied despondently.

But in my profound bewilderment, I scarcely heard what they were saying. I was still having difficulty accepting the bizarre notion that the Martians had not arrived on Earth hours before as I had thought, but had been living among us for who knew how long. Yet if this was some kind of Martian burial ground, then these children were . . . Oh, God . . . I contemplated them in disbelief. They were still standing in a huddle in the center of the crypt, a few yards away from us, regarding us with faint curiosity. They had done what we'd asked and seemed to be waiting with indifference to see what our next whim would be, perhaps hoping we would let them get back to their games. And to me they looked just like ordinary children, with their skin still smooth and unblemished and their young, miniature bodies. Children like ours: fragile, innocent, human. But they weren't. They only had the appearance of human children. And although I found this difficult to take in, doubtless because no Martian had yet mutated in front of my eyes, I noticed my companions were having the same difficulty: they were all staring solemnly at the children, trying to conceal the look of fear creeping over their faces.

"One of the children is missing," I heard Emma say beside me.

"Yes," Jane confirmed.

"Right," Clayton murmured in an imperious tone, ignoring Emma and Jane. "Let's not panic. We'll take advantage of the situation. Yes, that's what we'll do. Wipe that look of terror off your faces, we don't want to make these delightful Martians suspicious. I want to see calm smiles, everyone."

He said these last words in a gruff whisper that sounded like a threat. Then, clearing his throat, like a tenor preparing to go on-stage, he sauntered over to the children. The Martian children, I should clarify.

"Hey, Curly," he called out, crouching down in front of them. "Do you live here?"

Curly looked away from us, turning his ringleted head toward Clayton.

"No, of course not. What a silly idea!" the child declared. "We live up there. But he told us we couldn't play up there today, because it would be dangerous, that's why we came down here."

"Of course, of course, that way you could play safely," Clayton calmed the child. Then he gave us a sly smile before resuming his conversation with the boy. "And who told you that, Curly? Who is 'he'?"

"He's the Envoy, sir. The one we've been waiting for. The one they've been waiting for, too," said the child, pointing at the tombs.

"Oh, I see. And have you been waiting for him for a long time?"

"Yes, sir, a very long time. We almost thought he wasn't going to come."

"I see . . ." Clayton moistened his lips and exchanged a meaning-ful look with Wells, as though they shared some secret information. "And is he down here, too, Curly?"

"Yes."

Clayton swallowed hard.

"Good, good." He smiled. "And could you take us to him?"

"Why?" Curly looked at the inspector askance. "Do you want to kill him because of what he's doing to you?"

"Kill him? Why of course not, Curly," the inspector replied with a casual wave of his hand. "How could you think such a thing?"

"Why then?"

"Just to talk to him, Curly." The inspector shrugged, playing it down.

"Talk to him about what?"

"Er . . . well, about grown-up things, you know," Clayton vacillated. "Nothing very interesting, in any case."

"Do you think we wouldn't understand?" the boy asked in a faintly menacing tone, which struck me as all the more threatening for being cloaked in that innocent childlike voice.

"I didn't say that, Curly."

"Because I think we would."

"One of the children is missing," I heard Emma whisper again behind me, in a low, quavering voice.

I studied the group of children standing motionless, listening to the conversation between Curly and the inspector. There was something so malevolent and inhuman about their concentration that it sent a shiver down my spine.

"Of course, of course," I heard Clayton reassuring Curly. "I don't doubt it, but—"

"We're cleverer than you think," Curly insisted quietly, fixing his dark, terribly empty eyes on the inspector, who appeared to totter slightly, as if he was about to lose his balance, "and we understand things you could never comprehend."

"Oh for God's sake! That's enough!" Murray cried. He plunged his hand into my pocket and snatched my pistol. Before I had time to react, he leapt in front of Curly, placing the barrel against his head, and said, "Listen to me, kid: I don't know what you understand, or even what you are, and, frankly, I don't care. All we want to know is who is responsible for this damned invasion, and where to find him. And you, my dear little children, are going to help us do that. Otherwise, you can be sure I'll shoot you. If there's one thing I detest more than Martians, it's children."

We heard a laugh ring out from somewhere in the room. And a voice said, "Would you be capable of taking the most sacred life of all, that of an innocent child? Is it not written in your Holy Scrip-

THE MAP OF THE SKY

tures, 'Suffer little children to come unto me, and forbid them not, for of such is the kingdom of God'?"

As one, we peered into the dense surrounding gloom, trying to make out who had spoken. Then, the shadows seemed to congeal and we instantly discovered more than twenty people encircling us. For the most part, they were middle-aged men, who, judging from their apparel, came from every conceivable social class. Before we could react, the children scurried behind them, and Murray found himself pointing his pistol at air. The one who had spoken was standing a few steps closer than the others. He was an elderly, dignified-looking gentleman wearing a black cassock and a collar. Unlike the others, who were glaring at us menacingly, the old priest wore a smile of amused satisfaction. I noticed then that he was holding the hand of little Hobo, who must have gone to warn them while the others kept us occupied. Skipping and singing gaily, the children had led us into a trap. Out of the corner of my eye, I saw Murray aim his gun at the man who had spoken. Clayton, Harold, and Shackleton immediately followed suit. I simply piled close behind them with the others, cursing the fact that, stupidly, I had no weapon and was therefore unable to act.

"Oh, what a proud gesture, so touchingly human," the old man declared when he saw all our pistols pointing at him. "But do you really think shooting us will get you anywhere?"

Those brandishing the guns stared at one another, unsure what to do next, but they continued pointing at the Martians. Our pig-headedness amused the old man, who spread his wrinkled hands in a gesture of peace.

"Gentlemen, please. Don't make us kill you; you know how easy that would be. Put down your weapons and surrender," he urged in his melodious voice. "Those who do will receive His mercy: 'Be still and know that I am God,' Psalm Forty-Six, verse ten," he recited, with a smile of infinite compassion. "After all, I only want to take you where you want to go: He wishes to meet you as much as you wish to meet Him. One of you, in particular . . ." He stepped forward, stretching out his hands, palms upturned. "Let us go to Him in peace, brothers: 'My times are in thy hand: deliver me from the hand of mine enemies, and from them that persecute me. *Make thy face to shine upon thy servant,*' " he intoned, gazing at Wells with a strange look of tenderness, before adding in a whisper: "Psalm Thirty-One, verses fifteen and sixteen."

XXXVI

*C*HARLES AWOKE THE NEXT MORNING, HIS FACE IN A pool of blood. From the taste of blood in his mouth, he assumed he had hemorrhaged from the nose during the night. When he tried to wipe the blood off with the sleeve of his jacket, two of his remaining teeth came out. He pulled himself up laboriously, sweating and shivering at the same time. The simple act of breathing had become a torment: his throat burned and his lungs felt as if they were filled with hot coals. This was proof enough that he had little time left, perhaps even less than he had thought.

After breakfast, the Martians led them back inside the pyramid. The other prisoners in his work detail were all suffering the effects of having been exposed to the green liquid the previous day. Scarcely looking at one another, ashamed, perhaps, of their deplorable condition, or for fear of seeing their own wraithlike appearance mirrored in the others, they began trudging down the familiar long tunnel, though at one point Charles thought they took a different turning, which seemed to lead them deeper into the bowels of the Earth. He felt terribly weak and dizzy, but he knew this was not entirely due to the nosebleed or the occasional stabbing pains in his damaged lungs. The atmosphere inside the pyramid polluted his soul as well as his body. But he must conserve what little strength he had to keep walking, to stay in the line with his wretched companions as they marched forward in gloomy silence. Charles wondered where the Martians could be taking them now, what fresh atrocities awaited them after the terrible vision of the day before, an example of pure evil, of insane cruelty. What fresh nightmare of ingenious aberration could the Martians show him today to batter his benumbed soul further?

They reached the room at the end of the tunnel, and once more the green light flooding it forced them to close their eyes. When at last they opened them, shielding their smarting eyelids with their hands, they saw tanks that stretched up to the dark, distant ceiling, like those they had seen the day before. But the bodies they contained were not those of babies. This was when Charles understood that the nightmare was unending.

Floating inside the tanks, stacked one on top of the other in rows and columns like human bricks, were the bodies of hundreds of women. They were mostly young and tightly packed together to form these macabre layers, their heads brushing against the feet of the women in the next column. They looked as if they were sleeping, suspended in a disturbing limbo, their hair floating like seaweed in the abominable fluid, their flesh spongy and pale, their eyes closed. Their mouths were slightly open, yet he saw no sign of breathing to suggest a flicker of life. The most ghastly aspect of all was the tubes snaking out from between their legs, which seemed exactly like the cables he had seen sprouting from the babies' navels and descending into the holes in the base of their tank. This was where those cables ended up, he now realized, snaking between the legs of these women and defiling their sex, until they reached their dormant bellies. Hundreds and hundreds of cables descended from above, undulating in the infernal ocean like monstrous sea snakes wriggling their way into the silent interior of these slumbering women. *O Lord, why hast thou forsaken us?* Charles whispered, overwhelmed with horror as he stumbled toward the awful tanks. The women were floating motionless, their bodies rigid and pale, as though ready for embalming. He felt as though he was going to black out and made a superhuman effort to collect himself. He refused to let them send him to the funnel, not until he'd finished his diary, or at any rate until his heart burst, unable to take any more horror. He managed not to collapse as he listened to the Martians who had begun giving orders.

From what he could gather in his confusion, they were to carry out the same task as the day before: changing the liquid in the tanks. Driven on by the Martians' cries, the prisoners began trudging toward the storeroom containing the barrels. The hours passed with exasperating slowness. Working mechanically for what seemed like an eternity, Charles felt so dizzy and confused he kept thinking he was seeing himself from the outside. At one point he had a violent coughing fit and everything momentarily went black, making him fear he'd lose consciousness and collapse in front of the monsters' impassive faces. When he recovered, he stood contemplating a pool of greenish blood at his feet with two more of his teeth floating in it.

One of the guards ordered him to resume working with a sharp push that almost sent him flying. He took the barrel he had begun moving and rolled it down the passageway. But the coughing had left him weak and he felt feverish, and as he pushed, random thoughts began to assail him: snatches of memory, fragments of dreams, bizarre images that flashed through his delirious mind as in a half sleep. A chance connection in his subconscious transported him to the Chicago World's Fair, which he had visited in his youth, during the so-called Battle of Currents between Edison's General Electric, which advocated direct current, and Westinghouse Electric, whose founder believed passionately in the superiority of the alternating current as conceived by Nikola Tesla. The thrilled young Charles had marveled at the generators and engines that would illuminate the world, banishing forever the empire of darkness.

Electricity, Charles said to himself, pausing beside the tank, another of the great scientific advances that was to make Man master of all Creation. He gazed dolefully at the cables in the tanks reaching up to the ceiling and wondered whether this room really was beneath the one containing the babies' tanks. Were these women hooked up to their offspring in a kind of insane electrical circuit, transmitting energy-charged particles from one to the other like a diabolical multiple human dynamo? Had the Martians created a gigantic human battery, using the energy supposedly transmitted by their brains, by the age-old maternal bond, to drive their machines? Charles choked back sobs as he realized that what he had been thinking during his delirium might be true, that these parasites were robbing them of their purest essence. The Martians were forcing human women to conceive and give birth, then submerging mother and baby in this green liquid, locking them into an eternal cycle of flowing particles that might poison the world with its corrupt love. He wept silently as he worked the levers that emptied out the tanks, unaware that the tears rolling down his cheeks were green.

And then, in a corner of the tank, he saw her. The guards were distracted and so he was able to go up and look at her more closely, separated only by the width of the glass wall, against which his heart throbbed wildly. He recognized her, despite her long dark hair floating around her face like shreds of the night. He studied her elegant profile and recalled the adorable way she used to pout when she was alive, the delightful surliness that wrinkled her nose and curled her lips, the slight bashfulness that had made him feel strongly attracted to her the first time he saw her. That was when her friend Lucy introduced them, during the second expedition to the future, moments before they clambered aboard the *Cronotilus* like happy, excited children, on their way to see Captain Shackleton's victory. And now he remembered her as she was the last time he saw her in his uncle's basement, wearing an exquisite green silk dress she did not yet know would be the color of her shroud, standing on tiptoes, her arms around her husband's neck, and whispering a farewell in his ear that would remain with them forever, the last words they ever spoke to each other. And here she was, joined to a child some stranger had fathered. Charles did not know if in that state of limbo she retained any vestige of consciousness, if she knew where she was, if she perhaps dreamed of the child attached to the other end of the cord, far from her embrace, or of the captain, of seeing him again one day. All he knew was that the Martians had turned her into a beautiful mermaid whose eternal torment powered their machine. It was clear that in such a state, death could only be a deliverance.

That night, back in his cell, Charles knew he would not survive another day in the depths of the pyramid. And so he forced himself to write, despite spattering the remaining pages with drops of blood that glowed a soft green, smudging his already illegible scrawl. He doubted whether anyone finding his diary would be able to make much sense of the final entries, yet he kept on writing, trying to thrust aside the question that assailed him each time he paused to rummage through his memories: would he tell the brave Captain Shackleton that he had found his Claire?

DIARY OF CHARLES WINSLOW

17 February, 1900

For several minutes, the Martians, with the priest at the fore, led us through endless galleries until we reached a place where the tunnels intersected. On one side there was a closed gate. The priest walked over to it, still beaming at us amiably. He opened the door and ushered us through into a spacious room furnished like one of our offices: in the middle, standing on a soft rug, was a heavy mahogany desk buried in books and files. Among these a sharp letter opener glinted next to a globe with a gilt base, and a desk lamp; covering the walls were maps of the Earth's continents, and dotted about the room there were a few chairs in the Jacobean style, tables of varying sizes and shelves containing papers.

"Kindly wait here, please," our guide asked politely. "The Envoy will arrive presently."

After saying this, he gave Wells a look of profound admiration.

"It's a pleasure to meet you, Mr. Wells, even in such circumstances as these," he said courteously. "I'm a great admirer of your work."

His comment surprised us almost as much as it did Wells, who, once he had recovered from his amazement, replied with as much bitterness as he could muster: "Then I hope that when my work becomes extinct, along with everything else, you'll lament it as much as I."

The priest paused for a few moments, looking at Wells pensively.

"It will be one of the things I most lament, I assure you," he avowed at last, shaking his head sorrowfully. Then he contemplated Wells with a compassionate smile. "Grieving for the death of beauty is a very human idiosyncrasy. Do you know, Mr. Wells, when a star dies, the light from it goes on traveling through space for thousands and thousands of years? The universe remembers for a very long time whatever dies, but it doesn't grieve. It is natural for things to die. Yet I'll grieve for you when you've gone, for the beauty you are capable of creating, sometimes unconsciously." He cast a pained eye over the group. "I'm sorry I can't offer you greater solace, the solace a priest offers his flock. But all of us are subject to the laws of the Cosmos."

He smiled a sad farewell and went out, closing the door quietly behind him as if he had just tucked us all into bed. We could hear him outside giving orders, presumably to the men who were to guard the door, how many we did not know.

"I don't suppose you ever imagined you'd have such a universal readership," Murray quipped once we were alone.

Wells didn't laugh; in fact, none of us did. Instead, in what seemed like a rehearsed gesture, we all took a long, deep breath, as though testing our lung capacity, and breathed out in unison, in the form of a loud sigh. We all realized the game was up: we were shut in a room waiting for the Envoy, who was apparently in charge of the invasion and whom the others held in almost reverential esteem. We had no idea why he wanted to meet us, but we were clearly at his mercy. I wondered what he would look like, recalling the garbled description my companions had given me of the Martian they had seen. But I instantly realized any attempt to visualize his appearance was pointless, for he would certainly greet us cloaked in human form, especially if what he wanted was to talk to us.

"So, this is the hiding place used by those who had been infiltrated before the attack taking place aboveground," said Wells. "That explains how the Martian who fell into the blind alley at Scotland Yard could have disappeared without a trace!"

"Yes, he escaped down a drain hole," said Murray.

"Good, we're exactly where we wanted to be!" exclaimed Clayton, who, during what to me was Murray and Wells's incomprehensible exchange, had been pacing obsessively round the office, inspecting everything. "There couldn't be a more ideal venue for our plan."

"What plan, Inspector?" Murray asked. "If my memory serves me correctly, our plan was to flee London."

"It was, Mr. Murray, it was," replied the young man, jabbing a finger at him. "However, the paths we choose don't always take us where we want to go. Sometimes they take us where we *need* to go."

"Would you mind getting to the point, Inspector?" said Wells, before we all lost our patience.

Clayton nodded and gave a sigh, as though our continual demands were beginning to weary him.

"Naturally I was referring to the plan I devised while those adorable children were leading us here," he replied, beckoning us over while he glanced warily at the door. Once we had gathered round him, intrigued, Clayton raised his metal hand, pulling back his sleeve with the other one, like a magician wanting to prove he had no aces hidden up there. "Observe. This hand contains a bomb powerful enough to destroy the whole room if detonated."

The rest of us exchanged startled looks, wondering whether the inspector was intending to blow us all up forthwith, to spare us any possible suffering.

"Oh, don't worry. My plan isn't to kill you," he reassured us. "My hand also has a smoke capsule built into the forefinger. When the

Envoy arrives, I'll unscrew it, creating a smoke screen that will allow you to escape. Once you're safely out of the room, I'll detonate the bomb, killing the Envoy and myself."

A stunned silence descended on the room. In the end it was Murray who broke it, capturing everyone's bewilderment in a single question.

"Are you out of your mind, Clayton?"

"On the contrary, Mr. Murray," the inspector replied, unruffled.

Murray having opened the way, we all began expressing our doubts about this monstrous idea.

"For the love of God . . ."

"He's not serious, is he, Bertie?"

"Did he say he's going to create a smoke screen?"

"Of course he isn't, Jane. Honestly, Clayton, this is hardly the time for jokes!"

"I'm afraid he did, sir. And in my humble opinion, I don't think it's—"

"And he's going to sacrifice himself in order to kill the Envoy?"

"—a very good idea, because the smoke will get in our eyes and—"

The inspector suddenly raised his hands.

"Quiet, everyone! You heard me. I'll explode the bomb, killing the Envoy and myself instantly," he repeated, with an alarming display of disregard for his own life.

"But what about the guards in the passageway?" asked Murray, seemingly unmoved by Clayton's proposed act of altruism.

Clayton addressed Shackleton.

"You'll take care of them, won't you, Captain?" he said. Shackleton opened his mouth, but did not know how to respond to the inspector's exaggerated confidence in him. "If you move quickly enough, you can surprise them before they have time to transform themselves, which will make it easier to overpower them. They don't amount to much as humans, I've noticed. I suppose Mr. Murray,

Mr. Winslow, and the coachman . . . and even Mr. Wells can help you. After that you have to lead them all out of the sewers."

"For God's sake, Clayton!" Wells interjected, with a mixture of anger and frustration. "Have you forgotten your colleague at Scotland Yard? There must be at least five or six of those monsters out there . . . possibly more. What chance does Captain Shackleton have against them, with or without our help?"

"You'll just have to be quick," the inspector replied, shrugging his shoulders, as though this part of the plan wasn't his concern and he was doing us a special favor discussing it. "Remember, the element of surprise will work in your favor: the Martians won't be expecting you to break out of here; you'll catch them off guard. However, I don't think the difficulty of the plan lies in these details, do you? Not if you consider the role I'll be playing," he concluded, slightly dismayed.

Wells, Murray, and Shackleton sighed as one. Harold shook his head in the same way he might if Clayton had worn the wrong suit to a reception. The women seemed on the verge of tears or hysterical laughter. I simply stared at the inspector, bewildered. Part of me wanted to believe in him: wasn't this what I'd been longing for from the moment I discovered the captain in my uncle's basement, what I'd tried to argue for in the face of the others' skepticism: a plan that would halt the invasion? Yes, and here it was. At last, our path had been mapped out for us . . . but another part of me, the supposedly rational, intelligent part, was protesting loudly that this couldn't be the long-awaited plan, that we would quite simply be placing ourselves in the hands of a maniac if we did what Clayton suggested.

"Forgive me, Inspector," I intervened, attempting to clarify things a little, praying that Clayton's plan only appeared impractical on the surface, and that by digging deeper we'd discover the genius behind it, "but what good will come of killing a few Martians in the sewer when there's a powerful army up there, doubtless invading the entire planet as we speak?"

"We won't simply be killing a few Martians, Mr. Winslow. Among them will be the Envoy. Oh, please . . . Weren't any of you listening to what the children said? They've been waiting for him, for generations. The invasion didn't start until he arrived on our planet. Or should I say until he . . . woke up," he said mysteriously. "But that's not important now. What's important to us is that his presence is vital to the invasion. Therefore, we must assume that after his death the Martian army will be in sufficient disarray for any rebellion you might lead to succeed, Captain Shackleton." With these words, the inspector turned to me once more and, with what struck me as the smile of a madman, said, "This will be how we defeat the Martians, Mr. Winslow. And we both know my plan will succeed, because *it already has.*"

I looked at him, bewildered. What could I say, when my own words and arguments sounded like the ramblings of a madman when issuing from his mouth?

"Inspector Clayton," Wells cut in, addressing him with infinite calm, "I admire your altruism, but we can't possibly allow you to sacrifice your life in order to save ours. I'm sure if we study the situation carefully we'll find another way to—"

Clayton interrupted him with equal equanimity. "Mr. Wells, that night in my refuge, I could have chosen any one of my prostheses. As you'll recall, I have many of them, all with their particular advantages. And yet I specifically chose this exploding hand I had made a couple of years ago, because with my experience I knew that sooner or later my enemies would place me in a situation where I'd rather die than fall into their hands. I now see clearly why I had it made, and why I decided to use it today of all days. All our actions have a purpose; nothing is random, as Mr. Winslow has so rightly understood," he said, gesturing toward me with both hands, as though I were part of a freak show. "In fact, he's the only one of us who has seen our destiny clearly from the beginning. You've been an inspiration to me, Mr. Winslow." I shifted awkwardly under my companions' accusing gaze. "The fact we are here is no accident. I don't know what role each of you will play. You'll have to discover that for yourselves. But I know what I must do: clearly I must destroy the Envoy. And, as in chess, the game is over when the king falls. If I don't do this, the invasion will continue, and then I'm afraid no one will have the power to stop it. See for yourselves."

With these words, Clayton pointed at a pair of maps hanging on a wall. Mystified, we went over to take a look. One was of London and showed the advance of the tripods marked by numerous red crosses. This chart confirmed what we had already glimpsed from Primrose Hill: they had taken the entire city. But the other one terrified us still more, for it was a map of the world. Here the crosses spread like a red rash over the entire planet. The Martians hadn't only conquered the British colonies of Australia, India, Canada, and Africa, where the sun never set, but a host of other countries, too. Within a few weeks, they would have taken over the entire planet, and as Clayton had said, no one could stop them then. Paralyzed with horror, we stared at the map in silence. The Martians were destroying our planet. And I think this was when it really struck me. Despite all that I'd been through, despite seeing the mighty tripods spitting out their rays only yards from me, destroying buildings, ships, and people with preposterous ease, nothing made me more aware of what was happening than seeing that simple piece of paper. We were all going to be exterminated, wiped off the face of the Earth. The human race was going to vanish as if it had never existed.

Clayton contemplated us solemnly, as though defying us to continue raising objections to his plan, or possibly to come up with a better one, but we simply stared back at him forlornly. To some extent he was right. Yes, his plan was preposterous, but what else could we do? The inspector called our attention to a strange contraption on the far side of the room, and we all walked over to it, intrigued. On a small oak table lay a rectangular object, approximately the size of a book, from which a bluish mist arose, like smoke from a bonfire, forming a kind of vaporous egg. We gazed in awe at the shimmering indigo sphere, unable to believe our eyes, while inside it particles of light and strange phosphorescent squiggles darted about.

"What is it?" I asked.

"A map of the universe, if I'm not mistaken," Clayton said, still possessed by the blaze of inspiration that had come upon him since he entered the office.

We looked with amazement at the inspector and then studied the shimmering image. We were awestruck to discover that this wasn't simply a globe made of beautiful, ever-shifting smoke, but a replica of the Cosmos. Each speck of light inside the bluish vapor represented a galaxy with its thousands of millions of stars floating in rows or clusters. They were shaped like wondrous whorls of light, radiant purple roses, luminous sea snails, and some even looked like hats or cigars. Mesmerized, Wells stroked the object tentatively with his forefinger, and the gaseous map grew in scale. Suddenly, the firmament enveloped us like a glistening veil. We gazed at one another, our shoulders sprinkled with constellations, as we let ourselves be gently pierced by comets. I saw Emma balance a nebula on the palm of her hand like a sparkling butterfly, Jane with a star cluster snarled in her hair, Murray's jacket speckled by the Perseids. Like a curious child, Wells moved his finger in the opposite direction, and the map suddenly shrank, curling up like a frightened animal, until it reached a size that allowed us to admire the Cosmos in all its splendor and detail. I noticed our solar system, with its brightly colored planets orbiting round the sun, mere specks of dust dancing around a ball of light. And there we were, on the third speck nearest the Sun, in a backwater of the universe, believing ourselves to be the masters of something whose dimensions exceeded our imagination. I confess that when I saw the vastness of space, the immensity of the garden stretching beyond my window, I felt suddenly insignificant. Then Wells, apparently unable to keep still, stroked the object again, and a red line, like a silky crimson thread, emerged from the mist, joining each of the planets, which lit up, then dissolved before our eyes. We realized that this line traced the passage through the universe of the invading race as it conquered and consumed planet after planet in what seemed like an endless migration. A cosmic exodus, which, to our horror, ended on a small blue planet in our own solar system.

This was when we realized definitively that judging from their lengthy journey through the eternal night of space, the invaders did not come from Mars, but from a far more remote and unimaginable place. And yet to this day we still had been referring to them as Martians, perhaps out of habit, perhaps because this infantile refusal to recognize our conquerors' true greatness was a final act of rebellion, or simply because in order for Man to understand horror he has to contain it within familiar, nearby borders. Be that as it may, the word "Martian" represents everything we now fear and detest, and this is why I have used it to refer to them throughout this diary.

But let us return to the office where that pulsating universe revealed that crimson thread extending to the Earth, staining it red. It filled me with a mixture of fear and sorrow, yet, to be honest, what upset me more was a sense of what I can only describe as our cosmic humiliation. There we were on our insignificant planet, caught up in our wars, boasting of our achievements, completely oblivious to the majesty of the Cosmos or the conflicts that convulsed it.

"This is the true Map of the Sky," Emma said. "I think my great-grandfather would have felt very disappointed."

"No one could have envisaged it like this, Emma," Murray hastened to assure her. "Except Mr. Wells, of course."

"Only you envisaged such a universe, George." Murray addressed Wells with a hint of derision. "Do you remember the conversation we had two years ago, when I asked you to help me publish my novel? You told me the future I'd described could never exist because it wasn't credible. I had great difficulty accepting those words, because I longed to be able to imagine what the world would be like in years to come. Yes, I wanted to be a visionary like you, George. But I can tell you now, I don't envy your ability to—"

"I'd give my right arm to have been wrong, Gilliam," Wells replied coldly.

"And I'd give my right arm to be able to tell you that Man's imagination is considered one of the treasures of the universe," said a voice behind us, mimicking Wells, "but I'd be lying."

We turned toward the door where a dark shape stood. My companions shuddered as one, like a bush touched by the wind, for we knew this could only be the Envoy, entering the room in an undeniably human guise, just as I had imagined.

"I'm afraid no one but you considers it as such," he went on, without moving, "which is logical, for you have only yourselves as a reference. Yet the universe is inhabited by many species, which possess all manner of qualities, the majority inconceivable to you, and compared to which I can assure you Man's imagination isn't prized sufficiently for its loss to be a source of regret. You ought to travel more."

We remained silent, not knowing how to respond or whether the Envoy even expected a reply. And although he was still lurking in the shadows, I could see he had chosen to walk around on Earth in the guise of a rather feeble, emaciated-looking fellow. A weakling, to put it bluntly. But something made me uneasy: his voice sounded incredibly familiar.

"Even so, I confess that you, Mr. Wells, possess an imagination far superior to that of most men," said the Envoy, addressing the author. Then he stepped out of the shadows, at last exposing himself to the lamplight so that we could all see his face. "Or should I say *we*," he added.

We gazed with astonishment at the Envoy's appearance, for it was none other than that of Mr. Wells. Seeing him standing there, hands in pockets, smiling at us with Wells's familiar good-natured skepticism, we were suddenly confused. Not nearly as confused as the real Wells, of course, who stood staring at his double, pale and rigid as a statue, his face twisted in a grimace. Wells's amazement was quite understandable, for as the reader will appreciate, he was seeing himself without the aid of a mirror, and from angles a mirror would never reveal. He was seeing himself in three dimensions, gesturing, talking even. He was seeing himself for the first time in his life from the outside, the way others saw him. Wells's reaction made his reflection laugh.

"I suppose you didn't expect me to appear before you in the guise of Mr. Wells, given that he's still alive." The Envoy contemplated our bewilderment disdainfully. "I, too, was surprised when I discovered that the man whose appearance I had borrowed was asking to see me and had come all the way down here, to our humble refuge in the sewers of London." The Envoy stroked his whiskers, the way the real Wells sometimes did, and gave a contented smile. "Though by describing them as humble I don't wish to criticize this network of tunnels running alongside the real sewers, built by our brothers who infiltrated the teams of engineers and laborers of the period. A hidden world, secreted behind the other underground world that lies beneath London. As if your adorable Alice had followed the White Rabbit twice. A mirror behind another mirror, wouldn't you say? I believe you humans are fond of such ideas and images."

Wells went on staring at the Envoy with the same contorted look on his face, as though he was about to faint.

"How?" he managed to splutter.

His question appeared to move the Envoy.

"Forgive my rudeness, Mr. Wells. I expect you want to know how I managed to duplicate you," he said, stroking his whiskers once more. "Very well, allow me to explain. I imagine you've realized by now that we can adopt the form of various living creatures. Thanks to this ability, my brothers have been able to live clandestinely among you all this time. Apart from when we're born, of course, only in death is our true appearance revealed. Yes, death robs us of our disguise, which is why our ancestors decided to build a private cemetery down here. And in order to make the transformation, one drop of your blood is enough. After obtaining it we're careful to get rid of the donor. We don't wish to give ourselves away by producing a suspicious epidemic of twins."

"Good God," murmured Emma. "And the children, are they, too . . . ?"

"Naturally, miss," the Envoy replied politely. "It isn't the most suitable form for us, nor is it our first choice: a child's body has few advantages, but we've occasionally been obliged to duplicate them. And yes, the original children die, of course. But their parents have no idea and therefore don't lament their loss. They only think their children have become more intelligent, or more unruly." The Envoy gave a much more sinister version of Wells's familiar laugh. "However, in the case of Mr. Wells, he gave me his blood without my asking for it, and without my being able to kill him. This is why there are now two of us in this place that is so unworthy of him."

"He gave it to you?" Murray asked, seeing that Wells was still incapable of responding. "How the devil did he do that?"

"By chance—to use an expression only employed by your race," the Envoy replied, looking at Murray contemptuously. Then he turned his attention back to Wells. "But, as I just explained, the notion of chance doesn't exist in the rest of the universe. And so, from a loftier point of view, we might say you gave it to me because you *had to,* Mr. Wells. Because it was written, to use another of your popular expressions."

"Stop philosophizing and tell me how I did it," Wells demanded brusquely, rousing himself from his daze.

"Can't you guess?" Wells's double sighed and shook his head, half disappointed, half amused. "Of course you can't. Perhaps it would help if I told you I arrived on this planet sixty-eight years ago and spent the last eighteen years in an uncomfortable tomb in your Natural History Museum."

The Envoy's words once again stunned Wells, but not Clayton.

"I knew it! The creature wasn't dead!" the inspector exclaimed, taking the opportunity of placing himself before the Envoy. "Our scientists were mistaken. But how did you do it? How did you wake up?"

The Envoy raised his eyebrows, surprised by Clayton's outburst, but immediately resumed his disdainful sneer.

"I was about to tell you," he replied, while Clayton withdrew his artificial hand behind his back, so the Envoy couldn't see it. "Clearly I wasn't dead, contrary to all appearances, as the shrewd inspector has just observed. I was in a similar state to what you call hibernation. They transported me to London in a block of ice from the Antarctic, where I had inadvertently crashed my spaceship, and they thought I was dead, but I only needed a little blood to bring me back to life. Mr. Wells supplied me with that, unintentionally, of course. I assume he must have had an open wound when he touched me. In any event it was more than enough. And so I was able to launch the invasion, as you have seen. An invasion that would have started long ago had it not been for my untimely accident." He gave Wells a look of amused compassion. "Yes, Mr. Wells, thanks to you I was able to continue the mission that brought me to this planet. However, I'm not the only one who should thank you. All my people should thank you, in particular the brothers who have been living among you for centuries. Since the sixteenth century, to be precise, when the first volunteers arrived, charged with watching over the Earth and evaluating it as a possible future sanctuary for our race. A noble and often thankless task, in this case, because on this planet my brothers die." The Envoy gave a theatrical grimace of sorrow. "Yes, the excess of oxygen in the Earth's atmosphere is detrimental to us, which is why we never considered Earth a viable home. However, we have used up all the ideal planets and must be content to colonize those we can adapt. With the suitable transformations, we will be able to survive on your planet for several generations. This is why I came, to organize the conquest of Earth and prepare it for the arrival of our race. So, you see, if it weren't for your selfless gesture, Mr. Wells, I wouldn't have woken up in time and the clandestine colony on your planet would have died out, perhaps in one or two generations. Earth would have survived, at least until it destroyed itself."

The Envoy's words crushed Wells almost bodily, for he appeared to lean forward, suddenly pale and trembling. He stood there while Jane put her arms around him, and the rest of us gazed at him, more amazed than disapproving.

"Don't torment yourself, Mr. Wells!" I heard the Envoy say reassuringly, as I watched Inspector Clayton getting ready to unscrew his forefinger. "You aren't to blame, not in the sense you humans give to the word anyway. It is simply that, whilst you are an extremely inferior race, some of you possess more developed minds than the rest. And such is the case with you, Mr. Wells. Put in a language you can easily understand, your mind is capable of communicating with the universe, of tuning in to what we might refer to as a higher consciousness, the nature of which is beyond your comprehension, of course. This is completely inconceivable to the rest of your fellow men, with a few rare exceptions. Although, naturally, you yourself are unaware of it." The Envoy contemplated Wells, a tender smile on his face. "I know that you continually wonder why certain things happen to you, or why you make them happen. But you see, Mr. Wells, things don't happen to you, or because of you— *things happen through you.*"

"And what the devil is that supposed to mean?" exclaimed Murray, who must also have seen what Clayton was doing. "Are you insinuating that all of us here who don't look like H. G. Wells belong to an inferior race? Do you think we others don't understand what you're blathering on about? I think we all understand perfectly."

"Do you really?" The bogus Wells scowled at Murray, visibly irritated by his interruption. "You only understand me because I've lowered myself to your level, using concepts that are simple enough for you to comprehend. You could say I'm speaking to you in my sleep, or inebriated, if you prefer."

"And to what do I owe the honor of your wanting to talk to me, inebriated or not?" asked the real Wells in a feeble display of petulance.

I gave Clayton a sidelong glance to see how he was getting on, and my heart nearly leapt into my throat. The inspector was unscrewing his fake forefinger and with mouselike steps was moving away from us and imperceptibly closer to the Envoy. Damn it, Clayton, do it now! I wanted to shout, incapable of containing my tension any longer.

"I was curious," I heard the Envoy say to Wells, even as Clayton began surreptitiously raising his mechanical arm. "Your mind is unlike that of any of my previous hosts, and not simply because you are more imaginative or intelligent than other men. No, I'm referring to the fact that your mind possesses a . . . how can I describe it? A mysterious mechanism, and I want to find out what it is for. Although, judging from your face, even you don't know the answer."

Hearing the Envoy's words, Clayton stopped what he was doing and gave Wells a meaningful look, which I couldn't understand. Wells looked back at Clayton for what seemed like an eternity and then turned to the Envoy.

"Why all the interest?" he said. "You wouldn't be here if you weren't afraid of what I might do with it."

The Envoy gave a look of surprise, which he instantly masked with a smile of amused admiration.

"You're an exceptionally intelligent human, Mr. Wells. And you're quite right. Of course we're not having this conversation because I'm curious about you, but rather because I'm . . . afraid of you."

We all looked at Wells in astonishment, but the author said nothing. He simply contemplated the Envoy solemnly, and for a moment, the pair of them looked like reflections.

"Yes, Mr. Wells," the Envoy went on. "You have the privilege of making me afraid, of instilling fear into a being infinitely superior to Man in every way. And do you want to know why? Because not only do I replicate the body of those whose blood I steal. I replicate their minds and everything in them: their memories, their abilities, their dreams, and their desires. An exact replica of the original. That is why I only need delve into the recesses of your brain to know more about your childhood than you yourself, to discover the tepid feelings you pass off to your wife as love, to unearth your most shameful desires, to reason, even to write as you do. Because I am you, everything that you are, everything that is great and sordid in you. And the brain inside my skull, which is identical to yours, also contains the mechanism I mentioned. And I don't know what it's for, and that terrifies me. How can I explain it? Imagine if you dissected a simple cockroach and discovered in its tiny body something unknown and completely incomprehensible. Wouldn't it make you afraid, terribly afraid?"

"I'm not sure whether to be flattered or insulted," the real Wells retorted with icy calm.

The Envoy gave a rueful smile.

"I don't know whether this mechanism can be used to make the tomatoes in your greenhouse grow bigger, or to kill off our race," he said with a weary sigh. "But this doesn't concern me, Mr. Wells; what concerns me is what it all means. There's something inside your brain that no other species in the universe possesses. Something we know nothing about—we who thought we knew everything. This means the universe isn't what we thought it was, that it still contains secrets unknown to our race—secrets that could destroy us. I'm not sure if you humans can conceive of what that means, given the difference between your place in the universe and ours." The Envoy fell silent for a few moments, caught up in his own reflections, until finally he shrugged and sighed. "But perhaps I'm being unduly alarmist. Now that I've discovered you're alive and have survived the invasion, we may be able to resolve the matter. As soon as the rest of our race arrives on Earth, our scientists will dissect your brain, and we'll get to the bottom of the mystery. We'll find out what is hidden in your head, Mr. Wells, and we'll no longer be afraid of you."

As the color drained from Wells's face, the Envoy studied each of us, one by one, like a general inspecting his troops.

"As for you, I'm pleased to see you're all healthy, robust specimens, as we'll be needing slaves to help us build a new world on the ruins of the old one."

"In that case, I'm sorry to have to wreck your plans," Clayton suddenly declared.

We realized with a shudder that, like it or not, our mad escape plan was about to begin. We stiffened, ready to perform our role in it as best we could. The inspector raised his artificial hand, as if to stop a moving train, and a moment later, it spat out a stream of smoke into the face of the Envoy, who disappeared behind the opaque screen that fell between him and us.

"Quick, get out!" Clayton commanded, shouting over his shoulder at us.

As though we were carrying an invisible battering ram, we hurtled toward the door. First Shackleton, then Murray, who shielded the ladies with his bearlike frame, and behind them, Wells, Harold, and myself, relegated for differing reasons to a secondary role in this surprise escape: Wells owing to his fragile constitution, Harold because of his advanced age, and myself on account of my strong sense of self-preservation, which had always inclined me to avoid any physical combat outside of fencing classes. Unfortunately, I made the mistake of looking back, and, through the blanket of smoke, I was able to glimpse the Envoy's transformation. This made me stop, as if I were bewitched. With a mixture of horror and fascination, I saw the false Wells's body begin to swell up, distorting rapidly in a series of rhythmical convulsions. In a matter of seconds, he had changed into a monstrous four-legged beast the size of an elephant, with what appeared to be a long, thick tail. A thunderous roar showed me he also possessed a formidable throat. Suddenly, as I gazed in awe at the hideous transformation, the creature's thick spiky green tail emerged fully from the veil of smoke spreading through the room and flailed around in the air. As though searching for something to hit, the tail struck Clayton, knocking him to the ground, then snaked toward me. Mesmerized as I was, I couldn't even react. The tail wound itself swiftly around my throat, and, unable to comprehend what was happening, I felt my feet lift off the floor. The pressure of the tail around my throat made it difficult for me to breathe, and my vision became blurred.

Kicking in midair, I struggled to free myself from the slippery noose but quickly realized that my efforts were in vain. Terrified, I understood I was on the verge of choking to death. But before that could happen, I saw Harold enter my field of vision, brandishing the letter opener that had been lying on the desk. With a well-aimed blow that must have taken all his strength, the coachman plunged the knife into the creature's tail. The tail released me and thrashed around in the air while I fell to the ground with a thud, faint and gasping for breath, but able to see the tail now coil itself around Harold's throat with such force that he dropped the letter opener. I tried to pull myself to my feet so that I could grab it and reproduce Harold's exploit, but I felt too faint. And so, half kneeling on the ground, I could only watch as the creature dragged Harold inside the smoke cloud. There came the sinister crunch of bones, followed by a muffled scream, and all I could do was utter a curse. Harold had sacrificed his life for me, for someone who clearly didn't deserve it. I looked around for Clayton through the smoke screen he himself had created, but was unable to see where he had fallen when the monster's tail struck him. And so it was impossible for me to know whether he had been knocked unconscious and we were all still at the mercy of the Martian, or whether, on the contrary, at any moment a flash of light would illuminate the inside of the smoke cloud, revealing that the inspector had executed his plan and that we would all be blown sky high in a matter of seconds. I decided not to stay to find out.

I rose unsteadily to my feet, trying to overcome my dizziness, and stumbled toward the door, the swirling smoke blurring everything around me. Outside, it felt as though I had arrived at the theater after the start of the performance: Captain Shackleton was laying out one of the Martian guards with a fearsome blow. A few yards away, Murray was sitting astride the other, crushing him under his weight. He must have followed Clayton's advice and jumped on him by surprise, and now both of them were wrestling frantically, and aiming clumsy blows at each other. But just then, before the creature was able to transform itself, Murray seized the Martian's head and twisted it sharply, producing a snapping sound. Murray stood up, his back to us, gasping and reeling from the exertion. Flattened against one of the walls, Wells and the two women contemplated the scene, terribly pale, shocked by this dreadful display of violence. A quick glance told me there were no other guards, and I could only thank Heaven the priest had thought it enough to leave only two of them at the door.

"Quick!" I cried, running toward them. "We have to get out of here."

We all fled back down the tunnel that had brought us there, Shackleton once more leading the way, afraid that at any moment we would hear the terrible explosion that would blow us into the air, hurling us against the walls like so many rag dolls. But instead, what we heard was a deafening animal roar filled with savage hate, and alarmingly close. I glanced over my right shoulder and saw the Envoy's monstrous figure emerging through the doorway. Despite the dim lighting and the haze from the smoke, I was able to confirm the truly terrifying nature of his appearance. The powerful creature pursuing us looked like a dragon from a medieval bestiary: its skin was an iridescent green, it had a ridge of spikes along its back, and its mouth was crammed with huge fangs, from which hung shreds of bloody flesh.

"Run, run!" I cried, panic-stricken, turning again to look straight ahead.

"Run!" Clayton's voice repeated, to my surprise.

He overtook me on my left. I gasped, running after him, as we followed the others down a fork in the tunnel. "Inspector Clayton! What about your plan to detonate the bomb?"

"I've had a much better idea, Mr. Winslow! One that will solve everything! But I need Mr. Wells's help, and I didn't think I'd be able to ask him for it if I perished in there!"

Wells and Murray, who were scurrying ahead of us, turned around and looked at Clayton in astonishment.

"My help?" Wells managed to splutter, gasping for breath. "And you think now is the right time to start telling me this?"

"I'm only sorry I didn't think of it before, Mr. Wells!" replied the inspector, still running along with ease.

"Well, I'm afraid it'll have to wait, Inspector: we can't stop now, as I'm sure you can appreciate!" shouted Murray, who was clutching his stomach as he ran. "Hurry! Hurry!" he urged the women, who were a few yards ahead. "Keep running and don't look back!"

That was enough for me to turn around instinctively, to see the creature thirty yards behind us, advancing with great strides, followed by one of the guards, who had also begun metamorphosing into the same hideous species of dragon. I regretted Shackleton hadn't been as radical as Murray in dispatching him. It was obvious these creatures would catch up with us in no time. Would we all perish like Harold, ripped to shreds by their teeth and claws? The truth is I couldn't imagine a more grisly way to die. We turned a bend and came to a place where the tunnel branched into four. We hesitated, out of breath, and looked questioningly at the captain, hoping he would know which way to go, but Shackleton seemed as confused as we.

"Down here!" a voice said suddenly.

Emerging from the darkness of one of the tunnels, we made out the priest beckoning to us. We exchanged glances, unsure whether to trust him or if he was leading us into a trap. But what trap could be worse than the terrible fate that awaited us if the Envoy caught up with us? Then again, there wasn't much time to debate the matter: the sound of our pursuers leaping through the tunnel grew louder and louder, while their huge, misshapen shadows projected onto the tunnel wall warned us they would soon appear around the bend.

"Follow me!" Shackleton cried, darting into the tunnel from which the priest was beckoning.

We all ran after him, trap or no trap.

"Go straight down the tunnel," I heard the priest say as I ran past him. "It'll take you to the river, and it's clear, I've checked. Hurry, you've no time to lose! I'll hold them up while you flee," he murmured, glancing toward the bend.

"Why are you doing this?" I asked him in amazement, stopping automatically beside him.

Without looking at me, his face glowing with a kind of inner illumination, the priest said, "I am a priest. My name is Father Nathaniel Wrayburn, and I've never known anything else. I was born old, and I'm far too old to change now. Go in peace, my son. Go in peace." He stepped into the center of the tunnel, his back to me, and started to pray, projecting his voice loudly: "The thief cometh not, but for to steal and to kill and to destroy . . . I am the good shepherd: the good shepherd giveth his life for the sheep."

Clayton grabbed my arm, dragging me with him even as I yelled a brief "Thank you, Father." While I ran after the inspector, I looked back at the old man standing like a frail tree, trying to make his voice heard above the clamor of footsteps coming from the other tunnel. Then he opened his arms slowly, and his hands began to sprout claws, the prelude to the metamorphosis that would soon spread to the rest of his body. In the distance, the immense figures of his two fellow Martians bounded out of the other tunnel. I didn't want to see more. I turned round and followed my companions, splashing through the puddles of water on the tunnel floor. The deafening, otherworldly roars echoing ominously down the tunnel behind us announced the beginning of a fight to the death between these monsters from outer space. For a few minutes we ran for our lives, as the din of the combat grew fainter, gradually dying out. There was no way of knowing what was happening, although I don't think any of us would have wagered on the priest. Then Murray appeared to stumble and came to a halt, propping himself up against one of the walls. We all turned to look at him.

"What's the matter, Gilliam?" Wells asked between gasps.

"Don't stop, don't stop . . . I'll catch up . . . I just need to rest for a moment," Murray said, deathly white, grimacing as he tried to smile and clasping his stomach, almost doubled over.

"Are you mad, Gilliam? We're not leaving you here!" Emma declared, alarmed. "What's the matter?"

"It's nothing, Emma. I'm fine. I just need to rest for a few—," he began to say, but suddenly lost his strength and slumped to his knees.

Murray gazed up at us almost apologetically and to our surprise began unbuttoning his jacket, revealing the deep gash across his stomach, while he grinned sheepishly, as if he had just spilled wine down his front. Emma raised her hands to her mouth, stifling a scream. Through the awful wound a few bloody lumps protruded, which could only be part of his intestines. Blood was oozing copiously from the gaping wound, drenching his trousers. Only someone who was desperate to stay alive could have managed to run for so long in this state, I reflected.

"Unfortunately, the Martian I killed had time to transform one of his hands," he apologized, resting his faltering gaze on the girl. "I

was afraid to look before, I didn't want to see how serious it was . . .
I didn't want to leave you, Emma, forgive me."

Emma fell to her knees beside him, her horrified eyes fixed on
the terrible gash, reluctant to believe it was real. Her hands fluttered
around the mortal wound that had exposed Murray's intestines,
then she placed them over the wound, trying to cover it, as if she believed this simple gesture could dissuade Murray from his silly notion of dying. But his life went on trickling out of him through her
fingers. Emma gave a guttural cry of pain and rage and impotence.
Then she clutched hold of him desperately, in an embrace like none
I had ever seen before.

"No, Gilliam, don't die . . . You can't die!" she sobbed, frantically
pummeling his chest. She would have killed him if by doing so she
could have brought him back to life.

All of a sudden, we heard a thunderous roar of triumph in the
distance, which made us raise our heads, even as the blood curdled
in our veins. A few seconds later, thudding footsteps echoed down
the tunnel as the huge creatures bounded toward us. It didn't take
much intelligence to realize who had won the fight. In a matter of
minutes, the victors would be upon us. And it seemed there were
more of them, many more than two. I think we all knew we were
going to die at the hands of this frenzied pack.

"Inspector Clayton," Murray managed to splutter, blood streaming from the corners of his mouth and falling onto the hair of the
girl, who was still clasping him in her arms, "I don't know what
your new plan is, but there's only one way you'll have time to carry
it out. I'll stay here and when the Martians arrive I'll detonate your
accursed hand. That'll take care of a few of them for you, and at the
same time I suppose the tunnel will collapse, forcing them to find
another way through. It'll give you a chance to escape—"

"No, Gilliam, no!" the girl cried.

"Emma," Murray whispered with difficulty, "you know I

love to argue with you, but now isn't the time. Go, go with them, please . . ."

"I'm not going anywhere, Gilliam. I'm staying right here with you," the girl declared resolutely.

"No, Emma, save yourself, you must . . ."

"As you yourself said: now isn't the time—and I don't intend to argue. I'm staying here with you. Nothing you say will make me change my mind."

The dying Murray stroked her hair with an increasingly limp, trembling hand.

"I'm the most exasperating man on the planet with whom to survive a Martian invasion, but it's all right to die with me?"

"My good manners prevent me from answering that, Mr. Gilmore, and my honesty from lying. Draw your own conclusions," she replied with a catch in her voice.

Murray gave her a smile of infinite tenderness, and their lips met, his great paws sliding down the curve of her back, too weak to embrace her. We all looked away respectfully, moved by the scene. Unfortunately, there was no time for anything more: the monsters' thundering footsteps were drawing closer and closer. This time it wouldn't be the celebrated author or Inspector Clayton who interrupted their embrace.

"Inspector Clayton," we heard Murray say, his voice scarcely more than a rasping, urgent hiss as he separated his lips from those of the girl, who clung to him sobbing. "Don't get the wrong idea, but I'm going to ask for your hand."

The inspector smiled for the first time since I had met him. He swiftly unscrewed his artificial limb and gave it to Murray.

"Press this when you think the time is right," he explained, pointing to a button inside.

"Count on me, Inspector," Murray assured him with forced enthusiasm. He then bade us farewell, casting a feeble glance over the group before resting his gaze on Shackleton. "Take care of them, Captain. I know you'll get them out of here alive."

Shackleton nodded with an air of pained composure.

"I'm sorry I didn't reply to your letter, Gilliam," Wells apologized. "If I received it now, I assure you I would."

Murray smiled at him, astonished. "Thank you, George."

Wells stepped toward Murray and, with an abruptness that startled us, proffered his hand.

"It's been a pleasure to know you, Gilliam," he blurted out, in the tone of one who feels ridiculous when showing his emotions.

Gilliam shook his hand, relieved perhaps that his own anguished expression allowed him to conceal how moved he was by Wells's unexpected show of compassion. Then he turned once more to Emma in a final attempt to persuade her.

"Now go, my love, please. Live . . ."

"Not without you," the girl replied with anguished defiance.

"You won't have to, Emma," Murray assured her, stroking her hair with a trembling hand, controlled now by the strings of death. "I promise you, you won't be alone, because somehow I'll come back. I did it once, and I'll do it again, my love. I'll come back to you. You'll feel me embrace you, smile at you, watch over you each moment of your life . . ."

But his words only made Emma clasp the dying man even more tightly. Murray gave us an imploring look. He had done his best, but there was nothing more he could say to persuade her to flee with us. We all looked at one another, none of us daring to step forward and prise her away from him. Clayton glanced toward the end of the tunnel, where the monsters were bearing down on us. I suppose he must have figured that we had another two to three minutes at least. To our surprise, he knelt beside the couple.

"Miss Harlow," he said gently, "allow me to say that isn't just a metaphor. As you know, my department deals with all those things that defy reason, and so you have to believe me when I tell you that in some cases what Mr. Murray says is true. There have been loves so powerful they have even transcended death."

Emma turned and looked straight at the inspector in silence. Then she said, "If you'd ever been in love yourself you'd know this gives me no comfort, Inspector. And so, with all due respect, go to Hell."

For a few moments, the inspector gazed at her with an expression of sorrow and pain, an almost human expression I would never have expected from a man like Clayton. I didn't know whether he'd been telling the truth, whether he actually knew of loves that had transcended the frontiers of death, or had simply said the only thing he could think of to convince the girl to flee with us, a beautiful lie to save her life. Be that as it may, it clearly made no impression on Emma. Finally, Clayton stood up and gazed at Murray, as though asking permission to resort to force. But Murray shook his head with a smile of resigned defeat and clasped the girl to him with the last of his strength. At this, there was nothing more to say. Then, as if we were no longer there, Murray began whispering something in his beloved's ear in a lilting voice, like a lullaby, and although we couldn't make out his words, we all saw how the girl's sobs suddenly stopped. Her head still resting on his chest, Emma smiled as Murray kept whispering to her, calmly nestling in his embrace, lost in thought, oblivious to the closeness of death hurtling toward us, like a little girl smiling blissfully as she listens to a fairy tale. Because, from the snatches I could overhear, Murray was telling her a children's story, one I didn't know, about colored balloons floating through galaxies made of vanilla meringue, of orange herons and men with forked tails.

Clayton gave a solemn nod, as though this were the end of a story written by him.

"We have to go now," he said suddenly. "We should be as far away as possible when the bomb goes off."

And without waiting for a reply, he began running down the tunnel. We followed, our stomachs in knots. And as I raced through the London sewers, with so many conflicting emotions inside me I felt as if my soul had been turned inside out, I looked over my shoulder at the two lovers, still clasping each other in the middle of the tunnel, Clayton's artificial hand in theirs, growing smaller with each step we took. Then, just as the gigantic shapes of the monsters appeared behind them, I saw the lovers join in a serene embrace, as though they had all the time in the world to kiss each other and nothing mattered except the other's lips. And the touch of their lips made their hearts explode, producing a dazzling white light that spread through the tunnel, drowning it out.

I can think of no nobler way of illustrating Gilliam and Emma's love for each other than through the image of that blinding, powerful light. Two years have passed since it burned itself onto my retinas forever, and I'm proud to say that, although they died that day in the sewers of London, tenderly embracing each other, their love lives on. I made sure of that by remembering it each day, and now that I myself am about to die, I have tried to immortalize it as best I can in these pages so that it lives on after me. My only regret is not being able to write like Byron or Wilde so that whoever reads this, if anyone does, will feel his hands burn in the same blaze that consumed those lovers' hearts.

After the blast came a deafening crash, like a thunderclap. We were struck by a blast of hot air that almost knocked us over, and a moment later we watched with horror as around us great cracks appeared in the walls and ceiling of the tunnel. We ran as fast as our tired legs would carry us as the world came crashing down, helping one another as we dodged the rubble thundering down on us from the ceiling, with what, to our ringing ears, sounded like muffled thuds. Moments later, the tunnel filled with dust, and we could scarcely see where we were going, but amid shouts and splutters we managed to reach the tunnel into which our tributary led. With a rapid exchange of glances, we confirmed no one was injured. Shackleton, face covered in dust, tried to get his bearings, while the tunnel behind us began to implode.

"This way!" the captain yelled, stepping into another smaller passageway that led off from the main tunnel.

We could scarcely hear Shackleton but hurriedly piled in after him, stooping as we ran to avoid scraping our heads on the low ceiling. There was almost no light in the tunnel, and a good third of it was plunged into total darkness, so that we had to grope our way along, up to our knees in water. By that time I was so exhausted I was beyond caring; it no longer mattered to me where we were going or whether the Martians were chasing us or not. As my deafness began to subside, I could hear our tired, almost painful gasps resounding off the tunnel walls. I was overwhelmed by fatigue and dizziness, but most of all I felt crushed inside: I had realized that as a human being I was a fraud, that my soul was polluted by egotism and self-interest and nothing of any beauty could grow there. Everything that came naturally and spontaneously to others required an intellectual effort on my part, and in most instances some form of future compensation or personal pleasure. These were the thoughts that assailed me as I waded through the tunnel, panting for breath, finding each step increasingly difficult. And suddenly, I couldn't understand why, running began to seem miraculously easy, as if my feet had grown wings.

"The tunnel is sloping down!" I heard Wells cry behind me.

Then the gradient became so steep we found ourselves sliding down the narrow tunnel, dragged along by the water that was filling it. As I was being propelled toward God knew where, I heard the roar of water in the distance, growing louder and louder, and I quickly realized we were in one of the many pipes carrying the waste waters into the interceptor sewer, the vast tunnel beneath the streets that carried London's sewage to somewhere in the Thames. I imagined the tunnel would end abruptly in a chute a few yards high, a kind of miniwaterfall flowing into the basin fed by all the other pipes. I had no idea whether the priest from outer space had been aware of these hazards, and, given the circumstances, had considered them the lesser of two evils, but the fact was we were in grave danger, for I didn't think we would emerge unscathed from the imminent plunge. I positioned myself as best I could in the water and discovered Jane, terrified and pale, descending almost level with me, and a few yards behind us Wells frantically reaching out his arm in a futile attempt to grab hold of her. Without thinking, I grabbed her, clutching her to me, hoping to protect her as much as possible from the fall. All at once, the tunnel came to an end, and I felt myself gliding through the air, clutching the young woman's trembling body. It was an odd feeling, like floating in space. And it seemed the illusion would go on forever, until I felt my back hit something solid. The impact at that speed seemed to have cracked several of my ribs, winding me for a few seconds, but I managed not to let go of the girl.

When I had recovered from the shock, I realized I had crashed into the guardrail surrounding the huge basin where the pipes discharged the wastewaters. A few yards above me I saw the tunnel that had spat us out, dumping its foul cargo into the pool, and at least a dozen more doing the same. Emerging from the bottom of this pool, where London's excrement converged, was an underwater pipe leading out of the sewers, creating a gigantic whirlpool in the middle of the basin. However, it was impossible for anyone to be able to hold their breath for the fifteen or twenty minutes I calculated it would take to swim through it. If this was the good priest's plan, he had clearly overestimated our lung capacity. Next to me, Jane coughed. She was only half conscious, perhaps due to the fear that had overwhelmed her as we flew through the air, yet unscathed thanks to its having been my body that smashed into the guardrail. I noticed that Shackleton had fallen into the middle of the basin, but despite the huge whirlpool threatening to suck him down, he seemed unhurt and was swimming strongly toward the edge, where I could see an iron ladder embedded in the wall. I looked away from what I was certain would be Shackleton's successful escape from the deadly vortex and searched for the others. A few yards from me, I saw Clayton, his legs wrapped around the guardrail, his one good hand clutching Wells, whose legs were thrashing in midair. I realized immediately that if Wells fell into the water, he would be too weak to swim away from the whirlpool and would be irretrievably dragged down.

"Hang on, Clayton!" I cried, clambering to my feet to help the inspector hoist Wells up.

I dragged myself over to them as fast as my bruised body would allow, trying to ignore the stabbing pain coming from my ribs, even as I saw Clayton shout something at Wells, trying to make himself heard above the din of the water. A few yards beyond where Wells and Clayton were suspended above the pool, I saw the captain, who had managed to scale the ladder and was approaching them with his muscular arms. Even so, I was closer to them than he was.

"Try to hang on a bit longer!" I cried, gritting my teeth to stop myself fainting from the pain.

But they were too busy shouting at each other, and neither of them seemed to hear me. When at last I reached them, I could hear what at that very moment Clayton was shouting to Wells, his neck straining, the thick tendons stretched to the snapping point: "Do it! Trust me, you can do it! Only you can save us!"

Not understanding what the inspector was referring to, I also cried out. "Give me your hand, Wells!" I stretched out my arm, gripping the guardrail with my other hand.

The inspector looked at me and smiled, exhausted from his terrible exertion. Then his eyes rolled back and he passed out. Unable to grab the two men in time, I watched as they plummeted into the basin forty feet below. The captain, arriving from the other direction, dived after them and managed to grab Clayton before he disappeared underwater. But I realized he couldn't rescue Wells as well and so, without considering that I might lose consciousness as I hit the water, I leapt over the guardrail, plunging into that dirty, foul-smelling pond. The impact increased the pain in my ribs, but not so much that I lost consciousness. The water was terribly murky, and when I had managed to collect myself, I dived down, swimming desperately back and forth, struggling against the terrible power of the whirlpool threatening to suck me down to the bottom. Try as I might, I could not see Wells. When my lungs felt as if they were going to burst, I came up to the surface. And then I felt the tail coil around my neck and lift me into the air.

That was the end of our desperate flight. When one of the monsters fished me out of the water with its tail and hurled me onto the side of the basin, together with the rest of my companions, I realized we had been taken prisoner. The Envoy was standing before us, once more in the guise of Wells, leading us to deduce that Clayton's exploding hand must have annihilated only the few of his fellow Martians who were heading the chase. Two years on, I can still remember vividly the look of defeat on our faces as we glanced at one another beside the basin, breathless and weak, and our anxiety about our future, an anxiety that today seems almost laughable compared to the dismal fate that awaited us. But my clearest memory was of Jane frantically calling to Wells, crying out his name over and over until her voice cracked. But her cries paled in comparison to the Envoy's bellow of rage when his fellow Martians emerged from the depths of the basin to announce that the author was nowhere to be seen: his most precious cockroach had escaped, taking his secret with him. And, unfortunately for the Envoy, this changed the universe into an unfathomable place, where anything was possible. To this day, I have no idea what became of Wells. I assume he must have passed out when he hit the water and then drowned, his body flushed out into the Thames. And, although it might not seem so, he could not have wished for a better end.

Just now, beyond the gloomy forests that surround the Martian camp, the sun is sinking behind the ruined city of London, and in my cell I am hurrying to finish writing this diary, hours before my own life ends, for I am certain I shall not survive another day. My body is going to give out at any moment, or perhaps it will be my heart, this morass of despair and bitterness I carry around in my chest. Fortunately, I have succeeded in reaching the end of my story. I only hope that whilst I did not manage to be the hero of this tale, whoever reads these pages will at least have found me an adequate narrator. My life ends here, a life I wish I could have lived differently. But there is no time to make amends. All I can do now is record in these pages my belated yet heartfelt remorse.

From my cell I can see night gathering over the Martian pyramid, this structure that symbolizes better than any flag the conquest of a planet, a planet that once belonged to us, the human race. On it we forged our History, we gave the best and the worst of ourselves. Yet all this will be forgotten when the last man on Earth perishes, ending an entire species. With him, all our hopes will die.

And that is something that, although I still don't understand it, I have come to accept.

Charles Leonard Winslow, model prisoner,
the Martian Camp, Lewisham

XXXVII

LTHOUGH DAWN FOUND HIM STILL ALIVE, Charles had nevertheless hidden the diary in his trousers before descending into the depths of the pyramid, convinced this would be his last day. Having spent the whole night wracked with fever and convulsions, he was forced to confront the day's work, putting up with the inquisitive stares of the Martians, who were no doubt expecting him to collapse at any moment. But to his surprise, he managed to stay upright, transporting the barrels, willing his body not to give way, not to dissolve like a cloud unraveled by the breeze, reminding himself now and then to conserve enough energy to bury the diary.

When he reemerged aboveground, more dead than alive, he stumbled over to the feeding machines, where a line of prisoners was already waiting to be given their second ration of the day, before retiring finally to their cells. Charles walked past, averting his gaze, then came to a halt a few yards from where he believed the invisible ray that interacted with their neck shackles began to operate. He burrowed a hole in the ground with trembling hands, and, making sure no one was looking, buried the diary there. He wished he could have sent it by carrier pigeon, in a bold act of resistance, to a country in the old Europe where there might still be free human beings, but he had to be content with burying it within the confines of the camp. He spread a few stones on top and gazed at the tiny mound for a few moments. He didn't know for whom he was leaving the diary there. Conceivably no one would ever find it, and time would disintegrate the pages before they were read. Or perhaps a

Martian would stumble on it in a few days' time and destroy it immediately. On reflection, he would prefer this than the creature reading it aloud to his companions, making fun of Charles's lamentable prose, his banal meditations on the nature of love, or the futile attempts he and his companions made to escape the inevitable. But it made little difference whether the diary was found or not, he told himself, for now he felt ashamed of his reasons for writing it. He hadn't done it to celebrate Gilliam and Emma's love, or to document what he had discovered about the Martians, as he claimed in the diary. No, he had been compelled to write it, he acknowledged in a sudden fit of sincerity, by the same selfishness that had always motivated his actions: to show himself to the world in a good light, to record for posterity that despite having wasted his life, at least in his final days on Earth he had managed to act like any other dignified human being.

Well, if that had been his aim, he had fulfilled it and was now free to die. That was what his body yearned for: the absolute, peaceful, eternal rest that death offered. Charles smiled at the evening sky, exposing his wizened, toothless gums. Yes, that is what he would do. He would go back to this cell, lie down on his pallet, and wait for death, which before long would come knocking at his door. And the next morning at dawn, the neck shackle would interrupt his eternal sleep and take him for a posthumous journey through the camp, for his destiny would not be complete until he was turned into food for those who were still alive. And that would be the end of Charles Winslow.

His head spinning, Charles staggered back to his cell. He had no strength left for anything else, he told himself, and in some sense this relieved him of the burden he had felt since seeing Claire's naked body floating in the tank and wondering if he should tell Captain Shackleton his wife was dead. He was aware that by doing so he would take away the only thing that kept Shackleton alive. But didn't the captain also deserve some respite? Charles, with a few words, could grant him the right to surrender, to lay down his arms. Why did he not tell him, then? These doubts had been gnawing away at him all night. In the end dawn had come and he still hadn't made a decision. No matter how hard he tried to convince himself he hadn't the strength to go to Shackleton's cell, this paltry excuse did little to dispel his feelings of remorse. Weak as he was, he resolved he would make it over to where the captain was to tell him what he had seen, thus releasing him from his pointless purgatory. No doubt, when the captain discovered that Claire was inside the pyramid, he would try to go down there and the shackle would instantly begin to throttle him, to kill him even, if he persisted. But what did that matter now? Clearly there would never be an uprising, Charles reflected with bitterness; the Martians would be the lords and masters of the Earth. Things had gone much too far for anyone to be able to put them right. Their doomed planet no longer had any need of a hero. And so Charles decided the time had come to offer Captain Shackleton his freedom, the only freedom to which Man could now aspire: that of deciding whether he wanted to go on living. Filled with this resolve, Charles turned around and stumbled toward the barracks where his friend's cell was, on the other side of the camp.

However, he was weaker than he thought. The captain was forced to interrupt the exercises he was doing at the entrance to his cell when he saw Charles collapse a few yards from the barracks. He leapt down the steps, hoisted Charles's limp body onto his shoulders, and carried him back to his cell, where he laid him out on his pallet with the gentleness of an embalmer. Then he placed his hand on Charles's burning brow and realized he was too far gone for him to do anything: Charles would die within minutes. Shackleton sat beside him and clasped his hand. The young man appeared slowly to regain consciousness, groaning softly, his eyes struggling to focus on Shackleton.

When it appeared they had, Charles whispered, "I'm dying, Captain . . ."

The captain gave him a look of commiseration and pressed his hand but remained silent. Charles cleared his throat with a painful rasp and began.

"I'm sorry I took you away from Claire that afternoon," he said with difficulty. "I'm so sorry it was all for nothing. I should have let you spend those last hours together. They were yours, and I took them from you. I regret it more than you could know, Captain. But I promise I didn't do it out of spite or on a whim. I truly believed you were destined to defeat the Martians. It was written, remember?" Charles tried to smile at his own joke but only managed a pathetic rictus of pain. "And I still don't understand why it didn't happen, why the future you came from will not exist, even though both of us have seen it."

Shackleton shifted uneasily in his chair but did not break his silence.

"Luckily, I don't have much time to keep on asking myself why nothing turned out the way it was supposed to, and I suppose I've more than paid for all the wrong or mistaken things I may have done in my life. I'm so tired, Derek . . . all I want now is to rest . . ." Charles stared blankly at Shackleton as though a mist had descended between them, obscuring him. "And you must do the same, Derek . . . Yes, you must admit defeat, Captain. You've nothing left to fight for, my friend. Not anymore. I have to tell you something . . ."

Charles was seized by a sudden fit of coughing, causing his body to jerk on the pallet as several mouthfuls of blood oozed down his chin and neck, staining his skin an oily green. The captain hurriedly sat him up so he wouldn't choke on his own blood, holding him until the coughing subsided and gazing at him with infinite sorrow. When he had recovered, Charles closed his eyes, exhausted, and Shackleton once more laid him gently down. His breathing was so slight that for a moment the captain thought Charles had passed away, but when he moved his face close to his friend's bloodstained lips, he could feel his breath, light and fleeting, like the shadow of a dragonfly on the water. Shackleton looked at him for a few moments and shook his head slowly. Then he got up and walked over to the table on the opposite side of his cell.

"Captain Shackleton! Derek!" Charles called out suddenly, eyes wide open, frantically searching for his friend in the darkness slowly closing in around him. "Where are you, Derek? I can't see, I can't see . . . everything's gone black . . . Derek!"

The captain remained motionless for a moment, his back to Charles, his shoulders hunched, as though he were carrying an immense weight. At last, he took something from the table, went back over to the bed, knelt beside the dying man, and began to speak to him, his powerful hands caressing the object.

"Listen, Charles. I, too, have something to tell you," he said solemnly. "Much has happened during the three days since I last saw you. While you were inside the pyramid, I was in the women's camp—and I have some news. Important news."

Charles attempted to interrupt in a thin voice. "Derek, there's something I have to tell you . . ."

"Hush, my friend! Don't talk, save your strength, and listen to me," the captain insisted. "They brought a new batch of women from the Continent. And I was able to speak to some of them, Charles. They told me the Martians are having serious problems over there. Resistance groups have sprung up in France, Italy, Germany, and many other countries. Everyone is talking about a group of strange soldiers armed with powerful weapons. Yes, Charles, weapons no one has ever seen before, weapons almost as technologically advanced as the Martians'. And these soldiers move from camp to camp, freeing the prisoners, arming them, training them. And they are growing in strength and number. It is rumored they will soon arrive in England. And do you know what else they are saying, my friend? That these soldiers are searching for their captain, that they've come from the future to rescue him."

"From the future? Oh, heavens, Captain! But how can that be?" Charles managed to murmur, filled with wonder, afraid of surrendering to this miracle, to the intense joy threatening to engulf him and sweep away his pain.

"I don't know, Charles. I'm wondering that myself." Shackleton let out a loud guffaw, still mysteriously fondling the object he was holding. "But clearly these are my men, Charles. They are coming to save me, to save us. How could they have found out what was happening in the past? I don't know. As I told you, in the future we have time machines that are different from the *Cronotilus*. The one I used to get here was destroyed, but who knows, maybe there were others I didn't know about, and maybe other travelers saw the beginning of the invasion and went back to the future to raise the alarm."

"But if that's the case," Charles protested, making a superhuman effort to raise his voice so the captain could hear him, "then why did they take so long? And why did they turn up on the Continent and not here?"

For a few moments Shackleton remained pensive.

"I don't know, my friend," he said suddenly, recovering his enthusiasm, "but I can assure you that's the first thing I'll ask my brave men when I see them! Oh yes, Charles, you can count on it! I'll say to them, 'What the hell have you been doing while I, your captain, was rotting away in here? Baboons! Devil's spawn! Sodomizing one another? Impregnating your own mothers? Or do you suppose we've been enjoying ourselves in here, sons of bitches?' Yes, that's what I'll say. I can hear them laughing already," declared the captain, and he began to guffaw loudly. Charles felt his own lips forming a smile, exposing his naked gums, as he began to accept as true the captain's incredible story.

"But . . . are you sure, my dear fellow?" he asked. "Can you trust these women?"

"Of course, Charles. Look at this," Shackleton said, placing in his friend's hands the mysterious object he had been holding. Charles fondled it blindly, allowing the captain to guide his fingers. "One of them brought me this. It's from my time, it's a . . . well, we call it a marker. I knew what it was as soon as she gave it to me."

"What is it?" Charles's voice was scarcely audible now.

"We would use them after the battle to find survivors buried under the rubble. We all wore one around our neck. I took mine off before I traveled here, so as not to arouse suspicion among the people in your time. But now, thanks to that brave woman, I have this one. Many of the women who had escaped from the camps let themselves be recaptured, their mission to smuggle these markers in under their clothing and find me to give me one of them. And now I'm going to activate it and hide it under my clothing, Charles. That means my soldiers will reach me as soon as they land in England. It will only be a matter of months, my friend, possibly even weeks. But they will come, Charles, they will come. And that will be the end of the Martians. We're going to defeat them, my friend."

"To defeat them . . . ," Charles repeated with a groan.

"Yes, Charles, we're going to defeat them." The captain stroked his dying friend's thinning hair, plastered to his brow, then he gently retrieved the object from Charles's hands, which fell limply to his sides. His breathing was scarcely more than a rapid murmur now. "You were right, my friend. You were right all along. We're going to defeat them, because *we've already defeated them.*"

Because we've already defeated them, Charles heard as he crossed the murky threshold of oblivion. Yes, they were going to reconquer the Earth, he thought feverishly. He had been right all along, the captain had just said so. Yes, of course he'd been right, how could he ever have doubted himself? He had seen the future, he had been to the year 2000, and the brave Captain Shackleton had been there, defeating the king of the automatons, and there were no Martians, no . . . Claire. Charles's breathing quickened. Claire, he remembered. Claire was in the depths of the pyramid. Yes, she was there, dead, or worse. Floating in that repulsive green liquid. He had seen her, and he had to tell Shackleton, that's why he'd come to his cell, to free him. But he couldn't tell him now! he told himself, bewildered. If the captain discovered his wife was dead, it would destroy him. He wouldn't care about his men or saving the human race. Charles knew this because he had seen him before: Shackleton's love for his wife had changed him from a hero into a man, a man who wouldn't want to live in a world without his beloved in it. He would find a way to take his own life, and his men would arrive too late to stop him. And what would happen then? Would the uprising continue without Shackleton? Would his men save the planet without their brave captain, without the man who had rescued the world where they came from in the future? Charles did not know, but he could not risk allowing that to happen. And besides, what if by doing so he changed everything, caused one of those rents in the fabric of time that Murray had warned against? Could that happen?

Charles searched hard for an answer amid the increasingly murky shadows filling his mind, but his thoughts became tangled, forming a confused mass: the future—which he had seen, and which could thus be considered the past—and the present, in which he lived, had lost their natural order and been rearranged in a way that seemed odd, though the fact was he couldn't be sure of that either. Could the captain, who was meant to defeat Solomon, die inside the pyramid without the order of the universe being destroyed? Too confused, Charles resolved to remain silent, for fear of spoiling everything. The captain had to carry on hoping he would find Claire one day, he had to fight, driven on by this hope. Yes, he had to save the Earth and safeguard the future, the future where he would, once more, meet Claire for the first time, and from whence he would travel to be with her, to fall in love with her over and over again, to lose her over and over again, and to search for her forever, and no one must ever take away his hope of finding her, for the human race needed him to be lonely and sad, forever dreaming he would find his Claire.

Charles turned his head toward where he sensed vaguely the captain was and made a couple of grotesque faces before managing to produce the smile with which he wanted to accompany his joke.

"Because it's written . . . ," he managed to say, thrusting forever from his mind the naked body of Claire Haggerty, whom no one would rescue from the depths of the pyramid.

As he did so, Charles realized that his role in this story was none other than the deceiver, the king of deceivers, the trickster, the man whose task it was to conceal the truth from the hero so that he could go on being one. Yes, his role had been that of the man who lied to safeguard the future. And, embracing this minor role Fate had reserved for him, Charles Winslow allowed the darkness to penetrate him and his soul to dissolve into the void.

Captain Shackleton contemplated Charles for a few moments, then he reached out and gently closed his eyelids, giving his friend the appearance of finally being at rest, his ravaged face bathed in a deserving and infinite peace. He picked up the remains of the wax candle he had been pressing in his fingers while he was speaking, molding it into a shape that Charles, in his confusion, could believe was the marker that proved the existence of an army of the future that was coming to find him. Then he placed it on the table, wondering whether Ashton might get him another candle stub the following day, and whether it would be long before Charles's shackle activated itself and marched him off to the funnel, or whether he would have to lay his body on the floor so that he could sleep on the pallet. He needed to sleep. At dawn they would once more take him over to the women's camp, and he wanted to be as rested as possible, because, who could tell, tomorrow might be the day when at last he found Claire.

NATURALLY, THE CAPTAIN DIDN'T find Claire the following day, or the day after, or any of the many days that carried on silently piling up until they had become another year. But that is another story, one I hope you will forgive me for not having time to tell you now, because our story is about to take a different tack. Perhaps on another occasion, in which case I shall do so with pleasure. However, before we leave the brave Captain Shackleton in his cell dreaming of his beloved Claire, allow me to be so bold as to request that, despite the scene I have just described to you, you do not think badly of him. I am sure that during the course of this tale, many of you, just like Charles, will have been unsure what to think of Captain Shackleton. Influenced by Charles's incessant doubts, you will have asked yourselves over and over whether this man is the real Captain Shackleton, who in the year 2000 will save the world, or on the contrary whether he is an impostor, an opportunist who passes himself off as the captain in order to win the heart of a beautiful, rich young woman who would otherwise be unobtainable. Did this man travel from the future for love, or did love force him to invent a past? Is this the real Captain Shackleton, who made up a story so Charles would die a happy man, or is he a charlatan who felt pity for his dying friend? Is he a fraud or a hero? At the risk of upsetting you, I shall take the liberty of not telling you now. As I said, one day I may be able to tell you the captain's extraordinary story, and the amazing adventures that still await him, and if so, I promise then to reveal the mystery of his identity.

In the meantime, all I will say is whether or not he is an impostor, this man now sighing in his cell, imagining that he might find his beloved on the morrow, is obviously a true hero. But not because in the future he may or may not behead the evil Solomon with his sword, thus saving the human race. There are other, more subtle ways of being a hero. Is it not heroic to make a dying man dream of a better world as he has just done for poor Charles? As Charles Winslow was dying, through the veil of death he glimpsed a victorious planet Earth, rebuilt by the captain and his men, a world more beautiful than the one he had known. Ought we not to consider someone a hero who succeeds in creating a perfect world, if only for a single moment and for one man? And was not Murray also a hero for making Emma die with a smile on her lips? And so were Richard Adams Locke and many others who, through their imagination, have managed to save hundreds of lives. Indeed, and among these heroes should be included the false or the real Captain Shackleton, who chose to give his dying friend Charles his own Map of the Sky, a sky where the sunset would at last possess the longed-for colors of his childhood.

XXXVIII

ORE THAN SEVENTY YEARS BEFORE Charles's soul dissolved into the void, another soul emerged from the void. And although the birth took less than a second, Wells felt as though an invisible hand were reconstructing the whole of him piece by piece, hastily screwing together his various bones to create a skeleton, garlanding them with veins, arteries, and ligaments and then scattering a handful of organs around the improvised framework, finally wrapping it all up in the packaging of his flesh. Once the finishing touch of his skin was in place, Wells was suddenly struck by feelings of cold, tiredness, nausea, and other miseries characteristic of the body he had been dragging around with him for as long as he could remember, and which fastened him to reality like an anchor. Then he found himself submerged in murky, foul-smelling water, only to be ejected a moment later by the force of the current, which sent him flying through the air to land in a calm stretch of water.

Once he realized he was not going to be dragged anywhere else, Wells managed to swim up to the surface. He gasped several times and looked around, bewildered, unable to comprehend where he was or what had happened. Gradually, as he began to see and think more clearly, he guessed he had been spat out into the Thames through a sewage pipe, but try as he might he could see no sign of the others. Where the devil were they? He waited in case they floated up to the surface but soon found it too cold in the water. He felt suddenly dizzy and began vomiting copiously into the Thames. This was enough to make him abandon his role as guest of the river, and so, exhausted and shivering, he swam clumsily toward the nearest quay, hauling himself out of the water as best he could. Once on dry land, he tried to collect his thoughts. He had managed to escape the Martians, but this was no cause for celebration, because it was clear his victory was only temporary: at any moment they could emerge from somewhere and capture him once and for all and open up his brain, as the Envoy had promised.

Sitting on the quayside like a vagabond, breathless from fatigue and anxiety, Wells glanced about and was amazed to see no trace of the havoc wreaked by the Martians. Where was all the damage the tripods had caused? he wondered, studying closely what he could see of London. But the absence of any destruction was not the only oddity; there was something else. This was undoubtedly London, yes, but not his London. The majority of buildings were only one or two storeys high, and he could not see Tower Bridge. Not because it had been destroyed, but rather because it had not yet been built. Filled with disbelief, Wells saw that only a handful of bridges (Waterloo, Westminster, and one or two others) joined the two sides of the river. With astonishment he noticed that the new London Bridge was under construction some thirty yards away from the old one. Wells leapt to his feet and stared in bewilderment at the narrow, decaying structure of the original bridge, still in use while it was waiting to be pulled down. As if that was not enough, the Thames, which was navigated by paddleboats, now flowed past dark, gravelly beaches, with their small boat builders, private fishing grounds, and jetties belonging to a few luxurious mansions. The author heaved a deep sigh. Everything looked unfinished.

For a long time, he stood contemplating this incomplete London in a state of numb disbelief, until he realized this was no mirage resulting from mental exhaustion. His final conversation with Clayton started coming back to him, still tangled in his confused memories of the previous hours: the desperate flight through the sewers, the death of Gilliam and Emma, the awful fall through the tunnel. What had Clayton shouted to him before they both plummeted into the basin? Acting on an intuition as sudden as it was fleeting, Wells went over to a wastepaper bin, and from among the refuse he dug out a discarded newspaper to verify the date: it was from September 23, 1829. His discovery left him perplexed. He was in the London of 1829! he told himself. He shook his head, half horrified, half exhilarated. It would be eight years before King William IV died and the archbishop of Canterbury presented himself at Kensington Palace to inform the king's niece Victoria, who had just turned eighteen, that she had succeeded to the throne of the most powerful country on Earth. God, he himself would not be born for another thirty-seven years! How could that be?

God, he had traveled in time!

Like the inventor in his novel, only without any cumbersome machine. Apparently, he had done so using his mind, exactly as Clayton had told him he could in his basement only a few hours before. Well, to be precise it would be sixty-nine years before the inspector made this startling disclosure to him, while the Martians were destroying London above their heads. A London that looked nothing like this one, a London of the future. Then, like timid shooting stars, the last words he and Clayton had exchanged as Wells dangled in midair, held aloft only by the inspector's good hand, began to dart across his befuddled brain, slowly illuminating it. At that moment, terrified by the possibility of plunging forty feet and being sucked down into the furious whirlpool below, Wells had been unable to pay the inspector too much attention. But now Clayton's words came back to him with surprising clarity, as though the inspector were once more beside him, shouting above the roar of the water, even though it would be several decades before Clayton was born into that incomprehensible world, disposed to lose a hand in his eagerness to understand it.

"Wells!" Clayton had cried, as the author thrashed his legs anxiously in the air. "Listen to me! You're the solution! Do you hear? *You're the solution!*"

"What?" Wells had replied, puzzled.

"Remember what the Envoy said?" The inspector had resumed yelling, while the author became aware, panic-stricken, that his hands were slipping out of Clayton's.

Wells tried to cling on more tightly, but the moisture made it impossible. He was slipping, inexorably. Then he heard Charles's voice but dared not turn toward him, given the precariousness of his grip. In any event, Charles had sounded too far away: he would not arrive in time to seize hold of him.

"Clayton, do something! I'm slipping!" he cried, petrified.

But the inspector persisted with his absurd discourse.

"If you listen to me, damn it, you'll save all our lives!" he cried. "The Envoy admitted he was afraid of you. And I'm certain it's because of what I told you in my basement!"

"Don't let go, Clayton!"

"Don't you see, Wells?" the inspector went on. "The solution is in your head! The Envoy is afraid of you, Wells, because he senses you're the only one who can stop the invasion . . . by preventing it! That's what you have to do, Wells! *Prevent it from happening!*"

Clayton scarcely had a grip on Wells's fingers now. Out of the corner of his eye, Wells thought he saw the captain coming toward them from the other side, clutching the guardrail.

"Try to hang on a bit longer!" Charles's voice appeared much closer now. Hold on, yes. Wells made a supreme effort to tear his thoughts away from the roar of the water, from his physical discomfort, from the anguish beginning to overwhelm him as he realized he could not see Jane anywhere, and above all from Clayton's hysterical shouting. He tried instead to focus only on his hands, his two pale, slender writer's hands, which were ill equipped for their present task of clinging desperately to the inspector's one good hand, resisting the inevitable slide.

"You have to travel back to a time before the inevitable happens! Try to remember your dream at the farm, the nightmare that sparked off the journey I witnessed!" Clayton cried, his face turning purple. "Remember . . . and try . . . to do it . . . again!"

Then Wells lifted his birdlike face and looked at the inspector, the tendons of whose neck were stretched to the snapping point and who looked back at him for an eternal moment during which Wells knew he was about to fall, that Clayton was about to let go of him, because what he saw in the inspector's eyes was a farewell and an unspoken apology.

"Do it! Trust me, you can do it! Only you can save us!" he cried out for the last time.

Close by, Wells heard Charles's voice ring out and even glimpsed an arm reaching out to him.

"Give me your hand, Wells!"

But he was too late. The inspector looked at Charles, smiling, and at that very moment Wells felt Clayton's fingers go limp, releasing Wells's hands and letting him plummet into the murky water. And as he flailed in the air, trying desperately to cling to nothing, Wells must have remembered the nightmare he had at the farm. Or perhaps he remembered it later, after he felt the brutal impact of the water and the force of the whirlpool dragging him toward the Thames, or in that no-man's-land between the present and the past called the fourth dimension. He wasn't sure. All these events had happened in such a confused, dizzying, unreal way. But he certainly remembered it, and it was the same recurring nightmare that had tormented him over the past few years, in which he was falling through an endless space, yet without the feeling that he was moving. This sensation had always puzzled him. But not any longer, he told himself, for at last he had understood that his body was moving solely through time. He was falling through time.

Wells shook his head, smiling to himself as he remembered how he had resisted the notion that he could travel through time, despite Clayton's having assured him he had seen Wells vanish for four hours into the time continuum. However, he had no choice now but to accept it: he, H. G. Wells, author of *The Time Machine,* could travel through time thanks to the mechanism Clayton had assured him was lodged in his brain, the same one to which the Envoy had referred, something he must have activated because of all the accumulated tension, as he had done while asleep at the farm. But, whereas that time he had traveled only four paltry hours, now he must have activated it with the force of a colossus, for he had tumbled almost seventy years down the precipice of time.

Still unable to believe it, Wells threw the newspaper back into the bin and, like a bewildered ghost, began traipsing through the unfinished city, trying to assimilate the fact that he was now in the past, more than half a century before the time to which he really belonged. He ambled almost mechanically through the streets of his city, feeling the same fascination Murray's time tourists must have felt when he sent them to the year 2000. Captivated, Wells glanced around him with a strange feeling of incredulity and a certain unease, astonished to find himself in a London he knew only from history books and old newspapers. And his fascination intensified because he knew how the city would change over the years, into something that those now crossing its streets paved with Scottish granite or fired clay, where public transport was limited to a few mule-drawn omnibuses, could scarcely imagine. Wells walked for what seemed like hours, unable to stop, still refusing to accept the situation. He knew that the moment he did, his vague unease would give way to terror, because, much as this familiar yet alien landscape thrilled him, he could not forget he was stranded in the past, where things were very different from in his own time. London was reduced to the City and a few neighborhoods such as Pimlico, Mayfair, Soho, and Bloomsbury, and south of the river, Lambeth and Southwark. There were almost no buildings to the west of Hyde Park or south of Vauxhall Gardens. Chelsea was scarcely more than a village, linked to London by the King's Road, and like a green tide, the countryside reached in as far as Islington, Finsbury Fields, and Whitechapel, right to the foot of the Roman wall. From Knightsbridge to Piccadilly, Wells found signs of a rural London that was still clinging on: everywhere there were farmhouses, orchards, stables, and even mills. Trafalgar Square was no more than an empty lot where the royal carriages were parked.

Tired from walking for so long, Wells sat on a bench and tried once and for all to accept that what he was seeing was not a fake backdrop but the real 1829, where time ended, for on the other side was an abyss. Incredible though it seemed, the tomorrow he had traveled from had yet to happen. And now he was adrift in a time where he did not belong, where none of the people he knew had been born, and from which he had no idea how to return, or whether such a thing was even feasible. He had traveled there because of the tension that seemed to set in motion the strange machinery lodged in his brain. He was not sure he could reproduce this effect through suggestion. But even if he could, what good would it do unless he was able to choose his destination? He would be traveling blindly and might end up even farther back in time, something that horrified him, for the deeper into the past he ventured, the more alien and hostile the world would seem to him. It was best to stay where he was, in 1829, and wait for something, he knew not what, to happen.

But how was he to survive? To whom could he turn for help? He doubted anyone would believe his story, unless they had an extraordinarily open mind; perhaps a fellow writer. He searched his memory, dusting off his literary knowledge of the period. If he remembered correctly, Byron had died some years before, Charles Dodgson—better known as Lewis Carroll—had not yet been born, Coleridge must have been living by then in Dr. Gillman's house, recovering from his opium addiction, and the young, as yet unpublished Dickens had just started working at the offices of an attorney-at-law, where for the time being he was content to let his dreams of becoming a writer bubble in the cauldron of his mind. Yes, the future author of *Oliver Twist* might help him. He heaved a sigh, surprised at how quickly he had accepted that he would have to stay where he was.

Feeling calmer, he began to wonder about his companions' fate. What had become of them? What had become of Jane? He assumed the Martians had captured them. Suddenly he felt as if he had left them in the lurch, as if he had deliberately betrayed them. This thought made him miserable. He ought to be there, seventy years in the future, suffering with them, sharing their fate.

For a while, Wells was content to gaze at the passersby, a rueful smile playing over his lips. They all believed they were fashioning the future with their actions, unaware that the future had already been made, because this puny man shivering on a bench had seen it. As he gazed at the crowd, he recalled with a shudder that the Martians had for a long time been living secretly among them. According to what the Envoy had told them, the Martians had arrived on Earth in the sixteenth century. All that time they had been passing themselves off as humans, watching over the Earth, waiting for the Envoy to arrive and begin the invasion of the blue planet that they had been infiltrating for centuries. Could one of these people be a Martian? It was impossible to know, of course, and so Wells immediately stopped staring at them with the inquisitive expression he had almost instinctively adopted. With a feeling of bitterness he recalled that he was to blame for everything that had happened seventy years later. He wished he had not brought the Envoy back to life with his blood, since the Envoy's fellow Martians would have died one by one, poisoned by Earth's atmosphere. But he had. Or he was going to, given that he was now living in the year 1829. Yes, the Wells who would be born in 1866 would do everything he had done to the letter: he would write everything he had written, suffer in the same way he had suffered, fall in love the same number of times and with the same women, and when the time came, he would donate his blood to the Envoy, dooming the planet for all eternity. But this had yet to happen, which meant it could still be prevented, he thought, excited by the possibility of putting right his mistake. All he needed to do was talk to himself, convince himself not to enter the Chamber of Marvels with Serviss or, failing that, forcibly prevent himself. But this would not happen for another sixty-nine years, and Wells was already thirty-one and doubted he would reach a hundred, however well he looked after himself.

But, if he could not prevent the invasion, then why had he traveled back to this absurd 1829? And why the devil did this date sound so familiar? The answer came to him in a flash. He remembered that the Envoy had arrived on Earth in 1830, and as he himself had explained, his airship had malfunctioned, deflecting him from his mission and causing him to crash in the Antarctic. Wells felt his face draining of blood. Some-how, unconsciously, he had retained this precise date in a dark recess of his mind, and when Clayton had shouted to him that he had to travel back to a time *before the inevitable happened,* his memory had regurgitated it. Was this why he had emerged in this year and not another? Had he somehow managed to direct his journey through time, erring only by a few months? Clayton had suggested this was impossible, but apparently that was exactly what Wells had done: he had chosen his destination, even if he had done so almost involuntarily.

Wells stood up from the bench. If he really had traveled to this time by some means that could not be attributed to mere chance, then it could only be to try to stop the invasion before it happened, before the Envoy was shipped to London in a block of ice and the Wells who would be born in 1866 brought him back to life with a drop of his blood. He could achieve this only by joining the crew of the *Annawan* and kill-ing the Envoy. In the logbooks and cuttings he had been able to glance through during his visit to the Chamber of Marvels, he had read that this was the name of the ship whose charred remains had been discov-ered surrounded by her dead crew on an island in the Antarctic, close to where the Martian's airship and frozen body were found. No one, including Wells, knew what had happened during that tragic expedition, but everything pointed to their having received a visit from the Envoy. So, if he wanted to find him, he obviously had to board the ship that had set sail from New York on October 15, 1829, that is to say, in three weeks' time. Yes, this was the best way he could think of to put right his mistake, and the most feasible, even though it was, of course, the one that most terrified him. For a few moments, Wells toyed with the idea of forgetting this foolish idea and staying in London. He could begin a new life there, a life that, although he sensed it would be filled with misgivings and frustrations, would at least be a secure life, for he knew he would die a natural death long before the invasion began. Though tempted by the idea, he ruled it out before he had time to give it any seri-ous thought, for he knew deep down that if he shirked his responsibility and failed to board that doomed ship, he would feel too guilty to begin a new life. Alternatively, if he joined the *Annawan* and killed the Envoy, he would prevent the invasion and save the planet. His companions had all played their part, and now everything seemed to depend on him playing his. This is what he would do, he told himself. Only he must not delay, for he had just enough time to board a boat bound for America and join the crew of the *Annawan* the moment he arrived.

Staring into space, Wells stroked his whiskers for a few moments, as he had seen the Envoy do. He imagined his face showed an air of melancholy resignation, like heroes forced to sacrifice themselves to save their fellow men. A timid smile of contentment began to play over his face. For he was sure that wherever Jane was, she would be proud of him for embracing his fate with epic humility, and this made him discover within himself, if not the courage he needed, then at least something that helped him laugh in the face of fear. Wells nodded resolutely and strode valiantly toward the docks, ready to do his duty. No, his gift, this thing he carried around in his head, certainly wasn't there to make the tomatoes in his garden grow bigger. It had a different use altogether.

XXXIX

*O*FFERING TO WORK FOR NOTHING DURING THE
crossing, Wells had no trouble being taken on as a crew
member on a ship bound for America with a cargo of timber. The boat
crossed the Atlantic as leisurely as if it were being drawn by a pair of
mules, and Wells, understandably, spent the entire journey in a state of
considerable anxiety, afraid that if he arrived too late all his efforts would
be in vain. Finally the ship dropped him in New York, with only a few
hours to spare before the *Annawan* set sail, and so he was forced to use
all his powers of oratory to convince the captain, a fellow with a fierce
demeanor and a ruthless look in his eye, to let him join his already complete crew: Wells was not very strong but a hard worker, and he would
only take no for an answer if the captain could assure him the provisions
in the hold had been calculated to feed precisely twenty-seven mouths
for four months. If not, one more mouth would make no difference.
And besides, he had the appetite of a bird and if necessary could live off
the rats in the hold. As for the space he might take up, the captain could
see he was a small man who could curl up anywhere. He insisted he had
to sail on this ship and if need be he was prepared to make any number
of sacrifices. The captain appeared to find him amusing, or perhaps he
agreed to take him on simply to teach him a lesson. Perhaps he thought
the younger man would enjoy witnessing the everyday hardships of life
on the high seas, which had chiseled the captain into the brawny sailor
he was and would undoubtedly destroy this puny individual as soon as
he boarded ship. And so, less than an hour later, Wells found himself

surrounded by a group of rough and ready sailors who stank of rum, sweat, and wasted lives.

The time has come to reveal to you, dear reader, that, as a few of you already suspect, Wells did not give his real name when he enlisted on the *Annawan*. Instead, he gave the name of Griffin, the main protagonist of his novel *The Invisible Man*. For that was his mission: to remain invisible. And to do this he had to go unnoticed, avoid contact with the crew, and above all behave like a child in a museum and touch nothing, for fear that the slightest gesture, however trivial, could distort time, could change the natural order of events. And so it was that the *Annawan,* a whaler with a glorious past, whose hull had been reinforced with African oak to prepare her for the South Polar ice, set sail from New York with an extra crew member on board, a sailor who was as scrawny as he was reserved and who gazed at the horizon with a strange unease, as though he already knew what awaited them.

To go unnoticed and to touch nothing were Wells's priorities during the voyage. And he respected them, despite discovering to his astonishment that the author Edgar Allan Poe was also among the rabble on board ship. At that time, Poe was a pale young man who had not yet written *Al Aaraaf.* Apparently, he had joined the *Annawan* as a gunner in order to flee West Point, and while nothing would have pleased Wells more than to spend the tedious crossing conversing quietly with the man who would in time become one of his favorite authors, letting the gunner's every word and gesture enchant him, he limited himself to speaking with him only when necessary, so as to reduce the likelihood of being found out. For if anyone in that coarse crowd could discover that he came from another time, it was undoubtedly Poe, future author of the detective stories based on the deductive powers of Auguste Dupin.

His only distraction during the voyage consisted in drinking rum and forcing himself to laugh at his companions' crude jokes, and later, in contemplating Captain MacReady's strenuous efforts to steer the *Annawan* out of the ice, knowing in advance the ship would become trapped. When the old whaler finally did become icebound, Wells nodded to himself, like a theater director content with his actors' performances. The crew appeared to accept with calm resignation this misfortune that might well lead to their deaths. All they could do now was wait for the ice to thaw without wasting provisions or losing their grip on reality. Given the circumstances, there was little else they could do, even though Reynolds, who was in charge of this peculiar expedition, kept insisting to the captain that they explore the surrounding terrain for the passage to the center of the Earth, which he was convinced was hollow before Verne had even written his famous novel.

But Wells was not expecting any of that, of course. He was only waiting to see what—a week later, just when he was beginning to think nothing would happen—finally fell out of the sky. When it appeared, Wells had the strange sensation that he was the one who had arranged this air show to surprise his fellow crew members. He looked just as bewildered as they did, watching the ship fly through the air, then crash: after all, Wells had never seen it fly. And he realized that from that moment on, everything would happen as it had already happened, above all if he managed to stay sufficiently on the sidelines to safeguard events. The arrival of the airship in this desolate landscape made the crew uneasy, and the author could not help giving an amused grin when a few of them claimed it was a meteorite. The Envoy had arrived with British punctuality for their encounter on this remote, frozen island.

During their trip in search of the airship, he was obliged to invent an extravagant story to explain to Reynolds why he had insisted on enlisting on the *Annawan,* a tale so preposterous and unintelligible he almost thought he deserved to be expelled from the future Society of Authors on grounds of incompetence. Then he was forced to search for the possible pilot in the area around the spaceship, fully aware of what this pilot could do to him.

How alone and ridiculous he felt on board that ill-fated ship, unsure what exactly he had to do to prevent the inevitable from happening! During one of his exhaustive explorations of the ship in search of anything he might use as a weapon against the Envoy, given that he knew from experience that bullets could not harm him, he discovered several crates of dynamite in the powder store. He realized straightaway that this was the only thing on board the *Annawan* capable of finishing off the Envoy. Wells had never handled dynamite before, but he did not think it could be too difficult, though he realized the monster would not stand still while he threw a few bundles of it at him from far enough away so as not to be killed himself. He did not fancy sitting down and waiting calmly for the monster to come for him, as Murray had done seventy years later in the London sewers. Especially as there was no beautiful young woman on board who could embrace him at the crucial moment. This was when Wells's eye fell upon one of an assortment of harpoons in the armory. It occurred to him that if he strapped a few bundles of dynamite to it and hurled it at the Envoy with sufficient force and accuracy, he would have a slim chance of skewering him, and this was better than nothing.

Two days later, while Wells was busy trying to think up a more effective plan than the one involving the dynamite and the harpoon, Dr. Walker was disemboweled by the monster from the stars. He was attacked in the sick bay just as he was preparing to amputate Carson's right leg. This attack confirmed to Wells not only that the Envoy was inside the ship, but also which sailor's appearance he had usurped. Everyone was alarmed, and on the orders of an increasingly anxious Mac-Ready, the crew scoured the ship from top to bottom in search of the hole through which the monster must have slipped aboard: to no avail, of course. They concluded that, like the demon it was, the monster was somehow mysteriously able to enter and leave the ship unnoticed. But Wells did not believe in demons. What is more, he even considered denouncing Carson. In fact, he considered one by one the many possibilities opening up before him, none of which satisfied him. Informing his fellow crew members that Carson was not Carson, but rather a Martian who had taken on Carson's appearance, or killing Carson in cold blood at the first opportunity, perhaps by placing a stick of dynamite in his long johns while he was asleep, and then using the same argument during the trial that would inevitably take place once his crime had been discovered seemed to Wells the surest way to get himself locked up as a madman or a murderer, or both. Clearly he must carry on waiting, staying on the sidelines. The time would come for him to intervene. And so Wells tried to keep calm and watch Carson's every move as discreetly as he could, even as he wondered where the real Carson's body might be. No doubt it was lying somewhere out in the snow. As Wells watched him, he thought it strange that despite their conversation in the sewers of London the Envoy did not recognize him, did not pick him out from the rest of his companions. And he had to remind himself that none of all that had happened yet, however fresh in his memory it was.

The day he was on starboard watch and saw Reynolds running back shouting that Carson was dead, that he had stumbled upon his body close to the airship, Wells knew the climax was approaching. When Reynolds saw that the supposedly deceased Carson was at that very moment on guard duty aboard the ship, Wells observed the two exchange a few words while the dogs barked frenziedly. Wells realized that the Envoy, suspecting he might have been discovered, could put an end to the masquerade and adopt his true appearance. Following the conversation, the explorer had headed for his cabin without even glancing at Wells, leading the author to think that for some strange reason, he had foolishly decided to keep his discovery to himself. At all events, Reynolds's intended strategy mattered little to him. There was every sign that the slaughter was about to commence, for the explorer was playing with a time bomb, which would presently blow up in his face. And that, as you know, is what happened.

Later, after the apocalypse had been unleashed on that remote patch of ice, Wells had been incapable of focusing on anything except avoiding at all costs activating the mysterious mechanism lodged in his brain, which threatened to hurl him once more into the abyss of time to God only knew where. Perhaps it was the almost obsessive attention he applied to this that also helped him avoid being overwhelmed by panic. He was able to press his gun against the proud MacReady's temple, forcing him to do as Reynolds said, and afterward make his way to the armory, navigating the blazing inferno of the ship, as though the devil himself had assured him safe conduct. Once he had tied the sticks of dynamite carefully to the harpoon, he emerged on deck and leapt onto the ice without losing his astonishing composure, not even when he contemplated the final blast that reduced the *Annawan* to a twisted mass of metal surrounded by mutilated bodies and realized that, regardless of whether or not he succeeded in his mission, his slim hopes of returning to civilization had just been blown to smithereens.

Imagine him now, facedown on the ice, hidden among the victims of the explosion, dazed and in pain. The blast had deafened him, and the surrounding landscape now seemed shrouded in a primordial silence, the innate silence in which the world had dwelled before humans polluted it with their manmade noises. Slowly, the flames enveloping the remains of the ship began to die down. Wells remembered that in order to end up frozen in the ice, the Envoy must have survived the explosion, and so he carefully surveyed the debris strewn over the snow, until his eyes rested on a mound that was stirring imperceptibly. It was about thirty yards away from where he was, but even at that distance, the moment the figure rose to its feet, Wells could see that it was no human survivor. Flames were clinging to its strange casing, turning it into a kind of living torch, though it did not appear to be in any pain. Afraid the creature might see him, Wells rested his head on the snow and lay motionless, pretending to be dead, as he watched what the creature was doing. To his relief, the hideous insect begin heading in the opposite direction, where Wells could make out two other figures hurriedly standing up from the ice. It looked like Allan and Reynolds, who just then ran over to the dog cages. Wells smiled to himself. As soon as Reynolds unlocked the cage door, a pack of frenzied dogs hurled themselves at the Envoy, who retracted his armor, exposing his sharp talons, and with one fell stroke sliced through the first of the dogs. As soon as the Envoy had finished slashing through the rest of them, he directed himself toward Allan and Reynolds, who had apparently decided there was no point in delaying the inevitable and had given up trying to flee. Coming to a halt five yards from them, the monster let out a roar of triumph. Wells knew he would never have a better opportunity to try to skewer the Envoy with his harpoon. If he did not act now, the Envoy would end up somehow frozen in the ice by Allan and Reynolds, which would not ultimately prevent the invasion, as he well knew. He had to put the Martian out of action for good, not temporarily. That was why he had traveled through time and space.

Wells leapt resolutely to his feet, firmly grasping the harpoon, and that was when he felt it. He glanced about for a few seconds, slightly dazed, sensing that something was wrong. Everything looked exactly as it had a moment before—the burnt-out ship, the bodies strewn over the snow, the monster about to rip his companions to shreds—and at the same time everything seemed far away. Not the actual distances, which remained the same, but everything else: the pale dawn light was even fainter, the cold was sharper, his clothes were not damp from the snow, and there was no smell of charred wood or corpses, not even of his own sweat. There was a lack of intensity, vividness, color, of whatever it was that made things look alive. It was as if everything had become remote, while remaining exactly where it was. As though he were no longer in that place, but in the memory of that place, in the moment that had already passed. And suddenly, it struck Wells with a painful, unassailable certainty that it was about to happen again, he was about to travel through time. With trembling hands, he hurriedly lit the fuses, praying his body would remain in the present a few moments longer. He did not know how far in advance these symptoms, this subtle fading of reality, announced the actual leap, because he had been unconscious both on the farm and in the sewer basin, but he hoped he at least had enough time to throw the harpoon. He saw the monster's body tense, preparing to attack. Hang on, Wells told himself, don't leap through time, damn it, not yet. Taking a run up, he swung his arm back and launched the harpoon at the figure of the Envoy, convinced he would miss, and that he might even hit Allan or Reynolds. To his astonishment, he saw the harpoon plunge into the creature's back, easily piercing its bony carapace. The Envoy gave a terrible cry and tried hopelessly to pull the harpoon out as it writhed in agony, going through a frenzied series of metamorphoses that revealed to Wells the succession of bodies it had adopted until then. Then, with a muffled blast that sounded as distant to Wells as the mountains on the horizon, the creature was at last blown into a thousand pieces. Unable to get out of the way, Wells was sprayed with green blood and pelted with fragments of flesh and bone, which made him glow faintly as, exhausted, he fell to his knees in the snow. The smoke from the blast dispersed, and he was able to glimpse Reynolds and Allan gazing at him with a mixture of disbelief and gratitude, safe and sound on the ice, though oddly ethereal, as if they had been painted on a sheet lit from behind.

Realizing he had killed the Envoy, Wells finally gave in to that strange sensation. He had killed the Envoy, he told himself, as the accumulated fatigue and tension gave way to an increasing feeling of vertigo. Suddenly he seemed to become weightless, as though he had been torn out of his body and away from the painful weariness overwhelming him, which seemed to be keeping him in one piece. But this sensation was fleeting, and a moment later, Wells felt himself once more in his body, doubled over by his own weight. Suddenly he vomited, spraying a mouthful of bile over the snow. He coughed once, twice, three times, trying to recover from the dizziness. When his vision grew less blurred, he saw he was still kneeling in the snow, which seemed to have regained its proper consistency and was once again making him cold and wet the way snow always did. But when he could not see Allan or Reynolds in front of him, he realized he was in a different time.

XL

*A*ND YET, HOW COULD HE KNOW WHAT YEAR HE was in if he was surrounded by the same endless expanse of snow as before, devoid of any trace of civilization? He could just as well have traveled into the past as into the future, but either way it did not matter very much, he was still facing the same conditions, was just as vulnerable to exposure and exhaustion. When he had recovered from his dizziness, Wells glanced about mournfully and confirmed he was utterly alone: there was no sign of the *Annawan,* the monster, or his companions. And what did that tell him? Not a great deal, in truth. The ship not being there could mean he was in the past, in a year preceding 1830. Alternatively, it could mean he had traveled sufficiently far into the future for the remains of the *Annawan* to have disintegrated. Whatever the truth, he was alone in the middle of a patch of ice in the Antarctic, exposed to the harsh elements, without food or equipment, and with no hope of survival. This thought caused him to panic, and for a few moments Wells vented his rage, shouting into the silence. He could not have found a better place: shouting there was like not shouting at all. After a while, slightly calmer, gently cradled by his exhaustion, Wells finally felt ready to accept calmly that he would die there, either from hunger or exposure. In both cases it would be a horrible death. His only consolation was that he had killed the Envoy, though there was no way of knowing whether or not he had also prevented the invasion. He wanted to believe he had, and that the Envoy's brothers would one day become extinct, slowly poisoned by the Earth's atmosphere. Yes, he wanted to die believing he had restored peace to his time.

He began walking for no reason, simply because the cold was much more bearable if he kept moving. He drifted aimlessly, indifferent to where he was going, doubting if he could find his bearings or that there was any point in trying, immersed in the depressing gloom of the landscape, each step heavy with despair. Nothing Wells had ever experienced in life had terrified him more than the situation in which he found himself at that moment. For what awaited him was a slow, agonizing, lonely death, probably plagued with hallucinations and delirium, and no one deserved to die like that, forgotten by the world, forgotten by friends. He would die without dignity, alone, as though his death were a depressing ceremony no mourner wanted to attend. He would be the only witness to his own death. He would not even know when he was dying, what date would be carved on his imaginary headstone.

Then a snowstorm rose, violently whipping at him. Within a few seconds, Wells could scarcely see anything around him. The act of breathing felt like razors ripping through his throat on their way to his lungs. Snow began to settle on his clothes, weighing him down, slowing his unsteady gait, until his exhaustion, and in particular the futility of it all, made him sink once more to his knees. The cold was becoming more and more unbearable, and he knew he was going to die of exposure, to experience in his own body the terrible process of freezing to death. According to what he knew from his studies, tiny crystals would first form in his fingers and toes, where the blood would have difficulty circulating due to the narrowing of his blood vessels, causing unspeakable pain in his limbs, which would gradually stop obeying the commands of his brain. Next would come the arrhythmias, then his entire body would become insensible, to the point where he would urinate and defecate uncontrollably, after which he would suffer successive respiratory arrests that would bring him close to asphyxiation. His epiglottis and larynx would become paralyzed, and finally, after several hours submerged in a cruel numbness, he would lose consciousness and die without even real-izing it.

Horrified by this thought, Wells curled up in the snow, cursing, weeping, laughing, wishing he had never read about what he was now going to experience in his own body. Time went by out of inertia, or perhaps it did not go by at all, for there was nothing to measure its pass-ing, and the cold became so intense that it transcended its own meaning, becoming something else, until Wells no longer knew where the cold ended and he began, because everything was as one. He was the cold, and try as he might, he could not feel the limits of his own body, he could not discover the frontier of flesh that defined him. His numbness was such that he feared he might already have died at some point, with-out his body having told him.

Yet he was able to have thoughts: he could evoke Jane's smile, and so he must still be alive, though it would not be long before he slowly began to die out like a fire that cannot be rekindled. At that moment, he was seized by panic, and somewhere in his mind, which also felt fro-zen, he became aware of a familiar sensation, a sensation of dizziness that rapidly spread through his head. All of a sudden, the cold that was tormenting him vanished, because all of him vanished. Wells experi-enced an immense and wonderful feeling of relief, but a moment later, he found himself locked inside himself once more, trapped in the frozen sarcophagus that was his body. Something warm, his semithawed soul perhaps, crept up his throat, and he vomited onto the snow. But the diz-ziness did not stop. On the contrary, Wells could feel it becoming more intense, and again he felt as though he were being torn from himself, floating through the air, released from all suffering only for the pain and cold to return a moment later.

Nauseated, Wells vomited onto the snow, two, three, countless times, while part of his brain realized he was traveling back and forth in time, racing blindly through the years, perhaps through the centuries, scatter-ing his errant footsteps throughout eternity. His body yearned to escape death, that terrible, interminable numbness overwhelming him, threatening to freeze his guts. But what was the use of fleeing in time if he was trapped in space, always greeted by the same hostile landscape, this icy vastness intent on becoming his last resting place, at times plunged into darkness, at times barely illuminated by a weak sun shining in the sky like a bead of mercury. He could not escape from a place that seemed older than time itself. After a while, faint from the exertion, Wells noticed that his nausea had finally subsided. A soft light was making the snow sparkle, and the cold was not so biting. The temperature must have been three or four degrees, Wells estimated, and, exhausted as he was, he managed a weak smile of gratitude. For a while, he lay sprawled on the ground, expecting another leap through time, but nothing happened. On the brink of unconsciousness, he wondered whether the strange mechanism in his brain had been driven so hard it had burned out. Just like the *Annawan* in the ice, his body had finally become trapped in some unknown year, about which all he knew was that it would be the year of his death.

Then he saw the face of God.

It was a sallow face, with high cheekbones and almond eyes that radiated an intelligent simplicity. For a moment, they gazed at him fixedly, as though attempting to recognize in him a stray sheep, and, perhaps because he had atoned for his mistake and saved the planet, God decided he should live. He picked him up with his diminutive hands and stretched him out on a sleigh. Wells was conscious of something being laid on top of him, keeping him warm, and then he heard a sharp hissing noise, a kind of crackle, which a few moments later he realized must be the sound of the sledge gliding over the snow. God was taking him somewhere, and after a while, whether days, hours, or centuries he did not know, he heard voices, a swarm of words in varying tones the meaning of which he could not grasp. He felt hands examining him and undressing him, until finally the world stopped spinning and he came to a halt in a warm sense of well-being. And although, immersed in a fog of unconsciousness, Wells had no clear understanding of what was going on, he noticed that the cold had vanished. He was no longer caught in its terrible maw, and gradually he was able to perceive the forgotten contours of his body: he could feel his toes touching what he thought was a blanket, his back lying on something pleasantly silky, his head cushioned in a cocoon of softness. He was once more firmly defined in the world.

One day, he did not know how long afterward, he awoke in a bunk in a warm, cozy cabin. He was at what appeared to be a whaling station, alive and seemingly in one piece, although his right hand was bandaged. He was unable to tell what year he was in from the furniture or from the clothing worn by those drifting in and out of his cabin, and so, to everyone's surprise, he announced his emergence from unconsciousness by asking what year it was. He was told it was the year of our Lord 1865. Wells nodded and smiled weakly. He had not fled far. It was possible he had taken bigger leaps while he was dying on the ice, but he had no way of knowing. Now he found himself thirty-five years ahead in time from the day he had harpooned the Envoy's monstrous body and scarcely a year before the moment when, in a humble, bug-infested dwelling in Bromley, a man identical to him in every respect would be born.

When, a few days later, the surgeon at the whaling station removed his bandage, he discovered they had amputated his thumb and forefinger, but this seemed a small price to pay for being alive. He lay for at least a week longer in that rustic but comfortable-enough bunk, regaining his strength, silently savoring his remarkable victory over the Envoy, reliving every detail of the infernal expedition up to the final dramatic moments when he was convinced he would fail and everything would be in vain, that he would never be able to accomplish the heroic feat.

During this time he also remembered reading somewhere, perhaps in one of the many articles about the Baltimore author, that Edgar Allan Poe and the explorer Jeremiah Reynolds were the sole survivors of an extraordinary expedition that had culminated in a mutiny, which until then Wells had never thought to connect with the voyage of the *Annawan*. Clearly the two men had thought they managed to trap the Envoy permanently in the ice (perhaps by fleeing, after a sudden brainwave, to the stern of the ship where the ice was thinner?) and had somehow managed to return to civilization, where they had decided to lie about what had happened to them at the South Pole. However, now that Wells had seen with his own eyes what really happened, he did not blame them for having lied to the world. Would they have been taken for anything but madmen otherwise? Yes, it had been better to invent a mutiny and pray the matter would be forgotten, and that they could carry on their lives where they had left off. Wells did not remember what had become of Reynolds, but Poe had become one of the world's greatest writers. Wells himself considered Poe one of his favorite authors and had assiduously read all of his works, including *The Narrative of Arthur Gordon Pym of Nantucket,* that unwholesome tale permeated with a profound horror, the origin of which Wells had now discovered.

Once he had recovered, Wells set sail for New York and then London, a serene smile on his lips. He would be able to start a new life now, free from guilt. He had earned it. And although he could have settled anywhere in America, he had chosen to go home. He wanted to see London again, to make sure that everything was as it should be, in its proper place. But more than anything, he had to admit, he needed to be close to the Wells who would be born a year later, to see him live from afar, perhaps watch over him. Yes, he wanted to see what the life he could no longer live would be like, for he had to forge another life now, and his missing right thumb and forefinger, which he had once used to hold a pen, intimated to him that he must resign himself to an ordinary life. To being, simply, one among many.

XLI

H. G. WELLS ARRIVED IN LONDON A YEAR BE-
fore he was born.

During the long voyage, contemplating the vast, shimmering ocean
from the ship's deck, Wells had had more than enough time to make
plans: he would start a new life under the name Griffin; he might even
let his hair and beard grow so that no one could recognize him—though
there might be no need for that, for by the time the real Wells (why
could he not help referring to him as the genuine one?) reached his age,
he would be a venerable old man whose wrinkled face would be disguise
enough. There were other, more important considerations, he told himself. Where would he settle in order to begin this new life, for example?
After weighing up the various options, he decided on Weybridge, partly
because it was one of the towns around London that had most suffered
during the Martian invasion, but also because it was the same distance
from the capital as it was from Woking and Worcester Park, where the
other Wells would settle. Because he was clear about one thing: he had
no choice but to start a new life, even though it would be little more than
a mere existence, because he would never consider it his own life. His
true life, with its satisfactions and miseries, would be lived by the other
Wells, and only by remaining as close to him as possible, by becoming a
witness to the most significant events in the life of his double—those he
had already experienced and those he would never experience—could
he manage to endure life. He applied himself to this as best he could:
he settled in Weybridge, took employment at a chemist, and let each day

run uneventfully into the next, like a stream into which he had no interest in casting his line.

From time to time, he would take a carriage to witness parts of his real life: he saw himself as an infant in Bromley, where his parents owned a small china shop. He saw himself slip from the innkeeper's son's hands and break his leg as he fell onto one of the beer tent stakes, and then, in his convalescence, reading *The Narrative of Arthur Gordon Pym of Nantucket,* by Edgar Allan Poe. He saw himself dazzling Mr. Morley, who ran a college in Bromley, with his lively intelligence; wilting in the heat inside the Rodgers and Denyer draper's shop in Windsor, where his mother had sent him to work; and excelling at Midhurst Grammar School, from where, aged only fifteen, he was sent as an apprentice to Mr. Edwin Hyde's Southsea Drapery Emporium.

Wells observed all this from a safe distance, torn between compassion and nostalgia, taking great care not to alter the chain of events, letting his double do exactly what he had done, to the letter. But when the time came for his double to begin an apprenticeship at the Southsea Drapery Emporium, Wells decided this was the moment for him to show himself, because there was one thing in his life he had long wanted to alter. He had given the matter a great deal of thought, studying every possible ramification his intervention might entail, before concluding that it was probably not significant enough to cause any major change. And so Wells traveled to Southsea, where, planted opposite the drapery shop in which his twin was languishing, he allowed his memories to come flooding back. He remembered his unhappiness and bewilderment at his mother's insistence on keeping him out of school and university and forcing him to learn the accursed trade of draper, which he was supposed to exercise until the end of his days, as if it were the most commendable job in the world. Unless he ventured inside, or peeped through the shop window, Wells could not see himself, but he imagined his double smoothing out the fabric after showing it to the customers, folding and unfolding lace curtains, realizing how hard it was to roll up a bolt of linen, or dragging mannequins back and forth in accordance with

Mr. Hyde's enigmatic intentions, and doing all this with a book sticking out of his overall pocket, which would soon earn him a reputation as a daydreamer and an idler.

Wells was immersed in these memories one evening when he saw himself emerge from the building, exactly at the hour he remembered, and trudge wearily toward Southsea Pier, a downcast expression on his face. Quietly he followed the boy until he saw him pause before the murky waters, where he used to remain for almost an hour, toying with the idea of suicide, thinking that if this was what his life was going to be, then he preferred no life at all. He felt compassion for this pale, skinny lad whom life had cheated. In fact, if he remembered correctly, he had never considered suicide a very honorable solution, but the cold embrace of the sea, compared to the barren existence that awaited him, did not seem like such a dreadful alternative. Wells shook his head at the boy's suffering, which had been his own. He knew that happily, things would look up for him in a matter of months, when he at last resolved to rebel against his mother and wrote to Horace Byatt asking for help, where-upon Byatt offered him a job as assistant teacher at Midhurst Grammar School on a salary of twenty pounds a year. However, the tormented boy staring into the sea was as yet unaware he would succeed in escaping this tedious life as a draper's apprentice and construct a pleasant life as a writer. Wells strolled over to himself on the pier, preparing to burst in on his own adolescence in order to speak with himself. He hoped the fifty years that had left his face furrowed with wrinkles would prevent the youth from recognizing him, but above all he hoped his calculated in-trusion in the flow of events would not provoke a landslide bigger than the one he intended.

"Suicide is always a possibility," he said in a soft voice, catching his double's attention, "and so it's advisable to exhaust all others first."

The boy wheeled round, startled, and gazed at Wells suspiciously. And for the few moments his scrutiny lasted, Wells was also able to study himself. So this was what he had looked like aged fifteen, he reflected, astonished by the boy's eyes that had seen so little, his lips still devoid of their characteristic ironic grimace, his exaggeratedly tragic mannerisms. He found his earlier self painfully fragile and vulnerable, however much the boy, possessed of youth's absurd bravado, considered himself somehow invincible.

"I'm not thinking of—" Wells heard the boy start to say, only to break off abruptly and add, in a tone of puzzled defiance: "How did you know?"

Wells smiled at him as amiably as he could, hoping this friendly gesture would favor an easy exchange between them.

"Oh, it's not so hard to figure out," Wells replied with relaxed joviality, "above all for someone who as a youth entertained the same thoughts when gazing into these waters, with the same anguish you feel now." He shook his head vigorously, showing how painful it was for him to look back on that now. "But first you have to fight, to try other ways. If your life displeases you, my lad, try to change it. Don't give in to defeat so easily. Death is the only sure defeat. It is the end of everything."

For a few moments, the boy contemplated him in silence, still with some mistrust. What did this stranger want? Why had he come up to him and spoken to him like this?

"Thanks for the advice, whoever you are," he responded coldly.

"Oh, I'm nobody." Wells shrugged, pretending to be distracted by the gentle ripple of the waves. "Just a stranger who has watched you come here too often. You are an apprentice at Mr. Hyde's draper's shop, aren't you?"

"Yes," the boy replied, visibly uncomfortable to learn that this stranger whose intentions he could not fathom was spying on him.

"And doubtless you think you deserve more in life than to be a simple draper's apprentice," Wells went on, trying to sound as friendly as possible. "You shouldn't feel guilty about it. I had the same thoughts at your age, my lad. I was forced into an equally thankless job that neither satisfied nor fulfilled me. I dreamed of being a writer, you know."

The boy observed him with a flash of interest, though Wells knew at that age he had still not decided to be an author. He loved reading, yes, but he was still unaware of his talent for emulating his favorite authors. Not until he entered the Royal College of Science in London, where Professor Huxley taught, would he begin to draft his first stories, in that clumsy, graceless handwriting he would later improve when he went to teach at the Holt Academy in Wrexham. For the moment, the months he had spent at Midhurst, watching Horace Byatt deliver his classes, had aroused in the young Wells a vague fascination for the role of teacher, a vocation incomparably more beneficial to society than that of writer.

"And did you succeed?" the boy asked abruptly, rousing Wells from his momentary reverie.

"What?"

"In being a writer?"

Wells looked at him silently in the growing darkness, pondering his reply.

"No, I'm a simple chemist," he lamented. "I lead a very ordinary life. This is why I allowed myself to offer you some advice, my lad, because I know there's nothing worse than leading a life you don't like. If you think you have something to give to the world, fight for it tooth and nail. Otherwise you'll end up a sad, embittered chemist who never stops daydreaming, inventing stories he'll never write."

"That's too bad," the boy said, without bothering to appear sympathetic. A few minutes passed, and then he added, rather diffidently: "Why didn't you take your own life, then, if you don't mind me asking?"

The question startled Wells, though it should not have, for it was simply an early example of his own pragmatism.

"Oh, well . . . ," he extemporized, "books are what keep me going."

"Books?"

"Yes, reading is my only pleasure, and there are so many books left to read. For that reason alone it is worth going on living. Books make me happy, they help me escape from reality." Wells contemplated the sea in silence, smiling slightly. "Writers perform an extremely important role:

they make others dream, those who are unable to dream for themselves. And everyone needs to dream. Could there be a more important job in life than that?"

With these words, Wells fell silent, vaguely ashamed of the defensive tone in which he had spoken, which, moreover, did not seem to have overly impressed the boy. Wells deduced from the faint grimace of disdain on his lips that he could think of countless things more important for society than books, though he hadn't the strength or the inclination to challenge Wells. Perhaps he did not care what this stranger thought and limited himself to feeling secretly sorry for Wells. The boy picked up a small stone and tossed it into the sea, as though hinting to Wells that as far as he was concerned the conversation was over. At this point the author noticed that the boy had a small bandage on the side of his chin, which until then he had not been able to see properly.

"What happened?" he said, signaling the boy's chin.

"Oh, I tripped on the stairs this morning carrying some bolts of chintz. Sometimes I try to take more than I should so I can finish quickly, but I went too far this time," the boy replied, somewhat absent-mindedly. "I'm afraid it'll leave an ugly scar."

Wells remained silent for a few seconds, scouring his memory in vain for this accident. At any rate, the boy would clearly have no scar, for the simple reason that he himself did not have one beneath his bushy beard.

"I wouldn't worry about it, my lad," he said reassuringly. "I'm sure it looks worse than it is."

The boy gave a cold smile, as though deep down he did not care, and Wells decided it was time to steer the conversation toward the real reason why he wanted to speak to his earlier self.

"Do you want to know the last story I made up?" he said in a casual voice.

The boy gave a contemptuous shrug, as though this was of little interest to him either, and Wells had to make a supreme effort to stifle his irritation. He tried to appear nonchalant as he gestured toward the now starry night above their heads and said, "You see that sky, my lad? Have you ever thought there might be life on some of the millions of planets that make up our universe?"

The boy hesitated. "No . . . Yes . . . I don't know . . ."

"I have. On our neighboring planet Mars, to go no farther. Did you know that the Italian astronomer Schiaparelli discovered a complex system of canals on the surface of Mars that can only have been built artificially?"

Wells knew the boy knew, and so he was not surprised when he nodded, vaguely intrigued.

"Good. Now imagine there are such things as Martians, whose scientific knowledge is far greater than our own. Imagine, too, that their planet is dying, because in the course of their long existence, the Martians have exhausted all its resources. They are faced with a dilemma: they must move to another planet or become extinct. Earth is the planet with the conditions that are most favorable to them, and so they decide to invade it."

"How terrifying," the boy said, with genuine interest. "Go on."

"Imagine the Martians arrive on Earth," Wells went on, seeing the boy's expectant face, "crossing the forty million miles of unimaginable space that separates them from us, in cylinders fired from their planet by a powerful cannon, and once here, they begin to build fighting machines that could raze our cities to the ground. With machines like that, the Martians could conquer us in a matter of weeks, even days."

"I'd like to read that story," the boy declared with a mixture of fear and excitement.

"Then I'll give you the idea as a present," Wells said jovially. "You can write it whenever you feel like it. That way I'll be able to read it, too."

The boy shook his head and smiled uneasily.

"I'm afraid I don't like writing," he avowed.

"Perhaps you'll learn to in time," Wells said. "And who knows, maybe you're destined to become an author, lad. What's your name?"

"Herbert George Wells," the boy replied. "It's a long name for an author."

"You can always shorten it," Wells said affably, proffering his hand. "It's been a pleasure meeting you, George."

"Likewise," the boy said, returning the gesture.

And beside the dark waters on the front at Southsea, a man shook hands with himself, without the universe blowing up or seeming to register the anomaly in any other way. After Wells had said good-bye to himself with a nod, he headed toward the other end of the pier, still feeling the warmth of his own hand in his. He had only walked a few paces when he turned once more to the boy.

"Incidentally, one last thing," he said with a smile, pretending that what he had most wanted to say to the boy had slipped his mind. "If one day you write that story, don't have the Martians triumph, no matter how much you want to criticize British colonialism."

"But I'm not going to . . . ," his double started to protest.

"Please write an ending where the Martians are defeated. Don't take away your readers' hope."

The boy gave a skeptical chuckle.

"All right, I promise. But . . ." He paused. "What could defeat those powerful Martian machines?"

Wells shrugged.

"I haven't the faintest idea, but I'm sure you'll think of something. You have plenty of time left before you write it."

The boy nodded, amused by the stranger's request. Wells doffed his hat and left the way he had come, but that did not prevent him from also staying where he was, surrounded by the black murmuring water under the pier, an ironic smile appearing on his lips for the first time.

XLII

*I*T WOULD BE SOME YEARS BEFORE THAT BOY, whom stubborn Fate had made a writer, published his book *The War of the Worlds.* When at last he held a copy of the book in his hands, Wells contemplated the pages he knew so well with the same melancholy he had contemplated each day of his new life, for during those years, he had watched the boy on the pier happily leave the draper's shop in Southsea to work as Byatt's assistant, gain a scholarship to the Royal College of Science in London, marry his cousin Isabel knowing he would soon divorce her to go and live with Jane at Mornington Place, cough up blood on the steps at Charing Cross Station, publish *The Time Machine,* curse in front of Murray's Time Travel, and move to a house with a garden in Woking. And all this had happened exactly as it was supposed to, without Wells having perceived the slightest change in events. Now, with the novel in front of him, he would at last find out whether the precarious conversation he had held with himself on the pier at Southsea had been of any use.

The real Wells's novel was almost identical to the one he had written, but he was relieved to discover that it differed in two respects: the Martians did not attack the planet with airships shaped like stingrays, but with tripods that looked like sinister insects, which would shock the reader more because it brought the terror closer. Indeed, these pages even made him relive the fear he had felt as he fled the real tripods. However, the replacement of airships with tripods was an insignificant detail. The main reason why Wells had risked talking to his fifteen-year-old self was to convince him to change the ending, and he was pleased to see the boy had kept his promise. In his version the Martians had conquered the planet and taken the few remaining survivors as slaves; in his temporal twin's novel, they were defeated mere days after the invasion, though not by Man.

What defeated the powerful Martians were the humblest things God in His infinite wisdom had placed on the Earth: bacteria. When all of men's weapons had failed, these microscopic creatures, which had taken their toll on humanity from the beginning of time, invaded the Martians' bodies, invisibly, tenaciously, and lethally, as soon as they landed on our planet. Given the absence of microbes on Mars, the Martian organism was defenseless against them. It could be said that the Martians were doomed before they even set foot in our world. Wells was pleasantly surprised and had to admit that the boy on the pier had successfully risen to the challenge, inventing a rather original and unexpected way of defeating the Martians, in defiance of their powerful fighting machines. He had no doubt that readers of this novel, in contrast to his own, would finish it with a hopeful smile playing on their lips. Just as Serviss had wished.

AND SO, TWO MONTHS later, when his twin met Serviss for lunch at the Crown and Anchor, Wells was pleased to see that the steely glint of reproach in the American journalist's eyes had vanished. In the world Wells inhabited now, which was not his own, although it looked suspiciously similar, *The War of the Worlds* related an unforeseen and terrible Martian invasion, but one from which humanity was rescued at the last moment by the hand of God, which was as invisible as the microbes He had sprinkled over the planet. It was a much more relevant and subtle criticism of the excesses of British colonialism, Wells had to admit, even though the ray of hope his twin had added at the end had not prevented Serviss from writing *Edison Conquers Mars,* intended as a sequel to *The War of the Worlds.* In it, the insufferable Edison led an expedition to Mars in search of revenge. Wells had originally gone to the tavern with the aim of upbraiding Serviss for this audacity, as well as to demolish his work in no uncertain terms and even to tell him his true opinion of that scoundrel Edison. And hidden behind his beard, long hair, and wrinkles, Wells had watched the meeting between the two authors from his corner table. A meeting his twin had imagined would be like two stones knocking together and making sparks fly, but which turned out quite differently. By the time lunch was finished, the endless succession of beer tankards had worked its magic, and the two looked for all the world like a couple of old friends. Wells went after them as they staggered merrily out of the tavern. But once they were in the street, instead of taking a carriage straight to the museum, as Wells remembered, the two men bid each other a fond farewell and went their separate ways. From the doorway of the tavern, Wells smiled and felt an immense wave of relief. All these years he had been wondering whether he had changed the future, and now, at last, he knew that he had: the two men had not gone to the museum because the Envoy was not there. He had blown him to pieces on the remote icecaps of the Antarctic; he had obliterated him. It was possible his airship was still languishing among the hundreds of objects crammed inside the Chamber of Marvels, but clearly Serviss did not consider it as important as the Martian, which had brought so many consequences in its wake. Good, Wells said to himself, as he walked breezily toward the nearest station to catch a train to Weybridge. From now on, everything that happened to his twin would also be a surprise to him.

On the train, the author wondered whether, by killing the Envoy, he had also saved his companions. He knew his action had rescued Jane from that reality, for he had occasionally followed her through the streets of London when she visited her favorite stores, or rode her bicycle in the environs of Worcester Park, and when he saw her go home and fall into the arms of his twin, he could not help feeling a strange mixture of jealousy and contentment. Wells had saved Jane's life so that his other self could enjoy her, and more than once he had to remind himself that he, too, was this other Wells, and therefore he ought to be as happy that he loved her the way he did as he would doubtless be sad if, over time, he ceased to love her, which could still happen, regardless of his having risked his life to be able to spend the rest of his days with her.

He realized in time that he had also saved Charles, whom he liked to chance upon in theater foyers, simply to watch the elegant young man flash his dazzling smile and perfect teeth at his acquaintances, and even to walk by and overhear one of his droll comments on the state of the nation or other current affairs, as if by doing so Wells was trying to erase his last memory of Charles, filthy and bedraggled, fleeing through the London sewers, pursued by hideous monsters. He had saved Murray and Emma as well, along with Captain Shackleton and his beloved Claire, and Inspector Clayton, and the coachman whose name escaped him. Yes, wherever they were, happy or not, they could go on with their lives without having to suffer a Martian invasion.

But what of all the others, and their respective twins in the other reality; had he saved them, too? he wondered. Had that world disappeared, had it been erased when he destroyed the Envoy in the Antarctic, or had his action simply created a split, another branch on the leafy tree of time? Were his companions suffering the consequences of the Martian invasion in some other layer of the universe? Had the extraterrestrials captured them? Naturally, Wells liked to think they had not. He liked to think that his killing the Envoy had also made that branch of time wither to nothing. That if he pressed his ear to the walls of the universe he would not hear the cries of pain of those who had remained trapped in the adjacent Hell. In short, that none of it had ever happened.

But there was something that prevented this theory from being watertight: his memories, the memories of the invasion stored in his head. How could he remember something that had never happened? Wells had always fantasized about the possible existence of what he had called parallel universes, worlds that sprang from each choice Man took, however insignificant. If I decide to eat at home today nothing will happen, but if I have lunch at Coleridge's Tavern, I will get food poisoning from eating something that is off, and this trivial decision will cause my life to split into at least two different realities, which will exist simultaneously, parallel to each other, even though I will only experience one of them. But now Wells had no doubt that parallel worlds existed: if he had not destroyed the Envoy, the Martians would have invaded the planet, but by killing the Envoy he had prevented this from ever happening. Yet did this really mean that the other reality had ceased to exist? Was it not supremely arrogant to assume that because we could not see something, it simply did not exist? The world where the invasion had taken place had certainly existed. Wells had more than enough proof of this, so it was logical to assume that it continued to exist somewhere. Consequently, try as he might to feel reassured by reminding himself that he had saved his companions through his heroism, deep down, he knew this was only one way of looking at it, a viewpoint that was as biased as it was vindicatory. For those who had remained in the sewers after his disappearance, he had simply evaporated mysteriously, or had perhaps drowned in the basin and been washed out into the Thames. None of them would have known about his heroic deed, because it would not have affected them at all.

This appeared to be the sad truth, and Wells had to learn to live with it. He tried to console himself with the thought that at least he had managed to create a world in which the invasion would never happen. He closed his eyes, and, as was his custom since traveling in time, he abandoned himself once more to going over his store of memories about the invasion. He recalled with a fond smile how his opinion of Murray had gradually changed during the invasion, his hatred slowly turning into something he could only describe as respect. And it suddenly dawned on him that in a couple of days' time, the other Wells would find a letter from Murray in his mailbox. He would open it with trembling fingers, just as in the past he had opened Murray's invitations to travel to the future, trying to deduce the reason for this missive. But he could never have guessed it was a declaration of love, as Wells already knew. Yet he also knew that this perplexing discovery would make no difference to his twin, who would continue to be outraged by Murray's brazen request for his assistance in re-creating the Martian invasion described in his novel. He would read Murray's letter several times with astonishment and disbelief but would never reply to it. He would simply slip it between the pages of his novel and forget all about it. He detested Murray too much to help him in any way, no matter how in love he claimed to be. But Wells no longer detested Murray. No, after what they had been through together, he bore him no grudge. Love had changed Murray, ridding him of his selfishness, transforming him into someone who was prepared to give his life to save his companions. When he said goodbye to him in the sewers of London, Wells had apologized for not replying to his letter. *If I received it now, I assure you I would,* he had told him.

This was exactly what was going to happen two days later: the younger Wells was going to receive it again. And so, arriving home, Wells laid a piece of paper out on his desk, placed his pen on top of it, and contemplated the fateful arrangement as he pondered his reply. Clearly he had no means to help Murray re-create a Martian invasion, and besides he did not deem it necessary. He remembered how, as they fled the Martians, Miss Harlow had begun to feel a mounting affection for Murray, and in particular he remembered her laughter, her spontaneous laughter when Murray was trying to milk a cow at the farm where they had stopped off on their way to London. This, quite simply, was what Murray needed to do. Wells leaned over the piece of paper, and with the crooked, rather childish writing he had developed after years of practicing with his left hand, so different from his previous spidery, hurried script with its rippling plateaus and sudden peaks, he began filling the page with his scrawl. Of all the pages he had written in either of his two lives, this was the one that would give him the greatest satisfaction:

My dear Gilliam,

Strange as it might seem, learning that you have fallen in love fills me with joy. And yet, I can do little to help you, except to suggest that, rather than endeavoring to re-create the Martian invasion, you make her laugh. For if you succeed in making this girl laugh, if you make her laughter ring in the air like a fountain of silver coins cascading to the floor, you will win her heart forever.

Fond regards from your friend,

George.

He placed the letter in an envelope and, three days later, posted it to Murray's Time Travel. Back at his house, Wells could not help smiling as he imagined the look of astonishment on Murray's face when he read it. He knew Murray would be confused by the friendly tone of his missive, and by Wells signing off so warmly, but he had not wanted to deny himself this pleasure. It might even teach Murray that while finding true love was one of the most wonderful things that could happen to you in life, finding a friend was equally splendid.

XLIII

$\mathcal{O}$N AUGUST 1, 1898, THE DAY THE MARTIANS AR-
rived, H. G. Wells went to Horsell Common very early in
the morning to see the cylinder that had supposedly fallen from the sky
the night before. The carriage dropped him in front of a gaggle of vehicles clogging the entrance to the common, and after paying the driver,
Wells sauntered across the grass toward the crowd of onlookers in the
distance, who were obscuring the strange object. On his first trip there,
Wells had not been calm enough to observe things as closely as he would
have liked, owing to the presence of Inspector Clayton. But this time
he intended to savor every last detail of this scene, which he had already
portrayed in his novel. With the contented smile of someone taking a
carefree stroll, Wells made his way through the scores of people crowd-
ing onto the common, most of whom hailed from Woking and Chertsey, amused by some of the sensational newspaper headlines being cried
out. He even cooled himself in the morning heat by taking a ginger beer
at one of the many stalls dotted along the path, before approaching the
cylinder.

When he at last reached the site where the cylinder had supposedly crashed, making an enormous crater in the sand, he could see that
Murray had done an excellent job of re-creating the cylinder. The author stood for a long time, admiring the enormous ash-covered object,
at which a few children were timidly throwing stones. Now it only remained to be seen what was inside, for if Murray had finally decided to
drag the piece of junk all the way there, thus accepting Emma's challenge,

it was because he was intending to surprise her in some way. Would he forget about the Martian and try to make her laugh as Wells had suggested in his letter? He did not know, but whatever emerged from the cylinder, Wells did not want to miss it.

Although it was unlikely they would have recognized the old man he had become with the passing of the years, Wells remained at a distance from the throng, close to where some of the more timorous onlookers had retreated, and from there he gazed contentedly around him. He caught sight of his thirty-one-year-old self, standing at the front of the crowd next to Inspector Clayton. Just then, the inspector pointed with his metal hand at the cylinder, and Wells's twin, dressed in a garish plaid suit, shook his head with an air of skepticism.

A dozen yards to the right of them, he saw Emma, protected from the throng by the cocoon of her extraordinary beauty. The young American woman, who, unlike the first time he had seen her, was no stranger to Wells, was shielding herself from the sun with her parasol, solemnly watching the cylinder, forcing herself to hide how annoyed she was that Murray had accepted her challenge and organized all this simply to win her heart. The only person Wells could not see anywhere was Murray. He assumed he must be directing proceedings from somewhere, probably from behind the trees in the distance, waiting to make his entry.

But although everything seemed just as he remembered it, Wells felt a nervous flutter in his stomach. Suddenly, he had the unpleasant impression that something was not right, something was out of place, though he could not discern what it was. He surveyed the scene once more, in close detail this time, trying to discover what was amiss. A crowd had formed around the cylinder, Emma was watching from a distance, nervously twirling her parasol, Inspector Clayton was making his way through the onlookers to speak to the policeman in charge, exactly as Wells remembered he had the first time, and his twin remained dutifully in his place, grinning sardonically at the Martian cylinder, his plaid suit vibrant in the morning sun. Hold on! Wells said to himself, with a sudden pang of fear. That was it! It was the suit that was out of place.

The plaid suit his twin was wearing! With a shudder, Wells remembered seeing it in the window of the clothier's where he usually shopped, and how, after reflecting at length whether this daring pattern would look elegant or ridiculous, he had decided to play it safe and purchase a dark brown suit similar to the ones he usually wore, which would not upset the harmony that reigned inside his wardrobe. He had sported his new purchase for the first time that very day, but his twin had bought the plaid suit, proving he was more daring than his original self and had had the effrontery to turn up in this garb to see the Martian.

Wells gazed at him, puzzling over this small act of rebellion by his double, who had improvised instead of keeping strictly to the script. He wondered how this was possible without the universe exploding into a thousand pieces, or at least suffering some kind of ripple effect, similar to that caused by a stone hitting water. Then the author remembered the scar on his twin's chin, another anomaly, which to begin with he had considered unimportant. And these small differences, whilst changing nothing fundamental, disturbed Wells, for they showed that this was not his world. It was incredibly akin to his world, but certain details in it were different. He had already discovered two of these, but there were undoubtedly many more. All these years that he had been spying on himself, he had been so focused on the main events that he had paid scant attention to the details, which, like the scar on his chin, and now the garish plaid suit, had been whispering to him that this was not his universe.

But how could he not be in his world? He had traveled back in time to 1829, where he had made a change that had altered the future, and then had leapt forward to 1865, a year before his own birth, in the world that he himself had changed. He had thought that the only changes around him ought to have been those deriving from his destruction of the monster, and so he had difficulty believing that the purchase of a plaid suit by his twin was one of them. This could only mean that for some inexplicable reason, he had not come back to the same time line he had left. No, he had come back to a different world, similar but not identical. Wells shook his head as he watched Clayton take his place once more beside his twin. His conclusions had come like a bolt from the blue. But perhaps he was right, after all. What if these leaps in time did not take place in the same time line? And what if these parallel universes, as he called them, did not arise from each change made, but rather were already there, had been created beforehand? Wells imagined a universe made up of infinite versions of the same reality superimposed on one another like layers of pastry, an inventory of everything that could happen or be imagined, where each layer, depending on its proximity to its neighbor, could differ in details as insignificant as a plaid suit, or as transcendental as the destruction of a monster from outer space. Yes, there could be worlds where the steam engine had never been invented, or slavery had not been abolished, or cholera was unknown, or Shelley had not drowned when his schooner the *Don Juan* capsized, but Darwin had when the *Beagle* sank, or simply where Jack the Ripper had not murdered Mary Kelly on the night of November 9 but two days before.

The possibilities were endless. And in each of these worlds he would have a twin, there would be a Wells: there would be a Wells almost identical to him, but allergic to oysters, a Wells who would not have been a writer but a teacher, and a Wells who would have written the insufferable novels of Henry James, and, of course, there would also be a Wells who could not travel in time. There would be hundreds, thousands, infinite numbers of Wellses spread throughout a universe that was also infinite. And he would be able to leap from one world to another, possessing this . . . talent? this disease? Or was it truer to call it a curse? And so, he had not traveled back to his past, but rather to another past, a past that belonged to a parallel universe. But one where the Envoy had also crashed his airship into the Antarctic, and in which the *Annawan* had also become icebound (because, of course, there were thousands of worlds where these two events had not happened). In short, a past that was identical to his, except for a few details so insignificant he had failed to notice he had strayed into a different world. And then, after destroying the Envoy, he had traveled to another parallel future, to the future of a universe where his twin dressed with an audacity he had never possessed.

A universe, it suddenly dawned on him, where it was possible no one had destroyed the Envoy. A shiver ran down Wells's spine as he contemplated the cylinder and wondered whether it might not contain a real Martian after all.

At that moment, the lid of the object began to unscrew, and an awed silence descended on the crowd. Standing in the first row, Wells's twin and the inspector broke off their conversation and stared intently at the cylinder. If he remembered correctly, Clayton had been informing his twin that in less than an hour the army would have surrounded the cylinder, and his twin had been trying to convince him that such a show of force was unnecessary. But perhaps it was not unnecessary, as it hadn't been the first time, Wells said to himself, remembering the ray the machine had spat out, directly hitting four or five onlookers, who within seconds were enveloped in flames, turning Horsell Common into a slaughterhouse. Was this what was going to happen again? Had he destroyed the Envoy in vain? Wells watched the lid finally fall to one side with a clatter. He felt his heart racing wildly as he prepared to be burnt to a crisp by the heat ray.

For a few moments nothing happened. And then, from inside the cylinder a species of flare flew up into the early morning sky, only to explode with a gentle bang, sketching a brilliant red flower in the air. Almost immediately, there followed another, and then another, and another, until the sky turned into a garden filled with wonders. Wells contemplated it bewildered, and he scarcely had time to realize that the Martian cylinder was launching a stream of fireworks into the air before a flock of tropical birds emerged in a blaze of color, instantly scattering in all directions, flying over the hats of the amazed crowd. Then a lively melody started up, which at first everyone assumed was also emanating from the cylinder, until the sound became louder, and they turned as one toward a cluster of nearby trees, from which a troupe of musicians emerged, decked out in colorful uniforms, and proceeded to advance across the grass toward the crowd, filling the air with a cheerful blare of trumpets, drums, and cymbals. Behind them, to everyone's astonishment, there approached a troupe of a dozen horses with graceful ballerinas balanced on their backs. Before the audience had time to catch its breath, a handful of fire-eaters leapt out of the cylinder and began breathing balls of flame into the air.

Wells contemplated all this with a look of stunned disbelief, even as an immense wave of relief swept over him. Apparently, he was not going to die. No one there was going to die. He had ended up in a universe different than the one he had left, clearly a universe where the Envoy had never landed in the Antarctic but instead had crashed on a different planet or was still trapped in the ice, or perhaps another of Wells's twins from a different parallel universe had killed him in the same way he had in the other world. In any event, the cylinder before him was entirely Murray's work. The genuine Martian cylinders, if there actually were any in the world he was in now, must still be buried somewhere underground, where they would remain until corrosion and eternity eventually turned them to dust.

With a euphoric smile, Wells thrust these thoughts aside and tried to enjoy the spectacle taking place around him, though he scarcely knew which way to look, for a frenetic procession of marvels was streaming from every conceivable direction. And then, when it was far too late to cast fear into anyone, the Martian emerged from the cylinder. Its appearance was greeted with guffaws from the audience, for it was nothing more than a grotesque puppet, which immediately began to dance to the cheerful music with comical clumsiness. What really surprised the onlookers was the placard the Martian was clasping between its cloth tentacles, which in florid crimson letters said, *Will you marry me, Emma?* Amid laughter and applause, the crowd exchanged amused looks, trying to guess who this Emma in the message was, the woman for whom this mysterious suitor had arranged all this merrymaking. But only Wells was watching the girl with the parasol standing awestruck at a distance from the crowd, contemplating this spectacle put on in her honor.

The music rose to a thrilling crescendo of drumbeats as everyone glanced about expectantly, contemplating the cylinder, the cluster of trees in the distance, even looking at one another in bewilderment, searching for what the drums were heralding with mounting frenzy. Suddenly an enormous shadow, such as a storm cloud might cast as it passed in front of the sun, spilled onto the common like a dreadful omen. Everyone raised their eyes, including Wells, only to discover to their astonishment a huge air balloon floating above their heads. It was still too high for them to see who was in the basket, only the bottom of which was visible, but the vast balloon, painted bright green, yellow, and turquoise, had a gilt "G" emblazoned on it, embossed with gleaming precious stones. Seconds later, to loud applause from the crowd, the balloon began to descend. When it was a dozen or so yards from the ground, a bunch of colored ropes fell from the basket, and down them cascaded tumblers dressed in livery, performing dizzying acrobatics in the air until their feet touched the ground and they began preparing for the vast balloon to land.

Gradually, the audience was able to make out the lone figure in the basket, who greeted the crowd with a beaming smile as the balloon alighted with the lumbering slowness of an elephant sitting down. When it had done so, the man in the balloon stepped down, assisted by the liveried tumblers. He was impressively tall, and slimmer than Wells remembered him. Indeed, the author had to admit that, several pounds lighter, and with that neatly clipped beard disguising his features, no one could ever have identified him as the Master of Time, tragically killed in the fourth dimension a couple of years before. As a finishing touch to this unreal vision, Murray was wearing a shiny purple suit, a bright yellow bow tie, and a blue stovepipe hat out of which billowed an orange-colored smoke, undulating in the air like a vaporous caterpillar. After one last dramatic drumroll, there was silence. The stranger appeared to search for someone in the crowd. When he found her, he doffed his hat and gave a deep bow. The crowd understood, and parted, creating a passage leading from the stranger to the beautiful young girl, who was gazing dumbfounded at her suitor. Several tense moments passed, during which the crowd awaited the girl's reaction, until at last Wells saw a smile appear on her lips, a smile that Emma tried at first to stifle, but that spread swiftly, lighting up her face, and everyone present could hear the most wonderful, limpid laughter their ears had ever perceived. Or at least this was what Wells romantically liked to think, for although he could not hear her laughter above the clamor of the crowd, he remembered it perfectly from the farm at Addlestone. While the band celebrated the girl's gesture with gusto, breaking into another joyful tune, Emma walked with a beaming smile toward the man waiting for her beside the gigantic multicolored balloon. This outrageous, besotted man had somehow managed to see into her soul and to conjure up, with his ludicrous spectacle, the cosmic delight she had felt so long ago when she first saw the Map of the Sky. As she approached Murray, the excited crowd closed in behind her, surrounding the couple in a sea of cheers and applause, obscuring them from Wells.

But the author had seen enough. He knew the end of this tale better even than the protagonists themselves, for he had seen the girl curl up in Murray's arms like a sparrow in its nest, ready to die with him. A love like theirs seemed destined to blossom in all of the universes, however infinite in number.

With a touch of his hat, Wells took his leave of the lovers. He turned and walked away from the hubbub toward where the coaches were parked, hoping to find a driver to take him back to Weybridge. He had seen all he wanted to. On his old man's legs he struggled through the flood of people arriving to see the cylinder, surprised by the festive music emanating from where it had landed. Wells only hoped he could remain in this universe, where his old bones, tired of traveling between worlds, had finally come to rest.

Wells paused for a few seconds to rest his aging legs, dreaming of a pleasant world where there were no mysterious forces intent on sucking him into the whirlpool of events he himself prophesied. Perhaps there were many such worlds, inhabited by his twins, who enjoyed peaceful lives without all these cosmic responsibilities. He felt not a little envious of them, and yet at the same time he also felt sad for all those Wellses who lived in universes similar to the one he came from, and who therefore suffered from the same disease, the same curse as he. How many of them found themselves exiled from their world, like himself, foreigners in other worlds, Flying Dutchmen who would never return to their place of birth, because they had been condemned to drift for eternity in the myriad oceans of time? Many, undoubtedly.

In fact, it was hard for Wells to pin down exactly which world he came from, for in the first journey in time he had made at the farm at Addlestone, he must have leapt into a different universe, and then returned to the past, but to the past of a third universe, which another of his twins had just abandoned, leaving the bed warm for him. There must be hundred, thousands of them. Wells shuddered to think how many had made some change in the universes they arrived in, and he was convinced not all of them could be as positive as the ones he had been able to carry out in that other world, and that, it had to be said, owed more to good fortune than to any skill on his part. He had pulled it off, yes, but God only knew how. Yet in other worlds he might have messed things up or made them worse, unleashing a disaster. Perhaps, he reflected with dismay, this was where his age-old, obsessive fear for the fate of the human race came from, his lasting conviction, even from before he had experienced a Martian invasion, that mankind would inevitably become extinct. Perhaps, thought the author, despite not being acquainted with any other of his twins (except for the Wells who was a native of this world, and with whom he had spoken on the pier at Southsea when he was still a boy), everyone shared a kind of collective awareness, a multilayered knowledge, intuitive and unconscious, that made them fear such a thing.

He could not be so rash as to believe he was unique, not even in the matter of his accursed gift, for Clayton had already revealed that he himself had met other time travelers. So, there had to be many more who, like him, were infected with this strange disease, other unknown time travelers hidden among the branches of this tree of universes. Might they be at that very moment leaping between worlds, perhaps not always with honorable intentions? Wells shook his head slowly, perceiving through the fog of terror that familiar, yearned-for tingling in his fingertips: there was enough material there for a good novel. Undoubtedly. But he was no longer a writer, he told himself ruefully, as he moved off slowly again toward the carriages. He would soon be extinct himself, even if the human race survived.

Anything was possible in an infinite universe, he concluded, turning to contemplate for the last time the now distant balloon surrounded by the joyous hullabaloo. When he saw the lovers in the midst of the encircling crowd, Wells smiled once more, hoping that what he had thought moments before when he saw the smile appear on the girl's lips was true: that the love between Murray and Emma was permanent and unchanging; that in each universe, each reality, each and every world where their eyes met, they could not help but fall in love.

AUTHOR'S ACKNOWLEDGMENTS

I WOULD LIKE TO thank my publisher, Judith Curr, and my editor, Johanna Castillo, and the team at Atria Books in New York, from Mellony Torres onward, for their enthusiasm for my Victorian trilogy. Thanks for trusting in me and for bringing to the United States this humble homage to the books that made us dream as children.

I would also like to express my sincere indebtedness to my agents, Tom and Elaine Colchie, for their extraordinary work and support. It is thanks to them I can say that when I relinquish my work it passes into even safer pairs of hands. I thank Nick Caistor, too, for creating a wonderful translation of my work.

Yet, as anyone can see who leafs through the acknowledgments at the end of most novels, a book is read many times over before being published. Only a genius is capable of writing a novel entirely on his or her own, while the majority of us authors depend for guidance and advice on those to whom we entrust the reading of our manuscripts. In my case, Lorenzo Luengo is someone who, from the day we met, has been a tireless reader of everything that issues from my pen, helping me to hone my work with his ruthless sincerity, which in the long run is what always compels me to let him read my work in the secret hope that he will one day award a few of my drafts his seal of approval. I cannot thank him enough for his comments, and for the humor he injects them with to make them more palatable. Friends like him go a long way toward alleviating the crushing loneliness of being a writer.

And yet, I have discovered while writing this novel that it is possible to go even farther; that simply sharing this loneliness with another person can keep it at bay completely. Until recently I found this hard to believe—as I did many things before I met M.J. She willingly took refuge with me in this novel, providing a warmth that helped ward off the cold spells that habitually threatened. I now know I will never be alone when I write, and since the thanks I give every day scarcely seem enough, I would like to acknowledge here how indebted to her I am, not just for the infinite patience she has shown in the face of my moodiness, anguish, and insecurity, all of which are an integral part of the creative process, but also for the steadfast gaze I have awakened to each day, the unwavering assurance telling me that if I ever got lost, she would know the way. And so, in some other universe where we never met, this novel might have turned out completely differently. But what does that matter? I am convinced no universe exists where that did not happen.

TRANSLATOR'S ACKNOWLEDGMENT

THE TASK OF RENDERING Félix Palma's imagined worlds into English is often pleasurable, but also a lonely business. I have been privileged to share the task with the always scrupulous Lorenza Garcia, who has accompanied me throughout.

Nick Caistor

Praise for Félix J. Palma and the
award-winning *New York Times* bestseller,

The Map of Time

"A big, genre-bending delight. . . . Palma writes with shrewdness and glee."

—*The Washington Post*

"Wonderful, boisterous. . . . Compulsively readable. . . . Palma has steeped himself in the Victorian period and brings it marvelously to life."

—*The Boston Globe*

"Palma writes with panache and good humor, and he's cooked up a crackerjack story. . . . He uses the basic ingredients of steampunk—fantasy, mystery, ripping adventure, and Victorian-era high-tech—to marvelous effect."

—*The Seattle Times*

"Brilliant . . . an intriguing thriller."

—*Publishers Weekly* (starred review)

"Readers who embark on the journey . . . will be richly rewarded."

—*Booklist* (starred review)

"Lyrical storytelling and a rich attention to detail make this prize-winning novel an enthralling read."

—*Library Journal* (starred review)

"An imaginative novel. . . . Palma is a master of ingenious plotting. . . . Even the most careful reader won't foresee some of the twists here, and there are plenty of them."

—*Kirkus Reviews*

"'Intellectual thriller' is not an oxymoron in this case. Eccentric, informed. Spot on narration. Good clean fun."

—*Tulsa (OK) World*

"A luxurious blend of history, romance, mystery, and science fiction, this novel cleverly weaves fact and fiction, keeping the reader guessing to the end."

—*The Newark (NJ) Star-Ledger*

"After 611 pages, I was awestruck. All these plots, all these mysteries, all this lovely writing! By Jove, he's got it!"

—*The Cleveland (OH) Plain Dealer*

"A languorous, cunning mélange of historical science, science fiction, fantasy, and mystery, *The Map of Time* is agreeable escapist fare."

—*BookPage*

"An utterly fascinating and readable book. You won't want to put it down."

—*Bookreporter*

"Time travel, tragic love, murder and mystery all combine in what is nothing short of a surprising, satisfying and mesmerizing read."

—M. J. Rose, internationally bestselling author of
The Reincarnationist

"*The Map of Time* recalls the science fiction of Wells and Verne, and then turns the early masters on their heads. A brilliant and breathtaking trip through metafictional time."

—Scott Westerfeld, *New York Times* bestselling author of *Leviathan*

"*The Map of Time* is a singularly inventive, luscious story with a core of pure, unsettling weirdness. With unnerving grace and disturbing fantasy, it effortlessly straddles that impossible line between being decidedly familiar and yet absolutely new."

—Cherie Priest, author of *Boneshaker*

"Palma manages to be both fascinating and cozy, like having your favorite uncle telling you stories of his dangerous travels to far continents while sitting by your parlor fire. . . . A rollicking good adventure yarn that, with a nudge and a wink and a bit of sleight of hand, is sure to leave delight in its wake and a smile on one's face."

—*The Globe and Mail* (Toronto)

"A miracle from start to finish . . . a masterpiece."

—*Qué Leer*

"A bestseller any literature professor would be proud to say he's reading."

—*Público*